ALSO BY BILL FLANAGAN

New Bedlam

A&R

U2 at the End of the World

Last of the Moe Haircuts

Written in My Soul

EVENING'S EMPIRE

BILL FLANAGAN

Simon & Schuster

New York   London   Toronto   Sydney

Simon & Schuster
1230 Avenue of the Americas
New York, NY 10020

Copyright © 2010 by Bill Flanagan

"Willin'," by Lowell George, is quoted by kind permission of
Elizabeth George and Naked Snake Music.

First Simon & Schuster hardcover edition January 2010

SIMON & SCHUSTER and colophon are registered trademarks
of Simon & Schuster, Inc.

For information about special discounts for bulk purchases,
please contact Simon & Schuster Special Sales at
1-866-506-1949 or business@simonandschuster.com.

The Simon & Schuster Speakers Bureau can bring authors
to your live event. For more information or to book an event,
contact the Simon & Schuster Speakers Bureau at
1-866-248-3049 or visit our website at www.simonspeakers.com.

Designed by Esther Paradelo

Manufactured in the United States of America

1   3   5   7   9   10   8   6   4   2

Library of Congress Cataloging-in-Publication Data
Flanagan, Bill.
Evening's empire / Bill Flanagan.
    p.   cm.
1. Rock groups–Fiction. 2. Rock musicians–Fiction.
I. Title.
PS3556.L313E84   2010
813'.54–dc22   2009023871

ISBN 978-1-4391-4845-7
ISBN 978-1-4391-5880-7 (ebook)

For my daughters, Kate and Sarah

I don't know where my life has gone. I was a young attorney in London when the senior partner asked me to run an embarrassing errand for an important client. Next thing I knew I was in Barcelona, up a tree with a camera. That led to my stuffing a bunch of drugs in my pockets as the border guards came down. Then I was in California and I was rich. I was married and I was not married anymore. My children have no use for me. My oldest friends blame me for their self-inflicted failures. I look around and forty years have passed and I am old and I don't know where it went. Now I am a wealthy old man on top of a mountain in Jamaica and I don't understand how I got here.

I do know this, though. I know the poison that infected my life just by its proximity and that ate up many of my comrades. That poison was the pursuit of fame. I fell in with a crowd who had more than almost anyone—they were beautiful, they were loved, they had talent, and they lived like antique nobility. But, having so much more than others, they became obsessed with what they did not have. They wanted to be famous and if they got famous for a while then they needed to be famous forever. They made a terrible mistake. They assumed fame was the same as popularity. They thought if they were famous, everyone would love them.

They learned too late that fame does not mean everyone loves you. Fame means everyone knows you, and many of the people who know you dislike you. Fame means people mock and misunderstand you. Fame does not boost one's ego. Fame destroys egos. My friends who became famous grew bitter and mistrustful. They thought everyone leeched from them and they dismissed whoever disagreed with them. They dismissed their wives and their children and eventually they dismissed me.

The ones who did not remain famous spent their lives consumed with jealousy. They became more desperate with each year for something that does not exist. They thought that someone else had stolen their portion of glory, and that if they could fix that mistake all of the bad things they had done would be erased and their lives would be healed. The ones who had a little success and then lost it never forgave me for that, and they never blamed themselves.

I found a box of vinyl records yesterday. I put on a Van Morrison album that I bought in London in 1968 and which somehow has stayed with me ever since. I played it and memories flooded in.

I will stroll the merry way and jump the hedges first

It transported me to a flat in London, to a cottage in California, to a loft in Manhattan, to a hotel suite in Prague, to a glass room in Africa, and to the Paris apartment of a girl I have never been able to find my way back to.

And I will never grow so old again

I was raised in England but I have lived abroad for twice as long as I lived there. My English friends all say I talk and dress and carry myself like an American. I use American words. I have an American passport. My children are American. It is only Americans who consider me English. I live now in Jamaica, a former British colony. I feel like an old colonial, dispossessed of his land and left behind when the army withdrew. I don't know what the Jamaicans think I am. An old white man sitting on a hill. Perhaps they expect me to be dead soon. Perhaps they are right.

I don't feel old. I feel like the same young man whose life was all laid out for him in London in 1967. If only I had known then what it took me all these years to learn.

THE ONLY WAY TO BE

Mr. Difford was a senior partner and he wanted to see me. I was a young lawyer. Ah, but you see, I am transposing my memories into American. I was not a young lawyer then. I was a young solicitor. When I began dealing with Americans, they thought a solicitor was someone who hired a prostitute. A solicitor was not a lawyer; a solicitor was someone who needed a lawyer.

I was a young attorney with an old London firm called Difford, Withers & Flack. Mr. Flack had gone to his reward the year before I was hired, and when I saw Mr. Difford pass in the hall he looked to be only half a step behind him. I was just out of university and had an office the size of a storage closet with a narrow window and a view of a steam pipe. I was earning two thousand pounds a year. Mr. Difford wanted to see me.

I was shown into a brown office that seemed big to me then but would seem small to me now. Mr. Difford was there with Edward Withers, the partner to whom I reported.

"Here he is," Withers said when he saw me. "Mr. Difford, you know Jack Flynn." We exchanged handshakes and they gestured for me to sit. Withers spoke. Mr. Difford exuded the regret of a man watching a servant clean up after a sick dog.

"Do you know who this is?" Withers said, handing me an eight-by-ten-inch photograph of a smiling young man with long hair and a floral shirt and tight white pants and the beginnings of a mustache.

"Is it a Beatle?" I asked.

Withers looked at Mr. Difford and smiled and said to me, "Very close. Have you heard of a pop group called the Ravons?"

"Yes." I was pretty sure I had. I had heard the names of a lot of pop groups and a lot of animal species and they all blended.

"We represent the Ravons," Mr. Withers said. I would not have been more surprised if he had told me we represented Nikita Khrushchev. "You know we have always done a bit of theatrical work. Their manager is the son of Sir Carl Towsy."

I must have projected blankness. Withers was a bit annoyed when he had to explain, "The impresario."

"Oh yes."

"Towsy's son Dennis manages this pop band the Ravons. He also manages that girl, Tildie Gold. We look after Dennis and so we do a bit with his clients, too."

"I see."

Withers seemed bothered that he had to go into all this. Withers often acted as if he preferred subordinates to read his mind and save him the trouble of having to explain himself. Mr. Difford was sitting behind his desk with the casual alertness of a cat on a couch.

"One of the Ravons has a complication and we need to help him deal with it."

"Divorce case," Mr. Difford said. He was telling Withers to stop dithering.

"Divorce case," Withers echoed. "Ugly stuff. This young fellow, Emerson Cutler, is being sued for divorce by his wife on grounds of adultery."

I asked if we were contesting that claim and both of the older men looked at me as if I had belched.

"It would be awkward for us to claim that Emerson has been a faithful husband," Withers said.

"He's deflowered half of Piccadilly," Old Difford suddenly cried. "If there were a virgin left in Mayfair he would have ruined her, too!"

"We have been quietly settling up with girls wronged by young Cutler," Withers explained. "We cannot ethically maintain that he has been pure after marriage."

I said it sounded as if his wife had a good case. Here old Difford twirled and smiled and pointed at the ceiling.

"Except for one thing! Mrs. Cutler has not herself been loyal to her vows!" he said

"Ah." I began to dread where this was heading.

Mr. Difford began to softly sing an old army chorus: "Tramp, tramp, tramp, the boys are marching."

Withers said, "Mr. Cutler has informed us that his wife is tonight in Barcelona, in the arms of another man. If we can bring back proof of her infidelity, we greatly improve the prospects for a reasonable settlement of the terms of separation."

I tried to find a way back from the abyss toward which my superiors were nudging me. "So you would like me to hire someone in Spain to follow Mrs. Cutler . . ."

The two older men looked at each other with regret. Among that generation of Englishmen it was poor form to ask questions about touchy subjects. Instead one would tiptoe up to the edge of an uncomfortable topic and then declare, "Well, it needn't be said." For example, if you were a British soldier, an older officer might offer you a smoke and ask you to take a walk with him and tell you, "Damn tough thing about Pedro. The general's coming for inspection tomorrow and the silly bugger cannot learn to salute straight. It would be a good thing if you took him out and . . . well, it needn't be said." This left the subordinate unsure if he was expected to stay up all night training Pedro, hide him in a hamper until the general left the camp, or shoot him. I daresay that many the unfortunate Pedro got a bullet in the back of the head when all the officer intended was to have him sent to the kitchen for a day. That is the downside of discouraging underlings from asking questions.

I was of a new generation. I came right out and asked. "Mr. Withers, what exactly would you like me to do?"

Mr. Difford let some air whistle out from between his teeth. Withers said, "We would like you to fly to Barcelona this afternoon and take some photographs of Mrs. Cutler in flagrante."

All I had to qualify me for such an assignment was a camera. I said, "I don't imagine Mrs. Cutler will want to go along with that."

Here Withers gave me a look that suggested I was making him look bad in front of his boss and I had better fix that fast.

"Mrs. Cutler will not know about it, Flynn. We will give you a ticket and the name of the bungalow where she will be. From what her husband tells me, it is a place they have stayed before and security is lax. You should be able to get some pictures of her with her paramour and get out of there without announcing yourself."

I looked at the two old lions. To say anything other than yes would have been to consign myself to ten years of filing folders in a basement vault. I said I would buy a toothbrush on my way to Gatwick and be back with the pictures. They nodded.

But I was, as I said, of a new generation and I had to ask, "Sir, why me?"

Difford looked at Withers, who looked as if he were contemplating the dissolution of the British Empire. Withers said, "Because you are young, Flynn. You are part of this . . ." He waved his fingers as if looking for a word to pluck out of the air; he settled on, "new vogue."

I considered that all the way to Spain. I had not thought of myself as part of any vogue at all. I was a young man, certainly, born near the end of the war, brought up on rationing, pushed by my parents and teachers to take advantage of the opportunities purchased for me by the sacrifice of so many. It was quite a burden for a child to carry–to justify through his success the casualties of a long and brutal war–but, of course, one did not voice such rude ingratitude.

I was aware, of course, of the image of young London as a swinging hot spot of mods and dolly birds, but that seemed to exist only for a few dozen celebrities and attractive children of the very rich. It seemed to exist mainly in magazines. Swinging London was a marketing phrase that no more represented the lives of most young Londoners than Dodge City was full of gunfighters.

On that plane ride, though, I smoked a cigarette and looked at my reflection in the darkened glass of the window. Something in me began to change. It was as if Withers had by his assignment and assessment baptized me into a new idea of myself. Perhaps I was not as much like my superiors at the law firm as I had supposed. Perhaps I was more like Emerson Cutler than I had imagined.

If I tell you that I arrived that evening in Barcelona on a flight from London it will create a picture in your head considerably more pleasant than what I experienced. The airplane I arrived on was bulky and uncomfortable, driven by propellers and filled with cigarette smoke. We forget now that airplanes, restaurants, movie theaters, taxis, offices, and homes were all full of smoke then. There were ashtrays in every armrest.

The year was 1967, a long time ago. This was fascist Spain. Barcelona in the 1960s was living an alternative history: What If the Nazis Had Won the War? The new buildings were designed by men who thought ugliness bespoke virtue. The evening air was hot when I stepped down to the runway and I felt immediately uncomfortable in my blue suit, white shirt, and striped necktie. I felt like a man wearing spats on a beach.

I converted some money in the airport and took a taxi to a villa in the hills above Barcelona. We drove up a winding road out of a Hitchcock film and the full beauty of the illuminated city lying against the black ocean revealed itself. It said that governments come and go and don't mean anything. Franco might have imposed Spanish fascism on Catalonia, but Franco would pass. Barcelona was eternal.

The villas were a compound, a series of blond stone cottages linked by a web of gravel walkways and draped with ferns and palm trees. I heard the gurgling of a brook but I did not see it. Hidden floodlights made the grounds seem like a set from a play. I felt as if I had stepped out of the real world into a better idea.

My firm had booked me a room that turned out to be a suite. I suppose that it was small by the standards of the resort, but it was the nicest place I had ever stayed. I entered into a white foyer with a kitchen on my right and an arched doorway into a bedroom on my left. I found the light switch and lit up a large parlor with a fireplace; a bookshelf; an entertainment unit including a television, radio, and hi-fi system; and a dining table dressed with candles in glass bells.

The great window was opened, framing a swimming pool beyond, carved in curves to pass as a lagoon. I felt very much like James Bond. It was a bit of a disappointment to remember why I had come. I opened my traveling bag and took out a file with photographs of Mrs. Cutler.

She was a very attractive young woman with white-blond hair that appeared to be growing out long and straight after years of being puffed up and piled into a beehive. A lot of stylish girls looked that way that year. Standards of beauty were changing. In those days before cocaine, anorexia, and gym memberships, women did not worry if their arms were fleshy or their bottoms were broad. If a young lady had a pretty face and a nice smile she was beautiful to us.

What struck me even then was that Kristin Cutler looked too young to be married. She looked like a schoolgirl. Her face and arms were freckled. Her two front teeth were a little big for her mouth, as if they had just grown in. Her upper lip turned up to introduce them. In one of the photographs she was leaning against her husband, laughing, and though he was not more than twenty-four, he looked old and a bit unscrupulous with his arm around her waist.

I decided that the last thing I was going to do was sneak around taking pictures of this girl making whatever mistake she might be making. From what Withers had told me, her husband was a philanderer. What must it do to a sweet young bride to find herself married to a whoremaster? If she was now falling into her own infidelity out of pain, reciprocity, or the simple need to prove herself attractive, well, she would have a lifetime to regret that. I would not add to her sorrows by creating photographic proof of her adultery to be entered into the permanent record of the courts to haunt her for the rest of her life.

That was my intention as I walked from my room into the moonlit courtyard beyond my door. Our lives turn on tiny hinges. I was standing beside a small man-made brook that fed the sculpted swimming lagoon when I saw the girl from the photographs standing directly across from me, sipping a yellow drink from a long, thin glass. I was as startled as if Brigitte Bardot had stepped from the cover of *Paris Match*. In the moonlight Kristin Cutler was strikingly beautiful. What kind of husband would betray a woman like this?

Then she opened her mouth.

She brayed in a lower-class North London voice at a Spanish woman holding out a tray. "What is this farking crap? I told you I wanted a PLJ!"

The waitress, who spoke no English, was trying to figure out what she had done wrong. Mrs. Cutler decided that the way to bridge the language gap was to shout twice as loudly.

"This isn't PLJ! You got no Kia-Ora, you got no Tizer, and when I want PLJ you fob off some local spic juice! Are you trying to get me sick? Do you know who my husband is? I can get you fired!"

The waitress took back the glass and retreated. Mrs. Cutler looked up and saw me watching her. She rolled her eyes and said, "This place is full of farking foreigners."

I decided that perhaps I would snap a few shots of her after all.

A tall man with dark skin, straight black hair, a large nose, and black-rimmed eyeglasses came toward her, calling her name. She did not turn toward him. She struck a pose with one hand on her hip and studied the other hand's fingernails. She said, "I've been waiting here."

"Who were you shouting at?" He had some sort of Mediterranean accent. Not Spanish, I thought. Perhaps Greek or Turkish.

"Stupid maid tried to give me some kind of local pee and pretend it was PLJ. Where were you?"

The man put his arms around her waist from behind and leaned his head into the crux of her neck. He whispered something in her ear. She kept one hand on the hip and the other in the air. She stared straight at me, indifferent, while her lover nuzzled her nape and tightened his arms around her.

I was embarrassed. I averted my eyes and began to make my way back to my room. I took my time unpacking my camera and rolling in the film. I had a very good camera and a long lens. I would be able to shoot them in the moonlight without a flash.

I lay back on the bedspread for a moment and closed my eyes. I only intended to kill ten minutes before going back outside. I woke with the feeling I was falling and saw in a panic that hours had passed.

The lights on the grounds had been lowered. There was absolute silence outside my room.

I took my camera outside. The air had turned cold and the full moon was high in the sky. I circled the grounds like a spy, hugging the shadows and clinging close to the buildings. Blue television light came from a few windows, but otherwise there was no sign of life.

Until I heard a soft splashing. Staying in shadows, I worked my way around the grounds toward a small side lagoon, fringed with ferns and connected to the main pool by a man-made stream. I peeked over a frond. Mrs. Cutler had shed her bathing suit top (and for all I knew her bathing suit bottom) and was locked in a soggy clinch with her eagle-nosed lothario. I began to retreat. I remembered my mission. I raised my camera and snapped.

The camera's click sounded like a rifle shot to me. I almost ran. But the lovers kept kissing; they gave no sign of having heard anything. I was drowned out by their passion, or perhaps by the bubbles gurgling up from the underwater filters. I kept shooting. I was afraid of being caught, ashamed of what I was doing, and thrilled a little, too. My mission gave me permission to play voyeur. The assignment that had seemed so challenging this afternoon had turned out to be a snap.

After a while I stopped clicking and made my way back to a chair by a wall near the main pool, where I could see the shape of the whole courtyard under the bright sky. I knew I had my assignment in the bag and now I could relax, see if other opportunities presented themselves, and meditate under the Spanish stars like a poet on holiday.

I believe that all animals have the ability to sense when they are being watched. Humans do, too, but we clutter our minds with so many competing thoughts that we often miss or misread the signals. In the years since I went spying in Barcelona I have been in many situations where a famous person was being stalked—by fans, paparazzi, or subpoena servers—and there is a silent alarm that goes off to warn you that hidden eyes are fixed on you. I am sure of this. It is not supernatural, it is a mammal instinct we do not understand.

I think that something like that internal warning system buzzed for Mrs. Cutler and her Romeo, even if their hungry hormones caused them to take a while to respect it. I had been in my chair for only a few minutes when I heard them talking in low, excited voices. I think one of them wanted to stop and the other to keep going. A moment later I saw the pair of lovers wrapped in large brown hotel towels and headed into a two-story bungalow a little away from the other buildings, settled into the side of a small hill.

My work was done and I was glad they were gone. No more chance of discovery. I opened the back of my camera and rolled out the film. I stuck it in a small tin capsule in my pocket. I broke the seal on another roll and wound that into the camera like a real professional keyhole-peeker ready for his next assignment.

I took out a Woodbine and lit it and sat back to look at the constellations. A light came on upstairs in Mrs. Cutler's bungalow. I saw her walk across what must have been the bedroom, dropping her towel. I expected her to close the shutters but she did not. Naked, she lit a fag and exhaled a long plume of blue smoke. I felt like we were sharing a cigarette. I stood up to get a better look.

Her boyfriend came up next to her at the window. He seemed to want her to come away, to the bed, I supposed. She did not move. She smoked and stared outside. She must have known that anyone passing could look up and see her nudity. She must have liked knowing it.

The Greek began to nuzzle and caress her in front of the window, perhaps hoping to excite her into bed, perhaps daring her to stay where she was. She leaned her head back and kissed him on the mouth while keeping her body turned to the glass. As much as she was exposing to me, what struck me most was the length of her neck as she craned to meet his lips. She had a neck like a swan.

I raised my camera and took a picture. I framed the photograph in the viewfinder like a sniper looking down a scope.

Did she feel the shot being taken? Did she know I was out in the dark? Or did she see only her reflection in the window as her lover moved behind her and began to push? I had done my shameful job. I had gone up to the call of duty and down the other side. I lowered my camera and promised myself to go back to my room and draw the shades.

Even now, all these years later, after all the sexual, social, and psychiatric revolutions in which I have taken part, I cannot be certain why I did what I did next. You may laugh at that and say you know, but you don't. Was I following my orders or following my libido or—as

I believe I felt at the time—pursuing some artistic ambition to get the perfect photograph that I felt my subject, my model, my collaborator deserved and was enticing me to capture?

On my way from the chair in the courtyard to the door of my room I saw Mrs. Cutler's bungalow from a new angle, looking up the hill into which it was built, and I saw that a broad old palm tree leaned down from the high ground toward her bedroom window, tilting toward her like a gentleman bowing to his beau.

I intended only to walk by the tree, to see if what it suggested was even possible. I passed under Mrs. Cutler's window. There was a soft, rhythmic banging against it. I walked around the tree. It had bark like shingles—plenty of places to grip. I kicked off my shoes and scampered up the shaft like an orangutan. I settled in the first nest of branches, surrounded by large wet leaves. I pushed back a branch and there was Mrs. Cutler in a full panoramic view, achieving every aspect of ecstasy.

It was a startling scene. Not even the Swedish cinema dared show anything like this. I steadied myself, raised the camera again, and gave in to a frenzy of fevered snapping. I reached the end of my film as Mrs. Cutler and her lover achieved the finale of their passion.

I must have looked a wreck when I climbed off the train from Gatwick at Victoria Station early the next afternoon. On the way into the city two passengers who took seats next to me had got up and moved away. I was exhausted. I had been stuck in the tree outside Mrs. Cutler's bungalow for an hour while two groundskeepers swept and clipped the grass around the pool. The longer I clung to the branch, the more certain I was that either the caretakers would look up and spot me, or that Mrs. Cutler would see me and send for the police.

I hid there while my legs went numb. Eventually the groundskeepers packed up their tools and made to leave. I was sweating so profusely that I feared I would drip on them. As they began to go, one stood under the tree and called to the other. I shivered. They spoke for a moment in Spanish. I wondered if I could count on them to give me a chance to surrender, or whether they would shoot me off the branch like a duck.

They kept talking and talking. I could bear the suspense no more. I peeked out from between the leaves. The two men were not looking up at me. They were studying the shoes I had left below. They seemed to be arguing over them. At what seemed like great length, one of the men took the shoes and walked away. The other followed, carrying the garden tools. I counted to one hundred and slid down the tree, tearing my trousers as I went. When I made it to my room I locked the door, ran to the toilet, and passed what felt like the River Thames.

The next morning I hid my film in the bottom of my travel bag and went to the front desk in my socks to pay my bill and ask if anyone had turned in a pair of brown lace shoes. I said I had left them by the pool, which was not untrue. A check with the concierge and a search of the storage closet behind the desk did not turn up my shoes. The desk clerk said that if the maintenance staff had seen them, they would have turned them in. I bought a cheap pair of souvenir sandals and wore those back to London.

It is a measure of how young I was that I stopped at my flat just long enough to shave, bathe, and put on fresh clothes before I reported to Difford, Withers & Flack. I gave Mr. Withers a report of my activities, unsure if my success as a Peeping Tom would elicit congratulations or chastisement. He did not seem either impressed or bothered. One would have thought that this sort of thing was a normal part of the services of a solicitor, and that my taking secret photos of the wife of one of our clients having adulterous sex with a swarthy foreigner was no more remarkable than if I had won a motion in a local lawsuit.

I asked Mr. Withers if he wanted me to take the film to the chemists to have it developed. He smiled and said that was not a very clever idea—the firm had someone who did this kind of work quickly and discreetly. I was amazed. Apparently we did more of this than I would ever have imagined.

As I left his office Mr. Withers said—almost as an afterthought—"Good job, Flynn. I will make sure that Mr. Difford knows how well you did."

I went back to my desk and picked up the work I had put aside the day before. I was computing the taxes on the estate of an old woman who had passed away in Lewisham. I put down my pencil in the middle of adding a row of numbers. As I started in again, I felt disoriented, as if I were waking from a vivid dream in a strange bed. I stared at the numbers and they appeared to float off the page toward my eyes, levitate for a moment, and then return to the paper.

It felt like a month since I had stepped away from this work, and now the work itself seemed strange to me. It was like the dream in which you are standing at a school locker to which you have forgotten the combination. I felt as if I had been pulled out of my timid world, shown a Technicolor alternative, and was now deposited back in a black-and-white two-dimensional photograph.

Yesterday adding these figures and computing these taxes was as natural to me as taking the tube, and no more troublesome. Now it was a burden. It took a tremendous application of will to finish my calculations. When the work was done, I decided to take advantage of Mr. Withers saying I could leave early. I put on my raincoat and headed into the street.

The offices of Difford, Withers & Flack were just off Russell Square, near the British Museum. I lived a few tube stops away, in a small cluster of streets west of Euston Station. Most days I went home by train, but although it was winter the day was warm and the sun was still high in the sky. I wanted to walk. Even when I reached my dreary street, I did not want to go into my flat. I was sleepy but also restless. I kept walking until I came to Regent's Park.

The sun was lower now but the pedestrians in the park were clinging to the early scent of spring. I heard music coming from nearby, beyond a row of trees. I went toward it. I came to a small paddock where a group of perhaps two dozen boys and girls of college age were sitting in the grass listening to a man not much older than they were playing songs on an acoustic guitar. The guitarist was thin and tall, with long brown hair and the first indication of a wispy beard. He was singing with a southern American accent and fingerpicking with some skill. He was playing a Beatles song—"If I Needed Someone," I think. The young people at his feet formed an attentive audience. Together they looked like a Sunday school portrait, Jesus speaking to a gathering of disciples.

I stood on the edge of their group and listened to the music and studied them. The boys did not have long hair yet, not really. They were a little shaggy but not one of them had hair that covered his ears. One had a small goatee, the others were clean-shaven. They wore corduroy pants and what could have been school jackets. A couple had neckties. The girls wore skirts that did not fall much above their knees, and jumpers. Some of the girls wore hats. This was a moment before hippie clothes became easy to find. Most young people still dressed only slightly differently from their parents. Yet in spite of that, I felt a hundred years older than them. I felt I would look silly if I sat down on the grass and joined the audience. I was not sure I would be welcome, aged as I was.

I was twenty-three.

Monday afternoon I was in the office filing briefs when I was summoned to see Mr. Withers. I wondered what mission he had in mind for me this time. I was startled to find Emerson Cutler standing behind Withers's great desk, looking through a pile of eight-by-ten photographs. I am afraid I might have gasped.

Cutler was wearing a blue and white polka-dot shirt and narrow black trousers with fine gray pinstripes. He was studying the photos seriously. I felt ill. I saw one of the pictures lying on the desk. It was his wife in her full naked glory, pinned against the window by her exotic lover.

Cutler looked up at me with no interest and went back to going through the evidence. Withers saw me preparing to back out of the room and put a hand on my shoulder to steady me and cut off my escape. He said, "Emerson! This is Jack Flynn, the fellow who took the pictures!"

I decided that if Cutler struck me, I would stand and take it. But if he tried to hit me twice I would defend myself. The musician came around the desk toward me. I flinched. He broke into a wide grin—he had the straightest, whitest teeth I had ever seen in England—and embraced me, laughing.

"Flynn, you fucker!" he cried happily. "Heard you shimmied up a tree to catch me missus in the altogether!" He held out the photo of his wife in midcuckolding for both of us to regard. It was as if he were a proud father showing off baby pictures. "Nice pair on 'er, eh, Flynn? Cor, she almost took me eye out with 'em more than once!"

I glanced at Withers, who was indifferent to this bizarre reaction from a man presented with proof of his wife's infidelity. Was Cutler having some sort of breakdown? Was he in shock? Was he playing a game with me that would end in rage if I laughed along?

None of these. The young singer was genuinely delighted. "Fuckin' hell!" he cried to Withers. "I thought she was goin' to stitch me up good an' proper! Thought she had me dead to rights and would take it all away when we got in front of the judge." He looked at the photograph again. "Look at her! With a big old wog sendin' one in through the out door! That'll bring her financial expectations in line with her contribution to the dissolution of the marriage, I'd say! Wouldn't you, Flynn?"

I said that in my opinion Mr. Cutler's position before the divorce court had been greatly improved.

Cutler laughed merrily. He leaned back on the desk and smiled at Withers. "Nice one, Eddie. I wish I could be there when you wave this under the nose of her sanctimonious shyster."

I noticed that Cutler's working-class cockney was graduating to a more middle-class parlance. The difference, I supposed, between who he was onstage and who he was at home. As if sensing my observation, he switched back to Andy Capp speech and declared, "One up the bum—no harm done!"

Withers agreed that the negotiations over the division of property were now much more likely to be equitable and speedy.

"Fair play to ya, Withy!" Cutler said. "All right, that's it for me. I'm goin' 'round for a drink to celebrate me liberation."

He threw his arm around my shoulder and said, "You comin' with me, then, squire?"

I looked at Mr. Withers. He nodded. "Go ahead, Flynn. On the condition that you make sure Difford, Withers & Flack buys the first round."

And so I left my files on my desk and departed the offices early, in the embrace of a giddy pop star, to go drinking in Soho with the blessing of my superiors. As Cutler and I passed through the offices my co-workers looked at me as if I were parading in my underpants.

On the street, Cutler let go of my neck and waved to his driver to come and collect us. I asked him if he was not at all worried about how his wife would react to being presented with these photographs.

"Worried?" He flashed those impressive teeth again. "Nah, I got no worries for Kristin. She'll sulk for a weekend and then land another rich sucker with his brains in his knob."

We got in the automobile. He lit a black cigarette and offered me one. He said, "Kristin won't let any grass grow under her back."

It is hard to say from the distance of so many years, so many in-toxes, detoxes, and retoxes, but it does seem to me that I drank more on the first night I spent bar-hopping with Emerson Cutler than I ever had before or ever would again. We started with beers at a pub near his flat in Piccadilly, moved on to whiskey and Cokes at Blaises, switched to gin and Britvic at the Scotch of St. James, and then got rid of the Britvic. I have a dreadful memory of sharing a sticky bottle of Grand Marnier in the back of his car while two American girls with blonder hair than the British had yet to grow sat between us talking about their boyfriends at home. I could hold my liquor like any good English lad with an Irish mother, but by the time I sat watching Cutler kissing one of the girls while fondling the other I had passed through a wall of drunkenness into a garden of new insights.

I believe I was introduced to many celebrated lights of sixties Lon-don on that first evening of my initiation, but my memory is hobbled by the fact that at that point I did not know the names of so many people I would later know well. That I was pissed as a gibbon the whole time does not help me remember. What I can recall is that once the alcohol tuned down my inhibitions, I had the time of my life hob-nobbing with all sorts of glamorous girls and sharp-looking boys who seemed delighted to meet me as long as Cutler-the-cool said I was okay. Extraordinary women who would have avoided eye contact with me on the street—in the unlikely event such creatures ventured onto any street where people like me were allowed to walk—chatted with me and laughed as easily as if I were their brother's friend from school.

I was leaning against a rail watching these striking people dance when I felt someone pinch my bum. I turned and saw two fashion models walking past, giggling and looking back at me over their shoulders. I tried to picture how they would look from the top of a palm tree. It was a delightful perspective. I resolved that from then on I would try to be drunk as often as I possibly could.

Somewhere in the course of that long and slippery night, Cutler and I began exchanging confidences and booze-bonding. He talked to me about his insecurity, his lower-class background, how sensitive he was about his lack of formal education, and how nervous he felt around those who had been to the right schools and knew which fork to use. He admitted that he often felt his job was silly and juvenile, and that people did not take him seriously. He said he sometimes felt that way when he came into our office to meet with Mr. Withers.

I told him that I often felt the same way. He reeled back at that (or perhaps he was reeling from the young lady who was blowing hashish smoke into his mouth) and said that surely a well-spoken university lad such as I had no reason to feel uncomfortable around my fellow solicitors! Why, he would give a leg to be as smooth and assured.

Here I believe I launched into a speech I had been rehearsing in my head for years with no expectation of ever saying it aloud. I talked about growing up Irish Catholic in London and how the old prejudices had not changed as much as we'd like to think, how little money I made, and how the class system still ruled the law offices and courts of England. I ended my summation by declaring that the ghost of Cromwell murmured from behind the locked door of every posh meeting room at every firm in the City.

Cutler leaned forward, his blue irises floating in blood-red seas, and put his damp hand on the back of my neck to pull me close. He smelled like forbidden smoke. He said, "You're the one I've been looking for, Flynn. From now on, you handle all my stuff."

I nodded. This was a big opportunity. The small bit of my brain that was still sober banged against the neural roadblocks thrown up by my massive intake of liquor, searching for an open synaptic passage by which it could send the proper response to my tongue.

The proper response would have been, *I would very much like to work with you more closely, Emerson. On Monday let's make an appointment to sit down and discuss what that would entail for both of us.*

However, in the circumstance of my being—to use the Americanism—shit-faced, what came out of my mouth was, "I will, Emerson, I will, because you and I are the *same*."

Emerson Cutler and I were not the same in any way. Even in my drunkenness I knew that, but some part of me I am embarrassed to acknowledge wanted to believe we were. It was a mistake I would suffer for making, and make again and again anyway for years to come.

I dreamed I was on a television quiz program. I stood behind a wood podium from which a microphone on a curling metal neck extended toward me like a snake. A spotlight was in my eyes. I knew a studio audience was hanging on each word I said but I could not see them. A plummy BBC voice came out of the dark and asked me to name all of the British Prime Ministers of the twentieth century in sequence.

I smiled, took one step back, and rattled them off. "Robert Gascoyne-Cecil, Arthur Balfour, Henry Campbell-Bannerman." Each time I spoke a name correctly a buzzer rang and the audience cheered.

"Herbert Asquith, David Lloyd George . . ." The cheering grew louder. I knew that I was winning a lot of money. Everyone in England was cheering for me.

"Law, Baldwin, MacDonald, Chamberlain . . ." The buzzers kept sounding, the shouts of the audience approached pandemonium.

I paused dramatically. "Sir Winston Leonard Spencer Churchill!" The crowd roared its approval and support. I was aware of something else—a terrible pressure in my bladder. I needed to urinate very badly and I needed to do it right away.

"Clement Attlee . . ." I fidgeted and rubbed my left leg across my right. "Anthony Eden . . ." If I ran off the stage to find a bathroom I would forfeit my winnings and shame myself before the nation, but to remain where I was meant I might in my moment of nationally televised victory piss my pants on the BBC. "Macmillan." A loud buzz. "Douglas-Home." A louder buzz. "Harold Wilson!" A buzz so loud and long that it drowned out the cheering in the hall and cut through the pain of my knotted urinary tract and woke me from my sleep.

I was on the couch in the small front room of my flat. The buzzer was my doorbell, howling now in a single sustained whine such as had not been inflicted on London since the end of the Blitz. My head was pounding, my throat was raw, and while the podium, spotlight, and cheers of the crowd had all vanished with my dream, the need to pee was even more desperate in this world than it had been in the ether. I crouched as I made my way awkwardly to the door and opened it enough to see two young men with long hair, one of them dressed in what looked to be a woman's fur coat.

"You Flynn?"

I said yes, what is it?

"Emerson Cutler here?"

No, I said, he is not, who are you?

One man was small and one was tall. The small man spoke. "He's Simon, I'm Charlie. You sure Emerson's not here?"

"Look, do you mind? I really need to use the WC."

"I don't mind if you do or don't," Charlie said. "You mind, Simon?"

"I could not give a rat's sphincter," the tall man told him.

I opened the door to them and raced to the toilet, where I stopped a torrent that would have made Noah build a second boat. Relieved to the point of shivering, I stood over the bowl for a moment, took a breath, pulled the chain, and returned to the front room and my two strange guests.

The men were standing next to each other as if they were posing for a photograph. Charlie, the small one, was wearing a white fur coat that looked like a shag carpet. He had his hands looped over the enormous round buckle of the thick belt that held up a pair of tight purple pants. Beneath the coat he wore a green shirt with the top three buttons opened, revealing a chest of tubercular hue and boniness, offset by a rakish red kerchief drawn loosely around his thin neck. His hair was long and slightly feathered. Charlie gazed up at me with large sad eyes, breathing through his mouth like a puppy.

Looming next to tiny Charlie, tall and lanky Simon Potts looked Frankensteinian. He had thick brown hair drawn down across a heavy brow, and a long face descending into a very large jaw. He had the look of a man who was uncomfortable with his height and had spent his life slouching to be smaller. His large head leaned forward out of his broad shoulders like a vulture's. He wore brown corduroy trousers and a dark green jacket over a T-shirt decorated with a drawing of a nubile Tinker Bell, disrobing for a lustful crowd of Lost Boys at a Neverland stag party.

"Sorry about that," I said. "Rough night. You're friends of Emerson?"

The two men looked at each other. Charlie said, "More than friends, brother. We're his fellow Ravons!"

My mind was still moving slowly. I stared at him. The tall one, Simon, said impatiently, "We're in the same band. The Ravons! You haven't heard us?"

"Of course I have," I said, and it was true. Since my adventure in Spain I had purchased two singles by the Ravons and listened to one of them. It was not exactly my cup of tea but it was no worse than most of the songs on *Top of the Pops*. Bluesy rock with Negro affectations.

"You ain't seen Emerson?" the small one asked again.

I was about to tell him he was becoming a pain in the bollocks when to my astonishment the door to my bedroom opened and a naked Emerson Cutler strolled out, as poised as if he were walking onto his terrace to check on the gardener.

"Hullo, boys," he said to his friends. "How can we help each other today?"

He had a day's growth of beard and eyes hooded from sleep that made him seem languidly glamorous. His hair looked as if it had been windswept into perfect disarray. This I realized was the essence of charisma. While I came out of our wild night sweaty and smelling of piss, he looked like the fantasy poster from a homosexual magazine.

"We had a band meeting scheduled, Em," Simon said as if this were not the first time his plans had been sunk by Emerson's disregard.

"Did we?" Emerson said, unconcerned. "Well, did we decide anything?"

Charlie chortled. Simon glared. Emerson looked around for something. He said to me, "Say, Jack—you don't have any tea, do you?"

I hurried like a butler to put on a kettle. I had no memory of coming back here last night with Emerson or how I ended up on the couch and he found his way to my bedroom. He was completely at ease, as if waking up in new beds were an everyday occurrence.

I poured the tea and pulled down some biscuits from the cupboard.

Simon was complaining and Emerson was brushing him off. Charlie seemed to have forgotten what it was he'd come for. As soon as I went back in the room he grabbed two biscuits and stuffed them in his mouth while crumbs rained onto his fur coat.

Emerson took a cup of tea and sipped some without saying thank you. He and Simon had reached the end of their contretemps. He said to me, "Thanks for the bunk, Flynn. Let me get my shirt and I'll be out of your way."

Simon said nothing. Charlie looked around anxiously and, seeing no one else was going for them, grabbed two more biscuits like a boy used to swiping his supper from the corner grocer. Emerson went into my bedroom and came out a moment later fully dressed. Simon opened the door and the other two followed him out. Charlie said, "Thanks for the biscuits, mate," as a spray of crumbs came from his mouth. Emerson said, "Back to the press gang, eh? Talk to you soon, Flynn."

The door closed. The Ravons were gone. I took the tray of cups and the plate back to the sink and washed them, along with a couple of glasses and spoons. I set them on the rack to dry. My head was still kicking out from the inside and my stomach was doing that uneasy turning where you don't know if you're hungry, sick, or overtired.

Those were the last months when it would have seemed improper to me to sleep all day. I went in the shower and stood under the cold water a long time, trying to right my head. I came out with a towel wrapped around me, gathered my dirty clothes, and put them in a green cloth bag to bring to the cleaner. I tried to read a newspaper but I could not focus on the words. I turned on the television and the sound hurt my ears. I made myself a cheese sandwich and could not eat more than a bite.

The hell with it, I decided. I am going back to bed. I need to sleep this off. I went into my darkened bedroom and closed the door behind me. I stubbed my toe, cursed, and fumbled my way to my unmade bed. I climbed in and sank into the pillow. It smelled like Emerson Cutler. Sleep came to me quickly. I felt enormous relief.

A warm hand fell on my shoulder. I leaped. A woman's voice said sleepily, "Ready for another, Emerson?" Her fingers tiptoed down my belly.

I could hardly speak. I'd had dreams like this sometimes. I managed to say, "Emerson had to leave." My eyes were adjusting to the dark room just enough to get a sense of the girl's silhouette. She was slim, with a pointed nose. That was as much as I could tell.

"Did he, Jack?" she said. "What a bad boy."

She knew my name. If she was startled or embarrassed to find herself in bed with me, she managed to contain it. Who was this woman? Not one of the American girls I remembered from last night; she had a Scottish accent. I must have met her, I must have brought her up here with Emerson, I must have known her name. I had no recollection of any of that, though. She had not taken her hand away. She nuzzled against my shoulder and said, "His loss, then. You'll have to do."

I was young and inexperienced. I tried to be a gentleman. I said, "Listen, you're very kind, but we don't really know each other and I would not want to take advantage of you or put you in a situation you might regret."

"What? You a queer?"

That did it. I was prepared to be gallant but if she was going to *dare* me, well, what the hell? I proved myself to her once and then proved myself again. She seemed to accept this as a normal exchange of pleasantries, like inviting a stranger to a quick game of table tennis.

Before she left, I proved myself to her a third time.

Then I went out into London and had sausage and eggs and a pint of bitter. My headache was gone.

I once flew all the way from England to Australia sitting next to a French physician who had spent a lot of time working with Native Americans in the remote regions of Canada. Should I call them Native Canadians? It is hard to keep up. Given that this conversation took place twenty years ago, I suppose that on the plane we called them Red Indians. We don't call them that now. This fellow had spent a lot of time working with local tribesmen somewhere up in the area where the people we used to call Indians turned into the people we used to call Eskimos, and he told me something I never forgot.

He said, "This tribe was pretty poor, but they were happy. They hunted, they fished, they played cards and told stories and sang songs and made love and had birthday parties. They had a decent life. Until they got television. Suddenly they saw how other people lived. They saw families with big cars and fancy houses and nice clothes, doing things they'd never done and never would do. For the first time, they began to think of themselves as poor. The rate of alcoholism went up. Suicides among the teenagers went through the roof. They had a nice world going on up there, but as soon as they found out there was another world, they were miserable."

This was how it was for me going back to Difford, Withers & Flack after I met Emerson Cutler. I had been content in my tidy little universe, but now that I had visited the other world, I could never again be happy with my desk by the steam pipe. For two weeks I heard nothing from Emerson. Like a jilted boyfriend, I tried to put him out of my mind. The rational part of me said that his intrusion into my life had been only a brief interruption, a funny story I would tell over dinners for years ahead. But my work at the firm now seemed very banal indeed. I had seen the other world. I wanted to cross over.

I returned from lunch on a Thursday to a message inviting me to a party being thrown for the release of the new Ravons single at a discothèque near Piccadilly Circus. My heart began to pound like that of a fat girl invited to the dance. For the next twenty-four hours I whistled while I worked, and on Friday I left early to go home and bathe and get dressed in the new jacket and boots I had purchased on the King's Road. I was the first person to arrive at the party. I stood around drinking scotch and Cokes and tried to look swinging.

The room was red and white and oval-shaped, down a flight of stairs from the street. There were little cubbyholes with Islamic arches cut into the walls, in which sat plump red settees from which the poobahs of pop could survey their subjects. I watched as the room filled up. Everyone who came in seemed to know everyone else.

I was very surprised to see an actor known for playing soldiers and tough policemen in motion pictures waltzing around the room in a lavender Nehru jacket. I recognized a young model so famous that even I knew her name, and a boy with the longest blond hair I had ever seen on a male. Later he and I would become friends, then fall out when he stole from me, and reconcile not long before he died at the age of twenty-seven. Time moved more slowly then, and great events seemed to happen every week.

Incongruous in this young and glamorous company was a very large man at least ten years older than everyone else. He had menacing eyes, an enormous belly stretching the half-buttoned jacket of a dirty black suit, and shafts of hair from the back of his head spread across his bald dome like seaweed. He was at least three inches more than six feet tall, and he had long arms that left the cuffs of his jacket trailing behind his huge hands by a good four inches. He glanced around over the heads of the happy partygoers as if looking for an antelope to kill with a club.

After a while his gaze fell on a small man entering the room in the company of a taller and very exotic-looking woman. I was so taken by the woman—who had deep brown skin, a long Persian nose, and black-rimmed eyes—that it took me a moment to recognize her escort as Charlie Lydle, the bandmate of Emerson who had stood in my flat in his fur coat and stuffed his mouth with my biscuits. Charlie spoke to the huge man, who went to the bar and came back with drinks for

Charlie and his exquisite date. Then the big man led them to one of the cubbyholes, where he unhooked a velvet rope protecting one of the settees.

I was wondering if I should approach the rope when I felt a lunar tug on the room. Most of the people scattered across the floor gravitated toward the door, like the tide pulling toward the shore. This seemed to happen without conscious thought, on a herd level. As the crowd shifted toward him, Emerson Cutler, dressed in a sharp black suit and a red T-shirt, descended the stairs and came into the room. He was smiling but kept his eyes fixed ahead and moved straight toward the alcove where Charlie was waiting with his Cleopatra. The crowd followed him as metal filings trace a magnet.

Directly behind Emerson came lurching Simon Potts, who looked to me to be wearing exactly the same clothes he'd had on at my flat. Potts was moving behind Emerson, but was turning and nodding and showing his teeth to various people in the crowd. I decided he was trying to be starry and sociable. Simon smiled like he was going to the dentist.

The very large man with the long arms was behind them, looking back in expectation. Through the door, obviously running behind, came a fourth young man I had not seen before. He had even longer hair than the other three but somehow he did not look like one of them. He was loping, while they had lunged. He looked healthier, fit, and suntanned. Except for the hair, he might have come from a Hollywood hot rod movie.

I was seeing all four Ravons together in the flesh for the first time. If my eyes had been a camera, I would have had Charlie Lydle at the far right of my frame, perched on his red cushion like Charlie Chaplin's Little Tramp at a posh ball. Moving toward him was charming Emerson Cutler, the center of gravity. In the middle left came Simon Potts, showing the kind of tortured happiness displayed by Frankenstein's monster just before he threw the little girl into the river. On the far left of the picture was the robust-looking fellow who would soon be introduced to me as Danny Finnerty, the group's new drummer and an American.

Lumbering along behind Danny like the last Cro-Magnon on his way to extinction was the intimidating giant I would also be introduced to that evening—Tug Bitler, the Ravons' road manager. He hauled their equipment, guarded their bodies, selected which girls to let near them and which to keep away. If any promoter tried to shortchange them, he was available to hoist the cheater up by his ankles and shake out the money.

I would come to know each of those five men very well indeed. We would go through marriages and divorces together, have children and lose their love, change our jobs, our homes, even our nationality, and through it all remain attached, even though we would spend more time resenting each other than getting along. That night in the discothèque, enormous Tug Bitler came up and clamped his paw on my shoulder and told me in a voice that seemed to rise straight from his bowels that the boys wanted to see me. I followed him to the minaret-shaped hole in the wall and the rope was unhooked for me.

I was uncomfortable sitting on the settee with the Ravons as wave after wave of extraordinary-looking people came up to say hello, pay respects, and in the case of many of the young women shove forward whatever they considered their best feature. Over the course of the first hour, one or two of the girls were invited to join us. They slid in where they could, one even perching on the floor by glum Simon's large feet.

These were the strange in-between days, after the birth control pill and sexual liberation of the midsixties, but before the rise of feminism. This was that odd moment when beautiful young women thought that the road to personal liberation was traversed by making themselves into objects of adolescent sex fantasies for hip young men. The women coming at the Ravons that evening were striking, fashionable, and proudly docile.

It was the brief era of the political legitimization of the James Bond/ *Playboy* philosophy. Many of the young men who were in a position of celebrity during that short period never got over it. It caused them a lot of trouble with their girlfriends, wives, and daughters later on.

As I joined the group in their reviewing stand, Charlie's Eastern beauty excused herself quietly and never returned. He paid her leaving no mind at all. Perhaps, I thought, he has sent her home to sprinkle rose petals in his bath. All these years later I think differently. Now I suppose she was hired from an agency to complement his entrance and present the proper dashing rock star image to the Fleet Street photographers who snapped the group's arrival.

I tried to make nervous conversation, but Emerson, my sponsor, put a finger to his lips and made it clear that I was to sit back, be quiet, and enjoy the show. I caught on from watching the band that part of sitting on the throne of cool was to appear disengaged—not bored, exactly, but to give the impression of having one's thoughts on other things.

Each of the Ravons did this differently. Simon looked sulky. He nodded at each guest who presented himself, but left it to the others to shake hands or engage in brief conversations. Charlie was the friendliest. He greeted people by name and acted like he was genuinely delighted to see them all.

When he could not recall a name, he was even more cordial. "Hallo, you!" he exclaimed to a woman hovering along the rope like a nervous bird. "I was hoping you'd be here! Everything all right? Who are you with?" The fidgeting woman produced a sister who was giddy with delight to be meeting the pop stars her sister had told her about. Charlie made her feel like a million bucks: "Lord almighty—the two of you look like you stepped out of a film magazine! Are you gonna be around for a while? Yeah?" He reached into his pocket and produced what looked like a black credit card. He handed it to the first girl and said, "This will get you into the VIP room. If anyone gives you a hard time, ask for Eddie and tell them you're my guests. Go have some champagne on me, okay?"

As nicely as that, the girls were dismissed and Charlie turned his attention to the next supplicants at the rail.

Danny Finnerty, the American drummer, did not seem to share the Ravons' genetic code. If Emerson, Simon, and Charlie were a brotherhood, Finnerty was a friendly in-law. He was new to the group, a replacement for the exiled Ravon whose transgression against the band was not revealed to outsiders. While the three British Ravons were united in their sense of vague entitlement, Finnerty spent most of the time standing, engaged in a series of intense conversations with various men—other musicians, record label representatives—whom he would spot and invite into the private cubby for a chat.

Emerson Cutler was the center of the Ravons, the most charming and comfortable. He even seemed to be better lit than the others. He exuded the same sense of relaxed belonging on this couch, greeting well-wishers across a velvet rope, that he had parading naked through my flat. He looked like a man who felt at home everywhere. It was a very attractive quality.

After I had been sitting with them for about half an hour, during a break in the receiving line he turned to me and said quietly, "I want the lads to get to know you, Jack, to get comfortable having you around. It's a bit of a tough club to bust into, but you'll do well. After this is over I want the five of us to go out and talk for a bit. You okay with that?"

I said I certainly was. I sat back again as a big bald American in a blue suit and brown turtleneck shirt leaned across the rope to grab Emerson's hand. I was more comfortable now affecting the same half interest in the party that the Ravons projected. I knew why I was there.

A trio of pretty blond women came toward us. I was surprised that as they approached, Big Tug unsnapped the rope and let them right into the Ravons' domain. The girls already in the booth scattered like small birds. The tallest of the Valkyries leaned over and kissed Emerson. She moved in heading for his mouth but he turned and gave her his cheek. He smiled and said, "Kristin, have you met Jack Flynn?"

She looked straight into my eyes. Oh my God—the adulterous wife, the woman I had photographed naked and in full cuckold. I stuttered. She studied my face, trying to place me. She moved her mouth as if she were chewing gum.

"Very nice to see you," I said cautiously.

She said to her husband, "How do I know him?"

Emerson smiled brightly and said, "Why, darlin', Jack is a great photographer!" He winked at me and I almost ran away. It sailed over her head. Kristin simply turned her gaze back to me for a moment and said, "Oh yeah." She and her cohort of Nordic Amazons stayed a few minutes more, struck a couple of poses, drank some champagne, and then swung around and left the room abruptly, as if they had heard a summons to clear some battlefield of dead warriors.

I looked at Emerson, who seemed absolutely delighted at my unease. "Good going, Jack, you didn't crack!" he said. "Believe me, you and I are not the only men in this room who have seen Kristin in the pink."

There had been instrumental R&B music playing while the party moved along. Now it stopped and I saw a thin man a little older than the Ravons and me command a microphone in the center of the room and ask for attention. He cleared his throat several times and tapped the mike. The noise lowered, but there was still a bit of chatter by the bar. The thin man announced with unnecessary petulance that he would wait to begin until the bar stopped serving. Bit of a twit, I thought.

Charlie shouted very loudly, "Not that, Dennis! Don't shut down the barrrrr!" Everyone laughed and the thin man smiled and addressed our throne room: "Just for a minute, Charlie! This is important."

Dennis. The penny dropped. This was Dennis Towsy, the Ravons' manager. He was barely older than we were. He had shorter hair than the group—a thin fringe pushed down in front like Julius Caesar—which he compensated for by wearing a remarkable double-breasted brown velvet suit with a large black Little Lord Fauntleroy bow tie draped across a shirt with ruffles so pronounced it would have embarrassed a gypsy juggler. The word "gay" still meant carefree in 1967. We would have described Dennis Towsy as "artistic."

He spoke like a groovy schoolmaster. He said, "We are here tonight for the world premiere of the new single by . . . the Ravons!" Much applause. I noticed that Dennis pronounced the band's name not like Poe's bird but "Rave Ons," like the Buddy Holly song. I had not got that pun before. He said, "What you are about to hear is another original composition by the hit songwriting team of Cutler, Potts, and Lydle. And if I may say so, it is their greatest hit yet!" More applause, though a little less enthusiastic. Some part of the audience clearly wanted young Towsy to finish up so the bar could reopen.

"Now here it is for the first time anywhere—the Ravons doing 'Boston Uncommon.'"

The song played, nice-looking people danced and swayed. "Boston Uncommon" was a midtempo folk-rock tune with a strange Indian middle section that confused the dancers for eight bars before resolving back into a steady four/four. The lyric was a paean to the joys of Boston, Massachusetts, on a spring day. According to the catalog of attributes the song presented, one might come across on such an idyll, "a clown sharing wine from an old fruit bottle," "a motorbike girl letting down her throttle," and "kids with balloons filled up with laughter." The song was pleasant and seemed to my untutored ears as worthy of being a hit as most of what I heard on the radio.

When it ended the guests applauded and the Ravons smiled and

waved. Charlie grinned widely and put his hands on his heart as if asking for more. Emerson looked at me and cocked an eyebrow.

I said, "Good song, maestro. Why Boston? Do you spend a lot of
time there?"

"Never been to the States, mate," Emerson said with a grin. "But we
figure this might get us there. 'Barnsley Uncommon' just wouldn't do
the trick."

I was surprised that the Ravons had never been to America. They
were not quite as big a group as I had imagined. These were the first
people I had ever known who were at all famous, who were in show
business. I did not really have any way to measure where they ranked
in the pop hierarchy. "Boston Uncommon" was playing again. Simon
Potts was agitated. He was half sitting, half standing, trying to get
the attention of manager Towsy across the room. Towsy was elect-
ing not to notice. With a great demonstration of exasperation, Simon
climbed out of our alcove and made his way across the floor, where
he leaned in to the thin manager's ear for what looked like a very
intense exchange.

He made it back to our settee as the record ended. Young Towsy
took the microphone again—this time no one stopped talking for him—
and said, "And now, friends, the other side of the new single, 'Open-
Minded Friend.'"

Simon looked satisfied. Charlie and Emerson exchanged looks of
mild alarm, which quickly vanished as they regained their professional
expressions of half-engaged contentment.

A very slow song came over the loudspeakers with unusual jazzy
chords. A low, moaning voice began to groan about a "very liberal"
friend with a "heart so kind" who turns out to be a two-faced phony
and backstabber. I had boned up on the Ravons enough to know that
this was not the soulful singing voice of Emerson Cutler. We were
being introduced to the darker vocal stylings of Simon Potts.

"Open-Minded Friend" seemed to last forever, moving through section after section without ever landing on a chorus one could retain or
a melody one might whistle. As the song plodded on, the chatter of the
crowd grew louder, eventually drowning out the record. Emerson and
Charlie were part of that chatter, which only added more weight to the
anchor of burden pulling down Simon's face.

When the song finally finished, the club's disc jockey put on a James Brown record and the room began to heave with dancers. The party resumed. The Ravons abruptly made motions toward leaving, responding to some shared signal I could not see. Emerson took my elbow and said, "Stick with us, Jack. We're making our move."

Tug Bitler, the giant handler, moved ahead of the Ravons and me into the crowd like the prow of an icebreaker. The Ravons smiled and pointed and exchanged quick words with friends as they moved through the throng, but they never slowed down. I saw their manager trying to get their attention, apparently to introduce them to someone, but the Ravons did not lose their velocity. Only Simon Potts acknowledged young Towsy's entreaties at all, and he did so by shooting him a dirty look and a tight grin as we moved out of the nightclub and upstairs into the evening.

We were in the back of a large automobile heading away from the center of London. Emerson, Simon, and the new drummer they called Fin were in the backseat. Charlie and I squatted on two jump seats, facing them. Tug Bitler was in the front, with the driver.

"I want to work on this tonight," Simon said. He was stern.

"Kind of late to start routining a new tune, Garfunkel," Charlie said happily. "And I must confess, I may have had a drop too many."

"I want to do it tonight," Simon said again. "We're in the studio tomorrow and I don't want to put this one off any longer. It's what we need."

"We'll get to it," Emerson said. "We'll see what you've got. But first I want to talk with Jack."

They all turned their attention my way. I did not want to compete with Simon. He looked at me with no enthusiasm.

Emerson said, "We all know the hassles we've had with Dennis. He's a lovely bloke but he is not a businessman."

Charlie laughed merrily and said, "He's good on the business end of a tallywhacker, I reckon!" I heard a deep grinding noise somewhere behind me and thought for a moment that a rock had flown up into the car's engine. It turned out to be the sound Tug Bitler made when he laughed.

Emerson leaned forward and said to me, "Jack, could you look at our deals, our contracts, our business arrangements and tell us if Dennis is . . . doing an able job?"

"Well." I wanted to be careful in what I promised. "Of course I would be glad to read anything you want me to. Do you have copies of the documents?"

The Ravons looked at each other. Simon said, "What does that tell you?"

"Dennis keeps those things in his office," Emerson explained. "And if we ask to see them, it's going to get him all worked up. We were thinking there must be copies of all the contracts with the solicitors. Where you work. Couldn't you have a look?"

I considered that. It was a bit tricky. I finally said, "I suppose I could if you contacted Edward Withers and told him you want me to handle your affairs. I suppose that would be all right."

I was actually not at all sure how Mr. Withers would react to such a request. I suspected it would not make him happy. I saw this as my chance, though. It was worth risking Withers's annoyance.

I said to the Ravons, "What is your main concern?"

Emerson and Simon said nothing, Fin looked out the car window. Charlie said brightly, "We got no money, Jack!"

I was surprised. I said, "But this car, your clothes, that wristwatch."

Simon said, "Props. Bought on expenses."

"We don't own anything," Emerson said. "Six singles that have gone into the charts, two hundred shows, an LP that went to number seven, and none of us have more than a hundred pounds in the bank."

Charlie leaned in to my ear. He smelled like Johnnie Walker Black. He said, "But Dubious Dennis has golden rings on every finger and French perfume on his balls!"

Simon said, "You been near enough to smell his balls, Charlie?"

Charlie said, "I can tell by the way he walks."

Emerson said to me, "To be fair, Dennis does come from money. I don't think he's stealing from us . . ."

Simon snorted.

Emerson continued, "But I don't think he's very clever about these things. I wonder if the agents and record companies have taken advantage of him. We really need someone on our side in this, Jack. Someone who speaks our language, someone our age."

I was very happy that the Ravons saw me as being on the "us" side of the great *us* against *them*. I said, "You tell Withers and I'll find out everything I can."

The car stopped. We were in a barren factory district far from where we had started. The Ravons climbed out. I had no idea what we were doing. Tug Bitler went up and used a ring of keys to open the large door of a dark building. We all went inside. We walked down drab, badly lit corridors and up a flight of stairs. Big Tug wrestled with

another door and we entered a dull room painted black and insulated
with flattened cardboard boxes and egg cartons. Drums and amps were
waiting in a field of microphone stands. There was a large Hammond
organ covered with a piano tarpaulin against the wall. We had entered
the Ravons' rehearsal room. It was as depressing as a Russian army
barracks. A cracked radiator gasped out a stream of steam. The Ravons
took off their jackets and began plugging in and tuning guitars. Fin
took a seat behind the drums. There were a couple of cheap wooden
folding chairs, a plug-in teakettle and some dirty cups, and on the wall
a yellowed photograph of an 1890s burlesque queen, with a fifty-pence
price tag hanging from the cracked frame.

I was startled that the Ravons rehearsed their music in this shabby
and windowless room. I had imagined something much more grand, or
at least more mod.

Simon was sitting on an amp, hunched forward like a gargoyle. He
began playing a bass figure incessantly, clearly trying to focus the others on his new idea. They stopped doodling on their own instruments
and gave him their attention. He closed his eyes, leaned in to his microphone, and began to croon in the same deep voice that had ener-
vated "Open-Minded Friend" and almost sunk the record release party.

Simon sang:

He's at war with all the hypocrites
He's at war with the sexually repressed misfits
He's at war with the bullies of physically fit
He's at war with the ones who always quit.

It was an entirely unpleasant song. Simon's singing voice reminded
me of Boris Karloff. I was distressed to realize there was more to come:

He's at war with the military parasites
He's at war with their quaint historical sites
He's at war with the forces of permanent night
He's at war with the perfumed hermaphrodites.

At that last line, Charlie, strumming along on his electric Rickenbacker,
turned and said to Fin, "Rhymin' dictionary got a workout on that one!"

The song rumbled through another five verses like a dying trolley bus. It ended with a refrain of "He's at war with them all, he's at war with them all," repeated like the pulse of a toothache.

When it was over I studied the Ravons' reactions. Fin, the new boy, just sat tapping the foot pedal of his hi-hat. Emerson and Charlie leaned on their guitars and neither praised the song nor dismissed it. They went right to work.

"I think you got something there, Simon," Charlie said. "That idea of a war. I wonder, though." He strummed his guitar. "The 'he he he' makes it feel a bit heavy."

"It is meant to be heavy," Simon said. Emerson was fingering a new guitar part, a bit brighter than what he had played along to Simon's lugubrious bass. He was moving from minor chords up to majors while Charlie continued talking to Simon.

Charlie said brightly, "I'm just thinking, what if you said 'she' instead of 'he'? What if it were a girl? Where does that take us?"

Simon hesitated. He was listening. Whatever their differences in temperament, the Ravons respected each other's opinions. Charlie stopped talking and tuned in to the guitar riff Emerson was picking out. It was getting brighter by the bar, a vaguely music box pattern— what we would all soon be calling "psychedelic."

Charlie began to strum along with Emerson's guitar figure, and to sing in a high, cracking voice, "She's at war with 'em all, she's at war with 'em all." Simon looked a bit uneasy, but they had listened to him; now he had to reciprocate. Charlie kept strumming and humming, Emerson kept picking out the pattern, Fin tapped along—they were not going to give Simon an opening to drag them back into the tomb of his first intent.

Charlie began singing a new melody: "It's Mary vs. Mary vs. Mary, she's at war with herself." He looked at Emerson, who nodded. He sang again, "Mary vs. Mary vs. Mary—she's at war with herself / Mary vs. Mary vs. Mary vs. Mary vs. Mary vs. Mary vs. Mary, she's at war with herself." Fin played a drum fill. Simon fell in on the bass. The song was turning into something very different.

Charlie introduced a new chord into the pattern and sang, "Sometimes she wants to stay home / Sometimes she can't be alone / Sunday she likes to eat cheese / Monday she's covered with fleas / It's Mary vs. Mary vs. Mary, she's at war with herself." The band laughed and played with more confidence.

It was quite remarkable how deftly Charlie and the others had turned Simon's dirge into something more pleasant. Now Simon stopped playing and waved his hand.

"I think we might be losing the thread."

"We haven't lost anything, Si," Emerson said. "You know your version. It ain't going away. Let's play with this for a while and see if anything comes of it."

"I don't want to lose the intention," Simon said. "I like those lines attacking the greed of organized religion."

Charlie nodded and sang, "Sometimes she wants to believe / Other times she wants to be free." He kept playing and said to Simon, "That's the idea, isn't it?" He sang again: "Sometimes she's full of ambition / Other times she gives it all to the missions."

Now Simon wanted to get back into the game. He sang, "Sometimes she hates superstition / Sometimes she says an Act of Contrition."

I winced but Charlie and Emerson said "Great, man!" and kept playing the riff, speeding up a bit every time around. By the end of half an hour Simon's gruesome protest song had been polished into a hooky pop tune that one could imagine thousands of teenage girls taking to their bosoms. The grinding bass pattern that Simon had used through the whole song when it started had been relegated to eight bars between the second chorus and the third verse, where it could be covered with a guitar solo and do little harm.

Charlie reached under the seat of the organ and produced a cigar-box-sized cassette machine into which he plugged one of the vocal mikes. I had never seen a cassette before. It looked to me like something from the future. I remember being astonished that the tiny reels of recording tape inside that little cartridge could capture sound as well as the big spools I was used to seeing on conventional tape recorders.

The Ravons recorded several versions of "Mary vs. Mary," a song that would become their biggest hit yet when it was released in June 1967. You still hear it sometimes, on the soundtrack of movies anxious to re-create the mood of the Summer of Love.

Watching the Ravons collaborate in that cramped rehearsal space, turning a piece of sophomoric junk into a little bit of pop history, remains to this day one of my happiest memories. They really were a band then, a group of friends who knew how to work together to make something better than what any of them could have done alone. Emerson had the voice and the musical skill, but I saw that little Charlie had something, too: a gift for finding the bright spark in a dark idea and fanning until it lit up the room. Even Simon had the humility to allow his first musical draft to be broken down and reshaped by his collaborators. They were like brothers, working together to bring something beautiful into the world.

I often wondered in later years if any of them remembered it had ever been that way.

"Boston Uncommon" was not a hit. It did not make *Top of the Pops*. Neither did it make the bottom of the pops. Ten days after the record release party I found the Ravons seated in Soho's Alibi Club in a state of dissatisfaction. With whom were they commiserating? At this distance of years a hundred nights blend together, but let's say it was the fair-haired Bee Gee, the drummer in the Who, a girl who sang with Fairport Convention, and perhaps that boy with the long blond hair who later died owing me money. If he was there, he was with his frighteningly beautiful girlfriend, who always made me think of Ilsa, She Wolf of the SS. It is even possible that one of the Beatles' road managers was present. I don't recall exactly who was at the table that night, but it was a group like that.

I was now part of that circle, or at least accepted among them as long as I was in the company of one of the Ravons. I had begun dressing more stylishly, and although Difford, Withers & Flack looked askance at long hair, I let my sideburns creep southward. Mr. Withers tolerated it as a concession to my new role within the firm as liaison to the young pop world.

I had been nervous about Emerson calling Mr. Withers to say he wanted me to handle his group's affairs, but Withers could not have been more accommodating. He said it would be good to see if I could drum up some new business among this booming demimonde that the older partners did not understand. At the same time, I think he was happy to have responsibility for Cutler and his wronged women out of his in-box.

When I came upon the Ravons that evening, their spirits were low and drink was improving nothing. Their collective disappointment in the fate of their new single had turned to bitterness directed at the great success being enjoyed that week by the crooner who called himself Engelbert Humperdinck.

"What a load of old shite," Charlie groaned while stacking a pile of empty pint glasses. He began to sing in an exaggerated, hammy baritone, "Please release *meeeee*. Phew! Bollocks!"

"Rock and roll is over," Simon said with the attitude of a man speaking to a mob about to hang him. "It should have died with Buddy Holly and the Big Bopper. You can't reanimate a corpse."

It struck me that Simon looked like someone who might have tried.

"Come on, fellas," Emerson said. He was addressing his bandmates but I had the sense that he was actually speaking for the other pop musicians at the table. "The universe isn't going to melt because our new record isn't a hit. We just have to go in and make a better one."

Simon grimaced. He said, "We went with the wrong A-side."

The others looked at him with something hovering between amusement and disbelief. Finally Charlie spoke, laughing and spitting out a thin film of beer.

"Simon, me brother, you ain't gonna sit there and say we would have had a better chance with 'Open-Minded Friend.'" Charlie began to laugh and Fin, the drummer, joined in. From the look Simon shot him, I was pretty sure right then that Fin's tenure with the Ravons would be brief.

Simon said, "At least 'Open-Minded Friend' was something new and different. 'Boston Uncommon' was just a piece of toffee. It was not about anything."

Charlie looked very serious and declared, "Hold on right there, mate. 'Boston Uncommon' certainly was about something!"

Everyone was startled by the easygoing guitarist's fierceness. The whole table stared at him. Charlie looked straight into Simon's eyes and said, "It was about two minutes forty-nine seconds." Then he began to laugh and everyone except Simon did, too.

The night went downhill from there. I got a few pointed questions about what I was doing for the Ravons besides drinking their brandy, but it was a passing blow. The real venom was reserved for any band in London who was doing better than the Ravons and did not have a member seated at the table. In fact, after the Bee Gee left, he and his brothers came in for a little backbiting, too.

When the tedious evening reached its end and most of the table was gone and those who remained were drunk, Ilsa the She Wolf began whispering back and forth with her blond boyfriend. Whatever they were on about caused him some distress, but she was not letting up. Ilsa had a provocative habit of carrying knives and ostentatiously playing with them when she did not like someone. Now she withdrew from God knows where an ornate Egyptian dagger with a red stone in the handle. She began poking the edge of the table with the tip and said to her long-haired lover, "Tell them."

All eyes fell on the blond man, whose eyes were red and pouched. Finally he spoke: "There's someone you can see."

The Ravons stared at him, waiting for more. He reached out and took my half-full glass and emptied it down his throat. He said, "There is a spade up on Denmark Street. American. His name is G. T. LaSalle." This he almost whispered.

"What is he, then?" Emerson asked. "Some kind of bagman? Payola? Put the money in a brown envelope and he gets the record on?"

Charlie asked, "Isn't that the record company's job?"

Ilsa the She Wolf gave her boy a nudge in the sleeve with her dagger. He said, "It ain't like that. This guy . . . he's eerie. He can do things for you, abnormal things."

Charlie turned to Fin and said, "Right. New boy gets to cozy up with Mr. Abnormal. Come on, Finnerty, close your eyes and take one for the group!"

Ilsa was staring at the Ravons with a strange, fierce delight—like a fox studying a bunch of new-hatched chicks. Her boyfriend looked up at her as if hoping she'd let him off the hook. Ilsa never let anyone off the hook.

He said, "Here's the thing. This cat, he knows a lot about music. He goes back to, like, Charlie Patton and shit, the Stovall Plantation, Parchman Farm, real heavy stuff. Voodoo, potions, all that."

"Woo, wait up," Charlie said. "You're talking about a witch doctor?" He laughed but no one else did. Everyone looked at the blond, but it was Ilsa who spoke. She said, "These are things you know nothing about, stupid boy. But your betters do. They all do."

Simon asked her what she meant by betters and she told the blond to tell us.

"The Stones went to this cat," he said. "So did the Beatles. When everyone had turned them down, Epstein heard about him and went and they made a deal. Only Pete Best wouldn't go along. That's why they pushed him out and got Ringo in. Ringo was okay with it." He looked across the table at the drummer from the Who. So did everyone else.

"Yeah," the drummer said. "We met LaSalle. The Beatles told the Stones, the Stones told us."

"What the hell," Charlie said, laughing. "Pull the other one, it's got bells."

Simon said, "What does this wizard do? Sprinkle you with mojo root and you start to write hits?"

Now the drummer and the blond and the She Wolf all fell silent.

"What is it, man?" Emerson asked. "He take your publishing?"

"I can't talk about that," the blond man said. "You go or don't. Just an idea." He glared up at Ilsa. "Maybe not a good one."

The Ravons collected an address, no phone number, and the name G. T. LaSalle. The party broke up and everyone went home with inflamed imaginations.

Getting an appointment with G. T. LaSalle the voodoo song doctor
was like booking time with a ghost. Charlie tried to follow up through
Ilsa the She Wolf and her boyfriend but they would not take his calls.
He asked around the musical instrument stores on Denmark Street
and Shaftesbury Avenue and was told that LaSalle had gone back
to America, that LaSalle was dead, even that LaSalle was not a real
person, it was a joke name among the old jazz musicians. If a cop or
a bill collector or an angry father came along wanting to know who
was responsible for some trouble, the jazzers would blame it on "Mr.
LaSalle."

The Ravons had given up on ever finding this magician until a cold
Wednesday night when Emerson, Simon, and I went to see Mose Allison at Ronnie Scott's club. The show had begun when we got there
and we took a seat in the back, at a table against the wall. We became
aware of an elegant black man sitting with a beautiful young white
woman at the table next to us. He had his back to the wall and was
listening to her intensely while she whispered something that seemed
very important. He nodded, listened, put a long finger to his chin, and
finally wrote a number on a paper menu and passed it to her. She
grabbed the paper, stuffed it into the pocket of her raincoat, and left
the nightclub. The black man went back to watching the show.

When the music was over and people began to pack up and leave,
the stranger looked at us with the mild interest of someone who had
just noticed that his ice cream came with chocolate sauce. He opened
his eyes a bit wider and said, "Are you gentlemen the Ravons?"

Simon and Emerson nodded. It was unusual in those days before
music videos for young pop musicians to be recognized by anyone
older than a teenager, and unusual for black people to take much

interest in white rock and roll. The man was dressed in a perfect black suit with wide lapels, a white shirt with a starched collar, and a red necktie that matched the handkerchief in his breast pocket. He wore silver cuff links and a silver ring. He said, "I believe there was a message that you wanted to meet me. My name is LaSalle."

He was real after all, and nothing like we expected. The stories we had heard suggested a toothless old man with mud on his shoes. The gent who presented himself to us now was perfectly tailored, tall and robust, looked to be in his early thirties, and spoke with a gentle, exotic diction I would come to recognize as upper-class New Orleans. His hair was a little longer than most black men wore it in 1967 London, and he had a mustache and short sideburns that turned out to a point. He cut so striking a figure that I wondered how I had not seen him around before. He was not someone I would have forgotten.

"Coo, man," Emerson said, offering his hand. "We thought we'd never find you! Mickie Most said you'd left England."

"Sadly, my obligations abroad do sometimes force me to travel quickly without much notice," LaSalle said. "And I am oftentimes negligent in conveying news of my whereabouts to my various business contacts. I do hope my friend Mickie Most did not feel ill used by my absence. I will send him some small gift by way of apology."

"So what is it you do, exactly?" Simon wanted to know. "You're not a record producer?"

"Oh, my résumé is long and quite varied," LaSalle said. We would become familiar with his gift for gliding away from a direct question on a smooth flow of elocution. "I expect that were you to peruse my curriculum vitae you would find me accused of all sorts of dubious endeavors. I may have on occasion sunk to record production, when I was unable to find more respectable work as a forger or rumrunner, but it is not something I would wish to see in the first paragraph of my obituary."

The Ravons were charmed. LaSalle glanced around the room as if to make sure no one was listening and then lowered his voice and said, "My dear friend Cowboy Henry says, 'As soon as someone tells me he's a producer, I put my wallet in my boot.'" We all laughed and before we finished LaSalle had turned businesslike. "How can I help you fellows?"

Emerson was the leader. He fumbled around and said, "Well, we're not sure, really. Everyone says you know how to make ordinary songs into hits."

LaSalle smiled. "An ordinary song will never be a hit. A hit is always a hit. It comes into the world in a moment when a songwriter receives what is in the air unspoken that the public is leaning forward, waiting to hear. What I have on occasion been able to do is simply to clear away from a new hit whatever obstacles might be standing in the way of allowing the public to recognize it."

We were not sure what that meant but did not want LaSalle to lose interest in talking to us. Simon asked him, "What sort of obstacles?"

"Oh," LaSalle said, "there are as many as there are human foibles. It could be that the chorus is delayed too long, it could be that the song is being presented in the wrong key. I remember suggesting to my friends from Liverpool that they slow a number down to half its tempo. When they did, the hit that was always there emerged."

"You worked with the Beatles?"

"I'm sure you can appreciate that it would be indiscreet to share the names of any of my associates. It is a courtesy that they consult with me. I would never be so ungrateful as to compromise that courtesy."

The management of the nightclub turned on the house lights. Emerson said, "Right, then. When do we get together and play you some songs? Can you come by our rehearsal space?"

LaSalle held between his fingers a gold-trimmed business card that seemed to have appeared out of the air. He handed it to me and spoke directly to me for the first time.

"It is easier for me to work at my own office. I am not far from here. Perhaps Saturday at noon would be convenient for you and your partners. If so, I will be available. If not, don't fret."

"We can make Saturday," Emerson said.

"I look forward to it," LaSalle said, and he stood to leave. He was taller than I had thought, well over six feet. He wore crimson satin slippers and oxblood socks. We shook hands and he said to me, "You are an attorney, Mr. Flynn?"

The question threw me. I said, "A solicitor, yes."

"Ah," LaSalle said. "We have even more in common. I am not

licensed in your country, but I do take an amateur's interest in the ins and outs of contracts, leases, and partnerships."

With that strange announcement he was gone.

"Well," Emerson said, "we have met the mystery man. Wait'll we tell Charlie."

"Strange bloke," Simon said. "Likes to talk."

I was troubled by something I could not explain. I turned to the others and asked them, "How did he know my name?"

Simon said, "You introduced yourself."

"No, I didn't. I said your names and I said I'm Jack. I didn't tell him my last name."

Emerson smiled and said, "You just look like a Flynn, Jack."

That ended the conversation but it did not answer my question.

I was in my little office, going through the Ravons' files, reading their contracts and their management agreement with Dennis Towsy, studying their record deal and their obligations to their booking agency. They were thoroughly screwed.

Once I understood the disposition of the Ravons' finances, I no longer wondered that they had no money. The wonder was that they were not chained to the wall of a workhouse, licking their bowls for bits of gruel.

I called a band meeting at my flat to lay out the problems. I sensed it was better not to do this at Difford, Withers & Flack. I was not sure Mr. Withers would want me rocking the boat of the junior and senior Mr. Towsys, but my duty was to my clients. Emerson, Charlie, and Simon all showed up on time and serious. Fin, who was not a contractual member of the Ravons' partnership or a signatory on their management or recording contracts, was not invited.

"First," I said to them, "you understand that you are not signed to any record company."

"Well," Charlie said, "we record for Blue Knight Records, which is part of BEI, the big label."

"Yes and no," I said. "Blue Knight Records is owned by your manager, Dennis Towsy, and some business partners. Strictly speaking, you are signed—as recording artists, performers, songwriters, and for personal management—to one man, Dennis. Dennis then licenses your recordings to BEI, who press and distribute them."

"We know that," Emerson said. "Dennis told us this is a way for us to keep control and ownership of our records. Instead of BEI owning the masters and telling us what to do, we make the records our way, ourselves, and BEI has no say in the creative process."

I looked at him. "Well, that is right in all the particulars but wrong in the overall. You see, strictly speaking, you are not the artists in the eyes of BEI. Dennis Towsy is. You work for Dennis, supply him with recordings, and he is the one signed to BEI. The advances, royalties, all payments go to him. You are—technically—salaried employees of the record producer Dennis Towsy. All rights to the songs and the records are retained by him."

The Ravons absorbed this quietly.

"How do we fix it, Jack?" Charlie asked me.

"I can only tell you what some of your options are," I said.

Simon was starting to boil. He said, "So tell us."

"Well, you can go to Dennis and tell him you want to renegotiate your agreements with him. He might be open to it."

The Ravons looked at each other as if they were sharing a bitter joke. Simon said, "Let's imagine Dennis is not fair-minded. Can we break the deal?"

"It's not just one deal," I said. "It's about seven separate deals. The court might look at that as a point in your favor. What Dennis has set up is clearly unethical. The question a judge would have to decide is whether it is illegal."

"We're talking about suing Dennis," Emerson said.

"That would be the likely eventuality," I said, "if we cannot bring him around to our perspective through persuasion. Perhaps you have something you would offer him in exchange for his making the contracts more favorable to you?"

Charlie said, "Like what? I can tell you now, Jack, I might let him sleep with Emerson once or twice but that's as far as I'll go."

Simon resented Charlie making a joke of it. He said, "I want to push the little poof under a train."

Emerson wanted to know what they had to bargain with and I told them they could offer to extend their contract with Dennis—give him more years in exchange for a fairer deal.

"How much longer do we have with him as it is?" Emerson asked.

"Another five years," I told them. "But that can be extended by Dennis if you fail to deliver thirty-four releasable sides a year. Two LPs and three singles." I let them absorb that before I added, "You are already behind on your delivery by fourteen sides. As the contract is written, that means Dennis can extend the term of the deal almost indefinitely."

The wind went out of the Ravons. They looked like schoolboys dragged before a vengeful headmaster. Finally Simon said, "I don't want to make any further deals with Dennis Towsy."

Charlie nodded. Emerson said, "Get us out of it, Jack. All of it. File the papers, drag him before the court. I'll cut off my hair and stand in the docket for as long as it takes. Get us out of it. Do to Dennis what he's done to us."

We ended the meeting then, and I offered the band something to eat. "Don't talk about this in front of Tug," I warned them. "He may seem like a brick wall but he's got two ears and a devious heart. Always remember that he works for Towsy, too."

Dennis Towsy worked in a narrow tunnel of offices up three flights of stairs just south of Oxford Circus. It was close to Carnaby Street, where he roamed each morning in winklepicker boots and tinted spectacles. Dennis had an eye for the aspiring poor boys who picked through the trash bins for cast-off fashions from the trendy shops. He would invite them up to his office to discuss their prospects as singers, models, or nightclub managers and to calculate how open they might be to dropping the soap and furthering their career prospects.

It is difficult, in a different and more enlightened century, to talk accurately about how homosexuals were regarded in the 1960s. Attitudes had begun to change, but they had not changed yet. No one realized then that the American civil rights movement would provide a moral template through which women, immigrants, the handicapped, and gays would assert their claims on equality. At the time, the enlightened view was to think of homosexuals as persons with an unfortunate mental illness. The unenlightened view was to beat them and throw them in prison. It's shameful but it's true.

There had always been a certain protection for what we now call gay people in the world of theater, itself somewhat disreputable and beyond normal social mores. To call someone "rather musical" was a polite way of indicating that he might not be the marrying kind. In the early and midsixties a number of young men of a theatrical bent began to take an interest in the rough young boys who played rock and roll music. They dressed them in frills and tight trousers, cleaned them up, and encouraged them to grow their hair long. They taught them how to walk and talk and shake their fannies for the little girls, into whose tastes these Svengalis held great insight. Any list of the great English rock bands of the sixties will be a list of good-looking straight boys dressed up and promoted by homosexual managers. The Ravons were part of that tradition.

Dennis Towsy was only twenty-five, but he had the soul of a bitter old man. It was generally assumed that he had learned heartlessness from his father, the grand theatrical baron Sir Carl Towsy, but Emerson always maintained that this was not true. Old Sir T was a nice enough fellow, Em said, who had left Dennis's mother when the boy was five. Dennis did not know his father well, and contrary to the common wisdom did not share in much of the old man's wealth. Emerson said that the son had learned resentment and covetousness from his mother, who filled the boy with a keen sense of the easy life they had lost when Father left them to set up house with the second-best Stanley Kowalski to ever grace the London stage.

Dennis had viewed my coming into the Ravons' circle with reserved politeness and some suspicion. He allowed me to help out with the legal errands, but I had better never believe I was part of the inner circle. I thought it best to arrive at his office without notice, to try to catch him unprepared. I showed up at ten-thirty on a Friday morning. I was sorry when ugly Tug Bitler opened the door, eating an onion.

Tug looked like he had slept in his suit. The jacket was shorter than his arms and his shirt was half untucked. The top of his baggy pants was turned out at the waist, under his ballooning belly. He looked at me and said, "He's in the back there," and waved his onion toward an open office down a green corridor decorated with photos of pop stars and kohl-eyed ingénues.

Young Dennis had his back to his office door. He was facing out the open window with both hands in front of him and a phone cradled in his ear. He was shouting at someone in a voice that put inflections in all the wrong places.

"David, you *miserable* twat, I *don't* mind your lying to *me* but I am offended by your incompetence *at* it! You know *you* promised *full* pay for six nights for both *bands* if I got you the Black Snakes, too. I delivered *and* now you are attempting *to* renege. No, no, this *is* not a debate! There are not *two* versions of what you said and *what* I agreed to! There *is* the truth and then there *is* the lie you are trying and *failing* to maintain. Now, you *can* give Michiel the money you owe us and count *yourself* lucky or you *can* try to steal from me and know that I will *take* it out of your miserable ballroom and your *hairy* little balls. You and I *will* never speak again. But if you give Michiel the money today, at *least* you will still have teeth to *chew* with when this is over."

I coughed to let him know I was there. He turned halfway around from the window and I saw what he was doing with his hands. He had his willy out and was peeing into a beer stein. He had just about filled it.

He looked slightly distressed to see me, finished filling the stein, put his pride away, took one step toward the window, and poured his glass of urine into the alley below. He said to the person on the phone, "My bodyguard *has* just come in. If he *starts* out now he should be able to reach *your* door by the end of the day. Good-bye, David, and fuck you."

He was sweating. He looked at me and said, "Why are *you* here?"

"I need to talk to you about the Ravons, Dennis."

"You don't talk to me about the Ravons, Flynn," he said, sitting down at his desk and uncorking a small vial of pink pills. "When I want to talk to you I will tell you. Until then, go back to your little cell at Difficult, Withered and Fucked."

"The group has asked me to represent them, Dennis."

"Represent them at what?"

"They are unhappy with their agreements with you. They feel they could do better elsewhere. Given that you and they have all been disappointed by the failure of their recent singles, they feel this would be a good time for both sides to have a fresh start. They appreciate the support you have given them and would prefer that this not go to litigation. They have appointed me to negotiate a fair severance deal with you on their behalf."

Dennis swung around twice in his chair, swallowing pills as he rotated. When he came to a stop he was laughing.

"You didn't waste a moment, did you, Flynn? You dirty little papist, you Irish imbecile. You did not even have the good sense to ingratiate yourself with me for a month or two before attempting this clumsy blackmail scheme. I tell you, I knew you were stupid when I met you. That's the only reason I let you get close to the boys."

"We've all read your contracts with them, Dennis. They're completely illegal. Let's settle this quietly between us with no hard feelings and you can keep your little operation going. Keep all your other victims. But if the court gets a look at how you've conducted business with the Ravons, it's a safe bet your other clients will find out you've been screwing them, too. Then you will not only lose your business, you will spend the next ten years losing lawsuits from every artiste on your roster."

He put one of his pointed boots up on the corner of his desk and began chipping away at the wood with his Cuban heel. He said nothing, so I spoke: "You've lost the Ravons, Dennis. It's up to you whether you want to lose everything else."

While still looking at his shoe, Dennis began to scream, "Tug! Tug! Get in here!"

Big Tug Bitler came crashing into the room looking for someone to hit.

"He's attacking me!" Dennis shouted from his chair. "Stop him!"

Tug came at me and I jumped away. I did not want one of his ape hands to connect with any part of me.

"Stop it, Tug!" I told him. "Dennis is angry because the Ravons are leaving him. You and I have no quarrel!"

"Grab him, Tug!" Dennis cried. "Don't let him out of the room!"

Tug got one paw around my throat and grabbed the top of my hair with the other. He bent my head back and began shoving me toward the wall. I put both my hands on his chest and pushed, but it was like trying to stop a railroad train. I felt something slapping at my arm. It was Dennis punching me. Tug was grunting, I was choking, Dennis was screaming, and then Tug was pushing me over backward while I held tight to his wrist and I hit my head on something that I realized with terror was the frame of the open window.

Tug let go of my throat and it was I who now struggled to hold on to him. He heaved me back, Dennis pushing, too, and I was out the window and dangling upside down, three stories above a brick alley. The two monsters had me by one ankle and were shaking me like a fish on a line.

I would like to tell you that I kept my senses, but I was scared, disoriented, and saved from complete panic only by the fact that I could not believe what was happening to me. I was shouting as loud as I could for them to let me up, pull me in, save me!

Dennis was leaning out the window screaming, "No one steals from me! No one steals from me!" Even if I had possessed the presence of mind to consider that this was an intimidation routine he and Tug had practiced, I would have worried that the pills on which he was inebriated might cause him to kill me by accident, or in an amphetamine-fired burst of bad judgment.

In my distress I retreated to the vocabulary of a schoolboy: "I give up, Dennis! You win! You win, Dennis! You win!"

The swinging became less frantic for a minute. I tried to see some wire or drainpipe to grab. Then there was a heave as Tug hauled me up by my leg and back through the window. I collapsed onto the floor behind Dennis's desk, shaking. He stepped back and looked down on me, his face red and his eyes little black pinpricks. Tug, even more sweaty and disheveled than before, took two steps back.

My head was not right. I began to giggle.

Dennis tried to speak evenly. "Now you know, arsewipe. You get out of here and never, ever speak to my boys again or I *will* kill you."

I was at eye level with Dennis's desktop. There was his piss-stained beer stein. There was also a small curved Persian knife that he used as a letter opener. I grabbed the beer mug and threw it as hard as I could at Dennis's face and followed it toward him, taking the knife.

By the time the stein cracked his glasses and split open the ridge above his left eye, I had my hand on his shirt collar. I pulled him against me and pressed the little knife to his cheek.

"Don't move, Tug," I said. Blood was spurting from Dennis's forehead and he gurgled. I pushed the tip of the knife in enough that he would register what it was. I kept speaking to Tug.

"Little Lord Towsy here has just given me the legal right to kill him in self-defense." This was bullshit but Tug was no jurist. "You can be indicted as a coconspirator and go to prison or you can run away to Scotland and become a pig farmer. Depends on what you decide to do in the next fifteen seconds."

Dennis was gasping for Tug to save him but Tug had more experience with violence. He was not going to come at me until he had measured his options.

I twisted the knife against Dennis's face and addressed Tug: "Here's what you walked in on. The Ravons have fired Dennis. He is angry about that but he has no choice. He has broken a dozen laws and if they want to, they can prove that in court."

"It's a lie!" Dennis insisted. I slapped his eye with the heel of my hand and kept talking.

"Here are the cold facts, Tug. Dennis and the Ravons are finished. The group likes you and so do I. We'd like you to come with us. Work directly for the Ravons. We'll pay you five pounds more than Dennis and you won't have to beat up anyone." I was not certain Tug would view this as an enticement, but I was improvising. He looked confused. I sweetened the pot. "You would be associate manager."

At this Dennis let out a little cry and tried to pull away from me. I put my foot in front of his leg and tripped him. He went down on the carpet. I stepped on his back to keep him there.

I looked at Tug. It was impossible to read his face. He looked at Dennis, whimpering on the rug. Tug looked at me. He said, "Co-manager."

I was not sure I had heard him right, but Dennis started to wiggle violently.

"Say that again, Tug."

"I'm co-manager. With you. Equal partners."

I said that would be fine. I took my foot off Dennis's back and kept the knife, which I put in my pocket.

"Sorry, Dennis," Tug said to the figure on the floor. "But it's a chance for advancement." He looked at the papers I had brought, scattered on the floor. He said to me, "You want me to make 'im sign 'em?"

I said that was okay, we could settle the details later. Neither Tug nor I showed each other our back as we moved toward the narrow office door. Tug took out a lavender handkerchief and passed it to Dennis, who pressed it to his bloody face as he climbed to his feet. You'd have thought this was the sort of thing that happened in that office every day. Tug said, "I'll just pack up my things."

Towsy slid back into his chair and regarded me from behind his desk, with blood running down his face.

He said, "The Ravons are finished anyway. If you had asked me nicely I would have given them to you."

He looked ridiculous but I was impressed by his self-possession.

At noon on Saturday, the day after my battle with Dennis Towsy, the four Ravons and I arrived at a corner in Soho and tried to find the address of G. T. LaSalle, the rock and roll doctor from New Orleans.

"This is 22 Bricknell," Charlie said, looking up at a cobbler's shop. "And that is 26 Bricknell. I don't see any 24B."

"Let me see the card," Simon said. "Look, this is Bricknell Lane. He's on Bricknell Close."

Fin bore down on his *London A–Z* and announced, "Bricknell Close is just around the corner. Try turning left at the end of the block."

We did that and ended up on Bricknell Mews.

Emerson took the *A–Z*. "You've got it upside down. We need to go back down Curbisham Terrace. Bricknell Close is on the other side of these buildings." Emerson was right. We found a row of carriage houses that looked like they had not been visited since Jack the Ripper was a boy and followed the numbers to 24B, which was a different sort of building, a tall and narrow red brick house with steep stone steps and an ornate black railing filled with little curlicues, cement flowers, and silhouettes of cats. Above the black double doors was the sculpted head of a Turk, with wide eyes, a mouth open in surprise, and a bulging turban.

"Looks like Screamin' Jay Hawkins," Charlie said of the Turk's head as I read down the buzzers looking for LaSalle. I hit the button and the door clicked open. We entered the front hall facing a mahogany staircase, down which ran a frayed Indian stair rug. LaSalle appeared at the first landing and beckoned us to come up.

"Gentlemen!" he said. "So very nice to see you all. Welcome to my humble digs."

We climbed the stairs and introduced Fin and Charlie. LaSalle was dressed impeccably in a dark purple suit with very thin red pinstripes, a red silk necktie with a thick knot, and violet slippers with gold buckles. I was again impressed by his height. The physical command he projected almost contradicted the dignity of his speech and the cultivated softness of his voice.

"Will you gentlemen have some tea?" We followed him into a parlor filled with Victorian furniture, cherubs and gargoyles carved into every table, chair, and cornice. There was a silver tea service and a tray with bread and jam. Charlie and Fin availed themselves.

"You look settled in," I said to LaSalle. "Have you been here long?"

"Not as long as I would like," he said, giving me an answer that contained no information.

Emerson nudged Simon and the two of them regarded the photos on the wall. LaSalle with three very young Beatles and their manager Brian Epstein in what must have been the Cavern Club. LaSalle with the teenage Rolling Stones. The rest of us saw Emerson and Simon staring and followed their eyes to the wall.

"Holy hell!" Charlie said, almost spilling his tea. "You know Elvis?"

There, between LaSalle with Buddy Holly and LaSalle with Frankie Lymon, was our host with the very young Elvis Presley and his Sun Records mates Johnny Cash, Jerry Lee Lewis, and Carl Perkins. LaSalle's hair was slicked back with pomade and his suit was a little less perfectly tailored, but otherwise he looked exactly the same as the figure in front of us.

"It was my great honor to meet the young Mr. Presley in Memphis in 1954," LaSalle said. "And he remains today the same fine gentleman he was then."

"His new records are crap," Simon said.

"Perhaps he grew weary of the rigors of rock and roll," LaSalle said with a smile. "We are fortunate to have young enthusiasts such as yourselves to take up the mantle."

Charlie was bursting. "So, Mr. LaSalle, did you coach Elvis? Did you work with Buddy Holly? How do you know all these people?"

"I would not presume to call attention to my small contributions to someone as brilliant as Elvis Presley," LaSalle said. "He would have done just fine without me."

Even Simon was impressed by the wall of fame. There was Eddie

Cochran, Ritchie Valens, and someone Emerson recognized as Johnny Ace. "Is that Sam Cooke?" Simon asked, pointing to a group shot of LaSalle with a party of happy men and women in a nightclub or restaurant.

"Sam and his brothers," LaSalle said. "What a very talented family! And that boy Bobby Womack, why, he was almost like Sam's adopted son. Wonderful people. I suppose it's not bragging to say that when Sam got into a bit of trouble with some of the less enlightened representatives of southern law enforcement I was in the fortunate position of offering him some assistance." LaSalle looked at the photo. "My goodness, he was a handsome man."

LaSalle could at that moment have told the Ravons it would do their careers good to cut off their ears and they would have reached for the scissors. I was impressed, too, but I wished he would tell us what it was he actually did.

He led us into the next room, a dusty but elegant hall with high ceilings, tile floors, and long heavy curtains closing off most of the daylight from two tall windows. In front of a fireplace stood a piano, a small drum kit, three vintage amplifiers, three microphones on stands, and a variety of basses and guitars. LaSalle asked the Ravons if they would care to play him a couple of their songs.

The group looked like schoolboys called to the front of the class to recite. They did want to get a closer look at the instruments, which were rare American models coveted in London. They began fumbling and strumming and whispering to each other about the gear. LaSalle gestured for me to take a seat next to him on a crushed plush love seat facing the band. I sat and studied the room. There were hourglasses of every shape, size, and vintage on the mantel and shelves, even a huge glass the size of a barbell in the corner. Many had the sand running through them—LaSalle must have turned them over just as we arrived. I wondered if this was how he set the length of his tutorials.

The Ravons played a blues to each other as they got used to the borrowed guitars.

"My friends," LaSalle said in a voice more like a schoolteacher's than the southern butler he had been at the door, "whenever you are ready I would enjoy hearing one of your own songs. You are professional musicians, you should not be shy."

The Ravons got ready to play. Emerson was at the center microphone, with Charlie at his right and Simon wandering way off to his left, testing the length of the cord that tethered his bass to its amplifier.

Charlie called for their first hit, a song called "Good-bye, Gwendolyn." The boys performed it well, as they had hundreds of times before. LaSalle nodded and asked to hear another. They played one of Charlie's, a ballad called "Tomorrow I'll Be Going." LaSalle asked for something new. They looked at each other and gave him a song I had never heard called "People Will Talk."

Now LaSalle stood and walked up and down in front of the Ravons like a family doctor offering a diagnosis and prescription.

"You are very, very talented young men," he said. "I must say, I was unprepared for the level of musical ingenuity I detect in your harmonies and chord structures. May I ask if one of you in particular arranges the songs?"

The Ravons shared quick glances and Charlie said, "We all toss our bits into the pot. Best idea wins."

"A truly collaborative effort," LaSalle said. "Impressive. Don't lose that sense of commonality, gentlemen." He raised his first finger to point at the ceiling. "This finger by itself is fragile . . ." He folded it into a fist, which he held up defiantly. "But in concert with its fellows it cannot be broken."

Having fed them enough flattery, LaSalle changed tack and began to lecture: "Because you are all strong musical personalities with a surplus of ideas, you have a tendency to clutter your arrangements with unnecessary frills. Mr. Finnerty, you are a trained drummer, yes? You are not simply one of those children who banged on the pots and pans until his father gave him a pair of drumsticks. You read charts, you have studied the big bands, you are a professional."

Fin looked pleased that someone had noticed. "Yes, sir. I went to school for it. I did lots of sessions in the States. I did Broadway pit bands, too."

"A great deal of accomplishment at a young age. A drummer must be especially dedicated to his craft because he can only practice it in the company of other musicians. A guitarist or pianist can play alone, but a drummer must by nature be collaborative, as a player and as a person." He told the other three, "Any ensemble is only as good as its drummer. You fellows are very fortunate that with a percussionist of Mr. Finnerty's skill on the stool, your band's promise is unlimited."

Charlie, Emerson, and Simon looked at Fin, the adopted brother, with new regard. Then LaSalle told the drummer, "But you must be careful not to play everything you know every time you sit down at your kit. You are very good at playing the drums, Fin. Now you must learn to play the song. On the second number your attention wandered and you began tapping on the hi-hat as if you were playing in a jazz band. It drew attention to itself and distracted from the vocal line."

Fin looked sorry to be criticized and impressed that LaSalle had noticed. LaSalle went on, "You also have a slight tendency to speed up when you get excited." Simon smirked. LaSalle said, "That can be a very good thing in live performance, it builds excitement in the audience. But beware of bringing that habit into the recording studio."

He turned to Simon. "Mr. Potts, you have so many ideas, I am a bit overwhelmed. You must play other instruments?"

Simon said, "Guitar, piano, a bit of drums, a bit of sax."

This was news to Charlie, who laughed and coughed to cover it. LaSalle went on addressing Simon: "The bass is the border guard between the melody, harmony, and rhythm. The bass must hold the entire performance together. Without a good bass part played well, the guitars will become shrill and the drums unpleasant, all of the components of the music will be isolated from one another. You have a most important obligation to suppress your own ego to the collective good of the song, the arrangement, and the band. If the listener is aware of what the bass is doing, the bassist is not doing it well. I noticed that in the verses of the first number, you drifted away from Mr. Fin's kick drum and went for a stroll around the fretboard. The third time you did this, you barely got back in time for the chorus. That will get you the approval of the aspiring bass players in the audience, it may even make you look pretty good to people who don't know better. You have to be cautious, Mr. Potts, to hold the group together without seeking glory for yourself."

Simon said, "It's just that we've played that stupid song so many times, I get bored . . ."

"Understandably," LaSalle said. "But you are not playing the song for yourself, are you? You are playing it for the members of the audience, who are not bored with it, who may only get to hear it performed live this one time in their lives. When you step onto the stage you must play for them, not for you. That is the nature of the contract."

Charlie and Emerson were enjoying this tremendously. LaSalle turned to them. "You gentlemen exude great joy in singing and playing. Never lose that. It gives your audience permission to feel the same way. If we agree to work together we can talk about little changes that will help you bring forth what's best in your compositions, but for now I would only ask if you would do something for me as an experiment."

The guitar players looked at LaSalle. He said, "You are replicating a lot of unnecessary notes between your two guitars and Simon's bass. I know this is counterintuitive, but I would like you to practice that third song with both of you playing less. Emerson, while you are singing lead, strum only the downstroke, leave out the upstroke, and see how that lets the chord ring. Mr. Lydle, try dropping out of the chords the notes Mr. Potts is playing on the bass. If he's putting in the F, leave the F out of the chord. It will be awkward at first but you'll get used to it. When you play together this way, orchestrally the whole sound will be bigger and more united."

Charlie tried leaving out notes while strumming some chords. "It's hard to have to stop and think about it," he said. "I don't really think about the notes in a G chord when I play it. If I do, I might fuck up."

Emerson said, "I don't want to be up there playing triads all night. Make me look a bit lame."

"Gil Evans can imply a chord with two notes," LaSalle said. "As can John Lee Hooker. You must decide why you play music. Are you playing to impress people or to communicate with them? Are you serving the music or is the music there to serve some other ambition?"

Charlie said, "I want to meet girls, myself."

LaSalle laughed. "A universal motivation among musicians, I find," he said. "It kept us practicing scales when other boys were out playing football. These are only suggestions, gentlemen, based on a very cursory examination of just three of your songs. Don't give my first impressions more weight than they merit."

I could see it in their eyes, though: the Ravons might resist, but each of them would go home and try it LaSalle's way. He had planted ideas in their heads that would blossom. He was not out only to teach, he was looking for converts.

I spoke up. I said, "Mr. LaSalle, you are obviously someone we would like to work with. How do we proceed? And what do you charge for your services?"

LaSalle nodded and smiled without showing his teeth. "For now there is no charge for my advice," he said. "If you fellows would like, I could come to your rehearsal space and we could examine your music in more detail. Do you have a piano there?"

They said yes. He said, "Very good. I assume that your Monday evenings are quiet? Perhaps we should agree to come together again on Monday."

That sounded good to everyone. Charlie was strumming chords, practicing leaving out notes. I felt I had a fiduciary obligation. I said again, "Mr. LaSalle, at what point do we discuss payment?"

"Oh, you'll know when it's time, Jack. We all will."

That was all I was going to get out of him. We said good-bye and shook hands and I saw that all the hourglasses had run out of sand.

After our first session with Mr. LaSalle I said good-bye to the Ravons, packed an overnight bag, and took the train to Kingston to see my parents. I would arrive in time for Saturday night supper, go to mass with them in the morning, have Sunday lunch, and be home in London again by three. My father had bought a small house in the suburbs when I went off to university. It was a source of great pride to him.

I was an only child and we were close. I was used to their sharing my enthusiasms. My mother, Mary, greeted me at the door and tried to take my small bag from me. She told me my father was in the back garden and I should go help him clean the gutters before he fell off the ladder and hurt himself. My father, Gus, had worked as a house carpenter and construction foreman his whole life. He was in no more danger of slipping off a ladder than a bird is of falling off a tree limb, but I did as my mother asked. I found the ladder but not my father. I stepped back from the house and saw him on the crown of the roof, pushing a broom up and down in the chimney.

"Mum!" I cried in a high child's voice. "Stalin's on the roof!"

My father looked down and said, "I'm not Stalin, Johnny, I'm Father Christmas come to give you a lump of coal."

He pulled the broom out of the flue, tucked it under his arm like an officer's whip, and walked down the sloped roof as sure-footed as a goat. I winced when he stepped onto the ladder face forward and walked down it like a staircase. Mum was right, he could break his neck showing off like that. I thought my father was very old. He was four years younger then than I am now.

We didn't hug when he reached the ground. Irish men did not embrace one another in 1967. Irish men barely embraced women in 1967.

"How is our young solicitor today?" my father asked. "Have you brought justice to the oppressed? Have you found remedy for the afflicted?"

"I have had some interesting adventures lately, old mole," I told him, taking his filthy broom and leaning it against the house. "Let's go inside and scrub the grime off you and I'll tell you tales to curl the few remaining hairs on your ancient head."

I spent dinner telling my parents about my new clients the Ravons, describing how famous they were, how girls screamed when they performed, and what funny, endearing characters they were when they were at home. My mother said she was sure she had seen them on *Sunday Night at the Palladium* but from her description I knew she was talking about Cliff Richard and the Shadows.

My father seemed amused but cautious. "This won't take your time away from your other duties, will it, Jack? You don't want the authorities thinking you're not serious."

"The authorities" was my father's joking way of referring to my superiors at Difford, Withers & Flack. What he meant was, we don't want the Protestants to think the Irish boy is anything less than brilliant and dedicated. My father's instincts were those of an older generation, but so were the authorities'. I often wonder what all of those old men—my father, Mr. Difford, and all the rest in both countries—would have said if they had lived to the twenty-first century when it was proved that the Irish and English were genetically identical.

In fact, I know what my father would have said. I can close my eyes and hear him: "We are all descended from Adam, we knew that already. It only means that the crimes of the English are sins of volition and cannot be blamed on inherited shortcomings. I do expect, though, son, that examination of their craniums would find their skulls just a wee bit smaller, as excavation of their chest cavities must surely reveal their hearts to be a fraction less developed. If the distinctions between us cannot be blamed on heredity, then we must attribute them to the unfortunate ramifications of generations of inbreeding among their so-called noble class."

My mother would have tried to say something nice, perhaps about how tall and straight-backed young Prince Charles looked in his naval uniform. My father would have pretended to be outraged and said, "If he looks tall it is only because he is standing on the neck of Ireland!"

More and more as I get older I can hear my parents speaking. It is a great comfort. The people whose deaths we most dread when we are young never die to us at all.

My mother was born in Waterford, Ireland, in 1914. She was orphaned as a girl, came to London to live with an aunt, and worked as a servant. She met my father when she was nineteen and he was twenty-five, a carpenter on his way to becoming foreman with a construction company. My father had already been married and widowed when he met my mother. His parents were both from Ireland, but he was English-born. He was by the standards of the local community a man of achievement. She was an innocent provincial girl. His family thought she was beneath him. Her relatives thought he was too old and might treat her cruelly. I had one older sister who died at birth and another who died at age two of a fever in the early days of the war. I was their youngest child and the only one who survived. They poured all of their grief, hope, and gratitude into me.

Both my parents were self-educated. They were dedicated readers, naturally gifted storytellers, and could recite whole books of verse from memory. It meant everything to them that I did well at school and would not have to go into an apprenticeship at fifteen. University was always their ambition, and my becoming a solicitor was the fulfillment of their dreams and justification of all the sacrifices made by them and by their parents and grandparents.

The casual prejudice of the English Protestants was not even resented—it would have been like resenting the soot in the air. It stiffened our spines and demonstrated that the Prods were as thick as we thought. At university an especially old and imperious professor taught us that Darwin had ranked the ascending evolution of the human races from the ape up to the Englishman. The Irish race was at the very bottom of the scale, beneath the black African and just above the monkey.

To my father, Darwin, Freud, and Marx were the latest recruits in the procession of secular assaults against the invulnerable wisdom of the Catholic Church. They were the heirs of Luther, Henry VIII, and Cromwell, with whom they kept company in hell, unless the Lord in

His infinite mercy elected to burn off their sins with a few thousand years in purgatory.

My Catholicism was as much a part of me as my eyes and ears. It was not only how I saw myself, it was how everyone around me, Protestant and Catholic, identified me. I was born in England, my father was born in England, but to the Protestants I was Irish. To the Catholics we were Irish, too. When Difford, Withers & Flack hired me, it was a gesture of liberal magnanimity from them and a source of great pride to my parents, whose goal was for me to succeed in the English Protestant world without abandoning my Irish Catholicness.

As a young man I wore my faith lightly. I did not eat meat on Fridays and abstained from all food and drink from midnight forward on the one Sunday a month I took the Eucharist. I generally obeyed the rules of the church, but I was not dogmatic. I kissed girls and sneaked beers and did not enumerate all of my sins in the confessional. My father told me that when he was a boy he believed that if he went to the altar rail with a sin on his conscience, the host would turn into a snake in his mouth. He raised me with a less fearful faith. I believed that God loved me and had died for my sins. My obedience to the rules of His church was born more out of gratitude than from a fear of hell.

Looking back now, I understand that my generation's parents wanted to spare us the terrors that they had been raised with. They did not talk about the devil. They told us that we were God's children and He loved us. What ungrateful children we turned out to be! Assured of God's love, we forgave ourselves everything. Our parents had grown up in two great wars, divided by a period of deprivation. They wanted to spare us what they had suffered. It's an odd thing about demons, though. If you don't believe in demons outside you, you might create demons within. Over my lifetime I did a lot of damage to myself with drink and drugs, looking for the transcendence I felt as a child taking the host. I spent a lot of years listening to myself talk in the psychiatrist's office, looking for the absolution of the confessional. I learned too late that when you drive out your devils, you drive away your angels, too.

I know what my father would have said about that: "No one should belong to a religion because it's therapeutic. The only reason anyone should ever belong to a religion is because he believes it is true."

I left my faith behind in small increments, the way I left boxes in the basements when I moved flats, always intending to come back someday and collect them.

After dinner I carried the plates to the sink and my mother did the dishes. Then I found a 45 spindle and screwed it onto the record player and played my parents some 45s by the Ravons I had brought along. They were baffled. My father said, "It's not John McCormack, is it?"

My mother said, "The drum player is quite good. What's his name, Jackie?"

"Danny Finnerty."

My parents looked at each other with approval. "Irish."

They smiled and nodded through the second side. When I put on a third song, my father began to clap along as if he were at a Polish pub and I started to feel embarrassed. My parents understood my enthusiasm for the Ravons even less after hearing their music than they had when I talked about them. I took off the single and set the dial on the record player back to 78.

The next morning I went with my parents to nine o'clock mass. It started a bit late. We saw the priest peering out from the vestry looking for someone. When the mass began we understood why: there were no servers.

My father nudged me. "He has no altar boy, Jack. Go up there."

I whispered back, "I'm twenty-three years old, Pa, I haven't served mass in ten years."

"So what? You don't leave a priest alone on the altar, go up or I will."

The priest began reciting the Prayers at the Foot of the Altar, doing both parts: "I will go to the altar of God— To the God who gives joy to my youth."

I said to my father, "It's in English now, Pa, I don't know the responses. I was a Latin altar boy."

My father's face fell. He did not know the new English liturgy, either. His world was passing away. When it was time for the offertory I went up on the altar and brought the priest the water and wine. I stayed there to hold the plate during Communion. My father and mother were the first faces at the rail. He winked at me after he took the host, almost an impiety to one who took his sacraments so seriously. He was proud of his son.

It would not be long before I disappointed him.

After mass we walked through the village of Kingston, greeting my parents' neighbors. My mother made lamb chops for lunch and served a white cake with chocolate frosting for dessert. I made the two-fifteen train back up to town. At four I went to Emerson's flat to prepare the groundwork for our new relationship and to ready a defense against the inevitable challenge by Dennis Towsy, at whose face I had recently held a knife. Tug Bitler joined us in our conference, although I did not trust him. I needed him for this. Tug knew the ledger of Dennis's crimes.

We were a very strange trio, Emerson, Tug, and I. That evening we reached an understanding of how we would work together. I would endeavor to pry the Ravons' recording and music publishing contracts from Towsy's fingers. I thought I could convince the group's record company to support us in that effort, as long as they got something out of it. Tug would continue to serve as the band's road manager, but now instead of being paid a weekly wage he and I would divide between us 15 percent of the Ravons' income.

I also lobbied Emerson to make Fin the drummer a full member for purposes of recordings and live appearances, starting with the next record. It seemed to me to be fair to Fin and to the spirit of the group. As Fin was not a songwriter, he did not share in the music publishing. He deserved a stake. I was also worried that until we had cleared up the legal mess created by Towsy, we would not be able to pay Fin his salary.

We finished our work and Emerson sat back, lit a joint, and smiled. "Right, then, Jack, you are now my manager."

Tug loomed. Emerson said, "And you, Tug, are my other manager." He exhaled more smoke than my father's chimney. He looked at Tug and me and said, "All right, managers, we need money. We're skint! Go book some shows!"

I had no idea how to do that. That evening I began forty years of making it up as I went along.

I arrived at Difford, Withers & Flack very early on Monday morn-ing prepared for battle. Nothing happened. The office girls arrived on time talking about their weekends. The little rooms filled up. James Pillsley, another young solicitor, had the sneezes and kept asking me to help him decipher a deposition.

By noon I began to think that I had misunderstood the ramifications of drawing blood from Dennis Towsy. Perhaps Dennis had not told anyone what had happened. Perhaps his revenge would come with a pipe in an alley and not through the mechanisms of the legal system. Perhaps his revenge would never come at all. The only time I saw old Mr. Difford all day he asked me to help him find his hat.

I should have known better. At four P.M. one of the girls came and said that Mr. Withers needed me right away. I took a moment to run through the counterattack I had prepared. I went into Withers's office and found him standing with an imperial man of about fifty-five with unnaturally black hair, red cheeks, and a strong jaw turned up at a forty-five-degree angle. He wore a blue jacket and gray slacks, and had a short silk scarf draped around his neck. It could have been no other than Sir Carl Towsy, theatrical producer, friend of the Windsors, and father of Dennis.

I searched Sir T's face and form and could not see one aspect in which he resembled his son. Dennis must have taken after his mother.

"Sir," I said crisply.

"This is Jack Flynn," Withers told Sir Carl, pushing past me to close the door. "Flynn, this is Sir Carl Towsy."

"Sir," I said again, with a little snap of my head in the direction of the impresario.

"Flynn," Withers said, "what in the holy hell have you done with this pop group? We asked you to look after some minor details for one of the singers who works for Sir Carl's son. Your client is the Towsy family! Did you misunderstand that most basic fact? I am given to understand that you have gone over to the opposing team! You have fomented some sort of rebellion among the singing group against the younger Mr. Towsy? Is that true? And—and this I will tell you I have assured Sir Carl could not possibly be true—you have been accused of abusing your obligations as counsel in order to entice the group to break their contracts with young Mr. Towsy and replace him with you as their manager? I told Sir Dennis you would never do that, you are neither that stupid nor that corrupt. Flynn, what is going on here, what is this about?"

I was trained in the law. I did not fluster. I stuck to the script I had rehearsed.

I said, "Sir Carl, I wish no disrespect. I am sorry to say that when I began working with your son I discovered a number of irregularities in the way he has conducted business. His clients asked me questions about certain provisions in their contracts with him that on examination I found to be, well, questionable at best."

Withers began to interrupt but Towsy père nodded for me to continue.

"I went to Dennis to try to straighten things out and he became . . . defensive. Well, the truth is he had his man Bitler hang me out a third-story window."

Sir Carl smiled. I did not take that as a good sign. I plowed on: "Bitler himself has corroborated for your son's clients a whole litany of coercive, unethical, and illegal business practices Dennis has engaged in." I had been planning to hold this back but I felt I had the room, so I added, "Perhaps his judgment has been compromised by his use of prescription drugs, which I understand to be constant and that causes his moods to swing between the extremes."

Withers looked like he was about to stuff his handkerchief in my mouth. Difford, Withers & Flack protected their clients from this sort of thing.

Sir Carl carried himself like a man who had seen a lot and heard worse. He spoke for the first time. He said, "My son had you hung out a window?"

"Yessir. Friday."

"And how did you respond to that, Mr. Flynn?"

I looked at Withers. He did not seem imposing to me. He looked confused and scared. I liked him looking at me like that. I said, "When I was safely back inside I hit him with a beer mug and held a letter opener to his cheek."

Withers wilted. Sir Carl nodded. "Did you hurt him?"

"The beer mug cut him above the eye but he seemed all right. I think it actually shook me more than it did him."

Sir Carl said, "That would not surprise me. What would you like to see happen next?"

I had not been prepared for that. I had to improvise. I said, "Sir, the Ravons will not work with your son anymore, knowing what they know about how he has cheated them. If they choose to take this to court I will have to support them." I turned to Withers and said, "We have an obligation to our clients, of course, but we have a higher obligation to the law itself. We cannot collude in a criminal conspiracy." I was far from sure that Dennis's contractual shenanigans, unethical as they were, were criminal, but I could see that veiled threats and grand accusations were my only chance of coming out of this meeting alive.

I kept pressing. I said, "If the Ravons are allowed to walk away clean, to get out of their contracts with Dennis and start again somewhere else, none of the rest of this needs to ever come out. Dennis can keep his business going, retain his other clients, we don't care. I do have an obligation to the Ravons to free them from these unconscionable agreements. What Dennis does with the rest of his life and career is not any of my business."

Sir Carl looked at Withers, who had no idea what to say. Sir Carl looked at me and said, "I'm afraid that my son has left a trail of tears behind him since he was old enough to torture a cat. What will this cost me?"

I had hoped at best to get out of my fight with Dennis without being fired. It had never occurred to me that the situation might have left me with any new advantage.

Withers began to protest that of course Sir Dennis would never have to– I interrupted. I said, "Sir, your son owes the Ravons at least forty thousand pounds in back payments. Actually the number will be far higher if we look deeper, but just on his own books, he owes them forty grand."

"What about the rest of it?"

Suddenly I saw the picture whole. I said, "If we go to court this will drag on for a year and your son will lose everything, including his reputation. In the interests of a fast divorce, I would press the Ravons to give up all of the recordings and music publishing that your son already controls, in exchange for his surrendering any claim on their future work and earnings, from this day forward." I let that sit. No one said anything. I said, "And the forty thousand pounds."

Three hours later I was with Emerson, Charlie, Simon, and Fin in their rehearsal room. We were all laughing and drinking beer. Charlie cried, "He went for it!"

"He did!" I laughed. Beer was running down my sleeve.

"Fucking unbelievable!" Emerson said. "We're free! We're fucking free!"

Simon was happy, too, but he had to find some dark cloud. He said, "But he gets all our records."

"Just up till yesterday," I reminded him. "Yeah, he's got your past, he's got 'Boston Uncommon' and 'Good-bye, Gwendolyn' and the album. So what? He had those already. You've got your whole future! Tomorrow I start talking to publishers, talking to BEI, negotiating you the deals you deserve."

"Fuckin' Flynn," Emerson said, tipping his bottle against mine. "Done more for us in twenty-four hours than Dennis did in two years."

"Now, boys," Charlie said, "let's come up with a hit that will justify Jack's faith in us! Who wants to work on 'Mary vs. Mary'?"

"Should we wait for LaSalle?" Emerson asked. "He'll be here soon."

"Let's start now and get it so good Mr. LaSalle won't be able to think of any way to improve it," Charlie insisted. "I feel great! I want to play music!"

I left them there and walked all the way home. It had been a great day and I was proud of the way things had ended. The forty-grand check from Towsy Senior not only delighted the Ravons, but my percentage would fund my setting up an office for the new management firm Tug and I would undertake.

I had not told the Ravons what happened after Sir Carl left.

Mr. Withers had walked around his desk, shaking his head and looking at the floor. He stood there, leaning on his blotter until he was certain Towsy was gone from the building. Then he looked up at me and said, "You clever little bastard. The Irish gift of gab, the kiss of the Blarney Stone. Do you have any idea, Flynn, how lucky you are that Mr. Towsy is generous and that he is protective of his deviant son? Do you have any idea of the risk at which you put yourself and this firm? You assaulted a client! You used information you had gathered in confidence as his solicitor to blackmail him into turning over to you one of his assets! My God, I'd like to hang you out a window myself!"

It was no good to protest. I had enjoyed my triumph and now I would have to take a few kicks. That was the British way. I was no longer intimidated by Mr. Withers.

"Flynn, I would like you to take a leave of absence from Difford, Withers. I want you out of here for a while. Go manage your little combo. Grow your hair down to your knees and dress up like a girl if that is how you get your pleasure. Come back in September and we'll talk about whether you are serious about a life in the law, and if there is a place for you here."

By the time I got back to my desk I decided I had won the pools. Withers did not fire me, he had given me six months to devote myself to the Ravons. I had won my confrontation with Sir Towsy and come out with the cash I needed to set up my own business. If I failed, I would come back in six months and ask Withers for absolution and beg for my old job back.

I was not going to fail.

Tug Bitler was the man who knew a man who knew a man who could find you anything you wanted, from ketamine to office space to blue movies starring famous Hollywood names. He gave me the number of a Greek landlord who rented me a three-room office suite in Chelsea, just off the King's Road, at a very fair price. I wanted the lease in my name and I was willing to pay the whole rent for the security that afforded me. I was determined to establish a clear division of labor between Tug and me. Although we were co-managers of the Ravons, we did not form a legal partnership. I would write the rent checks, keep the books, and handle all contracts and negotiations. I would give Tug one of the rooms as his office at no charge and he would organize and oversee the band's touring. We would each take 7.5 percent of the Ravons' revenue. I was happy to do more than half the work to maintain control of what I considered the most important pieces of the Ravons' business.

Years later I learned that Tug took advantage of my innocence and his criminal instincts to earn much more than I did. While I was scrupulous about accounting for every penny that came in from royalties and advances, Tug was shaking down the nightclub managers, ballroom owners, and concert promoters who hired the Ravons to perform live. He was regularly demanding cash payments above the checks that he brought home from the road. When the group advanced to the point of staying in decent places and flying to shows, he also collected kickbacks from hotels and travel agents. Between the cash he was accruing in brown paper bags and the fact that I was bearing all of our office costs, I expect that Tug earned twice what I did from the Ravons in the years 1967 to 1969.

The band themselves, who lived ass by thigh with Tug in the vans and dressing rooms, had to know that he was skimming. Many years later I asked Charlie why no one had told me. Charlie laughed and said, "Ya really didn't know, Flynnie? Ho, ho. Mark it down in your ledger under 'The price of an education'!"

Once we had moved into our new offices we needed a corporate name. Playing on the Ravons, I called the new management company Nevermore Ltd. When I asked Tug what he thought of the name he grunted and asked if it was for the home of Peter Pan, "Where the Lost Boys never grow up." I said that was Neverland and he said, "Close enough for rock and roll."

It always unnerved me a bit to see Tug lumbering through the door, but he did not spend much time at Nevermore. Where he went and what he did was nothing I cared to know. I hired a sharp young woman named Allison Foster to run the office. She typed like a ticker-tape machine, brewed Jamaican coffee, and somehow kept up with every new band within a two-hundred-mile radius. Soon we fell into a pattern of my calling her name out from behind my desk and her running in to tell me who was who in the music business as I held my hand over the telephone receiver.

The first time I saw the band for more than a moment in those first weeks was at our office-warming party. The Ravons presented me with a framed Aubrey Beardsley print that struck me as too risqué for the workplace, but which Allison promptly hung on the wall of the front room, where she greeted visitors. I reminded myself to take it down when my parents came by.

The high point of the party was when the Ravons played us a tape they had recorded in their rehearsal space of "Mary vs. Mary," the song I had watched them write a month earlier. It was miles ahead of any music they had ever made before. I could not have explained it then, but what affected me, what affected everyone at the party, was the crispness and assurance of the performance, the feeling that every note, every beat, was in its perfect place.

Recently I listened to the song again, on an iPod, and I recognized how impeccably arranged it was—the way each instrument did exactly what it needed to do and no more—the way the pulsing eighth notes of an electric guitar on the verses reinforced the bass line and opened into a jangle of triumphant twelve-string on the bridge. Each time a section came around it gained something—a vocal harmony, a bit of maracas, a swell of organ—to make it sweeter. Every little bit was in concert with every other bit and together it all felt spontaneous and inevitable.

When the song finished playing everyone clapped and cheered and Allison ran to play it again. We must have listened to "Mary vs. Mary" twelve times that night. We knew what it meant. We had a hit, a real hit. The Ravons were going to get bigger and better. I could walk into BEI to renegotiate their recording contract armed with dynamite.

"It's all down to LaSalle," Charlie said of the group's new sound. "He's been working us like a boxing coach!"

Fin, who usually stood outside the Ravons looking in, was effusive about the magician from New Orleans.

"He made us sit and listen to all these R&B records," the drummer said. "Ray Charles, Motown, even 'Heartbreak Hotel' and 'Jailhouse Rock.' He makes us play along and he shows me stuff I never noticed—like how some of those drummers lift the stick off the hi-hat when they hit the snare on the four. At first I didn't get it, but he does things like make me and Simon play a whole song without guitars or vocals and really listen to our parts. He opens your ears."

Emerson told Fin to tell me about the Monkees. "That almost caused a rebellion among some of our more stubborn pupils," Emerson said.

Fin nodded toward Simon, who was across the room chatting up one of Allison's friends. The drummer said, "We're all digging this R&B stuff, and one day LaSalle makes us sit there and listen to the Monkees. At first we thought it was a put-on. Simon got mad. LaSalle says, 'That is an elegant drum part, Mr. Potts. Listen better.' Simon said he had nothing to learn from Micky Dolenz and LaSalle says, 'Do your ears tell you that is Micky Dolenz? Interesting. It may be the New Orleans in my upbringing causing audio illusions, but that certainly sounds to me like the great Earl Palmer.' As soon as he said that, we all started hearing the song differently. He makes us listen to just the tambourine and cymbals and, man, then he asks me to play just that percussion part, feel it from the inside. It was like a light went on for me, you know? LaSalle hears music more purely than anyone I ever met. It's like he has X-ray ears."

This reminded Emerson of another housewarming gift. He presented me with a small violet bundle tied with twine. "Monsieur LaSalle sent you a gift for the new office, Jack."

I opened it—an hourglass about the size of two teacups in a silver frame. The sand looked like brown sugar. I turned it over and sat it on Allison's desk.

"I will write him a thank-you note on our new Nevermore stationery," I said.

"He gave us each one," Charlie said. "Look, I'm wearing mine." He reached under his shirt and jacket and pulled up a tiny hourglass hanging across his heart from a thin chain around his neck. Charlie grinned and told us, "LaSalle says it will bring me luck."

He was right about that. LaSalle never said the luck would be good.

"Mary vs. Mary" was our ticket to glory. When BEI heard it they agreed to sign the Ravons directly to the mother label, on slightly better terms than what Dennis Towsy had negotiated for himself. We spent most of the Summer of Love in a recording studio in Barnes, working on the Ravons' second album. The Beatles were on television singing "All You Need Is Love" to the whole planet in the first global satellite broadcast. In America kids were packing up their Volkswagen buses and driving to San Francisco to put flowers in their hair.

There were probably days when we felt the party was going on without us, but the Ravons had a strong work ethic. They were determined to make an album that would earn them entrance to the upper echelon. Whenever the group's spirits got down, one of them would say, "Let's get Mary in here!" and the engineer would pump "Mary vs. Mary" through the studio speakers and the Ravons would cheer up. They knew they had a hit in their pocket.

During my leave of absence I developed a new relationship with Difford, Withers. I visited the office once a week. I no longer dressed like a middle-aged barrister. I wore the smart suits and colored shirts and ties appropriate to a young man comfortable in the London music world. The partners did not complain and the office girls liked it. I was the firm's ambassador to the new pop industry.

The Ravons' second album was finished in August and released in September. "Mary vs. Mary" became a top five hit. Offers arrived for the group to play on television, on BBC radio programs, and to tour Europe.

We spent September and October playing all over the UK, and doing every television and radio program that would have us on every corner of the island. We had a one-week break right after Halloween, two days back in the studio, and then a month-long tour of Germany,

Belgium, Denmark, and Holland, ending with three nights at a theater in Paris. The Ravons insisted I come along to learn the ropes and share in the glory.

The schedule was mad—we would arrive in a country and go straight to a radio station or newspaper interview or to sign autographs at a record store. Many days we would do all three. From there we might get to stop at a hotel long enough to have a bath, or we might go straight to the venue, where the boys would change into their stage clothes and play. There would usually be four or five acts on a bill, with the Ravons in first or second headline position in most of the towns. Often there would be two or three half-hour sets a night, with a new audience brought in for each. In Holland we played a matinee in The Hague in the afternoon, then took a train to Amersfoort for two shows that evening, after which we climbed in our van and barreled down the road toward Antwerp, Tug at the wheel.

In Dresden, Germany, the crowd seemed to be almost entirely boys, and testosterone aroused a passion that turned into aggression as the band played. From the wings I saw fists being thrown, and chairs pulled up and broken. I hoped the band would read the situation and play some slower songs, but they were boys themselves and the smell of violence excited them into playing louder, more aggressively. Angry policemen appeared at the edge of the stage holding back barking German shepherds. The dogs howled at the crowd above the band's amplified wailing. The boys in the crowd raged back at the dogs. The police struggled to hold the leashes, their own faces full of fury and confusion. Finally the theater's owner, appalled at what was happening to his old concert hall, raised the house lights and pulled the plug on the show. The fans responded by ripping up the rest of the seats and hurling them toward the stage.

In the dressing room I found the Ravons laughing like vandals. I went outside to a field in back of the venue to smoke a cigarette and saw one of the policemen dragging his dog on a chain across the muddy grass. The dog was barking frantically, spinning and pulling, getting tangled in its leash. When they were about a hundred yards into the meadow, the cop pulled out his pistol and shot the dog in the head. In my shock I imagined that the dog's frantic barking continued for a moment after the shot.

I stood in the dark and watched the policeman unchain the dog's collar and leave its body in the field. He came back toward the concert hall rubbing his hands as if he were over a sink. He was startled when he saw me.

He asked who I was in German and I told him in English I was with the band.

"The dog went mad from the noise," he said as if answering an accusation. "He was a good dog but your bedlam ruined him."

As the tour progressed, more police dogs were made mad and put down because of our din.

On the road the band lived on sandwiches, pills, and alcohol. They laughed all the time. Even Simon seemed like good company, his usual grumpiness flattened into a stoic determination to get to the gig on time, keep everyone on schedule, and play as well as he could.

It must have been Amsterdam where I took drugs for the first time. Simon and Charlie and I were sitting on a wall by the canal talking about the future when Simon took out a small pipe and lit a chunk of hashish. I became fretful, insisting he put it away. "No one here cares, mate," he said, offering me the stem of the pipe. I said no, thank you, and gave it back to Simon. Three young women who could not have all had red hair but that's how I remember them came up on bicycles and asked if they could have some. Simon passed them the pipe and the three girls inhaled like scuba divers and giggled and asked if we were a group.

The pipe went around and around. Not one passerby seemed bothered by the ritual. The girls wanted to know if they could come to our show. The hash did not seem to be causing them any problem. I wondered why I was being such a prude. The next time the pipe passed through my hands I took a little tug and passed it on. No one said anything about it. Charlie and Simon were competing to be worldly and charming.

When the pipe came back I took a longer drag and held it in. I did not cough or hack or have any adverse reaction. I was a natural. I did not feel high, but the girls certainly seemed to be getting prettier and the Ravons wittier and the twilight falling over Amsterdam more beautiful.

By the time we were all back in the hotel room Charlie was sharing with Fin, I was fascinated by the effect the hashish was having on my powers of observation. I noticed that the threads in the bedspread formed a pattern like a barbed-wire fence, and that the wrinkles in the fabric looked a bit like cows, bulls, and goats. It was not a hallucination, it was simply a playful observation. I felt like a child lying on his back on a summer day looking up at the shapes in the clouds.

I turned my attention to the wallpaper, which had a series of patterns that reminded me alternately of Greek urns and Navajo blankets. It came to me that there were many similarities between the American Indians and the Greek tribes. I thought this was an observation worth sharing with the room. I suppose I interrupted some other conversation to announce, "Did you ever think that the Spartans were a lot like the Apaches and the Cherokees were like the Athenians?"

The conversation stopped while Charlie, Simon, and the girls stared at me as if I had just levitated up through the floor. Charlie said, "No more hash for Johnny Flynn."

Everyone laughed and I felt annoyed. It was not as if I did not know I was high. When a stoned person makes an observation about, say, the fact that his thumbprint seems to be swirling like a whirlpool, he knows the ridges in his skin are not really turning. He is simply telling you what it looks like to him. It's no different from someone telling you about a dream he just had. It doesn't mean he believes the dream really happened. With more experience I learned that no one wants to hear about your drug insights or your dreams.

There were lots of girls on the road. It was as if they could walk through walls. They appeared in dressing rooms, in hotel rooms, at roadside restaurants. I had no idea that so many young women were eager to have sex with boys they knew only from photos in fan magazines. At first I looked down on the cavalier way the Ravons took advantage of these invitations, but I got used to it. The girls were more forward than the musicians. It was my first understanding of how great the change in our culture was going to be.

During a Ravons show at a ballroom in the suburbs of Copenhagen I wandered outside the venue to have a smoke and rest my ears. I leaned up against the van and thought I felt an earthquake. I jumped forward and realized that the ground was stable, it was the van that was shaking. For a moment I thought it was going to explode. I went around to the windscreen and peered inside. What I saw haunted my sleep for years. It was the naked, hairy, puckered, pimpled backside of big Tug Bitler heaving up and down like a dirty plunger struggling to clear a stuffed drain.

I stumbled away from the van and tried with trembling fingers to light another cigarette. I stood there inhaling smoke as the van door slid open with a bang and a tall girl in a miniskirt planted one go-go boot and then another in the mud and stepped away, straightening the brassiere beneath her jumper. She was not a pretty girl—few of the women who offered themselves to the band were beauty queens—but I could not imagine any woman with four limbs and functioning eyesight subjecting herself to the amorous attentions of Tug.

I kept watching as she strutted back to the hall to see the rest of the concert. At length, Tug emerged from the van and stood in the moonlight coughing and spitting, buttoning his pants and buckling his belt. He saw me looking at him.

"Tasty bit of crumpet," Tug said to me. He stuck out his tongue and wiggled it. Lord, I prayed, blind me now. Tug loomed toward me and spoke in a hoarse stage whisper: "I'm leaning on the van, having a nightcap. This bird comes up to me and says, 'Is Emerson Cutler in that bus?' I says, 'He was an hour ago, and he will be again as soon as they finish in there.' She says, 'Can I get in and see what it's like?' I says, 'Well, that depends. What would you do if you could be alone with Emerson Cutler?' She says, 'I'd let him put it in all the way.' I says, 'Well, I'm Emerson's best friend. If I let you come in the bus will you let me put it in all the way?' She says, 'Well, maybe just halfway, for a minute.' I says, 'Darlin', a minute's all I need.' I let her in the van, I give her one of the promo pictures of Emerson to look at, I put on the tape recorder with 'Mary vs. Mary,' and we have at it."

I felt the need to drink a bottle of rum very quickly to extinguish these details before they burned into my memory forever. Tug grunted and wiped his mouth and said, "The best thing is, I'm pounding away at 'er, sensitive to the time limit, when she starts groanin' and says, 'All right, put it in the rest of the way!' That gave me pause. I said, 'Darlin', it's in all the way already.'"

I congratulated Tug on his romantic conquest and got myself into the dressing room and started drinking. I was a quarter of the way into a bottle of red wine when the music ended and the band, sweating and happy, piled into the room. I had to convince myself of what I saw–the same tall girl in the go-go boots was now attached to Charlie. How did she intercept him between the stage and the dressing room? It was only twenty-five feet. Then I saw that Tug had given her a backstage pass. Method of payment.

I kept drinking and when it was time for us to pile into the van and leave I sat up front with Tug, away from the fresh stains I imagined in the back. Charlie was late joining us and we got caught in post-concert traffic.

"Where did you vanish to, then?" Simon admonished him as we sat stalled in a row of red taillights. "We been waiting half an hour!"

"Sorry, brothers," Charlie said with a smile. "I was introducing that young lady in the white boots to the ecstasies of Lydle's biggie."

Tug, clutching the wheel, laughed like gravel in a blender. I thought I would never have the heart to tell Charlie what polluted waters he had plunged into, although many years later, sitting on a patio in Barbados smoking ganja, I finally did. When I told him he had dipped his oar into Tug's puddle, he blinked and said, "I don't remember the Ravons ever playing in Denmark."

To be a group of young friends away from home in a foreign coun-try is a joy each new generation makes for itself. Middle-aged men of my father's time enjoyed a strange nostalgia for their army days, even if the war was full of horrors. People look back on university as if they missed taking tests and writing term papers. It is exhilarating to be on the road with your mates, far from Mum and Dad. It promises that after the insecurities of adolescence, the adult world is going to be full of new possibilities.

Years later, we would complain about the hardship of flying on private jets and staying in luxury hotels. You would have thought to hear us then that spending a week in a Tuscan villa was a burden like crossing the desert in a covered wagon. But in 1967 we were delighted to be bouncing through Holland in the back of a van that smelled of sweat, socks, and beer. We didn't need sleep and we could suck nutrition from a pack of cigarettes and a bottle of wine.

I was happy to be away from Difford, Withers, away from London, in such company and possessed of a reason to be there. I was the Ravons' manager! It did not take me long to assume an air of authority with the club owners and concert promoters I met on the road. Tug and the band knew most of these characters from previous trips. We all agreed that it was in the group's best interest for me to come on as assured and perhaps a bit aloof. None of us was certain what any of the locals' relationship with Dennis Towsy had been—victims, partners, or coconspirators. We did not want to be seen as pushovers. We wanted them to look at me and think, There's a new sheriff in town.

I look back now and know that they thought nothing of me at all. I might as well have been delivering beer, except the man who brought the beer supplied more of what made them money.

Rock groups did not play in many proper nightclubs in those days, as few rock fans were old enough to drink alcohol. We played ballrooms and theaters and once in Bruges in a circus tent. Many of the rooms where the Ravons performed were tawdry, not much more than skating rinks, but sometimes we found ourselves in a beautiful old theater or opera house. The girls usually screamed, the boys stood back with their arms folded, and the public address system was always inadequate. We didn't care. We were enjoying our good fortune, which I think we all assumed would last for a year or two if we were lucky. If a psychic had shown us that the ride we were on would last for forty years, Charlie might have been happy, but the rest of us would have been horrified.

We drove across northern Europe in one of a series of Commer vans that the Ravons would run into the ground. This was a sort of mutated milk truck in which we had piled an old mattress and a couple of blankets, along with the amps, guitars, and drums. I usually rode in the back with three of the Ravons. Tug drove. Emerson or Simon took the seat next to him.

Now Europe is unified by treaty, currency, and franchise restaurants, but in the late sixties the difference between each country was profound. Just ordering a glass of warm, bitter milk reminded you that you were far from home.

The Dutch were friendly, still grateful for England's role in the liberation. The Germans were wild, loud, demanding, and sometimes belligerent in a way that reminded me of Americans. I am not sure whether the young generation of Germans were shaped by the U.S. occupation, or if the German character influenced the American personality more than was usually acknowledged. When I got to know Texas and the Midwest, I understood how the English language has masked the profound German strain in the United States.

It was all new to me then. I put on a façade of sophistication that melted into wide-eyed wonder when we arrived in Paris. Paris made me feel like a hillbilly.

We were booked into a large and ramshackle hotel on the Left Bank. Tug navigated the van through the narrow streets with no regard at all to the automobiles he scraped as he passed. I was astonished that he found a parking place directly across the street from our destination.

I should say here that as a general principle Tug would park anywhere—in an alley, on a sidewalk, blocking a driveway—and simply rip up and toss away any tickets, notices, summonses, or warrants he found when he returned. These were the days before computers, when police departments in one city had no way of sharing routine information with other cities. The only chance you would pay a penalty for being a scofflaw was if you lived in the vicinity. If you lived in another country, you effectively had immunity from misdemeanor prosecution. I miss those days.

Paris was the end of the tour. We had three shows and a couple of interviews spread over five days. After the one-night stands of the previous two weeks, we felt as if we were on holiday. We dropped our gear in our rooms and headed out to see the town.

Emerson went to look up a girlfriend. Simon wanted Tug to drive him to some destination of which he would not speak. Charlie, Fin, and I set out to walk to the Eiffel Tower. Illuminated in the night sky, it looked like a close stroll. An hour later we were still tramping along. When we finally arrived we rode the lift to the restaurant, ordered chips and Cokes, and stood out by the rail looking at the city of lights.

"I can't believe I'm up on the Eiffel Tower," Fin said. "I mean, holy shit, right? My mom's never even been on an airplane, and look at me. Because I play the friggin' drums. Everything they told me in school was a waste of time—drums, cool clothes, chasing chicks, rock and roll—turned out to be how I make my living, and all the shit they told me would be so important—algebra, civics, biology—has never come up again."

Charlie looked at his American drummer and said, "French would have been good, though."

The next day we got up at one in the afternoon, determined to do something memorable with a free day in Paris. Fin had gone off with an Italian girl he somehow met while the rest of us were sleeping. Simon, Charlie, Emerson, and I had breakfast—coffee and a basket of bread—at a cheap café and then wandered up the Champs-Élysées. We stood in line to go up to the roof of the Arc de Triomphe. When we reached the top we stood heroically, as if we were posing for an album cover. Below us, hundreds of taxicabs and motor scooters rotated through the roundabouts and swept in and out of the tunnel through the arch. Charlie was hypnotized by the swirling traffic patterns.

"How can anyone look at that and not believe in an unseen hand?" Charlie asked.

Simon snorted. Emerson laughed and said, "Only our kid can find the hand of God in Paris traffic."

Charlie looked abashed but it was an act. He had a way of making cosmic pronouncements slowly, like a wondering child. He would emphasize the Cockney in his voice when he said these things, perhaps to defuse the ponderousness.

"But look at it, fellas," he said. "It's like a ballet. How do all those cars and bikes keep from colliding? How does the city function? Thousands of drivers, all lost in their own thoughts, seeing only what's right in front of them. Thousands of pedestrians crossing the roads, traffic lights changing, people darting out, bicycles, lorries. Yet the traffic flows, the cars don't collide, the people get home alive. And we don't even think about how miraculous it all is."

Simon said, "Smoke all the pot, then, did you?"

Charlie laughed. He was ever the urchin. As an adult he was only about five foot four and frail-looking, with big eyes so dark they often seemed black. I imagined an eight-year-old Charlie with holes in his clothes tugging at the sleeves of London tourists and asking for tuppence to feed the birds. With the young women who followed the band he could play either the rowdy rocker or the sensitive, wide-eyed boy, depending on how he read his audience.

I looked at the traffic. A small blue automobile slammed on the brakes to avoid hitting a businessman who had run out in the road to flag a cab. The driver of the car leaned out his window, hurling insults with the Parisian gusto for invective. Crediting God with French traffic patterns might be blasphemy, but I admired Charlie's sense of wonder.

Simon's attention fell on the great white cathedral dome on the hill overlooking Paris. He suggested we go up there, to Montmartre, the artists' colony, and blend in with the bohemians. Charlie said that was comfortably close to the Moulin Rouge, where he could perhaps rekindle a spark with a cancan girl he had met his last time through.

Tug was unreported. No one knew what became of Tug when he was off duty. I figured he was somewhere strangling a poodle.

The four of us took the tube to Montmartre, the great mount overlooking the city, and walked around glassy-eyed trying to make wise observations about the paintings, many of which made extreme use of black backgrounds and severe light, achieving an effect somewhere between Rembrandt and black velvet cheesecake pictures.

Simon had a fancy German camera with a leather strap that he wore around his neck. He snapped photos of the paintings as if he were a compatriot artiste studying the limitations of his fellows. Charlie suggested we go into Sacré-Coeur Cathedral and have a look.

As we walked into the basilica I blessed myself and Simon clicked his tongue. A colossal mosaic of the resurrected Jesus stretched out His arms to us. Charlie pointed up at the huge dome twelve stories above us. "It's great, isn't it?" he whispered. "Can you even think what it must have meant to a peasant a hundred years ago to come in here and see this glory? That's where equality and liberty really began, Jack. In the cathedrals. Common folks said, 'I am a part of this, too!'"

Simon scoffed. "So they gave up the coins that could have fed their hungry children for the glory of an invisible God."

Charlie shrugged. "Maybe worth as much as giving up their coins for the glory of rock and roll, eh, Simon? Nothing we ever do, nothing any musician ever does, is gonna move hearts the way this cathedral did."

Simon snorted and pointed his camera toward the marble altar, before which many rows of the faithful were praying and saying rosaries. A cleric stepped out of an alcove and reprimanded him, pointing to a sign on the wall in five languages: "No photographique!"

Simon scowled and lowered his camera.

"Come on," he said, pointing to an opening in the stone wall, "let's leave the sheep to their grazing and go upstairs and look at the view."

We followed him into a winding stone staircase that rose forever. We were young and strong, but after fifteen minutes I began to puff. We were turning up, up, up. Simon, his long legs spanning two steps at a time, refused to pause at any of the landings. Schoolboy pride kept the rest of us on his tail.

We came out, breathing through our mouths, at a thick wooden rail that protected tourists from falling out of a wide-open floor-to-ceiling vista framing all of Paris. I was dizzy as I looked down. I thought of Tug dangling me from Dennis's window and closed my eyes and took a step back.

The Ravons were wowing and whistling at the view when Simon said, "Look here! This door's open!" He pushed through a little hatch and we followed him out onto the roof of the building.

My vertigo was challenged by the greatest panorama I had ever seen. Sacré-Coeur was the highest point in the city, and we were perched on the roof.

It was as if we were in heaven looking down at the whole history of civilization. Webs of small white and sand-colored buildings that might have been from ancient Athens spun out toward the river, progressing into marble monuments that could have been raised by Rome to honor Caesar. Dark cathedral towers speared up from the pale architecture like the advent of the Christian era, to be challenged by the modernist icons, the Eiffel Tower and the Trocadero. In the distance, the skyscrapers of high capitalism erupted out of the landscape like metal volcanoes, threatening every opposing philosophy. It was a map of history but it was not sequential. All of these eras and ideas existed simultaneously in the Paris landscape, along with Egyptian obelisks, Arab mosques, and NATO antennae. I felt looking down on it as if all cultures and social systems were presenting themselves for our approval, inviting us to pick the politics we wanted to embrace, the ethics we wanted to live by, the kind of art we wanted to make, the sort of people we wanted to become.

We were young men of talent and potential and the world was laid out before us like a feast. I remember thinking, This is the best my life will ever be. Five years later I thought that enthusiasm naïve. Forty years later I believe I was right on the money.

Simon headed across the rooftop like the gorilla in the Rue Morgue, following a twisting one-foot-in-front-of-the-other walkway between the sloped eaves. We were young and stupid. We followed. We came to an unlikely set of metal fire stairs that clung to the outside wall of the dome. We climbed them, expecting to hear a police whistle at any moment. I had stopped looking down; to keep my balance I hung close to the wall and kept moving up, up, up on what was either Eliot's "Ash Wednesday" ascent or the stairway to heaven.

Simon called ahead of us, "I've got a way in!"

Sure enough, he had found another door, shorter than he was and made of water-damaged wood. He gave a shove and it opened and we found ourselves in a small belfry at the very pinnacle of the great dome of the Cathedral of the Sacred Heart.

Emerson put his fingers on the rail and leaned carefully over. I summoned the courage to do the same. We were ninety meters above the altar rail, looking straight down onto the tops of the distant heads of the worshippers. A choir was singing the "Ave Maria." Mass had begun.

"Oh–my–God," Emerson said.

"We ain't supposed to be here, men," I said. I began to silently say an Act of Contrition.

Charlie announced, "Boys, we have now truly made it to the top. This could be an album cover! Simon, give your camera to Jack and let's get a picture."

"Wait," Simon said. He was leaning over the rail at a dangerous angle, pointing his new camera down into the church below. "I don't think that annoying monk will stop me from taking a few snaps now!"

"Better not, Simon," I said.

"Don't worry, Jack," Simon said, one eye closed and clicking away like he was in *Blowup,* "you can blame this all on me when you go to confession."

There were four of us there and we all remembered what happened next the same way. There was a whoosh of wind through the door we had forced open and Simon let out a little cry.

"What's wrong?" Emerson asked him.

Simon was moving his lips but no noise came out.

Charlie wanted to know what was up. Simon squeaked out, "The camera . . ."

"Oh hell, he's dropped the camera!"

"Oh no!"

We all leaned over the rail. The mass was moving along, the worshippers were in their places below us, nothing had changed.

Simon gasped, "I had the strap around my neck, I was holding it with both hands . . . It was like someone pulled it away from me . . ."

"Where is it now?" I wanted to know.

"Must be down there," Emerson said.

"I didn't hear it hit," Charlie said.

"Well, it's a long way down."

"We'd hear it. Someone down there would react."

"What if it hit someone?" Simon was white. "From this height!"

Charlie looked over the rail. "No sign of that. Must have landed on a ledge or a parapet partway down."

That was the point at which the camera hit the floor. A crash rang through the cathedral like a bomb had come through the dome. It echoed all the way up to the small curved rail where we stood. We looked at each other and we began to run. We ran out the little door, down the metal steps, and over the steep roof. We were horrified. We entered the long stairwell to the ground floor and ran like we were coming down an avalanche, all the way back to the church. We tumbled out of the stone doorway expecting to be arrested or beaten by an angry mob, but the mass continued, the low murmuring of the priest's prayers and the congregation's responses filling the enormous room. We moved cautiously into the center aisle, like ushers, and crept along, looking down each crowded row, into each pew, until I came to an old woman in a head scarf and peasant black, bent over her beads. On the floor next to her was the flat, twisted remnant of what had been an expensive German camera.

I bent down to scrape it off the tiles. She glanced at me and asked, *"Qu'est?"*

"A camera," I whispered.

"L'appareil photographique?" she said.

"Oui, oui," I said. *"Appareil photographique."* She shook her head as if to say, *I don't think the warranty is going to cover that.* I nodded and hurried back down the aisle, gesturing to the others.

We met in the back, by the souvenir stand.

"She wasn't hurt," I told Simon, who was shaking. "No one was hurt."

"Unbelievable!" Charlie said, trying to hold his excitement down to a whisper. "All those people and it landed right between them! You got blessed with a miracle today, Simon! We all did."

"I swear, I had the strap around my neck," Simon insisted.

"Let's go," Emerson said. "Count ourselves lucky."

My father had told me as a boy to always try to light a candle when I visited a new church for the first time. I dropped some coins in the slot and took a long wick and lit a candle in Sacré-Coeur and blessed myself.

Simon did not object.

Shaken by the Miracle of Our Camera of Sacré-Coeur, we decided to walk back to our hotel. That turned out to be a terrible idea. After two hours we were lost and exhausted but could find neither a taxi nor a Métro entrance.

"I don't want to scare anyone," Charlie announced, "but I'm pretty sure we just crossed into Belgium."

"There's a cab!" Simon cried as a beat-up Paris taxi pulled over a block away from us and across the road. He lunged through the traffic to grab it before someone else did. We caught up with him by the door of the cab, forming a possessive quadrant. We waited for the woman in the backseat to pay the driver and get out. We waited a long time.

An argument broke out between the driver and the passenger. They were shouting at each other in a fast obscene French that none of us could understand. All we cared about was that no one else get the cab.

The driver threw open his door and stalked out into the street. He came around to our side of the car and yanked open the rear passenger door. He reached in, red-faced, and dragged the woman out of the taxi by her arm.

"Hey, hey, *ami*!" Charlie said, "no need for all that, now!"

The driver ignored us. The woman had her knee in the gutter, trying to regain her feet while the driver held on to her wrist and shook her, shouting. The woman was around forty and she looked out of whack, perhaps drunk, perhaps a bit crazy. Whatever she was, she did not deserve this.

Simon put his hand on the driver's shoulder. "Take it easy, man," he said.

The driver lashed around at him with his teeth exposed and his eyes bugging. "Piss off, fucking English!" He knocked Simon's hand away and went back to shaking the woman, whose belligerence had turned to panic.

Emerson said, "I'm going to go call a cop," and vanished.

Simon grabbed the driver by his hair and shouted, "Hey, shithead! Let her alone or I'm going to cripple you!"

The driver dropped the woman's arm and she scrambled to the sidewalk. He reached under the seat and came around with a six-inch chunk of pipe and waved it at Simon's nose. "You want to fight? Want to fight?" I was trying to get around the woman to slam into the geezer from the side before he could brain Simon when the taxi lurched forward. The driver got whacked by the open door. Simon and I jumped back.

Charlie was driving the cab. He pulled forward about ten feet, slammed on the brakes, rolled down the passenger window, and called, "Who wants to go for a spin, then?"

The driver forgot about the woman, forgot about fighting Simon, and ran after his automobile. Charlie let him get his hand on the back door handle and then pulled away again, honking the horn and laughing.

The driver was screaming in French for Charlie to get out of his car. Charlie kept letting him get close and then shooting away. He saw Emerson coming down the road toward him and pulled forward, honking the horn. Emerson looked up, saw Charlie in the cab, saw a mad Frenchman hurtling toward them waving a piece of pipe, and jumped into the taxi. Emerson and Charlie sped off down the road, the bellowing driver chasing after them.

I looked at Simon. He said, "They'll come back for us as soon as they ditch the mad frog." We helped the dazed woman to her feet, brushed her off, and escorted her to the doorway of an apartment building where she rang a buzzer and went inside.

We ordered hot chocolates and smoked cigarettes for about ten minutes, at the end of which Charlie and Emerson pulled up in their French taxicab and said they'd give us a lift back to the hotel. Eventually we got there, after breaking many traffic laws, fleeing a fender-bender with a lorry, and circling around the Eiffel Tower to get our bearings.

We parked the cab on a sidewalk near Notre Dame, just a short distance from our digs.

"I'm sure the cops will get Frenchie's taxi back to him," I said.

"Yeah, but the bastard will have some fines to pay," Simon said, nodding.

"Hey, you freeloaders!" Charlie shouted. "Who's going to settle this fare?"

He pointed to the meter. Someone owed fifteen hundred francs.

The Paris gigs changed the way the Ravons saw themselves. The band headlined a bill with Alexis Korner and two French yeah yeah acts in an ornate old theater where, the promoter promised us, Napoleon the Third used to attend the opera. By the time we got home we had dropped "the Third" from the telling.

There was a party in a saloon after the first show to which our French agent invited seven gorgeous girls of many nationalities, all of whom he introduced as his nieces. We invited them back to our hotel, where the party continued until morning. Each of the nieces ended up with at least one Ravon.

I spent an intense night rolling around with a beautiful young woman from Uganda. She had perfect ebony skin and spoke careful English. In the morning she asked me so many questions about how she could go about getting an entry visa for England that I began to feel ill-used. At breakfast she asked about which plane we were taking to London, what sort of house I lived in, whether I had a car, and if I would teach her to drive it. Her presumptuousness made me annoyed and nervous. She was as affectionate as if we were newlyweds and I began to worry that by the customs of her culture we might be.

I finally said, "Dora, you know you can't come home with us, right?" Her expression flattened; she let go of my hand, got up from the table, and walked out into the hotel to look for another sponsor.

All three concerts in Paris were wild, and the climax came with the final show. It was pandemonium. The Ravons had known screaming girls, of course. That was just ritual. But as 1967 began to descend toward 1968 the girls were growing up and the context in which rock was heard was changing.

Rock—no longer pop, no longer even rock and roll—was being

pressed into service as the telegraph wire for the student revolts, the anti-Vietnam War movement, the drug culture, and the advocates of Eastern mysticism. Musicians who were wholly unqualified to speak on any subject more complex than the mechanics of the wah-wah pedal aspired to earn credibility by paying lip service to all sorts of esoteric philosophies of which they understood nothing.

The Ravons were not intellectuals—although Simon aspired to an intellectual's pomposity—but they did have acute antennae for picking up waves of change. In the spring of 1967 they had all experienced a simultaneous widening of their belts, cuffs, watchbands, and sideburns, apparently without consultation, like a herd of deer who rush to high country just before a flood. It surprised me when they all came back from separate holidays having grown identical facial hair, and it impressed me more when a couple of months later boys all over Europe and America sprouted the same mustaches and sideburns.

When Emerson got an expensive new guitar, he started wearing his belt buckle on his hip, to avoid its scratching the back of his instrument. Charlie and Simon picked up on that and slid their buckles over, too. By autumn teenage boys all over England were buckling their belts on the side. The Ravons were not intellectuals, but they were very accurate weather vanes.

The group's collective compass was pointing toward seriousness of intention, leftist political rhetoric, and an illusion of social engagement. Their music began to lose some of its childlike melodiousness and drive harder. They were playing for the boys as much as the girls.

Many groups lost their footing in the rapids that rushed down between the shores of 1967 and 1968. It was a dangerous moment. Play it too safe and you were condemned to be thrown into kiddie oblivion with Freddie and the Dreamers. Take it too far and you would no more get on the radio than the Mothers of Invention. The Rolling Stones handled it perfectly, declaring themselves street-fighting men whose mission was to play in a rock and roll band. They grew in credibility as well as commercial success. The Animals began to lose old fans without picking up enough new ones.

Paris was a great place for the Ravons, in part because the newly radical kids there did not speak English very well and therefore drew whatever implications they wanted from the group's beat and attitude.

If they chose to believe the Ravons were revolutionaries shaking the walls of the Bastille, all they had to do was fix on Simon's sullen anger and Emerson's burning guitar. If they preferred to believe the Ravons were romantic rogues come to ravish them, it was an equally credible interpretation.

It was clear from the first song that the last French show was going to be the best. It was the final gig of the tour. The boys did not have to save their voices, spare their fingers, or conserve any energy for the next day. They howled through their repertoire with a mania that reflected the excitement radiating off the audience. The band performed what was normally a fifty-minute set in not much more than half an hour, waved a sweaty good-bye, and were brought back for three encores—at a time when encores at rock shows were rarities.

The audience was screaming—not the high-pitched shriek of little girls but the wailing of young men. The police were nervous. A perspiring captain of the gendarmes holding a police dog on a leather leash confronted me in the wings of the stage and told me the group must stop playing at once.

"You want to go out there and tell 'em, mate?" I said. "Be my guest."

The last song ended, the Ravons, laughing and soaked in sweat and adrenaline, moved offstage. They rolled by the policeman and me, oblivious, on their way to the basement dressing room. The gendarme captain shouted to the theater manager to raise the house lights at once and dismiss the crowd.

The lights came up and the kids responded by showering the stage with debris. They clapped and stamped their feet and shouted, "Ray-Vons! Ray-Vons! Ray-Vons!"

The gendarme ordered "La Marseillaise" to be piped into the hall at high volume. The crowd started climbing onto the stage. Tug appeared from the other wing and set about saving the drums.

The police captain's air of authority began to give way to panic. He asked me if the Ravons would come back out and tell the audience to leave quietly. It was my job to relay the request.

I made my way down a green and yellow corridor to a narrow and badly lit flight of stairs that descended into a damp basement with whitewashed stone walls and exposed electrical lines. I followed a trail of mounted steam pipes to the small room in which the Ravons were sitting on folding chairs, wiping their bare chests with their wet shirts and drinking warm beer. The sound of the crowd wailing for them to return was coming through the ceiling, which trembled under four thousand stamping feet. The band was giggling and twitchy.

I explained that the police had requested that someone from the group come back and ask the crowd to disperse.

Charlie said, "We're not going to side with the cops against the kids, Jack! The police want to treat our fans like juvenile delinquents, let 'em deal with the consequences. But we'll go back and *play* for 'em."

I looked to Emerson for common sense but he was wide-eyed and wired: "Tell the goose-steppers we'll go on and play another song for our friends and then we will ask them, with respect, to go home peacefully so no one gets hurt."

I relayed this message to the police captain, whose dog was becoming frantic from the noise of the banshee audience. The cop cursed and told me I would be responsible if a riot ensued. I told him the riot was under way already; he was asking my boys to save the situation.

The police refused to allow the Ravons to lower the house lights when they returned, which only added to the explosion when the fans saw them walking back onstage. I was on the stage now, too, along with eight or nine policemen and the captain with the barking dog. The cops held their billy clubs like conductors' batons.

Simon was hypnotized by the madness and noise in front of him. If he'd had a sword he would have marched his barbarian army out of the theater and started sacking. Charlie and Emerson were laughing uncontrollably as they plugged in their guitars. I heard Charlie shout, "What do we play? We've done every song we know!"

Emerson said, "'Ask Yer Daddy'!" and the band launched into a ragged, noisy, and exuberant version of a song they had written quickly and never played live, the flip side of "Mary vs. Mary."

"Ask Yer Daddy" was not much of a song, a fast boogie with lyrics at the level of, "Ask yer daddy if the Russians invade / Can I help pull the pins on his hand grenade." Charlie and Emerson had spent about as much time writing it as it took to play it.

To the radical university students of Paris, the mention of Russians and hand grenades signified acknowledgment of the poverty of the Western response to the challenge of Marxism. And you could dance to it.

Standing onstage next to the band looking into the heaving crowd gave me a perspective I never had watching from the wings. The kids looked up into the faces of the Ravons with unfiltered emotion. They opened up to them like lovers, revealing their passion, excitement, abandon, and a hundred variations of uninhibited honesty. I was struck by the intensity of their attention. Each face in the crowd gazed at the Ravons the way a new bride looks at her husband.

All the fans, grinning or grimacing, delighted or deranged, shared one quality. They were all desperately sincere. They were as sincere as an orgasm.

It filled me with electricity to stand next to that charge. What must it have done to the musicians to feel it flowing through them? I understood the anxiety that this show of uncurtailed energy inspired in the police. There was exhilarated fury in some of the faces, the raging intensity of the footballer or the arsonist. The police smelled anarchy.

I felt something else, even stronger—a signal carried on the current. I felt joy. Joy in being young and strong and tasting your power coming up in you. Joy in the ecstatic frisson of a community recognizing itself in the mirror of each other's faces. Joy manifesting itself as wild abandon. The Ravons were holding up metal rods in this lightning, calling down the storm, drawing it through steel strings into wire pickups and out of tube amplifiers back into the heart of the combustion. They were forming a loop with the crowd, feeding back their frenzy until everyone recognized his own voice in the roaring.

What chance did the police have against such a circular series of explosions? This blast had been building since World War II. The vibrations began shaking in the molecules of these war babies in the womb. The tuning fork started humming when the tanks rolled into Paris and the London Blitz chased our mothers down under the ground. If you send babies to play in bombed-out rubble you had better be prepared for them to want to upend the world as soon as they get the chance.

I remembered a joke from *A Hard Day's Night*. The stuffy old businessman on the train saying to the Beatles, "I fought the war for your sort!"

Ringo says, "Bet you're sorry you won."

The Ravons extended "Ask Yer Daddy" with guitar solos and

improvised additional verses until the captain of the cops and his dog both snapped their leashes. The balcony swayed as if a wave were passing under it. The applause when they finished exploded like Hitler's bunker.

Emerson thanked them all and asked them to go home in gentleness and peace. The fans cheered his request and dismissed happily.

"Ask Yer Daddy" went on to become the Ravons' all-time biggest hit in France and many years later enjoyed a lucrative second life as a popular theme song at American ball games. This would have nothing to do with references to Russians or hand grenades. It was because the third verse of the song went, "Rounded third, headed for home, boy wonder suffers a broken bone / Crowd explodes as he limps off the field, he's back next game completely healed."

I took it at the time as one more example of the Ravons' unfathomable ability to crowbar fake Americanisms into their lyrics. What did Charlie and Emerson know about U.S. baseball? It was only in the 1990s, when "Ask Yer Daddy" began to generate substantial revenue from American Major League broadcasts, that Emerson explained to me that they had nicked "Rounded third, headed for home" from a Chuck Berry song without knowing exactly what it meant. They were even lucky as plagiarists.

When the last Paris show finally ended and the captain of the gendarmes had left to execute his dog, the small cellar dressing room filled with fans. There was no security left, and the Ravons didn't care. Many of the strangers who crowded the basement room were young women, some attractive. Two very pretty girls who said they were students of political science invited the band back to their flat. We never considered saying no.

Thousands of days are lost to us completely. They pass out of our memories like songs half heard on restaurant radios. A few days stay with us forever. We recall every detail. We remember what people said and wore, what we ate and how it tasted, even the unimportant thoughts that passed through our minds before things got serious.

That's how the day of the bust is for me. No matter how many years go by, it remains vivid.

When that day began, at midnight on December 6, 1967, the four Ravons and I were at an impromptu party at the large apartment of two young women who had come to the last Paris show and their two exotic roommates. There were about twenty other young people there, all dancing in the living room and smoking and drinking wine out of water glasses. There were, in the words of the Beach Boys, two girls for every boy.

As it was the last night of the tour, as we had just played one of our best shows ever, as someone at the party had produced the single of the Ravons singing "Ask Yer Daddy" and had moved the tone arm so it would play over and over, as boys were dancing bare-chested and at least two of the girls had taken off their shirts and were doing the shingaling in their bras, we all drank more than usual. One of the last things I remember was knowing that I was drunk and getting a girl with a big jaw and a big chest to help me copy out four times, *11.OO– GARE DU NORD–PLATFORM 3–TRAIN TO LONDON–DON'T MISS IT!!* I stumbled up to each of the four Ravons and loudly insisted they place this message in their wallets and if they remembered nothing else in the morning, *Do not miss the train home.*

I knew that the five of us would wake up in five different locations while Tug was driving the gear to the English Channel. I would be responsible for making sure the band's effects were out of their rooms and the hotel bill settled. They had to promise to make it to the train station on time, or understand that they would have to get back to London on their own.

Each Ravon took one of my slips of paper and promised not to miss the train. I had performed my last official management function of the tour. I drank something the big-jawed girl promised was absinthe. After that my sequential memories give way to flashes of individual images, some pornographic and one distinctive—a picture of a yellow horse hanging on a blue wall next to a window with a view of the sun coming up over three television aerials arranged like the crosses on Calvary.

I have been to Paris many times since that night. I have never been able to find those three aerials or the flat of the girl with the picture of the yellow horse. If I ever knew her name, I don't know it anymore. For some reason I never understood, though, that image of the view from her room comes to me all the time. I can't remember anything else about it. I must have been happy there.

At ten forty-five the next morning I was alone with eight suitcases on the sidewalk outside the Paris train station. It was very cold and I was shaking from the low temperature and a cruel hangover. In fact, it would have been premature to declare it a hangover; I was still drunk. I was trying to force my mind to focus on my options. If none of the band showed up should I still get on the train with all the bags? Or as manager was I obligated to wait until I could shepherd at least two of them home?

It was a great relief when Charlie and Simon came around the corner, bearing coffees and croissants and the news that they had seen Emerson saying good-bye to the two exotic roommates over by the taxi stand. It is unkind but accurate to say that none of us considered Fin the American drummer a full Ravon. He was a nice kid but if he missed the train, tough shit.

Emerson joined us, as cheerful as if he'd slept twelve hours in his childhood bed. I had our tickets. The four of us picked up the bags and headed toward the first-class car. We found an empty compartment with four seats, two by two, facing each other. We shoved our suitcases into the overhead racks and lit cigarettes and I promised myself a good sleep all the way to Calais.

Charlie tapped the window glass and said, "Here comes Fin." He rapped harder and waved, apparently getting the drummer's attention. I did not open my eyes. Charlie said, "And look, here comes Mrs. Fin."

I leaned forward. Danny Finnerty was running along the side of the train, holding hands with a black woman. I focused. Why was the woman carrying a large duffel bag? It was not part of our luggage, I was sure of that. I lost sight of them. The train whistle sounded. There was a preliminary rumbling of the carriage as the power came on. A moment later, Fin, all smiles and American surfer bonhomie, leaned into our coach.

"Ravers!" He laughed. "Afraid I was gonna miss you guys! Good thing the traps keep me in top shape, I just ran the mile! You guys remember Dora!"

How Dora managed to track down Fin between the time I last saw him at the French girls' party and this morning was a mystery I did not care to fathom. But it was clear she had found a new pigeon to get her into England.

Dora looked at me cautiously. I said nothing. If Fin wanted to bring her home, that was her good luck and his business. I just wanted to sleep. Fin said, "Well, we better go find a place to sit." He and Dora moved down the corridor. The Frenchest of train conductors came through, gave us a suspicious sneer, asked for our tickets, and—seeing that we were not the vagabonds he took us for but really did belong in first class—punched our billets, clicked his heels, and touched his fingers to the bill of his cap.

"They do respect authority," Simon said with bleary contempt.

Charlie replied, "It's why they make such great collaborators."

I was not aware of sleeping on the ride to the coast but I must have, because it seemed like only ten minutes later that a different conductor came by and announced it was time to pick up our luggage and move to the boat.

My age is catching up with me again. I have to explain how we were traveling. There was no uninterrupted Paris-to-London train service in those days. The Chunnel was not yet dug or dreamed of and Europe was not yet a collection of borderless frontiers. In the sixties you purchased your ticket in Paris and took a train to Calais on the coast, then crossed the channel on a ferry, produced your passport and cleared British customs in Dover, and boarded another train to London. It was a long and unpleasant journey.

Space age as we were, we had elected to cross the waters not on one of the old ferries but on the super-modern Jetsons-here-we-come hydrofoil. Everyone was very excited by the notion that we would not be plowing through the water but rather shooting above it on a cushion of air. We were a hot young rock group riding across the waves on a hydrofoil! How bloody modern could you get?

By the time the boat shook off from shore I was feeling better and went looking for a sandwich. I saw Fin and Dora huddled against the windows of the second level, whispering and kissing. It bothered me a bit that he was still lugging around her duffel bag. He was welcome to play the gentleman but I hoped he had the sense to let her carry her own luggage through customs.

I found Charlie and Simon sharing a bench, playing cards and talking about the Paris shows.

"The psychedelic thing is over, man," Simon said. "Sixty-eight is going to be about hard sounds, blues, and power. We have to be on top of that."

"It ain't gonna be Eddie Cochran again, though, Simon," Charlie said. Charlie was holding his arm down while he made eye contact with Simon and slipping a card out of his cuff. "It's gotta be informed by all the new sounds that've come up in the last couple of years. Like, imagine Indian scales over heavy drumming. That's what the next thing will have to be."

Emerson was over by the cigarette machine, signing the notebooks of some schoolgirls who were trying to contain a nearly epileptic enthusiasm.

Nothing interesting happened on the crossing. The windows were steamy and the channel was foggy. The boat landed at Dover and all the passengers moved slowly into a long wooden customs hall and formed lines. My mind was set on standby. I was wishing I'd had a shave and looking forward to a hot bath when we finally got to London. I inched along in a row behind a French family with five children. I carried my suitcase and one of Simon's, as well as a shoulder pouch. The dull hum of bureaucracy lulled me into a half sleep. I was glad to hear English voices over the public address system.

At some point I came to myself and looked around for the others. Fin was one line over and had reached the front, the custom inspector's station. Dora was behind him like a papoose. I saw that Fin was still carrying her duffel bag. I should have cautioned him about that. Was it too late? I could not shout out; that would make things worse. I just hoped he was lucky. I had a bad feeling as I watched the agent talking to him, checking his American passport and long dirty hair. I began to feel like it might be quite a while until I got my bath.

The customs agent called to another officer to take the duffel bag and Fin into a side room. Fin seemed unfazed, loping after the inspector like a puppy. It was when I saw Dora fall back and move quietly away from the front of the line and into the crowd that I knew we were in trouble. I should have gone after her, but I got out of my line and went forward toward Fin instead. Emerson had already cleared customs and was waiting by the door to the train platform. I caught his eye and pointed toward the little room into which Fin had vanished.

I came to the customs agent who had sent Fin away. I interrupted him speaking to an old man and insisted, "Sir. I am a solicitor for Mr. Daniel Finnerty, the American concert musician you just pulled aside. May I ask whether there is a problem?"

The agent looked at me like a fisherman studies a worm. His skin hung off his neck.

He stamped the passport of the old man and waved him through and then spoke to me.

"What are you to the American?"

"I am his legal counsel."

The agent grinned. His teeth were yellow in the middle, brown at the edges. He said, "He brings his solicitor to go through customs? Why would he do that, I wonder?"

I tried to gather my thoughts. Emerson was now at the agent's back, asking me with his eyes what was going on.

"I must insist you let me into the room with my client," I said.

Emerson broke in, trying to help. "What's the problem here, then? Someone do something wrong, Flynn?"

It was the wrong thing to say. If anyone had done something wrong, the agent was going to make sure it was not he.

"You fellas all together, then?" He looked at Emerson's long hair.

He looked at his blue military jacket with epaulets and the yin/yang badge on his lapel and his skinny orange bell-bottoms. He looked at me, unshaven and unkempt. When Charlie in his rabbit-fur coat and Simon in his six-foot North African scarf and muttonchops came over to help I knew we were sunk.

There was a murmuring from the mob of travelers around us, the blunt opposite end of the sonic scream we had bathed in last night in the Paris theater. Two security guards with straps across their chests and nightsticks in their belts moved toward us. Through the fog of my hangover and anxiety and sleepiness I comprehended that, oh, we were in trouble now.

None of us ever saw Dora again, by the way. That girl must have backed up to the English Channel and swum home to Uganda. Or perhaps she was cleverer. Perhaps she took advantage of the diversion we created to stroll through customs with another tall story. I have even on one or two dark nights imagined that she was working with the Paris cops to set us up as revenge for making fools of them in front of our audience and forcing the captain to kill his dog.

Dora, if you read this—get in touch. I'd really like to know what your scam was.

The customs agents and security guards had twigged that they had a rock group in their flypaper. They must have felt like real undercover aces. The schoolgirls who had gotten Emerson's autograph on the boat were weeping and shouting for the authorities to let the Ravons go, they were not hurting anybody. This assured that the border guards would let no cavity go unexamined.

I kept making loud noises about being a solicitor and threatening all sorts of misery if my clients were not accorded the strictest measure of Her Majesty's legal protections in this insulting and grossly prejudiced harassment but I was scared pissless. We were all brought into a brown-paneled room with a large table and plastic chairs, illuminated by the sort of harsh lights one might see at a prison break.

It seemed that every person who owned a uniform within ten miles was in the room with us. The large duffel bag was laid on the table and unzipped by a mustached officer wearing the sort of thin gloves sold to housewives to protect their hands while washing dishes. He reached into the bag and fiddled around like a physician looking for a prostate problem. I could not fathom why he stared into the air and searched with his hands when it would have been so much easier to just empty the bag on the table and look at what was inside.

Finally he said, "Ah-ho," and pulled out a large plastic bag filled with little beads.

"To whom do these belong?" he demanded.

No one answered.

"Whose are these?" he said, louder, shaking the bag of beads.

Fin said, "Uh, sir, I was carrying that bag for an African lady. I don't know what's in it."

You would have thought from the examiner's reaction that Fin had told him those were poison pellets intended for Buckingham Palace. The examiner was showing off for his fellow customs agents. He said, "It's not your bag. You were just carrying it for an *African* lady."

The other agents and cops chuckled and shifted where they stood.

"And where, pray tell, is this *African* lady now?"

He reached over and ran a thumb down Charlie's fur jacket.

"This one dresses like a lady, but I don't know he looks too African."

The cops were really having a good time. The comedian reached back in the bag and pulled out a paper sack with half a loaf of bread, a chunk of cheese, and a little knife. He passed the knife to a guard at his left, who looked it up and down like he'd just pulled it out of the back of a corpse. The comedian said, "Smuggling foodstuffs into England from Africa is strictly prohibited. There's one charge. Concealed weapon is another."

Even if there were nothing illegal in the luggage, we were now at the point where it would be embarrassing for the authorities if they could not find a reason to charge us. I held my tongue and hoped we'd get through Dora's effects without finding a bladder full of heroin.

It took forever for the inspector to pull apart every item in that duffel bag. When he had, he had found various proscribed culinary and agricultural items, two gold wedding bands, and no narcotics. He had stopped making jokes as he got near the end of the survey. He even turned the bag inside out and ran his hands up and down the seams looking for hidden pockets or contraband sewn into the lining. It seemed for a minute that we were off the hook. Charlie made a joke to that effect. He should have kept his mouth shut. We were not in

England now, we were in cop country. Cops everywhere believe that the law is just an excuse.

"Whadyer got?" one of the guards asked the comedian.

"He got zilch," another guard said.

The comedian flushed. The Ravons chuckled. I clenched up inside.

The comedian said, "They must've passed it into their clothes." He raised his eyes toward the Ravons: "All right, you fancy little showers of shit. Put your effects up on the table and get yer kits off."

The fun washed out of the Ravons' faces. They probably could not even remember what pot, hash, or pills might be in the pockets of their dirty laundry. If the only illegal thing they had done on the whole tour had been to go to the party last night, that still would have left them with enough proscribed prescriptions to get them thrown in jail if the customs agents wanted to make a stink about it.

Here my life changed. I stepped forward and said in a voice straining to be both forceful and logical, "Hang on a minute here, sir. I'll remind you that I am legal counsel and these are my clients. We have gone along with this in good humor and patience up until now but be reasonable. There is nothing illegal in the duffel bag–which was the entire focus of your suspicion. My other three clients are in here only because they were concerned to see their friend being detained; they had already cleared customs when you pulled Mr. Finnerty aside. We do respect your mission and the difficult duty you have in protecting our borders, but let's all move on now. My clients have to be in London for important business meetings. Mr. Finnerty has certainly learned to not carry strangers' bags through border points. There's no need to extend this exercise by needlessly embarrassing all four of my clients. I promise you, sir, they have learned their lesson."

The comedian seemed to consider this carefully. I was giving him a chance to wag a finger at the boys and tell them never to joke around at UK Customs again. I was offering him a chance to save his pride in front of his comrades. He looked at the guard on his left, who looked back with a half smile that might have been read as, *You fucked up, mate. You let these nancys get past you.* The comedian flushed again. We were cooked.

"You think you're in a position to *negotiate*?" he said, leaning toward my face and exhaling sour spittle. "Who the fuck do you think you're talking to? Tell these pansies to empty their bags on the table and strip! You, too, *counselor!*"

The Ravons were white. How much were they holding? I raised my voice to match the inspector's: "This is harassment, pure and simple. Your own language and the epithets you use against my clients proves your motivation is personal and prejudiced. Every person in this room can be called as a witness against you. It's not going to be my clients who face a judge if you go through with this, Inspector. Are you quite certain you want to proceed?"

He pointed to Emerson. "You! Strip!"

Emerson began to struggle out of his high boots. Legal precedents were flying through my mind. There was no way to stop this; customs agents were granted enormous latitude. I spoke the words that would change my life forever: "Emerson, stop!" I turned to the furious customs agent but addressed the whole room.

"We will do exactly as you demand. However, before my clients strip naked and present themselves to you, I must insist that all of you leave the room for five minutes while I consult with them. I am their attorney, their sole legal representative and counsel. Under British and international law I have the right to confer with my charges in confidentiality. Five minutes, please. Then you may proceed with your strip search."

The comedian was confused. A white-haired guard came up behind him and whispered in his ear. They turned and murmured with another agent. It was the white-haired guard who spoke to me.

"You got five minutes, Borstal boy. Make the most of it."

With that all the customs agents filed out of the room. One or two looked back at the Ravons, smiling.

The door closed. I did not have time to worry if they were listening from outside or watching us through some peephole.

I said to the band, "Give me everything you've got. Everything!"

They were too scared to talk. They began emptying their pockets, their luggage, and their boots. Into my cupped hands came white pills, pink pills, two joints, a small chunk of hashish, and a bottle of Italian sleeping tablets, along with rubbers, a ten-inch nail, and a pornographic French magazine.

I tossed the nail in a dustbin, gave Charlie back his dirty magazine, and stuffed everything else into the pockets of my trousers, jacket, and overcoat. "Is that everything? Are you sure?"

The Ravons were perspiring, nodding, chastised. I stood outside of my body watching myself walk toward the door and open it and say to the guard outside, "All right, I've explained their rights to my clients. You can come in."

The guards must have had their own meeting, because the comedian stayed in the back when the officials returned to the room. It was the white-haired man who opened each suitcase, asked who owned it, and oversaw the scrutiny of every item by a team of three inspectors. He then told the Ravons to strip to their shorts and led a similar systematic search of their clothes. The body searches were quick and perfunctory. Then the white-haired man told the boys to get dressed, collect their luggage, and move on to the bench outside.

Simon was the last Ravon out of the room. He glanced at me with relief and gratitude.

"So that's it, then?" I said to the white-haired agent. "Everyone is satisfied?"

"I suppose," he said. He walked to a sink in the corner of the room and rinsed his hands. Why had I not seen the sink? I might have put the pills down the drain. The other guards now seemed bored, but none of them left the room.

"Well, then," I said. "I'm sorry for taking so much of your time. Do you need me to sign anything or are we done?"

"No need to sign anything," the white-haired guard said. He dried his hands on a rag.

I spoke to the comedian, whose expression was unreadable. I said, "Sorry I got short before, sir. It's been a very long tour and I'm just anxious to be home."

The comedian didn't acknowledge me at all. I moved toward the door. I said, "I better get along, then, before my charges wander off." The cops seemed to have lost interest in me. I put my hand on the knob, I opened the door. I saw the Ravons on the bench outside waiting.

"Ah, Mr. Flynn."

It was the white-haired inspector.

"Before you go, would you mind just emptying your pockets on the table, too?"

They knew they had me. I was out of tricks and rhetoric. I laid out marijuana, hashish, and pills.

The white-haired inspector looked at the comedian. The other guards gathered around. Hands were laid upon my shoulders.

Someone behind me said, "*Tsk tsk*. And you a solicitor."

My arrest as a narcotics smuggler changed my life profoundly in two ways. First, it won me the eternal loyalty of the Ravons, for whom I took the rap. We were joined in the marrow after that. Second, it got me disbarred. Even now it is difficult for me to say it. The hardest thing for a man to navigate is a challenge to how he knows himself. I thought of myself, with great pride, as a solicitor, which was bound up with knowing myself as a good son whose parents were justly proud. My taking the Ravons' drugs from them led directly to events that shattered how I was thought of by others and how I thought of me. I'm not sure I ever adjusted to it.

Of course my arrest made the papers. The story had everything the tabloids liked: drugs smuggling, rock and roll, celebrities, a bent lawyer, and a hero policeman whose ability to spot the criminal in a long passport queue became more supernatural with every interview he gave. It was brutal for my parents. They supported me but they were as confused as they were frightened. I told them I was carrying the drugs for someone else and left it at that. They took no comfort in learning that I had freely elected to dishonor myself and bring scandal to our family.

My colleagues at Difford, Withers & Flack declined to represent me at trial. They said they had no expertise at criminal defense in this sort of case, but I understood I had already visited shame enough on the firm. They referred me to a barrister named Ross Kleinberg, who specialized in narcotics charges. It was beautifully British; when the Irishman to whom they had given a break embarrassed them, they handed him off to a Jew. Kleinberg told me what I would have to do to avoid prison and I did it. I cut my hair, I wore the right suit, I looked frightened and penitent in court. He got me off with three years' conditional probation and a lecture that seemed directed at my entire generation of spoiled ingrates.

Much worse was to come. I was called before the Law Society and my name was struck from the roll. I was no longer a solicitor. I could no longer practice law in Great Britain. The life I had worked toward since I was twelve had been taken from me. From that day on I was not a rock and roll manager because I wanted to be. It was no longer a second career and certainly no longer a lark. From there on, it was the only job open to me.

Even before this scandal, the decision I had made to throw in with the Ravons had been hard on my parents. They had struggled to be kind about it. They tried to understand something for which they had no context. Their generosity toward my throwing away a future for which all three of us had worked and sacrificed made me appreciative and guilty. I loved my parents and felt I shared their values, but there was a divide down the middle of the century and we had grown up on different sides.

When I visited them in Kingston after the scandal, we stayed in the house. Their neighbors turned away when they saw me coming. I stopped sleeping over and joining them for Sunday mass. At dinner on one of those awkward Saturdays my mother said, "Poor Mrs. O'Neil. She always said her Kevin would say the mass at her funeral and now . . ."

I had grown up with Kevin O'Neil. He was the youngest of five boys, and his mother had had the Roman collar on him before he made his first Communion. Now young Father O'Neil had stunned the community by running off with the daughter of one of his parishioners. They had been civilly married and excommunicated. My mother spoke of Mrs. O'Neil's heartbreak with a sympathy that tore strips from my conscience.

I did not tell her that I had seen Kevin O'Neil and met his bride. He had phoned me at home in Chelsea and asked if we might meet for a drink. Exile that he was, he was looking for anyone who might not judge him harshly, and I was another fallen man.

After some initial awkwardness we passed a pleasant evening at a French restaurant in Notting Hill. O'Neil told his wife stories about our childhood that I barely remembered. He reminded me of arguments we'd had as teenagers about which Church teachings we thought were intractable and which allowed wiggle room.

"I recall you saying, Jack, that the Church relied an awful lot on context to decide what was sinful. It was a sin to eat meat on Friday, but the Pope himself would eat a plate of pork chops on Saturday. And you said how remarkable it was that the exchange of marriage vows transmuted a mortal sin into a sacrament. You had a head for legal argument even then."

O'Neil had taken these discussions more seriously than I had.

I reminded him of the time in catechism class when he asked a cranky old monsignor if God could do really anything. "Of course He can do anything!" the old priest had declared.

"Ah, then, Father," O'Neil had said, "can He make a rock so big He can't lift it?" O'Neil scored the point but the monsignor made him sweep out the church basement twice.

I tried to change the subject but O'Neil kept going back to our early theology. He clearly needed to talk about his leaving the Church with someone who understood the difficulty of his decision. I felt that his wife was indulging him, although it must have been murder for her.

"You remember how we plagued your poor mam with questions about free will?" he asked me, laughing. The wine was lubricating his nostalgia.

I explained to his wife, "Kevin and I used to torture my mother about why God gave us free will if not to encourage us to sin a little."

Kevin interrupted, "And his mam finally says, 'We have free will but we're not allowed to use it!'" He roared with laughter. "Jackie and I quoted that at each other for years!"

His wife and I chuckled along politely. Kevin stopped laughing. His eyes focused on something invisible and he said, "It was not a sign of lack of faith. It showed how deeply immersed in our faith we were."

He looked up at me, like he wanted me to forgive him. I put my hand on his arm and said, "We still are, Kevin. These are just different times. We have to live our faith in different ways." He mumbled. He was grateful, and he was getting drunk. For the rest of the dinner he hardly spoke, leaving it to his wife and me to talk about how she hoped to fix up their new flat, what movies we had both seen, and whether Richard Burton's talent as a great Shakespearean was being compromised by his passion for Elizabeth Taylor. By the time we finished dessert Kevin seemed to have disappeared.

I was not going to tell any of this to my mother. I relate it here because everyone talks about the sixties as a moment of change and liberation, but no one talks about what we were changing from. No one talks about what we gave up to embrace our new liberty.

The changes in attitude toward authority, money, sex, drugs, and the military have been well documented. But of all the revolutions of the 1960s, the most profound in our world and least recalled today was the Second Vatican Council, the ecclesiastical conference called by Pope John to open the windows of the Church and let in some light. The changes the council began to announce in 1964 shook the souls of the faithful. Coming at the same time as the upheavals in sexual mores, youth culture, race relations, and attitudes toward patriotism, Vatican II made it seem to Catholics of my parents' generation that all of the old pillars were collapsing, that the whole civilization they had fought to preserve in the Second World War was falling away.

The decommissioning of Saint Christopher was a blow from which my mother, an avid medal blesser, never recovered. My parents still went to mass on Sunday and on holy days, but they stopped going to First Fridays, stopped going to Monday novenas, and began leaving the church right after Communion, as soon as their technical obligation was complete. Their relation to the sacraments had become legalistic, like paying taxes.

I was young enough to roll with the changes. I liked the new collegiality, the fact that the priest now stood facing the people at a table instead of with his back to them at a great altar. I did not much like the folk songs and Protestant hymns that replaced the voiceless liturgical music of old, but that was mainly because we sang so badly. Catholics had no tradition of group singing and it showed in every atonal choir.

When I was a small boy and worried that I had sinned—I might have had an impure thought or taken the Lord's name in vain—my mother told me, "The Church sets the bar for holiness very high, so that even when we come up short we are still safe." As an old man I take comfort in remembering that, as I take comfort remembering my mother's kindness. Although I fell away from the faith, I never stopped thinking of myself as a Catholic and I never turned against the Church.

I believed it to be a force for good in a corrupt world. As I moved into leading a secular life I retained a sense of sin. I tried not to cheat anyone, or slander or steal. I gave myself more leeway with the sins of the flesh but I did not blame the Church for setting high standards. When I strayed I thought that I was weak, not that the Church's prohibitions were wrong. And, of course, I believed that like Saint Augustine I would have time to make up for the follies of my youth. It never occurred to me that I would not, like my father, marry a nice Catholic girl and stay loyal to her for life.

That is the world I came from. It is a world that does not exist anymore. Pope John opened the windows and in came a wind that blew down the house. I never spoke to my parents about drifting away from the Church. I had hurt them enough by getting involved with the world of rock music, by being arrested, and by carrying on with women and drugs in a manner that would have made them worry for my soul.

I hurt them by leaving the law to become a rock band manager, and when I was disbarred I embarrassed them before all their relatives and friends. As I still love their memory, I feel shame for the pain I caused them. They were not at all comforted that I became wealthy in my new career. They were not impressed with money; they did not think it had anything to do with virtue. They loved me but they did not pray for me to be rich. I do not think they would even have prayed for me to be happy, although I am sure they wished me happiness.

They prayed for me to be good. And it is the greatest regret of my life that they might have died believing I let them down.

I might be bending my memories of the environment around my own disposition, but it seems to me that the atmosphere among the musicians back in London changed after my drug bust. Perhaps the regulars now saw me as one of them and dropped the air of carefree youth they put on for company. Or perhaps I was now familiar enough with who was who to see through the happy veneer. It is also entirely possible I was simply in a shittier mood than I had been when I first arrived.

In 1968 and '69 the drugs would get much heavier and everyone's medicated attitudes would turn darker, but I don't think that had happened yet when I was arrested. We are all victims of nostalgia and show business, but it does seem to me that at Christmas of 1967 acid, pot, and hash still ruled. We had not yet embraced the false syllogism that if our parents and teachers had been wrong about the dangers of those soft drugs, they must also have been wrong about barbiturates, amphetamines, and opiates.

Not—here comes the public service announcement—that many of our fellow travelers did not make themselves plenty miserable with the soft drugs. The term "soft drugs" was itself a marketing pitch, like "low-tar cigarettes." LSD and marijuana brought out what was sleeping quietly in the psyche. Those with a basically pleasant nature often found the experience of getting high a happy one. But there were plenty of partygoers who had demons in their dreams, and LSD was especially good at dragging those monsters to the surface. Pot was not as powerful, but it did make the suspicious paranoid, the lazy slothful, and the slightly forgetful amnesiac. A lot of degrees never were finished and songs never were written because marijuana made it compelling to sit on the couch watching cartoons.

By the start of 1968 the soft drugs had become big business and in order to satisfy the market, the acid and pot began going downhill. There was speed mixed with the LSD, STP sprinkled into the hashish, shortcuts taken by the manufacturers. Remember that LSD was only then being made illegal. Up until the news reports about the hippie menace alerted the legislatures to the monster in the rec room, one could order peyote buttons in the mail. Prohibition brought in the gangsters, and the quality of the hallucinogens deteriorated even as the new dealers introduced our crowd to the sort of underworld characters who also handled heroin, guns, and prostitution. The road of excess was redirected through the palace of lowlifes.

Which is to say, we were fairly miserable at the Ravons' table at the Alibi Club when 1968 began, and it wasn't just because every man in the room seemed to have grown a beard while we were in France. I think a couple of Yardbirds were around that evening, and perhaps a Hollie. Not Jimi Hendrix but maybe one of his Experience.

I would like to imagine that a Beatle passed by and brushed us with the hem of his bell-bottoms, but the Beatles had been lying low since the sudden death of their manager Brian Epstein and the coming of their new guru, the Maharishi Mahesh Yogi. Emerson said he had run into Ilsa the She Wolf at the home of a pot dealer. She told him that Epstein's overdose had been a result of the band becoming involved in bad magic, and they had embraced the Indian mystic in an attempt to cleanse themselves. Charlie scoffed and said that Ilsa had a gift for finding the black lining in every dark cloud.

We were drinking in that room in 1968 but more than 1968 was in the room. If it was like most Mondays (Monday is for musicians what Sunday is for the rest of the race), there would have been one or two ghosts in there. "Ghosts" were what we cruelly called former stars who did not know it was over for them. There might have been one or two members of the Dave Clark Five, laughing and tippling, unaware that the hits had stopped for them forever.

The future would have been there, too, that night, sitting at tables by the door, hoping for a summons to come up higher, or standing by the bar nursing one drink all evening, smiling too quickly when the gaze of a star fell across him. It is not unlikely that a future member of Led Zeppelin was in the Alibi that night, a year or two away from their godhood. David Jones, not yet Bowie, might have been looking for a lighted spot to stand in, hoping to be seen. His deification was four years away. If the drummer from Pink Floyd was there, could he have seen six years ahead to the ascension of his band into the pantheon? Fleetwood and Mac might have gotten into the room as Bluesbreakers, but they were still ten years short of their season as biggest band in the world, which would be followed by the long-delayed triumph of our friends the Bee Gees, once disco was discovered.

Imagine that the little guitarist with his back to the mirror had been told his dreams would come true and he would play to a sold-out Shea Stadium with a group called the Police—but not until 1983. Would he have been willing to wait fifteen years for that distant glory? Or would he have thought it too long to hang on?

That London saloon in the first week of 1968 was filled with failure, success, and delayed gratification. None of us then could have imagined how many of those hotshots, those hopefuls, those has-beens, those hopheads would have a turn sitting at the big table, or in what sequence, or how many would find themselves pushed back to the bar before they were pushed out of the room. We didn't yet know the game we were playing. It was musical chairs.

Everything I remember about 1968 is ugly. Riots in Paris, London, and across the United States, brutal television images of the war in Vietnam, the rise of Nixon, the assassinations of Martin Luther King and Robert Kennedy, and the Soviet tanks rolling into Czechoslovakia to crush the promise of the Prague Spring.

In London, everyone had discovered barbiturates. My memory of that winter is of never seeing daylight. We lived like the undead, brooding, pale, and nocturnal.

The Ravons had no politics. Perhaps that's wrong. The Ravons gave no thought to party politics. After the drug bust, though, they began to understand that to the English establishment, they were political in spite of themselves. Young men who swanned about flashing money and taking drugs and sleeping with lots of girls and never getting up in the morning challenged the way things were done and always must be. After the bust, the Ravons knew that there could be a price for flaunting authority, but it had nothing to do with how they would have voted, had any of them been the sort who would ever vote.

If asked about the Vietnam War, Charlie would say something along the lines of, "Man, people have got to learn to love each other rather than shoot each other." Which is not to say that if Charlie came home and found a hippie stealing from his stash he would have hesitated to break a hookah over his head. The Ravons were working-class boys who grew up in a time and place when arguments were settled with fists and bottles. So was I. We understood each other.

It was Simon who first began to expound on the coming revolution. He was inspired by the Paris riots, where students and union members brought the city to a halt in the spirit of liberty, fraternity, and the three-day workweek. Simon saw something theatrically appealing in the photos of young longhairs on the parapets. I think it reminded him of *Les Misérables*. He began writing a song cycle called "The Dove and the Fist" that promised to achieve in naïveté what little it lacked in pretension. I have tried to block out my memory of "The D and the F" for many years, but I think at one point he wanted to devote a full hour of a Ravons concert to this opus, in which he would sing the voice of radical revolt, Charlie would play the part of pacifism, and Emerson would be the narrator, a young seeker torn between warring impulses. At the end their three voices would join in harmony in a song for justice that Simon, thank God, never finished.

It was important that the Ravons get into the recording studio and work on some new material. We had to capitalize on the success of "Mary vs. Mary" and the group's second album, *The Prince and the Pisces*, which had come out almost six months earlier, a lifetime in the reckoning of sixties rock. If the group were to keep the confidence of their record label and live up to their new, post-Towsy deal, they needed to make some music.

The trouble was that the Ravons were not sure how to proceed and the drugs were not helping. Charlie and Emerson had no interest in pursuing Simon's morbid concept album ideas, but their own instincts toward joyful pop were at odds with the tenor of the time. Heavy blues riffing was the new style and it was not the Ravons' forte. At one point Charlie suggested taking some of their old unfinished love songs and simply writing new lyrics about social injustice. They got as far as trying to turn a leftover called "Don't Trample My Heart" into "Don't Napalm My Brother" but conceded that it sounded like Johnnie Ray singing *The Communist Manifesto*.

Up a creative creek and frightened by the thought of turning the band over to Simon's operatic ambitions, Emerson and Charlie instructed me to negotiate terms with Mr. LaSalle to come aboard as their record producer.

I should confess here my own feelings about rock music. I didn't care much about it. When I met the Ravons my taste ran toward Rodgers and Hammerstein and "Danny Boy," standard stuff you'd hear on the radio or join in on at the pub. The score from *My Fair Lady* has never failed to bring a tear to my eye for reasons I do not understand. I didn't mind rock and roll, as a child I quite liked some of the early Presley singles, but I did not give it any more consideration than I gave to chocolate bars. Some were better than others and it was an occasional treat but there was no nutritional value there.

When I fell in with the Ravons I admired their skill at putting together successful pop singles the same way I would have admired their talents if they were making a best-selling candy. I saw that they did it well, and as I learned more about the business I came to understand the difference between a fine Swiss confection and a cheap jelly baby. But it was all still junk food.

I would never claim that Emerson felt the same way—he loved rock and roll enough to devote his life to it—but the only time I ever saw him express any suggestion that it was anything like art was when he was speaking into the tape recorder of a susceptible journalist or the ear of a gullible girl.

I approached Mr. LaSalle with the Ravons' request that he join their recording sessions in an official capacity. If he did not want to be credited as producer he could call himself anything he liked, but the band was having a tough time deciding on their musical direction and they all respected his ability to cut away the clutter and help them find the best in themselves.

LaSalle was, as always, cordial and mysterious. The two of us sat in a restaurant just off Soho Square discussing terms. It was a very old restaurant with heavy oak tables that looked like they had been there since Shakespeare's day. As I spoke with LaSalle about the Ravons' offer, I noticed that he was rubbing, almost petting the wood. He would stroke the surface of the table lightly and then sit back, as if listening for something. After a pause, he would do it again.

"Get a splinter?" I said finally. He looked up at me as if coming out of a trance.

He smiled. "Sometimes," he said, "you can get a vibration from old furniture. You can get impressions of the people who spent a lot of time here."

He saw me looking surprised and he smiled again. "I suppose this sounds superstitious to you, Mr. Flynn."

"I'm open-minded," I said.

"That is a virtue," LaSalle said. "Tell me, Mr. Flynn, are you a religious man?"

"In my way."

"Roman Catholic?"

"I am, actually."

"Then you believe in God, in the Immaculate Conception, in Adam and Eve?"

"I believe Adam and Eve might have been the first fish to crawl up on land."

"But you do believe in an all-powerful being who created the universe and rules over it still."

I was uncomfortable with this discussion but I supposed I had started it.

"Most days I do."

"Well, then"—LaSalle turned up his palms—"once we accept that, once we agree that the universe is in its essence supernatural, why should we be skeptical about any of the details?"

"Forgive me, Mr. LaSalle—"

"Do you believe in telepathy, Mr. Flynn? Ghosts and spirits? Communicating with the next world?"

"Not really."

"But why not? You have accepted that the universe is based on magic—why impose scientific logic on a magical construct? Science is always a hundred years behind. Scientists measured cranial capacity to discern criminal impulses and put leeches on the sick. Whatever the scientist says is true today will be proved nonsense tomorrow. Don't birds, deer, herds of buffalo all respond to signals we cannot in our science detect? Of course they do. They are tuned in to some psychic telegraph from which we are excluded. If we were to tell a nineteenth-century man of science that as we sit here there are voices, pictures, music passing through the air all around us he would say that is superstitious nonsense, but all we would have to do is turn on a television to prove him wrong."

I had never heard LaSalle speak so much and I had no idea why he had chosen this occasion to start pitching his loony metaphysics my way. I tried to steer the conversation back to his producing the Ravons but he seemed to think that his producing the Ravons was the subject at hand.

"What about brain waves, Mr. Flynn? Is it not possible that those electrical impulses are analogous to a television transmission? Some of us have the ability to receive them better than others do. What if ghosts are something like old reruns? Transmissions looking for a receiver? You believe the world is supernatural in its origins, Mr. Flynn. Why is anything far-fetched?"

"This is all over my head, Mr. LaSalle," I told him. "I am still trying to fathom why I can now eat roast beef on Friday. Let's talk about your working with the Ravons in the studio. I wondered what sort of fee—"

LaSalle interrupted me. "We are discussing my fee already, Mr. Flynn. I believe that music is a force that straddles this world and the world unseen. I believe that music is to us what the signal we cannot hear is to the lower animal. I believe that for anyone to wish to bend music to his service, he must be prepared to repay the debt."

"You have lost me, Mr. LaSalle."

"I do apologize, Mr. Flynn. These big ideas sometimes overwhelm my poor vocabulary. Perhaps it is best if I make my proposal to the whole group at once. Do you think they would consider that?"

Was all this double-talk some bargaining tactic? I did not want to embarrass the boys by having LaSalle hit them with terms they were unprepared to negotiate. I told LaSalle that it would be derelict of me to put the Ravons in the position of talking money with a man they so admired.

"My fee will not be financial, Mr. Flynn," LaSalle said. "That is why I feel I must present it to the Ravons as a group."

I had no idea what to say to that. I told LaSalle I would give the group his message and we finished our meal without saying any more about music, business, or the porous membrane between this dimension and the next.

We were at a television studio the next evening, where the Ravons were going to play a song on *The David Frost Show*, after which the host would chat with the band about music, revolution, and youth culture. It was a big break for a group who had been off the radio for months, exactly the sort of thing that could help the Ravons change their image from pop group to serious rock band.

We were standing in the wings waiting for Frost to finish his interview with a beautiful film star. The longer she charmed him, the less time we had.

The group was anxious to play. I had put off telling them about LaSalle wanting to discuss ghosts and ectoplasms before agreeing to produce their new record. One hurdle at a time.

I brushed a bit of dust off Emerson's shoulder. He was wearing an army-green Eisenhower jacket decorated with colorful badges and buttons instead of military medals. I fixed on the largest badge, which was a smiling portrait of Chairman Mao.

"I think you should lose that one, Emerson. Might offend some people."

Simon said sarcastically, "Ah, there's Flynn's Catholic conservatism showing its face again."

"Nothing to do with it," I said. "Mao is responsible for political suppression and mass murder on a scale that would embarrass Mussolini. Which does not mean he's not a groovy fashion accessory, but one whom you might not care to defend on national television if Frost decides to focus in on your decorations. Keep Bardot, keep Aldous Huxley, keep your Buster Keaton button, but I strongly suggest you put Mao in your pocket until after the broadcast."

Emerson gave me a goofy grin that told me he was stoned. He said,

"Don't censor me, Johnny. If David asks me, I'll say that I dig Mao's intentions but I'm not sure his methods need to be so heavy."

"Oh, for shit's sake, Emerson, take off the stupid button."

"Don't touch that badge, Emerson," Simon said. "We start censoring ourselves, the man has already beat us."

I was getting angrier by the second. Was every discussion from now on going to have to be conducted with people in a state of pharmacological illogic? First LaSalle with his brain-wave mumbo-jumbo and now the Ravons turning a wonderful promotional opportunity into a public defense of the Cultural Revolution. Wasn't staying in tune intellectual burden enough? When did every guitar player become a deputized political commentator?

I was seriously considering tearing the pin from Emerson's lapel when Charlie stepped forward with a Magic Marker and drew mouse ears on Mao.

"There ya go, Flynnie," Charlie said. "Problem solved."

Before any one of us could carry on the argument, David Frost announced, "The Ravons," and the boys hit the stage, picked up their guitars, and launched into "Turn Around Again," a track from the second album that we were lobbying the record company to release as a single, to tide us over until the next album was ready. In those days labels almost never put out 45s from albums that were already in the stores, let alone albums that had been out for months. But after the Frost show "Turn Around Again" became the exception to that rule and turned into a minor hit.

There were only two minutes left in the program when the Ravons finished playing, but Frost went over to them, asked who was who, and—sure enough—spotted Emerson's Mao button. He told the camera to come in close and asked Emerson the significance of the large round ears attached to the chairman's head.

Charlie piped up and saved the day. He said, "We're Mickey Maoists."

Frost laughed, the studio audience joined in, and the Ravons were established as fresh, witty social commentators. For the next month everywhere we went people repeated Charlie's joke to us. Many years later, in the "British Invasion" chapter of *The Rolling Stone Illustrated History of Rock & Roll*, Charlie's line would constitute the entire reference to the Ravons, lumped as they were between the Small Faces and the Kinks. By then the quip had been credited to Emerson.

At dinner after the Frost show, I told the Ravons about LaSalle's insistence that they all meet to discuss his terms for producing their next album. I further told them of his assurance that his requests would not be monetary.

"Sure, he wants to join the band," Simon said.

"You think so?" Charlie asked. "He's pretty old."

"Yeah, but he's a spade," Emerson added. "Might be pretty cool to have a spade in the band."

"Then we could get away with playing the blues," Charlie said. "Who'd dare correct us?"

"Be nice to have another American," Fin said and regretted it immediately.

I doubted very much that LaSalle wanted to join the Ravons. He did not strike me as desiring the spotlight, let alone as a musician who would enjoy the rigors of touring with a rock group. My concern was that he would demand a piece of the band's publishing or other profits, and whether he was a musical master or not, I had no intention of giving to LaSalle what we had wrested with such difficulty from young Towsy.

If I had possessed the imagination to dream of what LaSalle really wanted in payment from the Ravons I would have given him anything else.

We made an appointment with LaSalle for two nights later and I went back to the Nevermore office, which Allison had turned into an engine of efficiency. I began to put my legal training to use as I tried to comprehend why the Ravons, though freed of Towsy's usury, were still unable to bank anywhere near the money they earned on paper.

Almost everything they made—well over 90 percent—was going to taxes. This was the socialist England of the sixties, and this is why so many musicians and actors of the Ravons' generation were driven into exile. I know that sounds like we did not want to share the burden of supporting the less fortunate that our prosperity obliged. I was as progressive as the next sixties youthquaker, but when I began to study the tax code I saw what it really was—not a way to distribute the wealth more fairly, but a remnant of the old class system designed to keep those with inherited land and money untouchable and to drive the most talented of the lower classes out of the country.

The devious part of the tax code was addressed to those presumptuous commoners who dared to nurse ambitions above their station. If someone from the lower classes began to generate real money, it would be taken away from him *so long as he remained domiciled in England.* If, however, he went abroad and sent part of his revenue home, he could keep the bigger share of it. I began to understand that this system had been devised to drive the brightest and bravest of the lower classes out into the world to colonize, to captain ships, to set up trade routes, and to draw the diamonds, gold, and tobacco out of foreign lands. A talented British boy from the working class with ambitions to rise in the world was encouraged by the system to ship off to Jamaica or India or Australia, where his king would allow him to keep most of the fortune he made. But if he dared to stay in England, he would forfeit so much that he would never be able to rise far above his humble birth. What a kick my father would get out of this! The more I understood of how the system really worked, the less English I felt.

The four Ravons and I went together and rang the bell of G. T. LaSalle. He met us at the door and we followed him up the stairs to his drawing room. It was evening and the room was poorly lit. I could see all the hourglasses, with fifty-nine minutes of sand in the top of each one.

"Gentlemen," LaSalle said with great formality, as if he were speaking to a congregation, "thank you for coming. I am George Thomas LaSalle from the Orleans Parish. Are you each here of your own free will?"

The boys mumbled that they were indeed. I thought this ritual was a bit creepy but I held my tongue. God knows what combinations of drugs the Ravons had ingested; I did not want to trigger any bad trips.

"And you are all of age and free to enter into contracts?"

Here I began to worry again that LaSalle was looking to get his hands on revenue streams beyond what was appropriate for a record producer. The Ravons said sure, you bet.

LaSalle said, "Now I will ask each of you in turn to tell me what it is each of you wants. Mr. Lydle?"

Charlie cleared his throat and announced, "We would very much like you to produce our new album, Mr. LaSalle."

"That is too circumscribed a desire," LaSalle announced. "Tell me what you most want from the whole world, Mr. Lydle. Tell me what you most want from life itself."

"Ah, well . . ." Charlie looked at the floor and gathered his thoughts. LaSalle was pushing the guru vibe a bit too far. The Ravons needed a record producer, not a swami.

Charlie said, "To keep playing music, man. Buy some land in the country, have all me mates around. My dream for life is to be able to play music until I die, to never have to get a straight job, and . . . to never have to get out of bed before noon if I don't want to."

LaSalle moved on. "Mr. Finnerty? What is your heart's desire?"

"I'm American," Fin said, as if this explained what came next. "I want the nice cars, the cool pad, big house, chicks. I want to make a million bucks."

Simon snorted at Fin. Fin shrugged. "Just being honest, buddy," he said.

LaSalle called on Simon, who announced, "I don't care about any of that. All I want is to make my art with a minimum of interference from the gray men in neckties, the hacks and accountants and businessmen. I want an audience who will understand my music and support my experiments. I want to embark on a long and serious musical journey. I do not want to be a flash in the pan or a silly pop star."

LaSalle smiled and nodded and stroked the wall as he had petted the old table at the restaurant. This time it gave me the jitters. He turned his attention to Emerson but he did not say his name.

Emerson said, "I want everything we have now and I want more. I want the music and the success and the fame and the money and the whole thing. I want twenty times what we've had already. I want the women and to look good, I want to keep it all going. And I don't want to be a has-been at thirty. I don't want to be a has-been at forty or fifty, either." Emerson paused but he wasn't finished talking. LaSalle nodded at him.

Emerson said, "Whatever's on, I want more."

The Ravons stood in place and fidgeted. They had never spoken so frankly of their ambitions. They glanced at each other, defying their friends to question or mock what they had said.

LaSalle spoke again. "I believe you have each answered me honestly. If you had not, if you had told me what you thought I wanted to hear or what your friends wanted you to say, I would not have gone forward with this proposal."

Okay, I figured, here comes the bill. I was prepared to step in and stop the Ravons from signing away their rights as part of this psychological séance. I no longer trusted LaSalle at all.

LaSalle said, "All of the things you asked for are in your power to achieve. Music can deliver these blessings to you. Music has great power in this universe, and you have asked to control that power. To do that, it must for you be a matter of life and death. Do you understand why that is so?"

Simon said, "Better than you could ever know, my friend."

Charlie said, "Music is a matter of life, all right, I know that."

Emerson and Fin nodded.

"What I tell you now must never, ever leave this room. Can you agree to that?" LaSalle asked. The Ravons agreed.

"The proposition I will put to you is one I have made to many musicians over many years. Those who did not accept it went on their own way. Those who did are bound forever by the intentions they expressed. Do you want to hear the proposition?"

The Ravons wanted to hear it.

"Everything you asked for can be yours, and more than you asked for will be—if you are serious enough to agree that in exchange for music giving each of you your desires, one of you will give up his life for music."

I don't know what the Ravons were thinking right then—but I know exactly what I thought: This fuckery has gone far enough.

"Mr. LaSalle," I said, "we draw the line at human sacrifice. However, if you'd settle for cutting the head off a chicken I will run down to the poultry shop and be back with a hen."

LaSalle smiled as if of course this were all in fun. He looked up at me and said, "I don't mean to spook anyone, Mr. Flynn. That is not my intention at all. I simply need to know that our four young musicians take what they are asking for as seriously as they take life itself. For that is what we are discussing. We are discussing the disposition of the rest of their lives."

The Ravons had not said a word. I expected Charlie to make a joke but he was silent. I said, "By what authority do you make these promises, Mr. LaSalle?"

"Oh, by no authority except my own experience. I have been able to help other young men of similar gifts to make their dreams reality"—here he gestured to the famous faces in the photographs on the wall—"but I can undertake the odyssey only if I am certain that the intentions of my collaborators are fierce and unswerving. I will not work with artists who are not committed to music with their whole lives."

Now Fin spoke. "So the deal is, if all of our dreams come true, one of us will die. When?"

LaSalle said, "Well, my own understanding of these things is not unlimited, but in my experience it is enough to say 'prematurely'—sooner than you would die if you did not give your life to music."

"My life's already given to music," Simon said. "I'll sign your contract."

"There is nothing to sign," LaSalle said. "Your clear-spoken intention is all I need."

"Four to one is better odds than you get at the racetrack," Charlie said. "Count me in, Professor."

"Me, too," said Fin.

Emerson hesitated. "What if one of us dies before he gets what he asked for?"

"That is not the agreement we are making," LaSalle said. "Each of you will get everything he asked for or no one is bound."

"Count me in, then," Emerson said. "If music gives me all that, I owe her my life."

"When would you gentlemen like to begin recording?" LaSalle asked.

The Ravons smiled and laughed a little, glad the ritual was over. Charlie said, "We got the studio booked for Tuesday afternoon. You want to get together first and go over songs?"

"I am at your disposal," LaSalle said, "and on your schedule. Let's make some music together."

With that, the meeting was over. LaSalle seemed to shrink back down to his normal charming self and the Ravons found their usual personalities again. Our host led us out of the big room and back toward the stairs and out the door into the street.

We walked around the corner before Fin let out a laugh and we all relaxed.

"That was friggin' weird!" Fin exclaimed.

"Some serious voodoo," Simon admitted.

"You didn't want much, Emerson!" Charlie said. "And I'd like to live to be a thousand, and I want an antigravity belt, and twelve harem girls, and, em, could ya throw in a cherry without no stone and one of them new Corvettes while yer at it?"

Emerson smiled slightly but he looked distant. "The important thing is, he agreed to produce the album. He can dress us as leprechauns and have us sing 'Who Threw the Overalls in Mrs. Murphy's Chowder' if that's what it takes to get him to make the record."

They were laughing it off, but I knew that each of the Ravons was as shaken as I was by LaSalle's proposition, or would be when he got into bed and turned off his light.

I was not around much during the making of the third Ravons album with G. T. LaSalle. I had no business in the studio. The group needed to get their records in shape on their own. My place was in the office, working on the business that protected them and allowed them to make music in peace.

Very early in the sessions Charlie and Simon came by Nevermore to play me the first new song, a swampy vamp, quite unlike anything they had done before, titled "Voodoo Doll."

"I can see LaSalle's influence already," I told them. "It's great, guys. I think the record company will be very excited by this."

The label was. They wanted to release "Voodoo Doll" immediately, but Emerson pressed me to get them to hold off until they had a few more songs finished. He did not want a single to appear when the Ravons were too busy to promote it, and neither did he want to postpone recording to plug a new 45. The label agreed to wait.

I said before that all my memories of 1968 are dark. That is colored by my father becoming ill that spring. A persistent cough that he refused to tend to turned into pneumonia. He finally had to go to the hospital, where he got sicker. After weeks of coming home, getting worse, going back in, and coming out again, we took him to a new doctor, who told us he had lung cancer.

My parents took it as well as anyone could, but I was devastated. I was glad the Ravons were locked in the studio. Allison ran the office while I spent three or four nights a week in Kingston, trying to help my mother care for the old man.

The Ravons understood. We tried to meet every Friday to go over business. They would play the tracks from the LP in progress, which had a blacker mood than anything they had done before. Simon might not have won the day with his idea for a rock opera about the revolution, but he had certainly infected the band with his taste for the slow and ponderous. Emerson's guitar playing bestowed a certain majesty on the gloom, though; he had always been a gifted melodic player, but now, unconfined by the short solos allowed on pop singles, he was evolving an instrumental style of unexpected dignity. The album would redefine the Ravons as surely as "Voodoo Doll" would give us an opening with radio.

LaSalle did not come to our Friday meetings. As I never went to the studio, I never saw him.

"He doesn't want his name on the album," Charlie announced one Friday.

I said, "You're joking."

"He's adamant about it," Emerson said. "And he insists he does not want to be paid anything beyond a small per diem for meals and the car service back and forth between the studio and his house."

"That makes no sense," I said.

Charlie said, "He's an odd old bird. As far as I can tell he takes the deal we made very seriously."

I didn't like hearing that at all.

I did not get by the Alibi Club much in those months, and when I did I got out quickly. A London policeman had made it his mission to arrest rock stars for drugs. He began with Donovan and then started picking off the Rolling Stones. He got Jagger and Richards sent to prison before their convictions were overturned. He kept arresting Brian Jones until he began to crack. Then he went after the Beatles. John and Yoko were arrested at Ringo's flat. The mood in the London rock community turned paranoid. There were rumors that some among the musicians had cut deals with the police to save themselves, betraying their friends. It might not have been true, but that did not stop people from believing it.

The Ravons finished their album and we delivered it to the record company, which made plans for a big fall release. There was great enthusiasm and a sense of relief, as it had been almost a year since *The Prince and the Pisces* and the music world had been transformed in that time. Psychedelia and the Summer of Love seemed a thousand light-years away. We were entering the season of My Lai and Manson.

When we got paid for delivering the LP, I made a trip to LaSalle's house to try to give him a producer's fee, credit or not. I had trouble finding his building. I passed it twice before I realized that it had been painted and was filled with workmen who had taken out the windows, removed the ornate railings, and were sawing, scraping, and sanding the whole interior.

I came up the stairs and into the drawing room, where painters were on scaffolds turning everything the color of sky.

"Do any of you know where Mr. LaSalle is?" I asked. They had never heard of him. The foreman told me they had been hired by an Arab banker to gut and redo the house, which was to be a wedding gift to his son. LaSalle was gone and there would be no finding him.

I thanked the work crew and put his check back in my pocket. I started to walk out of what was now a sunny room, when my eye fell on an hourglass on the mantel, only half covered by a painter's tarpaulin. I reached up and took it out. The sand was all in the top, as if LaSalle had turned it over only a moment before. It was running down quickly.

My father died on the Feast of the Immaculate Conception in December 1968. Twelve years later John Lennon would be killed on that same day.

I was in New York when Lennon died, and although we had different lives by then, I heard from each of the Ravons that night. We talked around the subject for a while and at some point each of them said, "LaSalle."

Whether any of his implied associations with the legends of rock were true or part of some con or fantasy, in the years between 1968 and 1980 one member of every group in LaSalle's photo gallery died. One of the Stones, one of the Who, Jimi Hendrix of the Experience, even Elvis Presley. Now John Lennon of the Beatles. Each of those deaths caused my phone to ring through the night. Each of them brought the old gang together for a few minutes across the miles and wires.

In 1982 Charlie called me and swore he had just seen LaSalle in the French Quarter of New Orleans. He said he was standing in the road off Jackson Square at three A.M. trying to flag a taxi when a silver and gray Rolls-Royce Phantom appeared, creeping along the narrow street. The automobile passed in front of Charlie, who looked in and saw LaSalle behind the wheel.

"He had not aged a month, Jack. I called his name and he looked up at me and nodded and kept rolling right into the dark."

After all these years, I am still not certain what game LaSalle was running. He never made any money from the Ravons. Perhaps he was a grifter working on a long payoff; something unexpected came up and he had to split quickly and abandon the scheme. Or perhaps he was sincere. Certainly the musical advice he gave the Ravons paid off for them. Maybe he was simply an experienced musician passing along his wisdom to younger players. Maybe his demand for a blood oath was his way of insisting that his protégés make a lifetime commitment or go away and stop wasting his time.

I have at different times believed both of those contradictory possibilities. I have also, once or twice in times of personal despair, awakened in the night in an empty house certain LaSalle was the devil. Now that I am close to the end of my life I suppose that he was simply one more guru passing through town at the end of the sixties, when the occult was in fashion and every creative youngster with too much time, too many drugs, and too little formal education was hungry to be given a window into the paranormal and arcane.

LaSalle sailed into London on the crest of a metaphysical wave. Many more tides of the collective unconscious would follow it. With Lennon's death it became clear that history passed through psychic epidemics, where copycat patterns of mental disorder spread through the population of the unstable. Perhaps viral manifestations of dementia could explain clusters of child-murder at certain moments. Perhaps it could help us comprehend the infestation of anti-Semitism in Hitler's Germany and the genocidal rampages in Pol Pot's Cambodia.

In America it was believed that the Beatles' sudden explosion of popularity in February 1964 was a reaction to the winter of mourning that followed JFK's murder. Of course some lunatic would have to complete the assassination cycle by shooting Lennon. Yoko would then assume the oversized dark glasses of the widow Jackie. The circle of anguish was closed and the era of assassinations ended.

In December 1968 I buried my father and sat down to execute his will and settle his legal affairs. My mother's faith and her community sustained her in her time of grieving. The community I was a part of had different rituals.

The night after my father's funeral Emerson and Charlie took me to a private room at the Alibi Club for what they called an Irish wake. Charlie had come to the funeral, the others had not. They had sent a ludicrously large bouquet of flowers instead.

We were drinking and telling stories when there was a knock on the door and Ilsa the She Wolf entered. This was unexpected. She rarely came around without her boyfriend and she and I had never exchanged two sentences in a row. I guessed she knew my father had just died, although I could not be certain. Ilsa was a morbid woman. Perhaps she fed on grief.

She did not ask if she could join us, she just sat down. There was no glass for her, so I offered her a swig from our bottle. I vaguely hoped she would be insulted and go away. Instead she reached into a black leather satchel she carried and took out a vial of white powder. She made three lines on the table, like claw marks. She looked at the three of us, who looked back at her blankly. She took out a thin bamboo straw, held it to her nose, and sucked up one of the lines. Then she handed the straw to Emerson. He did the same and passed the straw to me. I took a draw.

Nothing happened right away. I expected a jolt, but except for the strange sensation of a gob traveling the wrong way through my nostril, I only coughed and swallowed and went back to my whiskey.

She laid out a second selection. Charlie took a snort and then Ilsa did a second. I began to feel ill. The liquor was coming back on me. I excused myself, went down to the gents', and puked up all the scotch I'd been drinking, along with my mother's buffet.

I was sick for a while and then with a drunk's aplomb I washed my face and fixed my shirt and went back to the private room to resume drinking. It was my father's wake and I was going to live up to every Irish cliché.

Ilsa was bent over the table like it was her cauldron. She was hectoring Emerson and Charlie.

"So now you know who LaSalle really is! Epstein thought he could kill himself and save his boys but it won't work, it must be one of the four who entered the bargain." She pointed at me. "This one cannot do it for you, it must be one of the four. The Maharishi could not lift the spell from the Beatles, that is why they turned their backs on him. Now Lennon has taken up with the witch, she tells him she can protect him. We will see."

I felt strangely content. I looked at Charlie and Emerson, who seemed puzzled. I took my seat, leaned over to Ilsa, She Wolf of the SS, and looked her straight in her eyes.

"May I ask you something, sweetheart?" I said. She glared at me. "Aren't you scared someone's gonna drop a house on you?"

There was a long silence and then Charlie and Emerson started to laugh. Ilsa reeled back, offended that we were not taking her sorcery seriously.

"You are stupid boys!" she shouted.

"How 'bout a little fire, Scarecrow?" Emerson said and tossed a lit match at her. We were laughing so hard we could barely breathe. Charlie was laughing and gasping and all at once a bucket of vomit shot out of his mouth and hit the wall. Emerson and I exploded, weeping, hysterical, almost pissing our pants.

Ilsa was disgusted. She left the room cursing us. With real curses.

Charlie staggered to the door and called after her, "Come back, darlin'! And bring yer mop!"

Whoever LaSalle was, he had found an opening in the collective psyche and set up shop there. A lot of self-ordained mystics did the same thing in the sixties. At least LaSalle had a good ear. If he appears at my deathbed I will thank him for the music lessons.

In 2005 Simon swore he saw LaSalle in the television footage of the evacuation of New Orleans after Hurricane Katrina. He said he was sitting on the roof of a house, impeccably dressed, calmly writing in a notebook while corpses floated past. It was an arresting image, but mitigated by the fact that by that time Simon was insane.

The third Ravons album, *Curses and Cures,* did quite well in the
UK, where it sat in the top twenty for six months, and even better in
France and the Netherlands. "Voodoo Doll" was a hit single; it got
to number two in Germany and number eight in the UK. My mission
as 1969 began was to break the band in America.

They were now, officially, "the band." When I met them in 1967
the Ravons were a "group." In 1968 they began to be a "band," at first
somewhat ironically insofar as "band" brought to mind Benny Goodman and Count Basie. By the start of 1969, however, a band was all
any self-respecting collection of young musicians could be. "Group"
denoted singers, "band" suggested players. It was something like the
simultaneous translation of "shows" into "concerts" and "pop" into
"rock." Pity the pop group in 1969 who failed to make the transition to
rock band. *Sic transit* Herman's Hermits.

The Ravons' first LP had never been released in the USA. The
American arm of our British distributor brought out two of the band's
singles there, and when they failed to perform, passed on issuing the
album. The second LP, *The Prince and the Pisces,* did come out, but
except for a bit of airplay in Boston and Philadelphia made no impression.

Thanks to LaSalle, *Curses and Cures* was the Ravons' most Amer-
ica-friendly work to date. The boys let me know that they expected me
to make sure that this one got them to the States.

I had no idea how to do that. I went and spoke with the British
label, which was well disposed toward the band now that they were
actually signed directly to it and the offensive Towsy was out of the
way. I did not go only to our A&R person, I made a point of getting to
know everyone from the art department to the PR reps. They all had

opinions about what the Ravons needed to do in the U.S. and they all knew someone over there I could call on.

When the American arm of the British record company seemed reluctant to give the Ravons another shot, I was counseled to take that as an opportunity. BEI's U.S. label was weak, I was told by the assistant to our A&R rep. She said I should take advantage of their lack of interest to bring the Ravons to someone in the States who would really get it. She gave me the phone number of a talent scout at Tropic Records, which she assured me was an altogether hipper label run by fellows with good ears and who never wore neckties. She even let me use BEI's phone to place the overseas call.

Within two weeks Tropic had secured U.S rights to the Ravons' records. The group and I owed our American career to that secretary. I am pleased to say that she later married one of the Moody Blues and got to live in the luxury she deserved.

In February 1969 I got on a plane to go to America for the first time. I was accompanied by two unlikely allies. Danny Finnerty, the Ravons' American drummer, was not only native but had experience playing U.S. venues with many bands and—according to him, at least—was chums with half the promoters, booking agents, and disc jockeys in the New World. Tug Bitler had road-managed U.S. tours by the Searchers, the Zombies, and the Animals. The three of us made an odd trio going up the ramp at Heathrow. We represented the less charismatic half of the Ravons' inner circle.

Emerson, Charlie, and Simon wished us luck and promised to use our time abroad to write a batch of new hits. Mostly, I later learned, they took advantage of my absence from the Nevermore office by taking turns trying to seduce my assistant.

That first plane trip to America is fixed in my memory as a moment of enormous anticipation and excitement. There is nothing as thrilling as setting off on a journey into someplace that has lived vividly in your imagination. We flew coach, of course, with Fin chattering in my right ear the whole way and Tug, across the aisle, splayed across two seats, the movable armrest sunk into the fat of his back, dribbling peanut juice down his chin and terrorizing the small man squeezed up against the window next to him.

By the time we landed in New York, eight hours and some circling of the airport later, Fin had finally exhausted his litany of cool guys he had hung with and cute chicks he had slept with in the New York/ New England corridor.

We were met on the runway—in 1969 one disembarked down a flight of stairs onto the tarmac and anyone who wished to could stroll out to meet you—by a pit band buddy of Fin's, a trumpet player called Tommy Wu.

"Doc!" Fin cried happily and threw his arms around the thin young man. Tommy Wu hugged him back.

Fin pulled his pal over to us. The wind on the runway was blowing Tug's shirt up, exposing a massive white and hairy belly. "Guys, this Jap bastard is Tom Wu, the best damn horn player in New York City! Doc, this is Tug and this is Jack Flynn, my managers! All right!"

Tommy Wu drove us into the city in a Cadillac convertible with loud soul music blasting from the radio. America was already living up to my expectations. I would not have been surprised if the Beach Boys had buzzed by us in a souped-up Woodie, drag-racing Chuck Berry.

I was not prepared for the long drive from Kennedy Airport into the city. I think I had expected the plane to land in Central Park. I craned to see what I thought were skyscrapers on the horizon, and realized that what I had mistaken for the Manhattan skyline were actually the elaborate tombs and mausoleums of an enormous cemetery. I was hit by a wave of grief for my father—these came upon me unexpectedly that year—wiped away as suddenly by the real New York skyline coming into view.

We were booked into the Howard Johnson's Motor Lodge in Times Square. Broadway was squalid and exciting. We checked into our rooms and I took a shower. I had never felt such a sustained and powerful burst of hot water. I stood under the torrent for fifteen minutes and it never ran out.

I went down to the restaurant to meet Fin, Tug, and Wu. Fin insisted we all have hamburgers and milkshakes. I had tried what passed for a real American hamburger at a wimpy stand in London, but it was nothing like this. This tasted better than English steak. I asked for a Coke and the waitress brought me a bottle and a glass filled with ice cubes.

I was easily impressed.

The three of us decided to fan out and connect with our separate contacts. I would go to Tropic Records and introduce myself to the American staff. Tug would meet with his connections from his touring days, with a special mission to try to get us on an American package tour. Fin would liaise with friends and acquaintances among the musicians of Manhattan and find opportunities for the Ravons.

Tropic Records was headquartered in Greenwich Village. I had imagined the Village would be a Disneyland of beatniks and hippies, and was surprised that so much of it seemed like a small Italian city, full of old women dressed in black, old men sipping coffee at sidewalk tables, corner fruit stands and churches. I don't know what I thought it would be—Phil Ochs leading a protest march while Joan Baez gave daisies to policemen, I suppose—but my first impression was that as a bohemian enclave the Village had nothing on sunny Goodge Street.

Fin and Wu dropped me off at the door of Tropic Records and told me to make my way down Bleecker Street to the Night Owl Café when I was done. They'd be waiting for me there.

Tropic Records was not posh. It was up a flight of stairs over a shop selling chess sets. But the offices were bright and covered with posters, and the girls who worked there were friendly in that very open American way. I felt I had landed in the right place.

I met Hal Allyn, our U.S. A&R man, in person for the first time. When we spoke on the phone I had pictured him looking like Jan or Dean. Instead Allyn, who laughed almost all the time, turned out to be a chunky black man with glasses and a goatee. I later learned that he had trained as a disc jockey to acquire that California voice.

"The Ravons!" Allyn said, clearing a pile of magazines off a chair so I could sit down across from his buried desk. "I have loved these guys since I first heard 'Good-bye, Gwendolyn.' I am so happy to get a chance to work with you. Wild Bill! Guess who's here!" A tall man stuck his head in the door. "This is Jack Flynn from London who manages the Ravons!"

The tall man smiled. "'Voodoo Doll'!" he said. "Love that record! Welcome aboard, Jack!"

Allyn was shouting out to anyone who passed by his door. "Hey, Wayne, the Ravons are here! Liz, come here a minute, I got someone I want you to meet."

I am good with names and I certainly wanted to make contact with as many people at our new American label as I could, but I was losing track of who was who and I was anxious to stop the meet-and-greet and actually talk some business.

When Allyn finally got down to it—and it was hard to get him down to it or to keep him there—his advice was: You're getting airplay in Boston and upstate New York, go there and work your ass off and every place in between. Don't try to break the whole country at once, it'll kill you. Start building a base in the Northeast. If the group could book a spring tour, the label would help out with some expenses, but most of the budget for the Ravons was going into posters, record store displays, and radio promotion.

Allyn promised to arrange a dinner for me to get to know all the Tropic crew better while I was there, offered me tickets to a hockey game, and gave me the phone number of their branch manager in Boston.

"They got a new thing going up there," he told me, like it was a secret code. "Underground radio."

The Tropic Records dinner never did materialize, but between the reconnaissance missions of Fin and Tug we got some good leads and a tentative offer to tour Ohio in midsummer as opening act for Tommy James and the Shondells. The good news was that it was a legitimate American tour, but the money was awful and the Ravons had no profile in Ohio. We decided it was a fine start but we should devote the remainder of our time in America to trying to better it.

Sometimes what turns out to be the most important thing you do during a busy period seems minor at the time. During our brief negotiation with Tropic Records for American rights to the Ravons, the solicitor in me became fixed on what seemed to be an insignificant contractual detail. Tropic expected their recording contract to include the right to manufacture and distribute Ravons cassettes and eight-track tapes, as well as vinyl records. I had no particular problem with this, as tape sales were insignificant, but when I inquired about it I learned that neither Tropic nor their distributor actually owned any tape manufacturing plant. They sublicensed their eight-track and cassette business to Ampex, a recording tape company, who distributed the finished tapes themselves and paid Tropic a royalty. What returned to the artist on tape sales was a fraction of a fraction.

I know this is arcane, but bear with me. I told Hal Allyn that I wanted each Ravons tape sold to pay the group the same royalty as an LP, or else I wanted tapes carved out of the deal altogether. After a little posturing, Allyn said, "Go ahead and keep your tape rights if you think you can do better." Tropic wanted the vinyl. Vinyl was where the money was. Hell, vinyl was what records *were*.

It seemed like a small point in a long afternoon of giving and taking. I was concerned about getting the band promotional support and

Hal Allyn was more concerned with sticking us with breakage charges, packaging deductions, and other tried-and-true means of making sure the label eats the whole steak and the artist is paid in gristle.

It was not until I was back in London that I even remembered to make a side deal for the Ravons' cassettes with 3M, an American tape company. A few years later, when cassettes began to outsell vinyl, the Tropic bosses were appalled to realize that they did not own tape rights to Emerson or the other Ravons. I was able to turn this to an enormous advantage for my clients, renegotiating their royalties and winning eventual reversion of their masters. I can't tell you how much money this meant to Emerson over the decades, and to Charlie and Simon, too, when CDs came along.

But in 1969 in New York City, it seemed like so small a detail that I did not even mention it to Fin or Tug. All of our focus was on deciphering the meaning of Hal Allyn's tip to get the Ravons on underground radio. On our third day at the Times Square Howard Johnson's we decided to drive to Boston and get to the bottom of this.

In New York we were three more hustlers trying to break into a city over its limit. But in Boston we were exotic creatures. Benny, the local Tropic Records rep, treated us like the Beatles. He took us around to meet every radio station programmer and college concert committee booker in a hundred-mile radius. We carried signed copies of *Curses and Cures* and played "Voodoo Doll" for anyone who would listen.

It felt in those days as if there were only about fifty people in the entire rock and roll business, and everyone you met—no matter how humble their position at the time—became part of your life for years to come. I would never have guessed then that the most significant acquaintance I would make in that whole first week in America would be a thin, toothy Boston University student called Ramon Castro. Castro was Cuban, and, his surname aside, was the well-heeled son of a wealthy family that had fled to Florida after the revolution.

"I would think being named Castro would open a few doors in Havana," I told him.

"Causes a lot of shit in Miami, though," he replied.

Unlike most American college students of that era, Ramon Castro was neither politically engaged nor laid back. He was a hustler. He had taken over the BU student entertainment budget and ran it like a bank. He had contacts at the local underground papers and with all the other college concert committees in the area. He got free records in the mail, too.

Castro knew all about the Ravons and agreed to book them at BU. More than that, he connected us with other colleges throughout New England, and for a small finder's fee persuaded them to hire us, too.

Castro took me to lunch at a delicatessen across the street from the Prudential Tower in the middle of Boston. We walked down five steps and past large jars of pigs' tongues and other internal organs offered as delicacies. There was a large jukebox playing a song called "Dirty Water." The small tables were filled with college students and local workmen on break from construction jobs.

Castro laid out his vision: "The Ravons can be major, Jack. They've got the tunes, they've got the chops, and they look great. Nobody talks about looking great anymore, it's not cool to say it, but come on—between you and me, this is still show business. The chicks want to look at cute guys and even the guys in the audience want to think the musicians are better-looking versions of themselves. Emerson looks the way all these kids in bell-bottoms and bad shirts want to think they look. That's important, but we never admit it."

I nodded and tried to signal the waiter to come take our order.

Castro went on: "It's important that every kid we play to thinks that he's discovering the Ravons for himself. See, you're actually lucky that they didn't have the pop hits in the States that they had in England. We're going to tell the Americans that the Ravons are underground, too hip for Top Forty. No teenybopper shit. We're going to build this so beautifully that every single fan will think the whole thing was his idea. Total credibility. Grassroots. You with me on that?"

I told Castro I was indeed and then he got us potato pancakes and applesauce and passed me the check.

It was worth it. The colleges Castro booked us into turned out to be a gold mine. There must have been fifty of them in the Boston area, each with a social committee flush with funds for bringing cool rock bands to campus. Benny the promo man helped us get an April booking at the Tea Party, a Boston rock club, which was prestigious but could not have justified transatlantic plane tickets for six people. We booked three weeks of campus shows around that Tea Party engagement, including a Spring Weekend concert on the quad at Yale, and a Sunday show as part of a series on the Cambridge Common.

Indulge an old man's nostalgia for a moment. The girls we saw on these campuses were the loveliest beings I had ever encountered. In my memory they all had long straight hair and long straight legs in startlingly short skirts or low-slung blue jeans. They wore peasant blouses or ribbed long-sleeve T-shirts with three-button collars that they kept undone. They wore sandals or sneakers (it was the first time I'd heard the word) or high, tight lace-up boots. They always seemed to be smiling and laughing and they all had perfect white teeth.

I never got over them.

Castro's system of college bookings was a new world to Tug, whose American experience was with Dick Clark and Murray the K package tours. He was annoyed at the idea of playing shows for university students and contemptuous of the kids who booked the concerts with their parents' money.

Fin and I thought it was great. The college students were just who we wanted the Ravons to reach, to get away from any association with bubblegum. We also discovered that each campus had a radio station, run by the students and anxious to get behind new sounds. Fin made it his personal mission to make pals with as many college radio programmers as he could find, and to evangelize for his British brothers.

If he suggested that the Ravons spent most of their time swapping ideas with Clapton and Hendrix, I always told myself that he believed it at the moment he said it.

I thought for a couple of days that college radio was the underground radio that Hal Allyn had steered me toward, but Benny disabused me of that. Benny had something I had never seen before—an FM radio in his automobile's dashboard. He turned it on, switched past the Mozart and Brahms, and to my amazement settled on the blaring harmonica of Little Walter and the bowels-of-the-earth voice of Howlin' Wolf.

"Holy shit, Batman," said Fin.

"What is that?" said I.

"That," Benny the promo man said with gravitas in a Boston accent, "is the sound of the future. That is commercial FM rock radio."

Fin repeated his earlier analysis: "Holy shit."

We were a strange company going to meet the wizard of FM radio.
Fin was a wonderful fellow but he had no brain. Benny was a record
company promo man—of course he had no heart. And Tug, with an
envelope of cash, a small bag of marijuana, and a large box of jelly
doughnuts, was the very picture of a cowardly lion.

I assumed the purpose of the cash was professional and the pot recreational. I was right and wrong about that.

The new Kingpin of Boston FM worked out of a Victorian house
on a leafy side street in Cambridge. He was a very tall fellow with the
open manner of a basketball coach. He had longish hair, perfectly
groomed. It was the first shag haircut I had ever seen on a man.

He led us through a series of rooms in which a dozen college girls
and two or three boys were talking on telephones, typing, and baking
cookies. The Kingpin was about twenty-four, the oldest person in his
operation.

He led us to a corner room with a view of the suburban street, several large potted plants, five short filing cabinets, and an old kitchen
table that he used as a desk.

"So," he said. "The Ravons!"

"They're so fuckin' good," Benny the promo man said breathlessly.
"You like Beck, you like Cream, you're goin' to flip for this!"

"I heard that other record they had. 'Along Comes Mary.'" The
Kingpin shrugged.

"'Mary vs. Mary,'" I said. "'Along Comes Mary' was someone else."

"Oh yeah." Benny laughed. "That's like mixin' up the Mamas and
Papas and the Mothers!" He seemed at once to be afraid he had insulted the Kingpin. He hurried to say, "Everybody got that confused,
it's probably why the USA is the only country where the good 'Mary'

wasn't a hit. But anyway, it's just as well because this new record the Ravons got is going to make everybody shit."

I wondered why that was a recommendation. The Kingpin said, hey, let's hear it. I pulled out a copy of *Curses and Cures* and passed it over the table to the Kingpin. He had a turntable separate from the rest of his stereo components, with a tiny little nub for a center spindle and a tone arm he lifted and placed on the vinyl himself. It was very space-age.

Speakers hung from the ceiling boomed and crackled to life and the first chords of "Voodoo Doll" pealed out with more volume and clarity than they had in our London recording studio. The Kingpin kept his bass and treble knobs turned up all the way.

We all rocked in our chairs to the swampy vamp and Emerson's passionate vocal. As the guitar solo ended the Kingpin lifted the tone arm and dropped it perfectly into the wide groove before the next song. This was one of Charlie's, and it sustained the southern American mood of "Voodoo Doll" while introducing a note of British melancholy.

"I dig this," the Kingpin said. "I'm going to add it to my overnight show and I'll bet the Woofer will want to put it on his International Hour, too. Of course, that's up to him." He looked at me and explained, "We're totally free form. No playlist."

I was very happy with the way this meeting was going. If America was this easy to crack, I was surprised it had taken the Ravons three years to get here. The LP kept playing and I wondered if we should excuse ourselves, offer to take the Kingpin to lunch, or stay put and groove to the whole platter.

"So," the Kingpin said.

I was missing something.

Benny was not. He got up and closed the office door. He came back and said, "Could we offer you a cocktail?" He reached into his shirt pocket and pulled out two thin and perfectly rolled joints. The Kingpin opened his window a crack and reached for the reefer.

Oh, I figured—that's it, a bonding ritual among the hipsters. I misunderstood. The Kingpin sucked in some marijuana smoke and exhaled it at a poster of Buddy Miles. He was waiting for something. Benny nudged Tug. Tug took a brown envelope out of his jacket pocket and slid it toward the Kingpin, who dropped a copy of *Rolling Stone* on top of it and took another suck on his cigarette.

Dawn broke on my innocence. We were paying the Kingpin to support our new record on Boston's breakthrough underground FM station. That was how the game was played. The icicles melted from my eyes. I wondered what the etiquette was for computing how much of the bribe money came from the record company and how much from the band. Benny and Tug seemed to have made that calculation without me.

I had seen the future of American rock radio. I had met the new boss.

Emerson, Charlie, and Simon were very happy to hear that they were finally going to tour the United States.

"It's good we didn't go sooner, actually," Charlie declared. "If we'd gone over as part of the Flower Power thing it'd be over for us now. Better we waited."

Despite their stated intentions, the band had not done any new writing while Tug, Fin, and I were in the States. They had been reveling in their new stardom. Emerson had been to a party at Paul McCartney's house, which he brought up at every opportunity, causing Simon to loudly predict that the Beatles were over anyway.

When they entered the Alibi Club now, the Ravons were sent free drinks from every corner. One night when we had all enjoyed too much liquor and most of the Rolling Stones were seated at the next table, I was startled to see Charlie reel back and throw a piece of battered fish at Keith Richards. In our circle this was equivalent to asking the Queen if she'd had a good bowel movement. I thought that either we would be ejected from the club or Charlie would end up with a knife in his pitching hand. Instead Keith looked down at the fish, which lay on the table in front of him, brushed it aside, and simply raised two fingers in the general direction of Charlie.

Charlie started grabbing at everyone else's plate for more ammunition. I told him to stop. The Stones' burly, jut-chinned road manager rose from their company and strolled over to our table. I prepared to take Charlie's beating for him but the road manager simply put both his big hands on Charlie's shoulders from behind, made a rubbing motion that was so far a massage but could quickly slip into a choke, and said, "Who's throwing his supper around, then? Must be a bad boy needs a beatin'!" He laughed and Charlie did the same and everyone at our table said hello, what's up, you blokes in the studio now, see ya, man, and he let go of Charlie's neck and gave him an affectionate slap on the top of the head and went back to his charges.

"Hell, Charlie," I whispered. "You don't throw food at the Rolling Stones!"

Charlie was delighted. He said, "That's funny, Jack, I could have sworn I did!"

Simon took having a hit record as a license to burrow into debt. He bought a flashy car that he drove all over town in first gear until he burned out the transmission. He moved into the upper half of a house in Mayfair that turned out to have a brothel on the first floor. He furnished his new rooms with bad taste from several cultures, each item overpaid for at antiques shops that I suspected were stocking their overpriced shelves from the secondhand stalls at Portobello Market.

Each of the band upgraded his stereo. Fin ordered a component setup like the one we had seen in America, in the office of the FM king. Emerson bought a great mahogany home entertainment center with a color television in its belly, a radio and record player in its shoulders, and speakers set behind what seemed to be medieval scrolling on either wing. Simon bought a hi-fi with a flip-down turntable, a shortwave radio, and speakers on hinges that either folded shut to make the whole console look like a drinks cabinet, swung out to allow the turntable to open, or detached and could be moved about the room on long wires to produce maximum stereo woof and tweet.

Eventually Simon hung those speakers from his ceiling, dazzling every guest who stepped into his parlor.

Charlie went for an expensive reel-to-reel tape recorder, which he ran through his old record player's amp and speakers. In those days audiophiles could buy albums on seven-inch reels of tape, which implied sophistication of a Hugh Hefner level. What attracted Charlie, though, was that not only could he record on the machine, but it had a feature that allowed him to record first on the left track, and then on the right. He could overdub at home.

"Check it out, Flynnie!" he cried while cueing up a tape he had made with guitar and lead vocals on one side, piano and harmony vocals on the other. "It's what I've always wanted! Permission to play with meself!"

When the royalty checks came in, Charlie presented each of the other Ravons and me with an elaborate gift. He had bought five sets of *Living Shakespeare*, a thirty-six-LP set of the Bard's plays, performed by the great actors of the British stage. Each disc was an edited forty-five-minute presentation of *Hamlet, Othello, Macbeth*, right up to *Henry VIII* and *King John*. They came six to a box in six wine-colored slipcases with gold leaf lettering that would sit on a bookshelf like thick volumes of prose. Each LP came with a booklet containing the text of the play and commentary. It was an impressive present.

"I got a set," Charlie said. "It's so good. You put one on the turntable, light up a joint, and lay back and let all that poetry float into your ears like smoke. Emerson, check out the sonnets. You see where Dylan gets it. 'Love Minus Zero' is right out of 'My mistress' eyes are nothing like the sun.' 'Tears of Rage,' it's *Lear*, man. Listen to these discs while you're falling asleep and you'll wake up with five new songs in your head!"

I think we were all touched by Charlie's generosity. It had not occurred to any of the other Ravons to use their new money to buy presents for anyone but themselves. I don't know about the others, but I did spin *Midsummer Night's Dream* and *The Tempest* a couple of times while working on tour-routing and tax forms. When I finally left England I donated my Shakespeare set to the local boys' school library, where I am sure it bailed many a student out of having to read *The Two Gentlemen of Verona*.

The Ravons having a hit record brought out every drug dealer in London. These furtive creatures—whatever their distinctions they all had cash registers behind their eyes—seemed to materialize out of the corners of nightclubs, dressing rooms, and parties. They knew all the doormen and ticket takers. They passed the Ravons endless pharmaceutical free goods in the hope of enticing return business.

I tried to advise moderation in all indulgences, but the Ravons had waited a long time for success and they wanted to eat it up. If this was the start of a long run at the top, they had no worries. If this was a short visit before a long fall, at least they'd have enjoyed the glimpse. They had no motivation to be moderate.

It was difficult for me to pull them out of their victory lap and get them back to writing songs. Without new material, the party would be over very quickly. Their taste of success had inflamed the Ravons' egos. They were no longer willing to compromise their own intuitions and desires for the good of the collective.

Simon's ambition to write socially conscious opuses with as many chords as possible was no longer a source of amusement to Charlie and Emerson. The two of them now found it easier to exclude Simon from writing sessions and to reject his attempts to revise the songs they came up with. The camaraderie was breaking down and the drugs they were being offered from every outstretched hand were not helping.

It was not that any of the Ravons were addicts. Far from it, their drug use was recreational and, by the standards of the day, moderate. The problem was that they were all taking different drugs now, which changed their personalities in subtle ways and broke down the bond between them. Speed was making Simon belligerent and egotistical. Hallucinogens were causing Emerson to become self-absorbed and aloof. A new blend of Turkish pot with enhanced THC content made Charlie silly and unfocused, and then he drank and his humor turned nasty. After a few brandies Charlie would poke at Simon's weak spots until Simon's nose started to bleed.

It was getting ugly in London. I held out the promise of the U.S. tour to the Ravons like a besieged parent using the coming of Christmas to get his kids to behave.

The band managed to squeeze out one single, a love song of Charlie's called "Leaving Time" that was slowed down and strung out to allow Emerson a long, rolling guitar solo. Somehow this languor made the implication of the song more cosmic—the leaving did not have to be a man walking out on a woman. It could be friends separated by the draft, earthlings lighting out for Alpha Centauri, or a band on the verge of breaking up.

It felt to us in the office—Allison, Tug, and me—that Simon might be out of the Ravons any day. He could easily walk on his own, or Emerson and Charlie could push him. I delayed a confrontation by insisting to a reluctant Charlie that "Leaving Time" continue the practice of crediting Charlie, Emerson, and Simon as cowriters.

"Look, Jack," Charlie said, "I wrote the whole song—all the words, the melody, every bit of it. Simon didn't even want to play on it. I don't mind putting Em's name on because he laid in a lovely solo but why is it fair that Simon does nothing and makes as much off the publishing as I do?"

"Because you're partners, Charlie," I reminded him. "You get your name on Simon's songs."

"I don't want my name on Simon's songs, Flynn! Fuckin' depressive tripe, it's embarrassing."

"As long as the three of you split the credit and the publishing money, the best songs win. As soon as you start saying, 'This is *mine,*' everyone's going to fight to get his songs on the records. Do you want that? Besides, I want each of you to be able to contribute to the other's tunes without worrying about who's getting a piece of your check if you take his suggestion. Believe me, Charlie, if you think Simon's a pain in the arse now, just wait to see what it will be like if you have to start competing for writing credits."

Charlie went along, but the bonds were fraying. I began to think it would not be such a bad thing if Simon left—as long as he waited until after the American tour.

What is unwise about building up Christmas is that the disappointment is so great when it is over. The Ravons did their tour; they played colleges from New Hampshire to New Jersey and club dates in Boston, New York, and Philadelphia. Tropic Records even got them on a bill opening for Joe Cocker at an outdoor show in Albany. It was three weeks of work, a foot in the door in America, and a great boost to their radio profile. By the time they left, they had offers of summer tours from two different booking agencies and a shot at playing the Fillmore East next time through.

But some part of them had expected to go to America and headline Shea Stadium. The fact that most of the audiences they played to did not know them dragged down their already low morale. For three years the Ravons had been working hard and getting better. Every time it seemed that they were about to achieve the summit they had labored for, they opened the door and found another staircase.

London that spring felt like it was falling apart. The energy that had descended on the city five years earlier was going elsewhere. Carnaby Street stores were turning into cheap tourist traps. Rumors were rampant that the Beatles were at each others' throats and delaying announcement of a divorce only until they renegotiated their record deal.

Cream was gone, Hendrix had moved back to America. What hit the Ravons the hardest was the firing and subsequent death of Brian Jones of the Rolling Stones. It reminded them of Ilsa's predictions and their own bizarre bargain with Mr. LaSalle. The drugs made the paranoia and recrimination worse.

They needed to make another album, but they were in no shape to do something good. We bought time with the American label by putting together a compilation of the best songs from the first two Ravons LPs, never before issued in the U.S., with the new single and a couple of B-sides, all tricked out with a new photo of the boys looking very hairy and 1969. Tropic Records was delighted to have the product, but it was a shoddy way to buy time and left the band depressed about their prospects in the States.

Simon could not have picked a worse time to begin agitating for the band to make a concept album about a rock singer who sells his soul to Lucifer in exchange for fame. He even had ideas for incorporating Emerson and Charlie's recent songs into the project, once Simon had rewritten some of their lyrics to fit his theme.

Emerson and Charlie kept making excuses to avoid going into the studio. I had to act. I suggested the two of them come to my flat on a Sunday afternoon to talk without Simon, Fin, or Tug. It would have been an unthinkable subterfuge just six months earlier. Now the pair accepted the invitation without question or objection.

I served tea and sandwiches and we put off getting down to business for as long as we could.

"How do you feel about the Tommy James tour?" I asked them.

"He's a bit wet, isn't he?" Charlie said.

"Huge in America, though," I said. "And the thing is, if we do the June dates on the East Coast and then want to stay around for Newport and the Fillmore at the end of July, we could use that tour of the Midwest as a bridge, rather than come back to England for eighteen days in between. I can't see any harm in it."

Emerson was not talking. I asked him what he thought.

"Makes sense," he said.

I plowed on. "So the question is, do the two of you feel that the band is going to be able to write and record a new album between now and those summer shows?"

This was an opening to talk about the Simon problem. Neither of them picked up the ball. So I said, "Are there changes that should be made before we go forward?"

"Is someone missing?" Charlie asked. "Is there an empty seat at our family gathering?"

"Look, fellows," I said. "I feel awful meeting like this but there is no question that something has to change if we're going to move forward. It feels lately like you two are uncomfortable with Simon's contributions to the band. I don't know how to handle that but there it is. Simon is our friend and I respect him, but the three of us need to talk about this."

Emerson had been staring straight ahead. He turned to me and his eyes were wet—something I had never seen—with either sadness or contained anger. He said, "You're right, Jack. Something has to change. Here it is. I'm leaving the band."

I was startled but Charlie was gobsmacked. His mouth fell open and his eyes turned black.

"You're fucking what, Em?" Charlie said.

"It's all gone miserable, hasn't it?" Emerson said to Charlie. I might as well have not been in the room. "We've tried the teen thing, we've gone psychedelic, we've done the social commentary and the jazzy progressive bit and the New Orleans R&B and the long guitar solos and it's all shit in the end, isn't it? Now we're sitting here calmly discussing tossing Simon out of the band. Just like we sacked Gino to bring in Fin. Simon, our friend. Well, what did we gain by sacking Gino, Charlie? And what do you really think we'll gain if we give Simon the boot? Then who's next? You? Me? And anyway, what are we doing it for?"

"Look, Emerson," I said, "if that's how you feel I apologize for bringing it up. Of course Simon stays. You're all overworked, let's take some time off and—"

"No, Flynn," Emerson said. "It's not about that. I made up my mind two weeks ago, I just didn't know how to tell you. I thought maybe I'd wait till after the summer dates but why prolong the torture?"

Emerson turned to Charlie, who looked like a wife whose husband had just announced he needed her out of the house because he was going to marry the babysitter.

Emerson said, "It's time, Charlie. We did everything we wanted to do with the Ravons, but come on, we all have to leave school sometime. I'm going to California. I met this promoter when we were in the States and he made me an offer. I thought it was just talk but he's followed up and it looks like he's got me a gig in Los Angeles with these cats who played on the Byrds albums . . ."

Little Charlie was an endless well of peace and harmony, but he had grown up poor on the streets of North London. He rounded on Emerson and punched him in the neck. Em crashed over the side of his chair and Charlie jumped up and began kicking him. I tried to pull him off and he rammed his elbow into my nose.

"Ya fuckin' traitor!" Charlie shouted as he put the boot into Emerson's ribs again and again. "Ya got this all planned out! Ya been linin' up gigs on the fuckin' coast, have ya?"

Emerson was five inches taller than Charlie and had twenty pounds on him but he pulled himself into a ball on the floor and took the kicking with his arms across his face.

Charlie stopped and looked down on him. Then he looked up at me.

"Tell the other two to meet me at the studio at five, Flynn," Charlie said. "I have to find us another guitar player. We gotta break him in for the American tour."

Which was what Charlie did. He recruited a session guitarist named Duf Mahoney, who learned Emerson's solos note for note and fulfilled all of the Ravons' obligations in the UK and abroad. Some of the big American shows dropped out—the Ravons never got to play the Fillmore or the Newport Jazz Festival—but the new Ravons limped on until August, when they gave their final performance at a fairground outside of Cleveland opening for Tommy James and the Shondells. It was the same weekend as the Woodstock rock festival in upstate New York.

Fin did not even bother returning to England with the band. He was American; he stayed behind in America to look for work.

In December Charlie, Simon, and the deputized Duf joined original Ravons drummer Gino Netro for an unofficial farewell show at the Alibi Club's Christmas party. The sixties were over; so were the Ravons.

ROUGH MIX

It is often said that there is a four-year lag between when a new decade begins and when the zeitgeist rolls over. According to this reckoning, the 1960s began with the assassination of JFK and the arrival in America of the Beatles, and ended when Nixon resigned. According to this view the early 1970s—the time of the invasion of Cambodia, the Kent State shootings, Patty Hearst, Angela Davis, and Crosby, Stills, Nash & Young—should be considered part of the sixties. The seventies began with Gerald Ford and disco.

While there is some wisdom in that way of measuring the periods through which we passed, there was one abrupt change between 1969 and 1970 that demarked the two decades as clearly as a barbed-wire fence. It still seems to me all these years later to be one of those psychic shifts that happen occasionally across large segments of the population without anyone organizing it, announcing it, or saying anything about it.

What reversed very quickly between May 1969 and May 1970 was the counterculture's attitude—a whole generation's attitude, really—toward the country and the city.

All through the sixties, youth culture, bohemian culture, rock and roll culture was urban. Young people left the farm, the small town, the suburbs, and came to the city to free themselves and become musicians, painters, writers, pickpockets, or drug addicts. We remember Swinging London, not Swinging Swindon. All of the explosions of the sixties—beat, mod, hippie—happened in cities: New York, Liverpool, London, Detroit, Los Angeles, San Francisco, Paris, Prague. To the freethinking new generation, the rustic was unwelcoming. The 1960s hippie view of the sticks is perfectly represented by the last quintessential sixties film—*Easy Rider*. When existential druggie bikers Peter Fonda and Dennis

Hopper venture into the countryside to look for the real America, the hillbillies shoot them dead.

Yet somehow, between the making of *Easy Rider* and the mass gathering at Yasgur's farm in August 1969, the counterculture all seemed to decide at once that the cities were dirty and corrupting and the countryside was where it was at. Like a subliminal signal alerting ducks to migrate, the radio filled with songs about abandoning the ugly urban for the cleansing rural. Suddenly we were "Goin' Up the Country" to "Share the Land" and eat "Country Pie" with a "Country Girl" because "Hey ho, want you to know, people in the country really let themselves go."

Downtown flats were abandoned and Volkswagen buses were loaded with hoes and fishing poles. Every album came packed with a fold-out sleeve and photos of the stars, their pals, old ladies, pets, and dirty blond children getting it together in the country. The images on the album covers said that Dylan, the Band, and Van Morrison were looking down from mountain ridges in Woodstock, the Allman Brothers were Georgia farmers, Led Zeppelin lived in stone cabins in Wales, and the Rolling Stones were lording over decadent castles in the English countryside and hunting for water rats around their moats. Berry Gordy packed up Motown itself and like Moses led his stars to the promised land of beachfront property on the Pacific Ocean. Neil Young made records in the barn on his northern California ranch. James Taylor beat that—handyman that he was, he built his own barn and farmhouse on an island off New England. Joni Mitchell sent dispatches from her stone hearth in British Columbia. McCartney had left the temptations of London and hot water to raise rams in a cottage in remote Scotland. The beards had all grown longer overnight.

I suppose I should have known then that the locus of power in the music industry would shift to Los Angeles, that strange quilt of country and city, with its canyons and mountains and beaches a short drive from nightclubs, recording studios, and top-line drug dealers. Emerson had got it right away—the magnet was moving and he followed it with the true star's automatic sense of the gravity shifting in his audience. But I never had Emerson's instincts. I never had his gift for obeying the part of the brain that does not translate into language. I suppose that was why I spent my life working for him.

Emerson had the guts to leave England and head six thousand miles west. The rest of us were not initially so brave. Charlie appeared in my office one day to announce that he had given up his flat in Kentish Town and had signed a two-year lease on a fifty-acre farm near Wales. He had met a wonderful woman named Margaret (aka Meg aka Maggie aka Magpie) who had made him see the benefits of the natural life. He was going to raise sheep and chickens and spend his days absorbing inspiration from the land and his evenings making wooden music on the porch.

I remember his using that phrase—"wooden music." I thought at first that it meant stiff and unswinging, but I came to understand it to mean something like music made with acoustic guitars and mandolins and the drummer beating on a cracker barrel with ears of corn. Charlie invited me to drive out to the farm with Meg and him to grok the homey vibes and have a gander at his geese. I could hardly say no.

We packed up and left London early on a Monday morning, as I remember. I am aware that our memories play tricks on us, especially memories that we have replayed over and over. The tapes get worn and other recollections bleed through and get mixed in. The way we tell the story begins to change the story. Compounding the confusion, we translate our experiences of long ago into the currencies of who we are today. When I recall being charged a shocking amount for a bad dinner in a good restaurant in 1970, I now think the bill was six hundred pounds. But that is impossible. The 1970 bill was probably thirty pounds. I have adjusted my remembered indignation for inflation, and to my circumstances today.

In the same way, even as I remember getting up at an ungodly hour of the morning to pile into the Ravons' Commer van—the mutated milk truck—with Charlie and Meg for an all-day ride to their new hovel in Chepstow, logic contradicts my memory. Our idea of an ungodly early hour in 1970 was probably noon, and the drive to Chepstow from Kentish Town could not have taken much more than four hours. I can, however, say with certainty that it felt like an eternity.

Meg was a short girl, and stout, with a very pretty open face and cascades of thick blond curls. She dressed in thirdhand clothes, high shoes and long granny dresses with the blouse opened to flatter her large bosom. She was nothing like the tall, skinny waifs in miniskirts who used to circle around the Ravons, and Charlie seemed to love her for it. I admit that after initially regarding her as dumpy and uninteresting, I warmed to her charms. She laughed easily and exuded a contagious joy in simple things. However, as the hours piled up, I did once or twice consider jumping out of the moving van to get away from her.

Our journey began with a lot of horn-honking and Charlie and Meg shouting good-bye to smelly London out of the van windows. As it takes a considerable while to actually drive out of London, especially on a Monday morning, these good-byes continued for a very long time.

"See ya later, DDT grocer!" Charlie cried as we passed the market.

"Good-bye, polluting petrol plant!" Meg shouted.

"Sayonara, dirty tube station!"

This went on and on. Every time we were stuck in traffic the two of them would jabber about how *this* was why they were leaving the city. If we passed a gasworks or a factory with a chimney sending out smoke or a row of small houses with TV aerials, Charlie and his Magpie would groan and point as if they were fleeing a war zone.

Their good-riddances competed with one tape that played over and over and over for the entire journey, a new album by the Grateful Dead that had become the leitmotif of their hippie hegira. I was vaguely aware of the Grateful Dead as a California band who played what we then called Freak-Out Music, long and ear-splitting jams. I was surprised that this new record was quite soft and old-fashioned, with country-tinged folk songs about railroads and coal mines. I was not certain it was not a put-on, but I didn't care and the music seemed homemade and pleasant. At least the first two or three times the tape went around.

By hour three of hearing Charlie and Meg sing along about riding that train high on cocaine, I was having a quiet freak-out of my own. My companions were harmonizing in at least two more keys than the Dead were using. They sang over and over, "Don't murder me, please don't murder me," while the option became ever more attractive. We had crossed the new Severn Bridge and could smell Wales when I asked if we could not please turn off the tape for a while. Charlie said sure. Then he and Meg sang the same song for another hour, unaccompanied.

As the roads got thinner and bumpier there were a lot of wrong turns and arguing about how they came last time. Charlie was all for asking directions of every yokel we passed, most of whom glared at us suspiciously and many of whom sent us the wrong way. Meg was more adamant about studying the map and navigating for herself. The more lost we got, the more she demanded to drive. Charlie laughed and tried to change the subject by pointing out birds or asking her what kind of tree that was.

Charlie and Meg had been passing a jug of wine back and forth for half an hour, which did nothing to make me more comfortable. Fumbling in the glove box for another set of directions, Meg came out with a rolled-up piece of newspaper which she shocked me by setting afire. Only when she put the other end to her mouth and sucked out a plume of smoke did I realize that this was no map, it was the biggest joint I had ever seen.

Now we were begging to be arrested, assuming that the combination of wine, marijuana, bad roads, and Charlie's dubious driving would not conspire to kill us first.

"Please put that out, Margaret," I said sternly. "We are not in London now. The authorities out here get very rough on drugs."

Meg looked at me like I had told her that her shoes didn't match her dress.

"I think you might be very surprised by the people out here," she told me with smoke following the words from her mouth. "People out here are real. They don't interfere with each other's personal decisions."

"It only takes one man with a badge," I said. Charlie was driving us up what seemed with every mile less a dirt road and more a ditch. "I know this from experience, I'm afraid."

"Jack used to be a solicitor," Charlie explained. "Got caught with drugs coming over from France and they took away his lawyer license."

Meg looked unconvinced.

"It was Charlie's drugs I was holding," I told her. "If we were to be stopped right now, you and he might get off with a few days in a country jail. But I will be sent straight to prison. You understand?"

Meg stamped out her doobie on the dashboard, sending fat sparks floating to the floor of the van. She squinted her nose like a child told to stop playing and set the table. She stuffed the still-smoking joint back into the glove box and reached for the jug of wine, which she tipped back and drank from until little red streams ran down her cheeks and neck. She wiped her mouth with the back of her hand, looked out the windscreen, and said, "Now where are we?"

There was no road left at all. We were driving in a grassy gap between two hills with sparse trees and very large rocks. Charlie said he was going to get out and take a pee. He parked the van and walked up the hill. Meg got out and sat against the bumper with her jug. I wondered whether we'd have to sleep in the bread truck tonight.

Charlie's voice came crowing down the hill, "I see the windmill! We're here!"

Meg was her smiling self again as Charlie ran into her arms. We backed up the van and turned onto a dirt road that gained some loose gravel as we continued down a steady slope. I saw above the trees a weather-beaten wooden tower shedding faded brown shingles. Charlie's windmill had no sails.

"We'll put 'em up again!" Charlie said. "The fella who owned the place was a drinker, end of the family line. Let it all go to pot a bit but we'll put that right quick enough!"

Meg was giggling now, bouncing back and forth between Charlie and me with her hands on both our legs. "Get out and open the gate, Charlie!" she said. "Let me drive in!"

Charlie bounded from the van and swung open a white wooden gate hinged on a stone column. Meg hit the gas and barreled us through, spattering dirt and gravel behind. On our left was a very large tan building, a big barn of some sort, with no windows. On our right was a dilapidated greenhouse with thin branches pushing through broken windows. The road slid downward until the gravel turned to hard mud in front of a horse barn that had been partly converted into a garage, and a farmhouse with a first story made of cement and two higher stories made of wood. I knew nothing about architecture and less about agriculture, but it seemed to me that to center a farm in the basin of a hillside, where water, sludge, seepage, and animal shit would all roll toward it, was perhaps a bad idea. I reminded myself that I was here only for a night or two.

Meg and Charlie showed me around the grounds. They did not see the farm as it was, they saw it as it would be when they had filled it with their dreams and labor. We all drank more bad wine and sat on a hillside and ate from a picnic basket Meg had prepared and drank more and smoked marijuana and retired early. I froze all night long.

I woke to roosters crowing, ducks quacking, geese honking, and the patter of what I hoped were only mice along the floor beneath my bed. The sunlight coming in through the yellow window gave me a better sense of the room in which I had spent the night. It was filthy. Bits of dust floated in the sunbeams like a slow-motion sandstorm. There was grime on the floor and on the old broken chest of drawers, above which hung a cracked mirror in a mottled frame. I was sunk deep into a mattress that had all the firmness of a coconut cake, in my clothes and overcoat, under a pile of musty quilts and blankets and one braided throw rug. I had shivered all night and piled on anything I could find.

Each time I had managed to fall asleep I had been awakened by the sounds of Meg and Charlie's exuberant and recurring lovemaking. Meg was clearly mad for it and she was a screamer. Perhaps that was one reason they were anxious to move far away from the city and other people. Here in the gullies of Chepstow she could holler like a ban-shee on the moors without neighbors pounding the walls with broom handles. I wondered if she frightened the livestock.

I smelled something cooking and wandered into the kitchen, where Meg was frying up sausages with lard and honey. She asked me to be a sweetheart and go collect some eggs from the chicken coop. I made my way outside, blinking in the light. The door to the coop was long gone and the chickens wandered freely in and out. I knew their domain by the trail of their droppings, which orbited out in wide circles from the yard around their domicile over broken fences and short stone walls to decorate an acre of ground. No one had enforced any boundaries on these birds in a long time and no one had cleaned up. I entered the coop itself and saw that seed was spilling out of big sacks in the closet next to the nesting room. The birds pecked freely and defecated where they dined. It was a wonder they had not all eaten themselves to death.

A fat red hen stared at me with black-eyed menace as I poked through the straw for eggs. I found two small gray eggs, then a fat white egg, and then three middle-sized tan eggs. I felt like a child on Easter Sunday. I tiptoed past the evil old hen and made my way back to the kitchen, where Charlie had joined his girlfriend, or, to use the terminology of the time, his lady.

"Mornin', Jackie!" he cried happily. Charlie was seated at the table. He wore a long-sleeve undershirt with a ring neck and three buttons undone and workman's trousers two sizes too big, with suspenders. "How'd you sleep, then?"

"Fine," I said. "I got some eggs."

"You hear that, love?" Charlie said, tipping his chair back and looking over his shoulder at Meg at the stove. "Jack's brought us some eggs!"

"Put 'em here, Jack," Meg said and tapped her spatula on the edge of the stove. She rolled her sausages off the frying pan onto a blue plate and began cracking the eggs and dropping them into the pan in a one-handed stroke. I was very hungry, which caused me to ignore a slight bad taste in the eggs when they came my way. Later, puking under a tree, I had cause to wonder how long some of them had been lying in the straw before I got there.

"Ain't this the life, Johnny?" Charlie asked me with delight. "It's like we're livin' in heaven's own cathedral. The sun in the mornin' makes everything look like stained glass. The birds are a choir. I never felt closer to God than I do right here, Jack, and that's the truth."

Charlie's professed love for God and religion had always been a puzzle to me, as it in no way impeded his enthusiasm for drugs, liquor, and frequent extramarital sex. With the full burdens of my Catholic upbringing pressing down on me still, I asked Charlie how he reconciled his spiritual longings with his love for the sensual world.

"Ah, but that's the beauty, Jack, doncha see?" Charlie laughed and waved at Meg. "God made this world a big ball of sex! Did you listen to them Shakespeare records I gave you? 'It is a bawdy planet.' Look around the barnyard, brother! The horses are horny, the hens are in heat, the rabbits are randy. Cor, Jack, Earth is the brothel of the universe! The plants are reproducing, the bees are balling the flowers, the trees are spilling seeds all over the ground, and the ocean is full of fish fucking! It's a throbbing hothouse God set us in! You think He thought we wouldn't notice? Mind-travelers from other planets must tell their kids to cover their eyes when they pass through *our* solar system! We're triple-X-rated, we are. A roiling globe of forests, beasts, and microorganisms sweating and heaving and fertilizing and repro-ducing like sailors in a cathouse! Sex is the engine that runs this world, Jack. The trick is to use it up while we're here and then graduate to the world of the spirit with no regrets."

"You have gone back to nature like Tarzan," I told him.

"Never left, mate," he said. "Never left."

Meg filled the sink and started doing the dishes. Charlie stood up from the table and announced, "We have one chore to do this morn-ing, Jackie!"

He was gone five minutes. When he returned he was lugging a rusty weather vane half as tall as his chest.

"How do you like her?" he said proudly, standing the weather vane on its pole and resting his hand upon the iron rooster at its crown. He gave the metal arrow a twirl. It spun slowly and came to rest pointing between my eyes. "When we mount this on the roof of the barn, Bom-badil Glen will be open for business!"

Bombadil Glen was what Charlie and Meg called their farm. Over the next few months Charlie would establish a publishing company called Bombadil Songs, record an instrumental called "Bombadil Boo-gie," and briefly brew a limited-edition beer called Bombadil Organic Ale. I didn't know what Bombadil meant then and no one ever told me.

Neither of Charlie's decayed wooden ladders was tall enough to as-cend the outside of the barn, so we ended up hauling a ladder and the weather vane into the hayloft and making our way up through a hole in the ceiling. By the time we were finally on the roof we were dragging the iron rooster on a rope that had been Meg's clothesline and trying not to slip and fall. I had no doubt that if I lost my footing I would manage not only to sail straight off the roof, but to land on a pitchfork.

With great difficulty the two of us forced the heavy weather vane up to the top of the turret and into the hole Charlie had sawn in the crown of the cupola. It sank straight down to the metal arrow and tilted forward. Charlie pushed it back to upright. It tilted forward again. The hole was an inch too big for the pole—which did not actually matter at all insofar as the arrow could not spin now anyway. It became apparent to us that in order to function, a weather vane needed to be mounted within a metal scabbard that would allow it to turn. We had worked very hard and risked breaking our necks to stick up a statue of a chicken on top of Charlie's barn.

Not that this failure of functionality bothered him at all. When we were back on the ground Charlie and Meg celebrated our raising of the wrought-iron rooster as if we had planted the flag on Iwo Jima. We spent the rest of the day smoking grass, eating cheese, and drinking plonk, toasting our mechanical accomplishments, while the weather vane on top of the barn tilted down toward the chicken coop like a *This Way* sign for mind-travelers from the outer cosmos looking for a party on this, the bawdy planet.

Nevermore Ltd. moved along, handling the solo careers of Charlie and Simon and administering the Ravons' music publishing. We communicated with Emerson through his new American lawyer. It was cordial and impersonal. I had arranged for all three of the ex-Ravons to deliver solo records to fulfill their obligations to Tropic Records in the U.S. and BEI in Britain. The U.S. label was willing to give Charlie and Simon one shot each. It was Emerson they were interested in.

Piece by piece it had dawned on me that my New York pal Hal Allyn had conspired with the boy concert promoter Ramon Castro to entice Emerson away from the Ravons. They had seen who had all the charisma and set out to separate him from the provincials holding him back. Castro had left Boston University and was now in Los Angeles with Emerson. The ambitious kid had teamed up with the U.S. label's A&R man to turn Emerson Cutler into a proper American rock star.

What annoyed me most was that it was working. Emerson had already brought out a successful LP in the States, a very Californian mixture of British blues and American country rock. The producer of that album was Tropic Records' own Hal Allyn.

I bought the *Melody Maker* from a newsdealer on Charing Cross Road and read "Potts Bans Pop in New Heavy Blues Outfit." Next to the headline was a black and white photo of Simon with a walrus mustache and a black hole where one of his lower front teeth used to be. I stared at the picture for a minute, trying to remember if I had ever seen Simon's teeth. Perhaps British dentistry and not his dyspeptic disposition was the reason for his sour puss.

I took the music paper into a café in Leicester Square and sat down with a sandwich and a cup of tea to read what Simon had said. He had treated me to a series of soliloquies about his ambitions for his new band, but I had not met the other players or been invited to rehearsals. I had advised him to be generous to the Ravons in his public statements promoting the new group, but Simon had a very small aptitude for generosity.

He used the *Melody Maker* interview to present the suggestion that Emerson Cutler and Charlie Lydle had been minor talents holding back the genius of Simon Potts and that his time with the Ravons had been a mere apprenticeship on the path to a mighty musical destiny, which Simon was now, with his new ensemble, ready to claim. That new combo would be called Blue Moon, and they would be no little pop group. Blue Moon would be an electric blues band of such back-breaking heaviness that stages would buckle under their weight. Blue Moon would rock like a Japanese destroyer in a typhoon and roll like a Sherman tank. Blue Moon's first album, now under construction in a studio in Pimlico, would contain three songs on one side and, on the other, a twenty-minute opus titled "Death Flowers" that would not only present a searing indictment of the military-industrial complex and a guitar solo of scrotum-shrinking intensity, but a stacking of explosive drum tracks rising into what Simon promised would be "a pyramid of percussion. It's like nothing anyone has ever done before and we actually may have to get permission from the recording industry regulatory board to extend the bottom range of the decibels past the current allowable frequency in order to release it."

The likelihood of said regulatory agency acceding to Simon's request for a special dispensation to plumb new sonic depths was immediately diminished by his prediction that "they'll probably try to say no. The British Phonograph Industry is run by exactly the same neutered bureaucrats who build radar devices for the American planes bombing the civilian populations of Vietnam. In a way, 'Death Flowers' is directed at them as much as any of the baby burners in uniform."

I sipped my tea and thought, Nicely handled, Simon. If this band fails there's a place for you in the diplomatic corps. I did not give a toss what Simon said about the BPI. I was worried about what he said about Emerson and Charlie.

"Not to put down the guys at all," Simon said, putting down the guys, "but they like that whole pop thing. You know, the little love songs and matching suits. That was never my scene. I'm an artist. I paint with music. The Ravons was like a little box of crayons. Blue Moon is a proper big canvas."

Asked about Emerson Cutler, Simon was quoted saying, "Emerson's gone to Hollywood now. He likes all that fun and sun, the American 'be my surfer girl' side of it. God bless him. I don't care about any of that."

I doubt Simon's slagging of his old bandmates ever made its way to Emerson in distant California. It did make it to Charlie Lydle in the Welsh hinterlands, who sent me a coloring book to forward to Simon along with three crayons—gray, black, and brown.

Blue Moon debuted as the opening act for Ten Years After at a weekend rock festival near Leeds University in the summer of 1970. They played a particularly unpleasant brand of bass-heavy hard rock in which I could find no trace of the blues so often referenced in their rhetoric. Still, they went down well with the crowd and by autumn were coheadlining a tour of northern England with Spooky Tooth. It was at one of those shows—at a student union in Manchester—that I first heard the lowing that would follow Blue Moon through their career.

An especially energetic climax resolved into a final splash of cymbals and closing crescendo. Along with the applause came a mooing sound as a thousand young male voices chanted, "Blue MOON, Bluuuuuuuuuuuuuue MOOOOOOOOOON."

I found this sound coming out of the dark hall unusually bucolic. It seemed to me that if Simon ran his hands up and down the bass neck a few more times his fans would give milk. More than a chant of approval and acclamation, the long, languorous *uuuuuuuu* seemed to soothe the mood of the barbiturate brood looming in the gloom of the student union, grooving to the music.

Over subsequent years I noticed a similar lowing coming from fans of Lou Reed, Bruce Springsteen, and the Who. When in 1980 I saw a small advertisement in the *New Musical Express* for a first record by a group called U2 I said to my assistant, "This band will be gigantic, crowds will gather just to coo that name!"

But in 1970, I was simply grateful that the audience remembered what Blue Moon was called. Their first album, *Funeral Florists,* got as far as number thirty-eight on the LP charts, its progress hobbled by

Simon's refusal to allow the signature track, "Death Flowers," to be edited down to three and a half minutes for release as a single.

"I won't hear of it," he maintained when I brought it up for the fifth time at the pleading of his record company. "Did Dickens allow them to pull one chapter out of *Oliver Twist* to sell by itself?"

"Actually, he did," I said.

"It's a theoretical question, Jack!" Simon insisted. He was in a state of constant emotional upheaval in those days, his always-hungry ego swollen in the honeymoon of the first days of what promised to be a successful new rock band. "The answer is no today, no tomorrow, and no forever."

As it turned out the answer was indeed no today and tomorrow, but forever turned out to be negotiable. In 1982, Simon would allow his opus to be trimmed to a snip under three minutes to fit into the final credits of a bad science fiction film. It appeared on the movie soundtrack album in that truncated form and even had a brief venture into the bottom of the singles chart. In 1970, though, forever was a border beyond the farthest horizon.

Blue Moon made it to the northeastern United States for two weeks, and even played the fabled Fillmore East on a bill with Frijid Pink and jazzman Ramsey Lewis. They returned to Britain with a hundred ideas for their second album, which was to be vaguely organized around a concept of telepathy as a means of interplanetary travel. I would not have discerned that theme from the lyrics, but I had the benefit of having Simon to explain it to me. The second album was called *The Mind Storm* and this time a single was designated, a five-minute opus for rock band and symphony orchestra called "Do You Know Me?" which struggled into the top thirty for one week before disappearing into what I can only imagine was a black hole opened by the collective will of the radio audience.

Here Blue Moon might have ended, were it not for a fluke. I have observed over the years that most of the stories in rock music—stories of unlikely success and tales of undeserved failure—hang on flukes. If a single disc jockey in Boston (or Cleveland or wherever he's telling the story this time) had not flipped over Rod's new flop and played "Maggie May," if comedy producer George Martin had known that the music division had passed on the Beatles, if Elvis had decided to buy his mother a bottle of perfume for her birthday instead of recording a song for her, how history would have been changed!

The flukes that lead to stardom are nothing next to the flukes that open the door to obscurity: If the A&R man who signed us had not been fired the week before our album came out, if the other band's roadies had not turned off our monitors when Ahmet walked into the room, if the car had not run off the road on the way to *The Ed Sullivan Show,* if I had known that the naked girl was the deejay's daughter, that would be me up there today. In 1970 I realized that I had dedicated my life to a business as fluke-based as professional blackjack, with far fewer rules.

The fate of Blue Moon was changed by the flip side of their failed single. It was a novelty number called "Oh! Oh!" that had been cobbled together by a weary recording engineer when the band had gone home, because someone from the label called me and said we needed a non-LP B-side for the 45.

The idea of a non-LP B-side was based on the premise that by putting a song that was not on an album on the back of a single, you could entice a group's most loyal fans into buying a record they would otherwise have no reason to buy. It did not matter that the song was no good. If the song were good it would have gone on the album. It was something new, a collector's item for the completist and a stinker for the sucker, the stench of which would not be revealed until after the purchase had been made. Thus did the record business routinely abuse the enthusiasm of its most loyal customers.

When I got the call asking for a non-LP B-side I phoned the studio to see if the band had any leftovers. Simon had gone home and so had the producer. I spoke with a junior engineer, who said there was just a silly little thing the group had fooled around with before they began work some evenings. He would see if he could paste together a decent version of it.

God bless that industrious engineer. He stayed up all night assembling different bits and pieces of a jokey riff with martial drums and an oompah-pah bass that Blue Moon had played while waiting for microphone levels to be set. I will try to separate the myth that grew up around this composition from what I remember happening.

Late on the day after I phoned the engineer, I went around to the recording studio to hear what he had done. He played me "Oh! Oh!" and it made me chuckle. The song sounded like a roomful of drunk children's show presenters on New Year's Eve. I asked where this odd ditty had come from and he explained that on one occasion, while the band was getting recording levels on their instruments, the drums, piano, and bass had rat-a-tatted this whimsical little figure and Simon had begun chanting in a Peter Sellers voice, "Yoko Ono went to Soho, took a photo with a hobo, combed her hair like Perry Como, drove back home in her DeSoto." That was followed by some off-microphone nonsense singing from other people in the room.

During downtimes and long overdubs in the studio after that, Simon and others added to a chalkboard on the wall other two-syllable *o-o* words: yo-yo, mojo, cocoa, phono, slow-mo, solo, no-go, no-show, bolo, dodo, promo, polo, go-go, so-so, no-no, logo, homo, and lobo, along with such dubious candidates as risotto, rococo, and majordomo.

The industrious engineer had made a loop of the musicians playing the silly riff and Simon's nursery rhyme about Yoko, and on top of that he had piled numerous voices—mostly himself, the tea boy, and the girl in reception, their vocals sped up and slowed down to make it sound like many different people—coming in and out around Simon, all chanting short lines that ended in that same *o-o* rhyme.

The engineer's greatest technical feat was to find a tape of Simon shouting, "Take a solo," from a session for a different song, and fly that in just before an eight-bar break. We would ask the guitar player to overdub a lead in that spot.

The only requirement for a non-LP B-side was that it not be available elsewhere; it did not have to be good. I thought this might pass muster. I played the song for Simon over the phone. He was indifferent, sounded distracted, and told me he didn't care if it came out on the back of his real song as long as he got sole songwriting credit. He knew that publishing money was split equally between the front and back of a 45.

I told the engineer he had done a terrific job and should take the next day off. I immediately registered the copyright to "Oh! Oh!" (I might have named it, no one can remember) in Simon's name, which caused some arguments when the song became the best-selling record with which anyone in Blue Moon was ever involved. We ended up buying the engineer who had assembled the song a motor scooter and giving him producer credit on later pressings.

"Oh! Oh!" was first played on the radio during the run-up to the news at the end of a popular afternoon show on the BBC. The phones rang like church bells on Easter morning. Pretty soon the silly ditty was a genuine hit single, and was being used on televised sports events, played over the loudspeakers at fairgrounds, and parodied in advertisements for Bromo-Seltzer, Howard Johnson's Motor Lodges ("HoJo's"), and an iced cake called a Ho Ho. At first Simon was furious that the good name of Blue Moon had been compromised by this commercial treacle and insisted I file legal orders to stop the use of his song in advertising. Then he saw the checks coming in and decided not to stand in the way of the public's appetite for novelty.

"Oh! Oh!" never stopped generating money. Later in the seventies a parody version about Led Zeppelin got significant FM play in America ("Check out ZoSo/ Page plays a solo / Plant is singing 'bout Gandalf and Frodo"). In the eighties it was credited—wrongly, I believe—with introducing the term "boho" into the vernacular. In the nineties it was sampled for a gangsta rap song called "No Mo' Mofo," and in the early 2000s it was used in a campaign for a new mobile phone from Moto.

Heavy as they alleged themselves to be, Blue Moon was not sure how to handle this unexpected windfall. Simon suggested to the underground press that he had written and recorded "Oh! Oh!" in five minutes to prove how shallow the pop market was, and how easy it was for a master musician such as he to manipulate the hit formula. Of course, Blue Moon's albums were where the real music was—singles were for children anyway.

I suppose it made some of the more morbidly authentic Blue Moon fans happy to believe that the success of "Oh! Oh!" was not in fact a sellout but a mockery of sellouts. It certainly made Simon happy to say that, as long as the checks kept clearing.

Simon was not the only Ravon on the singles chart in 1970. Charlie had a hit! It was wonderful. It paid for many improvements on the farm in Chepstow. Charlie had begun to gather a group of musician friends around him at Bombadil Glen. Some were fellow professionals looking for a break from the city, some were freeloaders and druggies who needed a place to crash, some were qualified hippies who actually knew how to function on the land. Charlie's house became something between a commune and crash pad and, while the chickens kept clucking, it did not seem to me when I visited to be a lot different from Charlie's life in the city. Every night was still a party, but now it was a party paid for entirely by Charlie.

In the middle of all this clutter he began to record an album on the farm. He had set up a four-track studio in a large cider mill on the property, though he ended up doing most of his musical work in the house with a couple of mike stands propped up in the parlor and cords running to a TEAC tape recorder on the dining room table. Dogs barking, children spilling drinks, and people passed out on the couch did not interfere with Charlie and any stray musicians he could deputize from bashing out the ballads that he composed as prolifically as he smoked, drank, and rolled in the hay with Meg.

He called me down to the farm one Sunday to hear his finished album. It was, I felt then and I feel now, delightful. Charlie had a gift for melody, and his lyrics managed to navigate the moment where one emotion turns into another—he wrote about love turning into regret, anger turning into forgiveness, and nervousness giving way to rowdy daring. Among the songs he played me was a lovely tribute to Meg called "Power Over Me," a sing-along drinking song called "Drowning," and a lament for lost love called "Fast as Sleep." I considered it then and still consider it the best work any of the Ravons ever did, and I told Charlie that. But I also told him I did not hear a hit single.

Understand, a hit single was not as important to a recording artist in 1970 as it had been before or as it would be again. Albums were the thing, and as the teenage rock audience turned toward their twenties they looked down on 45s as kid stuff. But the former Ravons were in a precarious position. Emerson had gone to America, and there was an assumption at the record company that he had been the talent in the group. Simon's novelty hit with Blue Moon had bought him time. The label still had to be convinced that Charlie was a viable solo act. They owned his contract and would not let him go, but if they did not hear a single they would not spend much money on promotion, either. I did not want Charlie to end up in professional limbo, bound to a company that considered him a minor investment.

He took my assessment graciously, but typical of Charlie he put it on me to find the solution.

"Them's all the songs I have, Jack," he said, propped on his couch strumming an acoustic guitar. "I suppose we could speed one up and put on some horns. You think that'd work?"

"I don't want you to change a note on any of these songs, Charlie," I told him. "They're great. I just wonder if there isn't something else that could go into the album, something that opens the door to all these wonderful tunes?"

Meg came out of the kitchen and said, "What about the one you sing to me all the time? That isn't on there."

Charlie looked up and said sure it was, all the songs he wrote for her were on the tape.

Meg stared singing, "Meet me at Maggie's place—oh!"

Charlie laughed. "I didn't write that one, Magpie. That's an old Sam Cooke song. I just modified the lyrics a bit to reflect my devotion to your lovely self." Here Charlie began strumming the song and singing along.

I said, "It's not the worst idea, though, Charlie. It's a good song, it's a classic, really, and no one's covered it since Sam Cooke put it out, what? Ten years ago. It might be the thing to get you in the door."

Charlie looked pensive. He strummed the song some more.

I said, "Look, it fits with everything else on the record. It's not like we're talking about adding some hackwork or something. It's a song you love, a song you sing, and part of the vibe here at Bombadil that you want the album to capture. It *should* be part of the record." I looked up at Margaret and told her, "You're a genius, Meg. You've solved the problem. Add that song to the album, Charlie, and the record company has to give us the backing we deserve."

Giving Meg the credit did the trick. Charlie came up to London to cut his version of "Meet Me at Mary's Place" in a proper studio, with good session musicians. He overdubbed some happy party noises in the background, to make it seem like part of the same album as all the homemade songs, but "Mary's Place" had a distinct pop sheen that the other tunes didn't have. It became the lead-off track on the album—which was credited to "Charlie Lydle and Lilliput," and a top ten hit on both sides of the Atlantic.

Charlie assembled a band to promote his record. He used the drummer and piano player from the "Mary's Place" session and three pals from his farm collective trading off on guitars, bass, mandolin, fiddle, banjo, and sloppy vocals. We spent the winter of '70–'71 playing every TV show, radio broadcast, university, free festival, and saloon that would have us, all over the British Isles, across to Canada, and down into the western United States. Meg was always there, serving Charlie's needs like a medieval wench and sometimes appearing for encores to shake a tambourine with the band. We all had a lot of fun, we all caught colds, and we were all delighted when the tour came to its conclusion in sunny Los Angeles in March.

We had two nights booked at the Troubadour, a nightclub beloved by the new West Coast singer/songwriters, as well as a lineup of television and radio appearances. Being a wise manager, I made sure that the band's first day in Hollywood was a free day. We checked into the Sunset Marquis Hotel and spent the afternoon lying around the pool like lizards sunning themselves on a boulder. Our whole rolling carnival entourage drank vodka and orange juice and waited for our pale skin to turn red.

I was half dozing when someone shook my shoulder and said in a somewhat American voice, "Please move along, sir, you're scaring the little girls."

I squinted up at a figure silhouetted by an intensely bright California sky. It was a bearded man with shaggy hair, brown skin, and luminous teeth. He was wearing expensive sunglasses and a red and blue floral shirt pulled out over white jeans. He was grinning at me as if I should know him, but I did not have a clue until he spoke again.

"Is that a hangover, Jack, or are you just unhappy to see me?"

"Emerson!"

"Welcome to paradise, you old parasite."

Charlie came splashing out of the pool and wrapped his former harmony partner in a wet embrace.

"Get a load of Mr. Flash!" Charlie said with delight, walking around and around Emerson. "Eating wheat germ or what, Em? You look like a new man!"

Emerson did indeed look like a different person. He looked American. His beard was trim and close to his face. It had been sculpted to enhance his best features, giving depth to his already impressive cheekbones and definition to his chin. He looked taller, stronger, healthier than I had ever seen him. Emerson had left England a beautiful boy; now he was a handsome man.

"I've been leaving messages for you two all day," Emerson said to Charlie and me with joshing admonishment. "I finally realized that busy pop stars and entrepreneurs like yourselves can't be bothered with old friends who knew you when, so I decided I'd better come down here in person and shame you into seeing me."

Charlie smiled and said, "I'm glad you did, Em! I never got the message. Guess I should think about getting a manager, eh? You know anybody?"

I took the ribbing. None of us had gone up to our rooms to check the pink message slips passed under our doors in those days before mobile phones. Emerson insisted that we all come to his home for dinner while we were in town, and as our only unbooked evening was that very night, that night it would be.

We drove up and down the Pacific Coast Highway for forty-five minutes, trying to figure out which gate was Emerson's. From the road it did not look like there could be anything but ocean on the other side of the white seawall that separated the highway from the beach. It also looked like pulling over to check the numbers on the doors cut into the wall would be an invitation to being rear-ended by all the other automobiles tearing around the winding thoroughfare. Our record company's Los Angeles promo man, who was driving, assured us that this was simply how it was done out here and coaxed us out of the limo and onto the asphalt, where we rang a few bells and talked to a few buzzers until we found Emerson's rented house.

Passing through that gate was like passing into another dimension. Everything before us opened up and spread out. The beach seemed to go on for a mile before it crashed into enormous waves rising out of an endless ocean into which was melting a red sun as vast as the whole sky. I looked at Charlie and Meg, who must have been thinking of their funky little farm and the various degrees of getting back to nature.

Emerson came to the door of his beach house, which was across a wooden bridge from where we stood staring at the sea. "Welcome to the ends of the earth!" he cried. "Now get your asses up here!" He said "asses," not "arses."

The house was as stunning inside as out. It was a transparent cube raised on pilings above the beach. At night when the lights were all on, anyone passing by could look in, an architectural manifestation of California's laissez-faire exhibitionism. Emerson had one great open room with glass walls on three sides–the Pacific Ocean was his wallpaper. A couple of thin, tanned men with long white hair mingled around with four or five startlingly beautiful women. Everyone was skinny, everyone was dressed elegantly but casually in desert colors. Drinks were poured, cheese and fruit dishes were passed around, joints were offered. We were all introduced and addressed by first name only. It was impossible to tell who were staff and who were guests. Charlie, Meg, and his band looked very rough and rustic among these sleek Californians. Emerson looked like he had been born there, clever and classless and free.

There was no ice to be broken, everyone was too relaxed for that. Charlie and Emerson told stories about their youth climbing over alley fences and stealing milk in post-Blitz Britain. They painted a picture of the two old friends as characters out of Dickens, mingling their separate childhoods as if they had grown up on the same street. The subtext of every tale told was of how far they had traveled from that black and white world of hardship to this glorious land of Technicolor.

I noticed that Emerson and in fact all the Californians in the room, men and women, were parting their long hair in the middle. Longhairs in London parted either from the back with fringe in front, not at all, or from the sides as men had for two generations. The hair parted on the side simply grew longer and longer with every year. The Californians had found another path, one that suggested that long hair was not a temporary trend but a permanent change with its own rules of grooming. If this observation seemed more fascinating to me then than it perhaps does to you now, remember that I was stoned. I could have become fascinated studying my toenails.

My gaze floated around the room, which seemed to me to have taken on the aspects of an aquarium. Charlie's band and Emerson's friends were getting on well together. Everyone was chatting and laughing. My eyes came to Meg, who looked uncharacteristically reserved. As always, she was sitting close to Charlie, but he was leaning forward on the couch and she had pushed herself way back, as if she hoped not to be noticed.

Was it possible that the country earth mother felt uncomfortable among the sleek Los Angeles women, the thin models and aspiring actresses who floated through the room like smoke? Or was it simply that she was used to having all of Charlie's attention, functioning as one four-legged, two-headed being with him, and it made her feel strange to share him with Emerson, who had known him longer and shared so much with him that was as intimate as sex and more rare?

Someone produced a guitar and asked Charlie for a song. He obliged, but this was not the all-hands-on-deck jamboree that he and Meg hosted every night at Bombadil Glen. This was a proper recital, with a clear distinction between performer and audience, star and supplicants. After two tunes Charlie passed the guitar to Emerson, who did one of his own. Before long a second Martin appeared and Charlie and Em were harmonizing on old Everly Brothers hits. The bond between them was never so tight as that evening in California, six thousand miles from where they began.

At the end of the evening Charlie, Emerson, and I were outside on his deck, leaning on the rail and looking up at a sky full of stars.

"You've figured it out, Em," Charlie said. "This is how it should be."

"You're right, Charlie," Emerson said. "So now that you know, when are you moving out here?"

Charlie smiled and looked into his wine glass. "It's tempting."

"Tell him, Jack," Emerson said to me. "He's a proper rock and roll star with a hit record. He can live anywhere he wants. More chance of making a million out here in the middle of things than off on a goat farm in Hereford."

"Chepstow," Charlie said.

"What do you think, Jack?" Emerson said. "It's better here. It's easier. Isn't that what we always wanted? And Jack, I would love to get your advice on some stuff I have going, too." Emerson looked a little misty. "I've missed you ugly geezers."

That was the moment Charlie and I began to detach from the UK and slide across the world. I looked at my two friends, grateful to be included in their company. I looked at the sea and the stars and thought how nice it would be to see this all the time. I looked back into Emerson's glass house, where party guests were sprawled on the carpet and couches in candlelight, and I saw Meg coming out of one of the bedrooms with an empty champagne bottle, followed by a tall young man in a cowboy shirt. I said nothing to Charlie, of course. For all I knew she was simply looking for the loo. I considered what moving to California might gain us, and what it might cost.

The business of leaving London for Los Angeles felt unreal. Charlie and I spoke about heading to the promised land the way boys lay plans to become football stars. Even as I filled out all the permits and papers I half believed it would never happen.

My sponsor with the U.S. government was Ramon Castro, the rich young Cuban American who had helped lure Emerson away from me. Castro had set up a touring and promotion company in Los Angeles and the plan was for me to join as a partner. Emerson confided that while Castro was a great hustler, they needed a grown-up to keep the clocks wound. I still resented Castro's role in seducing Emerson out of the Ravons, but I told myself that I had partnered with Tug Bitler— I could surely work with a little Batista.

Tug and I agreed to divide the assets of Nevermore. He would stay in the UK and manage Simon's Blue Moon. I would head to America with Charlie. We bought each other out by exchanging our interests in the two artists.

Allison was hurt that Charlie and I did not offer to bring her with us. If we could have, we would have, but we barely had enough cash to cover the costs of moving.

My mother's sister had moved into the house in Kingston, and the two of them buzzed around exactly as they must have when they shared a bedroom as children. I thought Mam would be heartbroken when I told her I was going to California, but she acted as if it were just another posh London neighborhood she had no desire to visit. I had already left her when I abandoned the law to join the rock and roll circus. To her this latest change of address was just one more manifestation of a transformation that had already taken place.

Simon, however, was aggrieved. He accused Charlie and me of

throwing in with the traitor Cutler, of selling out to the spray-on sun-tans and capped teeth of fascist Amerika.

"You're running after Emerson like an abandoned wife begging for the chance to be a weekend whore," Simon announced with all the subtlety that made his lyrics plop like turds into a bowl. "Fuck you if that's why you're in it. I hope you and Charlie have a good time pol-ishing Cutler's chrome."

And that, I thought, is why I'm happy to leave London. Bring on the sun, the surf, and the swimming pools filled with naked girls.

It was starting to get cool in England in September 1971, when Charlie, Meg, and I left, but in Los Angeles the summer never ended.

My most vivid first impressions of California were these:

The highways were filled with young people hitchhiking: hundreds and hundreds of kids between fourteen and twenty-five with their thumbs out, casually fearless.

There were almost as many motorcycles on the highway as auto-mobiles, many with the extended front wheels made popular by *Easy Rider*. A number of the young men piloting these bikes eschewed hel-mets for wool sailor's hats. They'd all come to look for America.

You could not order a sandwich, hamburger, or bowl of soup without being given a pickled cucumber, sometimes sliced, sometimes whole. I eventually accepted it but I never understood.

The record company found us two small cottages to rent on the side of a hill in Coldwater Canyon. Actually it was one cottage with a guest cabin made from what had once been a garage or barn. It was nowhere near as grand as the glass beach house they had leased for Emerson, but we were happy.

Charlie and Meg took the main house, a single-story white bunga-low with ceiling fans and the impression of being all one airy room. At the center of the house was a large wicker dining table. North of that was a kitchen area, all chrome and stools. West of the dining area was a high double bed with acres of quilts and pillows. East of the table was a parlor area with wicker chairs and couches.

The few feet of wall that delineated the borders between these areas stopped short of dividing them into rooms, but there were sliding doors within the walls that could be pulled out if privacy was ever required.

The house had been designed for occupants for whom privacy was not a priority.

South of the dining table were large glass doors that looked out onto a long, thin swimming pool with a tiled mural of a mermaid inlaid into the floor of the deep end. On the other side of the pool was the guest cabin, where I settled. The guesthouse was built with old planks that looked as though they had been sanded and salted in the side of a ship. There was a kitchenette at one end of the single long room and a small shower and toilet at the other, separated by the only interior wall from a soft old double bed. In the middle of the room sat a very large wooden table on rollers that served as my work desk, dining table, and on one drunken occasion the platform for a sexual encounter that left me with splinters and the clap.

Charlie and Meg made me a housewarming gift of a wooden chess set carved with figures from Robin Hood. I gave that pride of place under one of the nine windows that filled my cabin with light.

Although our little compound did not take up much space, and although it sat in a neighborhood lined with similar houses, we enjoyed monkish privacy. We were surrounded by high fences, which were lined and overgrown with palm trees, ferns, bushes, and shrubs. I had never seen such greenery.

"Wasn't Los Angeles built on a desert?" Charlie asked me one evening as we sat by our pool staring up at the constellations.

"I believe so," I said.

"Then how can it be so impossibly lush? I mean, look at this place, Flynn, it's like we're in equatorial Brazil."

"Must be over-irrigation," I told him. "When they worked out a system to bring water into the basin, they never turned down the tap."

"Well fertilized, too," Charlie reckoned. "Must be all that Hollywood bullshit."

Ramon Castro's wealthy father had secured a little house on Doheny Drive for his son, just below the Sunset Strip, which served as the business office of Dormammu Enterprises, the music booking agency and artist management company. I joined as a full partner. Although our roles were not officially defined, Castro and I agreed that he would look after the concert bookings and I would deal with the artist roster, Emerson and Charlie.

An experienced man of twenty-seven years, I sometimes thought of Castro as an overeager kid who should learn to muffle his enthusiasms when conducting business. Castro was a few months shy of twenty-three, a mere boy compared to me.

We got along well, though. After Tug, it was pleasant to engage with someone smart, and Castro seemed to have contacts in every city in the USA. He also helped put together a new group for Charlie, preserving the loose vibe of the Bombadil band.

Most of all I was glad to be back with Emerson, who had opened up as a songwriter in California. Unlike Charlie, to whom songs came unbidden at all hours, Emerson treated composition as a craft. He knew the rules, put in the time, and came up with the songs.

One Sunday afternoon I called on him at the glass cube by the ocean to hear what he had been working on, and he let me in on his songwriting secret.

"Look, Flynn," he said, hunched over a Fender bass while seated on his amplifier. He was squeezed between an electric piano, a small drum kit, and two guitars, with three or four large tape recorders framing his head on the shelf behind him. "Here's how we do it."

He played me a swinging bass line that conjured images of zoot-suited gangsters in 1930s Chicago. He said, "You know this?"

"Sounds familiar."

"'Green Onions,' by Booker T. and the M.G.'s. Now, that's a good bass part, a good bottom. So I get groovin' on this for a while"—he kept repeating the riff—"and then I say, What would happen if I tried to sing 'Johnny B. Goode' over 'Green Onions'?"

Emerson began to sing "Johnny B. Goode," varying the melody to fit the bass line. It did not sound like a revelation in songwriting innovation to me. It sounded like Emerson had been smoking a lot of pot before I arrived and I was, not for the first time, going to have to listen to the insights his inebriation had imparted.

He was still playing one song and singing another when he announced, "Now—what if, instead of singing it in my own voice, I were to try to phrase it like Harry Belafonte?" and here Emerson began to tell the story of the poor country boy who played his guitar like ringing a bell, as if J. B. Goode worked on a banana boat in the Caribbean. As he did this, the melody moved up toward a Jamaican call-and-response cadence and the bass followed, adding calypso to the groove.

I started to see some wisdom in the exercise. Emerson was still singing the lyrics to the Chuck Berry song, and he still had the rhythmic drive and confidence of "Green Onions," but the melody—struggling to stay within the walls of the bass line—was forcing itself into a new shape. The music was no longer recognizably "Johnny B. Goode," though it retained that song's structure.

"Now all I gotta do," Emerson announced as he repeated the altered riff, "is replace Chuck's words with my own," and he began to improvise:

I'm sitting in the basement
Flynn is looking at me
When I write some new words
I'll get a royalty.

The riff and melody Emerson came up with that afternoon eventually turned into "Give Cassie a Candle," a well-regarded album track and live favorite that no critic, fan, or litigator ever compared to "Green Onions," "Johnny B. Goode," or anything by Harry Belafonte. Emerson's formula worked. Most of his subsequent hits were composed by taking pieces of other people's songs and reconfiguring them so they would sound new.

In the middle of a night later in the seventies Emerson called me from some hotel in another time zone and said, "Hey, Flynn! Do you realize that you can sing the words to 'You've Got to Hide Your Love Away' to the tune of 'When the Saints Go Marchin' In'? Lennon must use the same trick I do!"

I told him it was also possible that there were only a limited number of cadences available to lyricists, and surely many hundreds would match each other if one wanted to waste one's time searching while the rest of us were trying to sleep.

My admonishment did nothing to curb his delight a decade or so later when he realized that Leonard Cohen's "Hallelujah" exactly fit the meter, structure, and rhyme scheme of Johnny Cash's "A Boy Named Sue." He tortured everyone on his tour bus by endlessly singing the "Sue" lyrics with the Cohen melody. Emerson's approach to songwriting was analytical and mechanical.

I have no idea if many rock musicians wrote the way Emerson did. I suspect that plenty of the most popular did something similar, consciously or not. I have come to believe over many years of seeing stars rise and fall that the true believers who consider themselves artists funneling a gift from God through their narrow esophagi may luck into success for a little while—but in the long run God gets sick of being blamed for so much bad music and withdraws His support. Long-term success goes to the craftsmen and the crafty, the ones who treat making music like building a car.

Over time I developed a professional admiration for craftsmanship. Motown songs were built like a Cadillac. Beatles records were Aston Martins. The Beach Boys made Mustangs—not much under the hood but fun for a summer with the top down.

In California in the 1970s we made a lot of Monzas, Crickets, and Dusters. They looked all right in their moment and sold a lot at the time, but they did not last very long.

I remember flying home to Los Angeles one evening not very long after I moved there. I had gone to New York to shake a larger recording budget for Emerson's next album out of the label. It was a ritual; they had so much money in those boom days that all you had to do was ask politely and laugh at their jokes and they'd add another zero.

I suppose I had some wine on the plane, but I was not drunk. Flying out of the desert and into the space above Los Angeles that night I was overwhelmed by the novelty of what I was doing. Here I was in a flying machine thirty thousand feet above the earth, looking down on a web of electric light. Humans had been on the planet for a million years but only in this century was this possible. Edison wired the world, the Wright Brothers untethered us from gravity. We took it for granted but it had all occurred within living memory. My father never rode on a plane. I flew as thoughtlessly as if the airport were a bus stop.

We descended into the field of lights. I was delighted to find a girl named Carey Cicola waiting for me at the terminal. We had gone on a first date the evening before I left for New York. We'd had dinner at a Spanish place in Santa Monica and seen a French movie. There was a little kissing in the car but I had to leave for the airport at six A.M., so no attempt was made to go further. She was a beautiful girl, Italian American with thick black hair and pale white skin. Between the Spanish food, the French film, and the Italian kisses, I felt I'd had the grand tour of the Riviera. Her showing up at the airport was unexpected and welcome.

She went to UCLA, and she worked in a bakery. She drove a red Thunderbird. She was a real California girl. I helped her lower the top of her convertible and settled into the passenger seat while Carey

Cicola drove us out of Los Angeles Airport and up La Cienega Boulevard.

"There's treats behind your seat," she told me. The wind was whipping through her hair and although it was ten P.M. she was wearing oversized sunglasses. I swiveled and brought up a small picnic basket.

"I figured you'd only had airplane food," she explained. In the basket was a sandwich, a bottle of wine, two glasses, and a plate of brownies wrapped in tinfoil. I poured us each a glass of wine and we drove along drinking it. People did things like that then—when the bars closed you'd see cars swerving up on the sidewalks and the police seemed not to care. She encouraged me to try the brownies she'd baked and we shared one of those. They were terrific. As a boy who'd grown up on postwar rationing I was astounded by the amount of sugar Americans consumed. Brownies and wine in a convertible flying up Mulholland Drive, piloted by a gorgeous California coed—the *Eagle* had landed.

We were climbing the winding road above Los Angeles when I began to experience what I hoped was not a first wave of nausea.

"You feeling anything?" Carey asked me happily.

"Umm, just a bit disoriented from the flight," I told her.

"Those are special brownies," she said. "Welcome home!"

She pulled the car over so that we had a panoramic view of the city. My head was flapping like a diving board. "Just enjoy the buzz," she said sweetly. "It's my special recipe."

I was determined to settle my stomach, to tune in to the high Carey had cooked up for me and ride it to a gentle landing. I looked across the illuminated grid of the city and tried to locate the airport I had just descended into. I found the blinking lights of the planes circling, landing, and lifting off like fireflies on a pond.

From that point on the horizon I traced the entwined lines of highway spreading toward us. The red taillights of automobiles shot along the yellow trails like photons. Spotlights shot upward from somewhere down in Hollywood, scraping white beams across the clouds to announce the premiere of a movie or perhaps the opening of a supermarket.

"Look at it, Carey," I told her. "The whole city is a field of light, shooting and pulsing like a massive circuit. Hollywood looks just like the inside of a television set!"

Carey laughed and I babbled on. "It's an open prairie of electric current, a vision belonging entirely to the twentieth century." Here I'm afraid I began to weep. "We are Prometheus, Carey. We have stolen fire from the gods. We have harnessed the lightning."

She took my hand and I leaned against her shoulder, sobbing.

"Well, well," she said gently. "No more brownies for you."

Because the seasons never changed, my sense of time gets shaky when I remember California. I sometimes feel as if my years there were one long summer. Sometime in 1972 I moved into Carey Cicola's apartment in Santa Monica. She proved her devotion to me by getting rid of a cat that made me sneeze.

I thought Charlie and Meg would be happy to have the Coldwater Canyon compound to themselves, although not long after I left they surprised me by subleasing the guesthouse to a male model who had come west to work on a soap opera. It was not that they wanted the company; they needed the money.

Charlie had so enjoyed the musical camaraderie of LA—the jam sessions, the parties, the nightclubs, sitting in on friends' recording sessions and jumping up onstage at their shows—that it was easy for him to forget that he actually was not making any records of his own. I booked him concerts around the West Coast, and as far afield as Austin and Aspen, but the gigs were getting smaller. It had been a long time since his hit single. I tried to impress upon him that he needed to take his songwriting and recording as seriously as he had with the Ravons. My great concern was that LA was too easy for Charlie. Left to his own devices, he would smoke and drink until he melted into the sand.

Emerson worked harder and did well. Already a fixture on FM radio, he was now nudging toward the AM dial. The underground sensibility was perforating the mainstream, and a couple of Emerson's songs made it onto Top 40 lists west of the Mississippi. It was encouraging.

One great advantage the U.S. rock audience had over the English was while the Brits valued novelty, the Americans rewarded persistence. The UK was agog over Bowie and T. Rex, a new style of rock

that Emerson and Charlie found confusing and slight. In the States, by
contrast, musicians who had kicked around for years as opening acts
were finally being granted headline status. Dave Mason, Boz Scaggs,
Linda Ronstadt, Peter Frampton, Fleetwood Mac, Steve Miller, Earth,
Wind & Fire, the J. Geils Band: they had all been touring and making
records since the Ravons first formed. They had hung in, formed alliances in the business, and earned the industry's support. Emerson fit
that profile. His new albums were mixes of original compositions and
a few well-chosen covers of country and blues songs. He could sell out
three-thousand-seat theaters under his own name from coast to coast,
and played high on the bill at festivals in Atlanta, Virginia, and San
Francisco.

The truth was that Dormammu Enterprises was using profits from
Emerson to pay advances to Charlie and cover his rent. Charlie did
not seem to worry about it, but Meg did. One day Charlie came home
from a two-night jam at the Hit Factory to find she had moved in with
the soap actor in the guesthouse. Given the beating he inflicted on
Emerson when he quit the Ravons, I worried for Meg's safety. Apparently Charlie took this as a lesser betrayal. He kept right on living in
the main house while Meg and her new lover took up residence on the
other side of the swimming pool.

That's how we did it in the seventies.

As Emerson's popularity grew, we all had to think about his image. In consultation with the Tropic Records publicity department, we agreed on a few ground rules. Emerson's good looks and sex appeal were never to be played up. He was a serious musician who lived for his art. He was not to appear in teen magazines or be photographed without his shirt or in anything that could be construed as a glamour pose. We knew that Emerson's being handsome sold records, but we never acknowledged it. At the same time, Wendy Ipswitch, our publicist, quietly selected just the right tight, worn jeans for photo shoots, and we had a Hollywood hairdresser come to the office on the weekend to groom him to look like he never thought of grooming.

We were very concerned with credibility in those days. FM rock sold albums to a college-age audience who read *Rolling Stone.* AM pop sold singles to junior high school girls who read *Sixteen* magazine. The FM audience was snobbish and protective. It was all right for an FM star to leak onto AM, that was a sign of the forces of light defeating the forces of darkness. But woe to the musician who was perceived as pandering to the AM crowd. He was excommunicated with bell, book, and bong.

Negotiating the perimeters of the AM/FM divide became an issue between Emerson and me when the head of his record company heard him playing the Supremes oldie "Come See About Me" at a sound check. Wild Bill came to me outside the dressing room and said, "I want Emerson to cut 'Come See About Me' right away. I'll pay for him to go into the studio tomorrow. We make that the lead-off track from the new album, we sell an extra million copies."

I waited until after the concert to mention it to Emerson. He refused to even consider it.

"It's bullshit, Jack," he said. "I've given them a brilliant album with twelve new originals, any one of which has more substance than 'See About Me.'"

"They agree, Em," I said. "But they think this would hit Top Forty in a way that would create an opening for two or three of the other songs."

"I won't hear of it. It's everything that's wrong with American radio right now. Have you noticed that they're all trying to run backwards toward the fifties? Everybody's either remaking oldies or writing nostalgic songs about 'Crocodile Rock,' 'Rock and Roll Lullaby,' 'Your Mama Don't Dance and Your Daddy Don't Rock and Roll.' What the hell is going on? They've got gas lines and the dollar's collapsing and they're all trying to get in a fetal crouch and return to their infancy. *Happy Days, American Graffiti,* Sha Na Na, *Grease.* One week I looked at *Billboard* and Elvis, Chuck Berry, and Ricky Nelson were all in the top ten at the same time. This country is confronting an ugly future by racing backwards toward an imaginary past of sock hops and teddy boys and I won't be part of it. Tell Wild Bill to suggest 'Come See About Me' to Johnny Rivers. I am an artist."

I knew when to shut up. I also knew that Emerson was an artist as long as the heat stayed on in the swimming pool. If I told the label he was rejecting the boss's idea, I would be inviting them to give his new LP minimal promotion, to prove the boss was right. I had to figure out a way to make Emerson think that cutting the Supremes song was his idea.

I found my way in through his new drummer, a black studio player named Baxter Selwyn. I pulled Baxter aside and told him that I wanted him to make sure the band had a tight arrangement of 'Come See About Me' rehearsed when Emerson was not around. Each time Baxter could encourage Em to play it as an encore number, Baxter would find an extra two hundred dollars in his per diem envelope. Baxter was a pro; he could be bribed.

Then I had to go to work on the soundman, to make sure that each encore was recorded using good audio equipment. This cost me a TEAC four-track tape recorder, a big box the size of a color TV with two large tape reels like the ears on Mickey Mouse. No doubt that TEAC was also the source of the many Emerson Cutler live bootleg records that appeared in the next few years.

My last solicitation was to the lighting director. Emerson routinely came back onstage to do one two-song encore. This was part of the set, he did it whether the audience demanded it or not. If the crowd was genuinely enthusiastic and kept cheering, he would come back a second time and do the Ravons' classic "Ask Yer Daddy." That was the end of the show—lights up, music on, back to the dressing room with whatever girls the roadies had selected to bring before the emperor.

So imagine Emerson's surprise when, in Phoenix, Arizona, he finished "Ask Yer Daddy," waved to the crowd, strolled back toward his dressing room, and heard the ovation through the walls continuing—building, in fact, in intensity. Halfway down the backstage corridor, Baxter the drummer put a hand on his shoulder and said, "Em! I think we gotta go back!" The local promoter, breathless as a schoolgirl, nodded and implored, "They're goin' batshit out there!"

Emerson was a generous monarch. He smiled, gave the band a *Tally ho!* expression, and reversed course for the stage.

What he did not need to know was that as soon as he had left, the lighting director had, at my instruction, cut all the lights in the hall, making it impossible for the audience to find their way to the exits and at the same time encouraging them to call for another encore. Some rapid flashing of the stage lamps goosed their enthusiasm. When Emerson reclaimed the stage, he thought he was being recalled by a spontaneous outpouring of adulation, when in fact the audience was responding to cues as rehearsed as the pedal pushed by a laboratory monkey to get his shot of vodka.

Strapping his guitar back on, Emerson smiled and looked around at the musicians asking, *What do you want to do?* Baxter hit the downbeat to "Come See About Me" and the whole band kicked in, sharp as the Motown rhythm section. In the high adrenaline of the moment, Emerson did not question it, he was glad for the idea and—if he had thought about it at all—would have simply assumed that they were picking up on a tune he had sung at sound check for fun. Was he startled when the bassist and keyboard player knew all the harmonies, the call-and-response background parts? No, he was Emerson Cutler rocking out for a delighted crowd of dancing fans. He expected things to fall together for him.

After Phoenix, "Come See About Me" became a regular part of the encore. Here the TEAC served me. I sent the three best versions to an LA recording studio and had them punch up a remix ready for radio, equalized, overdubbed, and generally polished like a whore's gold tooth. I had that pressed onto red vinyl promo singles with blank white labels and slipped those to Wild Bill. He passed them along to his promotion department, who relayed them—perhaps with cash or cocaine, I would never be foolish enough to ask—to disc jockeys and radio programmers at key stations in the South and West.

Well, guess what happened? I was able to report to Emerson with wide-eyed agog that, completely on his own and without authorization, some disc jockey in Baton Rouge had come across a bootleg tape of Emerson doing "Come See About Me," put it on the radio, and the phones lit up like Nero's Rome.

Emerson was not sure what to make of this; his first suggestion was a cease-and-desist order, but I told him that this was a *black* radio station. It seemed that the brothers really dug Emerson's take on Holland/Dozier/Holland. This flattered Em and gave him pause. He asked me to secure a copy of what they were playing. I came back to him two days later with a tape I had had in my briefcase the whole time. I told him that other stations, black and white, were demanding the song. He listened, nodded, and expressed enthusiasm for his own remarkable performance.

"God, I didn't know we sounded so good," he told me. "Let's get this thing out!"

I suggested that we did not want to legitimize a bootleg. We should quash it by going into the studio and producing a proper version of the song. Emerson agreed, the label paid, Wild Bill was delighted, and "Come See About Me" was a huge AM hit, which did grease the runway for two more songs—Cutler originals—from Em's next album, following it into the top ten.

And Emerson was very happy about the whole thing because it had all been his idea.

Charlie had become friendly with a rock journalist named Fred Zaras, who wrote a long and fawning piece about him in and after the Ravons for *Hit Parader* magazine. Zaras was anxious to profile Emerson. We felt *Hit Parader* was too much of a bubblegum publication for an artist of Emerson's profundity and turned it down. Zaras was persistent. When bugging the record company failed, he called the office. When I would not take his calls, he lobbied Charlie to plead his case.

"What are you doing, Charlie?" I asked him. "This guy's a loser, he's a freelance record reviewer. Probably lives with his parents. You shouldn't mistake him for a friend. He'd sell out your confidences in a minute to get a byline in *Playboy*."

"Fred's not like that, Flynn, he's a good egg," Charlie insisted. "He explained things about my music to me that even I'd never thought of."

"Well, presumably that's because they weren't true."

"Nah, that's the thing. They were true! He's like a shrink or something. He makes connections you weren't even aware of. Like, do you know how many of my lyrics mention fruit? I didn't, either, but Freddy did. Apples, grapes, melons, pears. Not sure if tomato is a fruit but there's one in 'Moonstone at Midnight.' Freddy says it's an image rooted in my ideas of sex and nutrition, how sexuality is part of nature and nature comes from God and that means it's all healthy."

I stared at Charlie. He was not making a good case for letting this nut in a room with Emerson.

"Don't you remember," Charlie pressed me, "back in Bombadil when we had that talk about how the world is a big green ball of sex? Well, Freddy twigged that whole philosophy from between the lines of my songs! He's like a psychic scientist or something. Plus, he's a really good writer. I know he'd do a great interview with Emerson."

It sounded like trouble to me, but I figured maybe we could get something out of it.

"Look, Charlie, here's the thing. We've been trying to get Em the cover of *Rolling Stone*. The label's been working on this and they think we've got a real shot when the new album comes out. Emerson showing up in *Hit Parader* could hurt his chances. Simple as that, really. But tell your friend Fred that if he can get a cover assignment from *Rolling Stone,* we'll give him unprecedented access to Emerson."

This was a suggestion along the lines of, "Bring me the broomstick of the Wicked Witch." I never expected Fred Zaras to call my bluff.

A week later Wendy Ipswitch called me in a fury.

"Did you promise someone named Fred Zaras unlimited access to Emerson for a profile in *Rolling Stone*?"

"Certainly not, he's the character who did the piece on Charlie for *Hit Parader*. He wants to interview Emerson and I sent word we'd only agree if it was for the cover of *Rolling Stone*. Why?"

"Well, apparently he went to *Rolling Stone* and they gave him the green light. Jack, do you know how long I've been negotiating to get Emerson this cover? I wanted one of the real writers to do it, Paul Nelson or Cameron Crowe. Now the magazine has given the assignment to this jackass."

"Are they offering the cover?"

"Maybe. They say it's under serious consideration for a cover but they want to see what Zaras comes back with. He's never written for them before."

"Well, Wendy, tell them that's not acceptable."

"You don't get it, Jack. It's too late. Once they've given this goon the assignment, we don't get to argue. They won't let the record company or management dictate the writer once the magazine has made its choice."

"Okay, we won't do it."

"Bad idea. At this point I think we have to put Emerson with Fred Zaras and hope for the best. It's our only shot at a *Rolling Stone* cover."

I hung up the phone wondering who made up these rules.

Charlie gave me Zaras's phone number. I called and invited him to come by the Dormammu office for a chat. I was not going to let him alone with Emerson until I had vetted him.

I was very surprised when he showed up with Charlie in tow. Charlie was taking an extraordinary interest in paving the lane for his new pal.

There was nothing obviously impressive about Fred Zaras. He was skinny, frail, and pale, with a receding hairline and a neck pitted with acne scars. He wore wire-rim glasses and had a patch of black hair growing out of the space beneath his lower lip. He was about six feet tall and stooped like a man who had been locked in the stocks. He wore an Allman Brothers T-shirt, painter's pants, and heavy brown motorcycle boots bound with straps and metal rings.

"Charlie tells me you're hoping to interview Emerson," I said after he declined a drink. He smoked cigarettes the whole time we talked.

"That is my desire, yes," he said, nodding. We each waited for the other to say something.

Charlie broke the silence.

"Fred knows more about the Ravons than we do, Jack. He even has bootlegs from that French gig with the police dogs."

"I'd like to hear those," I said.

"The Ravons were a completely underappreciated influence on British *and* American rock and roll," Zaras said as if he were stating that five times three is fifteen. "You can trace a direct line from Emerson's guitar arpeggios on *Curses and Cures* to what Pink Floyd are doing now. This thing Rod Stewart's got going with the mandolins and fiddles, that all goes back to Charlie's stuff. And these guys know it. They'll say it if you bring it up. It's just nobody's bringing it up. People think Emerson's career started with 'Lipstick Letter.' They have no idea how deep this guy is."

Well, he had me over a barrel, didn't he? It was clear that Zaras was knowledgeable, he was bright, he was a fan. Most of all it was clear that he was our only chance of getting Em on the cover of *Rolling Stone*. I told him I'd be delighted to put him in the studio with Emerson to watch him record and do an extensive interview.

It was the single worst decision I ever made.

Charlie had a new girlfriend. You had to hand it to him: when the money began to run out he would always find a way to engorge some poor woman's maternal instinct.

This time he hit the mother lode. Samantha Lipsitz was the daughter of a legendary Hollywood studio mogul and his second wife, a former bathing beauty who had given up the casting couch to marry the boss. Dad had moved on to another family, but Samantha had everything a girl could want, including a large house on a hill in Bel Air and a job as director of the Lipsitz Museum of Contemporary Art in Beverly Hills, one of her father's endowments and a place to hang the family's Pollocks, de Koonings, and Pousette-Darts.

This would have been more than enough to win Charlie's heart, but Samantha was also pretty and smart. Even Emerson was impressed.

"Don't know how the little elf does it, but he always does," Em said after the couple invited us to their mansion for dinner prepared by Samantha's personal chef. "Something about them big sad eyes and the way he picks the Gibson makes a girl roll over and forget her breeding."

Charlie living high on the hog made it tougher for me to scare him into writing a new album. In twelve months of intermittent sessions he had worked up rough demos of eleven songs, of which no more than four were good enough to play for the label.

"I'm not inspired, Jack," he told me while shooting pool on Samantha's antique table. "When the muse wants me, she'll tell me. No rushin' it."

When I could not stall any longer I presented three of Charlie's demos to the record company, lying that this was simply a random scoop of about thirty new songs he was sifting through, recorded very quickly to give them a taste.

The label did not buy it at all. They let me know that, much as they liked Charlie, I was free to shop the tapes elsewhere if I wanted. That scared my client into paying attention.

We came up with a ruse to try to interest other record companies. Emerson graciously agreed to overdub a harmony and guitar solo on one of Charlie's demos. I played that song for Warner's and A&M with the suggestion that if they signed Charlie as a solo artist now, they would be in a great position to get a piece of the duo album the two old Ravons were considering cutting next year.

It was a rotten thing to do but we needed a new contract. Warner's bit. They agreed to give Charlie a four-album deal with the provision that they would have first crack at any whole or partial Ravons reunion record. Given that Tropic actually had those rights, it was not strictly scrupulous of me to go along, but as I knew the Ravons had no intention of reuniting, I figured we would get away with it. I made Charlie swear not to tell any of this to Fred Zaras.

I was proud to have won Charlie a new deal, even if doing so meant sending my ethics on holiday. We had dinner at the Samantha mansion to celebrate. The three of us sat at a vast formal dining table and ate filet mignon by candlelight. Then Charlie hit me with his newest scheme.

"So, Jack, what's the advance, all in?"

"Two hundred grand for each of the first two albums, plus one fifty each in recoupable recording costs. If they activate the option for albums three and four, the price goes up to two fifty and two for recording."

"So the total dough that Warner's is laying out to me across this deal is"—he counted in the air—"one million six hundred thousand dollars."

"Don't think of it that way, Charlie, it's how you get in trouble. It's not as if Warner's is handing us a million and a half dollars. The recording costs, that's not real money. That's you making the records and them picking up the bills, bills they will then deduct from your royalty stream."

Charlie explained to Samantha, "Which is why there ain't ever any royalties."

I went on, "And we don't know if they will even execute those options for albums three and four. At the rate you've been working we won't even get to album three until about 1980. What you really have—to live on, tour on, pay your band—is four hundred thousand dollars for the next two or three years."

"After you take your cut, of course."

"And after you repay all those advances we've given you."

"Cor, man, good thing me old lady has a job!"

Samantha smiled and buzzed for more wine.

"So," Charlie said, grinning, "I have an idea."

"Oh dear."

"What if, instead of putting all that money into hiring some expensive LA recording studio, we get the label to buy me a studio of my own and install it right here?"

"What, in the dining room?"

"No, Jack, out in the pool house. Have you seen it? Sam's pool house is better than most people's homes. We talked about this, Sam and me, and we figure that for the three hundred thousand Warner's is putting up for recording costs for two fuckin' albums, they could *build* me a studio in the pool house and I could record for free for the rest of my life."

I considered this. "Charlie, you don't know how to operate a recording studio. You don't know how to run an electric can opener without cutting off your thumb."

"Oh hey, Jackie, you're too unkind. I been around studios since I was fifteen. And anyway, we get in an engineer, same as ever. Just this time we own the means of production. There's no clock ticking, no money goin' out the door, no pressure." Here Charlie turned on the urchin: "And think, Jack, if you been worried about me not recordin' enough, hell, with me own studio I'd be recording all the time. We'd make an album every six months, maybe more."

I turned to Samantha: "You'd be living over the store. Musicians coming and going at all hours. You sure you wouldn't get sick of that?"

"I like the idea of Charlie being able to be close to me while he's working," she said.

"Plus, Jack," Charlie went on—he'd been rehearsing this pitch—"let's take the worst scenario. Suppose my new albums don't sell, suppose it's two more for Warner's and then I'm done. If we do this deal right,

I'd still own the studio. I'd have me own business, utilizing all my con-nections, and I could live happily ever after and support my lovely lady in the manner to which she's accustomed."

There was strange logic to the proposition. I agreed to take the no-tion to Warner's, and although I had to make the pitch a dozen times up and down the company, they went for it. However, in order for Charlie to come away owning the studio—in order that it not remain the recoupable property of Warner Reprise Records—I had to agree to a reduced cash payment for each album he delivered. We dropped from two hundred grand a record to one twenty-five. I was against it, as was my partner Castro, who was thinking about our commission. However, I worked for Charlie and he signed away the money as quickly as I brought it in.

And so, one Monday morning I drove up to Samantha's mansion and found Charlie in the pool house with crates and boxes filled with several hundred thousand dollars' worth of state-of-the-art speakers, mixers, equalizers, microphones, cords, wires, plugs, circuit breakers, tape machines, and a beautiful new 1973 recording console.

Charlie took inventory of his equipment. "Bloody hell, Flynn," he said. "I don't know what plugs in where."

"You're getting someone in to take care of that, right?" I said.

Charlie looked as though he might weep. "I don't even know how to turn any of it on!"

Wendy Ipswitch, Emerson's publicist, telephoned me at Dormammu on my girlfriend's birthday as I was leaving to meet her for dinner.

"We lost *Rolling Stone*," she said.

It was the last thing I needed to hear.

"How could that possibly happen?" I demanded. "Emerson spent weeks with that lunatic Zaras! He had him in the studio, he went with him to the *Midnight Special* taping, he even invited him into his home! What more could they possibly want?"

"It's not the magazine," she told me. "Apparently Fred Zaras withdrew the story from them."

"How is that possible?" I asked. "Don't they have contracts? How can the writer withdraw the story?"

"I guess he turned in, like, a ten-thousand-word article and when they tried to edit it he flipped out, started making all kinds of demands. Said Emerson supported him and if they didn't run the article as he wrote it Emerson Cutler would never speak to *Rolling Stone* again."

"Oh my God."

Wendy the publicist went on, "They just said, 'Fine, take it, God bless you if anyone else wants to deal with this shit.' Life is too short."

"*Rolling Stone* said that?"

"Up to 'Life is too short.' I said that."

"Well, they should send another writer to interview Emerson!"

"It's too late, Jack, they've moved on."

"So who's getting Em's cover?"

"George Harrison."

"Again? Shit, George Harrison doesn't need another cover of *Rolling Stone*! Emerson does!"

"You want to hear the rest?"

"What more?"

"It looks like *Crawdaddy!* might run Fred's whole ten thousand words and give us the cover."

"That's supposed to make me feel better?"

"*Crawdaddy!* is very prestigious. But they'll need a new photo shoot."

"Fine, and right after that I want you to hire a gunman to put one between the four eyes of that simpleton Fred."

I put off calling Emerson with the bad news until I'd calmed down. I decided to drive over to his house and let him know in person. I phoned Carey to apologize for messing up her birthday and promised I'd be there as soon as I could.

Imagine my outrage—I rang Emerson's bell and Fred Zaras opened the door.

"Hey, Jack," he said.

"I'm surprised you'd be here, Fred," I told him. "You and I had an agreement that I would grant you extraordinary access to Emerson in exchange for a cover story in *Rolling Stone*. Imagine my shock to be told that you took it upon yourself to withdraw that story from *Rolling Stone* and peddle it elsewhere. I'm frankly amazed you would show your face after that sort of stunt."

Emerson's voice came from inside the house. "Come in, Jack!"

I stepped past Zaras into the living room, where Emerson was sitting on the couch with a pile of typewritten pages. He had a pen in his hand and appeared to be making notes.

"Don't be angry with Fred," he said to me. "He and I talked about it before he pulled the story from *Rolling Stone*. He did the right thing."

It was my girlfriend's birthday. I should have been enjoying a romantic dinner with her. Instead I had fallen through a rabbit hole.

I asked Emerson what he was working on.

"It's our article. Fred and I are going over some of the *Crawdaddy!* edits and putting back some bits *Rolling Stone* tried to take out."

"Is that normal?" I turned to Fred. "Is this standard journalistic procedure, Fred? The author and his subject go through and rewrite the article together?"

"I am very concerned with accuracy, Jack," Fred said. "Emerson has placed his faith in me, he's opened up to me. This is a reciprocal process."

"Read it, Jack," Emerson insisted. He shuffled through the papers on his lap and pulled out pages one through five and handed them to me. "Start on these."

I went to the wine cabinet and poured myself a glass and sat down to read. When I got through the first five pages Emerson fed me more, while he and Fred huddled on the couch conferring about edits and rewrites. The article was fifty-eight double-spaced pages, including inserts, handwritten amendments, and a number of paragraphs that had been marked for deletion by the *Crawdaddy!* editors only to be reinstated by Em and his Boswell with defiant *STET*s.

I read the article twice. It was compelling. Emerson opened up in it in a way I'd never known him to do. He spoke about his insecurities as a poor boy trying to pass among London's posh and educated. He talked very honestly about the decision to leave the Ravons and his frustrations with Simon. That surprised me. He spoke about music with an eloquence I had never heard before. I could understand why, having opened up this way, Emerson would not want to see it end up in an editor's trash can.

What caused me concern were the places where the quotes attributed to Emerson sounded nothing like him. I could not conceive of him saying, "Our generation has an obligation to use these new forms of communication to create a common mind-set that can bridge the chasm between the failed orders of market capitalism and totalitarianism and the coming age of postpolitical ecumenicism."

My worry was not simply that those words were not in Emerson's vocabulary. What bothered me was that none of those thoughts had ever been in his head.

I appreciated that the piece Zaras had written was flattering, that it appealed to Emerson to see himself portrayed as a deep thinker, but I was not going to allow my client and friend to be made into a mannequin for some pretentious ventriloquist.

"Some of it's great," I told Emerson. I did not look at Zaras. "But parts of it don't sound like you at all."

Zaras spoke up. "It is him, though. It may not be the man you see at business meetings but it is the true voice of the artist who writes the songs."

I cannot express how much I resented this interloper, this trespasser lecturing me about the true personality of one of my closest friends.

"We worked together to get the words exactly right," Emerson told me. "Fred helped me shape what I wanted to say so it wouldn't be misinterpreted."

"What did he do, Emerson? Stick his hand up your arse and move your mouth for you? This isn't journalism, this is creative writing!"

"Journalism is creative writing, friend," Zaras announced like it meant something.

I said, "This is half fiction."

"'Half of what I say is meaningless,'" Zaras told me. "'I say it that the other half might reach you.' You know who said that, my friend? John Lennon *and* Khalil Gibran. You make a common bourgeois mistake. You mistake literalness for truth. I am going for a higher truth."

"Look, Emerson," I said. "I think there's some good bits in here and some absolute rubbish. I wonder which parts *Rolling Stone* wanted to take out. What's done is done, we can't go back and do the interview over with a nonfiction writer, so if you want to see how much of this dissertation *Crawdaddy!* will publish, good luck to you both. I am now two hours late for Carey's birthday dinner, so if you will excuse me, I am going to try to get back to the real world. You know, Fred, the one ruled by facts."

Emerson made some vague noises about not getting bent out of shape and wishing Carey a happy birthday and was back to marking up his manuscript before I was even out the door.

I had never had much use for music journalists, but Fred Zaras was engaged in something other than music journalism. This was criticism as courtship. It gave me the creeps. I promised myself he would never get near Emerson again.

I doubled every speed limit on the way to the restaurant where Carey and I had had our first date. She was waiting for me alone at a booth in the corner.

"I'm so sorry, sweetheart," I told her. I had bought her a jade necklace but failed to get it wrapped. She put it around her neck without a word.

"I thought Adam and Mary were going to join us," I said.

"I decided it would be nicer if it was just you and me," she told me.

"Carey! You mean you've been waiting here all this time by yourself? I'm so sorry. I had no idea. What a birthday."

"It's okay," she said. "Jack, I have some news."

"When did you know they weren't coming? I wish you'd told me, my business with Emerson could have waited!"

"It's fine, Jack. I have something to tell you."

"You won't believe what happened with that *Rolling Stone* reporter who was supposed to do the cover story on Em. I just found out–"

"Jack? You're going to be a father."

I stared at her. She might as well have told me I was going to be a zebra. I smiled. I didn't speak. I was trying to figure out what she meant.

"I'm pregnant, Jack. We're going to have a baby."

I think I said, "Wow." She smiled at me. I hope I smiled at her. I would be ashamed if she knew the first thought that came into my mind.

I thought, And it's only Monday.

You would think that with my being Irish and Carey being Italian we could have had a Catholic wedding. Carey didn't want that. We went down to city hall and tied the knot in front of several of her friends and Emerson, Charlie, and Samantha. Then we all went to an amusement park and rode the Ferris wheel and squeezed into a twenty-five-cent booth to have our pictures taken. It was only a month later when I brought my bride to England to meet my mother that Mam insisted we go down to the rectory and get a blessing from the priest.

The old pastor almost declined to sanctify our union. He wanted banns of marriage posted and all the proper paperwork filed. I assured him that neither of us had any previous marriages or any other impediment to being made one in the eyes of the Church, but it was only when I took him aside and explained that my civil wife was with child that he relented and gave us a blessing. He made sure that I understood he was doing it only for the sake of my mother, on whom I had already visited so much heartbreak, and the unborn child.

I thanked him and slipped him a tenner and told him to buy some new candle wicks.

My mother and her sister took to Carey and began making lists of saints' names for boys and girls. I suppose it was something of a relief for them that I lived in America, as their neighbors would not be able to compute the difference between the date of the wedding and the birthday of the baby. Carey was great about it, but I know she was glad when it was time for us to leave. It made me sad, though. My parents and I had been so close for so long, and now my mother seemed like a distant relation. It was hard when I was with her to know what to talk about.

When we got home to California, Charlie had his recording system hooked up and working. He had found a wizard of a young engineer who was delighted to be given full run of a state-of-the-art studio. All manner of LA musicians were dropping by Samantha's mansion to make music in Charlie's pool house. A fair number of them seemed to end up swimming in the pool, sleeping in the guest rooms, and raiding the chef's reserves. I wondered how this invasion of freeloaders was sitting with Samantha.

Where musicians gather, drug dealers follow. And when musicians gather in a Bel Air mansion, drug dealers multiply like maggots on a dead dog.

Carey and I arrived for brunch one Sunday and found Samantha charming as always. She led us into the formal dining room, where the chef had laid out five lobsters on chipped ice along with platters of sliced fruits and vegetables arranged like dancers in a Busby Berkeley water ballet.

We sat and chatted and drank tea and finally Samantha said to her maid, "Marylou, will you tiptoe upstairs and tell the boys that lunch is on the table?"

A few minutes later Charlie wandered into the room, dressed in a T-shirt and track pants, his hair looking like a rooster in a windstorm and his eyes almost completely shut.

"Hey, Jack," he croaked.

"Top o' the mornin', your lordship," I said. Charlie landed in one of the chairs and looked at the lobster as if he were trying to remember its name.

He turned to Samantha and said, "Fin still here?"

"Marylou went to get him."

"Fin's here?" I asked. Charlie nodded. I had not seen Fin since he quit the Ravons after the last show in Ohio in 1969. "How did you get in touch with him?"

Charlie could barely speak. He managed to eke out, "He got in touch with me. Heard about the studio."

A moment later Danny Finnerty crept into the room. He looked worse than Charlie. He was wearing his hair shorter than he had when he was with the band. His fly was open and his shirt was buttoned wrong.

"What the fuck was that shit?" he asked Charlie. Charlie was pulling apart a lobster.

"I thought it was pharmaceutical cocaine," Charlie whispered. "That's what it was supposed to be. But I don't think that's all it was."

Samantha was passing fruit platters around as if we were at Windsor Castle and this was teatime chitchat.

Fin's red eyes fixed on me. "Hey," he said slowly. "Jack Flynn! How ya fuckin' doin', man! Hey."

"What a nice surprise, Fin," I told him. "Danny Finnerty, this is my wife, Carey."

Fin nodded stupidly. "Were you guys here last night?"

No, I told him, we were not.

"Right," Fin said. "'Cause we were jamming and this bald cat showed up with a briefcase full of what he said was pharmaceutical coke, but I don't know, I've had a lot of coke and this was something else . . ."

"So you're still playing, Fin," I said.

"Oh yeah, yeah . . . for fun, though, Jack. I manage a club now, down in Orange County. It's called Water Brother, it's very cool. We had Al Kooper in there last month. I want to do a Ravons reunion show, you know, for laughs. Not for bread, just for the music. We'll play under another name and then blow everybody's mind when they see who it is."

I said that would be great. Charlie was staring anxiously at the food in front of him. I had a feeling that he was afraid if he tried to spear it with his fork he might miss the whole plate.

I was breaking the tail off Carey's lobster when Fin turned to Charlie and said in what I think he intended to be a whisper, "Man, I shit my pants."

Charlie looked up at him intently. "Just now?"

"No, in my sleep. When I woke up there was a turd in my underwear."

Samantha went right on eating. She asked Carey where she'd registered for baby gifts.

"I did, too," Charlie said back to Fin. "I wasn't going to say anything, but when I woke up I smelled something and there was a big crap in the bed."

"Whoa," Fin marveled. "That coke must have been cut with laxative."

Carey had stopped eating. Samantha was soldiering through. I asked Fin how many people his nightclub held, and that worked for a couple of minutes. We rushed to the end of the meal and Samantha suggested we go outside and have lemonade on the terrace.

Fin and Charlie stayed stuck to their chairs.

"I've been very fucked-up before," Fin said as if he were describing a newly discovered ring of Saturn. "But I've never been incontinent."

Samantha buzzed for the maid, who took away all the plates.

At twenty-nine years old I was married, making some money, and expecting my first child. It was time to buy a house. Carey and I looked at half the homes in Los Angeles before settling on a two-story shingled storybook cottage in Laurel Canyon. You entered the front garden through a trellis and Carey undertook planting flowers all around.

We also agreed that we would use the term of her pregnancy to clean up our habits and get healthy for the baby. I promised to stop using all drugs, including tobacco, stop eating meat, and stop drinking.

Only the last of these gave me any trouble. I was surprised to find myself craving sugar all the time. I began to drink soda and eat chocolate bars. By the time the baby was due I had gained twenty pounds, which sent me into a spasm of running and swimming. The pounds were slower going off than coming on. I tried to wean myself from sugar, but that made me sleepy all the time. I was falling asleep at my desk. So I started drinking eight cups of coffee a day, which stopped any sleeping at all.

When my daughter, Lucy, was born I was an overweight, over-caffeinated, jogging homeowner. I felt like an American.

Into the pool of my new contentment paddled a little crab of anxiety called Fred Zaras. He had practically moved into Emerson's home and was exerting what I considered a dubious influence on him. In conversation Emerson took himself more and more seriously. The songs that I knew he composed using a mix-and-match formula he now talked about as gifts from some subterranean sea of the collective unconscious into which only he and a few other poetic champions had the gifts to dip.

What had once been blues clichés now became, in Zaras's lexicography, Jungian archetypes. Simple romantic metaphors became semiotic codes. I learned to be civil to Zaras when he was around but I would have paid a hundred dollars to see someone hit him in the face with a pie.

Charlie mentioned that the critic had stopped associating with him as soon as he'd won entrée to Emerson, which only furthered my suspicion that Freddy the freeloader was working his way up the food chain.

"You know my idea of an interview between Em and Freddy?" Charlie said to me one afternoon in his studio.

"Tell me," I replied.

"They're lookin' up at the stars and Em says, 'That one looks a bit like a dog, don't it?' And ol' Freddy gets out his pad and writes, 'Like the scholar kings of ancient Phoenicia, Cutler has an astronomer's eye for measuring the infinite and a painter's sense of order and celestial composition.'"

"Pretty good," I said. "You should try writing songs sometime."

"How's your little girl, Jack?"

"She's a doll. She has her mum's eyes and nose and my mam's ears and chin."

"Heartbreaker."

"She's already broken mine."

"Care for some weed?"

"Gave it up."

"Care for a drop?"

"Quit that, too."

"Hope you ain't gone off sex."

"Talk to the wife, she says it's a temporary thing till she's done nursing."

"I nursed till I was four and a half."

"That explains something."

"What can I tempt you with, then?"

"I don't suppose you have any cake?"

I hated the idea of never taking another drink. I missed the mending in the first glass of whiskey of the evening. I longed for my mind to again descend into that healing bath, rinsing away the troubles of the day. Looking back from teetotal sobriety on those infrequent occasions when I had chosen to drink to inebriation, I recognized those as times when I needed to take a short vacation from myself, to stop seeing and thinking as I otherwise did, to be a slightly different Jack Flynn for a while. The next morning I was back to myself with no harm done, ready to strap into my regular harness. To never drink again would be like saying I was going to remain locked in my quaint Laurel Canyon house for the rest of my life. It was a very nice house and I was comfortable there. But sometimes I liked to go out.

What no one talks about when they talk about Los Angeles in the 1970s is how much time we spent in a state of placid boredom. There was nothing on television, there was no theater, there was no place to see European football, and none of us followed American sports. All we could do when Emerson was not on the road was work and go to one of the three nightclubs that catered to a rock crowd over twenty-one. Other bars were either holdovers from the Sinatra era or workingmen's saloons that did not make us feel welcome. Once I stopped drinking and taking drugs, bars became tiresome. I remember sitting at a table at the Troubadour one night, watching the great stars of 1975 check out their reflections in each other's sunglasses. I was itchy and out of place, but I had to stick around. I was there for a meeting with Wendy to discuss the pernicious influence of Fred Zaras.

Wendy came in wearing too-tight jeans, too-high boots, and a too-small top. Only her hair was big. She had already worked herself into a fury when she got to my table.

"This must stop, Jack! It must stop!"

"Nice to see you, too, Wendy."

"Do you know what that creep is doing? He's selling exclusive interviews with Emerson to every alternative paper and music magazine from here to London. He must tape-record Emerson all night and then chop up the transcripts into little piles. This bit where he talks about his whammy bar goes to *Guitar Player,* this thing where he talks about fucking groupies goes to *Creem,* and the part where he talks about the influence of Lord Byron on 'Bust One for Me Mama,' well, that I'll just make up myself.

"I have had it with this guy, Jack. I called the *Village Voice* to pitch a piece on Emerson and they said, 'Oh, we're sitting on one already by Fred Zaras.' Same thing happened at *Penthouse*! Editors are calling *him* now to get interviews with Emerson. This is not good."

All of this made me unhappy but so did Wendy's whining. I said, "At least he's getting Em a lot of print. We never got these kinds of write-ups before Fred came along. People are taking our artist very seriously."

She looked at me like I had bad breath and knocked back a Kahlúa Mudslide.

"Well, if you're content with the situation, Jack, I guess we should just be grateful to have Fred doing both our jobs for us. Last week I sent you the press bio for Emerson's new album."

"Yes, I read it, it was fine."

"And then you sent it to Emerson."

"Sure, I always do. He never looks at 'em."

"Oh really."

Wendy reached into her purse and pulled out two sheets of xeroxed paper covered in scrawled revisions, arrows, and inserts.

"Here is the new press release, as rewritten by Freddy Zaras. It contains no mention of the album's street date or the upcoming tour or how many copies Emerson Cutler's last three LPs have sold. It does, however, contain a long dissertation on how Emerson's work with atonal scales recalls the similar experiments of Ornette Coleman and how he has incorporated into this music the polyrhythmic dynamics of New Orleans street musicians and the talking drums of West Africa. Have you heard Emerson's album, Jack? The only polyrhythm is when the kid banging the tambourine loses the beat. You want to hear what the lyrics are about according to this?"

"Spare me," I said. "I get the picture. Go ahead and send out the release I approved. I'll deal with Emerson."

"Who's going to deal with Freddy?"

"I'll deal with Freddy, too."

"He is a sycophantic slug crawling up Emerson's ass."

"If you exhibited that literary flair in your press releases, Wendy, Emerson would feel no need to roam."

"Fuck that slug, Jack. Freddy, I mean."

"I'll do my best."

"I hope he gets eaten by a prehistoric thesaurus."

I have reached the part of my story where I have to lay out for you the philosophy of Fred Zaras. If this seems tedious to you, imagine what it was like for those of us who had to listen to Fred unspool it one tangled thread at a time through endless stoned monologues, harangues, and diatribes. What I am about to summarize is actually more coherent than anything Fred ever said, but I have legal training— I can piece together an organized narrative out of random chunks of dissociative babble.

Fred's thesis began with the allegation that we can understand the tides of human history and behavior by studying the actions of amoebas. The human race began as a hundred million scattered, self-contained, and selfish cell clusters, each invested only in its own survival. Gradually, over millions of years (he sometimes had comets and/ or alien intervention acting as a motivating agent here but I will spare you) these microorganisms combined into families, then into species, and finally into races.

There was, according to Zaras, a raging genetic competition between the remaining racial clusters to see which would emerge triumphant, which would metaphorically absorb—Fred always said "eat"—the others. Here he would digress into a long exposition about the commonality of cannibal myths among competing ethnicities seeking to dehumanize their rivals.

Fred insisted that we could divide human civilization into seven ethnic clusters—Anglo (the UK, Ireland, Canada, the USA, Australia, and New Zealand), Latin American (Spanish-speaking America but also Brazil, the Caribbean, and parts of Florida, Texas, and California), non-Anglo European, Oriental, Indian, Muslim (from Morocco to Afghanistan), and black African. The rapid advancement of travel and communication in the twentieth century exacerbated the tensions and competition between these rival groups. Fred insisted that over the next fifty years all seven clusters would be drawn tighter together. Russia would break away from its alliances with China and Vietnam to reconnect with Europe. China, Japan, and Korea would overcome their old antipathies to form a new Pacific common market. The walls between England, Ireland, Canada, and the USA would dissolve, leaving one state with four flags.

One of the very troubling things about Fred's theory—and we have only stuck our toes in—is that aspects of it bordered on racism. Fred would happily maintain that the northern races, in adapting to long winters, had developed greater rationalism and intellectual attributes necessary for long-term planning and gathering nuts, while the East Asians had evolved superior collective and communal skills. American Indians (whom Fred counted as a lost tribe of East Asians) were most closely attuned to nature and, according to Fred, sub-Saharan Africans had superior physical and reproductive attributes.

I can't tell you how embarrassing it was when Fred started orating this way in mixed company. More than once I had to dissuade offended black people from demonstrating their superior physical attributes by introducing Fred's mouth to their fists.

When I asked Fred to tone down the parts of his theory that treaded closest to bigotry, he would laugh and say that of course he was no bigot! But stereotypes did not come from nothing—they were unarticulated instincts pointing back to our primal directives. Fred insisted that the only way to avoid a coming worldwide steel-cage death match between the seven emerging mega-nations was to recognize the biological roots of our rivalries and work together to speed the evolutionary conveyor belt toward its intended final consequence, the New Man.

In Fred's prognosis the New Man would achieve equal balance between the physical, the social, the instinctive, and the intellectual. He would be a poet, a warrior, an athlete, a scientist, and so sexually charismatic that both women and men would want to mate with him. His rallying cry would transcend language, ethnicities, and national boundaries. The New Man would meld the tribal drum of the African jungle with Oriental mysticism, European poetics, Native American shamanism, and modern technology to move mankind up the evolutionary ladder before our Neanderthal tribalism killed us all.

How would the New Man manifest himself? Well, what have we been talking about this whole time? Obviously the next evolutionary model for mankind was the enlightened rock star. According to Fred's laborious hypothesis, the entire donnybrook of human history had been a brutal genetic roller derby designed to end in the creation of Emerson Cutler.

Do you wonder that Emerson wanted this lunatic to write all his press releases from now on?

Emerson was going on a cross-country arena tour to coincide with the release of his new album *Bare Conditioned*. I had a thousand things to do, from approving the album cover (suntanned Emerson playing guitar in a shack on a tropical beach attended by two nearly nude fashion models–by 1975 the PR prohibition on overt sexiness was losing support) to arguing over advances with local promoters to filling out the paperwork for the Musicians' Union to checking the thread count in the Emerson Cutler T-shirts.

My business partner Castro had resigned to go to work for Bill Graham Presents. I had Emerson and Charlie all to myself again. I missed having someone to share the incoming calls demanding immediate decisions.

In the middle of this chaos Danny Finnerty phoned to say he was at a restaurant right around the corner and could he drop by for a minute. There was no getting out of it. I had not seen our former drummer since he had crapped his pants at Charlie's lobster brunch, but he swept into my office as if we shared a bunk bed.

"I like it!" he said loudly, looking around at my Doheny digs. "Very tasty, Flynn! A big step up from Nevermore down in Chelsea, I have to say. Although I did always have a little crush on that receptionist you had, what was her name?"

"Allison. Look, Fin, it's great to see you but I'm up to my nostrils in paperwork and phone calls for Emerson's tour. I really don't have time to reminisce."

"Hey, Jack, that's why I'm here! You and I are in the same game now! I'm a manager!"

"I thought you were running a nightclub."

"Well, guess what? That's where I discovered this band! And

they were so good I quit the whole frigging nightclub to take care of them!"

"What's the group called?"

"Izbushka! Isn't that wild? It's like Ukrainian or something, it means a house on chicken legs. These guys are so hip. They've got congas, a flute, a classical guitarist, and this kid who plays Coltrane solos on the harmonica. I mean, it's like a folk-jazz fusion with blues integrity."

"Sounds unbeatable," I said. I really needed Fin to leave.

"So, I'm thinking: Opening act!"

"For whom?"

"For Emerson! On this tour!"

"The support acts are booked, Fin. We have Pablo Cruise for the West Coast and Orleans in the East."

"Well, how about my guys get thirty minutes while the hall's filling up?"

"It won't work, Fin. Emerson's playing a very long set."

"You gotta at least listen to them."

"I'd love to, Fin, but right now I have to get back on the phone."

"Flynn! It's me, you crazy bastard. One song."

He was not going to leave until I gave in. "Fine. One song."

He put a cassette into my stereo and out came a rhythmic acoustic guitar over pounding bongos with a breathy flute in the right speaker trying to drown out a frantically fingerpicked acoustic guitar in the left.

A faux-bluesy white voice sang, "Love is an ointment, it can salve your wounds / Love is an ointment, just squeeze the tube." It proceeded from that premise for another four minutes. Fin played drums with two pencils on the side of my desk the whole time.

"What's it called?" I asked when it was almost over.

"'Ointment.'"

"An oddly mellifluous title. Did he say, 'It can solve your wounds'?"

"Salve. Salve your wounds."

"I never knew salve was a verb."

"It's an Americanism."

"Ah."

"I came up with 'squeeze the tube.' It needed a hook."

"Interesting juxtaposition of the sacred and profane."

"Like Ray Charles."

"The sanctified and sexual."

"Like Aretha."

"Eros and agape."

"I'm glad you like it."

"It's a gas, Fin, but it doesn't change that the support acts are already booked. I'm sorry."

Fin shrugged and smiled. I remembered that we had other business.

"Guess what?" I said. "Tropic Records is going to bring out a double-album history of the Ravons to coincide with Emerson's tour."

"Swell," Fin said. "Do I get paid anything?"

"Well, technically you've already been paid and this goes toward working off the group's old advances, but I put the arm on them and got a little money for you guys. Of course, it's prorated by the number of tracks you played on, but sometime in the next six months you should be getting a check for ten or twelve thousand dollars."

"Great!"

"But listen, I have to tell you one thing. They are billing it as 'The Ravons featuring Emerson Cutler.' You understand. Emerson is the selling point and, after all, having his name up front will move a lot more records."

"Doesn't bother me," Fin said. "Charlie cool with it?"

"He didn't jump for joy, but he understands. It's in his interests to have the songs he wrote with Emerson out there."

A coy smile trickled over Fin's face.

"What about Simon?"

"Remarkably enough, Simon signed off without a word."

"No kidding. I guess he's mellowed."

It would have been nice to think so. In fact, six months later I opened the mail to find a screeching foam-drenched tirade from Simon, who claimed to have known nothing of this double-pocket abortion until some unfortunate fan shoved it in his face to autograph after a show. Simon went on to promise lawsuits, litigation, and calumny unto the next ten generations of Cutlers and Flynns.

I went to the files and pulled out the release he had signed with the intention of xeroxing it and sending it back to him. Looking at it, I saw for the first time that Simon's name was signed not in his own crabbed hand but in the pen-snapping scrawl of Tug Bitler.

"Shit," I said to myself. "I'll bet Tug endorsed the check I sent Simon, too."

Emerson Cutler's Bicentennial Blues Tour was the biggest he had ever undertaken. The revenues were potentially enormous, but the expenses were intimidating. We had lighting techs, sound crew, roadies for each instrument, truck drivers and a cook, a nurse, and an after-show social coordinator to run interference with local press, retailers, and radio contest winners, and to buy drugs.

I signed off on all of it, but I paused when I saw that Emerson had submitted to the budget travel, hotel, and per diems for Fred Zaras.

"You want to bring Fred on the road?" I asked him. We were smoking a joint behind my house in Laurel Canyon. I was still off the booze, at least close to home, but under the pressure of preparing the tour I had backslid into pot.

"He plans to write a book about the tour," Emerson explained.

"Oh, he fucking does, does he?" I asked. Marijuana used to make me mellow; now it just exaggerated whatever mood I was in. "And when did he plan to submit this proposal to management?"

"He wanted to tell you right away, but I said I'd handle it."

"Oh, you're handling it."

"It's my life, Jack. I'd rather have Fred write about it than some hack."

"So let me understand. We are going to pay Fred's way across the United States so that he can write a book about you. Would it be unfair to assume that we will share in the profits from this book? I mean, if we're shelling out for Fred's living expenses while he writes it, if it's your name and face and music that will sell the thing, I assume we get a share of the revenue and the right to review the manuscript?"

"Fred would never agree to that, Jack. It would compromise his ethics as a journalist."

"Oh—sorry, wouldn't want to compromise Fred's journalistic ethics. I'm just happy they can withstand the conflicts imposed by our paying for his meals, travel, and sundries while he leans against the outer wall of your hotel room with his ear pressed to a drinking glass!"

"Come on, Jack . . ."

"I suppose by this point he's using a stethoscope."

Emerson smiled. It was all going to end up his way; he could afford to let me stamp my feet.

"You and I make a lot of money, Jack," Emerson said. And here we both knew he was referring to the fact that as his manager my 15 percent of the tour was commissioned off the gross whereas he paid the band, crew, and travel out of the net. We had argued about this before. From my 15 percent I also paid the whole costs of the office and everyone in it. Emerson absorbed more of the risk of touring because he made 85 percent of the profit. He still maintained it was inequitable and I still maintained, Tough shit.

"You and I make a lot of money, Jack," Emerson said. "Fred doesn't have a pot to pee in. You know what he gets paid for those articles he writes? One, two hundred bucks. And he works on each one of them like he's writing the history of the Roman Republic. This book will give him a chance to make a little bread, maybe put a down payment on a house or something. Get a decent car. It's the least we can do for him after what he's done for us."

It made no sense but it was beyond arguing. Emerson was going to get what he wanted, as always.

I had known Emerson now for nearly ten years. In some ways he had changed incredibly and in others he remained exactly the same. I had come to understand more profoundly our relationship and our mutual responsibilities.

Entertainers desperately want to be liked. I don't mean only professionally, to have the public buy tickets to their concerts and movies. They want you—you personally and you collectively—to like *them*. This has been true of every entertainer I have met in forty years. The performers who affect sullenness, moodiness, anger, and resentment toward the public for intruding on their privacy want to be liked most of all. They may have unresolved childhood issues with trust and need a lot of reassurance. They may simply be emotionally greedy. They test the public's affection by pretending to resent it. A star who says "I want to be left alone" is like an insecure girlfriend who says "Oh, I'm not very pretty." Both are begging you to disagree.

The decision to pursue a career in music has to be made when one is very young. If you have not started down the road to rock and roll stardom with a dedication bordering on obsession by the time you are fifteen or sixteen, you are too late. The rock business I worked in was filled with grown men living out the ambitions and fantasies of adolescent boys. Stars may wish they could switch off their celebrity when it is inconvenient, but if they had that power they would be too scared to ever use it. Tug was not far off when he confused Nevermore with Neverland.

The hunger for affection in the star is why the manager has to take on the roll of professional prick. The star needs someone to be his bad guy. In a restaurant Emerson would agree to anything. Sure, he'd play on your new album, of course he'd sit for an interview, he'd love to come out and see your beach house, score your movie, invest in your nightclub, play your fund-raiser, read your script, and listen to your daughter's demo tape. It fell to me, the square and money-grubbing manager, to put the kibosh on the deal.

When the personal home phone number Emerson gave you turned out to be no longer in service and you rang the office, I picked up your call and pretended that while Emerson had spoken with great enthusiasm about your project, I had to veto his participation because it might conflict with other deals I was in the middle of negotiating.

Jack Flynn was the villain, Jack Flynn was the obstacle, Jack Flynn didn't get it. You had no use at all for that rat Jack Flynn. But you went right on loving Emerson.

There are a few sacred rules in rock and roll. Don't leave your girlfriend with a drum roadie, don't touch Keith Richards's meat pie, don't step on my blue suede shoes. The greatest commandment, though, is this: never get married in the middle of a tour.

Everyone on a big rock tour is living in an alternative universe. Someone tells you when to wake up, when to go to sleep, when to get in the car, and when to go to work—work being a place where people you have never seen before and will never see again cheer and scream for everything you do. During a tour you never see a bill, you never wake up in the same city three days in a row, you never get enough sleep. After a month or so, you have turned into a different human being than you were at home and will become again when you return. Everybody knows you don't get married in the middle of a tour.

Emerson met a girl when the tour was in Miami, invited her along to Atlanta, stopped off in South Carolina to meet her family, asked her to marry him in Maryland, and told me to line up a minister for the night of our last show at Madison Square Garden.

Do I need to tell you she was a model? Cynthia Apple was one of the most gorgeous women any of us had ever seen. She was supernaturally long and thin. A man could cut himself on her cheekbones. Her hair fell to her shoulders in cascades of honey-colored curls and her lips always looked just-bitten. This was a girl who never had to wait for a table, who was always seated in the window, and who made velvet ropes disappear. Men saw her coming and walked into walls. I suspected that Cynthia had seen Emerson coming, too. She drove him wild and then pulled away. She made him chase her. She disappeared for days and did not return his phone calls. Then she would show up in the middle of the night—or the middle of a sound check—with her

hair wet and her cheek dramatically bruised. The woman was a walking emergency.

Cynthia dazzled me, too, but I kept my head enough to suggest to
Emerson that he wait to actually take the vows until the tour was over
and he could give Miss Apple the sort of wedding she deserved.

He was too far gone to get it. She told him she wanted to get married in Manhattan with all her model friends. Whatever reservations
any of Emerson's mates had about the nuptials pretty much went out
the window when they heard that.

Emerson told me to ask Charlie and Samantha to the wedding and
to try to locate Simon and convince him to come, too.

"I want all my best friends from my whole life there, Jack," he said.
"This is the one that's going to last forever."

I had premonitions of shimmying up another palm tree with a camera strap in my teeth.

I knew I was outnumbered when Cynthia Apple struck up an alliance with Fred Zaras. I had hoped that they would repel each other
like mixed magnets. I figured that if Cynthia drove Fred from Emerson's affections I would consider her a trade up. Zaras had been looming around the whole tour interviewing anyone who came near him.
Now he became Cynthia's confidant and confessor. Zaras explained
Emerson's unseen depths to her, and she was flattered by the writer's
gift for recognizing in her gifts he compared to those of Frida Kahlo,
Eudora Welty, and Amelia Earhart.

I figured that, first, Zaras was crafty. Get in good with the wife and
she'll talk you up to the old man. Second, he knew he had a scoop. No
matter what happened with the marriage, it gave his Emerson book sex
and drama. Third, she was probably the only beautiful woman who had
ever spoken to him. I reckoned he was hoping she had a blind sister.

As Madison Square Garden got closer I found myself in the unwanted position of wedding planner. We decided to keep the actual
service small. We could tie the knot at the Park Avenue apartment of
the president of Tropic Records one hour before Em walked onstage at
the Garden. He would announce the big news during the encore, bring
his bride out for a first dance—Cynthia's idea—and then we would all
limo up to the Rainbow Room for an all-night wedding reception and
end-of-tour party.

From there the golden couple would jet off to a honeymoon in the Caribbean. I wondered if Fred would go along to take notes.

My own marriage was taking a beating from my being away from home, keeping odd hours, and having to deal with both the hundred daily emergencies of a rock tour and now Emerson's engagement. All this took place in the days before mobile phones. It was always hard for Carey to find me and when she did I was usually distracted. She wanted my opinion on whether to fix the washing machine or buy a new one; what would I think of painting the bathroom blue; which of two competing preschools was best for little Lucy?

I tried to explain that I had faith in her to make the best decision and that right now I had to deal with a fire marshal threatening to shut down the venue and a keyboard player who had passed out from peyote. A few too many conversations like that and you find yourself not married anymore. Carey and I would hang on for another year, even go for counseling like real Californians, but the truth is that our marriage was over by the time Emerson's tour bus rolled into Manhattan.

New York in 1976 was at its nadir. If you had arrived on the is-land of Manhattan with the Dutch settlers and remained in a rent-controlled apartment until Hillary Clinton was your senator, you would have looked back and said, "The Civil War draft riots were a drag, that influenza epidemic sucked, but this place really bottomed out in the mid-1970s."

This was the era of municipal bankruptcy and the headline "Ford to New York: Drop Dead." The city was fixed in the popular imagination as a garbage scow of vice and crime. Times Square was squalid with hookers and tourist traps selling fake watches and cheap cameras. Drug dealers and pimps operated openly. Pay phones had been ripped out by their roots, garbage festered uncollected, vagrants pissed in the street. TV comedians had made "Central Park" synonymous with muggings, and the movies projected images of ruthless urban vigilantes battling against a tide of rabid dark barbarians.

The police? We knew from *Serpico* that the police were just a different class of criminal. Coming into Manhattan from California in 1976, our attitude was, *Lock yourself in the hotel room, put on some music, send out for room service, and pull down the shades!*

Was it really that much worse than it had been in the late sixties, when we were kids in from London thrilled to be eating real hamburgers and milkshakes and wandering around Washington Square?

Looking back, I doubt it very much. But we were different. Where we had once viewed every new experience as an opportunity, we now saw only threats. We now had something to lose.

Charlie was waiting for us at the Mayflower Hotel on the west side of Central Park. Samantha had elected to stay in Los Angeles—her museum had a big opening, Charlie said, although I wondered if he had really invited her.

We had two days until the Madison Square Garden show and Emerson's wedding. I had cleared as many interviews, meet-and-greets, and promotional activities from the calendar as I could, but we still had a busy schedule.

Everyone except Emerson was shocked when Simon Potts arrived on our second day in the city. He was clean-shaven and had had work done on his teeth, but he was otherwise unchanged. "You and I need to talk, Flynn," he said in a low voice when we all met for breakfast in the hotel coffee shop. "Tug ain't carrying his share of the load."

Oh, God help me, I thought, that's why Simon is here. He wants me to manage him again. I knew that Blue Moon was now a rotating title for any group of sidemen Simon hired, and I supposed that times had gotten tough for him as the audience for his kind of plodding and overwrought rock receded into what had once been the Austro-Hungarian Empire. If Fred Zaras's theories of genetic tribalism held up, Simon was composing the soundtrack for a dwindling Teutonic tributary a long way from the mainstream.

Here inspiration struck me. I went to the house phone and called up to Fred's room and invited him down to join us for scrambled eggs. I could tell Fred was suspicious. Any other time I phoned him it was to reprimand him for something to do with the minibar bill or underage girls. I had recently busted him for calling ahead to hotels on the itinerary pretending to be Mr. Cutler's assistant, making sure that Mr. Zaras got upgraded to a corner suite on a high floor.

Fred came into the coffee shop warily. He looked shocked when I warmly welcomed him to sit down with the closest thing to a Ravons reunion. I slid over to offer him a space next to Simon.

After some initial coolness toward the newcomer, Simon began to answer Fred's questions about the fratricide imagery in his early lyrics, how bass frequencies stimulate the recessive cortex of the brain, and why radio suppressed "Open-Minded Friend." The two of them got on like a pair of constipated seminarians, united in their tastes and grievances.

Why hadn't I thought of this long ago? Imagine the aggravation I could have saved myself if when Fred first showed up with his Ravons fixation I had bought him a ticket to England and sicced him on Simon. The two of them could have spent a happy life together, with spelunker Fred deciphering the hieroglyphics up Simon's rear end.

I was having a jolly time laughing at old stories with Charlie and Emerson when Fred made a disconcerting announcement: "Listen, men. Whatever you had planned for tonight, cancel it. I have been making some calls, and as my contribution to the wedding weekend, I have arranged for Emerson's bachelor party!"

There was a pause and then Charlie and Emerson cheered and Simon shrugged and raised his orange juice glass and I could see there would be no getting out of it. Whatever Fred Zaras had planned, I was going to have to pay for.

What would you expect the bachelor party of a seventies rock star to be like? Something between *Satyricon* and the inside cover of *Beggar's Banquet*? *Playboy* centerfolds cavorting to "Life in the Fast Lane"? Not with Fred Zaras in charge.

First we went for a lousy steak dinner at Max's Kansas City, a downtown joint that had once been the hangout of the Warhol crowd and now seemed to be nothing more than a place for tired drag queens to take a nap in the toilet. Zaras assured us that this was merely the first stop on a tour of New York's music demimonde. From there we went to the Blue Note to hear what I hoped would be jazz but turned out to be an electric group of white fusion musicians bringing out the worst in both funk rhythms and bebop harmony. Simon seemed into it, but Emerson started making faces and Charlie began making rude comments, so we got out of there and crossed Washington Square to the Bottom Line.

Fred did some fast talking to the woman in the ticket window and a short man with red hair appeared and led us to a reserved table in the center of the club. The act onstage was a three-piece band fronted by a young black folk-blues singer who recognized Emerson and invited him up to do a song. The audience clapped and shouted yippee. Em smiled and stood and made his way to the stage, where a roadie handed him an electric guitar.

Emerson and the bluesman traded guitar leads on a version of "Goin' Up the Country and Paint My Mailbox Blue" to the contagious delight of the room. Then the two of them whispered behind their hands, apparently conferring on which song to do next. The blues singer leaned in to his microphone and said, "I have some very special news. Emerson is here tonight with two other legends of British rock and roll."

He leaned back over to Emerson to make sure he had the names right, then said, "Could we put our hands together and see if we can convince Simon Potts and Charlie Lydle to join their old guitar player onstage?" Simon looked concerned, Charlie was delighted. The blues singer announced grandly as the audience climbed to their feet, "Ladies and gentlemen, for the first time anywhere since 1969, I give you– the Ravons!"

The crowd was shouting as Charlie and Simon made it to the front of the room and strapped on instruments. The blues singer graciously stepped to the wings to give his stage to his guests. He told his drummer to stay where he was.

The Ravons joked and shook their guitar cords and twiddled with knobs. There was an instant when it looked like it might become embarrassing, and then Charlie with his entertainer's instincts began strumming "Voodoo Doll," the drummer kicked in, and the room erupted. I looked over at Fred Zaras, who had his little cassette recorder out and a look of almost coital ecstasy on his face.

The reunited Ravons made it to the end of the song and whether it was good or not didn't matter. Everyone in the Bottom Line was delighted to have been part of a historic moment that would show up in "Random Notes" and *NME,* be described on FM radio from LA to London, and would cause the double-LP anthology credited to the Ravons Featuring Emerson Cutler to go top twenty in the USA the same week that Emerson's new album, buoyed by the media coverage of his Madison Square Garden wedding, would hit number one.

Seven years after they broke up, the Ravons were peaking.

For a moment when the song ended they seemed to consider doing another, but Emerson knew to leave the crowd wanting more. He also knew that the illusion would be better preserved if they came and went before anyone got used to them. He thanked his host band profusely, thanked the Bottom Line and his old and dearest friends, and said, "Now, if you'll excuse us, we really have to go home and sleep. You see, I'm getting married in the morning!"

It was not exactly true but it was sure a crowd-pleasing line. The place went completely nuts. Emerson, Charlie, and Simon embraced, bowed, and walked straight off the stage, through the audience, and out of the Bottom Line into the street.

Fred and I looked at each other. They weren't coming back. They were showmen. We quickly gathered our things from the table, paid the bill, and hurried out into the street to find the Ravons.

It was like they'd never been away.

Fred and I came out of the Bottom Line and looked up and down Fourth Street, trying to figure where Emerson, Charlie, and Simon had gone.

"They've probably jumped in a cab and said, 'Take us the Alibi Club!'" I said. I figured I'd give them fifteen minutes and then go back to the hotel.

"I have the opening for my book," Fred told me. "I am going to start it right there, at the Bottom Line, but I'll make you think at first I'm describing a Ravons show in London in the sixties, then it will be a surprise when you realize it's New York and it's today. The whole book will then happen in flashback and end up tomorrow at Emerson's wedding."

"Sounds like a plan, Fred," I said, standing in the road looking up and down for any sign of my three little lambs. "Ah! I think I know where our comrades might be holding the after-show."

One block east of the Bottom Line was Tower Records, a looming vinyl supermarket at the intersection of Fourth Street and Broadway. The windows were filled with posters of superstars—Wings, Elton John, the Commodores, Tavares, Barry Manilow, Chaka Khan, Bette Midler, Dolly Parton, Diana Ross, Jackson Browne.

We walked into the neon temple. Music was blasting—"Rock the Boat" by the Hues Corporation was segueing into "Kung Fu Fighting." We found the Ravons at the "R Assorted" bin, checking out their oeuvre.

"Thought you'd be here," I told them.

"Wasn't that fun, Jack?" Charlie said. "I dunno, Emerson, think we might have to do it again at the Madison Square?"

Emerson was charming and noncommittal. Simon accosted a passing boy in a Tower Records T-shirt.

"You, clerk!" Simon called at him. "Where do you keep your Ravons records?"

"Ravons?" the kid said. He was burdened with a stack of albums that came to his chin. He said, "Check the Emerson Cutler section."

Simon looked like he needed a guillotine. Charlie laughed and said, "Easy, Potts, our lad's gettin' married tomorrow!"

I wish we had gone home then. For random and unexpected reasons of bad fusion and good fortune, Fred had steered Emerson toward the perfect bachelor party, a triumphant onstage reunion with his old mates.

We should have quit there and returned to the hotel, or taken up the road crew's offer to meet them at a strip club in Times Square for a real celebration.

That's what Emerson wanted to do, but Fred insisted that now we go back to his original itinerary and finish the night at the hippest new hangout in New York, a club just down Bleecker Street called CBGB's. I could tell that Emerson did not want to go. It was his night, and I stepped in to play the bad cop. But Fred whined about how much grief he had suffered to convince the recalcitrant and unimpressed owner of CB's to reserve us a table. Apparently they did not reserve tables for anyone.

Emerson was still buzzing from the Ravons' reunion. He said, "All right, then, if Fred went to so much trouble. We'll stop in for one drink, then back uptown."

CBGB's was in a bad neighborhood even by the standards of seventies New York. The bar was beneath a flophouse on the Bowery and the sidewalk was crowded with winos, junkies, and the homeless. Bleecker Street was the main thoroughfare of the Village, along which sat many legendary folk, jazz, and rock clubs. If you followed Bleecker Street all the way to its terminus, you arrived at the door of CBGB's. This was where the music ended.

I have heard people talk about the Ravons' visit to CBGB's in ways inaccurate and sometimes impossible. Contrary to what you might have read elsewhere, we did not roll in accompanied by a dozen fashion models and record executives. We did not loudly demand that a group of patrons be cleared out so we could take their table. None of us was drunk and no one heckled. There was no fistfight.

We did not, as is sometimes reported, see the Ramones, Talking Heads, Blondie, or the Dictators. When we walked in, the group playing was Television. Their unannounced surprise guest was Patti Smith.

I said to the fellow at the door, "Hello, I manage Emerson Cutler."

The doorman replied, "Do I come to you with my problems?"

I want to also say—and I am not defensive about this, I just want to be accurate—that we were not frightened or offended by CBGB's. The Ravons had played in much tougher joints. The crowd was not arrayed in Mohawks and safety pins. There were all sorts, including men with beards, women with Farrah Fawcett hair, and lots of people in flared trousers. They were perhaps a bit on the young side, but the drinking age in those days was eighteen and I did not get the impression the doorman was being scrupulous in checking IDs.

The five of us were directed to a small table, two of us on a bench along the wall, three on chairs. Fred went to the bar and came back with five beers in plastic cups. We toasted each other, and Emerson said, "One drink and home."

Television came onstage. They were set up like a beat group—two guitars, bass, and a small drum kit.

"They have short hair for a band," Charlie noted. "Maybe this is Young Republican rock."

They began their first song. The singer seemed awkward, wary. He had a somewhat strangled voice by our standards. We were not used to white singers who did not try to sound black.

"They should get a chick singer," Emerson said.

"They should get a keyboard player," Simon said.

"Just listen," Fred insisted.

The two guitar players launched into an extended solo section. The Ravons stopped talking; this was of interest to them. The fair-haired guitarist drew out strange lead lines that would build lyrically and then interrupt themselves to scratch and cough. It was something like seeing a bird in beautiful flight abruptly fall to earth.

"Reminds me a bit of the guy from Fairport," Charlie said.

The group returned to the top of the verse and the second guitarist, dark haired and sweet-faced, stepped forward. He revved several times like he was kick-starting a motorcycle, and then shot off down the road, firing muscular lines, melodic and confrontational. Charlie said it reminded him of Mick Taylor, with a bit of the abandon of Neil Young.

"What do you think?" Fred said when the song finished.

"It's okay," Emerson said. "I like the guitar-playing more than the songs. Or the singing. They need a chick vocalist and maybe a conga player, something to make it groove."

"You got your cassette machine, Fred?" Simon wanted to know. "Give it here."

Fred passed his tape recorder to Simon, who pressed RECORD and placed it on the table.

"What are you doing, Simon?" I asked him. Years of chasing bootleggers out of Emerson concerts had made me sensitive.

"Just want to keep a record," he said. "Might get some ideas."

After a few songs there was a great stirring in the club. I could tell that Emerson thought he had been recognized. Perhaps he was considering whether the Ravons would honor a request to get up here, too.

Instead it turned out that the excitement was for Patti Smith, who had appeared at the side of the stage. She was a local poet and rock critic who had released an album that was the new underground sensation. I had heard one song, a cover of Van Morrison's "Gloria." I preferred Van.

The Television singer did not announce her. He said something to her in a low voice and she climbed up to take command of the microphone with the authority of an Apache brave stepping into a war dance.

"I don't mess with the past but I fuck plenty with the future!" she declared as Television vamped and throbbed behind her. With a snap of the snare they were off into an extended riff—I can't call it a jam because I had the impression that they had done it before—that allowed Smith to improvise a stream-of-consciousness poetry that reminded me of William Blake, Allen Ginsberg, and Lenny Bruce. She talked about radio being holy because it was "the ray of Dio, the ray of God," and then began evoking Rimbaud and Verlaine alongside Jimi Hendrix and Jim Morrison.

No matter what Fred Zaras or anyone else claims about that night, we were neither offended nor impressed. What made the biggest impression on me was that here was a new generation for whom Hendrix and Morrison were historical figures. They had been dead only five years, but they were ancient history to these kids. That was when I felt a shift was coming on.

We stayed until the end of the set. I think the general feeling among us was that it was okay, interesting, better than the fusion band at the Blue Note, not as good as the blues singer at the Bottom Line. Emerson was certainly not, as Fred later claimed, shaken by a confrontation with the future.

We were getting ready to go find the roadies at the strip club when two of the members of Television came up and stood in front of our table.

"Hello, there," Emerson said, grinning broadly. He probably thought they were going to ask for his autograph. "Really dug your set, man. What kind of delay do you use?"

The dark-haired guitarist spoke grimly. "You were taping us. Hand it over."

Emerson laughed. I looked at Simon. The cassette recorder was nowhere in sight.

"I think you've been misinformed, boys," I said. "This is Emerson Cutler. We're playing Madison Square Garden tomorrow."

"Would you like tickets?" Emerson said. "We enjoyed your show, you should come to ours."

"Hand over the tape, buddy," the guitarist said again. He leaned forward. Other members of the group's fraternity began to gather around us. I thought, Well, they're pretty frail-looking, I bet we could take them, but we've got to keep Emerson pretty for the wedding and the Garden show.

"Let's not be silly, lads," I said. "No one taped your songs."

Simon said, "Don't flatter yourselves."

Charlie added, grinning, "We might have wanted to tape your mouths—"

"Stand up," the guitarist said to Simon, and now the crowd around him was egging him on, enjoying the confrontation. "I'm going to pat you down."

"Like fuck you are," Simon said. He stood up. He was four or five inches taller than his accuser, but the guitarist did not back away or blink an eye.

"I have the tape!" Fred announced. He pulled out his little recorder and yanked the cassette from it and handed it to the guitarist. "Here, no one was trying to steal anything from you, we just liked the music and wanted to hear it again."

"You want to hear it again, you can come back tomorrow," the guitarist said, yanking the tape from the cassette casing and then breaking it under his foot. "Oh, that's right, you can't. You're playing Madison Square Garden." He said the name of the arena like it was an insult. The people standing around him all laughed. I got up from the table.

"Thanks for the hospitality," I said. "I'll be sure and tell my friends in the record industry all about you." We walked out of CBGB's to the sound of jokes and catcalls.

"What a dump," Emerson said when we were back on the Bowery, dodging the weaving bums. "I don't think we'll be hearing any more about that dive."

Our passing through CBGB's was not even a big part of our evening out. It was only later that it was painted as a shocking moment of revelation and confrontation for Emerson, after Fred had turned against him.

Say what you will about the greedy capitalist record chiefs of the 1970s, they sure knew how to throw a party. Emerson got married to Cynthia Apple at the expansive and expensive Park Avenue duplex of Wild Bill, the head of Tropic Records. New York might have been rotting from the Red Death outside, but the nobles were living high.

The groom's side stuck to the idea of the actual vows being celebrated with just a few close friends in attendance. Emerson's only guests were Charlie, Simon, Fred, two of the crew, Baxter the drummer, and the head of Tropic and his wife. I was best man.

The bride's invitation list was a bit more generous. It seemed she had invited every model in the Ford book, as well as a generous selection of hair and makeup people, talent bookers, and photographers. As a result we were half an hour late getting Emerson to the Garden, which we roared into with a full police escort, sirens blaring. Cynthia and her cortege raced through the backstage tunnels to a VIP room I had arranged to serve as the bride's chamber, while Emerson was handed his guitar and rushed to the stage by a cordon of men with flashlights and walkie-talkies.

I stood on the side, watching the show with Simon and Charlie. Talk of a Ravons reunion tonight had been vetoed by the new Mrs. Cutler, who reminded Emerson that he was to announce their marriage during the encore and then bring his bride onstage for their first dance.

She would not have the Ravons steal attention from her wedding! Emerson relayed this to the boys, who said of course they understood, what were they thinking? Charlie asked if it would be appropriate perhaps for Simon and him to join the backing band for the wedding dance but Emerson said, "You know, it's a great idea but at this point I think I need to just let the matter rest."

We were quickly learning to appreciate Cynthia Apple Cutler's instinct for the dramatic. Emerson came to the conclusion of his set, an extended version of his hit "Lipstick Letter," thanked the crowd, and said good night.

On the side of the stage Charlie leaned over to Simon and said, "What do ya say, Si? You slip the soundman a twenty, I'll give the lighting guy the same, and as soon as Emerson walks offstage, the house lights come up, the music goes on, and there's no encore tonight."

Simon laughed. They waited. The audience made their ceremonial demand for "Mooooore!" as if the encore numbers were not printed onto the set list. Emerson was a long time coming back. Cigarette lighters were illuminated and held aloft, making the hall look like a Christmas tree.

Emerson returned to the stage in a new white suit. "Sorry I took a while," he said. "You see, I just got married!" Now the ovation exploded. Emerson grinned and said, "Would ya like to meet my new wife?"

Cynthia Apple Cutler came onto the stage at Madison Square Garden like she was on a catwalk in Milan. She had taken her wedding vows in a short white dress, but now she had donned a full va-va-va-voom wedding gown cut down the front to her navel. She walked past Emerson to the lip of the stage and turned, giving all the photographers two or three angles, then spun toward her groom and tossed her bouquet over her shoulder into the crowd, who roared and fought over it. I saw a fat photographer wrest the flowers from a weeping teenage girl. Many years later, I saw the bouquet again, on eBay.

The band broke into an instrumental version of "When a Man Loves a Woman" while Mr. and Mrs. Cutler slow-danced like the junior prom. Photos of this romantic moment ran in newspapers that had never covered rock and roll before.

"I'm glad I didn't bring Samantha," Charlie said to me as the dance ended and the couple bowed to the crowd. "After this she'd have made me marry her on live satellite from the Hollywood Bowl."

Simon said, "Or at least from the bathroom at CBGB's."

Having blown some marriages in my time, I think I have gathered some late-life wisdom about why these things go wrong.

Many women think they want a marriage when all they really want is a wedding. Ours would be a happier world if every girl were given a wedding on her twenty-first birthday with no marriage attached. Give her a day to be the center of attention, to walk down the aisle with Daddy, to wear a beautiful white dress, and to have all her friends ogle her and weep. Stop dragging us men into it.

Many men subconsciously use marriage to try to freeze a moment when they are satisfied in their lives, when they have achieved some career breakthrough, when their dreams are finally coming true. The aspiring author gets his first book deal—he gets married. The medical student gets his doctorate—he gets married. The journeyman rock musician goes to number one on the charts and sells out Madison Square Garden. Here comes the bride.

Watch how often this is true among ambitious men. Signed to the pros/named partner/makes his first million—gets engaged. Why do we do this? I think when we have worked for something a long time and we finally get it, we want to stop time. We say, all right, I've finally reached the mountaintop, I want to stay here—time to tie the knot and start reproducing.

Of course, we later learn that we cannot freeze that moment. The wife we took on the mountaintop follows us right back down to the valley and starts complaining about the view.

My first marriage ended the year after Emerson's big tour. I suppose the truth is that Carey got sick of my being married to Emerson. She soon remarried, to a cabinetmaker. In spite of my doing my best to show up for birthday parties and school plays, it was he who raised my daughter, Lucy, and it was he whom she asked to give her away when she grew up and became a bride.

The Madison Square Garden wedding had given Emerson a level of celebrity with the general population—non-rock fans—he had never known, and had brought him an offer to return to New York in the fall as musical guest on the season premiere of *Saturday Night Live*. In anticipation of that PR coup, Tropic Records was releasing a third single from the album *Bare Conditioned,* which had now sold two million copies.

Amid all this attention *Rolling Stone* came back, promising a cover. Emerson was delighted. Obviously they would be sending one of their staff writers. I suggested to Emerson that he avoid mentioning this to Fred until the interview was complete. We had all begun tiptoeing around Zaras, whose endless demands for more and more access had begun to try even Emerson's patience.

"When is he going to stop interviewing you and start actually writing this great book?" I asked him. "He has the opening, the Ravons onstage at the Bottom Line. He has the ending, your royal wedding at Madison Square. I dare say that he has the middle from about ninety different angles."

"I don't think he can face transcribing all those tapes," Emerson said.

"Good, maybe he'll give up on the stupid idea and go get a useful job as a mattress inspector."

While I was in New York negotiating for a double live album, Emerson would entertain the writer from *Rolling Stone*. To get rid of Fred I offered him a thousand dollars to write a two-page press bio celebrating Emerson's platinum sales, new single, and *SNL* appearance. This was a total gift. It was a one-hundred-dollar job that the label usually did for free. Fred should have been able to sit down and write it in half an hour, so I gave him a week.

Emerson and Cynthia moved into a faux-Italian villa in the hills above Malibu. They had a swimming pool built into their patio that lined up with the horizon line of the Pacific Ocean and seemed to go right over a cliff. I got vertigo when I tried to paddle across it.

I would never accuse Cynthia of having married Emerson because of his Hollywood connections. I'm sure she married him for his money.

However, given that he did have Hollywood connections, she would have felt silly not taking advantage. Cynthia pressed Emerson to press me to get her go-sees with casting agents, auditions with directors, and meetings with studio chiefs. I did as I was instructed. Everyone agreed that Cynthia was charming, bright, and beautiful. No one thought she could act. The only parts she was offered were as arm candy, third girl at party, and roles that required on-screen nudity and simulated sex. Strictly speaking, Cynthia was not against that, but Emerson made it clear to me that if I put his wife into a naked sex scene I could expect to find myself back in England, working under Tug.

A drama coach who worked with her told me that Cynthia's personality was too vivid to submerge. She could not convincingly play a role because she could not stop being herself. What made her a very successful fashion model impeded her as an actress.

At the same time Hollywood was letting Cynthia down, the New York fashion world was beckoning her back. Marriage to a rock star and her own gift for publicity had raised her profile. Ford, from whom she had gone on detached service, was calling daily with offers for perfume contracts, jewelry sponsorships, the cover of *Vogue*. Cynthia began to lobby Emerson to buy them a place in New York. He asked me to fly there and line up some apartments for them to look at when we went back to do *Saturday Night Live*.

"Okay," I said, "I'll do your house-hunting for you."

"Thanks, man," he said.

"But Emerson? This is why I commission out of the gross."

One good thing about a city in social disorder and financial crisis: you can find some real estate bargains. In New York I looked at Fifth Avenue condominiums, West Village brownstones, Upper East Side townhouses, and Central Park West co-ops. Given that I expected Emerson and Cynthia to spend only a little time each year in Manhattan, I hoped they would be sensible and go for a midsized apartment in a doorman building, not a house that would require constant upkeep and security. My duty, however, was to show them the range of possibilities.

I knew Cynthia's tastes were grand. I hoped we could keep the budget under half a million. At that time one could buy a nice corner apartment with high ceilings and good views for twenty-five thousand dollars. If I could go back in time I would buy a hundred of them.

The first thing I did when I returned to California was go to Emerson's house to see how the *Rolling Stone* interview had gone.

"Fine, I think," Emerson told me. He was dressed in tennis shorts and a T-shirt–Cynthia had introduced him to aerobics. "The guy, Timothy, was really smart. He knew more about my stuff than I did. Quite easy to talk to, didn't ask any rude questions. I guess he was at the Garden show."

"Great," I said. "Any land mines?"

"Nah. He wanted to know about Dennis Towsy; I said he was a great guy, helped us a lot, but got a bit out there at the end."

"You didn't mention drugs or his being gay."

"Nope, I know–grounds for libel. He asked about the early Ravons shows and I said, ah, they were great, let on we had a bit of a friendly competition with Hendrix."

"That's a stretch."

"Well, he can't call Jimi to fact-check, can he?"

"Sounds like it went well."

"Yeah. One thing struck me as odd. He kept asking me about punk rock. He must have come back to it five times."

"What did you say?"

"Well, I said I liked some of it, some I didn't. I'd been to CBGB's, checked out Television and Patti Smith. I think that really impressed him."

"Great."

"I said it reminded me a lot of the Ravons when we started out. A lot of energy, anger, young kids from the wrong side of the tracks ready to take on the world."

"That's good, that should be your line all the time."

"Yeah, I think so. Listen, did you tell Fred about the *Rolling Stone* thing?"

"No, did you?"

"No, and I haven't heard from him all week."

"I gave him a job for us, writing a new bio. Paying him a thousand bucks."

"Oh, that's good, Jack. He could use the bread. Listen, will you tell him about this thing?"

"*Rolling Stone*? Sure."

"Will you tell him in person?"

"Emerson, he's a grown man."

"He gets sensitive, Fred does."

Emerson getting Cockney in his locutions meant he needed a favor. "Okay, Your Eminence. I will drive out to Fred's hovel and tell him of your adultery. And, Emerson?"

"I know. This is why you take your percent off the gross."

Cynthia breezed in wearing tennis whites, too. "Hi, Jack," she said. "How did the house-hunting go?"

"Very well. I saw five places I think you should look at, and the realtor has a folder full of others."

"That's so exciting," Cynthia said. "Listen, Dustin invited us to the premiere of his new movie Saturday night. I'm putting together a group of people to go. Want to join us?"

"Love to, Cynthia," I told her. I knew I would never hear about it again. Cynthia loved planning dinners and announcing expeditions and if you made the mistake of taking her seriously you would find that when the day came she was not taking phone calls. It didn't hurt my feelings. She meant it when she said it.

I drove back to my office and went through my mail and phone list. A week of work had piled up and I resented having to drive over to Echo Park to tell Fred Zaras that Emerson had spoken to another journalist. I resented it twice as much when I learned that Fred had not turned in the simple two-page bio I was overpaying him for.

I took Fred's address and directions and drove east down Sunset toward his house. "I'm not a manager," I told myself, "I'm a butler."

I had been to Fred's apartment once before, when I had put him in my car and driven him home after he had overstayed his welcome in Emerson's guest room. Cynthia saw eye to eye with me on that one.

I rang his bell. No one answered. I pounded on his door, I called his name. I walked to the corner and put a dime in a pay phone and let it ring twenty times. Then I tried something else. I called back, let it ring once, and hung up. I waited and did the same thing again. Then a third time. The fourth time I did this Fred grabbed the phone.

"Hullo?" He sounded like he was in the last stages of chemotherapy.

"Fred? It's Jack Flynn. I'm right downstairs, come let me in."

I went back to the house and waited. Fred appeared in a filthy T-shirt and sweatpants, barefoot and unshaven. Even his eyeglasses were dirty.

"Jack?"

"Where have you been, Fred? You never turned in the bio, no one's heard from you. Emerson was concerned."

I followed him into his apartment. It was gruesome. You could walk across his living room and never touch your foot to the rug, so thick were the piles of newspapers, magazines, writing pads, record sleeves, typed pages, paperback books, cassettes, fast-food wrappers, and articles of clothing.

"Maid's day off, then?" I asked. Fred had pulled the mattress from his bedroom into the living room and was sleeping on the floor of this recycling center. My allergies alerted me that cats had taken over his bedroom.

"What day is it, Flynn?" Fred asked me, falling onto his mattress.

"It's Friday, Fred. Do you really not know?"

"Friday? Oh fuck. I took some mescaline mixed with acid. You know, I sometimes fast for a few days to cleanse my system of toxins and go on vision quests and tape-record my insights."

"Oh sure," I said. "My mother does the same thing."

Fred continued, "And this time something transcendent happened. It was not a dream, Jack, it was a breakthrough. A bird was sitting on that window, right there, singing. And I was lying here listening to it. And Jack, this is going to sound strange but I swear, my mind went into the bird. And I was on the windowsill looking into the room at my body lying on the mattress. And I was drooling."

I was not going to get my press bio.

"So get this—I should actually record this." Fred dug through a mound of paper and came out with his cassette machine and turned it on and spoke into it: "I entered the bird, and I had to make a decision about whether I wanted to go back into my own body. I was scared, but I knew this was a onetime opportunity. So I gathered my courage and I spread my wings and I took off into the air. Jack, this was frightening and exhilarating. I was flying all over Los Angeles, I flew through the Hollywood sign, over the Capitol building, out to the ocean. I flew over Emerson's house." He clicked off the tape recorder and said, "I saw Cynthia naked." He clicked the recorder back on: "And I had insights. I could hear the signals animals hear, I was getting impressions, not through my ears but almost through my skin, of wavelengths telling me to fly this way, where food was, to avoid a hawk that was waiting in a big eucalyptus tree. And I felt like if I could learn to read these signals, they went back and forth in time, too. If I stayed in the bird I could learn to translate these vibrations and see back through history."

I didn't know what to say. I made a joke about wanting his prescription.

Fred laid down his tape recorder and put his head in his hands. "Finally I felt the bird's mind trying to get me out of there. But we were flying really high and I didn't want to let go. So there's a rumbling in my belly and all of a sudden the bird just pooped me out. He pooped me out and, zoom, just like that I was back in my own body, back in this room, but it was days later, and my cats had shit on everything."

I promised myself not to repeat this story to anyone, though it would be very hard. I said, "Well, the main thing is you're okay. You want to get cleaned up and I'll take you to get something to eat? You must be starved."

"No, that's okay, Jack. I have a bag of Oreos. Emerson was worried?"

"Yes, he was."

"I need to give him a call. Don't say anything about me seeing Cynthia naked, okay?"

"Not a word. Anyway, you were a different species at the time. By the way, you know that *Rolling Stone* cover that didn't happen in the spring? It came back."

Fred was suddenly fully alert. "What do you mean?"

"*Rolling Stone.* They're giving Emerson the cover after all."

"They haven't called me."

"No, well, you did tell them to fuck off last time, didn't you?"

"When do they want to do this?"

"They did it. Tim White came out and interviewed Emerson day before yesterday."

"Behind my back?"

"Fred, you were flying over Emerson's house at the time. I'm surprised you didn't see them."

"This is not cool, Jack. This is not how Emerson and I communicate."

"Well, Fred, then blame me. I set the whole thing up. I'm sure it did not occur to Emerson any more than it occurred to me that you would be anything other than supportive of our good fortune."

"You betrayed me, Jack."

"How exactly do you figure that, Fred?" Here my discretion began to slip. I should have given him the bad news and slipped away, but this resentment had been building for months.

"We have given you hours and hours of access to Emerson. You have sold articles about him to every half-wit rag and fan magazine in the United States. You allegedly got an advance for a book about Emerson that no one expects will ever be written, and we paid all the expenses for you to follow us all over the United States on a three-month tour. How much more do you calculate we owe you, Fred? Because it seems to me that by your mathematics every time we do you a favor, we now owe you another favor!"

Fred became almost catatonic. His eyelids fluttered. He said in a low voice, "I regret that I will not be able to write Emerson Cutler's new press bio. Under the circumstances, I think it would be inappropriate."

Now I felt bad. I said, "Look, Fred, I'm sorry, I just got off a long flight and everyone was worried about you. Now come on, let's get some food in you."

"You can leave now, Jack," Fred told me. He stood there rigid. I left.

Fred following Emerson around all the time had been a real drag. Fred hating Emerson's guts was going to be much worse.

Charlie was having trouble at home. Wealthy Samantha Lipsitz was getting tired of the endless stream of musicians rolling through her lavish mansion to use Charlie's studio. She was getting tired of the drugs in the house. She was probably getting a little weary of Charlie telling her that he loved her too much to ever ask her to marry him until he was as rich as she was.

It was becoming clear, as Warner Bros. Records declined to pick up Charlie's option, that the only way Charlie would ever become as rich as Samantha was if Samantha gave all her money away.

"Maybe you should marry the girl, Charlie," I told him. "You're not likely to do any better."

"Ah, I can't be married, Jack, you know me."

"Yeah, yeah, you've got to be free to swim around in the great globe of sex. Boy's got to grow up sometime, Charlie."

"Not this boy, Jackie. Not yet anyhow. Besides, Samantha's nuts."

"And that's a real impediment in our world? Go ask Fred Zaras how it feels to be crapped out of a passing bird and then tell me Sam's crazy."

"You know the art museum she runs?"

"That would be the Lipsitz Museum, named after her incredibly rich family?"

Charlie lowered his voice. "You know what she does there at night, Jack?"

"You sure you want to tell me?"

"She goes in with her paints and fixes up the masterpieces."

"What does that mean?"

"I mean, the girl adds a few dribbles to her Pollock. Slaps another coat on de Kooning."

"Wait. You're telling me that Samantha defaces the artwork in the museum?"

"She don't consider it defacing, Jack. She sees it as collaboration."

"How long has she been doing this?"

"Since Daddy brought home his first Picasso, I reckon. I've added a few streaks myself from time to time."

"Jeez, Charlie, that really is nuts. And no one's noticed?"

"Quite the contrary. Art critics and teachers with tours have often commented admiringly on Samantha's innovations. Giving credit to the original painter, of course."

"Well, they're her pictures, I suppose. If someone wants to buy one of your albums to burn it, they're entitled."

"More than one copy of my albums, Jack. I need to get out of there."

"You've thought this through."

"But you need to help me get the studio out of the pool house."

"Ah, for God's sake, Charlie!"

"What do you think of us renting a little house up in the Holly-wood Hills and running the studio out of there?"

"When did this become 'us'?"

"You're my manager, ain't ya, Jack? I want you to share in the rev-enues from my recording venture."

"For God's sake, Charlie. We don't know anything about running a studio."

"Speak for yourself, man, I can fly that baby blindfolded."

"Look, work out your issues with Samantha. I'll talk to the guys at Sunset Sound about how real this is when I get back from New York with Emerson. You don't have any money, you know."

"Not yet we don't! But once we get a little house in the hills and set up our studio . . ."

Emerson, Cynthia, and I flew to New York for the season premiere of *Saturday Night Live,* and to look at apartments. Cynthia found something wrong with every place I had selected. She wanted to live in a loft in SoHo. I pointed out that if she had told me that before send-ing me on the initial goose chase we both could have avoided a lot of aggravation.

SoHo in those days was still no-man's-land, half deserted and half industrial. The idea of climbing into a freight elevator to haul yourself up to a chilly brick hangar seemed to me absurd. But it was what Cynthia wanted, so Emerson said he loved the idea. She dragged him around to the lofts of her friends in the neighborhood to show him what they could do with a bohemian address and a whole lot of Emerson's money.

"You're going to be paying for this forever, Em," I warned him. "And the work is going to take years. Look at this place. I'm not even sure it's legal to live here. The contractors and architects and plumbers and carpenters are going to stitch you up."

"I just want her to be happy, Flynn," Emerson told me. I shut up and did as I was told.

I was at *Saturday Night Live*'s **Thursday music rehearsal when a** page came up to me with a message to please call Wendy Ipswitch. It was an emergency.

I went into an empty office and used the phone. She was hysterical.

"I told you that worm Freddy Zaras would screw us in the end!"

I asked her what happened.

"*Creem* magazine is about to come out with a ten-page cover interview with Emerson Cutler, written by guess who. In it Emerson talks about his promiscuity, drug use, blackmailing his first wife with sex photos–which, by the way, he says you hid in a closet and took. Oh, and there's a very long scene set at CBGB's in which Emerson makes an ass of himself and gets slapped by one of the Voidoids."

I was stricken. "It was Television," I said. "And nobody slapped anyone. Can we stop this? I'll pay for an injunction."

"It's on sale Monday, Jack! I'm holding a subscriber copy. Do you know that *Rolling Stone* may pull their cover when they see this? We guaranteed them an exclusive."

"Oh God." I hung up the phone and sank to the floor. For the first time in my life I missed Tug Bitler. How I would have loved to hang Fred Zaras out a high window.

I made a risky decision to not tell Emerson until after the *Saturday Night Live* performance. I could not risk his blowing that.

I called Wendy back and we went into triage mode to save the *Rolling Stone* cover. Their issue was about to go to the printer and I considered letting it go, but it turned out they already knew about *Creem* and were meeting to decide what to do. I swore to them that if they would stick with me and let us get through *SNL*, I would put their writer back with Emerson for the entire day Sunday and they could get the *real* story.

That's what we did. I hardly remember anything about the TV appearance. I spent the whole time terrified that someone would tell Emerson about the *Creem* story, which I read over and over, finding new slanders and insults each time.

To say Emerson was outraged is like saying that the Rape of Nanking was a bit out of order. He understood that he had to use the *Rolling Stone* story as a corrective, but it was very difficult for him to trust any journalist after Fred's betrayal.

We got through it, that's about the best that can be said.

A few weeks later Emerson found a long letter from Fred in his mailbox. There was no stamp on it. Fred had crept up in the night and stuck it there. The letter went on for about twenty pages in tiny printing. When Emerson showed it to me I said it reminded me of the diary of Sirhan Sirhan.

What jumped out was the conclusion, which was printed twice as large as the rest:

> I hope you understand how betrayed I feel. Not by your petty deception to win the affection of a corrupt and irrelevant fan magazine–but by your abdication of responsibility as an evolutionary avatar. You could have moved us forward toward the sun. Instead you have chosen to retreat into the slime. Everything I predicted will come to pass without you. Russia will rejoin with Europa. Islamistan will rise in a suicidal fury against the west. Asia will become a totalitarian manufacturing superstate. Latin America will move north into the lower USA and the Anglo Atlantic community will reunite. Africa will be the pivot which will tip the balance. The food supply is shrinking and each embryo is reuniting with its own kind to build strength for the final confrontation. You could have been a force for peaceful transition but you do not have the guts. I will become the New Man in your place. My writings will be the beacon in the night that your songs will never be. I wish you a peaceful decay–
>
> Frederick Zaras

Emerson was shaken. Cynthia was furious. "This maniac knows everything about us!" she declared. "He knows things about my husband I never knew. He has been in our home a hundred times. And he's insane! I can't live here anymore. I want to sell this house."

"Darlin'," Emerson said, "let's not go crazy, now."

"Someone has gone crazy, Emerson! Someone has gone crazy and it's the same awful little man you told me was a trustworthy friend. I want back all the tapes he made of me telling him things! Jack—tell the lawyers. No, hire some thugs. I don't want that little monster listening to my voice on his headphones and doing— I don't want to think about this anymore."

Cynthia wanted to go back to New York, where she was successful and famous. She wanted to be in a loft in SoHo and on posters for fragrances and going to discos and dancing till dawn and then going to a *Vogue* cover shoot with dirty hair and bags under her eyes and letting the makeup people worry about it.

She was heading that way with or without Emerson. He said sure, darling, if it makes you happy—let's try New York for a while.

I remember 1977 through a scrim of exhaustion, anger, regret, and jet lag. Once Emerson and Cynthia were settled in their New York loft, they hardly set foot in California except when he had professional obligations there. Having been cut out as Emerson's manager once, I would not let it happen again. I began traveling to Manhattan every two weeks, working from a desk at Tropic Records or out of my room at the Gramercy Park Hotel. At the end of each trip I dropped my dirty clothes at a laundry on Lexington Avenue, flew home, and collected them when I came back ten days later. I didn't carry a suitcase.

In California, Carey and I were dragging ourselves toward divorce across the burning coals of marriage counseling. Once a week we would sit next to each other in the office of a psychologist named Theresa and the two of them would explain to me what a repressed, guarded, emotionally crippled, and withholding block of self-serving ice I was. I figured that was a good excuse to clam up and watch the wall clock until my fifty minutes of abuse had elapsed. I was very sorry Carey did not love me anymore, and if it were up to me I'd stay married anyway for the sake of the baby, and besides, why not? She did not see it that way. She wanted to reform me on her way out the door so I could see how it was all my fault.

I was happy to let her think anything she wanted. I could agree that everything that had gone wrong in our marriage was because of my shortcomings and that I would lie awake kicking myself for the rest of my broken-hearted life. I just didn't see why we had to pay Theresa the therapist to beat the confession out of me. I was willing to sign anything, admit to anything, if we could just call it a day and go our separate ways.

I was ashamed to realize that, while losing my marriage was painful, it did not hurt as badly as Emerson quitting the Ravons and firing me back in London had hurt.

One good thing about getting divorced was that I could go back to drinking openly again. I imbibed, smoked, and snorted, and dated flight attendants and nightclub hostesses like a man just let out of jail. I often hit the town in company with Charlie, who was living the bachelor life since Samantha the Hollywood heiress had rolled him and his recording equipment out of her estate in a U-Haul.

"I've found a partner for my studio," Charlie announced to me one night when we were drinking rum at a Mexican restaurant on La Brea. "Fin!"

I waited to see if a warning bell would go off, but in my boozy state I had to admit it made a certain sense. Fin was nothing if not a hustler, and he knew anyone in LA that Charlie did not. The two of them running a recording studio together might actually work out.

"Fin still managing that silly band?" I asked.

"Nah, he gave up management. But you know, he put his Ravons money into a waterbed company back in 1970 and I guess he got out with a lot of cash."

We stared at each other and Charlie said before I could, "Before the bottom fell out of waterbeds."

"Where are you going to hang your shingle?" I asked Charlie while trying to decide if the dark-eyed, black-haired, pale-skinned waitress was smiling at me because she really liked me or because she was working for tips.

"Fin's bought a big old house in Burbank," Charlie said, "just over the hill. Cozy little four acres with a kidney-shaped pool, three-hole golf course, and plenty of guest rooms. Kind of joint a band can work in nine-to-five, or move into for four months."

"You want me to look at the paperwork? Make sure Fin's not playing fast and loose?"

"You're me manager, mate," Charlie said happily. He emptied his glass and walked up to the waitress I had been trying to contact mentally and said, "Darlin', you've got the sweetest knockers I've ever seen. How about you clock out early and we go for a ride?"

I was sure she would hit him with her tray but she smiled and batted her eyes and ten minutes later had handed me the bill, dropped her apron, and was driving into the hills with Charlie.

I paid up and went home alone. Next morning I was on the first flight to New York to check on the progress of Emerson's new album, a record it was costing a fortune to record at Manhattan's Hit Factory. I had pleaded with Em to find a less expensive place to record—which would have included anywhere—but he refused. He had fallen into the Manhattan life like a tiger falls into a covered pit.

My flight got to the airspace above New York at three P.M. New York time. We then circled over JFK for two hours, waiting for fog to lift and the constellation of planes in orbit to set down ahead of us. I was to meet Emerson for dinner at nine and had hoped to have a chance to shower and get a nap, but it was looking more and more like I would have to go straight to the restaurant.

The pilot came on and said, "Folks, we are still waiting for the weather to lift over Kennedy but right now our fuel is getting a little low so we may have to fly up to Boston, set down, refuel, and then come back into this pattern."

Here the passengers groaned with the impotent fury of a shipload of prisoners being told a typhoon was brewing and some of them would have to be tossed over the side.

A few more minutes and the captain said, "Looks like we can refuel in Newark. We are going to get over there right now before the opening closes up again. I apologize for this, folks, but there is nothing we can do about Mother Nature."

No, I considered, but there is something you could do about letting us off the plane in New Jersey rather than land us there and then haul us back into the air again. As soon as we were on the runway at the Newark airport I stood up in the aisle and demanded the attention of the flight crew.

"Attendant!" I said to the purser, loud enough that everyone else in business class could hear. "I have urgent business in Manhattan. I insist you let me off the plane here so I can get into the city in time to close my deal."

"I'm sorry, sir," the attendant said as if he were speaking to a senile patient in a nursing home, "we cannot legally discharge passengers in Newark. Now please sit down. We will be in the air again shortly."

"Young man," I said, not moving, "I am an attorney due to plead a very important case in federal court in less than two hours. As you should know if you are familiar with FCC regulations, you absolutely can request a passenger discharge from the Newark tower. The only reason you would not is if this airline is trying to avoid paying a second gate fee. And on behalf of all the other passengers who have been stuck in a holding pattern for two hours and have no desire to be returned to that pattern for two hours more, I think this airline should just swallow the gate fee and let us off!"

Here a rumble of agreement from my fellow prisoners swelled into clapping and a couple of hearty "Yeah!"'s. The purser looked as nervous as the last mate loyal to Captain Bligh. He tried to argue with me some more but I started making up legal precedents –"*Simon Potts vs. TransWorld Airlines, 1959,*" "*Lydle vs. United, U.S. Supreme Court, 1967.*"

The plane was resting on the tarmac; ground crews were pumping it full of fuel. I ripped a page from the notebook of a reporter sitting across the aisle and scribbled a hasty petition for our release and circulated it among the passengers. The purser took it to the cockpit and after ten minutes the pilot, a straight-arrow air force type in short-sleeve dress shirt and black necktie with airline tie clip, came out to negotiate.

He spoke to me as representative of the mutineers.

"Weather control expects the fog over Long Island to dissipate shortly," he said evenly. "Once we get up again all indications are we'll be landing quickly."

The solicitor in me said then, "The key phrase there is 'all indications,' Captain. When we finally get down is beyond your control. We know this is as frustrating for you as it is for us. All we're asking is that you cut a break to those of us who are in time-sensitive situations. Pull up to the gate. If your bosses give you a bad time, explain you had a cabin full of angry attorneys looking to stir up a riot and you did the smart thing and calmed it down."

The captain chewed that over. He said, "You check any luggage?"

Here I was grateful to know that my laundry was safely in the Lexington Avenue dry cleaner's.

"Just this briefcase," I said.

"Let me see what I can do," the pilot said and went back to the cockpit.

Ten minutes later his voice came over the speakers. "Okay, folks, we are fueled up and ready to fly, but before we take off, we have had a request to let those passengers who wish to, and who checked no luggage, to deplane here at Newark. We are going to pull up to the gate and let off anyone who wishes. Again, only passengers with no checked luggage can disembark here at Newark. We will have the rest of you in the air and on the ground at JFK very shortly."

I was amazed I'd pulled it off. The aircraft dragged its tired frame to the farthest gate of the Newark airport and the purser gravely opened the door.

Only four other passengers got off with me. Checked baggage or the Stockholm Syndrome? I did not care, I had beaten the system, I was free.

"Good luck with your case," the purser said as he handed me my coat. "Must be something big."

"Son of Sam," I told him. "I think I can get him off on an illegal wiretap if I file by five P.M."

A gasp went up from those passengers who heard me. I ran down the gangway and out of the airport before my fellow travelers caught me and beat me to death with their shoes.

With rush-hour traffic from Newark to the Holland Tunnel, I barely had time to check into my hotel and brush my teeth before heading out to meet Emerson for dinner. He had asked me to meet him at an Afro-Cuban restaurant a friend of Cynthia's had opened in Chelsea. Coming from Los Angeles with tribulations along the way, I still managed to get there on time. Coming from two miles away, Emerson was forty-five minutes late.

"Flynn, how are you?" he said when he finally showed. "Cynthia can't join us, has some friends in from Milan. You'll see her later."

That meant this night was going to stretch on past supper.

"How's the album going?" I asked.

"Sixteen days in and we can't get a drum sound," Emerson complained. "I'm starting to think the touring band is useless in these situations. We might have to bring in session cats."

I saw the recording costs multiplying. I tried again to broach moving somewhere cheaper and my employer shut me down.

"You don't get it, Jack," he told me. "Times have changed. We can't just go in and bang out twelve sides and expect to get it on the radio anymore. Standards have been raised."

Emerson was twitchy, talking fast, sweating. He'd been in the wife's Peruvian cornflakes. I wondered if the reason that everyone was having so much trouble getting drum sounds lately was that all the engineers had lost the top end of their hearing from years of wearing headphones and all the musicians were high on coke.

Emerson and I had some serious talking to do. Before we could get to it, a short young man with curly hair and a handlebar mustache came to the table and greeted Emerson like his lost son.

"Carlos!" Emerson jumped to his feet and shook the interrupter's hand while grabbing his shoulder. "This is my manager, Jack Flynn. Jack, this is Carlos's restaurant!"

There went any attempt at serious conversation. Carlos asked where Cynthia was, Em made her excuses, Carlos began telling me the tedious story of how he met Emerson's wife when they both were modeling in Rome and they had both had affairs with the same roguish photographer and when he first came to New York he stayed in Cyn's little studio and how he had always loved Emerson's music even though he was mostly into black groups and disco—and as he talked he took a seat at our table and told the waiter to bring us some of the special boiled goose eggs and some sugarcane salsa and he kept jabbering on and Emerson laughed and listened and the staff kept bringing over dishes of inedible food that he insisted we try and I just gave up and started drinking.

After about an hour I had knocked off three whiskeys and Carlos finally said good-bye, kiss kiss, come again.

"You're moving in new circles," I told Emerson.

"He's a sweet guy," Emerson said. "Cynthia cosigned his loan to open this place. She doesn't forget her friends."

Emerson then launched into a pitiful soliloquy about how hard it has been for him to hang on to any of his old mates, as they all want something from him.

"I'll tell you what, Jack," he said. "People I used to know call me all the time, begging to take me to lunch to pitch me on this or that. And when I say okay, they always expect me to pay. Always. They invite me, they ask me for some favor, and then when the check comes they act like, well, of course, the rock star is going to get it. Pisses me off, I'll tell you."

It was clear I would be picking up the check tonight. I signaled our waiter, who presented me with the bill. I was insulted to see that Emerson's dear buddy Carlos had charged us for every unwanted appetizer and sampler he had insisted be sent to our table, all of which now sat cold and uneaten on their dishes, along with all the booze he drank. I paid.

Emerson demanded I come with him to the studio, where his producer and engineer were continuing to turn knobs and move microphones in an attempt to capture the perfect drum sound. Baxter sat beating the skins like a weary woodchopper, while the rest of the band played Ping-Pong and Space Invaders in the outer lounge and calculated their hourly pay.

At about one A.M. I was ready to nod off on the studio couch when Emerson announced that Cynthia had just called and invited us to meet her and some of her pals at Odeon, downtown. After a couple of hours of listening to drum tests I would have jumped at the chance to go to the animal shelter and watch them gas cats. We got in a taxi and headed south on Ninth Avenue.

When people ask me about New York in the very late seventies, this is the sort of thing I remember. I didn't care about Studio 54 or hanging with Belushi or any of that. I had been in the London Alibi Club with the Beatles and the Stones; standing in the VIP room of a crowded disco with Liza Minnelli and Truman Capote did not thrill me at all. What I mostly remember is the sort of thing that happened when we got to Odeon and met Cynthia Cutler and her crew of emaciated models and fashion industry hangers-on. It was Thursday night. They had all begun the evening promising each other they were not going to do any cocaine tonight. They were staying healthy.

Then, as the evening went along they drank wine with dinner and then champagne. As they got tipsy, their resolve weakened. They each began thinking, A little coke would be nice. But no one said it because they had all promised each other to stick to drink.

By the time they got to Odeon for dessert, they cracked. Someone said it would not be so bad to have just one little toot and–zoom– everyone was off to the pay phones, calling their connections, dialing up a friend of a friend who knew a guy who lived around the corner . . .

Dessert came to the table as the delivery boys arrived. People began peeling off rolls of bills to pay and slipping little packets into their purses and pockets and then sliding off to the toilets to snort the first snootful.

Oh, but they came back to the table happy. Bubbling, smiling, talking a mile a minute. This was where the real trouble began. It was almost two A.M. and for everyone at the restaurant except me, the evening was just getting started.

By three we were all trooping off to the loft of some painter who had a big place on Broome Street that was always open to a party.

Then we were in a cage riding up three flights to his loft. Then our group of eight merged into about six of the painter's cronies who had already been elevating their metabolisms for some time and were ready to make new friends.

I stuck with my whiskey. I had quit cocaine. This was never a social impediment. If you did not drink among drinkers, they grew resentful and suspicious. If you refused a joint among potheads, it hurt their feelings. But cocaine users were delighted when you declined to join them. You know why? "More for meeee!"

I watched Emerson carefully. He was subdued, in control, chatting with a French hairdresser friend of his wife. I monitored Em in case the Other Guy came out. This was the name Charlie had given to the personality Emerson sometimes exhibited when the balance of stimulants and depressants in his system let loose the werewolf of egotism that lurked beneath his charming manners. The Other Guy was the unbridled id, the maniacal me me me me me. There is little in this world as ugly as the creative face without its skin on.

I had met the werewolf before. Late in a tour, when Em was overworked and undernourished, when the next gig was Buffalo and it was snowing and he had a cold and the bus broke down again, then the Other Guy came out. Everyone in his eyesight was a parasite. The miserable roadies, the incompetent soundman, the freeloading record company rep—oh, those regional label reps could really get their balls chewed off by the werewolf—and the greedy musicians in the band who acted like they were the stars, not just replaceable hired hands.

Anyone who works closely with a rock star for a sustained period of time meets the beast. To be a rock star a boy must be driven and ambitious and ruthless in his pursuit of success, which he must achieve on some level by the time he's—at oldest—twenty-four. Anyone who sustains that dedication and develops his performing ability to such an advanced degree by so young an age will have to leave other aspects of his personality undeveloped, even retarded.

If that young person is lavishly rewarded for his musical precociousness, indulged and pampered, he will proceed down a narrow path and never develop interpersonal skills. By the time he is thirty-five he will have the ego of a spoiled prince attached to the social incompetence of a mentally handicapped child and the appetites of a sybaritic sheikh. However, if he is to maintain the success to which he has dedicated his development, he must learn to imitate basic manners and politeness. He must learn to smile and be friendly to people who can help him. He must figure out a way to pretend he cares about what others have to say. He must fake acting normal.

As he drank more liquor and inhaled more cocaine, I watched Emerson carefully to see if the werewolf might come out. If it did, it would need to be subdued so my friend could return. The trouble was that the werewolf liked it out in the moonlight. The werewolf would not want to go back in.

I got lucky. The other revelers hit the wall of fun before Emerson did. The Other Guy stayed caged inside him.

At five-thirty in the morning the sun was creeping up over the water towers outside the windows. I watched the partygoers begin to turn. We were coming to the hour when it always got ugly. We were coming to the edge of the big crash.

These people had been drinking since eight o'clock. By the time Emerson and I joined them after midnight they were good and drunk, a half hour or so shy of the time when the tide of liquor would overcome them and they would pass out, puke, or run over someone in their automobiles as God intended.

But the cocaine hit their systems just in time to head off that alcohol blitz. At the very edge of dropping into stupor, they lit up again. The coke set their clocks back to eight-thirty or nine. They felt great once more, lively and social. So they kept drinking.

At about three-thirty the second crash came. Some of the happy, chatty people began to look stricken. A pretty red-haired model in a retro minidress slurred her words. A French boy nodded back his head and gurgled. Time for more coke! They stumbled toward the bathroom. Those locked out said fuck it and laid out their lines on the dining room table. They all snapped to life again, but this time with more of an edge. They had seen the abyss. They were running across a rope bridge and the lines were fraying.

In the next sixty minutes the chatter reached a higher pitch. The red-haired model rubbed her gums with her finger. Men grew aggressive, women got nervous, Cynthia became weepy, and Emerson was antsy. They all drank now like sailors at closing time, trying to take the edge off the tooth-grinding buzz.

And at five-thirty—ring the bell! Time, gentlemen! Ring the bell—it's a knockout in the ninth! Ring the bell—we have a winner. The French boy is having sex in the bathroom with the painter's wife. The painter is down in the street screaming at one of Cynthia's fashion friends who he chased down the stairs trying to steal a leather coat. The gay photographer is upchucking into the toaster. The pretty red-haired model in the retro minidress is going into convulsions on the couch while the nightclub talent booker attempts to get his hand under her shirt.

All of the booze hit at once as the cocaine wore off. The drugs kept them drinking long past the point when they should have passed out from liquor. Now the alcohol was landing on them like an avalanche. In the morning they would have hangovers of such magnitude that the only way to make it to the toilet to be sick would be to snort some more coke.

In my experience, that was how cocaine killed people. Not by stopping their hearts, although I suppose it eventually did that to a couple of them. Cocaine killed people by keeping them awake so that they could drink in excess of their physical capacity. Years later, when their livers gave out or they died of hepatitis or alcoholism, no one credited it to cocaine. But I was there, Your Honor, and I can testify. I knew those people when they were young and pretty. They may have strangled on booze's noose, but it was cocaine that built the scaffold.

The sun was up and I was in the back of a taxi on my way to the Gramercy Park Hotel. The city was peaceful. I was finally going to get some sleep.

You know where I was happiest in New York as the seventies gave way to the eighties? In the backseat of a cab. This was my one island of solitude. It was peaceful. No one could find you. Someone else was driving. And you were moving forward, you were going somewhere, so there was no guilt that you were shirking off. The back of a Yellow Cab was the one place where no one could get at you.

That peace does not exist anymore. The mobile phone burned down that oasis. Now when I get in a New York taxi my phone is vibrating, my BlackBerry is dinging, the driver is shouting in a foreign language to whoever he's talking to on his earpiece walkie-talkie, and a horrible little TV screen mounted in the seat back in front of me is blaring commercials. The driver's radio is turned up loud to a rap station to drown out the advertisements on the TV, which is why he has to shout at his phone.

Once those technical improvements came into my life I never had a moment's quiet reflection again. Mobile phones did away with contemplation. We were all leashed.

But there was a time, and not so long ago, when riding in a New York taxi was a quiet interlude in an otherwise frantic day.

It was on the cab ride to my hotel that night that I conceded that I would have to move to New York. This was where Emerson had settled. Charlie didn't need me, he was going into the recording studio business with Fin. My California marriage was over. I had to go where the work was. When the taxi dropped me off I wandered in the peaceful morning around Gramercy Park. Here was a New York square that looked like London. The park itself was a city block filled with greenery, beautifully manicured, and locked behind high iron fences. Residents got a key. Outsiders were excluded. How very un-American, how very English, how delightful.

The park was surrounded by old brownstones, townhouses, and prewar flats. On the south side were stuffy old private clubs with leather chairs and dust on the paintings of founders with muttonchops. I told myself that if I lived here I would be halfway between Los Angeles and London, psychically as well as physically.

The seventies were over. It was time to start again.

THE SOUND OF THE SINNERS

With the money I made from selling my house in Los Angeles I was able to buy an airy three-bedroom apartment with French doors opening onto a brick balcony on the east end of Gramercy Park. I rented an office nearby, on Union Square, and hired two assistants who were young, bright, and had no interest in rock and roll. I had learned how much that helped.

In April 1980 I went to London for label meetings and to visit my mother. Each time I saw her I was initially shocked at how old she looked, and then relieved by how young she acted.

She and my aunt were still in the house in Kingston. I had tried many times to convince her to let me buy her a bigger home but she would not hear of it. On this trip, I learned that the little cottage next to my mother's was for sale. It was a five-room wooden house with an old stone fireplace and a large garden that abutted my mother's back-yard. On a whim, I bought it. If I could not convince Mam to move into someplace bigger, I could at least expand the property around her. I invited my cousin Mary, my aunt's daughter, to live in the new house and keep it occupied.

Mam's reaction was, "Oh, how lovely, Jack. Now you'll have a place to live when you settle down." I thought that was funny at first, but later wondered if she did not know me better than I knew myself. There probably was a part of me that thought all this living-in-America stuff was temporary and I would eventually want to have the option of moving home. To marry a nice English girl, have children, and grandma next door? It didn't seem like the worst idea I'd ever heard.

For the worst idea I'd ever heard I could count on my old comrade Simon Potts. He had learned I was in London and phoned me incessantly to meet with him.

I called on Simon at a Bayswater hotel where he was living. After a decade of spending three hundred days a year on the road, Simon had become institutionalized. Living in a house or flat unnerved him. He hated having to clean up after himself or hire someone else to. He hated being responsible for his own security, laundry, or decorating. When his telephone rang he wanted someone else to answer and give him the message.

Tug Bitler had worked out a deal with a second-rate hotel north of Hyde Park to lease Simon a small suite on a month-to-month basis. This was all done through Tug's management and touring company, so Simon never saw a bill. When he explained the arrangement to me I warned him that somewhere in the bowels of Tug's business a meter was running. Every time Simon called down to room service for an omelet, a charge was ticking over.

Simon said that was why he wanted to see me.

"I need you to look into things with Tug," he said. "I've got a feeling he's taking more than his share."

Christ, I thought, this is where I came in. I had not seen Tug in years, although we corresponded about Ravons catalog business and the fifty or sixty compositions on which our clients shared publishing. I knew that he had artists other than Simon, all of whom were of roughly the same professional disposition: heavy rock bands, metal acts, and Thunderjug, a Swedish progressive rock unit who rarely got played on the radio, sold moderate numbers of albums, but made money on the road pounding out loud and repetitive riffs for frustrated young men of many nationalities. Among this legion of vulgarians, Simon was the most senior and, by the standards of the genre, the most intellectual.

"As your friend, Simon," I said, "I am happy to look through your contracts informally and advise you about any monkey business. But let's try to find a way to do this without alerting Tug, all right? He'll set fire to the paperwork and then set fire to me."

Simon nodded. "I have copies of everything," he said.

"Good. Here?"

"No, in the office."

"You mean in Tug's office?"

"Well, he is my manager."

"Of course. See if you can borrow them when he's out on the road with one of his other bands, will you? I'm too old to be hung out any windows."

Simon told me something that surprised me: "Tug doesn't go out on the road. Ever. He hasn't in years. He barely comes out of his house. You should see it. Big pile out by Heathrow. He has guard dogs, an electric fence, the whole thing. When he does come into town he rides in an armored limousine he bought from the Soviet embassy. Gets about nine kilometers to a tank of petrol. He's not the Tug you knew and loved."

This does not sound promising at all, I thought. If I had any sense I would have told Simon to find another auditor. But I did not have it in me to turn him away. Although I came very close when he added to my burdens by announcing, "I want to play you my new album."

Spare me, I thought. "Love to hear it," I said.

We took the lift to Simon's rooms, where he cued up his latest concept record, which was titled *Synthenesia*. It was long, lugubrious, and painfully self-referential. There is nothing wrong with writing a suite of songs in the first person, if there is a reasonable opportunity for the listener to see himself in the "I."

"I Can't Turn You Loose."

"I Wish It Would Rain."

"I Want You."

"I'll Be There."

"I Want to Hold Your Hand."

Nothing wrong with any of those. Simon, however, had pretty much eliminated any possibility of the "I" in his opera being mistaken for anyone other than Simon Potts. Beneath the usual Dungeons & Dragons metaphors, *Synthenesia* was the story of a legendary rock star who goes to war single-handed against an army of incompetents, sycophants, and corporate villains who want to keep the great man (who shares Simon's birth date, birthplace, disposition, and given name) from reaching the audience who are hungry for his heroic message.

We listened for almost an hour and then Simon said, "Now here's the second half." At that point I began drinking.

When it finally ended I had entered the tranquillity of the whiskey brain bath, which perhaps made me a bit more honest than I otherwise would have been. Or perhaps not—I had been kissing Emerson's ass all week. Simon was not my client and he had pretty much put a pistol to my head and demanded my opinion.

"Some of it's quite good," I said, tiptoeing to the lip of the dragon's cave. "I like the instrumental very much, it has a sort of majesty."

Simon waited for what was coming.

"I'm not certain you're doing yourself any favors making it a double album," I ventured. "Seems to me that if you took the ten best tracks you'd have a very strong single LP."

Simon sneered. "Then we'd lose the story, wouldn't we?"

"Screw the story, Simon," I said, refilling my glass. "No one will understand it but you anyway."

"Which is the whole point, Flynn. It details exactly what I have gone through in this corrupt business. It is my journey. To begin editing it to make it more palatable to the simpleminded would be to make it a lie. I am a truth-teller. That is my job."

I was so sick of hearing this kind of tripe for so long that I am afraid I took it out on Simon a little. I said, "Fancy that, I thought your job was making music. I thought people paid you to entertain them."

Simon took umbrage. "I am not an entertainer. I am an artist!"

"Forgive me," I said, "I am a Philistine, but don't artists get to be artists by expressing something the public can relate to or aspire to or at least find compelling?"

"You don't find *Synthenesia* compelling?"

"I find some of it compelling, Simon. I find some of it a bit annoying, to be honest. All I'm suggesting is that you might profit by taking out some of the annoying bits. Like when you say, 'He traded it all for a corner office and a color TV.' You know, all TVs are color TVs now. They haven't made black and white TVs in a long time. And the bit about you knowing pain and the rest knowing only self-pity. Forgive me, but it's the most self-pitying thing I've ever heard. You're painting a big fat target on your head with that one."

"Maybe it's not for you, Flynn," Simon said. "Maybe you are not my audience."

"No argument there, mate. But perhaps your"—here I almost said "dwindling" but I stopped myself—"audience doesn't need to see *every* side of you. Show 'em your best face, by all means. Show them your wit and your smarts and your diligence. Show them your righteous anger, Simon, that's fine, that's your gift. Just don't show them your arsehole, that's all I'm saying."

Simon looked down his long nose at me and passed sentence. "My arsehole is part of who I am, Flynn. That is the difference between entertainment and art. Art does not deny the arsehole."

I thought, You said it, pal, but what I said was, "Well, then, art better be a comfort when your audience is gone."

We parted on bad terms that night. I had hoped to be an honest friend by telling Simon what he needed to hear before the label and critics sent him the same message in a cascade of poison arrows. It was hopeless. Simon had signed onto the new solipsism. Creative integrity meant singing your diary and if your diary that day consisted of a bad case of the trots, that became your next libretto.

When I returned to New York, Emerson was in a foul mood. He had finally released his new and overbudget album, *Rock & Roll Criminal,* to the worst reviews of his career.

He was in my office on Union Square pacing up and down and reading aloud from a pile of clippings that our publicist Wendy had been stupid enough to collate and present to him. She should have put them in her mouth and swallowed.

"'Pathetic attempt to be modern by laid-back dinosaur.'"

"'Emerson Cutler has stayed on the train way past his stop.'"

"'That this sort of tired shit is on a major label while the most vital new bands in rock and roll toil in obscurity shows why the old record corporations are destined for the junk heap of history.'"

Wendy said, "That's really more about the label than you, Em."

"I spent half a million dollars on that album!" Emerson erupted. "What the hell do these little twits want from me?"

Wendy said, "I think you've got to lose the beard."

"Here's what I'd like to know," Emerson declared. "Have any of these jack-offs ever made a record? Entertained an audience? Written a song? I'd like to hear it! What qualifies them to piss on my work?"

"They're supposed to represent the audience, not the musician," Wendy explained.

Emerson looked at her, astonished. "Oh really! Oh, are they? Oh, do they? They represent all those people filling my sold-out shows and buying my albums? Is that who they represent? Eh, Wendy? Because when I look through these rags"—here he grabbed a copy of *Trouser Press* magazine from the top of the pile—"I see that these self-anointed representatives of the audience are very enthusiastic about"—he began reading off names from the table of contents—"Fripp and Eno. The

Modern Lovers. The Damned. Gang of Four. Oingo fucking Boingo. Yeah, there's the vox populi, all right. There's the taste of the average fan reflected!"

Emerson fell into a chair and began flipping through the magazine. He stopped at a feature story extolling a punk band called the Tin Pagans. He held it up. "Get a load of this," he said.

I looked at the black and white photo and said, "So what?"

He pointed to the byline on the article. "By Fred Zaras." He began reading. "Lead singer Bob Hymen explains the almost feral response he solicits from the crowd by opining, 'We are tuned in to something shifting in the mass unconsciousness. The tectonic plates are moving under the collective psyche and we have tapped into that evolution.'"

Emerson looked from Wendy to me to Wendy. We all burst out laughing at once.

"Fred has found another mouthpiece for his theories," I said.

"Creep," Wendy snapped.

"We should have kept him in our camp, Flynn," Emerson told me, his mood lightening a little. "He's the reason the press turned against me."

"Come on, Em," I said. "He was a tosser, and besides that, he was insane. You think Cynthia would have put up with him hanging around anymore?"

Emerson threw down the magazine.

Except for some daily newspaper reviewers who were older than we were, most of the rock press had turned against Emerson after punk rock seized their imaginations. Say what you will about punk, it was easy to write about. It's a lot simpler to come up with copy about a singer who runs a razor blade down his chest than it is to talk about the unexpected introduction of a minor augmented chord into a major progression.

Emerson was no longer being evaluated based on whether he made a good Emerson Cutler record or a bad Emerson Cutler record. Now the record was prima facie bad because it was Emerson Cutler, who played blues-based music with lyrics about love, lost and found, containing conventional guitar solos and studio musicians. Plus, he had been around since the sixties and was nearly forty years old.

All of these predispositions and antecedents condemned his record before it ever reached the stereo. On the other hand, the Tin Pagans, the new favorites of Zaras, played short songs with simple chords, a straight beat (no swing), very occasional solos (and those incompetently executed), and descended from the Stooges, the MC5, and the Ramones. They had the right pedigree. Anything the Tin Pagans did was lauded and their record need not be played to ascertain its quality, either. These new rock writers were not reviewing music, they were reviewing ideology.

"I'll tell you one thing," Emerson announced before he went home. "I would never criticize anyone for doing something I had never done myself. That's my point. If they've got some songs to share, let's hear 'em. Otherwise, shut up and sit down. If I had never done something myself, I would keep my uninformed opinions to myself."

We nodded assent. Still, I considered how many things I had heard Emerson offer opinions about that he had never done himself, sometimes from the stage or in interviews. Emerson had vivid opinions about politics, though he had never run for office or in any way gotten involved in any social action. He could hold forth at great length over dinner about the shortcomings of various actors, directors, authors, TV presenters, painters, designers, and, God knows, journalists, though he had never practiced any of those trades. We were all critics. The difference was that we did not all get paid for it.

When Emerson had gone, I asked Wendy if we had any other business, or whether she had come over only to make my client miserable. Wendy had left Tropic Records and started her own independent public relations firm. We were paying her two thousand dollars a month to make Emerson look good in the press. Based on today's news, she owed me a refund.

"I want to talk to you about this new opportunity," she said. "It's a cable TV music channel Warner's is starting up. They're looking for rock stars to do promos and I think Emerson should consider it."

Wendy really was on thin ice today.

"I can't tell you how unlikely he is to do that," I told her. "Wendy, he's sensitive about looking cheesy and you want him to be a huckster on cable television? My God."

She passed me a cardboard folder filled with hype about this new music service. "Check it out, Jack. I really think Emerson should consider it. He needs to connect to a younger audience."

"Christ, Wendy, you better tell him. I'm not going near this one. What do they call it?"

"MTV."

I repeated the name. It sounded far-fetched to me but I told her she could try to convince Emerson when he calmed down.

There is a song I love by Pete Townshend called "Somebody Saved Me," which details all the times in the singer's life when by rights he should have met with disaster, and through no merit of his own he was delivered. Some greater power, some unseen hand, stepped in and prevented the tragedy toward which his own designs had steered him. I often think that Emerson and I were beneficiaries of a similar benevolence.

Just when it looked like the Ravons' brand of adolescent beat group was over, along came FM rock radio and gave Emerson ten years of renewed vitality. Now, with the power of FM waning and the new wave gnawing at our ankles, we were about to be saved again.

In spite of our having parted on bad terms, Simon continued to send messages begging me to audit his deals with Tug. After John Lennon's murder, a new paranoia had invaded his communications, which came to me not over the phone or through the mail but in sealed and taped letters delivered to my New York office by strange German friends of his who were passing through town on mysterious business.

I sent back word that if he got me the documents, I would read them when I could. Some time passed and two cardboard boxes arrived, filled with copies of letters and contracts and royalty statements. These were presented to me by a young Indian man, nervous as a spy. He said Simon had told him I would pay him a hundred dollars when he brought me the boxes. How could I argue?

My assistant put the boxes in a closet until I could bear to dig into them.

Simon was three thousand miles east of me. Three thousand miles west was Charlie, who had sold his share in the recording business in Los Angeles, including all of his expensive gear, to Fin for a hundred and fifty thousand dollars. He had used his free studio time to record what he promised me was the best album of his career and wanted me to get busy selling it to a record company.

I listened to the tape. It was pure Charlie—rustic, cheeky, melodic, and sentimental. I liked it very much, but there was nothing I could hear that would interest a major label in these New Wave days.

I did my duty to my client. I tried. When all else failed I put the arm on Wild Bill, who had moved up the corporate ladder to run the international conglomerate that had purchased Tropic Records. He praised the music and kicked me back downstairs to the A&R staff, who said it was lovely but not what the kids were into anymore.

Of course, Charlie was disappointed. We finally arranged to release it through a folk and bluegrass label in Nashville, who paid only a tiny advance and had no promotional machinery. Diligent fans of Charlie's who lived near a well-stocked record store would be able to find it, and he would get copies to sell at gigs, but that was about it.

To salvage the situation I set out to get Charlie some new publishing money. There was no interest in the States, but I managed to put together something in the UK, with a Denmark Street song merchant we had been friends with back in the days of the Alibi Club. He agreed to pay us twenty-five thousand pounds for a two-year lease on twenty of Charlie's new songs, twelve from the new album and eight more that we had to come up with.

Charlie always had plenty of songs on hand. The trouble was that most of them were not very good. He went through his boxes of cassettes and demos and came up with another eight, one of which was called "I Never Could Believe I Wouldn't See You Anymore" and would cause us a world of trouble a few years down the line.

But for now, Charlie was content. He had the publishing money. His new record was at least coming out, which meant he could do a club tour. He had a hundred and fifty grand from selling his share of the studio to Fin. By any reasonable standard of 1981 living, Charlie was doing quite well. He would eventually find a way to turn his good fortune into misery for both of us.

Simon was three thousand miles to my left. Charlie, three thousand miles to my right. I had Emerson standing right in front of me.

He looked as unhappy as I had ever seen him. Wendy the publicist had talked him into shooting a promo saying, "I want my MTV," in exchange for which the new music channel would play a clip of him performing his new single "Bed of Nails" seven to twelve times a day for three weeks. The video had cost us almost nothing to make—we booked a surprise show at the Bottom Line and filmed the whole thing with two video cameras. Emerson did "Bed of Nails" four times and we edited the best bits from each together. It took three days from start to finish.

That was not why Emerson was upset. He was dressed in new clothes Wendy had bought him—a shiny black jacket of which she told him to roll up the sleeves, a skinny red necktie, and some badges to decorate his lapel. That was not why Emerson was unhappy, either.

Wendy had finally succeeded in convincing him to shave off the beard he had worn for ten years before they went to MTV to tape his promo. That was why Emerson was unhappy.

"Look at my face, Jack!" he cried. "I'm fat!"

Emerson was not fat. If his enormous ego had not seen to that, his fashion model wife would have. His newly pink and puffy cheeks, however, did suggest a chipmunk stocking up for a severe winter.

Wendy was right behind him. "Jack! Tell him he looks fine!"

"I look like a cream puff!" Emerson wailed. "I look like a plump forty-year-old man!"

The big birthday was looming. It was a spider crawling up Emerson's subconscious.

"I think it's common for the face to swell up after the first shave in a long time," I said calmly. I had no idea if this was true but it was reassuring. "You just have to give it a couple of days, Emerson. Once the skin gets over its sensitivity it will go back to its normal shape. You do look years younger."

Wendy piped up, "That's what I told him!"

"Because I look like the fucking Gerber baby!" Emerson wailed.

"Listen," I told Wendy. "Tell MTV that Emerson had to fly to London for a funeral and reschedule this thing for next week." She began to protest but I gave her a look that shut her up. "Emerson, take Cynthia down to Key West. Go swimming, get a tan. See how your face looks then. I can arrange for you to check out a studio in Miami so we can take the trip off your taxes. Maybe don't shave the last three days you're there so you get a heroic stubble. Then, if worse comes to worse, we'll bring in that French makeup guy who painted Cynthia's cheekbones for that *People* magazine piece about the two of you at home last year."

Emerson nodded. He was off the hook for now. Wendy went to call MTV. I told my assistant to start making travel arrangements for the Cutlers in Florida.

Emerson was still sitting across from me. He made no motion to leave. We were alone for the first time today, so I figured he had something else on his mind.

I said, "What?"

He got up and closed the office door and came back to his chair.

"Cynthia wants us to go to this doctor in Nashville," he said.

"For what?" I asked.

"Our nostrils." He tapped his nose. "This guy rebuilds the septum, the wall between."

"Christ, Em, have you eaten a hole through the inside of your nose with cocaine? Think it might be time to switch to quaaludes?"

"Cyn's got the real hole," Emerson explained. "She can stick a Kleenex in one nostril and pull it out the other."

"Wow. If a less beautiful woman did that it would be off-putting."

"I'm just clogged up all the time. It's affecting my singing."

"Well, get some nasal spray! Lay off the drugs! Shit, there must be some way to deal with this short of surgery!"

Emerson leaned forward. "Well, what I hear is that this same cat in Nashville also shaves the vocal cords. He's done it for a lot of country guys. They say it makes you sing with natural reverb."

"Listen to yourself, Emerson. Cynthia's a model. If she needs cosmetic surgery for her career, she should get it. Her voice is not necessary to her earning a living. Your voice is. I would be very, very wary of letting anyone get near your nose, mouth, or throat with a scalpel, at least until things deteriorate to where that is necessary. Let's hope that day is a long time away."

"What about the natural reverb?"

"Shit, Emerson. Add the reverb in the bloody studio."

After a week in the sun and a three-day stubble and some discreet rouge, Emerson looked every bit the roguish rock star. He shot the promo for MTV and they began to play the clip of him singing "Bed of Nails."

We could not believe the response. MTV was not yet on the air in New York City, but in the places where it was carried, radio stations were besieged with requests for "Bed of Nails." Emerson's album *Rock & Roll Criminal* began a climb up the charts that ended at number four.

"What did I tell you?" Wendy asked me.

I was amazed. "You were right, Wendy," I said. "This thing is going to mean more than all the reviews put together."

"It's bringing him a whole new audience," she said. "Jack, kids are buying this album. Teenagers. They never heard of the Ravons, they never even heard of Emerson before this. It's a whole new generation."

She insisted that we take advantage of our momentum by making a proper video for Emerson's next single. None of this cheapskate live-in-concert stuff. Hire a hot young director, hit up the label for a big budget, and consolidate this advance.

Over the next week Emerson, Cynthia, Wendy, and I looked at reels from all sorts of directors. People who had done TV commercials, short films, recent NYU graduates, suggestions from the record company, from our booking agency, from photographers we knew. We looked at everything from shampoo advertisements to avant-garde collages. We could not achieve consensus.

Finally the wife played her card.

"Use Antonio," she insisted to Emerson. He would have agreed to use Walt Disney if it meant he could get out of that room.

"Who's Antonio?" Wendy and I wanted to know.

"He did Cyn's jeans ad," Emerson explained. "Italian dude, really smart. He did the Renault campaign. He might be good."

"Okay," I said. "Give me his info and I'll ask for a reel."

This insulted Cynthia. She said, "You do not audition an artist like Antonio. We will be lucky if he agrees to even consider this. I will call him."

Oh dear, I thought, Mrs. Cutler slept with the director of her dungaree ad.

For someone who was supposed to be hard to get, Antonio sure made it to New York from Italy quickly when he heard about Emerson's video. He was a short man with an eagle nose, long black hair, and tinted eyeglasses.

"This song, 'Take It Over,' it is political, no?" Antonio asked us. Emerson, Cynthia, Wendy, two promo men from the label, Antonio, and his very tall and sexy female producer were seated around the conference table in my office.

"Uh, not overtly," Emerson said.

"The song is called 'Talk It Over,'" I told Antonio. "Talk, not take. It is not political."

Antonio conferred in Italian with his producer. He returned to us smiling.

"Yes, 'Talk It Over.' Communication, yes? Miscommunication. Everything today is a jumble. How do I know if you mean what you say? Does the word I pick match the meaning you hear?"

"You've drawn up some storyboards?" I asked, trying to break through the semiotics seminar.

"See, this is what inspired our treatments," Antonio explained. He produced three large drawing pads. Each had sketches for a possible video.

In the first, Emerson was dressed in a white sailor suit, rowing a lifeboat filled with beautiful women up and down great rolling waves. A Nazi submarine appears—we see the periscope—and shoots a torpedo at them. Before it can connect, a white whale emerges and swallows the small boat and all aboard. A match is struck in the darkness of the whale's belly and Emerson sees a guitar, amplifier, and microphone resting on some sort of natural bandstand within the whale's stomach.

He has been singing the whole time, but for the last chorus he jumps from the boat, slings on his Stratocaster, and drives the female refugees to strip down to their underwear and boogie madly. The final shot is of the whale pursuing the fleeing U-boat, Emerson's guitar still rocking from the leviathan's digestive tract.

There were a number of objections to this scenario. The label thought it would be too expensive, Cynthia did not want her husband off on a location shoot with a boatload of models, and Emerson was resistant to wearing a sailor suit.

No one brought up the fact that it was plain stupid.

Option two involved Emerson playing his song at famous landmarks all over the world. He would begin it on top of the World Trade Center, dissolve to the Eiffel Tower, cut to the Pyramids, and so on from the top of the concrete Christ in Rio to the Wailing Wall, the Forbidden City, and finally to a riotous ending with Emerson stopping traffic for a concert in the middle of London's Tower Bridge.

"Are you planning to do this with blue screen?" I asked. Antonio did not understand. "Special effects," I explained. "You would shoot Emerson in a studio and drop the locations in behind him with trick photography?"

Antonio and his producer conferred. He corrected me.

"No, no, that would have no value. We must go to all of these places and Emerson would rock out. This is why we make history."

The record company representative could not contain himself. "Buddy," he said, "do you have any concept of what that would cost? The travel? The licenses? Getting permission to shoot in Peking and finding crews? Get a grip!"

Antonio shrugged. "I thought Emerson was big star, this was priority for American record group?"

Wendy said, "Yes, Antonio, but we need to stay within a budget of perhaps two hundred"—she looked at the label rep, who shook his head—"thousand dollars. That is more than almost anyone gets for a music video."

Antonio shrugged. He said he and his producer would have to brainstorm on this overnight. I said we were in a bit of a rush, and Antonio's producer spoke for the first time.

"You can have fast, you can have good, or you can have cheap," she told me. "Two out of three. You want good and you want cheap, so you don't get fast."

Two days later we convened again. Antonio presented us with a new scenario, designed around the limits of our budget and the lyrics to Emerson's song.

Emerson would be in a carnival, a freak show. He would be a ventriloquist with an Emerson dummy on his lap. He would begin singing to the crowd, and then the dummy would take over. The crowd would applaud and cheer, part of the show. Then, during the guitar solo, we'd see Emerson in his tent that night with a beautiful woman from the audience. They are kissing, about to make love, when the dummy's eyes spring open. Now Emerson and the dummy trade lines of the song, dueling for control. The girl between them is frightened; she tries to run but the door is sealed.

"I thought they were in a tent," Wendy interrupted.

"Okay, a circus wagon," Antonio improvised. He was flipping pages of drawings as he spoke. "Anyway, Emerson defeats dummy by hurling lantern at him. Emerson and girl escape into night as circus wagon burns behind them."

"That still looks like a tent in the drawing," Wendy said.

"We'll change it to a wagon!" the producer said.

Antonio flipped to the final drawing. "At sunrise girl awakes under a blanket in a pile of leaves in the woods. She is smiling. She leans over to kiss Emerson good morning but when she pulls down blanket . . . it is dummy!"

We looked at each other. No whales, no submarines, no international travel, and no sailor suits.

We all agreed this was the one we liked. We shook hands and kissed cheeks and Antonio and the label reps went off to argue about the budget.

We had to go to Los Angeles for Emerson's video shoot. We were inexperienced enough to believe Antonio that only Hollywood had the costumes, props, and equipment he needed to do this on the budget we had given him.

The three-hour time change worked in our favor, as we all had to be up at five A.M. and on set at six-thirty. We were scheduled to shoot a small film in one very long day, with a nonactor in the lead. We knew it was going to be hard work.

Inside a TV studio on the Warner Bros. lot, Antonio was supervising painters, riggers, and lighting technicians as they completed detail work on the sets—the carnival midway, the inside of Emerson's circus wagon, and the glade in the woods where the final scene would take place.

Everyone shared the giddy mood of a school holiday. Cynthia picked out a ruffled gypsy shirt for Emerson from the wardrobe woman, and a fortune-teller outfit for herself.

We had talked her out of playing the girl whom Emerson loses to the dummy. Instead Antonio had promised a close-up of her holding an ominous tarot card.

Extras were being outfitted as midway gawkers, carnies, or freaks. It certainly seemed we were getting our two hundred thousand dollars' worth.

At nine A.M. Antonio announced he was ready to begin principal photography. Emerson took his seat on a wooden chair in a wagon in the middle of the midway.

Antonio called into an electric megaphone, "Dummy!"

The sketches had suggested that Emerson would have on his lap an elaborately carved wooden mannequin, sculpted to resemble him.

Imagine his shock when instead of being presented with an Emerson doll, he watched a midget strut onto the set wearing a costume exactly like Emerson's and a bad Emerson wig, with a cigarette in one hand and a ham sandwich in the other.

" 'Bout friggin' time," the midget said, strolling up the steps to Emerson's stage and climbing onto his lap. He looked up at the astonished rock star and said, "Hey, I'm Tony. Nice to meet ya."

Emerson looked out into the crowd. His eyes found me. He was horrified. I leaned over to Antonio, who was staring into the video monitor and pointing to shadows.

"Um, Antonio," I said softly.

"Yes, Jack?"

"You didn't tell us there was going to be a midget in this."

Antonio kept studying his monitor. He called over an assistant and asked her to have a lamp moved slightly to the left. He did not look up at me. He just said, "Of course a midget to play the dummy. What did you think? A real dummy that can walk and talk and sing?"

"No one cleared this with me or Emerson," I said as softly as I could.

I looked back. The midget was trying to get in a last puff of his smoke while sitting on Emerson's leg. Emerson looked like he was going to cry.

Antonio looked up at me. "Tony was listed on all the call sheets. You approved it. Now come on, Jack, we have to start shooting."

I walked up to Emerson and whispered to him, "Just go with it. We need to start filming. We'll talk soon."

The midget said, "Who the fuck is this douchebag? Your nurse?"

Emerson said to me, "I am a musician, Jack."

"Hey, what do you play?" the midget asked him. "I got a tape of my tunes with me, you want to hear it later?"

I have rarely spent so long and sorry a day doing any kind of work as the day we spent on that set.

During lunch Emerson dragged me outside into the hot noon sun.

"That midget is a creep!" he told me. "First of all, he weighs a ton. Holding him in my lap all day is like sitting under a pony. My leg is asleep, my balls are crushed, he's sweating through his costume, and he farts every time Antonio yells, 'Cut'!"

"It's lousy, Em," I said, "but come on, it's almost over. We're done with the bit with him sitting on you. The scenes in the trailer will be easy. I don't think they even need you for the bit in the grass."

"Look at me, Jack. I'm a clown! I'm dressed up like a moron in a pageant, singing with a dwarf on my lap! However many records you think this will sell, it's not worth it. I'm a musician, not some twat who puts on makeup and makes an ass of himself for the camera."

"You look great, Em," I insisted. "Just get through this, okay? If you don't like the final result no one will ever see it."

"Tell that to the label! They're paying for it!"

"If you don't like it, we'll buy it back. No, I'll buy it back. Fair enough?"

Emerson took off his pointed Robin Hood boot and pulled out a joint. He asked me to light it and we ducked behind a parked pickup truck and shared it with our backs to the passing extras.

Emerson got control of himself. He said, "All right, Jack. I'll see this through, for you. But I don't like that creep Antonio, he keeps flirting with Cyn. And I hate that fucking foulmouthed, farting, sweaty little miserable midget!"

Emerson stamped out the joint and went back inside to get some food. I heard something rattling behind me. I looked into the cab of the pickup truck we had been leaning on. There, eating his lunch from a paper plate, was the dwarf, still dressed as Emerson. His makeup had sweated off and he had removed his wig to reveal a bald scalp dotted with flat warts.

I was embarrassed, of course. But before I could apologize, he made a spitting sound at me from between his teeth and a chunk of chicken flew out of his mouth and landed on my shirt.

"Fuck you if you're going to be like that," I told him and stalked away.

I always thought Emerson needed a lot of hand-holding in these situations, but his surliness had nothing on what that dreadful dwarf displayed for the remaining fourteen hours of the endless shoot. No one on the crew understood why Tony the midget had become so un-cooperative, but the video hinged on him. There was no backup midget in reserve.

I was not about to say anything.

Tony did everything he could to delay, screw up, and sabotage the rest of the filming. He drove Emerson to distraction and the shoot into double-overtime.

When we finally limped out of the hangar at two in the morning, the time change had caught up with us. Emerson was beaten past complaining and even Antonio was sick of filmmaking. Tony the midget, though, was like an adrenalized fighter anxious to battle on.

I said good night to Emerson, who climbed into the back of a limo to be driven home. Cyn had given up hours before. I made it to my rented car, unlocked it, turned over the engine, and began to back out. The wheels squealed and the whole automobile lurched. I put the car in park and climbed out to see what I'd run over. All four tires had been slashed.

I looked toward the set to see if there was anyone who could give me a lift. Headlights came toward me and someone honked the horn. I lifted my arm to wave hello. The oncoming pickup truck hit the high beams, almost blinding me, slowed down as if it were going to stop, and then sped forward as I stepped toward it, forcing me to jump out of the way.

As he passed I looked into the cab to see Tony the dwarf, giving me the finger.

Back in New York, I got down to the gruesome business of going through the boxes of Simon's agreements with Tug.

The first part of what I learned was what I had expected. Simon's recording career had not kept up with his touring career, which was no surprise. Good relations with a record label required intellectual diligence, of which Tug had none, and the ability to charm and be cordial, of which Simon hadn't any, either. Faced with this deficit, Tug had simply followed his own skill set and kept Simon working on the road, which was what Tug understood.

Luckily, Simon's old novelty hit "Oh! Oh!" continued to generate healthy royalties. Here I saw an opportunity. I called Tug as if out of the blue and asked if he and Simon would like me to explore licensing that tune for commercials and motion pictures. All Tug wanted to know was whether it would cost him anything.

Simon was initially appalled but soon rationalized that there was no artistic compromise in whoring out a novelty song that had no artistic integrity to begin with and which, anyway, he never played live.

Over the next twenty-five years "Oh! Oh!" would become the flotation device of Simon's finances, providing him with an annuity that allowed him to retain an illusion of fiscal health when the public stopped buying his records and coming to his shows. I eventually introduced him to a good accountant and secured him a healthy flow of income.

I have said some bad things about Simon but he was never extravagant or money-hungry. He could live within his means if that meant not having to do things he resented. He never expressed his gratitude directly to me, but he did once say, "Good thing you and I looked into this, Tug never would have sorted it out." That was as close to saying thank you as Simon was capable.

Getting involved with the business on "Oh! Oh!" gave me entrée to other people in Tug's orbit. As I was someone who had brought money into the company, and an old friend of Tug and Simon's to boot, they opened up to me. I was able to piece together what a rotten game Tug had been playing. First, he had formed a holding company called Wormwood Inc. and based it in the Cayman Islands. That got me sniffing.

Simon's own publishing company was called Wormwood Ltd. This gave me pause. I went back through the papers in the boxes. Sure enough, over the years Simon had signed all sorts of rights and income over to Wormwood Inc. Surely he had believed he was assigning these assets to his own company, not Tug's.

I tried tracking Simon down by phone but he was, as usual, on tour. I finally reached him at a hotel in Antwerp. It was four in the afternoon there. He answered the phone in a low, disguised voice.

"Simon?"

"Wrong number."

"Simon, it's Flynn. Can you talk?"

The voice changed. "Flynn? How did you find me?"

"I got your itinerary from your office, Simon, how do you think?"

"No one's supposed to have that!" He was obviously frightened. "Where are you?"

"In New York. In my office."

"Stay there. I'll call you back."

Well, I thought, this is getting a little weird. I went back to reading tour offers for Emerson. Twenty minutes later my phone rang.

The hushed, disguised voice. "Flynn?"

"Simon, you sound like you're at the circus."

"I'm at the train station. I don't think anyone saw me."

"Simon, what are you frightened of?"

I thought I had lost the connection but just as I was about to hang up he spoke.

"It's LaSalle, Flynn, he's back."

"You're joking. You've actually seen him?"

"I don't know. I mean, someone's been outside my window. I can't get a good look."

"Calm down, Simon. Why do you think it's LaSalle?"

"He's been leaving notes! *Mr. Potts—your time is close. LaSalle . . . Mister Potts—we have a rendezvous. LaSalle.* Flynn, I find these in my hotel rooms, under my pillow, in my bass case at gigs. No one could get into these places! He's the devil, Flynn. We never should have mucked around with voodoo. Now I'm going to pay the price for all the money you and Emerson made!"

"Simon, listen to me. This isn't LaSalle. It's Tug. Or someone who works for Tug. Someone on your road crew is doing this, but I promise you Tug is behind it."

There was another long silence. Then, "Why would Tug do that?"

"To keep you scared, Simon. To keep you isolated and paranoid and to stop you from asking questions. I'll bet your roadies are feeding you drugs, too."

"Fuck off, Flynn. Who do you think you are? I'm in control out here."

I bit my tongue. "That's only because you have a powerful mind and a lot of backbone, Simon. Another man would have cracked under these circumstances. I've been going through the files you sent me. Tug has been ripping you off, and I think I know how. Do you know what Wormwood Incorporated is?"

"It's my publishing and holding company," Simon said. He was regaining his composure. His panic was cooling into recrimination.

"I thought you'd say that. Actually, your company is Wormwood Limited. Wormwood Inc. is owned by Tug Bitler. I think you've been signing your assets over to Tug's company. I think you've probably been doing that for a while."

Now Simon was filled with the rage that could come only from a paranoid who has discovered the source of his anxieties. "I am going to slit that fat thief's throat!"

"Hold on, Simon," I said. "Don't play this wrong. Remember, you are out on the road surrounded by people who work for Tug. You don't know who you can trust, and we don't want him to know we're on to him. When you get back to London at the end of the tour, we'll make arrangements for a writ to get all of your materials out of Tug's offices. We want to go into court with all the proof we can gather. And God knows we don't want to give Tug a chance to destroy evidence."

"He has all my master tapes!"

"We will get them all back, Simon. But you have to play it very cool. Okay?"

Simon sighed. He said, "I understand. We're only out for another six days. I can get through this."

"Of course you can."

"Jack?"

"Yes, Simon?"

"It is good that you and I will be working together again."

I said good-bye and hung up the phone. "Oh my God in heaven," I said out loud. "I have Simon back."

"Talk It Over"–the midget video–was a smash. It worked its way up to heavy rotation on MTV and pushed the single up the charts. Emerson found himself famous in a way he had never been famous before. In the past he had enjoyed radio celebrity, concert celebrity, and LP celebrity. Radio celebrity was anonymous–the public knew your voice and your name but did not know what you looked like.

Concert and LP celebrity was very pleasant. The only civilians who recognized you were those who liked you enough to buy a ticket to your show or buy your album and spend so much time staring at the cover that they could identify you in the unlikely event they ever saw you on the street.

But with MTV success, Emerson had something new. He had television celebrity. That is a wholly different level of recognizability. TV celebrity is indiscriminate. People who hate you and laugh at you know what you look like, too.

I remember not long after "Talk It Over" began airing twelve times a day, Emerson and I were in Chicago for a radio convention. We had an hour to kill and we went into a mall to get him some underwear. He was wearing a baseball cap and a pair of glasses. From years of experience, we know his chances of being recognized were remote.

Our experience was inoperative. A group of teenage girls passed us walking through the mall, turned around, and began to follow us, chatting excitedly. When we went into a men's store they stood staring in the doorway.

By the time Emerson came out with his T-shirts and shorts, a crowd had gathered. Kids were pointing and squealing. Adults were coming out of the stores to stare.

A man's gruff voice shouted, "Hey! Where's the midget?" and the girls screamed. Emerson took off his cap and put his glasses in his pocket and waved. Flashbulbs popped, girls charged toward him, housewives came pushing forward with pens outstretched for autographs.

Em began to sign and I got the sense that this was not going to ease. More and more people were crowding in. Mall security and police began trying to create order. The kids were alerting their friends. Emerson stopped signing and posing and said, "Okay, gang! I have to go! Gotta catch a plane!"

The crowd only pushed in tighter. We looked at each other. Even the brief heyday of the Ravons' chart success was not like this. Then the fans were our age. Now we were twenty years older than most of them. What were the rules?

Other voices could be heard above the happy shouts and calling of Emerson's name. An adenoidal boy yelled, "You suck, Cutler!" An older voice called out, "Queer!" Someone else shouted, incongruously, "Down with disco!"

A security guard, an older man, pushed through the crowd and told us to follow him. We did, back into the men's shop and through a storeroom at the back and out into the parking lot.

"Do me a favor, Ringo," the guard said as he stood in the door. "Next time you want to pull a stunt like that, call us first and give us a warning."

He slammed the door and we were abandoned in the parking lot, with no idea where we'd left our car.

"Well," Emerson said.

"Yeah," I replied.

"Been a while since we've had one of those."

We tracked down our car and went back to the radio convention. We both knew something profound had shifted: Emerson's relationship with his audience. His old listeners had grown up with him. He could count on certain shared assumptions and experiences with them. These new fans were young enough to be his kids. What could he and they possibly have in common?

Up until that day we had assumed, without ever talking about it, that rock music was something that would sustain us until we were, at the outer limit, forty. Then we would quit the field with our winnings and live out our twilight years in quiet retirement. Of course, these were the vague intentions of young men who imagined that once we reached forty we would be halfway in the grave already and grateful for a nice porch swing and money for Metamucil. When we actually got close to forty and found ourselves still fit, energetic, and sexually alert, we were bound to have a rethink.

Before that day was over I was on the phone with Emerson's agent booking a national concert tour. I wanted to go to arenas in every major city that had MTV, especially towns where Emerson had not played before.

Then I got on with the head of legal affairs at Emerson's record company. I told him I wanted a guarantee of three videos for each of Emerson's albums, to be paid for by the label, nonrecoupable. We did not get it settled that day, but they gave in within a couple of months.

As Emerson's new wave of success became apparent, I would even get the label to raise his royalty rate to $1.55 an album. I had given up wading through the briars of deductions and surcharges the record industry imposed to make sure that the artist got, if he was lucky, half of the figure he was promised on paper.

My new line was, "Here's what I want. You go ahead and take out all your levies and hidden taxes and licensing fees and manufacturing costs and packaging deductions and advertising charges and sales to military bases. Compute all those little frauds and double deals any way you like. But after all that is taken away, I still want Emerson to get a dollar fifty-five an LP. How you get there, I don't care. But that's where we have to end up."

They were reading the same sales reports I was. Emerson Cutler was not going to fade away in the new age of video stars. Emerson Cutler, sixties legend, was in the game forever now. They paid what I demanded.

I was always on an airplane in those years. While Emerson was adjusting to his new level of celebrity, I was in London with an old solicitor friend serving Tug Bitler's office with writs demanding the immediate surrender of all contracts, paperwork, records, and master tapes belonging to Simon Potts.

Tug was not there. As Simon had informed me, Tug remained locked away in his fortresslike mansion by the airport. His office was filled with frightened employees who seemed less reluctant to honor the court's orders than genuinely incompetent to do so. None of them knew where the keys were, what was filed where, or indeed which of the subpoenaed materials they even possessed.

Simon had refused to come to the office with the solicitor and me. After a frustrating standoff with the bodyguard of idiots, I went to Simon and told him we had to go to Tug's house and let him know that we were onto his scam and it was up to him whether he wanted to sit down and work out a settlement, or get into a fight that could only end badly for him.

I had to play on Simon's resentment to pry him out of his hotel suite, and even with an experienced driver we got lost four times on our way to Tug's suburban hideout. It was designed to be hard to find. Simon had been there before, but he was little help until we got to the walls of the estate. Then he remembered that there was a side gate closer to the house than the main gate, which looked as if it had not been opened since the death of Vlad the Impaler.

We rang the buzzer. No one answered, but two large black dogs began barking at us from the other side of the well. I leaned on the button for a full minute.

When I finally relented, a deep, gargling voice came out of a field of electrical interference: "Who the fuck are you?"

"It's Simon, Tug," Simon said. "Let us in."

"Who's with you?"

"Jack Flynn, Tug," I announced. "Want to call off the dogs?"

The gate buzzed open. We hung back, unsure if we wanted to step through into the jaws of angry Cerberus. A bellow came through an open window and the dogs turned tail and ran away.

"Well trained," I said to Simon.

"With a cruel whip, from the way they ran," Simon replied.

We climbed six broken rock steps to a large stone patio, wild grass sticking out of every crack. We approached the heavy front door, which showed no sign of opening. We stood in front of it hoping the dogs would not come back.

"You think you should ring the bell?" Simon asked.

"He knows we're here," I said.

"Look at the mail slot," Simon said.

I looked. It had been crudely nailed shut with a piece of broken fence board. Whatever paranoia Tug had fostered in Simon must have been a weak reflection of his own.

The door opened. A dead-eyed old man in frayed sleeves looked through us, turned, and walked back inside. We glanced at each other and followed.

Tug was looming in the dark at the far end of an entry hall. I could see half of his face in the shadows.

"We meet again!" I called out as nonchalantly as I could. I knew this would not be a pleasant encounter but I hoped we could get through it without bloodshed.

I put out a hand toward Tug. There was an explosion of electric chimes and buzzers. Tug had installed a metal detector in the entrance of his home. Tug jumped back into the shadows, and the old man who had opened the door rushed toward us with a sharpened fireplace poker.

"What the hell?" I demanded.

"Empty your pockets!" the old man cried. He waved the poker in Simon's face.

Simon and I took a step back. The old man pointed his poker at a wooden sideboard. I went through my pants and coat and deposited my wallet, passport, spare change, and a pen on the table.

Simon grimaced and turned over a money clip, his metal studded belt, and a thin steel link chain from around his neck.

The old man motioned for us to back up and come through the doorway again. I came in first, to no alarm. Simon followed and the bells and buzzers exploded.

I looked to him with the universal expression of *What now?*

Simon made a dyspeptic face and pulled off his high brown boots and placed them on the doorstep. He then passed through the force field without tripping any alarms.

"Steel toes," he said with a shrug.

I wondered. So did the old man with the poker. He moved past us, weapon cocked and pointed, rang the alarm himself approaching Simon's boots, and turned them over. Out rolled a switchblade knife. The old gnome cackled and grabbed the knife and held it aloft to show us he was smarter than we were.

"What were you thinking, Simon?" I snapped.

"Thinking I'm going into the fortified house of a violent, demented thief," he shot back.

I walked into the front hall, which was dirty and dark.

"Come on, Tug," I called. "You've done quite a number on Simon with the fake threats and messages from LaSalle. Now let's settle this like adults. We know all about your Wormwood setup in the Caymans. We can prove in court that you breached your fiduciary duty to Simon and defrauded him out of millions of dollars. You don't want to go through that and neither do we."

I walked around the room as I spoke, not sure where among the various doors, stairs, and large pieces of heavy furniture Tug was hiding. I was sure he was close enough to hear me, though.

"Come out and let's figure a settlement. You've got a good business going without Simon. You will still have your other acts. No one needs to know if you just negotiate with us here."

A voice like pebbles in an outboard motor came from the top of a staircase.

"That's what you told Dennis, in't it, Flynn?"

I looked into the gloom for Tug. I could not see him.

"You told Dennis Towsy that if he let you take the Ravons you'd leave him in peace. He could still carry on with his other groups. You know what happened to Dennis, Jack? After you got done tellin' the tale to everyone at the Alibi of how you outsmarted him and stuck a blade in his face and made him cry like a baby?"

"I didn't do that, Tug."

"I was there, Jack, remember? Oh, the story got better every time you told it. And Dennis got worse. Dennis wasn't a bad boy, Jack. A bit theatrical, maybe. Took too many pills but he'd have settled down eventually. If he'd had a chance. All his groups left him, Jack. You did that to him. You made him a laughin'stock. Even his own father turned on him."

"Dennis was a very troubled young man," I said. Not being able to figure where in the room Tug was hiding was starting to spook me. "He would have ended badly no matter what choices you and I made."

"He hanged himself, Jack. Hanged himself in his boyfriend's toilet in Mexico in 1975. Didn't even make the papers here. Nobody remembered. Nobody cared."

"Tug, 1975 is a long time after we last saw him. His death has nothing to do with me, or with you." I rotated as I spoke.

Now Tug was right in front of me. I lost my breath when I saw him. He was twice the size he had been the last time we met. He must have weighed four hundred pounds. His nose was bulbous and scarred. He had a large growth, more than a boil, drooping from his left eyebrow. His face was scabbed. All of this I registered in my first startled look, but what took a moment for me to comprehend was what was sitting crooked on top of his bald dome. It was a toupee that looked like it had been hacked out of a piece of carpet and stuck to his head with the rubber underlining still attached.

I gathered my self-control and extended my hand in greeting.

"It's good to see you again, Tug," I told him. "It shouldn't have taken us this long."

Tug huffed, Tug puffed. I thought for a moment he was going to keel over. Instead he began to slowly raise his left hand.

"Look out, Flynn!" Simon screamed.

"Jesus, Mary, and Joseph!" I shouted, my mother's voice coming upon me as I saw the hatchet in Tug's hand.

"I should have dropped you from that window, Flynn!" Tug roared as he swung his weapon toward my shoulder. I jumped out of the way and began running for the door.

The old man who had the drop on us did not know what to do. Simon grabbed the poker from him and threw it to me. Did he expect me to snatch it from the air and whirl around and harpoon Tug? The poker hit my arm and bounced to the floor and I kept running. Simon did, too. He made it out of the house first; I was an inch behind him. We got all the way to the gate and stopped. No one was chasing us.

We looked at each other. Were we in mortal danger or not? The car keys were back on the sideboard in Tug's front hall with our money, pens, my passport, and Simon's boots. We mulled it over for a couple of minutes and then I went back and knocked on the door and called to the old man to give us back our billfolds, or at least our car keys so we could leave.

I waited there. There was a loud creak and a window above me opened a few inches. Our wallets and my passport and the keys came down. Not Simon's boots or knife, though. He had to go home in his socks.

One thing I will say for my negotiations involving Tug Bitler. I always got some exercise. I left the disposition of Simon's legal case with a solicitor friend in London. I doubted he would ever get back any of the money Tug had secreted in the Caymans, but at the same time I was certain Tug would not come out of his castle to try to enforce any further contractual obligations between himself and S. Potts.

Simon was all mine again.

I stayed in London for a week to visit my mother and try to promote interest in Simon's new album with some of the big record companies.

We went together to a party Virgin was throwing for their hot new signing, a ten-piece rockabilly band with full pompadours from the cotton fields of Sussex. It was an elaborate and expensive celebration, held at London's new Hard Rock Cafe.

I will tell you the difference between American rock managers and English rock managers, as I observed at this soiree. American managers always want to tell you how busy they are, how hard they're working, how early they got up, how late they'll go to bed.

English managers are entirely opposite. They brag about how little they are doing, how they work only twenty minutes a day, how much holiday time they are taking while their acts drag themselves around the world making the managers rich.

The English and American managers work exactly the same amount. The difference between them is in how they choose to lie about it.

The party was all right, as those things go. The rockabilly band performed only four songs, which was just within the limits of what anyone attending could tolerate.

I introduced Simon to Mercer Ambridge, the managing director of a record label, whom I had earlier talked into giving Simon's new album a listen. Perhaps Ambridge had even done so; he certainly pretended he had.

Ambridge was already inebriated, but I figured that could work in our favor. I stepped back and let him bond with Simon.

"I love *Anesthesia,* Simon," Ambridge insisted, leaning in close. "I would like to sign you." Simon nodded. "But I played it for the radio promotion department and they need a single. We have this songwriting/production team we've been working with. They call themselves the Chop Shop. You know them? They've worked with Annabella, Adam Ant, Bananarama. What would you think if we teamed you up with them to see if they could work up a single for you?"

Simon was holding a flute of champagne. I watched, horrified, as he kept his gaze locked on Ambridge's eyes, nodding as if absorbing his advice, the whole while gently tilting his glass forward so a thin stream of wine poured onto the executive's black suede shoes.

Ambridge kept talking, Simon kept nodding, and he graduated the stream up to the executive's pants leg. No reaction. Ambridge was hypnotized by the melody of his own rap.

Simon raised his wrist and now he was pouring wine down the front of his victim's jacket, and still Ambridge rolled on with his spiel, until finally Simon lifted the almost-empty glass to his lips, swigged the last drop, and said, "Oh fuck it, then, Ambridge, if those asswipes can't hear it. I'm going to get some more champagne."

Simon strode toward the bar, still straight-faced. I followed him with my eyes a few feet, and then looked back to Ambridge, who seemed surprised to have gotten away so easily with delivering the bad news.

He looked around for a waiter, grabbed a crab cake from a passing tray, and only then noticed that his leg was wet. He traced the damp up to his jacket and hurried off to the men's room, flustered and confused.

Simon had accomplished a cruel private joke with remarkable aplomb—although if he had been capable of considering how to give the unfortunate Ambridge a single, he might instead have had a new deal.

I returned to my office in New York to find mischief and disaster. Wendy Ipswitch, publicist and perpetual nervous wreck, grabbed me as I walked in the door and told me that while I was off having fun in the UK, Emerson's career had been hit with a crisis that would have caused Churchill to throw in the towel, the Spartans to run screaming, and Davy Crockett to desert the Alamo.

"The dwarves hate us!" Wendy cried.

I asked her what she was talking about and was there any chance this could wait until I had a cup of coffee or, better yet, a drink?

"How could you not have heard about this?" she demanded. "It's been all over the trades, all over the radio. This is terrible."

"What is it?"

"Well, the Television and Motion Picture Union of Professional Little People is urging a boycott of MTV over Emerson's video! How could you not know this?"

I made it to my desk. It was papered with message slips.

"Who are you talking about? The professional young people? Who is that?"

"Not young people, Flynn—little people! Dwarves! They say Emerson's video is disgraceful, disrespectful, and discriminatory."

"Nice gift for alliteration. Should have expected that from the Lollipop League."

"See!" Wendy said, slamming her hand on my desk. "Those kind of cheap jokes are just what you need if your aim is to have this scandal follow Emerson forever. Take this seriously, Jack! MTV is certainly taking it seriously!"

"Oh, come on, Wendy! Why is Emerson to blame for this? When has Emerson ever muttered a derogatory word about any m—any little person? He was in a video cooked up by some crazy Italian director. The little people want to picket someone, tell them to go after Antonio."

"Not gonna happen, Jack. It seems the vice president of the TMPU-PLP is Tony Wharton. Name ring a bell?"

"Why would it?"

"He's the midget in Emerson's video! He is going on all the radio call-in shows saying that Emerson was insulting, nasty to him on the set, and openly mocked his size and made disparaging and rude comments about the dwarf community."

"Oh, for heaven's sake. Wendy, as far as Emerson knows, the 'dwarf community' are at the North Pole making toys! I was there on that video shoot. Tiny Tony was a little prick! He was the one who was being rude and insulting, not Emerson. He gave me the finger! He slit my tires! Now that the video's a big hit he's coming out from under his bridge to raise a stink and get his name in the papers! Tony Wharton can climb up on a ladder and kiss my ass!"

My assistant came in with word that MTV was on the phone. I picked up. They were not going to take the heat for this. They had pulled the video and wanted Emerson to come on the air to make an apology to the midget community.

"Fat fucking chance," I explained.

In that case, I was told, we could pretty much kiss good-bye any future video play for Emerson Cutler.

I wished I were back at Tug's house.

"Okay," I told my blackmailer. "But if I get Emerson to do this—and I don't know if I can—I want a promise in writing that his next two videos get maximum rotation for four weeks each! Otherwise, he's going to recount all the midget jokes your staff made when we delivered the clip!"

I hung up the phone. Let them come back to me. They needed us to take the heat on this enough to give Emerson some play down the line. Maybe I could talk Em into believing this was a net positive.

Yes, sure I could. And then I could convince him I was a little black girl.

Wendy worked with MTV on scripting an interview Emerson did with one of their veejays in which he talked about how uneducated he had been about the traumas experienced by and prejudices directed toward Little People until this video controversy had opened his eyes.

He was forced to sit there while the veejay cued up examples of other bigoted images in the history of popular entertainment, from minstrel shows to Stepin Fetchit routines to Yellow Peril stereotypes directed at Asians to Hollywood westerns in which Apaches spoke like Frankenstein's monster and sitcoms with limp-wristed gay men in pastel suits. All of this was delivered by the veejay—who referred constantly to an autocue—as a lesson he had to teach the delinquent Emerson.

The whole exercise was condescending and insulting. What surprised me most was that after intercutting shots from Emerson's midget video with scenes of panicking natives from a Tarzan movie, the veejay introduced, as an example of sexism and prejudice against women, several American TV commercials from the 1960s and early '70s, including the White Owl cigar girl, a shaving cream commercial in which a husky-voiced woman demanded, "Take it off, take it all off," and an airline stewardess purring, "I'm Judy, fly me."

I was willing to accept that our abuse of dwarves was part of a continuum with stereotyped images of blacks, Asians, Indians, and homosexuals, but if MTV wanted to teach their teenage audience about images that objectified women, they would have better directed them to any of their video hours.

Wendy and I stood in the wings of the small studio waiting for it to be over. The veejay had one more trapdoor to spring under Emerson.

"We thought to clear the air on this once and for all," he said to the camera. "It would only be fair to offer Tony Wharton, the star of

Emerson's 'Talk It Over' video, a chance to give us his perspective on the controversy."

Emerson looked into the dark around the set in horror. I grabbed the MTV producer next to me by the arm. "No one cleared this with us!" I snarled in his ear. "This is a total ambush!"

He grinned at me from behind designer spectacles. "You want a promise of video rotation? Take your medicine."

I took a step forward to stop the taping but Tony the terrible did not appear.

The veejay said to the camera, "We invited Tony to be here but he is in California rehearsing for the opening of a new production of Shakespeare's *Richard III*, in which Tony plays the title role of a mighty general who goes on to win the throne of the UK. For those of you in the greater San Jose area, tickets are available through all the usual outlets or by phoning the San Jose Actors' Playhouse at the number on the screen. However, our cameras did catch up with Tony in rehearsal and he had this to say."

Now the video monitors lit up with our dwarf nemesis in a cape and crown, cradling a broadsword. An off-screen voice asked Tony what the scene was like on the set of Emerson's "Talk It Over" video.

"Pretty grim, man, I have to tell you," Tony said with rehearsed regret. He tilted back his crown. "I'm a working actor, you know. For me, it's all about the integrity of the role. I went into this shoot with Emerson expecting a collaboration. When the director pitched me on this he explained it as a meditation on identity, duality, the struggle of competing aspects of a single personality. That's what I was there to do." Tony shook his head.

I had never heard such malarkey in my life. Antonio the director could barely order lunch in English and this opportunist creep had been hired—without audition or consultation—from a casting book.

Tony went on as if it were painful for him to part with each word.

"Emerson is not an actor, let's put it that way. He's a rock singer, okay? He needed three people to show him where to sit down and he had trouble lip-synching his own song. Maybe he was under pressure, maybe he was flustered because he was out of his element, hey, maybe he was high. I don't know. All I know is that he was as abusive to me about my height, my looks, my body density as anything I have ever experienced. I mean, I can take a joke but this guy would not let up. All day. It was brutal. The crew were appalled, the director took me aside and tried to apologize. Then later, when I saw the finished video, I realized that Emerson had got them to cut it in a way that made him look all cool and me look like a clown. I started getting calls from actor friends saying, 'Man, why did you let them do this to you?' That's when the trouble started."

The off-screen interviewer asked if Tony had any advice he wanted to offer Emerson.

Tony looked into the camera. "Get over your preconceptions, man. People are people, okay? We all have hearts, we all have feelings, we all need respect. Okay? Emerson?"

The monitors went black and the veejay turned to Emerson, who had almost burst out laughing when he saw Tony in the crown but was now angry enough to focus.

"What do you think, Emerson Cutler?" the veejay said. "Have you learned something from all this?"

I tried to communicate with Emerson telepathically: *Please don't say anything insulting here, just take it and put it behind us.*

Emerson was so angry his eyes were wet. He gathered his breath. He looked at the veejay. He said, "All of the music I have ever made has been devoted to tearing down prejudice and the barriers between people. This has been a great lesson for me. From now on I will try even harder, and I will always practice what I preach."

The veejay gave Emerson the reassuring smile a coach would give a Little Leaguer who had just screwed up an easy play and reached over and squeezed his hand.

"Thanks Emerson," he said. "I think we've *all* learned something. Now, you told me a moment ago you wanted to make an announcement about the 'Talk It Over' video."

Emerson looked at the veejay blankly. Wendy, at my side, was hissing something. Emerson remembered his script.

"Yes, I want to announce here that I am withdrawing the 'Talk It Over' clip from MTV and in fact from all video outlets everywhere in the world. As far as I'm concerned, that video will never be seen again."

Except under the credit bed for this MTV apology special, I noted.

The producer rushed forward to hug Emerson and thank him for being so brave. "Loved the tears, Em," he said. "Showed real remorse. I think we've begun to put this behind us."

I reminded everyone in the room that Emerson had been promised heavy rotation on his next video, which would be delivered the following Tuesday, in exchange for sitting through this flaying, and we got out of there.

MTV lived up to their side of the bargain with the next two videos, which led to greater record sales, more radio play, and sold-out shows all over America. You could not turn on the television in the first half of the 1980s without seeing Emerson playing guitar on a strip of highway lit with bonfires or Emerson in moody black and white under a swinging lightbulb or Emerson as a lonely World War I infantryman on the eve of battle writing a love letter home.

During that time we had to learn to deal with an entirely new kind of fame.

For Emerson, going out to a club or concert or restaurant now meant having his hand pumped, his shoulders squeezed, his arms grabbed by persons he did not recognize who were experiencing delight to see him again, who had been just about to phone him, who had only yesterday been telling this gorgeous girl about him, who wanted to know if he had gotten the package. He didn't remember any of them. Who were these people who seemed to know him so well? They talked about shared dinners he couldn't recall, meetings he didn't remember, mutual acquaintances he was certain he had never known. These anonymous confidants were much tougher to face than fans. He understood his relationship to the fans, and for the most part they did, too. He was a beneficent czar, they were grateful serfs. But these back-pounding alleged acquaintances shook him up. They suggested that great swatches of his memory were turning to smoke.

I recognized some of these chummy strangers. They were passing acquaintances who refused to pass. They were a woman who had been seated at Emerson's table at a charity dinner and spoke with him across the centerpiece, a man who had been introduced to him by the side of a hotel pool, the former assistant to a Chicago concert promoter, the sister of a TV producer who had shared a crew meal with Emerson during rehearsals for an awards show.

Emerson had chatted with each of them and forgotten them before the end of the day, but they nurtured and stoked their encounters with Emerson, embellishing each retelling to imply an ongoing intimacy that they came to believe was real by the time they saw him again.

"Emerson Cutler told me once over dinner how he loves Peter Sellers movies."

"That Emerson is a terrible flirt—he goes on and on about this necklace of mine."

"You know how Emerson Cutler does that thing where he doesn't say a word for half an hour and then he says one sentence that sums up the whole conversation?"

Meeting Emerson was important to them, and so they came to believe that meeting them was significant to Emerson. When they saw him again they were like lost lovers recalling a brief encounter.

"Emerson! Did you get that new Sellers box?"

"Emerson, look! I'm wearing that necklace!"

"You're making notes on all this, aren't you, Emerson? You're storing it all up!"

Emerson had no idea what they were talking about.

The most aggressive of them did not leave it at the after-party. They would attempt to force intimacy by writing Emerson letters, sending him gifts, asking him to write college recommendations for their children. If the fellow across the table at an industry dinner saw Emerson ordering penne pasta, he would seize on that detail and inflate it. Anytime Emerson's name came up he would say, "I'll tell you one thing about that guy—he loves penne pasta! Cutler could be in the best veal restaurant in Florence and he'd just want the penne!" Boxes of pasta would arrive at the office with ingratiating notes for Emerson: *Found this great noodle joint in Milan—thought of you. Call you when I get back—Alex.*

We never forwarded these unsolicited gifts to Emerson. The secretaries took them home and fed them to their dogs.

Being constantly approached by strangers who acted like old friends made Emerson nervous. Hearing the snap of little cameras when he was trying to enjoy private moments made him moody. Feeling spied upon all the time made him edgy. And he swore to me that every time he saw a midget, he got a dirty look.

People don't remember now that when Ronald Reagan ran for president in 1980 he never mentioned personal morality at all. He did not condemn sex, drugs, or rock and roll whatsoever. He preached laissez-faire government, every man a king, your home is your castle, no draft, no taxes, no one snooping into your bedroom, your wallet, your pharmaceutical files.

Reagan was a smart politician. He saw that greed and hedonism did not need to be adversaries. By uniting the right wing that wanted wealth with no obligations with the left wing that wanted pleasure with no consequences, he built a new American majority. From 1981 to 1985, a high tide of self-indulgence engulfed the Western world.

But as his reelection campaign grew near, the door began to close on illicit fun. As the autumn of 1984 got close, the club-goers, drug users, wife swappers, and social deviants began to wonder if Reagan really had their backs.

First came a series of magazine covers, TV news specials, and newspaper exposés announcing that the cocaine epidemic in the United States had metastasized to a size that was impacting the economy. Wall Street was apparently filled with hopheads who were crashing en masse and jeopardizing the stock market every day around two P.M.

I was visiting Charlie in Los Angeles when one of these panic reports came on television. "Say what you will about cocaine," Charlie said while lighting a bowl of hashish, "you can't knock it for making people work hard. Give a gal a little flake, go out for an hour or two, and see if you don't come back to a clean house. If the productivity of the American worker is at issue here, I think Uncle Sam should hand out a packet of coke at every factory in Detroit. Might lose a few fingers in the gears, but boy, they'd build a lot of automobiles."

The big headline was that cocaine—"long championed as the non-addictive high," in newsman-speak—was in fact "psychologically addictive."

"Never would have guessed that from watching those lawyers crawl around the toilet floor at Area," I observed.

I asked Charlie if he had any new music to play me. He said he was working on some things. I suggested he might want to get off the weed and on to something more stimulating himself.

The second blow to the pleasure culture was the announcement of a herpes epidemic. This was old news to those who trafficked in the world of groupies, but it came as a shock to the civilians. Suddenly every newsmagazine was announcing the end of the sexual revolution and rise of the New Monogamy. Television news specials were filled with weeping young women with blacked-out faces bemoaning that their thoughtless seconds of pleasure had condemned them to a lifetime of shame and discomfort.

During a phone conversation with Simon the subject came up. I asked him if he was taking precautions.

"For herpes? Shit, Jack, I've had it for years. It's just a rash, I get it when I'm worn down. Put on some ointment. It's not like crabs. Crabs is a misery."

The third plague was the bomb. With the coming of AIDS, disease stepped forward to assume the duty religion had abdicated. New prohibitions on personal behavior were laid down. There was real panic in the music community. Headlines announced it every day: "Sex Kills." The fun was over.

Fatal illness is a mood dampener anytime, but this was made more unbearable by the long media elegy for the end of innocence. The wild abandon, drug addiction, and sexual omnivorousness of the Studio 54 era was painted as a passing summer of childhood freedom from care, before the heavy burdens of adulthood descended. Speedballs and orgies were dappled with the retrospective glow of Tom Sawyer wooing Becky Thatcher.

It was strange for me to imagine New York at the turn of the eighties ever being described as an age of innocence, but I should not have been surprised. The sixties, with all its murder, riots, and war had been repurposed as tie-dyed nostalgia. The Great Depression and World

War II had been turned into "Those Were the Days" retrospectives, situation comedies, and collectible mugs. No matter what traumas are afflicting the wider world, the time in which you grew up becomes a happy, simple, optimistic era when you get older and look back on it.

Everyone went off to be tested for HIV. The initial fearmongering news reports insisted that the virus was whipping through the heterosexual population as well as the gay community. That turned out not to be the case, but we did not find that out until later. Most of the people I knew were listing their sexual partners on notebook paper and worrying about which one had brought death along to bed.

Emerson came into the office one February morning panicked by a trip to the dentist. This was unusual. While my client was not heroic in most matters, he was like a Spartan at the Gates of Fire when it came to enduring dental work. It was this stoicism that had allowed a snaggletoothed British teenager to become a man with the gleaming white grillwork of an alabaster racehorse.

"What's wrong, Emerson?" I asked when I had closed my office door.

"You know Dr. Sullivan, right? You go to him?"

"I do, though not as often as you."

"He ever wear rubber gloves with you?"

"No, that's the proctologist."

"He did with me this morning! Before he went in my mouth he put on surgical gloves. Because of AIDS, he said! Dentists are worried about getting AIDS from the blood when they work on teeth!"

"That sounds reasonable."

"It was like he was wearing ten little condoms! It felt disgusting."

"I'm sure it's for your protection, too. Think how many mouths a dentist's fingers go into in the course of a week."

"That's the problem, man. Now that he's brought it to my attention, it makes me sort of sick."

"It's a new world."

"I mean, this is New York, odds are he's worked on guys with AIDS, right?"

"Odds are."

"Shit!"

Emerson asked me for some stationery and he began making a

list of names of women he had slept with in the last five years. It was a very long roster. From many of these names he drew arrows to the names of men whom he knew to have shared the affections of these women. He soon had enough names to fill the student directory of a small college, with a sidebar for the department heads. Some of the names he circled, others he underlined. Even allowing for the women whose names he did not know or could not remember and the obvious limitation of his knowledge of who each had bedded down with before him, it was a far-reaching and eclectic social register. I saw that Emerson was connected by common knowledge to a number of prominent film stars, television personalities, moneyed layabouts, and politicians.

"Strange bedfellows," I said as he turned to the third sheet of paper.

"You ain't off the hook, Flynn," he muttered. "You've dipped your wick in a few of these candelabras. God knows how many you didn't tell me about."

"You're the rock star, Emerson," I said. "I have no reputation to uphold or live down. Say—you slept with Jenny Rosen? When did that happen?"

"When she and Mike were separated."

"When were they separated?"

"When he was on jury duty."

"I thought you liked Mike Rosen!"

"I do like Mike! Christ, Flynn, stop being such an altar boy! I went by the house to drop off some papers for Mike, and Jenny was there alone. She was in the mood and I went for it. It didn't mean anything. I'm sure Mike does the same thing when he's on the road. No one got hurt."

"Well, we'll find out, won't we? What are you going to do with this index you're compiling?"

"Just trying to see where the gay connections are. Like here, Amy Bless. Remember her? She was living with that hat designer who left her for the golf pro. What if they were already at it when she and I commenced?"

"I think there has to be more than an exchange of fluids. I think there has to be blood."

"That's not what the dentist says. He says they don't know anything, they're just trying to avoid a panic. He says half the people who got blood transfusions in New York in the last five years could be infected. Gay guys sell their blood more than any other group."

"This is starting to sound hysterical, Emerson. Homosexuals are not vampires."

"That's right. A vampire bites you, you live forever."

During this winter of test results and recrimination Emerson's wife Cynthia confessed that she had had a chain of affairs throughout their marriage, most seriously with Antonio the video director, who himself had been profligate with both male and female partners.

If Emerson did not suspect that Cynthia had occasionally strayed, he was a fool—but this was something more than adultery. This was the introduction of potentially life-threatening indiscretion. There was no coming back from that. Emerson kicked Cynthia out of their SoHo loft and told me to serve her with divorce papers.

He then instructed me to book him the longest tour of his life, with as few days off between shows as possible. He was going to hit the highway, leave his blues behind, bury himself in his music, and seduce every virgin between the oceans.

He told me to amend his tour rider to require that each venue provide him with two dozen prophylactics.

Emerson's tour obligated him to play eighty-five shows in seventy-six cities in the U.S. and Canada in 110 days. It was a backbreaker. We had to hire double crews, the first to set up and execute one concert while the second was breaking down last night's stage and driving to tomorrow's.

It was a logistical challenge, and we needed a top-of-the-line road manager to make sure the thousand small decisions and dozens of sudden emergencies were handled efficiently.

Here an old acquaintance returned to our lives. Ramon Castro, former Boston University hustler, seducer of Emerson away from the Ravons, and my former Los Angeles partner, came to me looking for a job.

Ramon had spent some years working for the concert promoter Bill Graham in San Francisco and had road-managed tours for Starship, Santana, and other big names. He owned a ranch in Utah where he bred horses. He seemed in every way older, settled, less quick to talk and more ready to listen.

I asked him if it would be awkward for him to take orders from me, his former equal, or to be a road manager after having once been Emerson's manager full stop.

"Not at all, Jack." He smiled. "Hell, you were always the senior partner anyway. And the way I look at it, being road manager to Emerson the superstar is a much bigger job than the one I quit when Em was just finding his feet. This is what I do. I like it a lot. I'd love to do it with old friends."

We shook hands and drew up a deal memo and Castro was back on the bus. We rehearsed and launched the tour in Florida and worked up the East Coast before heading into the heartland. I flew out for important dates and joined for a day or two when I could, but my work was in New York. Castro ran things on the road.

Two months into the operation, I began to see the signals that Emerson was sinking beneath the workload and the delayed onset of grief for the end of his marriage. The tour had left behind Miami, Washington, New York, and Boston, exciting cities where old friends and celebrities showed up backstage and the crowds were attuned to every nuance of the music. The renewed charge that would come when they got to the West Coast was a month away.

They were now dragging themselves through the secondary markets—Toledo, Cincinnati, Knoxville, Lexington. Emerson was tired and bored and taking it out on the crew and the band. Castro asked me to come out and hang with him for a few days.

I booked myself out of the office for a week. I would connect with the tour in Scranton and travel aboard Emerson's bus through Pittsburgh, Cleveland, Bloomington, and St. Louis. It was hardly a vacation on the Riviera, but that's why we call it work.

I arrived too late to catch the Scranton show, but was at the hotel waiting when Emerson and Castro and the band returned. Emerson was still high on performance adrenaline. He hugged me enthusiastically and said he was delighted I was there.

"All right, you little liggers, gather 'round," he called to his backup musicians as he put me in a headlock. "Some of you know him, some of you have only heard of him, some of you fear him! This is Jack Flynn, my manager going back to a small van in the north of England, and the meanest man who ever held a knife to a promoter's neck! Jack's going to be with us for a while, so no more stealing shampoo or he'll kick your teeth from here to Shepherd's Bush!"

The musicians laughed with the forced camaraderie of hired help. "Good to see you again, Jack," said Baxter Selwyn, Emerson's drummer and the only holdover from his previous touring band.

Emerson went off to shower and change. The musicians dispersed. I asked Selwyn, "How's he been, Baxter? Edgy?"

Selwyn was diplomatic. "Been through a lot with the divorce. And we haven't had many nights off. He's been pushing his voice."

I said I had warned Em about that but he had insisted I book every possible date.

"Yeah, well," Selwyn said, "he's paying for it now."

"How's the band holding up?"

"They're pros. They know the rules."

"Well, I'm glad you're here, Baxter. You going to join us for dinner?"

"Sure thing." He hesitated and then said, "Hey, Flynn?"

"What?"

"This thing with the midgets. It really preys on his mind."

"I think that's over and done with," I said.

"Yeah, well. Try to convince Emerson. Everywhere we go, he thinks he sees dwarves. Sometimes it's just little kids. Sometimes just short people. But Emerson is sure they're all cursing him and making faces and saying things behind his back."

"Okay, Baxter."

"It really messes him up."

"Got it. I'm on it."

"Okay," Selwyn said. "Let me go drop my bag and we'll meet up for dinner."

There were not a lot of late-night restaurants in Scranton, but Castro had found the best and arranged for them to stay open to accommodate us.

It was an Italian place, small and dark with candles. Considering that it was past their usual closing time when we arrived, it was still fairly crowded. From the looks we got when we entered, it was clear a large part of the late dinner crowd had come from Emerson's concert.

Castro, Baxter, and I knew the routine. We took our table and Emerson sat with his back to the room, to avoid eye contact with strangers. We formed a tight phalanx around him, sitting uncomfortably close on either side to discourage fans from trying to squeeze in. If we were in a nightclub, we would have brought extra crew members to sit on the arms of his chair. If Emerson wanted to allow an attractive woman to join him, he would tap the roadie and a place for her would open up. But this was just dinner. The object was to provide no opening at all.

People did come over, of course. They were polite. They wanted to shake Emerson's hand, get a photo with him, tell him how much they enjoyed the show, ask him to sign their tour programs. Castro moved them along but Emerson gave them each a moment, smiled, thanked them.

When celebrities behave badly in public situations–and of course when you are famous every situation is public–they are chastised for being ungrateful and reminded that they chose to live in the spotlight–"This is what you wanted."

There is some truth in that but mistaken assumptions, too. Emerson certainly set out to be a successful rock and roll musician; there is no doubt about his ambition. He wanted the freedom and the money and, yes, the fame.

But when Emerson began his pursuit, rock and roll stardom was not what it would become. It did not entail being a television star or a mainstream entertainer. He did not know he was inviting the world to look at him all the time. He did not understand that celebrity was not something that could be turned off.

Have you ever been at a family birthday party where someone, let's call him Uncle Jim, shows up with a movie camera? He starts moving around the table, filming all the grown-ups and kids singing "Happy Birthday" and eating cake and playing games. Everyone waves at the camera and says, "Hello, Uncle Jim!"

But perhaps Uncle Jim has a sadistic streak. Sometimes he takes that movie camera and holds it on one person's face for five seconds, ten seconds, sixty seconds, and won't turn away.

Let's say Uncle Jim turns the camera on shy Cousin Carol. How does Carol react? First she waves and says hi and makes a funny face. Then she says, "All right, Jim, that's enough." She tries to go back to eating her ice cream but Jim's still got the lens on her and Carol is self-conscious about how she looks with her mouth full. She holds her hand in front of her face and says, "Come on, Jim, cut it out," but Jim keeps filming, his little camera whirring away.

Now Cousin Carol starts to lose it. She gets cross. She tells Jim to leave her alone. Childhood resentments begin to fester. Jim the bully. Carol the victim. She is not having fun anymore. She tries to wiggle out of the frame. She is angry now. Jim is ruining the party. The camera keeps whirring and turning and Carol gets up from the table and storms into the kitchen.

Should Jim pursue her, still filming, she will crawl under the table, run out the door, hide in a closet to escape from his camera.

Now imagine being a pop star, or any kind of modern media

celebrity. The camera is on you all the time. You go out to a movie, someone films you. You go to dinner, snap, there's a photograph. You bring your children to Disneyland—every tourist in the park comes running to get a shot of you. Is it any wonder that after a while pop stars begin to react like abused guests at a birthday party? They begin by waving and smiling. Then they turn away, then they say stop now, then they lose their temper and either fight or flee. The more you shine those lights in their faces, the more anxious they become.

You would, too.

The last fan to speak to Emerson was a woman who was no older than we were but whose face bore the baggage of years of bad diet and disappointment. She managed to lock him into an intense and whispered conversation before Castro put a hand on her shoulder and eased her away.

When she was gone Emerson leaned toward my ear and said, "That woman told me that her daughter had an abortion and if her husband knew, he'd kick her out of the house. I don't even know her name and she grabbed my hand and blurted out her greatest secret."

"She must feel intimate with you through your songs," I said.

"They're just songs, Jack."

"That's like saying, 'It's just an abortion.'"

"You remember that party for Bowie we went to in New York? The girl from the TV news? She came up to me at the bar and told me very anxiously that she was torn up because she was carrying on an affair with her fiancé's brother."

"She was coming on to you."

"I don't think she was. This was something else. She wanted to establish some sort of confidentiality with me. She was offering me a secret to create some bond between us."

"This has been happening a lot?"

"Yeah, and I don't understand why. Something's changed, Jack. I mean, we always got fan letters torn from kids' diaries. I get that. The fantasies of lonely teenagers. But these people are adults. They seem together, well adjusted. I don't know what they want from me."

"Absolution."

"Jesus."

"Tell them to make a good Act of Contrition and go bother Tom Petty."

I did not understand then the shift that Emerson detected. Over time I saw it. Listeners who relied on his albums for consolation and companionship wanted to continue the conversation they imagined they were having with him face to face. They wanted him to hear their side, too. When they encountered their late-night confidant in the flesh, they attempted to jump-start a personal relationship with him by pulling him into their private revelations.

Every time Emerson stepped into a room with more than fifty people he found himself a reluctant recipient of lamentations about miscarriages, auto crashes, dying parents, abused childhoods, chemical dependencies and recoveries, and crises of faith and marriage.

Is it any wonder that he began to travel in a cordon of employees? He needed a bubble of inconsequential chatter as protection from the intrusions of the penitent and aggrieved. Eventually Emerson began going out after concerts to loud discos and sitting close to the loud-speakers. The volume of the music made talking impossible. Drink orders had to be screamed at the waitresses. It was murder on his ear-drums, but it was the only way he could drown out the sorrows of his supplicants.

The last patron had left the Italian restaurant in Scranton and the door was locked. Emerson told me, "I've written a new song. I want you to hear it tonight. I think it's the best thing I've done in a long time."

"Great, I can't wait."

Emerson began to tap on the side of his coffee cup with a knife and hum a low ominous tune. Baxter picked up the implied groove and began drumming his fingers on the table. Castro closed his eyes and nodded.

Emerson sang to me softly, "You got to gimme some privacy. Pri-yi-yi-yi-yi. Gimme some privacy. Pri-yi-yi-yi-yi. 'Cause this is killing me."

I told Emerson it sounded very strong.

"It's the first thing in a long time I've written from here, Jack," he said, tapping his heart.

I said that perhaps his gifts as an artist would allow him to al-chemize the pain of his divorce into music that would heal himself and others. What I was really thinking was that no kid watching MTV wants to hear a rich rock star complain about how miserable he is. That was not what Emerson was supposed to be selling.

Broken hearts, lonely roads, getting high, sexual discovery and jealousy, traveling around, resentment of authority—those experiences resonated with the fans in the stands. But when the musician's experience became too rarefied, when his diary let slip that he stayed in expensive hotels and flew first class and collected art and Italian shoes, that he spoke a foreign language and had some money in the bank, well, then the listener resented the singer's affluence, his luxury, his difference.

Let the fans see your room service bill and the gig was over. Now you were a jet-setter, a sellout, a deserter, a traitor. And then you were a has-been.

I should not have worried. Emerson knew his music and his audience better than I ever would. When paired with a throbbing bass line and an ominous synthesizer, "Privacy" would become one of Emerson's signature hits. He still had the knack for turning his personal obsessions and high tax bracket problems into universal laments with which the common man could identify.

When we finished eating we walked back to our car and Emerson said to me quietly, "It's a miracle if your dreams come true, Jack. I know that. But I have to tell you, it's a misery when they come true wrong."

Emerson's self-image would not allow him to admit that the over-scheduled tour was beating the shit out of him. He took too much pride in his professionalism for that. Emerson saw himself as a superior being, more gifted than other men, able to work harder, and therefore not bound by the rules that protected them but would only hobble him.

As we worked our way across Ohio and Indiana, I saw his exhaustion and frustration leak out. We were at breakfast west of Cincinnati when a foolish member of the crew, a T-shirt vendor, approached our table with a tray. He sat down across from Emerson, whose eyes were clouded.

"Mornin', boss," the T-shirt man said. "That was a pisser you played last night! Holy moley! That solo you did on 'Criminal' gave me a woody!"

Emerson looked up from his oatmeal and stared into the happy face of his employee. I saw that a fuse had been lit and all I could do now was wait to see which way the roof blew off.

"Listen, Em, I was thinking," the vendor went on, talking with his mouth full. "What if tonight you did 'Criminal' as a medley into 'Who Do You Love?' I mean, it is kind of the same song."

Emerson summoned a smile of pity for the poor ignoramus. The suggestion in his expression was, *Take offense? A nobleman like me? Of course I don't take offense at the charming naïveté of this lovable peasant presuming to advise me—ha ha, ME—of how I should perform my music or indeed suggesting that one of my signature compositions is in any way derived from the work of another artist. Isn't that adorable? I love this simpleton!*

That was what his expression suggested, but I knew Emerson very well. What he said was, "That's a pretty interesting idea, Tommy."

The T-shirt vendor beamed. Emerson went on.

"You should take notes during the shows of any ideas like that that come to you, man. You know, song order, interesting covers, things that might not be working. Keep a log and when you've filled up twenty or thirty pages, type it up and let me have a look at it."

Tommy nodded, happy the boss took him seriously. Baxter the drummer came toward us with a plate of eggs and home fries, saw the way Emerson was looking at Tommy, and did a U-turn.

"That would be good," Emerson went on, "because then people on the tour can't say, 'Tommy doesn't do anything, Tommy just sits on his prat all day and lets his crew do all the work, we should send Tommy home and save the per diem.'"

The vendor's face fell; a bit of chewed banana crept out of his slack mouth.

"Who's saying that about me, Emerson?" he asked.

"Nobody, man!" Emerson flashed his lightbulb smile. "Everybody loves you! That's what I'm saying!"

Tommy the T-shirt guy slunk away. Emerson's eyes went dark again and he finished eating in silence.

Emerson was charming, glib, talented, and good-looking. It would have been enough to ruin anyone.

Emerson had suffered fewer knocks growing up than most of us do. I could see him as a small child making a drawing of a dog and his mother praising it and saying to all the family, "Look what Emerson has done! Isn't that good! Look, everyone, we must hang this up on the wall!"

A few years later when he made a little poem I'm sure the teacher read it aloud to the class and gave Emerson a gold star. These were common and healthy acts of encouragement such as most children experience and all children deserve. However, for most children life provides some leveling of this sort of praise. The boy whose poem is read aloud by the teacher may find himself troubled after school by a resentful bully. The small child may see his dog drawing replaced by the work of a younger sibling. These tribulations help us keep life in proportion.

From what I know of Emerson's childhood, his dog drawing never came down. If there was a school bully, Emerson deputized him and made him his bodyguard and valet.

Emerson grew up a leader to other boys and a valentine to every girl. How could such a youth produce other than a charming monster? Is it any wonder that when he encountered the rare dissident who expressed disapproval of anything he did, Emerson attributed it to envy, ignorance, or some other character flaw?

Emerson credited any negative review of his work to stupidity on the part of the critic and any personal rebuke as jealousy. Of course he did! He'd been bred that way from birth.

Emerson was already grown up, married, and a well-known pop star when I met him, but now I was the oldest friend with whom he had any contact at all. Oh, he saw Charlie once a year for dinner, if I arranged it. But no one from his childhood, his teenage years, and almost no one from his family. He had a sister, who told me that the last time she visited Emerson's home his maid kept her waiting in the parlor for forty minutes before she was escorted into the room where he was eating his lunch.

Most of the rich and famous, no matter how good their initial intentions, fall out of contact with old friends who are poor or middle class. They start out trying to stay in touch, of course. They pretend to be the same boys under the skin. But years pass, their friends' lives become mundane, they marry women with whom the star has nothing in common. Soon socializing becomes awkward for everyone. The old friends can't afford to pay their own way at the restaurant, the star resents being treated as a bank machine, they misplace all their common references. How many times can anyone stand to listen to the same old stories about school?

So the old friends and cousins and nephews and nieces are relegated to free tickets when the star's concert comes to town and sticky passes for the backstage potato chip room.

Emerson's coffee had gone cold in the restaurant. The crew bus had left, the band bus had left. "Em," I said, "time to hit the road."

He nodded and got up from the table. Castro had already settled the bill. I followed him onto his bus, a Greyhound-sized mobile home with a bedroom in the back, bunks in the center cabin, couches, a kitchen, and a state-of-the-art sound system. Castro and I were the only other riders on Emerson's transport.

"How long to Indiana?" Emerson asked the driver. Five, six hours.

"Shit," Emerson said. "I think I'm running a fever."

I told him to go take a nap. He crawled toward the back of the bus. I could hear him coughing for the next hundred miles.

I asked Castro if he had been partying much.

"Not to excess," Castro said. "But you know, he doesn't sleep. This thing with Cynthia has really fucked him up. After every show we have to find someplace to go look for chicks, which usually means some crappy disco or covers club. Once we get there, he's unhappy. So he drinks too much. The show buzz starts wearing off and the liquor kicks in and he starts getting moody. Closing time he points to some girl with Loni Anderson hair and too much makeup and brings her back to the hotel room. They probably do some blow. In the morning I have to find her a ride home and get her out of there. I don't think he's taking any pleasure from any of it. I think he's beating his head against a wall to drive out the pain of his marriage breaking up."

"Perhaps he'll meet the next Mrs. Cutler out here," I said.

"Then we better find a better class of bars," Castro said. "Last week he complained all day about how he got no rest the night before because the woman he picked up took three hours to climax. Didn't she know he was a busy man? Didn't she understand he needed his sleep? He went on and on about inconsiderate she was."

Emerson came out of the back of the bus and we stopped talking. His eyes were red and his nose was running.

"I feel like crap," he said. "How much farther?"

"Four hours," the driver said.

Emerson slumped down in the seat beside me. "Look, Ramon," he said to Castro. "When we get to this hotel I don't want to talk to anybody or see anybody until one hour before showtime, okay? I want you to go in and get my key and come out and tell me which way to the lift and what floor I'm on. I don't want to sign any autographs, pose for any pictures, or meet the desk clerk's daughter. Right? I'm ill. I need to get straight to my room with no stops."

"Got it, chief," Castro said.

We had a very unpleasant ride the rest of the way to Indiana. Emerson drank half a bottle of NyQuil, which did nothing to improve his mood. He began complaining about how much we were overpaying the instrument wranglers. Why couldn't one man tune all the guitars and the bass? Why did the keyboard player need his own roadie? I kept hoping he'd drop off to sleep but he never quite did.

Finally we pulled into the Bloomington Comfort Inn. It was a nine-story building just off the main highway. The parking lot was crowded with cars and buses. Emerson insisted our driver pull as close as he could to the front door. Castro climbed out on his mission to clear the way for Emerson to dash straight to his room.

Ten minutes later the road manager was back. He handed Emerson a key to room 904 and me a key to room 902. "Top floor, Em," Castro said. "The elevators are straight in the front door and hard left, there in the lobby. You get off the lift at nine and turn right. You have the room at the end of the hall."

Emerson put on his sunglasses. "Don't call me till six-thirty," he said and began to bolt from the bus.

"Wait, Emerson!" Castro said. "One thing you should know . . ."

Emerson was not listening. He was off the bus and charging toward the hotel entrance. He shouted over his shoulder, "Flynn! Come now!" as if he were calling a dog.

"Jack," Castro said, "I wanted to tell him—"

"Call my room," I said and ran off the bus following my master's voice.

I caught up with Em passing through the glass doors of the hotel. Emerson was repeating under his breath, "Hard left, ninth floor, hard right, end of hall, hard left, ninth floor, hard right, end of hall."

He was in a battle of wits against the NyQuil. There were three elevators. Two had people standing outside their doors, waiting. The last one dinged and opened. Emerson led a passing maneuver around the outside of the queue and we slid in.

He was puffing like he'd run a mile. "Hard left, ninth floor, hard right, end of hall."

Someone put a hand in the door of the lift to stop it from closing. Emerson looked at the floor. He did not want to talk to any fans.

The elevator filled with people—five, then seven, then twelve. They all knew each other. They were holding the door and laughing and saying in high voices, "Come on, one more, you can do it!"

The door finally shut and I looked around and I thought I was hallucinating. The elevator was filled with midgets. I put my hands on

Emerson's shoulders to steady him. He raised his eyes slightly behind his dark glasses. Then he lurched and made a gulping sound. I put my hand across his mouth.

This aroused the attention of a four-foot man who had a face very much like the old comedian Jimmy Durante.

"Yer pal don't look too healthy," he told me.

All the other midgets looked at Emerson. "Hey!" one of them said. "That's that dickhead English singer who makes fun of dwarves!"

"Holy shit, I think you're right!"

"Hey, asshole—why don't you go back to Limeyland, ya bigoted creep?"

Emerson was shaking, he was sweating, his hands were flapping. A couple of the midgets reached out and poked him. The elevator door opened on four and he bolted down the hall. I chased after him. "Emerson! This is not our floor!"

The midget voices followed us down the hall: "Emerson! Oh, Emerson! Come back, Emerson, come back and lick my balls, you English faggot!"

Em got to the last room in the corridor and shoved his key in the lock, trying to force the door to open. I caught up with him. He was panicked. He slumped down to the carpet.

"I think I'm having a nervous breakdown, Flynn. I really mean it."

"No, Emerson, it's fine. You're just ill. You need to sleep. Come on. Let's get another lift and I'll get you to your room."

"I don't want to go back in the lift, Jack."

"Emerson, it's five floors up."

"Get me a room on this floor, Jack."

"Come on, Em. I'll check the elevator to make sure it's empty and then you get on."

He looked up at me bravely. "Okay. Okay, man. I'm just sick, you know? I have a fever."

"I know, Emerson. We're going to get you right into bed."

"Okay, Jack. Thanks, man. I love you, you know."

"I love you, too, Emerson."

We made it to the ninth floor. Castro was waiting, pacing up and down. He saw Emerson looking like a wet rag doll and knew what had happened.

"That's what I was trying to warn you about, guys," Castro said. "They're making a movie out here with, like, a hundred professional dwarves. The check-in clerk said they've been here for three weeks already. We were lucky to get rooms."

When Emerson had slept for five hours and put on a lackluster concert, we got him to a doctor who gave him B_{12} shots and a vitamin stew. The next day was free and the physician suggested that Emerson stay in Bloomington to sleep and fly on to his next stop, gain a day of rest.

Emerson would not even consider it. He wanted to be on the road and as far from Munchkinland as fast as possible. He refused to ever accept that it was just coincidence that he had been booked into a hotel filled with little people. He said that Castro must have done it on purpose, must have thought it would be funny. Castro swore up and down that was not true. I mostly believed him. But Castro was off Emerson's bus for the rest of the tour.

A full year before he turned forty, Emerson had begun announcing that he wanted no party, no gifts, no mention of that dreadful day. He said it so often, so loudly, and to so many people that it was obvious to me that I had better set up a super shebang.

How to do this, though, without violating the letter of his orders? Here was where I earned my money. After Emerson recovered from the miserable American divorce tour, I arranged for a one-month series of European concerts with three days off each week and ending at Montreux, Switzerland, just two days before Emerson's birthday. The end-of-tour party became the first ovation in a series of unofficial commemorations of the Cutler nativity.

In Scandinavia Emerson had begun an affair with a woman named Uta Lindberg, a former Miss Norway who worked as poetry editor of an Oslo literary magazine. She flew in to Montreux to surprise him by jumping out of a cake.

The day after that, Emerson, Miss Norway, Baxter, Castro, and I moved up to Paris for twenty-four hours of rest and ostentatious luxury. Two younger couples, friends of Miss Norway, joined us there. A dinner at Le Vieux Bistro included many toasts to Emerson. At the end, we were all served chocolate tarts with candles.

His actual birthday began with an elegant private breakfast for our whole company at a three-star restaurant called L'Ambroisie. From there we were driven to the airport and boarded a private plane for the west of Ireland, where we had roast goose in the dining room of a castle. Here telegrams of congratulations were read from friends around the world and bottles of gift champagne were popped like Gatorades at a football game.

We stumbled out of the castle and back onto the plane. We crossed the Atlantic with much revelry, a few elaborate gifts being presented. Then we settled back to view a long film documentary of Emerson's life, complete with testimonials both sincere and silly from two dozen pals and colleagues.

When this cinematic tribute ended, Emerson and Miss Norway moved to the private cabin in the back of the plane for a bonk and a nap. Upon our arrival at a private airport in Westchester, we were all ferried to an elegant candlelit dinner at the New York Players Club, a Gramercy Park institution where Booths once rubbed shoulders with Barrymores, organized by our old record company boss Wild Bill.

When I entered my apartment at three A.M. (nine A.M. European time, which was what my body clock was set to) I knew that Emerson was happy. He had had a three-day fortieth birthday celebration culminating with breakfast in Paris, lunch in Ireland, and dinner in Manhattán, while maintaining the illusion that we were not really celebrating his birthday, merely the end of a successful tour and his being such a beloved and humble fellow.

My own fortieth birthday passed less eventfully. I received flowers from my daughter, Lucy, obviously arranged by her mother. Carey, my ex, encouraged Lucy and me to stay in touch. I was all for it but Lucy was reluctant. She called Carey's new husband Daddy and resented being reminded that she had a different father than her younger brothers did.

I was dating a gallery owner named Stephanie Berkowitz. She organized a small dinner party and we had a cake. Emerson was there. So were a couple of Stephanie's friends. So, to my surprise, was Danny Finnerty, whom I had not seen in two years. I later learned that he had pressed Emerson to be invited, and Emerson had pressed Stephanie. I had no problem with that, I liked Fin well enough, but he was not a close friend. He was not someone who had ever come to my home.

When we opened gifts, I began to understand Fin's motive. I was sitting in a big chair in the living room. After all the other presents were opened, Fin presented me with a wrapped box. It appeared to be some sort of stereo receiver. I thanked Fin very much and prepared to move on but he insisted on setting it up right there, plugging it into my sound system. He had brought all the necessary mounts and wires. I could hardly object, and the truth was that if Fin did not set it up the thing probably would have gone into a closet. So I let him go about his work while the rest of us continued our chatting and joking, and pretty soon Fin was done and demanded everyone's attention.

He reached into a leather bag and presented me with another gift, smaller and elaborately wrapped. I opened it and found three plastic cases about four inches square. Each contained a small silver disc.

"These are compact discs!" Fin announced with delight. He pointed to the unit he had just wired into my stereo. "This is a compact disc player! Philips came up with it and it's going to change everything!"

Fin took one of the discs from my hand and slid it into the new component he had bestowed on my living room. I caught Emerson's eye. He smiled and winked—another of Fin's world-changing get-rich-quick schemes. Steely Dan came booming out of my speakers at a volume that hurt my fillings.

"You know this album, right?" Fin shouted. I nodded. The whole captive company of friends gave up on doing anything but listening to Fin's demonstration.

My resentment toward Fin for hijacking my party receded as I listened to the music. I knew this album quite well, but I had never heard it like this. The bass seemed to have been doubled by a herd of tubas, the piano was so bright that it sounded as if there were tacks on the hammers. The background vocals, a vague choir on vinyl, became three distinct personalities. I could hear Donald Fagen drawing in his breath before each chorus and the pick scraping the strings of the guitar. It was as if every instrument had been dipped in silver.

I looked at Emerson. He was mesmerized. We had heard the future and we knew it. Fin said, "I'm in charge of new technology for the label now, and I tell you guys, no one there knows how big this is going to be. It's going to start as a high-end thing for audiophiles but once that demo is saturated, these things are going to be mass-marketed."

I was interested in all that but I said to Fin, "Wait. You're working for a label? I thought you were running that studio you and Charlie set up."

"Oh, man, Jack." Fin laughed. "We have been out of touch! After Charlie left we started getting a lot of work at that studio, a lot of heavy producers found the place. Started getting us involved in all this cutting-edge audio. Two years ago I went up to Canada with Quincy to hear a demo of this digital reproduction and I was gone! Came back and started evangelizing. Polygram offered me a position as head of new technologies."

Amazing, I thought. Once more Charlie sells out too cheap and too soon, and hustler Fin is on the inside again.

Fin held up a CD. "Here's what no one's saying out loud," he whispered as if he were ratting out the Rosenbergs. "They're cheaper to make than records! Vinyl is a petroleum product, you remember how shitty the quality of records got during the oil embargoes? No more. These silver beauties are made right here at home. And there's no loss of sound quality no matter how many generations you go down! They don't scratch, they last forever! Fellas, I swear—I believe that in five years, vinyl records will be a thing of the past."

"I kind of like vinyl," Emerson said.

Fin smiled at him. "Yeah, but tapes already outsell records! Vinyl is going to go anyway. But with CDs you have a beautiful replacement and—now wrap your heads around this, boys—everybody is going to end up buying their whole record collections all over again. Think of that. All your albums, Em, are going to sell new copies to everybody who bought the old copies. Which is why I am imploring you two to come in on this early. Take advantage of the hunger that's going to be out there for CDs while there is still a scarcity in the market. Let's go in with the original tapes and remaster every Emerson Cutler album for compact disc and hit the market with a big campaign that sells the concept of the CD to America while reselling the entire Cutler catalog!"

Stephanie and the other guests had gravitated to the kitchen. I knew she would resent Emerson for bringing Fin to dinner and turning my party into a business meeting. But I did not mind anymore.

I thought that Fin was right about compact discs and we should do the deal he suggested. I saw it as the best fortieth birthday gift I could have got. Emerson's American record contract retained the arcane clause I had demanded years before, when the label wanted to subcontract out their right to market cassettes and eight-tracks. We were signed to Tropic only for vinyl. We had a year-by-year side deal for tapes. Compact discs were not included at all. Theoretically, Emerson could take his compact disc rights to whichever company offered him the highest advance. We would not do that to Tropic, but we would make sure that they paid us handsomely for staying in the family.

It occurred to me that being forty was going to be great. I had dreaded it on some level because I suppose I always thought that the jig would be up. When I started with the Ravons, I figured we would be lucky if the jig lasted until thirty. That would be a hell of a run for a pop group manager by the standards of the 1960s.

All through our thirties, through California and marriage and divorce and money and hits, I vaguely imagined that if things went really well we could stretch this out all the way to forty. Then it would be time to get a real job.

Now, holding that shining disc in my hand like an Olympic medal, I knew that I was never going to have to get a real job. I could see Emerson and me continuing until we were fifty, and then taking our loot and living like pharaohs for the rest of our days.

Every time it felt as if our natural trajectory was headed down, some new technology provided an updraft that carried us to new heights. When the beat group craze was petering out and Emerson was getting a little long in the tooth to be a teenage pinup, FM radio emerged and opened a whole new audience to us. Ten years later, when the tickets were moving a little less quickly and punk rock was demanding we be put out to pasture, MTV came along and the whole thing got bigger and more lucrative than it had ever been.

And now, while we were still riding the winds of MTV, here was a little silver disc that was going to make it possible to resell everything we had done for two decades to the kids who watched MTV and to their parents. I was not always a good prognosticator, but I knew as soon as Fin played me the compact disc that we were all due for a windfall.

Emerson and I told him that we were aboard with his plan. Let's remaster the Cutler back catalog and take a seat on top of the coming digital volcano.

At thirty-nine I had experienced a vague dread about getting old. Now I felt great. Better to be in prosperous, healthy, and early middle age than clinging to the last strands of youth. I was very happy to be forty.

That night after the guests had left, Stephanie and I made love energetically and athletically. A dozen years later, almost a dozen years after we had split, I saw Stephanie at a dinner party in Beverly Hills. By then it was the 1990s. She had married and divorced a successful film editor. We reminisced about our time together over dinner and most of a decanter of red wine. When the other guests went into the media room to watch a film, the two of us stayed by the swimming pool, talking. I could tell there was something she wanted to tell me and I had begun to flatter myself that it was that she had always loved me and wanted me back.

That was not what it turned out to be. "Remember your fortieth birthday party, Jack? When that awful huckster showed up and made us listen to compact discs all evening?"

"Fin. Yes, I thought I was getting old! I had no idea what old was."

"Well, Jack, I chickened out that night, I have to confess."

"How did you chicken out, Stephanie?"

"I was pregnant, Jack. I was going to tell you on your birthday."

I looked into the illuminated ripples of the swimming pool. I felt panic rise and subside. I said I did not understand.

"I couldn't tell you unless I was sure I wanted to keep the baby. I mean, even then you were such a Catholic, Jack. You pretended you weren't but I knew you. You would never have let me have the abortion."

"You said you were planning to tell me. What stopped you?"

"Well, don't think badly of me, this is all a long time ago and I was young. I had been telling myself that you and I should stay together and raise the child. But that evening I realized it could never work."

I was calculating how old our daughter or son would have been by now. I tried to imagine a parallel life in which Stephanie and I had stayed together and raised a family.

"Why could it not have worked?" I asked her.

"You were already married, Jack. You were married to Emerson."

I resented hearing it, but I knew it was true. As the years went by, my partnership with Emerson had taken on all the stresses, strains, and resentments of a bad marriage, without the mitigating sex.

As I have suggested elsewhere in this reminiscence, even those who should know better like to think that a rock star is a prisoner of his manager. Filmmakers, magazine editors, political operatives, and other adults from whom one might reasonably expect some degree of sophistication want to believe that if they can get around the manager, sneak a message to the star through his barber or dentist or auto mechanic, the great man would love to play on their demo, donate to their charity, write a song for their movie, or be interviewed for their book about the effects of psychedelic drugs on the creative process. According to this attitude, my life was devoted to blocking Emerson from doing all the noble things he would jump at if he only knew. Of course, my actual job was to get him out of promises he had made in restaurants, dressing rooms, and boudoirs. But no one wanted to believe that the star was a selfish creep. It was my job to creep for him.

I bring this up not defensively, but to explain that if it had been up to me, Emerson would have performed at Live Aid. I started getting requests from London in the spring of 1985. I raised it with Emerson several times and each time he told me he had no interest. He was spending a lot of energy hiding from Bob Geldof and his haranguing minions.

"I hate that 'We Are the World' thing," Emerson told me. I said this was coming from the "Do They Know It's Christmas" people. Emerson said, "I hate that one, too."

The only social cause that aroused Emerson's passion was his outrage when a hotel mixed shampoo and conditioner in the same bottle. It was not that he was insensitive. Emerson enjoyed playing Father Christmas for friends who had fallen on tough times and was likely to have a sudden burst of generosity toward a homeless woman huddled with her baby on a grate. He could be magnanimous with the afflicted when he stumbled upon them.

Like many sensitive people, especially those who consciously cultivate their sensitivity for professional reasons, he was enormously attuned to his own feelings but less acutely focused on the feelings of others. His sensitivity, his generosity, and his charity were in the end manifestations of his highly developed self-regard.

Still, as the July date of the Live Aid concert grew close, I sensed that we might be missing a major promotional opportunity. The week of the show I dropped a hint to a Live Aid rep that perhaps I might persuade our boy to show up at Philadelphia with an acoustic guitar and do a solo version of "Bed of Nails." She told me to get in the back of the line, she had already had calls that day from Carl Perkins, Robert Palmer, and Bachman-Turner Overdrive.

The evening before the big event, Emerson, Miss Norway, and I had reserved a table upstairs at the Lone Star Cafe to see the blues and rockabilly guitarist Lonnie Mack, an early influence on the Ravons. When we arrived, the room was crowded. We stopped to pay our respects to Doc Pomus, the Brill Building songwriter who held residence at the center table, and then made our way upstairs to our reserved spot in the crow's nest over the stage.

Every rock legend headed for Live Aid the next day was in the upper box of the Lone Star that night. There was Mick Jagger, Keith Richards, Ron Wood, Bob Dylan, and Paul Simon. I could see Emerson's face tighten, that he alone among them had failed to answer starving Africa's appeal. I asked a busy waitress to help us find our table and said Emerson's name. She pointed to a spot by the rail, in which two intruders were squatting and trying to get a conversation going with Jagger. I told Emerson and the women to wait back here, I'd go kick them out.

The table was covered with empty beer bottles, the men were loud and rowdy. I walked over and put one hand down on the table, pointing to the cardboard Reserved sign with my name on it.

"Sorry, gents," I said. "Emerson Cutler's here for this table, I have to boot you out."

The man closest turned to look at me. "Hey, Jack Flynn!" he said happily. "Tell Emerson to come on over! Hey! Emerson!"

It was the MTV producer who had dragged us through the horrible Midget Mea Culpa Special. I hated him.

"Sorry, boys," I said with cordial firmness. "We've got ladies with us and we're expecting more guests. I have to ask you to move over." I could not resist adding, "I think Dylan's got a couple of empty chairs."

The producer stumbled to his feet. He waved at his companion to finish his beer and come on.

"Fine, pal," he said to me. "And say good-bye to your video rotation."

Missing Live Aid was a mistake that Emerson tried to make amends for by playing every poorly organized, badly executed, and dubiously intended charity show for the next three years. He played for every suffering ethnic group in the third world, as well as for sharecroppers, landslide sufferers, earthquake relief, and victims of bad haircuts. No one ever suffered the charity fatigue Emerson suffered.

Of all the aspects of Live Aid that have been analyzed, one that I have not seen discussed is that it seemed to be the day when the breach between the old rock dinosaurs and the new wave was finally healed. U2 and Boomtown Rats and Elvis Costello and the Pretenders shared the stage with Queen and Led Zeppelin and McCartney and Mick and Keith and everyone got along fine and cheered each other on and joined hands at the end and sang off-key as one.

I wish Emerson could have been part of the event just for that. Although the rise of MTV had disemboweled the rock critics who had turned against Emerson with such venom at the end of the seventies, he still resented that dismissal. On some level he still wanted critical approval.

Live Aid served as the Appomattox of rock's great late seventies civil war between the old guard and the new wave. By sitting it out, Emerson missed the chance to lay down his sword. Instead, like Jesse James, he remained unreconciled, and nursed his resentment for years to come.

Charlie Lydle burned through money as if it were twigs in an in-cinerator. He came to New York to invite me to lunch and ask me to please see if Emerson would be interested in buying his share of the Ravons' music publishing.

"For God's sake, Charlie, don't do that," I said. "That money is your retirement! You don't know what it will be worth someday—one of those songs could get covered by Linda Ronstadt and be a hit all over again. I almost got my neck broken getting your publishing back from Dennis Towsy. Don't blow it to buy a new Jaguar!"

"I ain't gonna blow it, Jack," Charlie said while eating the potatoes from my plate. "I'm gonna invest it in a better opportunity."

"Let me guess, Charlie. You met some Peruvians who are going to bring a submarine full of drugs through the Panama Canal, they just need to make the last payment on a periscope."

"Not at all! This is a big thing; Fin's already made a fortune and he can get me in on it."

"Oh well, in that case," I said, "let's amend my earlier opinion from 'no way' to 'absolutely no fucking way.' You and Fin went in on your studio, didn't you? He came out with a million dollars and a big record company job and you ended up with nothing, as usual."

"Hey, that one was my fault. Fin told me to stay in and I wanted the cash. I say good on him for getting one over! And good on him for offering old Charlie another shot at the prize."

"What is he letting you in on, Charlie? I understand that Fin is now the king of the compact disc. Too late to get aboard that train."

"Yeah," Charlie said, "but that's where he's smart. He always knows the next technology. Like, I remember Fin telling me how big Betamax was going to be, that everyone would have a taping system hooked up to their TV by 1990, and look, it's already happening. I bet you got one, don't ya, Jack?"

"Yes, I do, Charlie. I have a VCR. So does everybody else. If you had sunk your money into Beta you'd be broke now."

"Jack, I'm broke now anyway! But Fin was right in essence, wasn't he? He said, 'Home video, movie rentals,' and he was right."

"So what is the great prognosticator prophesying this time?"

"DynaTAC, Jack." Here Charlie reached in his shoulder bag and placed on the table between us a two-pound white walkie-talkie with twenty-one push buttons on its face and a long antenna, like the aerial on an automobile, ascending from its crown.

"You want to sell your publishing to invest in walkie-talkies?"

"Not walkie-talkies, Jack. Mobile telephones! They're gonna open up all this bandwidth that the government's been sitting on since Marconi did the mambo. Fin reckons that in the next ten years, every family is going to want a mobile phone."

"Why?"

"You take it with you! Outside watching the kids, on a camping trip, to the beach. Say you got someone in the hospital. Or someone's expecting a baby. Say you want to take the kids on a cross-country car trip but you don't want to be cut off. Mobile phone!"

I told him I thought it was very risky. Even if he and Fin were right and Americans were going to start lugging around communications devices the size of a shoe box, he could find himself with Betamax all over again. He could invest in Sony phones and then General Electric could turn out to have the winning patent.

Charlie was adamant, though. He insisted that if Emerson did not want to buy his publishing he would sell it somewhere else. He knew this would quiet my objections. The last thing I wanted was to have Emerson suddenly saddled with some unknown and unwanted partner.

Wily little Charlie acted sweet but he knew how to play hardball. With my back to the wall, I suggested a new idea. "Look, Charlie, hold on to your songwriting money. There's something else you could sell. You could let Emerson buy your share of the royalty stream on the Ravons recordings and your piece of the group's name and likeness."

Charlie was intrigued. He made about fifteen thousand a year from

Ravons' record royalties, far less than he made from the music publishing. Name and likeness had never earned him a cent beyond a small piece of a T-shirt advance that had never earned out.

Delight moved across Charlie's features. It was as if he had learned there was a silver deposit beneath his chicken coop.

"How much do you reckon them Ravons royalties are worth, Jack?" he asked.

"I don't know, Charlie, I'm not even sure how we'd calculate it. Take the average for the last five years and see how they're trending, up or down, and make a projection based on what we might reasonably expect them to generate over the next ten, I suppose. Something like that. You have to understand that if you do this, you may regret it. What if one of those records gets used in a movie or something? 'American Graffiti 3' or 'Star Wars Goes to Carnaby Street.' It could happen."

"Well, then, I'd still make money off the song publishing, which under this plan I would hold on to. I like it, Jack. Make me an offer!"

I explained the idea to Emerson, who must have been stoned. He seemed to have trouble remembering the difference between his recording royalties—money made from the sale of records and CDs—and his publishing income—songwriter's fees.

"What it comes down to," I explained, "is that if we do this, you will get twice as much money from Ravons record sales for the rest of your life. Also, you will own two-thirds of the Ravons' name, which means you will have controlling interest, with Simon as minority partner."

Emerson liked the sound of that. We agreed that we should pay Charlie more than market value, and arrived at a figure of $325,000. I wrote Charlie the biggest check he had ever seen. He was ecstatic. He told me later that he kept aside $100,000 to maintain the standard of living to which he had become accustomed and plowed the rest into Fin's mobile phone scheme, which made him nothing for a long time, and then a little money for a little while, and then nothing again.

Charlie later claimed he lost his shirt on the investment but with Charlie you never knew. It is possible that he put only ten thousand of his windfall into Fin's cell phone enterprise, buried twenty in his back garden, and sank the rest into a Peruvian submarine.

An ironic aspect of my negotiating such a good deal for Charlie was that the next professional move he made was to fire me. Given that I had made no money from representing him for almost ten years, it was no blow to my business. He could not have been nicer about it. He explained that he was in love with a new girl, Melissa, and she was a manager herself. True, she had up to now managed only show dogs, but she was very smart and anxious to apply her skills to the music industry. Anyway, there I was all the way in New York and Melissa was in the bed right next to him.

"No hard feelings, Jack?" he asked me.

"None at all, Charlie. Now that I don't work for you we can just be good friends."

"I love ya, Jack."

"I love you, too, Charlie."

The next time I saw him he had a poodle haircut.

From Emerson's point of view, the best thing about buying out Charlie was that in later years his control of the Ravons' name and likeness would turn out to be important and lucrative. The worst thing was that a revisionist myth would grow among rock critics that Emerson had taken advantage of Charlie when he was down and out to rip off his share of the Ravons. There was no doubt where that story came from. I could imagine Charlie with a rueful smile, whispering it off the record to a sympathetic reporter. I loved Charlie, but he sometimes had the manner of the college boy who implores the older woman to take him to bed and then laments that she stole his virginity.

After Stephanie left me—but years before she told me about her pregnancy and abortion—I resolved to get fit and take better care of myself. I began working out with a trainer and once again swore off drugs and drink. This time it was much harder. The drugs I could do without, but alcohol had a hold on me.

With Emerson's blessing, I spent a month at a clinic in Montreal and came out sober. I would remain that way for more than two years. While I was away, Castro had supervised the office for me. It was an easy fit. As Emerson's tour manager he knew everyone I dealt with and was already seen as a sort of vice admiral. Wendy the publicist also stepped up. Although she had other clients, she made it clear that Emerson was her favorite. We put her on staff as a "management associate." I felt very settled. I had a family at work.

Among the offers that had arrived while I was away was a proposal from an editor at Byblos Books, a division of the international NOA media corporation, for Emerson to write his autobiography.

I called the editor to get the lay of the land, see what his offer might be. He was young and seemed to be a real fan. I got the impression that he had just graduated to the position where he could sign new authors. I said we'd need a million dollars to consider it. I thought that would shut him up.

He came back the next day with an offer of five hundred thousand for the U.S. rights, hardcover and paperback, and another four hundred for the rest of the world. The kid was enthusiastic and he had come through with the money fast. The hundred thousand shortfall was an obvious negotiating tool. I was sure his boss had told him to offer half that but he was hungry for this deal.

I ran the idea by Wendy, who thought a lot of good could come out of it.

"It could be a great opportunity for Emerson to shape his own image, Jack. He still doesn't get the respect he deserves. I think this is a very interesting proposal."

"I don't think Emerson could write it himself."

"Of course not. We hire someone to do that. Emerson talks into a tape recorder and then we go over the manuscript to make sure it's how we want it."

"How much do we have to pay the ghostwriter?"

"Oh, you know, you get somebody from *Billboard* or *Guitar Player* who likes Emerson to do it. I don't know. We offer them twenty-five grand and maybe for the right person go up to fifty."

"That leaves Emerson with nine hundred and fifty thousand dollars."

"It's his name and story that will sell the book."

"I know who he's going to want to have do it."

"Who?"

"You, Wendy. Come on, it's obvious. You know him better than any writer, you have shaped his image, you work for him. It's got to be you."

"I wouldn't consider less than a fifty-fifty split."

"Bitch."

We pitched the idea to Emerson and he was unimpressed. He said autobiographies were for old men and he was just getting started. Miss Norway agreed, although her opinion was compromised by the fact that she wanted to collaborate with Em on a volume of poetry.

I brought it up several more times, as did Wendy, with passion, and eventually Emerson agreed—on the condition that they go somewhere warm to write it. I said okay but the cost of the holiday had to come from the million-dollar advance.

Everyone was happy with that and after signing the deal with Byblos, we carved out an eight-week period early in the next year for Emerson and Wendy to go off to the Caribbean and collaborate. Miss Norway decided to work on her first volume of children's stories at the same time.

While Emerson was off on his literary sabbatical, I would go to England and spend time with my other client, the brooding Simon, whose career had not advanced beyond plodding through the Sudetenland playing his opuses for rooms filled with baying proles, but who was at least now getting the money due him for his troubles.

I will recount a few of my bad times with Simon in the next chapter, but before we set out on that long winter journey, let me flash forward a few months to when Byblos Books announced the upcoming autobiography of rock legend Emerson Cutler. The announcement itself got more press than I expected, a good sign. Much of that press made mention of the advance Byblos had paid Emerson, which was reported, accurately, barely, as "seven figures."

Emerson and Wendy and Miss Norway were off in the sun working on the book when I received a lawyer's letter from a firm I had never heard of in Pasadena, California. In my business you get sued for everything. Lunatics claim they wrote Emerson's songs. Con men claim Emerson promised to invest in their new project and then reneged. Women insist they have Emerson's children (those we check out). Failed concert promoters try to shake us down to return advances we never got. Photographers want money because they saw a picture they took of Emerson in a Portuguese tour book. We got lawsuits and threats of lawsuits every day.

This one knocked me off my stool.

I had promised not to disturb Emerson and Wendy in the tropics, which was a deal I intended to honor. They were in the Caribbean but as far as I was concerned I was the one on holiday. But for this I had to phone.

Wendy answered. I said, "You won't believe who's suing us."

"Who?"

"Fred Zaras."

"I don't believe it."

"You won't believe why."

"Tell me."

"Because Emerson is writing his autobiography."

"I don't get it."

"Zaras claims that he has an exclusive contract to write the biography of Emerson Cutler."

"That was ten years ago! He never wrote it! The publisher sued him to get back the advance. That book was canceled in 1978!"

"I know."

"He's nuts."

"I know."

"Should I tell Emerson?"

"Nah, I don't think so. How's the writing going?"

"It's going. Miss Norway is doing a lot of skinny-dipping. Diverts our boy's attention from his mission."

I heard Emerson's voice in the background saying, "Tell Emerson what?"

Wendy told him, "I'm on with Flynn."

"Tell Emerson what?"

"Jack," she said, "I'll call you back."

I read the letter from Fred's lawyer again. I was going to have some real fun composing a reply to this one. I resolved not to bring up Fred's demonstrated inability to meet deadlines when in the body of a bird. Or maybe I would.

The phone rang. My assistant said it was Emerson. I picked up.

"Hello, Mr. Hemingway," I said.

"Wendy told me about Fred's letter," he said.

"Um," I said. "I'm just meditating on my response."

"How much is he looking for?"

"Oh, I don't know." I looked at the letter. It was full of misspellings. My name was spelled "Jon Flinn."

"He's asking for seventy-five grand, which he claims is the fifty thousand advance he lost for his book, plus half that again in personal damages. It's bullshit, Emerson, don't think about it. A total fishing expedition from some shyster Fred met at the Kinks convention or something. It's completely groundless."

"Look, Jack," Emerson said, "I want you to pay him."

"Yes, Emerson, and I want to pass rubies from my rectum every time I eat ice cream but I don't think either is likely to happen."

"I'm serious, Jack. Fred doesn't even write in the music magazines anymore. Wendy says he's really down and out. He's living off what he can get for selling promo copies of the records he gets mailed. Let's slip him seventy-five grand for old times' sake."

The idea made me angry. I said, "That's a very generous impulse, Emerson, and if Fred had come to you and pleaded for charity I would say God bless your beneficence. But that is not what is happening here. Fred is threatening to sue you for writing your own life story! Doesn't that offend you just a little?"

"Hey, Jack. If Fred had ever written that book he was supposed to, maybe my book wouldn't be worth so much. Let's cut him a check."

We argued about it but Emerson was determined. The sun and the sex were making him soft. I stalled a couple of days, hoping he'd change his mind, but he never did. In fact, he checked up to make sure I did what he told me to do.

So we paid Fred Zaras $75,000 as a "settlement" for interfering with the Emerson Cutler biography to which he had exclusive rights.

I never heard a word from Fred. I'm sure his Pasadena lawyer fainted when he got the check. I'll bet after that he sent shake-down letters to every author in *The New York Times Book Review*.

Fred used part of the seventy-five grand to privately publish his long-threatened opus, *Tectonic Shift: The Coming Realignment of the World into Seven Super-States and What It Means for the 21st Century*.

Snappy title, huh? Here's the punch line. After the USSR collapsed, Fred's book got some serious attention, He was invited to go on C-SPAN and CNN a couple of times and his book got picked up by Random House, who shortened the title to *The Rise of the Super-States*. It was written up in *Commentary* and *The New York Review of Books*. For a year or two Fred became respectable. He went on the lecture circuit, got hired for a college teaching job but never showed up, was assigned articles by some prestigious political journals but never turned them in, and eventually faded back into obscurity.

Fred had attempted to explain his thesis years earlier, sitting by the pool of the house Charlie and Maggie and I shared when we first moved to Los Angeles.

"It comes down to this," he insisted an hour in. Charlie, Maggie, and I were smoking and giggling.

"In a world where all people are thrown into close proximity to all others, groups will cluster around their genetic partners. So the

Russians will pull away from their countergenetic alliance with China and Vietnam and move back toward the West. China, Korea, and Japan will overcome their antipathies and forge a common market. The lines will blur between England and the United States, who will begin to absorb Canada and Ireland . . ."

"England's been trying to absorb Ireland for some time now," I said. "It's not going well."

Fred said, "That's only because the Irish are too loyal to the chains of Catholicism to accept England's leash, but as the next generation grows out of Christianity, those issues will be forgotten."

Fred insisted that the big shift would come in the Far East, where Beijing would have to face off against a forced alliance of the manufacturing nations—Japan, Taiwan, and South Korea. Those three would overcome their mutual animosity to avoid being absorbed by China.

"As the old Maoists die off," Fred proclaimed, "I believe China will retain the autocratic façade of communism but use it to create a manufacturing superstate where the West will go to buy cheap shoes and radios. They will out-Japan Japan, by turning the gulags into factories and arrest as many workers as they need to run the conveyor belts."

"I don't think the West will go along with that," I said. "It's not like our unions and workers and manufacturers are going to let their jobs be shipped off to Chinese dungeons."

Fred snorted. He said, "The capitalist will sell us the rope with which we lynch him. Lenin said that."

Charlie, emptying a bottle, wanted to get us out of this dissertation. He piped up, "Lennon also said, 'I am the walrus.'" Meg started laughing.

Charlie said, "And I believe he went on to add, 'Goo goo ga joob.'"

Fred gave up on trying to explain his prophecy to us potheads.

"I don't think you're considering what Marx said about this, Fred," I told him.

Fred looked at me suspiciously.

"Time flies like an arrow. Fruit flies like a banana."

I remember that Charlie laughed so hard he rolled into the pool.

Emerson's autobiography never came out. The young editor who commissioned it had been fired by the time we delivered the manuscript, which his successor disliked on the old publishing principle of

NABM—Not Assigned By Me. Emerson had no interest in making the extensive revisions the new editor demanded and after some routine recriminations we agreed to shake hands and go our different ways. Emerson got to keep the two-hundred-fifty grand he'd already been paid and we forgave the remaining seven-fifty. When other publishers did not jump at Emerson's memoir we chopped it up and used it for the CD booklet copy for a series of Cutler reissues. I even got the label to pay us an extra twenty-five thousand for Emerson's extensive notes.

When his literary sabbatical in the Caribbean was over, Emerson showed up at my office to ruin everyone's afternoon. He hated the new publicity photo the record company had sent over.

"Who told this girl she was a photographer?" he asked the whole office staff, waving the offending picture at two interns who were alphabetizing invoices. "My eyes look like I'd been up for two days, the cheeks look like I have an abscess, and my skin tone is all bleached out and spotty. Why does this keep happening? Can no one take a picture anymore?"

I whispered to my assistant Judy to go to the files and pull out the shoot we did three or four years ago with the Dutch fellow. I assured her that we had never used any of those, go take a look.

She did and—did I know my boy?—Emerson loved them.

"This is more like it!" he said loudly. "Where did you get these, Jack?"

"Ah, we did them when you were in the UK last year. Took a while to get the prints in. You want to give these to the label instead?"

"Hell, yes! Look at them! There's no comparison! The crap they sent over is like a bad Polaroid. These here are proper photography! Why did we never use them?"

"Umm, I think we were going to save them for the tour book and then we went with live shots instead. So we go with these?"

"You shouldn't even have to ask, man! These are great shots!"

The interns all nodded. Everyone in the office agreed with Em. He reacted as we all hoped—he said good-bye and went away.

I then explained the way the world worked to my assistant Judy:

"Take these photographs he just rejected and file them away. In five years he will love them. He hated those Dutch shots when I showed them to him four years ago. There is a fifty-month lag between what Emerson looks like and what Emerson thinks he looks like. When his appearance has deteriorated some more, he'll think the ones he hates today are wonderful photos."

Judy said, "So it's like planting potatoes?"

"That's right, we bury our seeds with faith in the eventual harvest."

Emerson was supposed to be working on a new album. He had fallen into the thrall of a super-synthesizer called a Synclavier, which allowed him to record and play back any sound on all the notes of a piano keyboard. He could load tubas, French horns, or the honking of geese into this digital treasure trunk, along with Jimi Hendrix's guitar, Buddy Rich's snare drum, and the basses of Charles Mingus, Jaco Pastorius, and the London Symphony. The Synclavier gave Emerson access to any sound he could imagine and allowed him to make his records right in the machine. He spent hours locked in the studio he had erected in his SoHo loft, examining the sonic possibilities of adding Charlie Parker's saxophone to chords harmonized from his own whistling.

Lost as he was in the endless audio possibilities, Emerson was not writing any new songs. He had begun collaborating with various sidemen and studio musicians in a fashion that I conceded was brilliant in its cunning.

Emerson would invite players over to jam and record their improvisations on his Synclavier. Afterward he would listen to what they had played, until he found a riff or groove that he liked. He would loop that into something resembling the verses of a song and match it with the bed for a chorus, although at this point there was no melody and no words.

Then Emerson would invite some other musicians over—single-note musicians now, saxophone or lead guitar or even flute players—to solo over the rhythm sections he had assembled. When they went home, he dredged their improvisations until he found something that struck him as usable for a vocal melody. He would appropriate that melody, perhaps modifying it as he proceeded, and sing it over his track with nonsense syllables until a song began to take shape.

By now he would have some little lyrical phrase, a cliché from everyday speech, which he would repeat in the chorus: "Keep it up" or

"Don't be a stranger" or "Just say no" or, on one occasion, "Workers of the world unite."

Here is where the crafty crossed over to the nefarious. Emerson would construct a demo of him singing nonsense verses with a two- or three-word hook and send that to the English professor sister of one of his girlfriends, who it turned out knew how to turn a phrase and had a head full of romantic poetry. Emerson would tell her, "Here's a song I'm working on, got any ideas for lyrics?"

The lady professor would send back reams of poetry, some of it original and some sampled from the masters, all of whom rested in the public domain.

From this, Emerson would put together what he passed off as an original song. He would offer his "co-lyricist" 10 percent of the publishing or a flat fee. If he felt that his appropriation of the main melody line was so blatant that the soloist who actually came up with it might notice, he would instruct me to cut him in, too. In the end, Emerson would have 70 or 80 percent ownership of a song to which he had contributed two or three words.

While I admired his industry, I had to ask him if it would not be easier to simply pick up his guitar and write some new songs from scratch.

"That's old thinking, Flynn," he told me. "You don't expect the sculptor to mine the marble. Anyway, as soon as I pick up a guitar I'm a victim of muscle memory. My hands go to the same places, make the same chords, I write the same old song over and over. This frees me up to explore new areas. Every creative person benefits from bouncing ideas off other artists."

"Sure, Emerson, but you're not really collaborating, are you? You're editing a lot of other people's ideas together. You're just keeping them all in separate rooms so they don't realize that you're not really doing anything."

I had intended this to sound joshing. Emerson and I had been together so long that I sometimes made the mistake of thinking that if we both knew something, it was all right to say it out loud.

"Not doing anything?" His eyes darkened. "Really, Jack? You think I'm not doing anything? Gee, must break your heart to take fifteen percent of *nothing*."

I told him I was only joking but he was off, the werewolf was out.

"Fucking sycophants! All around me. Critics! Who wrote these songs, then, Jack? The poetry teacher? She only put words from an old book to the melody I supplied her! The fucking flute player who tooted along to a riff I played him? The nitwit session musicians who came in here and played bad funk for two hours? Which of them could have written this song, Jack? Hmm? Oh, I know—none of them! Only I could have done it! Only I spotted the ten seconds in a fucking eight-minute sax solo that might with work and polish and digital modulation be turned into a singable melody! But I guess to you that's nothing. I guess to you an artist is someone who sits under a tree in the garden waiting for the apple of inspiration to fall on his head and then runs inside to write it all down before the fleeting glimpse passes back into the ether. And then, of course, he goes and lies down with a towel on his dainty brow while his fucking manager comes and peels off a fat percentage for the effort of taking it to town!"

He fell into a chair sulking. I waited fifteen seconds and then said, "Gee, Emerson, did I tell you your hair looks terrific?"

Who do you suppose had introduced Emerson to the Synclavier?
Why, it was that maven of modernity Danny Finnerty, who had maneuvered his experience working with the new technology department of a record company into a position of real power in the corporation. Fin was lucky enough to be sitting at the right desk when CD sales exploded. Because it was his department, he got credit for an influx of income that would have happened even if the desk had been empty. Big corporations do not worry about such things. They promote the fellow who brought in the most money. Fin was the right man in the right place at the right time.

Newly flush, Fin had invited Emerson to stop by the National Association of Music Merchants trade show in Anaheim, California, to receive an award that Fin had cooked up, and to see how new technology was going to revolutionize everything from the way music was recorded to how it was distributed.

First Fin flabbergasted Emerson with an exhibition of new MIDI technology, which allowed a musician to use his personal computer as a recording studio, to input all sorts of sounds and instruments and sync them together as if by magic.

What flabbergasted me was how Fin was dressed. Once a long-haired leisure-suited dandy, Fin was now dressed in a red track suit with black piping, Adidas sneakers (untied), a silly fur hat that looked like he had swiped it from a Russian grandmother, and what appeared to be a Mercedes hood ornament on a silver chain around his neck. When he smiled, he exposed a gold tooth.

I knew that Fin had been using his authority within the record label to advocate for signing rap acts, but I was not aware until I saw him that he had taken to dressing as an Apache to go among the Indians.

Emerson was dismissive of rap music, certain it was a fad that would quickly fade. The evening we arrived in Anaheim, Fin insisted we visit a small studio nearby so he could show us how rap records were put together. We imagined driving into some ghetto, but it was nothing like that. We went to a factory district that reminded me a bit of where the Ravons used to rehearse in London. Several young men, black, white, and Latino, greeted Fin with hugs and invited us inside.

The studio was, to us, all control room. In the outer room where the band would usually gather there was only an empty drum booth and a closed piano. The engineers went about their business like NASA scientists, sampling sounds, recited rhymes, and music pulled from a stack of vinyl records and mixing and altering them all in the first Synclavier we had ever seen. Emerson was like a little boy spying his first electric train. Fin handed Emerson an acoustic guitar and asked him to play something. Emerson gave him a little blues lick. Fin's scientists synchronized it so it came back four times in a row, over three different beats, and then began altering its pitch and key. Before we left California, Emerson had ordered two Synclaviers, on which I have no doubt Fin took some sort of commission.

The next morning we went back to the trade show where Emerson was to receive his award. On the way over, Fin mentioned that Emerson was expected to say a few words of acceptance. Emerson had nothing prepared. Fin pulled out a two-page speech he had taken the liberty of composing and typing up. When we arrived, Fin installed Emerson in a backstage greenroom with wine and cookies. I wandered out into the hall in which a thousand people were waiting. A poster mounted on an easel read, *10 A.M.–KEYNOTE ADDRESS by legendary rock guitar legend EMERSON CUTLER.*

Fuckin' Fin, I thought, never misses a scam. There was no sense upsetting Emerson, we'd play it out. Emerson came onstage after a long introduction of Fin by one of the NAMM organizers and a shorter introduction by Fin of Emerson. Emerson gave the speech Fin had written for him to the assembled guitar manufacturers, drum makers, recording studio personnel, and musical instrument shop owners. When it was over Emerson posed for photographs with the event organizers, who told him what a thrill his appearance was for all these music lovers who adored him.

That turned out to be half true. What most of the attendees really
wanted was to force Emerson to take their demo tapes and résumés
in the hopes that they could join his band. He was already sorry to be
there when we found out that Fin had also booked a special NAMM
concert performance by himself and Charlie. Emerson walked into the
trade show expecting to pick up a gong and shake some hands. Instead
he was very nearly waylaid into a Ravons reunion. I pulled him out of
there with a lame excuse. Let them say that the artist wanted to play
with his old mates but the greedy manager stepped in and stopped it.
Like many explorers in Indian territory, we had walked into an ambush.

After that I thought Emerson would never speak to Fin again, but
within a couple of weeks he was calling him at all hours to ask for help
making sense of his Synclavier.

What I took away from the event, aside from a vow never to trust
Danny Finnerty again, was the sheer audacity of his dressing like a hip-
hopper.

"Fin," I had said when I first saw him, "why are you dressed like
2 Live Crew? You're a forty-year-old white boy from New Jersey. If
you can't act your age, at least act your ethnicity."

"You're gettin' old, Flynn," he told me. He turned to high-five a
passing brother and asked the man if he had any weed by saying, "Yo,
my glaucoma's acting up! You help me?"

The African-American musician said he might know a man who
was holding, at which point his girlfriend berated him for making a
drug deal in a public place with a bunch of old white men.

Fin stepped in between the unfortunate couple to explain to her,
"Listen, sweetheart, if your man ain't cheatin' on you and your man
ain't beatin' on you, he's a good brother—cut him some slack."

I have been witness to a lot of embarrassing moments in my career in popular music, but that was top three of all time. Not for Fin,
though. He sailed happily on as the offended woman dragged her boyfriend away from us.

"Come on, Fin," I said to him. "I appreciate you're making money
off this but we've known each other for twenty years. You're not going
to tell me you really like rap music."

"Jack," he said earnestly, "I'm a drummer, remember? My whole life has been spent with rhythm! Do I like what's going on now a *lot* more than I liked tapping along to would-be Dan Fogelbergs? Of course I do!"

I said to him, "But it's not really music, is it? I mean, someone puts on an old record and someone else talks over it. I suppose that could be a kind of art if the lyrics were any good but they're about at the level of *The Cat in the Hat,* with obscenities."

"Ah, you are too old for me to talk to, Flynn," Fin insisted. "Drop your teeth in a jar and say good night."

"Look, this Synclavier, this sampler you've got Emerson sold on. All it is, is an elaborate, very expensive tape recorder. You call it sampling, I call it stealing."

"What do you think the trumpet player said when he saw the first piano, Jack? Really. Think back to the powdered wig days, when you were a boy. 'This is not a musical instrument! You don't blow in it, you don't bow it, you don't pluck it—you just touch your little finger and the note comes out! What artistry is there in *that*? It's so easy! The notes are all lined up for you! Any monkey could make music on one of those!' Right? I mean, what's a piano but a machine that puts all the notes at your fingertips? What's a sampler but a piano for the twentieth century?"

Fin always had his rap down. Now he had it down in the service of rappers. Soon he would be chasing something else. I was tired of listening to him, I wanted to get out of there, but he launched into a speech with the closest I ever saw him come to genuine passion.

"People tell you that rock and roll was the big revolution in popular music in this century, Flynn, but it's not true. Rock and roll was just a shift in technology, from acoustic to electric instruments. Rock and roll was just jump blues with an electric guitar taking over for the horn section. It was technological and it was economical—suddenly a four-piece band could make as much noise as a big band. It was cheaper, that's why it caught on.

"The real revolution came before rock and roll. It was when swing came in, when big bands and jungle rhythms replaced a ponce with oil in his hair singing 'Bicycle Built for Two.' European music was all about melody and harmony. African music was all about rhythm. European America in the early twentieth century was sitting around the piano singing 'I Dream of Jeannie with the Light Brown Hair.' Rhythm hardly even came into it. Rhythm was a slight technical concern, like intonation. It was all melody and harmony.

"Now comes Prohibition, the Roaring Twenties, black populations moving up from the plantations to work in the cities, that African rhythm starts catching on across the railroad tracks, across the rope line, across the *No Colored Allowed* signs. White kids start diggin' that rhythm. Radio comes in, no one can tell what color the musician is. Depression, Duke Ellington—what did they call it? Jungle music. Jungle rhythms. Duke Ellington is the most sophisticated composer America ever produced but to the white audience, that shit is African. Scary. Picture cats with spears and bones through their noses. Kids like it, though. So they try to white it up, promote Benny Goodman, Glenn Miller. Kids know the difference. They want to hear Duke, they want to hear Basie.

"Now, all through this, what's getting bigger and bigger? The rhythm. So what's getting squeezed to make room for more rhythm? The melody. Duke leads to Louis Jordan. Simplified, funny lyrics. Harmony shrinks so the beat gets bigger. Louis Jordan, he is rock and roll, but no one calls it that until Chuck Berry plugs in an electric guitar and starts playing those horn lines through an amplifier. You English kids, you know all you did was whiten up Chuck Berry and sell it back to the little girls as something safe with cute boys in matching suits and bowl haircuts. But the music keeps moving, the rhythm gets bigger, the harmony gets smaller until you hit on James Brown.

"James Brown! Holy smoke! This guy plays one chord for a whole song, but the rhythms are outrageous. He's got different beats laying on top of each other, shifting around, kicking up against the groove, laying in opposition to each other, blending and breaking apart and coming back together. And melody? James is so far beyond melody. He's grunting—he's shouting—he's threatening—'Get up! Get on the good foot! Say it loud, I'm black and I'm proud!' That's it, Flynn. That's the revolution right there. James Brown is the start of funk, James Brown is the start of rap. James Brown is more important to the development of modern music than every British band put together, no offense meant.

"Rap is the logical continuation of James Brown's innovation. Let's grind that rhythm down to pure power—let's not just play drums and bass, let's play steam shovels and pistons and turntables and pile drivers. Let's play bombs going off and gunshots in the middle of the night. Let's play reality. And let's make the voice a percussive instrument, too.

"So you see, Flynn, when you ask me if I really like rap, that just tells me that you missed the point of this whole long experiment we call twentieth-century popular music. The European values have been on the wane since 1918. The African values have been expanding since the doughboys drove the Kaiser out of France. You might not like it, that's your business. But if you're going to try to continue to work in rock and roll it would probably do you good to at least attempt to understand it."

I had never seen this side of Fin before. I suppose one should not be surprised to learn that a man has some passion driving his life's work, but I admit that in Fin's case it had never occurred to me to consider it. I was impressed, but I was not about to tell him.

Instead I said, "Be that as it may, man, the gold tooth looks ridiculous."

The compact disc tide lifted all boats in the second half of the 1980s. The baby boom, that swollen pig in the demographic python, bought all their albums a second time and labels, music publishers, and even musicians enjoyed the rewards.

By the end of the decade, though, CD sales were leveling out and everyone looked for new sources of income. Here we entered the heyday of the box set—fat anthologies of the recorded work of heritage artists annotated with thick booklets and packaged to sit proudly on the bookshelf.

Charlie and Simon were anxious for Emerson to allow the compilation of a Ravons box, buying the band a bit of the historical respect they felt they deserved and putting some cash into their pockets. No part of me looked forward to shoveling through the load of legal entanglements, paperwork, and old licenses such an undertaking would require, and Emerson was indifferent to what he saw as a minor and juvenile corner of his oeuvre. But I knew that Charlie and Simon needed the money, so I pushed it through.

It has been, as I write this, seventeen years. I am still waiting for a thank-you.

The immediate problem with compiling a Ravons box was that the Ravons only ever made three rather short LPs and a few loose singles. Those fans who cared already had them, probably in several formats. We needed rare and unreleased material, demo tapes, and remixes.

Emerson said he had nothing. Simon had a couple of turgid and badly recorded demos that he claimed were made for the Ravons but which I was sure came from the Blue Moon era. Simon did offer to remix some of the tracks, which resulted in his raising the levels on his bass throughout and, according to those with keener ears than mine, also overdubbing unwanted extra instruments.

It was Charlie who hit the treasure trove, coming up with a shoe box full of cassettes of what he swore were early Ravons demos. I had not only not heard most of the songs, I had never heard of them. There were at least five titles we had to register for publishing for the first time, which caused headaches because if they were written in the midsixties they were owed to the estate of Dennis Towsy rather than to Charlie's current music publisher.

"How come you fellas never cut these songs in the sixties?" I asked Charlie. "Some of them are better than a lot you did put out."

"Ah, who remembers, Jack?" Charlie said. "Everything was movin' so fast. I think these were written just before the group broke up. They were intended for the fourth album that never happened. We might even have played some of them in America on that last tour, after Emerson was gone."

"I take it, then, Emerson is not included in the composing credits?"

"Ah, not that I recall, Jack. No. No. Now that you mention it, I'm sure I wrote these right around the time Emerson split, so he would not have had a hand in them."

"And Simon?"

"Well, Simon played on them, but no, I think by that point we were all writing separately."

"Um-hum. I guess that means more money for you, then."

"Well, I would have liked to have kept the band together and all of us stick as a three-way. Emerson was the one who broke it up, not me. He's a tight old bastard but I can't imagine he'd want a piece of songs he didn't write."

"No," I said, "of course not. Tell me this, Charlie. Did they have synth pads back in '69? Because my ears, and more to the point my engineer, tell me there is a faint synth pad under the acoustic guitar on this song 'Wake Up and Apologize.'"

Charlie looked at me with a cracked half grin. "Ah, that ain't a synth pad, that's just a bit of old Hammond organ under there. I think Simon played it."

"Charlie, I'm not going to bust you. When did you record these songs? Really?"

"Found 'em in an old shoe box, Jack."

"Yeah, well, when did you put them in that old shoe box?"

"My mind gets foggy after all these years."

"Yeah, yeah. Keep up that act, Brando. We have enough material for a box set. That's the important thing."

"You think I could get a little advance on the advance, Jack?"

"From who?"

"From you, mate. The money all comes through your office, don't it?"

"Not yet it don't. Anyway, I'm not your manager anymore. Ask Melissa the dog trainer."

"I'm afraid Melissa and I have split, Jack. If you sleep with your manager you'll ruin two good relationships. That's why I never sleep with you."

"How did you blow this one, Casanova?"

"She became great with child."

"That's not funny, Charlie. I hope you were a gentleman."

"You bet I was! I stepped aside. Her husband is over the moon."

"Melissa is married?"

"I told you that."

"You didn't. So she's having your baby and her old man thinks it's his."

"You can see why we both thought it best to reconsider our business partnership."

"I don't know how you get away with it."

"I'm in the market for new management, Jack. What do you say? Want me to take you back?"

"Do I get to commission these new songs?"

"Hell, no, man, those go back to before I retained you."

And so I was Charlie's manager again. Given that he had almost no work and very little money, it was not a gig I took for the revenue.

Soon after I reenlisted, Charlie went behind my back and did the one thing I had always begged him not to do. He took advantage of the hype around the release of the Ravons' box set to sell his share of the Ravons' publishing to the sheet music company April-Blackwood. Having already sold Emerson his record royalties and rights to the Ravons' name, he had now cashed in all that remained of his future Ravons income.

When I found out—and not from him, by the way; April-Blackwood notified the record company that they were due payments for the box set—I was furious.

"Bad enough for yourself that you did it, Charlie," I shouted down the phone. "But if you were going to be stupid enough to sell off your future in the band, why did you not at least come to me and offer to sell to Emerson? He'd have paid you whatever April-Blackwood paid you and at least the band's rights would have remained with the band!"

"Ah, Jack," Charlie said, "you'd have just talked me out of it. We both know that. Anyway, Emerson has enough."

Charlie sold those rights for $200,000. If he had hung on to them another fifteen years, he would have earned five times that. I eventually acquired the rights Charlie had sold to April-Blackwood for Emerson for three times what April-Blackwood paid. Charlie had again sold himself too cheap.

Simon had written a good song. It was titled "Evangeline," and although he had not yet recorded it, whenever he performed it in concert his audience rose to their feet and held up matches and lighters like they were all auditioning to replace the Statue of Liberty. It had a two-steps-down, one-step-up melody that stuck in the head and it kept coming around to a majestic refrain: "In a smoke-stained world, I'm just making out, I'm just making out."

Although the song plodded like the rest of Simon's repertoire, it had advantages over his other tunes. First, the title was a girl's name—so even though the lyrics were obscure there was some suggestion of human interaction and emotional connection. Second, the recurring refrain induced the audience to sing along; Simon's stuff did not usually invite participation. "Evangeline" was by Simon's standoffish standard inclusive. Third, the audience liked singing "I'm just making out," both as a declaration of endurance and a celebration of sexual foreplay.

The song went over so well that Simon started performing it twice at each show—two-thirds of the way through as a change of pace from his bombastic catalog, and again during the encore as a torch-lit valedictory.

My trouble was that big new song or not, no established record label wanted to give Simon a contract. He had been signed to five different companies over the preceding fifteen years, the last three had lost money on him, and every one of the five had found working with him to be a miserable experience. I was unable to find a label at which Simon had not personally insulted at least one executive. He was to my knowledge the only artist who had been asked by Amnesty International to stop speaking out for them. Each time he did, they lost members.

It was 1989 and Simon's brand of progressive paleo-metal was not only out of fashion, it was out of the last four fashions. Combined with his enormous personal dislikability, it meant that one good song was not going to be enough to hoist Simon back into the big league. More than a couple of the A&R men to whom I pitched it enjoyed telling me so.

"Struck out again, man," I told Simon after a third try to convince Emerson's label to cut me a favor. "We may just have to do a one-off singles deal with that Manchester indie I told you about. There are potential advantages. If the song hits you can write your own ticket."

Simon's voice came back from the speaker box on my desk.

"Bullshit, Flynn! They are a novelty label! Have you heard the crap they put out? I am an album artist. This song must anchor a full-length CD. If they cannot hear that, then they really are as pathetic as the dismal state of the charts suggests."

"We're running out of options, squire," I suggested. "There is the notion of adding 'Evangeline' as a bonus track to a best-of collection. Rhino expressed interest, if they can clear the rest of the catalog."

"I am not ready to be remaindered or retrospected into oblivion, Flynn. Thanks for your faith in me."

He hung up. I ordered lunch. God deliver us from old friends fallen on hard times.

Nine days later he called me back. "Flynn! We have a record deal!"

"Do we?"

"Don't worry. You'll still get your commission. I have been approached by a German businessman named Gunter Kempner. He has big money behind him. He and his partners want to get into the music business. They are starting a record company and they are fans of mine. They offered me a stake in their new label as well as a two-hundred-thousand-pound advance and recording budget to be their vanguard artist."

It sounded improbable to me but not impossible. There was a tradition of wealthy continentals, often the children of aristocrats, spending their way into show business. Daddy usually turned off the credit card eventually. Still, Simon had no other offers.

"Sounds promising," I told him. "You want me to check out these Krauts for you? Read through the contracts?"

"I need you here, Flynn, actually," Simon said like an admiral ordering a midshipman to the wheelhouse. "Gunter is hosting a dinner party for me Saturday evening at which you and I can talk through the deal points and impress his investors."

Bloody hell, I thought, it's already Tuesday. "Not sure I can make it to London this weekend, Simon," I said. "Lots going on here."

"It's Labor Day in America isn't it, Flynn? Nothing's going on. Listen, old chum, you're my manager, aren't you? You spent the last year unsuccessfully trying to get me a new deal. Now I have come up with one on my own. I need you here."

I have never had the aplomb to tell any of my clients to blow it out their buttocks. He had me. He knew it. I booked my flight.

Gunter Kempner's flat was south of the Thames, in Greenwich, close to the *Cutty Sark* and Greenwich Observatory and overlooking the campus of stone buildings that housed British Naval Intelligence. It was an unusual place for a German businessman to set up housekeeping, far from the city's financial center and even farther from the chic London nightclub neighborhoods where wealthy immigrants usually settled.

I walked along a row of brick walls until I came to an arched doorway and pressed the buzzer. I was invited to climb to the third floor, where I was greeted by a bleached blond butler dressed in a purple sport jacket with the sleeves pushed up to his elbows.

"Hullo!" he called out happily in an Eastern accent. "You must be Jackie Flynn! You look just like Simon's stories!"

I stepped inside. The happy servant had a thin mustache bleached to match his hair. He took my coat and offered me wine. I could see past him through a wallpapered parlor into a large formal dining room with a mahogany table big enough to host an armistice. The walls of that room were wood-paneled, deep brown, and decorated at every join with carefully carved flowers blooming out of cresting waves. The flat was enormous. It took up the entire third floor of a large Edwardian townhouse.

I followed the butler through the dining room into a library dominated by upholstered love seats and a four-foot-around wooden globe of the earth resting on its axis in a half-moon cradle. Three men stood there chatting in German. Simon was not among them.

"Hello," I said, "I'm Jack Flynn."

A very tall man with a long face and a high forehead stopped talking and shifted his eyes to a small, moon-faced fellow, who also clammed up. The third man had his back to me. He wore a striped sport shirt that showed off broad shoulders and a wasp waist. He turned and looked at me. He had a boxer's face, not unhandsome but with scars above the eyes and a nose that had been broken and reset. He wore a flattop crew cut that descended unexpectedly into long side-burns that looked painted on. He spoke to me past a cigarette fixed to his lower lip.

"Famous Jack Flynn, welcome! I am Gunter. This is Horst and Maynard."

The other two men nodded and protected their drinks.

"Nice to see you all," I said. "Great place, Gunter. You been here long?"

"Simon is not with you, Jack? I thought you would come together."

"I came straight from Heathrow, told him I'd meet him here."

"Very good. We'll have a chance to get familiar. You met Leon?"

I was unsure who Leon was. The bleached butler sidled up to me.

"Hello," I said.

"Party, party, party," Leon said, giggling and topping off my drink. He skittered away.

"Old family retainer?" I asked.

"Leon keeps everything running," Gunter explained. His eyes followed the butler, who was no more than thirty. I reckoned Gunter to be ten years older than that, almost my age. Leon wore a tight black cashmere jumper with a V-neck under his purple jacket. He was shorter than Gunter, but like him had the physique of a bodybuilder.

A cathedral doorbell gonged and I heard Simon's deep voice greeting Leon.

"They've all arrived, then? Flynn, too? Lead on, Leon." He was, for Simon, in a jolly mood.

There was the requisite conviviality over drinks and then Leon tinkled a bell and told us dinner was ready. We ate what seemed like acres of venison and drank buckets of red wine. Gunter held forth at length on the business openings available with the new perestroika between East and West, and there was an extended dialogue between Gunter and Simon over whether the progressive opportunities offered by Mr. Gorbachev would be embraced by the new American President George Herbert Walker Bush. I was buzzing from wine and jet lag. I let Simon chatter on.

"At least that right-wing imbecile Reagan is out of office," Simon announced. "Not that Bush is much better. He ran the CIA, you know. I have been told he had something to do with the Kennedy assassination but we'll never prove it."

The Germans did not rise to the bait. Gunter said evenly, "Reagan turned out to not be so bad. Like many provincials, he matured when he ventured into the wider world and saw that other nations were not devils with horns. The Soviets like Bush. He understands that it is in both sides' interests to allow commerce between the two spheres."

"You are an optimist," Simon said.

"No, I think I am a realist," our host replied. "The ideologues of both sides are very old now and dying. The new generation is not married to political purity. Everyone wants to make a little money and be secure."

"Well, here's to artistic purity," Simon said, standing and raising his glass. "May music raise a bridge between adversaries!"

I am sure he did not intend to say "raise" a bridge but everyone was too tipsy to notice, except perhaps Gunter, who seemed unaffected by the wine. He smiled and closed his eyes and nodded agreement. Leon the butler had joined us at the table and was flitting and giggling like a girl. He was extravagantly gay, which made me wonder about the true nature of his relationship with his austere boss.

Over dessert and schnapps, Leon began to reminisce about his boyhood in what sounded like an Arcadian idyll of horseback riding, ski vacations, and summers on lakefront estates. By the time he recounted harp recitals in a marble ballroom, the two of us were sprawled on a plush love seat and I had moved beyond ordinary drunkenness toward an almost psychedelic level of inebriation.

"Did you grow up in a family of servants, Leon?" I asked him.

He laughed. "Oh God, no! It was my grandfather's estate. My father left us when I was very young and I grew up with my mother and my aunts in Grandpapa's house."

This confounded me. "So, pardon my rudeness, you come from money?"

Leon murmured and looked across the room to make sure Gunter was not listening. "We were taught to never speak of our advantages."

"Forgive my asking, but if that's the case, then why do you choose to work as a butler?"

"I grew up surrounded by servants, Jackie. It's the only job I know how to do."

It took a lot of booze for me to buy that explanation. In times to come, Simon and I would have occasion to look back and speculate about the true nature of Gunter and Leon's relationship. Every time we thought we had it worked out, we would stumble on some indication that we were exactly wrong.

There were many tipsy nights at Gunter's while Simon recorded his new album on the German's budget and we laid plans for the launch and promotion of both Simon's CD and the new label, which would be called Hidden Records. Simon lobbied strenuously to call the new company Schadenfreude Music, but Gunter explained that he was interested in making inroads in England and eventually America and did not wish to emphasize the German financing of the new venture.

The recording went very quickly, as Simon had worked up the material with his road band and wished to spend as little time as possible in the studio so that he could pocket the rest of his advance. Leon kept the wine flowing as we interviewed local publicists and promo men and assembled a team who promised to make sure Gunter's investment resulted in a top ten album. There was a belief abroad in the British music industry that the old multinational labels were too big to respond to the quick and fluid tastes of the English record-buying public. The energy was all with the indies now. Hidden Records was going to plug into that current.

One evening when we had swallowed half of Gunter's wine cellar and everyone else was in the parlor smoking and listening to rough mixes, I elected to make the grand gesture of clearing the table for Leon. The butler was with the guests, dancing to Simon's latest. I took a tray from the kitchen and gathered up our glasses, stealing a sip or two from the dregs. When I came to Gunter's glass I saw that it was still full. I tipped it toward my lips and nothing came out. I tipped it back. Nothing.

I held out the glass and studied it. Gunter had been drinking from a trick goblet, the kind you might find in a joke shop. A red liquid sat locked between two thin layers of glass. It appeared from the outside to be full of red wine and when you tilted it the liquid moved as if it were emptying, but when you set it down it returned to its original filled position.

I put the trick goblet on the tray and continued to pile up glasses and dishes. Leon swanned into the room and said, "Jackie Flynn, don't touch a thing!" He almost shoved me aside. I had offended him. He piled as much as he could onto the tray and charged into the kitchen.

I said nothing to Simon about any of this. It was he who raised suspicions to me.

"Do you think Gunter and Leon are spies?" he asked me one night when we were driving back from the recording studio.

"What makes you think so?" I asked.

"Well, you know—I'm not sure they're really gay."

"I don't know about Gunter," I said. "Leon's fruity as a mango farm."

"He acts so, doesn't he?" Simon said. "You remember Philip Keefe, my friend from school? He's bent as a periscope. I invited him over to Gunter's thinking they might hit it off and he got a very weird vibe from Leon. I thought it might be that Gunter and Leon are monogamous and saw Phil as a home wrecker but he said it wasn't that at all. Phil thinks they are straight men passing as gay."

"Why?" I asked.

"Because they're spies! You know, one or the other of them is always going on weekend trips to Germany."

"Well, they are German."

"But they often come back beat up, with bruises and bandages. Once Leon was gone for days and when I saw him again he had stitches in his forehead."

"Rough trade?"

"It would be a great cover, wouldn't it? Two men living together, very fit, coming and going at odd hours, secretive, flying all over, cuts and bruises. Well, if they're gay—that explains it."

I was accustomed to brushing off Simon's conspiracy theories, but this one intrigued me. I had not told him that I thought I had seen Leon through a taxi window, late one night in Soho, negotiating with a prostitute. The cab had moved on before I could be certain and, of course, I might have misunderstood what I saw. I would continue to keep it to myself.

"Why the record label, then?" I asked Simon.

"Flynn! What a perfect cover! Music executives! They go everywhere, they hire planes, they move big freight cases of gear across international borders . . . think of it. Perfect cover for secret agents."

"Do you think they are ours or theirs?"

"How do you mean?"

"They're Germans, Simon. Are they East or West? KGB or CIA?"

"No way to tell, is there?"

"They have digs near Naval Intelligence. Suggests they are ours."

"Unless they're spying on us."

I had been associating with Simon too long. My mind was beginning to run down the paths of paranoia he treaded.

"You really worried about this? You want me to get you out of the record deal?"

Simon was shocked. "Are you joking? If it's CIA or MI6 or flipping KGB, do you know how much money they have? Infinite resources, Flynn! Unsupervised budgets! Columbia Records in its heyday did not have expense accounts like this!" He leaned in to my ear and whispered, "I hear that the CIA has their own mint. They just print as many dollars as they need. I want to take full advantage of this. I've never had a proper promo budget."

Simon had political principles but his main creed was that virtue lay in whatever advanced the work of Simon and its just compensation.

When Simon's album was almost finished and I had helped Gunter hire the staff he needed for Hidden Records and we had retained publicity and promotion professionals, I went back to New York to renegotiate Emerson's recording contract. I promised to return to London for the launch party and release of Simon's album and the public debut of Hidden Records.

When the big night came I was there, in a hotel ballroom south of Hyde Park with two hundred socialites, disc jockeys, journalists, and models. Leon was in his full glory, dressed head to toe in gold with his hair ascending into an inflated pompadour. Gunter and his unseen partners must have spent a hundred thousand pounds on the party, which climaxed with Simon standing on the bar to make a speech about showing the old brontosaurs of the major labels the doorway to extinction. He thanked no one and cued up the first public play of his new album, which he had titled *Karma Suit Ya*.

It sounded great in the room. In my experience it always sounds great in the room. Everyone's drunk and stuffing their faces with free food. There are beautiful women and big speakers pushed up too loud. At the expensive party, the record always sounds like a hit.

And sure enough, *Karma Suit Ya* entered the charts the following week at number twenty-eight. A nice start. Gunter toasted Simon with his magic goblet and they made bets on whether it would go straight to number one or linger awhile in the top ten before the single release of the undeniable "Evangeline" pushed it to pole position.

I was back in New York when the screaming started. In its second week, Simon's album did a reverse backflip down to number seventy-seven. By week three, it was gone. I flew back to London and Gunter's apartment in Greenwich.

When I got there, the Germans were standing over Simon like interrogators in Stalag 17, telling him that while the album was dead in the UK, it was showing life in Germany, Austria, and Eastern Europe. Simon had to pack his suitcase and get over there and promote it.

It was not an unreasonable demand, but Simon—his eyes so recently fixed on triumph at home—had fallen into a black mood that rendered him unwilling to work, play, or even hold a conversation. He was sunk on the sofa groaning while Gunter marched up and down the rug waving fistfuls of paper that enumerated the pounds spent on this project.

"My partners are out a lot of money, Simon," Gunter said like he had nothing to do with it. "They are not happy. They expect to see you working. This is no time for you to lie down and moan."

"The album's dead, man," Simon muttered. "Let's just let it go."

Gunter leaned in to Simon's face. "These guys don't let anything go, Simon. Someone fucks with their money, they take it back other ways." He raised his voice toward the kitchen. *"Isn't that right, Leon?"*

Leon entered the room carrying a tea service. His eyes were black and swollen, his upper lip was cut and scabbed, and he wore a bandage around his head like a bandanna.

"Cor, Leon, what happened to you?" I asked. Leon said nothing; he laid down the tea and went back to the kitchen.

"That was nothing, Simon!" Gunter shouted. "Leon they *like*. You they have no sympathy for. Now get up and go pack your bags, you're going to Romania."

"You better show me the itinerary, Gunter," I said. "I don't know who your partners are but if they know as little about booking a tour as they obviously do about releasing a record there's no reason for Simon to go play for them. Did you all think the pop business was easy? Did you think all you had to do was throw a little money around and hire some whores and bribe some radio stations and you'd establish yourselves as players? Now you're going to blame Simon? You heard the music, you said you loved it. Where were your critical faculties then, amateur? If you took money from the Mafia and gambled it on something you knew nothing about, that's your tough luck. It's not up to Simon to work off your debts."

Gunter straightened up and looked me in the eye. He was not

angry. He was remote. He said, "Don't bring the Mafia into this, this is nothing to do with any of that. You are right, this is my fuckup. But Simon is in it with me. He is contractually obligated to promote his album in all the territories where we release it. We can still make money in Eastern Europe. All of us. We need to show my backers good faith and that means Simon must live up to his contractual obligations."

I took the itinerary from him. I said, "I'll look this over. We will want to go with promoters we have worked with in the past, people we can trust to know what they are doing. No more dilettantes. Yes?"

"We want the same thing," Gunter told me.

"That," I said, "would surprise me very much. Come on, Simon."

I had a car waiting. I told Simon I could get him out of this, show a judge that Gunter had failed to live up to his professional obligations, make Simon look like a victim of incompetent foreigners stumbling into a business of which they were ignorant. He would not have to go on this tour.

"No, Jack," Simon said with a miserable determination. "I'm going to do the tour for them. I'm going to play every date. I don't want to have to lie awake nights waiting for Gunter or some spook to come through my window with a garrote."

"That's not going to happen, Simon," I told him.

"It's not just that. Jack, you said it yourself. No British or American label would sign me. I've had some good press with this record. That's something. If I pick a fight with the Germans now, if this ends up in court and we have to go public with what inexperienced suckers they were—where does that leave me? It makes me a laughingstock, doesn't it? It makes me out to be the old tosser who was so desperate he signed with a bunch of foreigners who don't know which side of the CD is up. I'd be finished, Jack. I'd be finished for good. No, look at this tour schedule and make it the best it can be and I'll go out and do it. I'll play wherever they want me to play, I'll do every local newspaper interview they can arrange, I'll shake hands, I'll pose for photographs, I'll visit radio stations. You set it up. I'm going to see this through."

There was no argument to make. Simon was right. He did not have to do this tour for the Germans but he had no place else to go, and if we went public with his humiliation there would be gloating among his many enemies. Simon was awful in many ways, but there was a grim nobility in his willingness to sacrifice his comfort for what he saw as the greater virtue of his art. In this he was unlike Emerson, for whom everything came easy and who therefore valued very little.

I spent the next two weeks on the phone with my contacts among local promoters and made sure that Simon would have clean accommodations, proper visas, a working van, and a couple of decent warm-up gigs in Oslo and Stockholm before he jumped the Iron Curtain to play the dates lined up for him by Gunter's dubious connections.

Gunter's itinerary looked like it had been lifted from Hitler's to-do list: Warsaw, Minsk, Brest, Budapest, Vienna, Prague, Belgrade, Bucharest, and Sarajevo. I consoled Simon that the middle part of the tour took him to three of the most magnificent cities in Europe, and the rest would be culturally stimulating. Perhaps this would not be so bad after all. The people of the Eastern Bloc were passionate rock fans, what with most of it having been proscribed by the Reds for so long. Now that Glasnost was leaking out, the lid on that passion was coming off. Simon might get in ahead of the stampede and put his stake in Eastern Europe early.

"I wish you would not use the phrase 'putting a stake in' until I get out the other side of Transylvania," he said. I could see that he was getting engaged. Simon's belief in his own great destiny was not long hindered by either adversity or reality.

"Why do we end the tour in Yugoslavia?" he wanted to know. "No one has ever heard of Sarajevo."

"It's a beautiful city," I told him. "A cradle of progressive attitudes where Serbs, Croats, and Muslims intermingle without prejudice."

"Why can't we end in Prague?"

"The truth, Simon? We can't end in Prague because Czechoslovakia is landlocked."

"Are we planning on swimming home?"

"I would like you to come out of this tour with some money. Sadly,

Eastern European currency is virtually without value in the West. Even if we get you a good fee, there is nowhere to spend it but in Eastern Europe. Therefore, when the tour ends in the relatively prosperous and liberal Yugoslavia, I have arranged for you to buy a boat."

"Flynn," Simon said, "I don't want a boat."

"Nor shall you keep it. Bear with me on this, Simon. If you come back through Heathrow with a suitcase full of rubles and dinars, you will be lucky to exchange it for enough quid to pay your taxi fare home from the airport. Within Eastern Europe, however, you will be holding a tidy sum. Therefore, when the tour is over the two of us will spend a couple of days in the beautiful and historic city of Dubrovnik on the coast of the Adriatic. While there, we will take delivery of a beautiful double-masted sailboat built by the craftsmen of Montenegro. We will pay them with your tour earnings and then sail that schooner across to Italy, where we will sell it. You will thus return from your travels with your knapsack stuffed not with worthless communist currency but with good Italian lire, which you will bring to the bank and magically transform into even better British pounds. That is why we are ending your tour in Yugoslavia."

Simon stared at me. He said, "Did you think this up?"

"It's been done before. The Italians have a regular business in buying up pleasure craft from across the Adriatic. It's a semi-secret currency exchange that benefits both sides without fucking up the Cold War. Obviously it's not the kind of thing to which anyone wants to draw attention. Word of it gets in the papers and there will be shoes banging on rostrums at the UN and American PT boats patrolling the straits off Venice."

Simon grunted. "Mustn't scare the gondoliers."

"Quite right. You in?"

"We'll sing some chanteys as we sail."

"Quite right."

Simon set off for the East with an Irish road manager and a cut-rate band of only a guitarist and drummer. Economics had induced him to try rocking out with a power trio. I made the shows in Oslo and Stockholm, which were successful enough considering there seemed to be no women in the halls. Simon had always done well in the Nordic countries. His music went over best in places with high rates of alcoholism and suicide. I said good-bye to him and his small crew as he shipped off to Poland, where Gunter had promised to be waiting.

I went back to America for twelve days to deal with my other business while Simon rocked beneath the hammer and sickle. When I rendezvoused with him again it was in Czechoslovakia and his luck had run out. We met at the mellifluously named Hotel Rott, just off Prague's Old Town Square where the ancient Astronomical Clock tolled the noon hour while a procession of clockwork replicas of the twelve apostles rolled around on hidden levers and gears.

"I hate that clock," Simon told me by way of greeting. Simon's threshold for hatred was very low, but this seemed extreme even for him.

"How can you hate a mechanical marvel of the medieval world?" I asked him as he slumped into the only good chair in my room and lit a cigarette.

"Have you gone and looked at it, Flynn?"

"I just got here, Simon. I have unzipped neither my suitcase nor my pants to pee. What insult am I missing?"

"It is not just the twelve apostles who march out of that clock. There are also figures of the deadly sins."

"How ecumenical."

"There is a skeleton . . ."

"I'd think you'd like that."

"And a vile Turk with a long nose and dagger."

"Well, they have suffered many occupations, not counting the one going on now."

"And a usurious Jew."

"Ah. They never get bored of that one, do they?"

"My band quit," Simon said. "I have had to make do with a horrible Slovakian wedding band for the last two gigs."

"I got your message," I said. "Gunter set that up?"

"Gunter is in a general panic. It's more than this dreadful tour, too. He is genuinely frightened by something. He jumps at every sound, he smokes five packs a day, and he's no longer even pretending to be homosexual. Last night he went off to the toilet with a whore in the middle of 'Open-Minded Friend.'"

"The fact that he's not gay doesn't prove he's a spy, Simon. He may just be a genuinely incompetent businessman who knows his investors are going to come looking for him with crowbars."

"I think it's more than that. I think it's all coming apart. The whole system. All the people here are talking about Havel, the playwright they had in prison. I think we're in the middle of a revolution, Flynn. You know how this always ends—the Russians send in the tanks."

"We'll be sailing to Italy by then."

"Or lined up against a wall."

"The hell with tomorrow. We're in Prague. Let's live it up among our fellow Bohemians."

It took me only the bus ride to the gig to become infected with Simon's depression. It turned out his show was not *in* Prague, it was somewhat *near* Prague—an hour away in the factory town of Ústí nad Labem. I had rarely seen such a desolate place. Everything was brown or dust-colored. The buildings were concrete blocks in the Soviet style.

Simon's new organ player, the only member of the Slovakian wedding band who spoke any English, gave us the background: "Ústí was on the Allied flight path after Dresden," the organist explained. "They dropped their leftover firebombs here. The town never recovered. You can't drink the water, it's full of chemicals. The Nazis pillaged it, the Americans bombed it, and the Russians used it to dump all their poisons."

"And now," Simon said, "I get booked here. The procession of historical indignities grinds on."

Simon's show was to be played in a venue called the Metronome, which turned out to be an abandoned factory with tables set up at one end as a bar and a rickety wooden stage at the other. The part of Simon that saw himself as a noble voice of the proletariat raging against the encroaching dictatorship of a brutal conformity took a sort of doomed romantic energy from this environment. Part of him liked the idea of rallying the subdued spirit of personal liberty in a brutalized population.

A crowd began to convene quite early and by eight P.M. there were four or five hundred people—young women as well as young men—lined up outside the mill waiting. When the doors opened they bought their drinks and stood expectantly in front of the low stage. The wedding band came out first and played a few tunes to warm up the audience and earn whatever pay the vanished Gunter had promised them. They executed—and I use that word deliberately—versions of "Brown Sugar," "Whole Lotta Love" and the theme from *Ghostbusters* before the organist leaned into a gothic dirge that signaled the entrance of Simon Potts, British Rock Legend.

This might have been a remote and miserable corner of the world, but here was Simon's constituency. He had come a long way to find several hundred people who cheered when he stepped into the spotlight and raised their fists in solidarity when he raised his.

"We are not the authors of your failure," he sang in the lowest part of his deep baritone. I had not heard this song before; it seemed to have been written during this tour. "We won't be your victims anymore!"

The crowd seemed to be digging the sentiment. I looked to the last survivor of our original British contingent, an Irish roadie named Kenny Thomas who was serving as soundman, lighting director, and road manager. Kenny had few tools to work with, but he was making the best use of what he had—using his right hand to raise the wattage of a single yellow spotlight until Simon's shadow stretched across the wall behind him, while with his left he twisted the level of the bass volume knob until the ominous droning of Simon's mordant low notes made manifest the intentions of his lyrics.

"It is our turn to rise! It is our turn! Our turn! It is our turn to rise! Our turn! Our turn! Our turn to watch you fall!"

This was going over. I began to consider that Gunter might have accidentally gotten something right. Maybe Simon did have a market here in the hinterlands. These people had been under the boot of the Soviets for so long that they were attuned to Simon's musical mixture of misery and grandiosity. Their unarticulated ambitions were amplified by their miserable conditions. They were hungry for support and sympathy. Simon might just do very well here, at least until the Russian army or more talented musicians arrived.

The applause was loud and sustained. Simon basked. He turned to the band and counted off a quick beat. They launched with a roar into the Ravons' old hit "Ask Yer Daddy," a song I had never heard Simon play. The fans jumped up and down, raising their hands and spilling their drinks on each other. Kenny the Irish roadie cranked up the volume—and then there was a loud *pop* and the whole place went black and silent.

It was not the Russians who had shut down Simon; it was the rusty and burdened fuse box overloaded by all this hard rock amplitude. Matches were struck and held aloft. Someone from the Metronome made his way to the stage with a large flashlight and shone it on Simon's face. Simon shouted to the fans, "Anyone got an acoustic guitar?"

No one did, so Simon, lit like Nosferatu, began slowly clapping his hands over his head and singing, "Ninety-nine Soviet tanks on the road, ninety-nine Soviet tanks. You blow one down, you turn it around: ninety-eight Soviet tanks on the road. Ninety-eight Soviet tanks on the road, ninety-eight Soviet tanks. You blow one down, you turn it around . . ."

Christ, I thought, he is going to get us sent to the gulag. Simon's band picked up his chant and so did the audience, although their ability to count backward from a hundred in English was unsteady. Simon made a *Keep going* gesture and climbed off the stage. I met him there, as did the concert promoter and Kenny the soundman.

"They say they have a small backup generator in the boiler room," Kenny shouted in Simon's ear. "They are going to try to get it working but it is bolted to the floor and they don't know if the power lines will reach from there to the stage."

"Well," Simon said, "I guess you have about ninety-six Soviet tanks to get it worked out."

The audience kept singing and clapping while the managers of the hall and Kenny the roadie fired up the spare generator. They were plugging power cords and boxes one into the other to stretch from the boiler room to the stage. Everyone in the crowd made a path to let the lines through. They came up two feet short. At that point Simon's latent military ambitions came to the fore. He directed his band and several of the fans to clear a space on the floor and move all the musical equipment off the stage and into the center of the room. Now the power box reached, but there were not enough inputs for all the gear. Simon put the power box on the floor in front of the drums and plugged his bass amp into one slot. He put the guitar amp into the second and put his vocal mike through the guitar amp. He handed the organ player a tambourine and told him to pretend he was Davy Jones.

Kenny ran a snake lamp through the room and hooked it to a pipe above Simon's head. It cast eerie shadows. Fans formed a circle around the reconfigured rock group like primitives at a campfire. Some climbed up on the abandoned stage to get a better view. Simon began plucking his bass and singing again, and while it sounded brittle and low-fi, like a teenage garage band, there was no denying the excitement generated by this improvised Mad Max approach to rock and roll. What the next half hour lacked in sonic fidelity it made up for in the intensity of Simon's performance and the wild enthusiasm of the audience. After six songs, including a raucous, extended "Louie Louie" with lyrics about "Give my finger to the brutal regime," the backup generator caught fire and the show was over.

The crowd carried Simon around on their shoulders while the Slovak wedding band scurried to protect their instruments.

I thought the promoters might blame us for blowing up their factory but they were delighted to have been part of what they clearly considered a brilliant revolutionary experience and paid us with a small check for half of the contracted fee and a large paper bag of cash for the remainder. I knew we would never redeem the check, but the cash allowed me to pay the wedding band and Kenny the one-man road crew.

On the way back to Prague, after the excitement and recountings and mutual congratulations had worn off, I asked Simon quietly where the money from the rest of the gigs had gone.

"Gunter collects it and locks it in a metal suitcase," he whispered. "He paid the hotel bills but nothing for me or the band yet. That's why the other two players pissed off back to England."

Abandoned as we felt, we were surprised to find Gunter waiting in the lobby when we got back to the Hotel Rott. He was smoking a cigarette and had the metal suitcase Simon had described handcuffed to his wrist.

"Jack Flynn, good to see you," Gunter said. "Simon, how was the concert?"

"We played a blinder, man," Simon said. "Sorry you couldn't make it."

"I've been watching the news."

"What news?"

"You have not heard? How is that possible?"

Simon said, "We've been off the electrical grid. What's the news, Gunter?"

He walked into a side lounge where what looked to be the entire population of the hotel was gathered around a black and white television. I could not understand what the announcer was saying but mobs of people were pouring down a wide urban avenue. Everyone in the room was watching in silence, as if they were witnesses to a miracle.

The organ player said, "Jesus God."

I recognized the city now—Berlin.

"The communists have opened the Berlin Wall," Gunter said. "The citizens of the East are pouring into the West. There are reports of men with sledgehammers and pickaxes knocking through the concrete."

Simon stared at the images. "And no one's shooting them?"

"No one is shooting," Gunter said grimly. "They are having a party."

"Surely," I said, "the Russians will come."

"If they do," Gunter said, "it will be too late. The Poles, the Czechs, the Hungarians, they are all coming through."

Gunter looked Simon in the eye. "We must leave for Bucharest in the morning."

Simon said, "What about Belgrade?"

"Fuck Belgrade. The Serbs will be digging up the guns their grandfathers buried. We need to get to Romania."

An old woman watching the television shushed us. We stepped out into the corridor.

"Listen, Gunter," I told him, "we're in the middle of a revolution now. I'm not sure any local concert promoters are going to be honoring contracts made under previous regimes, and of all the places we want to be when the heat comes down, the worst dictatorship in Europe seems a poor choice."

Gunter let out a long plume of cigarette smoke. "What do you know about who is the worst dictator?"

"Why are you in such a hurry to get to the palace of Nicolae Ceauşescu?"

Gunter looked like he was considering whether to stamp out his smoke or break my nose. He said, "I am a businessman. I only intend to see Simon fulfill his obligations."

Simon piped in, "That works both ways, Gunter. I've dragged my arse through eight countries for you and played a dozen of the worst shitholes on the map. The only time I got paid so far is tonight when you didn't show up to sweep the loot into your metal briefcase. Now I'll tell you what—you unlock that valise and pony up what you owe me and the band and I'll go to Dracula's castle with you. Short of that, you can fuck off back to S.P.E.C.T.R.E."

Gunter rolled his eyes like a weary schoolmaster. He said, "Be in the lobby at nine A.M. I will arrange new transport. Once we are on the road I will pay everyone what they are owed. If you skip out on me, you are on your own."

We all returned to our quarters that night and were in the lobby at nine, but we never saw Gunter again. He and his handcuffed suitcase vanished in the night, by his own volition or against his will. I paid the band out of my own pocket and tried to buy tickets back to London for Simon, Kenny, and myself. Half of Prague seemed to be heading west before the wall could close up again.

Failing to get through to any airline or travel service, we stuck to an abridged version of our original itinerary. We took a train to Dubrovnik, checked into a beautiful old stone hotel out of a fairy tale, and booked passage on a boat to take us across to Italy. We were not sailing on our own magnificent schooner, of course. We were huddled on the wet and windy forward deck of a fishing boat. But we got home, with Simon broke and me having run up six thousand dollars on my credit card.

A few years later the beautiful old hotel where we stayed in Dubrovnik would be set on fire by the missiles launched out of Montenegro, the idyllic town next door. Freedom did not come to Eastern Europe as easily as we sometimes pretend to remember.

When we were home Simon phoned and insisted I turn on the BBC right away. He swore he saw Gunter in the middle of the Romanian mob that was calling for the execution of the dictator Ceaușescu and his wife. I could not be sure, but I admitted to Simon that the furtive figure moving one way while the lynch mob moved in the other might have been Gunter.

We never found out for sure if it was and we never found out which side he was on.

While I was in Europe with Simon defeating communism, Emerson had fallen in love. Miss Norway and he had parted when she accepted a teaching position at Bennington College. Into the opening stepped Delilah Grath, a twenty-two-year-old movie actress with underground credibility from her work in independent film. She was also a fantasist. She would have been appalled and insulted to be called a liar. She believed whatever absurd tale she was spinning at the time she told it. She had short brown hair, enormous brown eyes, pale white skin, tiny bones, and a small boyish frame. In the past Emerson had gone for tall, buxom women but as soon as he met Delilah, he was lost to us.

A student of the sixties counterculture and self-styled expert on classic rock and roll, Delilah pursued Emerson, twenty-five years her senior, like a girl with daddy issues who was used to getting everything she wanted.

Her mother, who was two years younger than Emerson, had been a sexually liberated yoga teacher and enthusiastic drug taker who sent the young Delilah to a communist summer camp where the children celebrated Holocaust week by wearing yellow stars and treating each other like dirt.

At least that's what Delilah told us on Tuesday. By Thursday she had grown up in a commune in Oregon and when the weekend came she had been a virtual prisoner of a cruel stepfather in a gated community near Beverly Hills. The identity of her birth father progressed from Greek fisherman to fugitive radical to one of the Eagles.

Emerson lapped it all up. Sleeping with this young bombshell made him feel like a boy again. The rest of us tolerated the tall stories but became concerned that Delilah might supplement her lies with thieving. Small valuable items seemed to vanish when Delilah was around. Wendy from my office swore that a jade bracelet she had left in her bathroom when Emerson and Delilah came to call went missing and later showed up on Delilah's wrist.

"She was raised by hippies," Wendy shouted. "She's got no scruples!"

Delilah followed Emerson everywhere. She had strong opinions about his music and made them known in the recording studio.

Emerson's producer called me in frustration in the middle of the night, after the new sweetheart had commandeered a session.

"There's no sense in my coming back tomorrow, Jack!" he said. "She's producing the sessions now! We get a great take and she tells Emerson she heard mistrust in his voice and he has to do it over. He's in the middle of putting down a guitar solo and she walks into the room and starts beating on the amp with a drumstick. She's producing now by *dancing*."

I rolled over on my pillow and asked what that meant.

"I mean she stands in the middle of the room and does the hully gully or some such bullshit and if the music moves her to dance well, she announces it's a take and if the music causes her to dance badly, she makes us do it over. I can't take this. I'm out."

I went by to see Emerson the next morning and explain that he had to separate work from courtship. He came to the door of his apartment in the nude and let me in and offered me juice.

Delilah bounded out of the bedroom, naked, too.

"Jack Sprat!" she shouted. "Don't talk to Emerson about anything that will interrupt his creative flow! He's in touch with his inspiration this morning!"

"Perhaps he could also get in touch with a bathrobe," I suggested.

"Ah-hah, old Flynn is very conservative you know, 'Lilah," Emerson said with a laugh. "Go cover yourself before you give him an infarction."

"Booo." Delilah laughed and bounced back into the bedroom.

Emerson picked up a glass of some organic blend and plopped down naked on his davenport.

"God, she's rejuvenated me, Jack," he said softly. "I feel like I'm eighteen again."

"I'm happy for you, Emerson," I said. "But listen, you don't need to rub your good luck in the faces of the less fortunate. Hal wants to quit the album. He says his suggestions are all being overridden and contradicted by Delilah."

Emerson began to protest and I said, "Look, I know. You respect her advice, that's fine. But solicit her opinions at home, away from the crew. You know how it feels to the pirates if the captain has a woman on board the ship. Try going down to the studio without her and see if we can't get this album wrapped up. Take her ideas, sure, but present them as your own. They'll be accepted quicker. What do you say?"

Emerson scratched his crotch and considered. He was a pragmatist. Clearly he was enjoying some great sex but he was not the type to start a war if one could be avoided. He said, "I don't appreciate Hal saying this to you instead of coming to me directly."

"Yeah, I agree. I told him that, too. He was just upset, he felt he wasn't being given a fair listen—"

Delilah must have been eavesdropping, that's all I can figure. Just when Emerson was ready to go my way, an ear-piercing whoop came from the bedroom and she came leaping toward us like a burned rabbit. She was now dressed in knickers and a T-shirt and was waving a tiny plastic baton.

"I'm pregnant, Emerson! We're pregnant! We're going to have a baby!"

Emerson leaped up and threw his arms around her. "Darling," he said, "I'm so surprised . . ."

Delilah reached out and pulled me close to the two of them, still shouting. "We're going to have the most beautiful, talented baby in the whole world!"

My face was an inch from Emerson's. He was confused but smiling. This was as much a shock to him as it was to me.

"If it's a girl," Delilah said, "we'll call her Lilith—do you like that, Emerson? And if it's a boy . . . Jack Flynn Cutler, after your best friend!" She whooped again and squeezed our heads together.

Emerson had been conscripted. The two of them were married within the month and Emerson got a look at his new bride's extended communal family and at least three of his possible fathers-in-law. The couple's daughter—who ended up being named Autumn but as a teenager called herself Nancy—was born ten months later. An unusually long gestation? I am no obstetrician, but I suspect that the pregnancy was imaginary when Delilah announced it. After the wedding she had to make it come true.

Simon's recording career had collapsed with the Berlin Wall. He be-
lieved passionately that the album he had made for the Germans could
be a huge hit in the U.S. if I would simply take a break from wiping
Emerson's nose and get out there and sell it to an American record label.

I reminded him that we had been down this dead-end road before
and ended up recording for the spies, but Simon insisted this was a
new circumstance.

"They don't have to advance me any money, Flynn," he insisted
across the ocean. "They don't have to speculate. The album is all finished! All they have to do is put it out!"

I had been diligent in trying to track down Gunter or anyone else
associated with Hidden Records, but they had shut down and ab-
sconded. In doing so they had breached all their contracts with Simon,
voiding his obligations to them. He was indeed a free agent and I had
no concerns about our taking the master tapes and making a new deal
with them. If Gunter ever showed up to protest, contract law was on
our side. My problem was not legal, it was musical. No label I could
find wanted to deal with Simon.

"I'm coming to New York," he told me. "I want to meet these people myself. I will show them they need not be frightened of me."

"Fine," I said. Fright was not the issue but let him try. Then I realized that if he came to New York he would expect me to put him up.
I booked him a room at the Gramercy Park Hotel, right around the
corner from my flat. I would happily pay to ensure our mutual privacy.
Simon did not want that. He had a notion that the two of us should
renew our youthful friendship by eating, sleeping, and bathing in the
same abode. I tried to talk him out of it, the one way to ensure that he
would not back down.

"Look, Flynn," he said, tracking mud into my apartment and dropping a large wet valise on my carpet. "You and I have spent too much time as voices on the phone. Prague was the most time we've spent together in twenty years and it was good, wasn't it? We need to connect again at a"—he punched himself in the belly—"gut level. Let's recommit to our alliance."

"Okay, Simon, fine. You can stay in my daughter's bedroom. It's through there, don't mind the New Kids pinups. There's a bath right next to–"

He stuck his head in and out of the doorway. "No, I can't sleep in that room," he announced. "Where do you sleep?"

"You're not putting me out of my own bedroom, Simon."

"That's right, I'm not."

He went into the room I kept for Lucy's visits and came out dragging her mattress. He deposited it on the floor next to my bed.

"What the hell are you doing, man?" I demanded.

"This will be fun, Flynn," he said with an unconvincing grin. "Like Boy Scouts. We can lie in the dark and talk, share ideas."

"What? Like Eric and Ernie? We're nearly fifty years old, Simon! All we have to share is snoring, tooth grinding, and sleep apnea."

"If it doesn't work out we'll both know. Don't be a fuddy-duddy, man, try new things!"

Even as a child Simon had never said "fuddy-duddy." Either he was throwing himself full-force into becoming social in the hopes of convincing the record companies they had misjudged him, or he had suffered a nervous collapse.

That night I went to sleep with Simon on a mattress on the floor next to my bed. It was my good fortune that he was weary from the flight and faded quickly. I woke around eight and heard him working in the kitchen. He had cooked us both waffles and fried eggs. He had also rearranged my dishes.

"Good morning, Felix," I said. "You've been busy."

"Just making this bachelor pad livable," he said. "We need to get some whole-grain bread in here, and some fruit. It's amazing you are mobile, the way you eat."

"I don't actually eat at home very much," I said and then told myself not to get drawn into his arguments.

"I threw out the butter and salt," he told me as he sat at the table and tucked in. "Poison. And you had an old empty box of cake mix from years ago. I chucked that as well."

"Where did you put it, Simon?" I demanded, getting up from the table and finding the trash bin empty.

"I bagged all the crap and put it down the incinerator," he said. "New York needs to ban those, you know. Breeds poison."

"You burned the Betty Crocker cake mix box?" I opened the cabinet.

"It was ancient."

"Yes, Simon. See, I keep a couple of hundred dollars in cash in that old cake box and my passport. In case the apartment is ever robbed, I thought that was a safe spot. Wrong again."

"Sorry, man," Simon said as I sat back down and poked my egg. "Silly place to leave money, though, isn't it?"

"My fault entirely." I wondered why, if I had to lose my passport, it could not have been before Simon dragged me off to Eastern Europe.

Simon was prepared to move on. He said, "Where do we go today?"

"I am going to my office to deal with my business, which includes trying to get Charlie another publishing deal and convincing those promoters who lost money on Emerson's last tour to give him more money for the next one. You, I think, should visit the Metropolitan Museum and look at their crossbows."

"No, no, mate," Simon said. "I didn't come all this way to play tourist. You and I are calling on the record labels."

I did not fight him. Simon was in New York and I had already realized that there was a subtle threat in his taking up residence next to my bed. He was going to haunt me until I either got him a new record contract or proved to him that there was none to have. The hell with it, I figured, let's get out there and test the hypothesis.

Over the next four days we called on Mercury, Geffen, Atlantic, Epic, Elektra, Arista, Sire, Island, A&M, and I.R.S. Everyone we met with was cheerful and flattering. Each yanked out some mutual association to establish that they and Simon trolled the same waters. Each sat and listened to two tracks from *Karma Suit Ya* with furrow-browed intensity, nodding sympathy, and pencil-tapping enthusiasm. Each asked Simon specific tactical questions about how he saw the roll-out, the marketing campaign, the live shows, the videos. You would have thought that they were sold on the music, sold on Simon, and ready to whip out the contract right there on the company blotter.

I knew the routine. I tried to convince Simon that these people did this for everyone, he should not get his hopes up. He was certain, though, that his new-minted optimism and willingness to sit down and talk to the suits as if he respected them had overcome whatever unfair obstacles had slowed his deserved momentum. He was sure his ship was coming in.

We lay in our shared bedroom staring at the dark. When he spoke it did not matter if I pretended I was asleep, he would keep talking anyway.

"I think Atlantic is the best fit for me right now," he announced from his mattress. "I'm not a kid anymore. I should be on the label of Ray Charles and Aretha. Play the dignity card."

"Let's see what they come back with," I cautioned.

"I don't want to be with Epic, I'll tell you that. They're not in the music business, they're in the Michael Jackson business. I don't want to have to worry that I'm second priority to some song-and-dance man."

"God forbid," I said.

"Warner's could be good, but I don't see myself as an LA label act, you know? All that sunshine and surf, that's Emerson's thing, not mine. I think my fans expect me to be with a New York company. Something urbane and gritty, something real."

"Warner's has great distribution," I said. The first rejections had already come in. I had decided to keep that from Simon for another day or so. If we got lucky with someone—anyone—I would sell him on that being the best possible choice and let's reward their enthusiasm by signing with them immediately. I felt like the parent of a student with poor grades waiting for the college rejection letters to arrive.

A week later Simon was still living in my apartment and the novelty had worn off. His self-imposed conviviality had lapsed with his optimism. He knew that Epic and Atlantic had passed. We could not get anyone from Warner's on the phone. The old paranoia was creeping up into his ganglia and it made for a most unpleasant roommate.

"Jack," he moaned one night in the middle of a thunderstorm. I decided that if he wanted to climb into bed with me I would stab him. I pretended to be asleep.

"Jack? Jaaaack? *Jack!*"

"What is it, Simon?"

"My bum hurts."

I let that resonate. Weary as I was, I could not think what response was appropriate, so I said nothing.

"Jack? Did you hear me? My bum hurts."

"Simon, what can you possibly expect me to do about that?"

"My bum is all red and sore. It's that coarse toilet paper you use."

"For fuck's sake, didn't you grow up in postwar London? Since when are you so delicate?"

"Do you have any nappy cream?"

"Fuck off, Simon. I don't have any nappy cream. Go to sleep."

"You don't have any nappy cream?"

"Simon, my daughter is a teenager who lives with her mother in California. Why in the holy fuck would I have fucking nappy cream in my house?"

"What do you do when you get a sore bum, Flynn?"

"I suffer in silence."

The rain pounded and the thunder ripped and I lay there vowing to myself that I would not go out in the storm to look for nappy cream for Simon goddamn Potts, who was groaning on the floor by my bed like a dog with kidney stones. But he kept moaning and he kept whining and the rain kept pouring and the wind kept pounding and my temples beat with a mounting fury and finally I said, "All right! All right, you miserable twat, if you really want me to get out of my bed at four in the bleeding morning in a monsoon to walk the streets of New York City looking for a deli or convenience store or all-night pharmacy that will sell me a tube of fucking nappy cream to squirt up your red-rimmed asshole, I will put on my boots and coat and do it! Is that what you want, Simon? Is that what you want?!"

"Thank you, Flynn."

So I did. I got dressed and walked in the freezing rain from Twenty-second Street to Union Square looking for someplace that would sell me a gel or ointment for skin rashes. The sixth place I tried was a bodega near Sixth Avenue.

"I hope you can help me," I told the old man behind the counter. "I need a cream for diaper rash. It's a bit of an emergency."

The old man dug under his counter and came up with a tube of Johnson's cream decorated with a picture of a smiling infant.

"You have baby at home?" the man said as he rang up the price in the register.

"You bet I do," I said.

When I got back to my apartment, Simon was asleep. I stood there cold and wet and astonished. I considered discharging the tube all over him but I'd only have to clean it up later. I laid it next to him and went and showered and shaved. Might as well get to the office early. There were more of Simon's rejections coming our way.

A&M had bailed, Sire was out. As Simon's infestation of my apartment on Gramercy Park entered month two, the mood at our sleepover camp was turning from paranoid to murderous.

Now, to be fair, I had palmed him off for a night or two on Castro, Wendy, even one weekend with Emerson and his child bride. They all sent Simon packing back to me. He had at least moved from my bedroom to my living room, although that made me a prisoner in my own boudoir.

"Fuckers!" Simon sneered when I came in from work and found him lying on the floor in his underpants. "That nice girl from Mercury who *loved* 'Evangeline'—you remember her? Acted like she wanted to shag me there in her office. I just called and they said she wasn't in. So I called back and said I was her doctor with the test results and she picked right up. Ha! I said, 'Betty, it's Dr. Simon Potts and the prescription is for Mercury to put out *Karma Suit Ya.*' A joke, right? Well, she gets all pissy and says I have no right to harass her. Harass her! And then she claimed that she spoke to marketing and radio promotion and they don't think my album would fit with their current initiatives. What the hell kind of double-talk is that? I said, 'Look, you little hypocrite, are you telling me you have no actual authority of your own? Or are you just saying you don't have the balls to back up your taste?' Well, she gets all up in arms like I'd called her a slut or something, which I absolutely did not do, and she says, 'I just didn't like the record very much, Simon.' Can you comprehend that? You were there, Flynn—she acted like she *loved* my record. What kind of bullshit con game are these eunuchs running? If you didn't like it, why the bloody hell did you not just say so to my face and save us both a week of misery?"

I said, "I wish you had not made that call, Simon."

"Growing out my toenails waiting for you to get an answer."

"Yeah, well, believe it or not you are not their only priority. These people all talk to each other. Word gets around that you tore into Betty like that and suddenly you're the miserable bastard all over town."

Simon, still lying flat on the rug, began to punch the side of my couch with his left hand.

"Have you got anything for me, Flynn?"

"Last shot, old man. It's still midday in Los Angeles and I'm hoping to hear from Elektra before they leave. You remember Bruce Gilbert, the rocker with the tattoos and earrings? He was going to take it out to California with him and play it for his boss. I hope to hear from him before"–I looked at my watch–"nine tonight."

So Simon and I began a ghastly vigil. We waited for a phone call like condemned men hoping for a last-minute reprieve. I made some soup. Simon strummed his guitar and worked on a new song:

The cheaters in their jealousy
For anyone fearless and free
Who must tear down what they can't understand
Whose lives and emotions are perfectly planned . . .

Boy, I thought, if they hear that piece of toss they'll rescind Simon's passport. And it was here that an idea spoke to me. Surely Simon had entered the United States on a temporary visa. He was not legally allowed to work while he was here. He had just gone by the thirty-day mark. If someone were to drop a dime with the Department of Immigration, my burdens would be over. I stopped myself. What sort of man was I, to think such a thing? This was my friend of more than twenty years, this was my client! I had a duty to protect his interests, not conspire against him. A deportation would put a red flag in his passport forever. All his future travels would be burdened, opening him to searches and detainments. I could not seriously consider it.

He whacked his guitar and bellowed:

I will not be a cookie cutter
manufactured peanut butter

artificially sweetened snack
for their corporate heart attack machiiiiine.

Well, I figured, it was not a sin to merely consider it.

The phone rang. I grabbed the receiver. It was Elektra A&R man Bruce Gilbert calling from Los Angeles.

I greeted him. We made small talk. I looked up and saw Simon slinking into the kitchen. He picked up the other phone to listen in. I waved for him to hang up. He put a finger to his lips. I could see how badly this would end.

"Did you play Simon's record for Sherry?" I asked the innocent Gilbert.

"I did, man. I gotta tell ya, it's not lookin' positive."

I could hear Simon breathe in sharply. Gilbert did not notice. I said, "Well, okay, let's talk tomorrow, then . . ."

Gilbert said, "It's like I warned you. Nobody here thinks Simon can do it anymore. He's old, he's not great-looking. Most people never heard of him. Plus, you know, his reputation is not for being an easy date."

"Let's talk about all this later, Bruce," I pleaded. "There's still the option of talking to the Canadians."

Bruce plowed on like an automated grave digger. "Nah, you know that ain't gonna happen, Jack. I mean, the one thing is, I've got this girl I've been working with—Nell Tanco. She's twenty-one, she's really hot, almost six feet tall. You gotta see this girl, Flynn, you'll explode. Anyway, I've been working with her and we need to put a band together. I was thinking maybe Simon becomes part of that project, they try cowriting. He brings some musical weight to what she's doing and she brings some youth and sex appeal to his—"

It was the best and only offer we had landed in a month of trying, but of course the eavesdropping Simon could not hear that. He exploded into the telephone and into my ear.

"You ignorant miserable fucker!" Simon screamed. "You expect me to prop up some pea-brained bimbo you want to parade in front of the paparazzi? You expect me to give my songs to some empty-headed pole dancer you hope to promote into the next skin-rag sensation for sexually frustrated teenage boys? Who do you think you are, you ridiculous, coked-up, ear-ringed, bribe-taking little pimp?"

"Simon?" Bruce Gilbert said. "Hey, Jack, is Simon on the phone?"

"I am going to call every journalist I know and tell him you tried to pull this behind my back, Gilbert!" Simon screamed. "I am going to ruin you!"

"Buddy," Gilbert said, "I'm trying to throw you a lifeline. You know the only thing I should be saying to you? 'You're welcome.'"

Simon kept screaming but Gilbert had hung up. Simon was banging the telephone on my ice maker when I excused myself and said I was popping out to the liquor store. I did, too. I bought two bottles of scotch whiskey and a carton of cigarettes and then I went to a pay phone and called the Department of Immigration. I gave them Simon's name and birth date and passport number and told them where they could find him.

The next day I went to the office as usual and did not take his panicked calls when they came. I told Castro to tell Simon to go along with the authorities, we'd meet him shortly with a lawyer. Then we did nothing until they had put him on a plane and shipped him back to England in steerage.

I don't know if Simon ever knew for sure that I had turned him in, but he certainly knew I had failed to get him loose. I knew he would never forgive me. I counted on it.

Want to get a lazy aging rock star back on the road? Get him a young wife he wants to impress. He won't resist playing all the old hits. He wants to show her an audience standing up and singing along. Emerson threw himself into his new tour with an athletic dedication. He had not played so much lead guitar in years. The band noticed a real change for the better in him. Baxter the drummer told me, "I wish Emerson would get married to a hot young chick before every tour."

Delilah had taken full advantage of her celebrity wedding and the birth of her beautiful baby girl. She had signed for two mainstream movie roles, and *Vanity Fair* had called her the next Julia Roberts. This at a time when the previous Julia Roberts had not even been around very long.

It must be conceded that marriage to a young starlet helped Emerson, too. At a moment when MTV might have been losing interest in him, he was back on the hot list. As one video executive said to me, "He's married into our demo." That was great for our new album, especially when the sexy young wife showed up shimmying in a black two-piece bathing suit in the clip for the new single, "Random Man."

The strange thing was that as Emerson acted so rejuvenated, he seemed old to me for the first time. We were both closing in on fifty, the first birthday that had ever scared me. Fifty is when our head finally convinces our gut that aging and dying is going to happen to us, too. Emerson was a youthful and handsome man, but when he stood onstage wiggling his ass for his young bride he looked to me like a foolish old bugger.

This was also the tour when he started using a teleprompter. He explained that there were just so many songs in his repertoire now that he needed a quick reference source so he could pull out unexpected oldies and mix up the set list. Emerson never mixed up the set list. When I pointed that out to him he said, "Well, it's easier for me to concentrate on my guitar playing if I don't have to remember all those words."

Delilah was aboard for the first month of the tour, baby Autumn in her arms when she wandered to the side of the stage to let the photographers snap their shots. After that, mother and child retired from the road so that Delilah could supervise the rebuilding and interior design of the mansion she and Emerson were renovating in Sagaponack, Long Island. Delilah took great pride in making elaborate sketches of the ballroom, guest suites, and solarium she intended to create on their fifteen oceanside acres.

Emerson's tour looped around the USA once, hopped to Japan, and then came back for an extended run of secondary American markets. I was out for part of it, home for much of it, and always in contact. There was a two-week break after a June concert at Jones Beach. Emerson and Delilah threw a party at Sagaponack after the show for the band and about twenty friends. Everyone had a wonderful time; Delilah had memorized everyone's name and she and Emerson were perfect hosts.

The exchange of the evening came when the very elegant ex-wife of a Hamptons publishing mogul swept into the party and up to Emerson in a low-cut gown with a high-slit skirt.

"Lambshanks!" she called to Emerson coyly. "Take me away from all this!"

"Denise," Emerson said, kissing her hand. "I want to introduce you to Delilah, my wife."

Delilah swooped to Emerson's side and put out her hand. Denise took it and looked down at her. She looked back to Emerson and said, "Well, this is a surprise, Emerson. You told me your wife was dead."

The Cutlers had invited me to stay in the guesthouse that night. When the last guests had left I said good evening and headed across the lawn to my quarters. It was a beautiful, clear June night with a full moon and a steady breeze coming off the Atlantic.

I was settled in before I realized that I had no toothpaste. All the lights were still lit in the mansion. I put on my shoes to go back.

I walked up the steps onto the patio and looked through the opened French doors at Emerson and his young wife. I was about to call out a greeting when I realized that she was reprimanding him fiercely.

"I just want you to stop talking about yourself so much, Emerson!" she shouted. "Listen to other people! Say their names when you speak to them! And stop making those lame references to old movies that nobody but you remembers. It's so boring! It makes you seem like an old man."

Emerson was tipsy; he thought he could rely on his charm. He reached out to embrace her and she shoved him away.

"Get your hands off me, don't touch me, you don't own me. What? You think I *owe* you something, Mr. Rock Star? I don't owe you any-thing! Get a rubber doll!"

I should have got right out of there but I was startled. In all the years I had known Emerson, the one constant was his easy sense of control. Women loved him, he had power over them. I was surprised to see the reality behind what had looked like a permanent honey-moon, but I had been there myself and I knew that no one outside any marriage knows what really goes on.

What amazed me was that Emerson, the sex symbol, a man who was always romantically aloof and emotionally disengaged, a man who would walk away from a relationship if he didn't like the way she ironed his shirts, was putting up with this.

"Baby," Emerson implored, "what are you cross about?"

"What am I mad about, Emerson? I'm mad about the way all your friends talk to me, the way they all look at me. I'm disgusted that people think I'm the kind of woman who would be with somebody like you!"

Delilah bolted up the stairs. A door slammed. Emerson stood there gently swaying from side to side. He looked out into the evening and recognized me standing on the patio.

"I'm sorry, man," I said. "I came back to get some toothpaste."

"That's just how she is, Jack," he told me. I made a gesture to him to hush but he came outside to talk to me.

"She's sweet as pie when other people are around, but the sec-ond we close the door behind them, she turns angry. I understand it, though. She has this terrible need to be loved, to have everyone think well of her. She is charming morning to night with everyone she meets, no matter how rude or unpleasant they might be. Then when we're alone she takes out on me all the frustration and anger and insults that build up in her from all the people she turns the other cheek to. Because I'm the only one she trusts to love her no matter what, to love her when she doesn't play America's sweetheart. She trusts me to see her dark side and still love her. In a way, it's the most intimate thing we do."

What can you say to something like that? I told Emerson that he was a good and wise husband, but I believed that his turning himself inside out trying to translate these insults into a strange manifestation of love was no behavior I would have expected of him. It was the alibi of an abused child.

When Emerson's tour passed through Los Angeles I called on Charlie Lydle. His money had run out again and I had pretty much used up every method of swindling advances from foreign publishers to keep him afloat.

Charlie now faced a prospect he had devoted his entire life to avoiding. Charlie was going to have to get a job.

"I can't work in an office, Jack!" he explained to me with great passion. "It would be like putting an eagle in a canary cage! I'll pull out all me feathers!"

"Who said you're qualified to work in an office?" I replied, attempting tough love. "I was thinking maybe we could put you on a road crew, working side by side with convicts. That would have to open the songwriting tap."

He looked at me with his big pathetic eyes and in spite of myself I let up. "Look, Charlie, how about if I get you some temp work? That's easy and flexible. Some executive's secretary calls in sick, they call the agency, who call you. You go sit at a desk all day, take phone messages, read a book, write some lyrics, come home with a paycheck. It's easy money till you get back on your feet."

"I'd rather die, Jack. I'd sooner go back to London and go on the dole. You talk to Emerson about my big idea?"

"I don't have to, Charlie. Emerson does not want to do a Ravons reunion."

"But it's for charity, Jack."

"Yeah, the Charlie charity. Come on, man, you try to pull off a scam like that, they won't just deport you, they'll send you to jail. What is so horrible about taking a job for a few months?"

"Listen to you, givin' out with the schoolmaster speech. 'Don't go puttin' your faith in the guitar, Charles, there's no living in that.' I showed 'em!"

"You showed them, Charlie. You don't have to prove anything to anyone. For heaven's sake, you've been supporting yourself as a musician for thirty years! Take a sabbatical and recharge."

Charlie would not be persuaded. He borrowed forty dollars from me and said he was going to talk to a boot designer who had an in with George Michael.

For neither the first nor last time in his life, Charlie was rescued by a woman. This time, however, it was not because she fell for him and took him in and paid his steerage. This woman had already fallen down that rabbit hole. Samantha Lipsitz, Charlie's ex, daughter of California affluence, used her father's connections to get Charlie a job working at Walt Disney Pictures, writing songs for straight-to-video sequels to their big box office animated musicals.

Disney animation was enjoying a creative rebirth. They had hit big with *The Little Mermaid, Aladdin,* and *Beauty and the Beast.* They were working on *The Lion King.* These were jewels to be polished and protected, brought out in theaters with great fanfare and then withdrawn for several years.

In the meantime, they kept the lights on with direct-to-video spin-offs on which they spent much less time and money. *The Little Mermaid Meets the Lucky Lobster. Beauty and the Beast's Haunted Halloween. Jungle Book 4: The Leopard Ghost.* These knockoffs were put together fairly quickly and ran only about thirty-five minutes each, their brevity and low purchase price a selling point for the stressed young mothers who used them as pacifiers. Each sequel needed three new songs, written in a style as close to the original scores of the mother movies as possible. It was hackwork, but Charlie excelled at it. He told me that he enjoyed the easygoing atmosphere at the Disney Animation Studios, the company of the talented young writers, directors, and cartoonists, and the fun of writing songs for hire, under deadline, in a given style and to a very specific length.

That summer and fall Charlie brought home a regular paycheck and lived scam-free in California. He often called to sing me his newest children's song over the phone, and I appreciated that while

I was living three thousand miles away he made sure that my daughter, Lucy, got invited to all the big Disney movie premieres and events.

November was the month when Charlie swapped the contentment of the tradesman for one last swipe at wealth and glory.

It started when he called me at dawn in New York—the middle of the night in Los Angeles—to say that he was up for a major gig.

"Have you heard about *Timewar,* Jack?"

"Another of Simon's rock operas?"

"It's only the biggest movie of next year! Everyone out here knows about it. *Timewar.* This squad of World War II soldiers tracking a Nazi super-weapon go through a rip between dimensions and come out a million years ago."

"You sure Simon didn't have a song like this?"

"They have to get back, but along the way they must fight saber-toothed tigers and primitive half-human tribes of ape men."

"Yeah, I get the picture, Charlie."

"And just when it looks like they have a way out, they realize that the Nazis are there, too, and they're training dinosaurs."

"This animated?"

"No, it's not bloody animated, Jack! This is a big, big movie. That director who did the meteor hitting the earth and the one about the five people trapped in a lift with a time bomb. It's got all these young superstars. There's a scene at the end when an American fighter plane goes up against a dozen Nazi pterodactyls. This is going to be bigger than *Alien,* all right?"

"All right with me, Charlie. Can I go back to sleep now?"

"Listen, Jack. I been talking to this girl at the studio. There's a good chance I could write the theme song for this picture! Think about that, Jack! It's big!"

I reached for a pen and piece of paper. I needed to be clear on what Charlie was telling me and I was only half awake. I wrote down the name of the film.

"Who is the woman telling you this?" I asked him.

"Her name's Robin Charbusser, she's vice president of production at Disney."

"Don't they have a dozen of those?"

"Who cares, man, she's a powerful person and she really digs this song I wrote. She thinks it could be perfect for the film."

"Which song?"

"'I Never Could Believe I Wouldn't See You Anymore.' You heard it."

"For a dinosaur movie?"

"It ain't just a dinosaur movie, man! It's a love story. It's about a guy and girl separated by war and the time barrier and everything he has to go through to get back to her."

"Okay, my mistake."

"Don't make light of this, Jack."

"Sorry, mate, didn't mean to impugn the integrity of the jets vs. pterodactyls scenario."

"It's World War II, Jack. They don't have jets."

"Well, I figured if they had dinosaurs . . ."

"I need you to take this seriously."

"Couldn't they just go like ten years into the future and get some jets?"

"You still my manager?"

"At your beck and call, Charlie. At your beck and call."

"Okay, look, Robin is really pushing to get my song in the movie, but there's this real dick at the studio, guy named Leroy Bjerke, who is lobbying for one of those stupid big schmaltzy ballads written by the same team that writes all the big schmaltzy ballads for all the movies. We gotta get the director and producers to pick my song over Bjerke's."

"You need me to fly out for a meeting?"

"No, man, I need you to get a big superstar to sing my song."

Now I was fully awake. I was sitting on the edge of my bed looking at the sunlight on the building across the street. I had to make sure I had all my facts straight.

"We need to get a superstar to commit to sing this song before the studio commits to use it?"

"Yes, that's what Robin says. She says that the director wants to use my song but he's not going to war with the producers over it. The producers just want something they know will be a hit. That's why they will probably go with the safe choice, the established hit-maker. But if I come in with Whitney Houston or Anita Baker singing my song, the arguments against me will collapse."

I rubbed my eyes. "You've worked this all out."

"Jack, this is my big shot. This is the one. The goal kick at the buzzer. I get this, I'm on top. I can get a new record deal, I can write more movie songs. Jack, you know how many tunes I have stored up! I been lookin' at the movies in production. There's going to be a Spider-Man movie. Remember my song 'In Your Web'? I mean, come on! And get this, the cat who did *The Terminator* is making a movie about the *Titanic* going down. How about my tune 'Drowning'? Jack, we get this, we're in."

"Well, I don't know about the chances of getting Whitney or Anita to cut a song on spec. We don't have any relationship with them, really. Clive practically tastes Whitney's food before it reaches her fork . . . I suppose I could ask Emerson if he would do it at least as a demo."

"They won't go for Emerson," Charlie said quickly. "I asked. Too old, and anyway, they want a chick."

It bothered me that Hollywood studio people were dismissing Emerson as too old but I let it pass.

"What about Barbra Streisand?" Charlie asked me.

"Don't be crazy, Charlie, she lives in a different universe than us."

"Aretha?"

"I don't know, let me figure out if I have a way in there."

"Tina Turner would be great. Everybody knows Tina."

"I'll try, Charlie."

I hung up and tried to go back to sleep but it was useless. I was excited for Charlie. If his optimism was not getting the better of him, if this was true, it really could change his life. Taking that job at Disney was the best thing that had ever happened to him, I thought.

Wrong again.

I tried to get to Anita and Whitney, I tried to get to Madonna and Tina, I tried to get to Aretha and Mariah. None of their emissaries were interested in Charlie or his song or jumping through hoops to audition to get a track placed in a monster movie. These were singers whom movie studios wooed and lobbied, not the other way around.

I called on Wild Bill, the Ravons' old label boss, who was chief of the conglomerate that owned Emerson's record company. He had a soft spot for Charlie and I thought he might help me get to Cher.

"Cher has left us on unpleasant terms," Wild Bill informed me while trying to put a mini-basketball through a full-sized hoop in his enormous office near Times Square. "She has no love for me or my minions."

He scooped up the ball and passed it to me. I threw it and knocked over a vase.

"Well, Bill, you have a huge roster . . ."

"That's what she said." He sank a shot left-handed.

I continued, "As well as extensive social connections. Don't you serve on a civil liberties committee with Bonnie Raitt?"

"Can't poach another label's artist. Hey, if you use one of our acts do we get the soundtrack?"

"That's certainly something to consider."

"Don't kill yourself making this enticing to me, Jack."

He ran down his carpet and leaped into the air, stuffing the ball through the hoop. He turned to me, winded.

"Hey, I got it. Lydya Hall! We're cutting a new album on her right now! Got three big producers doing four tracks each. Costing me a freaking fortune. Maybe this song would fit. Help set up the record. Widen her demographic reach."

I hesitated. Lydya Hall was a big name, a soul singer who hit in the disco era, had won Grammys, been on the cover of *Rolling Stone*. It had been six or seven years, though, since she'd had a song on the radio. She had changed labels a couple of times, changed managers. At this point she was more famous than she was popular. I told Wild Bill that I was not sure that getting Lydya Hall to sing Charlie's song was the coup he needed to impress the studio.

"You're wrong, Jack," he insisted. "This album we're making is going to put her back on top. You gotta hear this stuff."

He called for his assistant to bring him Lydya's new demos and played them for me at brutal volume. I had to admit, they were exciting and her voice was strong and seductive.

"Whadid I tell ya?" Bill said, glowing. "I'm taking a personal interest in this, Jack. We're pulling out all the stops. One thing we don't have right now is a movie tie-in. You got Charlie's song with you?"

Of course I did. I played it for Bill, although after the power and glory of Lydya's tracks it sounded frail. Wild Bill saw past that.

"It could work, man! Don't say anything to Charlie yet. She's in Los Angeles. Let me put this in front of her people and see if they bite."

"I can't thank you enough, Bill," I told him.

"No one can," he said happily.

I went back to my office to three messages from Charlie. When I rang him back he talked a mile a minute about how he had spotted Stevie Nicks on Rodeo Drive and chased her car out of Beverly Hills and over Mulholland Drive in a futile attempt to give her a copy of his song.

"You're lucky you didn't run her off the road," I said. "You have to ease up a little, Charlie. Listen, this is far from a done deal but we might have a chance of getting your song cut by Lydya Hall. I'm working on it."

"Lydya Hall? She still around? I don't think so, Jack. I don't think she's big enough. You know what I was thinking would be good—a onetime reunion of Diana Ross and the Supremes. The key to that is going to be getting Berry Gordy excited."

"Charlie," I cautioned, "you need to take a breath. Lydya Hall is in the middle of recording a very expensive and from what I have heard very good comeback album. Hers is a famous name. Getting your song on this record would be good even if there were no movie. I think we need to focus on this opportunity."

I waited. Charlie stopped dreaming the impossible dream and came back to earth. He said, "She did have a lot of hits."

"She certainly did," I assured him.

"Okay, Jack, but don't stop trying with the others, right?"

"Of course not, Charlie."

Wild Bill was a good ally to have. Within the week he phoned to say that Lydya had heard Charlie's song, liked it, and would try cutting it at her session at Sunset Sound on Monday evening. I asked if Charlie and I could go by to pay our respects. Bill said of course. I told Charlie that if ever his sweet-natured charm was called for, this was the occasion.

When the evening arrived he was as nervous as a rabbit. He was not the usual Charlie. He wanted to get his song in the dinosaur movie very badly.

We arrived at Sunset Sound and found a space at a parking meter at the front door.

"Hey, Jack," Charlie said, "you pulled a Kojak! Empty spot right out front! It's good luck!"

We told the receptionist our names and were ushered into a comfortable recording studio with the lights set as dim as a teenage petting party.

A small group of men in worn jeans and expensive untucked shirts were huddled over the mixing board. They did not rush to greet us. I said, "I hope we're not interrupting," and a very thin, fair-skinned black man with a tight goatee reached a long hand out to brush my fingertips.

"I'm Cain," he said. This was one of the hotshot producers of the moment whom Wild Bill had hired to sprinkle hipness on Lydya Hall.

"Nice to meet you, Cain," I said. "I'm Jack Flynn. This is Charlie Lydle. He wrote 'See You Anymore.'"

"Right." Cain nodded as if he were trying to remember a dream he had last night. "We're going to see if we can do something with that."

One of the men sitting near Cain was fooling around with a fretless bass. Charlie went over and admired it. They began talking about the relative merits of different necks and thickness of strings. Soon Charlie was playing the bass, which was too big for his small hands, and asking for tips. He had broken the ice.

Lydya Hall appeared then, and with her the glacier.

If Lydya was no longer having big hits, no one had told her. She entered the room like an Amazon general, an entourage of female soldiers spreading out before her with Filofaxes and bottles of mineral water. The crew in the room clambered to their feet. Charlie stopped playing his bass.

Cain spoke: "Lydya, good evening. We were just listening back to 'Razzmatazz.' We dropped that second bridge and it sounds better, sounds very good."

"That's nice," Lydya said, and she looked at Charlie. "Who are you?"

"Charlie Lydle," he said, smiling broadly and then snapping the bass to his side like a rifle and making a little bow. "And I know who you are."

I said, "Charlie wrote 'I Never Could Believe I Wouldn't See You Anymore,' Miss Hall. Our mutual friend Bill said it would be all right if we came by to say hello."

"I don't mind," Lydya said, handing her jacket to one of her attendants. "We ain't promised to cut that track, you know."

I said, "We presume nothing."

She said, "We'll give it a shot."

Cain reminded Lydya that they had something else to work on first, a leftover from the last session. Lydya dismissed him with a brush of her hand.

"That can wait. These gents have come from England to hear us sing their song, let's give it a shot."

There was some shuffling of papers as the musicians found the lead sheets for Charlie's song and scurried into the studio to set up their instruments.

Lydya entered the recording booth like a queen ascending to her throne. An assistant handed her headphones. She cupped one can over her left ear and left the other dangling. She cued the drummer to count off. The producer did not object. The song began.

Charlie had written and performed "I Never Could Believe I Wouldn't See You Anymore" as a slow folk rock song, not a million miles from Hank Williams's "I'm So Lonesome I Could Cry." Lydya—or Cain, it was impossible to tell who was in charge here—had sped it up a hair and changed the key. Lydya was taking it as a blues song with a touch of gospel. When she got to the middle section, a rolling build toward "Bridge Over Troubled Water" majesty, I cold imagine kettle-drums, choral swells, and flying aces in dogfights with dinosaurs.

I looked at Lydya, who was lost in her performance, pushing every word as if she were reading her diary. I looked at Cain, who was nodding as if in prayer. I looked at Charlie, who seemed to be itching to rip off his clothes.

The moment Lydya finished singing, Charlie jumped up and said, "Cain, can I get on the talk-back?" He reached down on the mixing board and pressed a small square button. "Lydya? Hey! That was very nice but you might be emoting too much too early. If you go back and listen to my version, I hold back until the refrain. Like, I'm going about my day and then it hits me, right? I remember she's gone. You come in grieving, you have to build up to it . . ."

Lydya, still in the glass cocoon of her vocal booth, stared back through the window in disbelief. Cain pushed Charlie's hand away from the talk-back button and glared at him. I put my hand on Charlie's shoulder and reminded him, "She has to make the song work for her, man."

"I know that," Charlie said, "but I wrote this tune, I know how it should go!"

"Charlie," I whispered directly into his ear. "Sit down."

Cain was on the mike talking to his artist. "It was beautiful, L," he said. "I did not know that song had so much in it. You want to come in and listen back?"

"Not yet," she said, satisfied that the infidel had been banished. "Let's run it down one more time. And you—piano."

The pianist looked up from behind his Steinway. She told him, "No trills. Just play the chords."

He nodded. They began the song again. I was holding Charlie down on the couch as he struggled to climb up on the console and conduct. I dug my elbow into his ribs.

Lydya finished take two. I said loudly, "That was beautiful. Thank you, Cain. We should go."

Charlie shrugged to his feet like a delinquent. I said, "Please tell Miss Hall how thrilled we are that she is considering Charlie's song."

"Yeah, sure," Cain said and began setting up the faders for a playback.

Lydya stayed in the vocal booth until she saw us leave.

Lydya Hall's version of Charlie's song "I Never Could Believe I Wouldn't See You Anymore" did what we needed it to do. It convinced Disney to take the track seriously as a contender to be the theme for their big summer action movie. Charlie's advocate at the studio, Robin Charbusser, was doing all she could to move the song forward. She played it at staff meetings, sent copies to the cast of the film, and demonstrated with survey data how it could bring women and over-twenty-fives to a movie already secure with the young male demo. Surely, I thought, Charlie must be sleeping with her.

Playing mongoose to Robin's cobra was Leroy Bjerke, her rival at the studio and a man determined to get a proven Hollywood hit-maker to compose a song for *Timewar*. Every time Robin got a clear shot at the goal, Bjerke blocked her. He argued against using Charlie's song to the studio chief, the movie's director, and members of the Hollywood Foreign Press Association.

"Why does this guy Bjerke have it in for you?" I asked Charlie.

"He's just a dick, man. He can't stand to see anyone else succeed. He'd rather that the movie tank than Robin get credit for bringing in the theme song."

"So he has nothing against you personally? You didn't seduce his wife or something?"

Charlie tried to change the subject. I dragged him back. He said, "Well, she wasn't his wife at the time."

The best way to get Charlie's song selected for the film was to make it Disney's easiest option. To that end I went along with all their boilerplate demands regarding their ownership of Charlie's song if it was selected for their film. To my great frustration, Charlie was not helpful.

"It's a very good sign that they are even talking to me about the publishing, Charlie," I told him. "Let's not get in a fight with them over this. Let's do the deal quickly and hope the momentum carries us over the finish line."

"I won't do it, Jack!" Charlie insisted. "I will not give those creeps the publishing on 'See You Anymore.' Fuck them! It's my song and I am keeping the rights."

"Charlie, you know I am a great advocate of the artist keeping his music publishing." This was a dig; Charlie had ignored my advice about selling off his rights in the past. "But for God's sake, look at the big picture. Getting this song in this film could change your life! If this takes off you will make more money on the writer's share than you have seen in twenty years. Disney always takes the publishing! It's the price of getting your song in their film! Give it up!"

"I will not do it, Jack. Not this time. I can feel in every bone of my body that this is the big one. This song is great. It is a masterpiece. No one can deny it. Even these movie hacks recognize it. It will elevate their silly dinosaur movie. It will sell millions and become a new standard. I am not giving up my publishing or anything else concerned with it. If Disney wants it, they will take it on my terms."

Charlie was getting power-mad. All the years of smiling in the face of disappointment, being a good sport, and acting humble had taken their little bits from his skin. He had been suppressing his artist's ego for a long time. This was an awkward moment for it to come roaring back to life.

I got on the phone with Robin Charbusser at the studio and told her that I insisted on Charlie holding on to his publishing.

"Christ, Jack, are you *trying* to kill this deal?" she asked me. "This asshole Bjerke is fighting me right up to the chairman of the board! Next thing, he's going to go down and defrost old Walt and lobby him to reject Charlie's song. If you guys won't play ball on the publishing you're giving him a hammer to beat us with!"

I often found myself arguing for positions I did not believe. That is what a manager does: represent the client's wishes even when you think him deluded. In this case, though, my client was sawing a circle around himself, so I said, "How about this, Robin—we split the publishing. Either fifty-fifty or domestic-overseas. Can you sell that to your bosses?"

"This is not where I should be spending my energy," she told me. "It's not the fight I need to have right now."

"Just try."

"All right, Flynn, I'll try. But I hope Charlie understands that your taking this position is putting his song at risk."

I said he understood and put down the phone. Charlie called every fifteen minutes to see if there was an update. Two days later there was. Disney agreed to a sixty/forty split on the publishing with Charlie owing them five additional songs for future projects at the same rate. I said yes without checking with him.

When he called again I said, "They caved. You've got half the publishing and all the writer's share. Congratulations."

"Half the publishing?" Charlie said. "Good, they're retreating. I knew they would! Now call them back and say, nope, Charlie keeps it all."

"Too late, man. I accepted."

Charlie hit the roof. He cursed me as I had not heard him curse since Emerson quit the Ravons. He informed me that I had no right to do that without his okay and instructed me to call them right back and say I had made a mistake.

"No, Charlie," I said. "I took the deal and you have to live with it. Now listen—keep your eyes on the prize. It looks very much as if your song is going to be the theme of a big-budget, heavily promoted summer blockbuster. You are set to take home more of the money than any other Disney composer gets to keep. This will lead to a new record deal for you, other scoring assignments, and likely more cash than you have ever earned in your life. Charlie? Don't fuck it up."

I would not say he became contrite, but he stopped complaining. It was as much as I could ask for.

I had lingered too long in Charlie's Hollywood drama. Emerson was barreling around the country on a tour that was going very well and making him rich enough to let Delilah tear down and rebuild their seaside mansion as often as she liked.

I caught up with Emerson in Houston. I arrived at the venue during his encore, just in time to scamper into his sport-utility vehicle as the band ran from the stage to haul out of the arena before the traffic jams formed. Castro was in front next to the driver. He had a stack of clean white towels in his lap.

"Flynn!" Emerson shouted when he saw me sitting next to him in the SUV. "Where the hell did you appear from? Did you hear the show?"

"Of course I did, man, I was at the mixing board. You were great!"

"I am having the best time of my life, Jack! The best time ever! How about the band? How about Baxter? I love these guys, Jack!"

Emerson was drunk on adrenaline, elated and talking a mile a minute. He was always like this immediately after a concert. It is a profound physical experience for a performer to go out onstage in front of twelve thousand cheering people. No matter how many years he does it or how often, the shock to his nervous system is intense. On a purely primal level, when he hits the stage and the lights go up and the audience screams, there is a rush of fight-or-flight chemicals into the bloodstream and brain stem. Then, emotionally, there is the addictive shock of having thousands of strangers drench you with love and admiration. Most of us begin life as babies, pampered, adored, and assuming we are the center of the world. Most of us are disabused of these illusions by the time we start school. Some part of our psyche never gets over the feeling that a mistake has been made and that the way we were treated as infants is how it's supposed to stay. For rock stars, it does.

A tour doctor from North Carolina once told me that a performer at Emerson's level goes through adrenal shocks and emotional upheavals on a nightly basis that most of us would experience only once every few years—winning a sports championship, being arrested or questioned in court, facing the death of a loved one, getting married or divorced, having a baby. The doctor said to me, "Humans are not built to absorb so many jolts. No one who does could possibly remain normal."

Emerson was many things good and bad. Normal was not among them.

When we reached the parameter of the arena grounds, an escort of motorcycle policemen formed around our caravan and turned on their lights and sirens to clear our way to the airport.

"All right!" Emerson laughed. "The Klingons are with us! Good job, Ramon!"

Castro nodded and handed him a towel. Emerson wiped his face. He said, "Hey, man, bequeath me a ceremonial swizzle stick."

Castro popped open the armrest and passed Emerson a tightly rolled joint. He then dug out a thermos of vodka and began pouring it into three glasses that he held between his fingers by the stems. We were flying along at eighty miles an hour and he did not spill a drop.

Emerson took a long drag and let the blue pot smoke whistle out. He then accepted a glass of vodka and raised it in a silent toast to both of us.

"Great audience tonight, man," he said. "I love Texas."

We hurtled down the highway, Emerson letting the marijuana medicate his mood. I was aware that the other vehicles in our motorcade had dropped away. We were the only car left. One of the motorcycle cops pulled up alongside Emerson's window and blasted his siren to get our attention. He was pointing and gesturing. Emerson's mood flipped over.

"Fuck! He sees the joint! He's telling us to pull over!"

Emerson's affection for the Lone Star State suddenly slipped. "This is a setup!" he said. "Driver, keep going!"

The driver, a large Mexican man, said, "Got to obey the law, sir."

Emerson dropped the joint onto the floor and ground it into the carpet. Castro snapped up the armrest pocket and directed us to pour in our drinks. He then reached in his leather travel bag and came out with a small tube of air spray that he squirted all around. It was a resourceful but futile gesture; the car smelled like a Cheech and Chong movie.

The driver rolled down the window. The cop leaned in.

"Mr. Cutler," he said. "You went by the turn for the private airport. You need to go back and get off at 42E."

The driver said to Castro, "We're not going to Hobby?"

"No, man," Castro said. "The private field. That's why all the other cars went left back there."

"Sorry," the driver said.

"Shit, man," said Castro.

"We'll turn you around and take you back there," said the cop. He made a little salute and returned to his motorcycle.

Emerson looked at me and started laughing. "You should have seen your face, Flynn! You were having a flashback to the English Channel, weren't you?"

I smiled. Castro glared at the embarrassed driver. "Not cool, man," he whispered.

We found our way to the landing field and climbed onto Emerson's private jet for the short hop to the next stop, New Orleans. As we ascended I looked down at the countryside. It was a clear night and all the electric grids were illuminated. In the twenty years I had been living in America the flat glowing orange web of Los Angeles had spread east. Villages and woods and white fences and stone walls had fallen to endless tracts of malls and housing developments, big box stores and double-wide streets. Every place in the country looked like LA now.

"Is there any shrimp on the plane?" Emerson asked the attendant. She went to look. Emerson turned to me and said, "I'll tell you why I have to stay out on the road, Flynn. It's my fucking hippie in-laws. Delilah has more godparents, half siblings, and ex-stepfathers than Simon has enemies. The house on Long Island has become Total Loss Farm, you've never seen so many freeloading bead-makers, I Ching readers, and wind chime designers."

"Couple of bullshit artists, too?" I asked.

He smiled. "The thing that kills me is, she keeps telling me to send the *plane* for them. I say, 'I don't mind your mum and her boyfriend moving into my house and drinking me dry for two months but do I really have to send a private jet to pick them up? Are they really so posh they can't fly commercial if we buy them first-class tickets? I mean, we are talking about people who live in a camper, am I right?' She won't hear of it. Sixty grand—poof. And they always eat all the fuckin' shrimp."

We had barely leveled out after takeoff when we began our descent into New Orleans. We landed and we loaded into a van and motored to our hotel. Emerson wanted to meet in the bar for a nightcap. One drink led to five others and soon we had decided that while we were in the Crescent City we would track down our old witch doctor, G. T. LaSalle. It was only midnight when we lit out—lunchtime in the French Quarter.

LaSalle was not listed in the phone directory. We made it our mission to ask up and down the Quarter. We inquired in saloons, outside musical instrument shops, and at nightclubs. We asked buskers on Dauphine Street and cornet players at Preservation Hall. It being New Orleans, no one said they did not know. Everyone suggested he knew *something*, although specifics were as rare as snowdrifts.

"Oh yes, I know George LaSalle, he teaches music at the high school in Baton Rouge."

"LaSalle? He played with Ernie K-Doe. Got fired for sleeping with the police chief's wife over in Mandeville."

"He drowned down in the Gulf. His body washed up near Biloxi and all his teeth were gone."

"That song 'Long Tall Sally' was originally called 'George LaSally,' you know. Oh yes, the record company made Richard change it. Richard and George were an item."

The stories were contradictory and circular. By two-thirty in the morning we gave up. Emerson had the next day off and we determined to use it to track LaSalle, but a whole afternoon of inquiries and false leads left us disappointed. We had thrown in the towel and gone for dinner at the Rib Room at the Royal Orleans Hotel when Emerson was approached by an African-American valet.

"Mr. Cutler, would you sign this picture for my daughter? Her name is Daphne."

By that time in his life Emerson was often impatient with white fans who bothered him in restaurants, but he was flattered when black people recognized him. He asked if Daphne had a favorite song.

"I think she likes that one you had out about the girl going away to college. She played that for me."

Emerson had sung a song called "Good-bye, Good Luck, Sally G," which was used in a Molly Ringwald film. He wrote on the photograph, *Good-bye, Good Luck, Daphne—from your friend Emerson Cutler.*

The valet took the picture from Emerson and studied the inscription. He thanked us and he said, "I heard you gentlemen were looking for G. T. LaSalle."

We said we were indeed. The valet said, "I know where Mr. LaSalle lives. Out in the Garden District."

Emerson said, "How do you know him?"

"My Uncle John played bass guitar on a lot of record sessions. He and Mr. LaSalle worked together for a long time. He used to deliver groceries out to Mr. LaSalle's house and then I did it for a while."

I looked at Emerson like Watson looking at Holmes. "Is there any chance you can get us a phone number?" I asked.

"No, sir, but I can tell you the address."

I got out a pen and wrote what the valet told me on the back of a drinks menu: 161 de Lille, between Euterpe Street and Terpsichore. We called our driver to head over there right away.

New Orleans' Garden District was verdant and sweet. Big-trunk weeping willow trees twisted out of wet grass on thick lawns that crept up to houses with long low porches and white globe lights above the doors. The lawns were not cut as tight as they would be in another American city, the tree limbs not sawn back. Everything was a little lazy, dangling and dripping in the night breeze.

We crawled up and down de Lille looking for 161. Many of the houses had no numbers. We finally figured out that a four-story brown wood tower was number 157. And we learned from ringing the bell that the brick house on the corner was 165. Therefore, the Spanish-style hacienda with the chipped cement wall and the wrought-iron gate had to be 161. It was like a little Alamo, a locked compound set back behind an untended yard of large fronds, with moss climbing up the walls.

We tried the gate. It felt like it had been locked for years. Emerson located a call box with a button. He pressed it. There was no response. There was a light on behind shutters on the second floor. I called up hello. Nothing. He pressed the buzzer again, holding it down. No reply.

We had nowhere else to go, so we sat down on two large rocks and leaned our backs on the wall and shared a joint. Once in a while Emerson reached up and gave the buzzer another push.

We were talking about old divorces when a face appeared between the bars of the gate. We dropped the joint and climbed to our feet.

"Hello," I said, "I'm John Flynn and this is Emerson Cutler. We're old friends of Mr. LaSalle."

A black woman who looked as ancient as the stones stared back at me with narrow eyes and said nothing.

"Emerson is playing at the House of Blues this week. Mr. LaSalle produced one of his early albums, he'd like to say hello."

The woman turned away from the gate and shuffled back into the house. We waited for the gate to open or someone else to appear. After five minutes we realized that nothing was going to happen. Emerson took out a cigar and lit it and sat back down on his rock, pushing the buzzer as he passed.

After a while a shutter opened upstairs and a younger woman with American Indian features leaned out to have a look at us.

"Hello, there," I said. "I'm John Flynn from England. I'm here with Emerson Cutler the famous recording artist. We'd like to see our old friend Mr. LaSalle."

"He's sleeping," the woman in the window said.

I thought about that. "Well, perhaps you could knock on his door and ask if he might not like to get up to see Emerson." She looked at me as if I had suggested setting the roof on fire. I said, "Emerson wants to invite him to his concert at the House of Blues."

The shutter closed. I sat down on a stone next to Emerson, who said, "We're running out of things to smoke. You don't have your crack pipe on you?"

The iron gate squeezed open and the Indian woman glared at us. We got back on our feet and dusted off the seats of our pants. She walked into the house. We followed her.

We stepped into a long and dingy hallway, half lit, at the end of which stood what I first took to be a gruesome statue and then realized was a living man. He was old, tall, and thin as a corpse, with a filthy black suit and a twisted gray necktie. His skin was albino and his eyes were rheumy. There were white hairs sticking out of his chin where his razor missed, and it looked like he had stuffed gray spiders up his nostrils. The Indian woman passed him without acknowledging him, as if he were a grandfather clock, and took a sharp left at the end of the hall.

Emerson said hello to the ghoul as we followed. He let out a gurgle and sank back onto a wooden stool. We went into the room the Indian woman had entered. It was a parlor filled with dusty chairs draped with antimacassars and tables and sideboards crammed with knick-knacks—souvenir plates, china teacups, candlesticks, glass birds, and at least a dozen hourglasses of various sizes and materials.

"LaSalle is here," I said to Emerson.

"You may look around," the woman said.

"Thanks," Emerson told her.

"Will you go tell Mr. LaSalle we're here?" I asked her. "It's Jack Flynn and Emerson Cutler, from London."

She left the room. Emerson nudged me and pointed to the walls. There were plaques with LaSalle's name, citations from chambers of commerce in Muscle Shoals and Memphis, and a gold single from the King Records label. There were photographs, including the one with Buddy Holly I remembered from London and a picture of LaSalle with Stevie Ray Vaughan.

Also on the wall was an Elvis Presley novelty clock with the King's legs swinging like pendulums, a black velvet painting of a horse, a dart-board missing the bull's-eye, and the sort of signed pictures of obscure entertainers one sees along the walls of diners. The faded yellow wall-paper was interrupted by square patches where the paper was brighter, as if frames that had hung there forever had recently been removed.

Emerson and I were getting seriously spooked when a narrow door at the end of the room opened and a tiny man entered, grinning and bearing a tray.

"For you," he said in a woman's high voice. He held out two foam-ing drinks overflowing from dirty coffee mugs.

I took mine and nodded thanks and took a swig. It tasted like warm coconut laced with iodine. I tried to swallow enough to be cordial. Emerson did not even put his lips to the rim.

The servant grinned up at us with large, infected gums. His teeth looked as if they were about to fall into the beverage cups. It was impossible to tell what race this creature belonged to. He had a high forehead and long oily black hair that was falling out in patches. There were sores on his neck. His fingernails were long and cracked. He kept grinning at us and never blinked. I took some more of the potion and my throat constricted. So much for manners. I placed my cup back on the tray. He smiled again and went back through the narrow door.

"What the cripe is this, Jack?" Emerson whispered.

"It looks like they've been stealing his awards and photographs from the wall, doesn't it?" I whispered back. "I don't think LaSalle would ever hang up these silly clocks and posters. I think these ghouls must be ripping down his gold records and autographed Beatles pictures and fencing them. They put up this crap to cover the thefts!"

The Indian woman was back in the room. She barked at us, "He's not coming down!"

Emerson opened his mouth to speak and closed it, considering.

I suggested, "If Mr. LaSalle is unwell, we could perhaps go upstairs and pay our respects."

The Indian woman was a mighty fortress. She said, "You got your drinks, you looked around. Now you go home."

The tall bag of bones by the door loomed into the room. The leper with his tray reappeared, delighted. We were facing an escort of the ghastly. We had no more excuses for stalling.

"Please tell Mr. LaSalle that his name will be on the guest list at the House of Blues Thursday. Or if he wants to reach us before then, we are staying at the Royal Orleans."

The three spooks stared at me. I became aware that their coconut drink was boiling in my belly and threatening to come rising up my throat. Now I wanted to be out of this haunted house. Emerson and I went down the corridor and through the front door to the road and heard the wrought-iron gate clank shut behind us.

We wandered through the Garden District looking for our car and driver. I puked behind someone's lilac bush. I was feeling feverish.

"I think they've fucking killed him, Flynn!" Emerson announced.

"I think LaSalle is dead and these half-human hyenas are keeping it a secret to keep his royalty checks coming in! Fucking hell! That was like the children of the damned in there, wasn't it? I can't believe LaSalle is alive."

I was down on all fours, vomiting into someone's clay garden pot. I said, "Get me back to the hotel and phone a doctor or I'm going to join him."

That visit to the Garden District was as close as we ever got to seeing G. T. LaSalle again.

Emerson's New Orleans concert suffered from his carrying a two-ton hangover. He cut it short by three songs and we lit out for the airport and, I expected, Tennessee.

When we had been in the air two hours I asked the flight attendant how much longer it was to Nashville. She told me we were going to New York. I nudged Emerson, who had dozed off.

"We're going to New York tonight?"

"Yeah, man. I got tomorrow off. Why spend it sitting around a hotel in Nashville when I can pop home and surprise my babies?"

"Fine with me," I said, "but no one told me. I need to arrange to have a car pick me up at the airport."

"Come out to my place with me, you can stay in the guesthouse."

"No, thanks."

"Come to my place anyway, I'll lend you a car."

"Fine."

We landed at East Hampton Airport on Long Island. Castro was heading to Montauk for twenty-four hours. I rode out to Emerson's house with him. It was after three A.M. The estate was dark. He whispered that it was much too late for me to start back to the city, I should take one of the guest rooms. He was right and I said so, although my last experience sleeping over at the Cutlers' had ended with my promising myself not to do it again. I wish I had kept that promise.

We were looking for an unlocked door—Emerson never carried keys—when we heard splashing coming from the swimming pool. Emerson put his fingers to his lips and motioned for me to follow him.

"It's freezing out, Emerson," I whispered. "Who would go swimming on a night like this?"

"Heated pool, man," Emerson whispered back. "'Lilah loves the way it feels to slip from the cold air into the warm water."

We walked around a pool house and peeked over a fence. The blue lights inside the pool were on; the ripples in the water made flickering shadows. Stretched across the green lip of the pool were the tanned arms and shoulders of Delilah Grath Cutler. The back of her wet hair tilted languidly to one side and we caught the soft edge of her fine profile. She was resting in the water, hovering like a painted angel, holding on to the side of the pool for support while she slipped between sleep and waking.

"God, Jack," Emerson whispered. "Look at her. Look at my beautiful wife."

"Hello, darlin'," he called out softly.

Delilah cocked her head like a doe. "Who's that?" she asked.

"Surprise!" Emerson said, stepping through the gate. "I hope you're naked, because I'm about to be."

That was my cue to exit. Before I could go, Delilah said, "Emerson! What are you doing home?"

"Missed you and Autumn," Emerson said, pulling off his shirt and unbuckling his belt as he moved toward the pool.

"You should have called," she said.

I heard a warning in her voice. Emerson was still marching toward her, shedding his duds. A second head emerged from the water. It was covered with hair, crown to chin. A wet and confused young hippie came up for air and found a load of trouble.

"What the hell?" Emerson stopped cold.

"Hey," the hippie said. He spit water into the pool.

"Emerson," Delilah said, "this is Jude, my cousin."

Emerson absorbed what he had walked into. Delilah and Jude were both naked, and from their position and the rigidity of his manhood, he had not been cleaning the filters.

"Get the fuck out of the water!" Emerson shouted.

Jude straightened up. He was long, wiry, and hairy all over. His wet beard reached his clavicle. "Chill," he told Emerson.

"Oh, okay," Emerson said. He marched down the steps into the pool. Delilah scampered over the side and rolled onto the paved path.

Emerson reached out his right hand to Jude as if to shake it and then belted him with his left fist. Jude wobbled and Emerson punched him with his right. Jude went down, not for the first time that evening but almost certainly for the last.

"Emerson!" Delilah screamed. Every time I visited their home I got to hear her scream and see her naked. Most people had to buy a movie ticket for that. "Don't hurt him! What are you doing here? Your schedule said you were in Nashville!"

Jude the obscene was doing the dead man's float. Emerson gathered a handful of his lank hair and hoisted his face up out of the water. He dropped it again and Jude stirred and came up gobbling for air. Emerson was climbing out of the pool now, moving in on Delilah.

"Why are you acting like a crazy monster?" she shouted. "He's my cousin!"

Emerson snatched her wrist. "You're into incest, too? Do you have any sense of decency at all, Delilah? I walk in and catch you having sex with some tramp and you're going to try to lie your way out of it? Are you completely mad?"

She yanked her hand away, indignant and furious. "Oh, come off it! You of all people! Mr. Bring-On-the-Groupies! You are not going to tell me that I am not allowed some recreational sex while you are out chasing all the sluts your roadies collect for you! Don't even try to sell that one!"

Emerson stopped cold. He stared down at this strange, fierce, shivering girl who looked as if she might jump on his neck and try to bite him to death.

"You are mentally ill," he said. "You have until suppertime to get out of my house. Tell all your horrible friends and fake relatives the bad news. Flynn!"

It was the first time Delilah realized there was a witness. I stepped forward and said, "Yes, Em?"

"Call Kelleher and start the divorce. Tell him to get tough if she fights it. Tell him this marriage is over."

Jude the damp and hairy gigolo was crawling into the pool house. Delilah switched personalities. She became contrite and imploring.

"Baby," she murmured to Emerson, draping her arms on his shoulders. "I didn't mean to be bad. I was just lonely. Let me make it up to you."

Emerson stared down at her. He said, "You're really not a very good actress, are you?"

The end of his previous marriages had spurred Emerson to work.
This divorce made him quit doing anything. He finished his tour
with perfunctory performances and refused to let me book any more
dates. He bought a large house on the side of a steep wooded hill in
Woodstock, the Valhalla of old rock stars, and retreated there.

I sympathized with his pain and humiliation, intensified by the
added insult of Delilah's winning custody of their daughter. All the
same, it was a terrible moment for Emerson to drop out. The rise of
Nirvana and the grunge bands did what punk had failed to do fifteen
years earlier—it drove classic rock off FM radio. American broadcast-
ers had spent two decades locked in 1971—"Brown Sugar," "Won't Get
Fooled Again," and "Maggie May" had arrived that summer and did
not go away until "Smells Like Teen Spirit" and "Jeremy" stormed the
Bastille in flannel shirts and baggy shorts.

Since the seventies, Emerson had almost always had a song on the
air. That changed in a month as radio abandoned the old rock stars for
Pearl Jam, Smashing Pumpkins, and Green Day. MTV followed suit.
They pushed any singers over thirty to VH1, and from there to oblivion.

I tried to convince Emerson to do something to remind the public
he was alive, but he would not even leave his house. Emerson had
been a rock star for a very long time. He did not understand that he
was being dismissed. Punk had been a press movement only; it did not
affect radio or ticket sales. Grunge was different. It knocked him off
the airwaves. Those radio stations not playing new rock bands were
devoted to rap and hip-hop, forms he detested from the distance of his
mountain in the Catskills.

Faced with trying to keep his income flowing and his music playing, I made deals for Emerson we would not have considered before. I

licensed his songs to B-movies and television commercials. I let his old tracks be used on compilation albums sold on late-night TV. He agreed to everything. The only question he ever asked was, "How much?"

Talking to him was a chore. He dismissed all invitations and well-meant suggestions out of hand. Any idea I relayed from the record company about how he might update his image and extend his career was rejected. He had never been comfortable listening to others' suggestions, but now anyone who dared offer a criticism was, to hear him tell it, displaying a failure of integrity and probably evidence of dishonesty. No one was allowed to simply not care for one of his songs; they had to have a low motive. To not love and support everything Emerson did was a failure of character.

Emerson needed a manager less than a psychiatrist, which meant that I had more time to deal with Charlie's exploding ego. Summer was coming. Previews for *Timewar* were already running in movie houses. Charlie's song had made it to the finish line. All he had to do now was not find a way to screw it up. The cuckold Leroy Bjerke was still lurking in the shadows of the Walt Disney Company, hoping for an excuse to replace "I Never Could Believe I Wouldn't See You Anymore" with the song he had commissioned from an established hack, "Forever and a Day."

Knowing that somewhere out there an enemy plotted to sabotage his dream was driving Charlie crazy. I got my first mobile telephone that summer. Charlie called it every time I crossed my legs.

"Jack!" he cried one morning as I was sitting down to breakfast at Balthazar with the head of Arista Records. "Have you heard the crap songs that win Academy Awards? I am definitely going to get nominated!"

"Don't count your pterodactyls before they're hatched, Charlie. I'm in a meeting, I'll call you back."

"Wait, this is important! What if they want Lydya to sing my song on the Oscar telecast?"

I smiled at the Arista chief and told Charlie, "That would be a nice problem to have."

"I'm not going to get set up, Jack! I want you to get this in writing with Lydya's people now or I'm pulling the song. I will *share* a duet with her on the Academy Awards but that is as far as I will go, and I think that's very fair given that I have written the song that is going to put her back on the map and give her the biggest hit of her career!"

"I'll call you back, Charlie."

The fever was upon him. He had subsumed his ambitions for so long that now they were crawling up his spine and infecting his brain. My job was to keep him locked in his room until the movie came out with his song attached.

For the next week all was calm. I checked my calendar. The release date of the film was moving closer, the posters were in the theater on Twenty-third Street. Surely Charlie could not blow it now.

My new mobile phone erupted six times while I was trying to take a bath. On the seventh I grabbed it. I was pretty sure it would not electrocute me. I soon wished it had.

"I've been reading the bylaws, Jack," Charlie wailed. "We're cooked!"

"What bylaws?"

"Of the Academy of Motion Picture Arts and Sciences! To be eligible for Best Original Song a composition must have been created specifically for the motion picture for which it is nominated! Previously existing compositions are not eligible. Jack! They're going to take back my Oscar!"

"Charlie, you don't have an Oscar. What in God's name are you talking about? 'See You Anymore' is a new song, you never recorded it before, no one else ever recorded it before. You did write it, right?"

The misery of the voice on the other end of my telephone was like that of banished Adam.

"Of course I wrote it! But, Jack, it's not new! I said it was, but I wrote it ten years ago!"

"Charlie, listen to me. One: no one knows. Two: no one cares. Okay? Many, many Oscar-nominated songs began in someone's scrap pile. Have you told anyone that you did not write this song for *Timewar*?"

"Just you."

"Wonderful. Now just make sure you *never tell anyone else*. All right? Can you do that? You read this script and you were so moved by the plight of these brave soldiers stranded a million years in the past that you sat down at the piano and this lament poured out of you as if a Tyrannosaurus rex had just eaten your one true love."

There was a gurgling down the wire. Shampoo was drying in my hair. Charlie finally spoke: "Jack, remember when you got me that money for the dozen songs we licensed to that publisher in England? Remember, Jack? This song was in that package! They can prove I didn't write it for the movie!"

I considered this. It meant nothing. "Charlie? Listen to me now. That was a short-term deal. Two years. It came and went without the British publisher placing a single song. No one recorded any of those tunes. The deal ended, the songs reverted to you. No one else has any claim. Nor will anyone at that company even remember the name of the songs in that portfolio. Trust me, Charlie. The only way this will ever come out is if you tell someone."

"I can't take the chance, Jack! I can't! This song is going to win the Academy Award and then some jealous creep in the UK is going to pop up with a lead sheet proving that I wrote it ten years ago and they're going to try to take my Oscar away!"

"Charlie! Charlie! Have you got some marijuana? I want you to roll a big joint and put on *Kind of Blue* and mellow the fuck out! What did we talk about before? Keep your eye on the ball. What is our main objective? Our main objective is to get your song in the movie. That will get you a lot of money and tremendous exposure. If that happens and the song is a big hit, you have already won! You have already won, Charlie! Now, if all that happens and you are lucky enough to be nominated for an Oscar your first time at bat, it's gravy. It's a bonus! If you win the Oscar, you are the happiest fella in the world. But, Charlie, please, *don't count on it.*"

There was a long silence. I thought I'd lost him. Finally he said, "All right. I'll smoke some weed and think this over."

I thanked him and hung up. I had to get to California at once. I wondered if I dared take the time to rinse.

By the time I got to Los Angeles, fifteen hours had passed and Charlie had made a big step toward ruining everything. I landed at LAX and rented a car. Robin Charbusser, the production executive who had fought for Charlie's song, was looking for me.

"Are you here, Jack?" she demanded when I called her back. "Are you in LA?"

"Just arrived. How's Charlie?"

"Charlie is a putz! He wants to pull 'See You Anymore' from the film and he won't tell anyone why."

"He's having a panic attack, ignore him."

"He's gone to the director, he's gone to the producers, he's even chased down the actors. He's telling everyone that 'See You Anymore' is not specific to the story of the film and he has a much better song he's just written that actually mentions being lost in time. Jack, this is a disaster. Bjerke is still pushing to get his song in. The producers do not want to have to deal with Charlie's shit—they are still editing the movie and it comes out in three weeks!"

"I'll get him to stop, Robin."

First I had to find him. I called his number and left a dozen messages. I drove to his house, called everyone who knew him, and phoned people at the studio I had never met before, most of whom had heard from Charlie recently and made it clear to me they would appreciate never hearing from him again.

I felt like I had missed a turn, I had gotten off on the wrong exit, I was not where I was meant to be. My self-image was of the detached and ironic grown-up who swoops in at the last minute to sort out all the trouble, but this time the kids had fallen into the deep water and I could not get there in time. I was standing on the side of Santa Monica Boulevard pounding numbers into my mobile phone when I thought of Charlie's ex, Samantha Lipsitz. It was her connections that had got him the job at Disney. Her phone number was unlisted. I called my office in New York and had them patch me through.

"He's here, Jack," Samantha said. "I'm up in Beverly Park, come over."

I made my way to Samantha's house. She was living in what looked like a small Mediterranean hotel on a brand-new street with brand-new mansions designed to look old. The old cliff dwellers of Laurel Canyon had exchanged their funky little cottages for gated grandeur.

In the way of Los Angeles, the front yard was small and gave the illusion of modesty, an illusion immediately vanquished by the size of the home. Samantha opened the door herself. She led me through a foyer with Greek and Roman sculptures into a large library decorated with sets of antique books and out the back door to a swimming pool big enough to scrub down a herd of cattle and sentineled by topiary sculptures the size of radar dishes. Charlie was on the lip of the pool, hunched over his guitar and a notebook.

"Listen to this, Jack," he said to me as if I had been there the whole time. "It's the same chords as 'See You Anymore,' the same feel, but a much better song."

He began to sing a slow song in a warbly voice. The central idea was that our love would carry on through the smoke and flame.

"They gotta like that one, eh?" Charlie said. He smiled and sounded happy but his eyes were ringed with purple. He looked awful. "I figure if they love 'See You Anymore' they can still use that on the soundtrack, maybe for the scene when Cannon gets the radio signal to work so he can talk to Kara across the time barrier. But this should be the big song, this should be the credit theme."

I sat down next to him on the edge of the pool.

"Charlie," I said. "Robin at Disney is freaking out. She says you told the producers you were pulling the song."

"I told them I had a better one! Come on, Jack." He looked around secretively to be sure Samantha was not listening. "You know the issue with 'See You Anymore.'"

"Charlie, remember. Eyes on the prize. Let's make sure we keep your song in the movie."

"That's not in question, Jack," he said.

"Can we drive over there and see Robin and calm her down and assure her that you are just offering the producers a second option? You are fine with them using 'See You Anymore' if that's their preference?"

He began to protest but stopped short. He said, "She's freaking out?"

"Oh yeah."

"Okay, sure. You know what this means to me, Jack."

"I sure do, man."

I opened my cell phone and called Robin Charbusser to say that everything was fine and Charlie and I were on the way over. She told me not to bother.

"The song's out, Jack," she said. "This went all the way to my boss's boss and he said, 'Why are we dealing with this bullshit when the movie is not finished?' Bjerke was right there with his big-time film composer piece of crap on a CD for them. The theme from *Timewar* is going to be 'Forever and a Day' performed by Whitney Houston. Charlie's out. They don't even want him back at the animation factory. We all tried our best but he blew it. I'm sorry. Good-bye."

I felt like the boy in the children's movie who has to go out and shoot Old Yeller. I went over and gave Charlie the bad news. He did not understand what I was saying. He kept insisting that he could fix it and I had to get pretty rough explaining that he could not, the song was out of the movie and no one at the studio wanted to talk to him. He finally stopped protesting. He quietly took his notebook and stuffed it into the sound hole of his acoustic guitar. Then he placed the guitar into the swimming pool as if it were a boat and pushed it away. We watched it sail a little, take on water, and sink.

I left Charlie sitting there and went into Samantha's kitchen and found some liquor. I was drinking it when a short handsome man in a sweat suit came upon me.

"Who are you?" he asked.

"Jack Flynn. Charlie's manager," I said. "You?"

"Gil Andrews, Samantha's husband."

I said, "Thanks for the drink."

"Don't mention it. You think your boy's going to be camped on my deck much longer? I'm open-minded when it comes to Samantha's old boyfriends but—pardon me for saying so—this dude is a drip."

"No," I told him. "We won't be around much longer."

On the day I turned fifty Emerson was in seclusion, Charlie's career was sunk, and Simon hated me. My daughter would not come to the phone when I called her mother. My aides, Wendy and Castro, were frantic to have projects to work on and so were engaged in all sorts of dubious outside activities, which they ran from the offices I continued to pay for. I would have said I was experiencing a midlife crisis but that would have implied that I expected to live to be a hundred.

With time on my hands and depression sniffing at my transom, I decided to take the advice of every friend I had left and push myself into meeting a new woman. I had never felt less romantic, but Wendy warned me that my looks were fading and this might be my last chance.

Let me tell you about dating after age fifty. It's horrible. When you're married you meet all these charming women and think, Wouldn't it be fun? Then you are unmarried and you get out there and it's no fun at all. They're drunks or they're damaged or they're desperate. When I was younger if I went out with someone once and didn't feel anything special, I simply never called her again. Cruel? No doubt, but so were all the alternatives, and anyway, there was a good chance she felt the same way. Now, however, a new technology appeared and knocked down that wall of civilized deniability—e-mail.

It was the latest intrusion on privacy and civility to be promoted as a time-saving miracle for the fast-moving elite. When e-mail was brand-new, early adapters took childish delight in sending each other messages. Power brokers who would never return a phone call jumped to respond to e-mails like children talking into tin cans down a length of string. It was the latest status symbol, and who grabs on to status symbols faster than the well-off and over-thirty-five single women of Manhattan?

Before I was even home from the bad date, an e-mail had arrived saying, "That was fun, when do we do it again?" A gentleman was obliged to reply. I would take refuge behind a brief and noncommittal non sequitur: "Didn't expect the movie to be so violent! Looking under my bed for assassins!"

Would that end it? No. "Next time I'll come check under your bed for you."

Shit, quick reversal. "Thanks for the support." Can she leave it there and say good night already? Not at all.

"Or maybe we'll just stay on top of the bed."

O Jehovah, pull me out of this nosedive: "Fun night, take care now." Surely that ends it.

"Melissa Etheridge is here next weekend. Can you get tickets?"

Now, how could I answer that? I was a rock manager, she knew I could get tickets–but if I did, would that mean I had to go with her? Shit.

Answering machines were bad enough, that was the equivalent of the introduction of the Gatling gun into infantry warfare, but e-mail was the arrival of aerial bombardment.

One woman, one date, a setup, was named Greer. She was very nice but nothing clicked for me. I knew a half hour in. End of the evening, peck on the cheek, so long, thank you very much, got an early flight. She didn't even let me get two steps away.

She yanked me back like I was a dog about to piss on the carpet. She said, "When are we going out next?"

I said, "I'm pretty jammed up the next week or so, let me call you."

"What's your cell number?" What can one say? I gave it to her. Now she could appear in my pocket at any time. If I did not pick up, I got a series of text messages. Finally I agreed to see her for lunch. I tried to keep it light but she was hell-bent on keeping it heavy.

She said, "So, do you want to keep seeing me or not, because I want to keep seeing you."

I replayed a favorite from twenty years before. "Greer, I think you're fantastic but I have to be truthful. I'm just not feeling that special something. I don't know what else to say."

She knew what else to say: "I don't think you're giving this relationship a fair shot." It was like an experienced fighter being smacked by a jab he never saw coming. I flummoxed and fumbled. Of course, what I should have said was *This relationship? What relationship? We had one dinner and heard some bad jazz, and now we've had one mediocre lunch. I've had deeper relationships with my ophthalmologist.*

Easy to think of that now. At the time I said, "Um, well, I don't—okay," condemning myself to two more horrible and now tension-filled dinners served with the pressure to have sex and garnished with a sprinkling of recrimination. I understood for the first time how Carey must have felt in the last days of our marriage. Greer gave every indication of wanting to skip over the days of attraction, happy lovemaking, serious courtship, engagement, wedding, honeymoon, and period of settled contentment and speed right to the vindictive run-up to an ugly divorce.

I knew if she got me into bed I would be giving her a psychological bludgeon with which she would beat me silly, but she was determined to have her way. When we got to her apartment she asked me to come upstairs because her neighbor had been burgled recently and she was frightened. It was a line with a hook and a barb. I saw her to her door and as soon as she slipped the key in her lock she had her tongue in my ear, her left leg wrapped around my knee, and her hand on my zipper. It was like playing Twister with a bag of eels. I tried to pull away and she grabbed my belt buckle. "Come on," she said, "I need this now."

I kissed her lips and after a decent moment said, "Greer, I have to leave. I told you, I have to make a call to Tokyo at one A.M."

She said, "It's not even midnight. You can call from here."

"I need my notes."

"I finish fast."

"No, Greer, I don't want our first time to be like that."

This stopped her a minute. I was offering to trade escape tonight for a future commitment, but she saw it for a feint and snapped back, "This is a rehearsal. I need to see how you measure up."

Let's go back to our corners for a moment to contemplate that last innuendo. It was another thing I hated about dating in middle age. In the sixties we had a lot of sex with a lot of people but there was not this obsession with size, stamina, and duration. By the nineties sex had been quantified and commoditized; it had been reduced to a system of weights and measures. This burden was not only on men. You could look at the cover lines on any women's magazine to see that females were being held to at least as many sexual standards and obligations. No one was excused from the burden of performance rating.

It did not used to be this way. In the sixties we just jumped on top of each other and rolled around until both people stopped having fun. No one had the tape measure out or the stopwatch running. Now, a skeptic might say it was because we were young and good-looking and unselfconscious and could go all night anyway and still get up for work. The skeptic would say it has nothing to do with "the sixties." It is true for young people of any generation, just as old people of every generation feel that the world has gone wrong when in fact it's simply that they no longer have the juice they once did. Be that as it may, such speculation is theoretical and my problem was actual. I was determined to get out of Greer's love nest. This was a desperate woman. I was tilting into the sort of situation that leads to teary cries of "I'm keeping the baby" and an angry judge and a daddy with a shotgun.

I finally fell back on the most despicable of all ploys: "Greer, I'm gay."

This was the equivalent of picking up a stool and breaking it over your opponent's head in the tenth round. Greer knew I had an ex-wife and a daughter. She knew also that I had been trying to wiggle away from her since the night we met. As a tactic, this was pure desperation. But she hesitated. She said, "That's what Joyce said, but I didn't believe it. Look, come inside. I can help you." She rubbed the front of my pants. "I don't think you're *all* gay."

I should have kept my mind on the mission but I had to know: "Who the hell is Joyce?"

"Ramon Castro's girlfriend. She told me you were closeted."

"Oh, she did?"

"It's okay, Jack. I knew what I was getting into."

How stupid was I? I was sparring with a heavyweight and I walked into a sucker punch. Insecure fifty-year-old Irish Catholic that I was, I then had to prove I was not gay, and Greer had me where she wanted me. Knockout! We had miserable sex on her polar bear rug and then she made me date her for a month. When I finally broke it off she called me a heartless creep who had convinced her I was in love with her in order to take advantage of her in bed, and she sent me vicious e-mails for two months as well as text messages saying that everyone agreed I was a bitter misogynist closeted homosexual and when I admitted it I would be a healthier person and happier.

THE DRUGS DON'T WORK

Emerson had not written a song for two years. There was no prospect of getting him into the studio to work. He was not even interested in firing up his assembly line. I had experience sitting out his dry spells, but this drought was becoming a desert. If he didn't come up with something soon, our orchard would wilt. Worse than the record company calling me to complain was when they stopped calling. They did not care about Emerson anymore.

The problem was greater than his depression over the end of this third marriage. The bigger issue was that as the twentieth century limped toward its finish, Emerson had fallen out of love with contemporary music.

I knew the list of grievances. He hated the *sound* of new music, the icy digital production like jackboots marching on breaking ice, keyboards like heart monitors, bass like the rumbling of a subway train through a basement wall, and mewling keyboards stuffing aural rugs and blankets into every open space, leaving not a breath of air between the instruments, suffocating every note.

Still, he contended, he might have overcome all that if the lyrics contained one original thought. No one understood better than Emerson that rock songs speak to adolescent concerns—first love, lost love, frustration, rebellion, and an inchoate longing for justice and a better world. The reason the best rock songs were written by people in their twenties was because after that age you knew how unoriginal these ideas were. Declaring clichés with passion and conviction demanded a lot of naïveté. You had to not know they were clichés.

What wide-eyed kid could tell Emerson anything he did not know? What new song could move his heart of stone?

So he went backward into old music, music he had missed or

misunderstood when he was younger. He went deep into the country blues he had brushed past as a trendy boy in London, into esoteric R&B from forgotten southern labels, into jazz, into the sort of early bluegrass that he had dismissed as corny before he was old enough to know better. In his fifties and orphaned, Emerson was looking for elders, looking for wisdom, listening for anything he had not already heard.

Everything that had ever been out on vinyl was now out on CD, often in expansive box sets that included lost treasures that a record collector would have spent years trying to find. As much as Emerson relished this discovery, archaeology can only look backward. I knew that if Emerson did not keep up with what was new in music, he would fall behind forever. Across the radio and retail landscape, rock was in retreat. The latest generation of guitar heroes had abandoned the field. Kurt Cobain had killed himself. Eddie Vedder, Sinéad O'Connor, and Axl Rose retreated from the spotlight. Nine Inch Nails declared war on the conglomerates that distributed CDs. Unwilling to sully themselves with the taint of commercialism, rock's new leaders raced toward self-inflicted obscurity like nuns fleeing a brothel.

From my jaded perspective, they seemed ridiculous. Rock and roll was supposed to be commercial! It was intended to reach as many ears as possible. The idea of rock as being something obscure, only for the cool kids, was antithetical to the purpose of the form. Jazz could be arcane, modern classical music could be obscure, but elitist rock and roll was as silly a notion as elitist chewing gum. Rock was for everyone who wanted to listen or it was useless.

Still, that was what had happened. Unlike Emerson, who had had twenty years to adjust to gradations of celebrity, the new recruits went from bar bands to television stars in six months, and it shook them. Once Nirvana, Pearl Jam, and the other sensitives quit the court, the game was left to pure pop acts—to the Spice Girls and Backstreet Boys and 'N Sync. Those bubblegum singers, signed up straight out of the Mickey Mouse Club and as polished as Vegas strippers, had no problem with being popular. The demons of self-doubt that plagued Kurt Cobain did not trouble Christina Aguilera. She knew what game she was in.

It was a treacherous environment for rock and roll, and especially for an over-fifty musician. I warned Emerson that if he did not find some way to connect with contemporary music, the temperature in his heated pool would soon be dropping.

"The hell with it, then, Flynn," Emerson said to me while watching a video in which Mariah Carey sang on a roller coaster. "This is what we got into it to destroy. If the public wants to go back to 'How Much Is That Doggie in the Window,' it's time for me to bow out."

"So which of your homes should I sell?"

"Don't try to bullshit me, matey, those houses are paid for."

"Yes, but the staffs who maintain them still have to pick up their checks every week. The electric bills come in every month. The property taxes are due every quarter. You need a hundred grand a month just to maintain your homes, Emerson. Unless you intend to start cutting the grass and rolling the tennis court yourself."

"I could cut back."

"Where would you like to start?"

"Well, for one thing, who says we have to fly first class everywhere?"

"You're willing to fly business?"

"Not me, but Castro and Wendy, for example."

"They do fly business when they're not with you. When they're traveling with you, they fly in whatever class you fly in."

"Who made that rule?"

"It's in their contracts."

"Well, why do we even give them contracts?"

"Among other reasons, because we don't want them to be able to write books about working for you or in any other way betray the thousand confidences to which they have access."

"As if they would!"

"As if they wouldn't! Get real, Emerson. Half the time you treat them like crap and don't even know it. Do you know how many bouquets I have sent to Wendy under your name to apologize for some unintentional insult? She's a publicist, for God's sake! She deals in hype and bullshit for a living. If you ever fire her or someday humiliate her once too often, she'd write a book in a minute. That's why we have contracts and confidentiality clauses."

"Well, maybe. But not Castro. He barely speaks."

"Did you know that Castro now has a contractual clause that says he gets a producer credit on all your long-form videos and TV appearances?"

"Why?"

"Because he wanted it and what do I care? It's cheaper than giving him another raise."

"He's not a producer, though."

"Maybe he figures it looks good on his résumé. Maybe it's to impress his grandmother back in Havana. Don't care. His lawyer pressed for it and we gave in. Only thing I didn't anticipate was that giving it to him would set off Wendy. She now wants executive producer credit on anything on which Castro gets producer credit."

"You going to give that to her?"

"I don't know. It's like satellite missile defense. The escalation never ends. The truth is, they've both been in their jobs too long. They resent that there's nowhere up for them to go, so they become obsessed with perks and titles. Castro has already gone from road manager to tour manager to co-manager. Wendy's gone from publicist to management associate. Every time I cough they look up anxiously to see if I might be dying. It's their only avenue for advancement."

Emerson was already bored with the topic. He said, "I should fire the lot of you and bring in a bunch of bright young college girls. Then I'd have money to keep my hedges trimmed without having to make idiotic pop records."

"I dare you. Put me out of my misery."

"Put you out of my misery, too."

"You need to listen to some new music, Emerson. Did you listen to that Smashing Pumpkins CD I sent over? Their producer would like to meet with you."

"I'll get to it."

"Don't treat it like a burden."

"Don't pretend it's a pleasure."

Emerson had fallen in love with music through Elvis, Buddy Holly, and the Everly Brothers and had moved forward through Smokey Robinson, the Beatles, and Aretha Franklin. Discovering rock and roll was for Emerson like boarding a rocket ship that would blast him away from his working-class neighborhood and mundane destiny. As long as he kept moving forward through pop music—from Aretha to Sly to Stevie Wonder to Bob Marley to Steely Dan to Prince to Annie Lennox, as long as there was something new to inspire him to stay in the game—his trajectory outward increased. The past kept tugging back at him, though, like the earth's gravitational field. Eventually every musician finds his tolerance for new music waning. He knows the tricks, he recognizes where that riff was lifted from, he spots the swipe. He knows too much to hear new music with fresh ears. This is inevitable and it is dangerous. "How can I pretend to care about this silly little band on the cover of *Q* magazine when I have all these great old Muddy Waters reissues to listen to?"

The musician who starts to love going backward more than moving forward will inevitably forfeit his momentum and begin the long fall back to earth.

When I pressed him to write new songs, reminding him that he had in the past worked out clever ways to trick the muse into cooperating, Emerson tore into me again.

"You still don't get me, do you, Jack?" he groaned. "If it were that easy, everyone could do it. I am an artist. My job is to uncover the hurts that people like you spend your whole lives working to bury. Amateurs think that my talent is playing the riff. They're wrong, a monkey could learn to play it. Check the studio musician's directory for examples. The hard part is not playing the riff, the hard part is thinking of the riff!"

I was following him around his living room while he gestured with a bottle of gin.

"When Charlie and I started, we wanted to be the Everly Brothers. Simple as that. It was Charlie who came up with the notion of writing our own songs. I never would have been arsed. But I figured it out the same way I figured out tricky chords and Carl Perkins solos, and I loved the songs we wrote. But you know what? No one else did. No one else wanted to hear 'em. We'd do one of our originals in the pub and everyone would talk through them and tell us to play something they could sing along to. Couple years go by, beat groups become the rage. We only hooked up with Simon because his mother was rich and he had all the gear we coveted. We get a break, get on the telly, play those same songs—now everybody loves them. The same todgers who hated them in the pub are screaming for 'em now. You know why, Jack? Coincidence. That's all success in music is. The song they ignored in '61 is their favorite in '65 because of an accident of timing. Bring out the same song in 1970, it would be a flop. It's the coincidence of what I write and sing happening to line up with what people want to hear at that exact moment. A different moment, I'm washing dishes. Right now, I don't think coincidence is working in my favor. Right now, I got nothing to say that any of the tossers buying Soundgarden records would want to hear."

It was Baxter the drummer who provided a fresh infusion when he got Emerson stoned and played him some new records from Africa. The next time I saw my client his lights were back on.

"Flynn!" he said, running around his Sagaponack beach house like a teenager in love. "You have to listen to this!"

He put on a CD that filled the room with languid, tropical guitar blues over a rolling rhythm.

"It's a player from Mali called Ali Farka Touré! Listen to that! It's the mother lode, it's where the blues began! This cat is who they left behind in the village when the slavers came through and dragged the rest of the tribe in chains to the Mississippi Delta!"

I looked at the CD cover. An African man in a long dashiki and a black beanie sat with an electric guitar in his lap, staring at the camera like he was about to bite it.

"He doesn't look that old."

"He's playing ancient traditions, nutbag. He's like a griot of the blues."

"Emerson," I said, "this is lovely music but come on—he probably learned his licks from John Mayall records, same as you did."

"You're not a musician so you don't get it, Flynn," Emerson explained. "This is the wellspring. This is going back to the source of the hidden river we've been drinking from all these years."

He began pulling out other CDs. "This cat Fela Kuti—he builds and builds like Isaac Hayes and then—boom—he busts out like James Brown! And check this." He opened the CD player and replaced the blues with what sounded like drawing room harp music. "Toumani Diabaté—master of the kora. It's like a guitar with twenty-one strings. Listen to that! Roll over, Leo Kottke, and tell John Fahey the news!

Flynn, there's so much to hear! It reminds me of when I was a kid and I first heard Little Richard and Bo Diddley. It's all here and it's all great and it fills me with inspiration!"

I was happy to see Emerson excited by music again. Perhaps he would find a way to incorporate some of these melodic and rhythmic ideas into new songs of his own. Anything that made him want to pick up a guitar and start writing was good news to me.

"We've found the Nile, Jack," Emerson told me as he put on a Salif Keita album and began doing the hippy-hippy shake across his twenty-five-thousand-dollar carpet. "Now we have to sail up to the source!"

"You want me to see if any of these acts are touring the U.S.?" I asked.

"Come on, Jack! This isn't a trip to the museum! You don't discover a new continent by sitting in the map room of the library! I already told Baxter. We're going to Africa!"

We were fifty years old. Should this not be getting easier?

"Who we?" I asked.

"Us we." Emerson smiled, playing congas on his teak table. "You, me, Baxter, and Castro. Men only! We're going to do the whole thing–Senegal, Mali, Mauritania. We're going *out there*, Jack. And we ain't coming back until we've been vaccinated with the primordial needle of rock and roll."

"Ah, Christ," I muttered, but there was no getting out of it. I had wanted to reanimate Emerson's enthusiasm for music and if it was going to take some pilgrimage into the heart of darkness to engorge his inspiration, well, I just hoped we would not all end up boiling in some jungle stew pot.

Right after New Year's we flew to Paris and from there took a chartered jet to Senegal to begin our trek. We landed in Dakar early on a Sunday morning in January. A delegation of local musicians met us at the airport and moved us through customs with efficiency. There were four older men in the group, and one young man who served as their translator. "We are honored to have as our guests fellow ambassadors of the nation without walls or boundaries." We said it was a great privilege to be in the land where so much of the music we loved had its source. A van brought us to the best hotel in town, which would have been nearly the worst hotel in Amarillo, Texas. I put down my bag in a dreary little room with a nightstand and cot that reminded me of a television program I once saw about the minimum-security federal prison in Connecticut where they send convicted congressmen and judges. It would do. We were in the wilds of Africa, after all. We were on safari to stay.

Our hosts had arranged a full day for us, which was wonderful news, as none of us wanted to stay in his hotel room and there wasn't much of a bar. We drove into the Dakar marketplace, a hive of merchants in their stalls selling shoes, cosmetics, cassette tapes, rugs, mirrors, fruits and vegetables, sunglasses, baseball caps, and a disconcerting assortment of Gaddafi T-shirts. The Libyan dictator appeared to be ahead of Bruce Lee in the number of souvenirs decorated with his face, but behind Bob Marley.

"If anyone asks," I cautioned Emerson, "say we're from Iceland."

The people were genuinely warm, and as curious about us as we were about them. I told one young man I was from Reykjavik, and felt guilty when he asked me so many questions about Iceland that I had to spin out increasingly elaborate lies. I hope he never goes there looking for the igloos I promised.

A woman approached and asked if we would like to visit her family, who were drum-makers. Emerson agreed at once and Castro decided it was safe. She got in our van and directed us through a maze of low white houses like the adobe homes of the Southwest Indians until we turned down an alley and she told us to stop. She led us through a narrow door into a low, wide house divided by half walls into four rooms of equal size. One or two men, all apparently brothers or cousins, were working in each of the rooms. Two boys brought dried animal skins in from what looked like a clothesline in the backyard and stretched them across the tops of wooden tubes. In the room behind them, a young man sat at the edge of two dozen knee-high wood barrels, stumps, vases, and umbrella stands, carving into them intricate patterns. In the third room, an old man and a boy were wetting the skins and pulling them taut over the mouths of the carved wood. The fourth room was filled with their handiwork—a forest of new drums, from bongos to congas, each slightly different in its size, shape, and color. All beautiful and ready to be played.

Emerson insisted on buying one to bring on the plane. He had me take several photos of him with the drum-makers and hoisted the conga on his shoulder to take back to the car. "Someday," he said, "I will play this at my daughter's wedding!"

As we climbed into the van, the woman who had brought us ran up and insisted we come back. Her father wanted to honor us. We tried to beg off but did not want to offend local custom, so we trooped back into the house. This time she led us past the drums and out into the backyard, through the curtain of drying skins, to a circle of lawn chairs. She indicated we should sit down. Her father, the old man who had been stretching drumheads, came and sat opposite us in a lawn chair of his own, as if he were on a throne. He did not speak to us but assumed a new formality. He called out two words in Senegalese and all the young men from the house came out carrying their drums, sat on the ground in a half circle, and at some unknown cue began pounding out a complicated pulse.

Em looked at me as if to say, *Get a load of this*. The old man cried out again, and his daughter and three other young women, one a girl of about eleven, appeared in brightly colored ceremonial dresses and leaped into a dance that would give Madonna a hernia. The talent of this family was astounding, more so for having jumped out spontaneously in the middle of a working day.

"It's kind of like an Elvis movie," Castro said, "where Elvis leaps up on the hay wagon and suddenly everybody on the farm starts doing the frug."

Children from the neighborhood began climbing over the back fence, laughing and trying to imitate the dance routines. Some of them picked up sticks and drummed along with the men. This was a culture where there was no barrier between the musician and the audience. Everyone seemed to be able to put down their tools and play or dance, with the grandfather as maestro and the smallest children learning to find the beat.

When the performance was over we thanked the family profusely, bowing and clasping our hands as if in prayer. On the way out I indicated to the daughter that I would like to offer some money as a thank-you and she made clear it was inappropriate.

Our driver/translator was waiting in the van. "I want to record these people!" Emerson declared. "I mean it, Flynn, that is real music, that is the stuff. Everything we do in the West is a version of the thing; that is the thing itself."

I thought it was a very good sign that Emerson had found his El Dorado on the first day of the journey. Perhaps we could rework our itinerary to head straight to Morocco. Leave out all that dragging through the Sahara. It might well have gone that way, too, if I had had the foresight to shoot our translator.

"Those are some very super musicians," our guide said as we passed three goats chewing on a Coke carton between the pumps of a filling station. "Benjamin records with Peter Gabriel."

Emerson's heart was broken. "He's recorded with Peter Gabriel?"

"Yes, Peter Gabriel lives in big house right along ocean. We will pass it on our way to dinner."

"Ah," Emerson said. We would have to press on farther to find the source of the river of soul.

We spent two more days in Dakar. It reminded me of Southern California. The land was ripe and green, the long ocean beaches were white and seductive, the people were friendly, and the restaurants were superb. We went to a football match in which Senegal defeated South Africa, for which we were grateful. We didn't want to be the only whites in a stadium crowd full of black Africans who just got beat by the last Dutch team on the continent. We visited Youssou N'Dour's nightclub and caught a show by Baaba Maal, Emerson's new hero, who sat cross-legged weaving languid, lilting melodies for two hours and then suddenly leaped to his feet and became a young Otis Redding.

The last place we visited was Gorée Island, where slaves had been brought and loaded onto ships for the New World. A small sunny village in the sea just west of Africa's westernmost point, Gorée still had a few of its old "factories," tiny concentration camps with dungeons where captured families were divided into men, women, and children. The backs of the factories opened onto great stone wharfs–loading docks where for generations human beings were stuffed into the holds of ships and dispatched to Cuba, Brazil, and the United States. Standing looking into the rock-and-earth holding pens, one heard mothers screaming for their children. There were punishment rooms where men who would not stop resisting were beaten to death. Imagine if Auschwitz floated in clear tropical waters. That was Gorée Island.

I wondered if Emerson felt any unease about being a wealthy white musician who had made his fortune off of imitating the music of Africans. Probably not. I think he was just annoyed that Peter Gabriel had got there first.

We revved up the plane for a flight east to Mali. We would soon

learn that the farther you went into Africa, the more assured the inhab-
itants were that their land was where blues began. Malians we spoke
with talked about Senegal the way people in Memphis talk about
Branson, Missouri.

We touched down in Bamako, the capital city, and I felt like we
were running out of water. Senegal was lush and green, Bamako was
brown. A sprawling, dusty city, it had begun as a camp for crocodile
trappers, and our new guide—a local named Sundi who looked a bit
like Chris Rock—claimed that you could still have your hand snapped
off at the wrong bend in the Niger River, which ran through the belly
of the city.

Our hotel in Bamako was no worse than the one in Dakar, and
they had a restaurant serving eggs and bread. I count myself an experienced traveler; I knew to stay clear of fruit, salad, anything that was
washed. Foolishly, I ate a lot of bread, which is usually the safest thing.
It did not occur to me that bread that sits out for a long time after it is
baked makes a natural nest for parasites. I became more and more ill
over the next days. Upon our eventual return to New York I suffered
through months of colonic irrigations and excavations with the legendary poop doctor of the Upper East Side.

But that was still in my future; I had many other miseries to live
through before the worms of Bamako would be stalking through my
large intestine. We went out into the town and the sunlight was so
bright I had to cast my eyes on the ground. The streets were full of
bicycles, farm animals, mopeds, and busted-up minivans. Everything
around the edges of my vision turned white. In late afternoon I was
back in my hotel room, looking across the river as the sun began to
go down. A long industrial bridge and one thin row of greenery on
the opposite bank were the only substantial shapes. Everything above
or below those two straight lines was misty and indistinct, like an im-
pressionist watercolor in which earth, water, and sky all blended in a
luminous fog.

We planned a big night out in Bamako, visiting the legendary Ogun
Club, a venue run by Toumani Diabaté, master of the kora. A kind of
frontier fort, the Ogun put me in mind of the half-indoor, half-outdoor
ribs venues where bands play in Austin, Texas. The master was in
the house and moved over his harp strings like rain on the crocodile

river. Drunk on good music and bad liquor, we moved on to the Hotel Wakadodo, a resort owned by and dedicated to the Aretha of Africa, Oumou Sangaré. I suppose this is analogous to the Las Vegas venue constructed around Céline Dion (or is that like comparing the Queen of England to the local butcher because they both live upstairs from where they work?). We stayed almost until dawn, dancing and eating roasted goat.

Emerson could not want more than this, I thought. We had found our way back to musical Eden. I was astonished when he went off for a piss and came back moody and anxious to leave. "We have to get out of Bamako," he insisted.

"Because you have reached Nirvana and are prepared to go home?" I asked.

"Go home, no. We need to go deeper. This is just a tourist trap."

I was dumbfounded. We were swimming in extraordinary music. I decided that retracing my charge's steps might reveal the source of his unease. I went down the hall toward the bathroom Emerson had just emerged from and saw the instrument of his discontent—a photograph of Miss Oumou on this very stage, performing a duet with Robert Plant.

I promised myself that if this expedition led to us trudging through some equatorial jungle I would go fifty steps ahead of the group, in case I needed to hide any photographs of Sting.

The next day at noon, Castro, Baxter, and I were eating a breakfast of eggs, bread, and parasitic worms when Emerson appeared with his guide Sundi to announce that he had decided on our next destination: Timbuktu.

I laughed. I had thought Timbuktu was a make-believe place, like Shangri-la or Krypton. Emerson rolled out a map and disabused me.

"Of course it's a real place, Flynn! Christ, you're provincial. It was once a great trading city. The Sahara was exactly like a sea, and the caravans were ships. On every edge were port cities—Marrakech, Cairo, and here in the southwest Timbuktu. It was the gateway city between Arab North Africa and the sub-Sahara."

"The Liverpool of the sands," I said.

"Timbuktu is very sandy now, boss," Sundi said. "The Sahara is eating it. In a hundred years the city will be gone."

"Well, then, we have no time to waste, do we?" Emerson said. "Are the pilots in this hotel?"

I took out the little cards with cell phone numbers that private pilots hand you before you go your separate ways. There always seems to be an unspoken deal—leave me alone unless the arrows are actually in the air. I phoned our captain, pilot Dave, who answered in the exact same slightly southern, slightly military voice that aviators must practice for hours in the flight simulator. "Yes, sir, let me make a few calls, work up a flight plan, and with the help of the Good Lord and clear skies we could be wheels-up as soon as fifteen hundred hours."

"A.M. or P.M.?" I asked. I told Emerson that when I said I'd follow him to the ends of the earth I had not expected him to take me up on it.

We had been in the air only a short time when what little foliage there was disappeared from the terrain below us, and the brown earth of the land around Bamako turned to a cracked egg-yellow. Our plane followed one narrow red road, like the mercury rising up a thermometer, north toward Timbuktu. We touched down on an arid airstrip with a single modest terminal building. Heat vapors rose from the tarmac; everything on the ground looked like a mirage.

The pilots informed us that they would be flying back to Bamako, and we should call them by satellite phone when we were ready to leave. They got out of there fast. Three local merchants had their wares unrolled on the runway. They implored us to consider their selection of hunting knives, switchblades, and daggers.

Baxter observed, "You don't often get a chance to buy weapons between the security station and the airplane. We'll have to pick up some pigstickers on our way out of town."

Sundi had arranged for a van missing its windshield and front grille to ferry us into town. Timbuktu reminded me of one of the desolate Mexican villages in a Clint Eastwood spaghetti western. The streets were dirt and the buildings had been pressed from the same mud, making it hard to tell where the structures ended and the earth below them began. It's one thing to hear that the desert is claiming a place; it's another to see the architecture actually melting back into sand. Tough-looking nomads rode in from the surrounding dunes on camels, looking for a place to put up for the night. Lazy men taking siestas on the porches looked out with slit eyes from under turbans and broad Chinese hats. Donkeys were tied to posts and fed from wooden buckets. Timbuktu made Bamako look like San Francisco.

The best hotel in town was the sort of two-story clay and straw structure from which Mary and Joseph are turned away on Christmas cards. We checked in and I found my room, a small cell with a bed, one sheet, a blanket apparently sewn together from distressed handkerchiefs, and a brutalized toilet with a rusty chain. Dozens of tiny legs skittered into the dark corners when I pulled the string that lit the bare bulb. I would be sleeping on top of the blanket, fully clothed and lightly.

There was nothing to do but stroll around the town. I found Castro and we wandered down the dirt street to a web of markets, crowded and filled with merchants chatting up their wares. Some had stalls, some had wagons and tables set up in the narrow alleys. They were selling shoes, weapons, and food, but also a great assortment of out-of-date paraphernalia decorated with photos and drawings of the stars of old fads. There were *Dukes of Hazzard* lunch boxes, *Saturday Night Fever* platform shoes with likenesses of John Travolta on the toes, *Charlie's Angels* dolls, *Star Wars* plastic ray guns, and *Starsky & Hutch* track suits. T-shirts hung on lines like the flags of a hundred forgotten nations–*Six Million Dollar Man,* David Cassidy, Jackson 5 (animated cartoon version), Sonny & Cher, Bay City Rollers, *Police Woman,* the Captain & Tennille.

Castro studied the T-shirts like a sailor deciphering the semaphores of a strange armada.

"My God, Flynn," he said. "We have reached it at last. The end of the retail trail! You know how last season's styles move out of Beverly Hills and show up in the malls in Reseda? And then, a year or two after that, you can find them in discount stores in Compton? Then, maybe you see them a few years after that in Salvation Army shops or at garage sales? Now we know where the last stop on that train is. Twenty years after they get flushed out of the flea markets, they end up in a stall in Timbuktu."

I said, "I hope we don't see any old Emerson swag in here."

Castro said, "There's a tribe of Dogons in the desert who worship Fonzie as a god."

After an hour of wandering we came to one of the oldest mosques south of Sahara, a sort of caked-mud mound rising about three stories from its base, with wooden branches protruding from all over its surface, like the back of a porcupine. A neighborhood radiated out from the mosque. The buildings looked like they had been poured out of overturned flower pots. The whole city seemed like an elaborate sand castle on its second day, after the night tide had washed away all its corners and edges. Everything was sinking back into the soil.

We returned to the hotel and found Emerson, Baxter, and Sundi sitting on the roof, drinking Coca-Colas and negotiating with a nomad.

"This fellow says he can lead us to the music," Emerson said happily. "His brother has a jeep with a windscreen, and for fifty dollars they will take us into the desert, to an oasis where the great Tuareg musicians gather and play!"

I said, "I don't suppose we could just pick up some CDs and listen to them on the plane?"

"We're almost there, Jack!" Emerson said. He was enthusiastic. "The Tuaregs are the real deal, the Lords of the Atlas! They are the Apaches to the Malian government's General Custer. They have their own tribes, their own laws, their own army. They roam the desert on camels and horseback and come sweeping into towns brandishing scimitars. But they are the greatest musicians in Africa. They travel the sands with guitars and rifles strapped to their backs and are masters of both."

"You memorized that from some tourist book, Emerson," I said. "You would never use the word 'brandish' on your own."

The son of the man who ran the hotel came out on the roof looking for us. He indicated that we had a visitor.

"Probably Fred Zaras," I said to Emerson. "He heard there's a free buffet." I looked over the edge of the roof to the road in front of the hotel and was startled to see three bull-necked white men with the manner, wardrobe, sunglasses, and gum-chewing demeanor of American undercover cops.

"Concert security?" I said to Castro. He came up next to me and looked down at the visitors.

"Shit, Flynn, that's gotta be CIA. Don't go down there."

"What are we going to do, bolt up like the Alamo? I have to see what they want. Tell Emerson discreetly that if he's holding any dope he might want to stick it somewhere safe until we see what these musclemen are after."

I went downstairs and greeted the Americans, who had the same accents as our pilots.

"Can I help you?"

"Sir, are you with Emerson Cutler and his band?" one asked me.

"I am his manager, John Flynn. Who are you?"

"Major Glenn Buckmaster, U.S. Army," the first man said, extending a hearty hand. "This is Sergeant Kino and Sergeant Brandstein."

"Gentlemen." I nodded. "You're a long way from home."

"We're out here digging wells for the locals," Major Buckmaster told me. That was all he intended to say about their mission.

"Really," I said. "How is that going?"

"Sir, it would mean a great deal to our commander, Colonel Nahod, if Mr. Cutler would consider being his guest for a traditional Timbuktu dinner this evening. We don't get many celebrities out this way, we're all big fans of Mr. Cutler's music, and I know many of the locals admire and would love to meet him."

I did not expect that any of the locals would know Emerson from Paula Abdul. I was fairly certain this was the CIA station chief's attempt to get a photo with Emerson, and perhaps inveigle him into singing a song for his dinner party.

"Emerson is very weary, and we depart in the morning for a long journey, so while I know he will very much appreciate the invitation, I think it's unlikely he will be able to come," I said. "However, I will of course ask him. How do I reach you fellows?"

"We'll find you, sir," the major said. "Again, the colonel would very much appreciate it."

"Come back in an hour," I told them. I went back up to the roof and passed the word along to Emerson.

"Screw the CIA," Emerson said, not unhappily. "I'm not goin' to dinner with any spooks. I am departing at dawn to join the Tuareg tribesmen at the lost oasis. Tell the spies to fuck off back to Virginia and leave these wonderful people alone."

Baxter spoke up. "Might be a bad move, Em. We don't know what we're getting into out there. Might not be the worst thing to have some friends with machine guns and a helicopter. You know, just in case."

Emerson shrugged. He understood the logic. When the three soldiers returned I told them that Mr. Cutler would be delighted to dine with the colonel, provided he was able to be back in bed by ten o'clock and there was no expectation that he would perform. The grateful soldiers said absolutely and thanked us briskly.

At sunset they returned to drive us far out of Timbuktu into the desert, where the colonel had set up a tent and an elaborate meal. The only locals there were servants, and of course once we had all relaxed and had some wine, Major Buckmaster produced a guitar and pressed Emerson for a song. He managed a medley of "Sitting in Limbo," "Rock the Casbah," and "Midnight at the Oasis," while our hosts took photos to wire back to Langley.

At the end of the evening, the major pulled me aside. "Don't go out among the Tuaregs," he said. "They're allies of Gaddafi, enemies of the Malian government. You get in some kind of trouble out there, we can't protect you."

I told this to Emerson back at our hotel. It made him want to go even more.

We set out from Timbuktu at sunrise, heading into the Sahara to find the elusive oasis of the Tuaregs, where Emerson intended to dip his bucket into the hidden spring of African roots music. There was Castro—our Cuban-American road manager; Baxter—Emerson's African-American drummer; Sundi—our translator and driver; the nomad guide who promised to lead us to the oasis—whose name I have forgotten but who for purposes of this journal I will call Moronus; Emerson—wrapped in a blue turban and four-hundred-dollar sunglasses; and me, in a baseball cap with a kerchief hanging out of the back to cover my neck and swathed in enough sunscreen to baste a goose.

If it had been a World War II film we would have each been expert in some deadly skill, but I'm afraid that between the six of us we would have had difficulty finding the jeep's gas cap. We were exactly the sort of rich Western adventure tourists whose only legacy after they get themselves killed is a long *tsk-tsk*ing *Vanity Fair* article that details all the mistakes they made on their jolly way to disaster.

We were about ten minutes out of Timbuktu when the jeep got stuck in a sand dune. Five of us got out and pushed while Emerson sat gunning the gas pedal and spinning the tires. At great length we heaved over the hill and regained traction, but five minutes later we were pushing again. Ten minutes after that likewise. This seemed like the long way to find the roots of the blues.

In the second hour the terrain flattened out and we cruised through what appeared to be hills of sugar, plains of baked clay, and dunes patched with prairies of green grass that made you imagine the ocean was just over the hill. In the fourth hour of our journey we rattled over fields of broken stone that suggested that some prehistoric meteor had shattered here and we were bumping over its fragments. At noon we were driving through acres of red dirt laced with thin white grass like stray hairs spread across an old man's sunburned head, which gave way to fields of cracked hard soil that looked like the surface of Mars.

Baxter finally said it out loud: "Do we know where we're going?"

Emerson and I had been wondering the same thing. We looked to Sundi for assurance. He spoke to the nomad guide, who was hanging on the outside of the jeep, riding on the running board.

The nomad shouted something back, which Sundi translated as, "No problem, we're almost there."

An hour later we stopped in the center of a dead salt seabed and put the question to our nomad one more time.

This time he and Sundi exchanged sharp words, and then the nomad stepped back from us, much in the manner of a dog who knows you're about to discover he wet the carpet.

"He doesn't know where we are!" Sundi said with theatrical anguish. "He thought he could find the oasis but now he admits he has never been there. I think perhaps he intended to take your money and run away, but he has realized there is no place to run to."

"Balls!" Emerson said. "Our nomad's no good!"

"He is not even a true nomad," Sundi said grievously. "He is a Bozo."

"I'll say," I said.

Emerson looked at me as if I were an incompetent bellboy. "Bozos are a major ethnic group in Mali," he said.

"I'll say," I repeated.

"Bastard," Castro said. "Let's strap him to the fender like a deer."

The nomad-cum-Bozo looked miserable indeed. "All right, Sundi," I said. "Tell him to grab on to the roof rack and let's try to go back the way we came. If he falls off we're leaving him."

Part of me was glad that we had an excuse to cancel this fool's adventure and go back to Timbuktu. My relief faded as another hour went by and nothing in the afternoon desert resembled anything we had seen in the morning. Castro tried to get a satellite phone signal, fruitlessly.

I felt illness coming upon me like the plagues of Egypt. It started with a cough, and then my lungs began to fill with phlegm. I was hacking up wads of gummy green pus and spitting it out the window of the jeep. The more sand I breathed in, the thicker it got, until I was spewing up little balls of gluey green dirt and shooting them out of my mouth like Demosthenes at the end of elocution practice.

That was only the first visitation. Next I realized that my hearing was half gone. I could hear people's voices but not make out what they were saying. It was as if someone had put a hose in my ear and filled my head with Jell-O. Pressure lined the inside of my skull. I tried shifting my weight to one side and then the other, bopping up and down in the jeep as one does to pop a bubble in the ear. All that did was allow me to feel the fishbowl in my head shift and splash from one side to the other. If I tilted my head as far back as I could, the whole tide would move and my ears would clear for a moment. But as soon as I brought my neck back to the forward and locked position my hearing would close again. This was bad, I told myself. We were lost in the desert and something ghastly had invaded my body.

We saw a few trees on the horizon and headed toward them. There were people there. For a moment we told ourselves we had found the oasis. It was no such thing. It was a cluster of three single-room houses made of baked clay bricks, with a few chickens and goats. The houses were arranged around a well made of rocks that looked like sandbags, which was being slowly circled by an ox bound to a long pole. Two men stood by the well, smoking. Four children were chasing the chickens. The scene was biblical—this could be the well where Jesus spoke to the Samaritan woman. This could be the home of Abraham and Sarah. Except for us in our jeep.

Sundi asked the men about the location of the Tuareg oasis. They conferred, debated, and then pointed toward the horizon, zigging and zagging their arms to indicate various turns and maneuvers that would get us to where we wanted to go, assuming we could decode what they were telling us with no landmarks except different-colored rocks. After going through it with them three times, Sundi pronounced himself satisfied and thanked them. We got back in our jeep and noticed that our Bozo was running away from us, ducking behind one of the houses with a goat in pursuit.

The men by the well did not seem bothered that the incompetent

Bozo was hiding behind their hovel, so we slipped them some money, said thanks four or five times, and rolled on down the trail.

The sun was low in the sky when we next saw human beings. Two men, identical and vaguely Palestinian in their features, came toward us driving a little orange truck. We stopped nose to nose, neither of us wanting to turn off into the soft sand at the side of the worn track. Sundi got out and greeted them and asked what they knew of the Tuareg watering hole.

Here our luck turned. The brothers said they had just come from the very place we were seeking, and began to unflap a map.

I did not think we'd survive another goose chase. I said, "Look, Sundi, tell them we'll pay them a hundred dollars if they turn around and lead us there." This prompted a quick negotiation, which ended with the men saying, more or less, "You bet!" They backed their truck into the sand, reversed it, and led us on a short ride over four dunes into a flat dirt field where several dozen desert tribesmen wrapped in blue were camped around dinner fires with their camels, trucks, and rifles.

The first thing I noticed about the oasis was that there was no oasis there. This patch of sand did not look substantially different from all the other desert we had driven through on our sunburned exodus. There were two or three scrawny trees close to a stone well, and three rows of tents. There was also a half-opened one-room wooden shack with a few card tables and folding chairs set up outside, and a makeshift saloon selling soft drinks and bottles of water, and serving rice from one iron cooking pot and some kind of yellowish meat from another. It looked like we would be sticking to our imported rations of energy bars and Evian.

I left Sundi and Emerson to bond with the Tuaregs, who seemed neither impressed nor bothered that we were there. I wandered into the shack. Two nomads were playing dominoes while a bartender stood behind a plank stretched between two sawhorses. Lined up on the plank were a variety of canned sodas and plastic bottles. I asked for a can of Pepsi, which looked at that moment like the most delicious elixir in the world.

The proprietor handed me the can and I handed him a bill. He made change and I indicated he should keep it. I looked down at the can to pull the tab and saw that the whole surface was coated with sand. I pointed to it, hoping the barman would offer me some sort of napkin to wipe it off. He nodded apologetically and took the can back from me. To my horror, he gobbed a long stream of spit onto the top of the can, rubbed it in with the palm of his filthy hand, and popped the top, handing it back to me with a proud smile. The two players looked up from their dominoes, studying my reaction. I drank up and said thank you.

When I rejoined my party, Sundi the guide was negotiating with the Tuaregs to set up a couple of tents for us. When they had settled on a price, one of the Tuaregs walked over to two goats roped to a stake in the ground. He cocked back one of their heads and slit its throat in a single quick motion. The other goat looked up at him with a startled expression of *Holy shit!* The butcher began slicing the dead goat's belly open and gathering its organs to pour into a dinner pot.

Sundi explained, "He will use the skin to make you a tent roof. His cousin is gathering sticks for poles. The rest of the goat will be our dinner."

Baxter said quietly, "You know how sometimes back home I refer to myself as an African? I ain't. I am very, very American."

Emerson was enjoying the otherness of the atmosphere. "Listen!" he said happily. "Listen to that music, man! Come on, let's follow that sound!"

We climbed a sand dune and came down the other side. A Tuareg was sitting in the shade of his camel, playing a beat-up blue Fender guitar through a Pignose battery-powered amp. He was churning out a hypnotic, driving riff on a single chord.

"I want to record this," Emerson said. "This is the deep stuff, this is the umbilical link."

Baxter listened for a while and said, "He's playing a James Brown song, Em."

"This is where James Brown got it," Emerson insisted.

Baxter said, "No, I mean he's literally playing a James Brown song. This is 'Let a Man Come in and Do the Popcorn.'"

"It's an ancient taproot," Emerson said.

"I swear to God, man," Baxter argued, "he got this off a James Brown record."

"I would have thought that once myself, Baxter," Emerson said with just enough of an edge that Baxter realized this was employer talking to employee. "Then I realized that all of our funk, soul, and blues traditions can be traced back to here, to the old Bamana Empire."

Baxter stopped protesting. We had all learned to clam up when Emerson adopted his "I used to think that, man, but then I learned . . ." locution. Disagree with Emerson about anything–that pigs were smarter than dogs, that the Chinese found America before the Spanish, that calf's liver was good for the sperm count–and he would smile a patronizing smile and explain that he *used* to be as misinformed about the subject as you were but then he discovered the truth, which was the position he now held. Emerson was not disagreeing with you. He was *helping* you by sharing his hard-won experience. If you continued to misunderstand, you were ill-mannered and ungrateful. It was a form of condescension that brooked no objection.

By dinnertime the camp was full of Tuaregs. They appeared on camels, horses, and the occasional motor vehicle. Many carried rifles; all had long knives. One group arrived on a jeep with a mounted machine gun. They built a fire and passed around rice and goat meat.

I crawled off to lie under the goatskin that had been stretched for me across a spine of crisscrossed sticks and branches. The sun was setting on the desert. The Tuaregs were playing electric guitars. The fires glowed. As the moon came up I was shivering. I put on all the T-shirts I had with me and wrapped myself in a Tuareg cloak and still I felt like I was in an icebox. I climbed into my state-of-the-art Lands' End Inuit-level sleeping bag and shook like the last woolly mammoth. Cold sweat poured out of every pore while the liquid flooding my head seemed to boil and bubble. I slipped between hysterical dreams and hacking wakefulness.

I crawled down into a gully behind my tent and vomited into the sand. When I was empty I covered up the puddle of sick. I heard a voice crying in sympathy and looked up from my misery into the sad face of the surviving goat.

What followed was the most abject night of my life. By two A.M. there was nothing left to expel and I fell into a fit of dry heaves. All the time I could hear electric guitars, drunken voices, and bursts of gunfire. As I lay on my side burning up, I saw boots and hooves passing along just outside my hovel.

Finally I passed out and fell into fever dreams of dying there in the desert and being buried in the sand, a bleached skeleton next year at this time. Perhaps I would receive a special dedication on Emerson's next CD, which would include a morbid violin-backed song about the pain the great man felt at the loss of his friend, written and sung in the manner of Lawrence of Arabia. In my dream I resolved that if I were going to die out here I would find a way to take Emerson with me. I would negotiate his tenure in purgatory and take 10 percent of his royalties in the celestial choir. The image gave me some comfort in my distress.

I woke once, suddenly, and opened my eyes to see a blue-faced Tuareg staring down at me, his loose turban falling away from an impassive face. I wondered if he would smother me and take my watch and money belt. I was too weak to protest. I passed out of consciousness again.

Somewhere in the middle of the night I came to myself. I felt very weak, but the demon had stopped chewing through my guts from the inside. I sat up and peeled off the layers of T-shirts, all wet and stinking, and huddled back down in my sleeping bag for what I hoped would be a peaceful recovery.

When I woke I was buried alive. My eyes were full of dirt and the weight of the desert pressed down on me. I tried to scream and sand filled my mouth. I was filled with a vision of being trapped inside one of LaSalle's hourglasses. I struggled and heaved and managed to sit upright. The sand poured off me. I looked around my tent. Two feet of desert had blown in during the night. I pushed through it and staggered upright. It was morning. The fever had receded but I was still shaky. My body was caked with dirt where the sand had mingled with sweat while I slept. I dug around in the dune and came up with my backpack and a bottle of water, half of which I drank and then poured the rest over my eyes and rubbed into my nose and cracked lips.

As my heart rate came down I was aware of shouting outside and more gunfire. There was also a sustained mechanical moaning getting louder, like a generator about to explode. I pushed myself out of the tent and saw a large brown military aircraft with indistinct markings flying very low over the encampment. The Tuaregs were screaming and throwing things at the plane. Someone was shooting at it from behind the tents. A couple of the younger men were trying to unlock and turn the machine gun turret on the jeep.

Castro and Baxter came running toward me, carrying their knapsacks. "Jack! We're leaving! Now!"

"Where's Emerson?"

"He's in the jeep. Now, Jack!"

Each took me by an elbow and directed me down the sand dune behind the tents and up another incline to where Emerson sat behind the wheel of our transport with the motor running.

"You look terrible, man," he said to me.

"Let me drive, Emerson," Castro ordered. Emerson slid over, while Baxter settled me in the back.

I said I had left behind my backpack and my money belt, and they told me to forget it.

"That plane is our CIA pals," Castro said. "The Tuaregs are displeased."

"How do you know?" I said, gasping as the jeep lurched over the dunes and toward the flat hard clay of the road out of camp.

"Let's put it this way," Baxter told me, his arm around my shoulder holding me in the vehicle. "The Tuaregs are sure it's the CIA. That's good enough for them and bad enough for four American men who just happened to wander into their camp last night claiming to be tourists."

"I'd like to see us down the road before those hopped-up kids figure out how to fire their machine gun," Castro added.

As we hauled down the track away from the oasis, we could hear rapid gunfire receding behind us. Were they shooting at us? Perhaps not, but when we tell the story we always say so.

In our panic to evacuate we had left Sundi our guide behind. In this we were much like our colonial ancestors. Castro was driving like a man who knew where he was going and I was too ill to worry about becoming lost in the desert again. Hot juices shot up my throat, a warning fusillade from my uncertain bowels.

"Jeez, Flynn, you're a rag," Baxter said to me. Then he said to Castro, "We need to get Jack to a hospital."

Castro and Emerson looked over their shoulders from the front seat. Their faces did not reassure me.

"Working on it," Castro said. "Hold tight, Jack, I'm working on it."

We drove for about four hours, with regular stops for me to heave into the landscape. Ladies, please forgive my vulgarity here, and skip to the next paragraph. Gentlemen, I was now expelling streams of bloody brown soup from both ends of my body. I was using my underwear as toilet paper and limping back to the jeep with my ass and legs pinned with burrs and brambles. Castro was getting satellite phone reception, which meant we were moving in the right direction. He managed to reach some American military station, who fixed our location and talked us back to Timbuktu. The ancient desert city, which had looked like a sand castle to us just three days before, now looked as cosmopolitan as Chicago.

We tore straight through the town and on to the airport, where our pilots and plane were waiting with the engines running. Emerson paused on the tarmac to purchase a jewel-encrusted knife from one of the merchants.

"In case we need to operate on you during the flight," he said.

I crawled onto the airplane's couch and trembled with gratitude to be out of the desert.

Castro announced that he had made contact with a legendary rock and roll doctor in Tangier.

"He's taken care of Zep, the Stones, all the way back to Burroughs and the Beats," he assured me. "This guy's going to fix you up, Flynn."

I lost consciousness as our plane craned into the air.

Dr. Tommy Crocker of Tangier was an extravagant white-suited homosexual of the sort I thought existed only in the plays of Tennessee Williams. Banished from his wealthy Alabama family for the sin that dares not speak its name, Doc Crock had roamed the fleshpots of Paris and Spain until he landed in Morocco, where traditional morality holds little sway. He was about sixty when I found myself naked under a ceiling fan on his examining table, listening to his florid tales of buggery and the relative talents of Spanish, Arab, and black rent-boys.

It is a measure of how frightened for my health I was that I did not object to this unsavory litany, even when he told me to roll over on my belly so he could check my prostate.

"Good God, you've got a tight ass, man," he complained while probing me with what felt like two fingers and a thumb. "You'd never make a living in a Greek whorehouse!"

"Sorry, Doc. I haven't been dating much."

He lurched over to his ornate medical cabinet and pulled out an antique Jules Verne hypodermic needle long enough to pick up radio signals. He raised it and squirted out a glob of yellow liquid. Satisfied, he leaned over me and injected into my ass a series of antibiotics, morphine, steroids, saline, B$_{12}$, and liquid ether.

"I mix it up myself, right here in the basement," he bragged. "I used this same needle to cure Allen Ginsberg's malaria. Go back to the hotel and sleep now. You'll wake up either cured or dead."

Castro was in the waiting room. He paid the doctor and thanked him and drove me back up the hill to luxurious Villa Josephine, a former private estate perched on the rise where the Atlantic Ocean meets the Mediterranean Sea. Between Timbuktu and here we had fast-forwarded through ten thousand years of human evolution. In my ornate suite I sank into the greatest bubble bath of my life. I bought a new wardrobe in the hotel men's shop and threw away my soiled desert rags. I then slept on the soft mattresses for two days straight.

On the third day I rose and walked out on my balcony. Emerson and Baxter were eating breakfast on a patio on the rolling lawn below. They saw me and waved.

"Lazarus is risen!" Emerson shouted. "Come on down here and eat something, you skinny wretch."

I joined Emerson on the terrace and tried some toast and tea, enjoying my fragile rehabilitation. My head was clear for the first time in days and the food tasted great. The garden around us was bursting with blooms. Sweet fragrance of roses mingled with the sea air blowing in from beyond the cliffs. We studied how the green waters of the Mediterranean churned into the deep blue Atlantic. It was a very clear morning. I could see Spain on the far horizon. Europe was in sight. I was greatly relieved.

That did not last long. Castro came to join us and said to Emerson, "It's all set. Got the reservations, got a driver, we can leave this afternoon."

"I've got a surprise for you, Jack," Em said.

I hoped it was that we were flying to Cannes to recuperate in a grand hotel for a few days before heading up to London. Or perhaps a chauffeured car was going to meet us across the strait and drive us up to Barcelona. That would be pleasant.

Emerson said, "We're going on safari! We're flying down to South Africa and heading out to the Limpopo Reserve! Hippos, lions, giraffes—all roaming in the wild, and us camped out among them!"

I felt like a lost sailor who sees land in the distance just as his sinking boat drags him under.

"Emerson," I said, "South Africa is thousands of miles south and east of here. Do you understand? *Thousands* of miles. Sitting here in Morocco we are nearer to Miami than we are to Cape Town. Europe is right there, you can see it! We don't really want to turn around and go *back* into the jungle, now, do we?"

"Listen to this lazy old fart!" Emerson laughed and Castro laughed right back at him. "Flynn, we are not going into a Tarzan movie! This is one of the fanciest resorts in the world. Tell him."

"The whole place is the size of a small country," Castro said, reciting like a tour guide. "And it's ecologically impeccable. You stay in these elegant glass rooms so you're right in the terrain. Every few years they completely dismantle the hotel and move it to another location in the reserve, so there's very little negative impact on the environment. Every nail, every screw, every paper cup is carted off as if it had never been there."

I said, "The only thing better than that would be to actually never go there at all. Then we'd really be environmentally impeccable, wouldn't we?"

"You're still soft from the brain fever, Jack," Emerson told me, getting up from the table without signing for the food. "This will fix you right up. I'm going to my room to pack. We didn't come all this way to quit and go home."

I watched him leave. Castro gave me a shrug. He said, "If you really don't feel up to it . . ."

He let it trail off. Of course I did not feel up to it and of course that did not matter. Emerson had snapped his fingers. We all had to jump. I thought of the scene in *The Last Emperor* where the boy king orders his teacher to drink ink.

We rolled out of the beautiful Villa Josephine before dawn the next morning and went back to the airport and climbed onto our private jet. I was surprised to find four other people already on board, and taking the good seats. There was a small, thin, and nervous African-American man with headphones in his ears bent over a computer. There was a very large African-American man in a long leather coat whose demeanor and metal knuckle dusters said *Security*. There was a very beautiful young woman of, I computed, mixed Asian and Latin genealogy. Seated next to her, resplendent in his rehearsed indifference, was the U.S. hip-hop impresario who called himself Big Mak. We had met a couple of times at industry functions, but he looked through me as if I were fog.

Castro, behind me, stretched out his fist to Big Mak and they brushed folded fingers.

"What up, Mak?" Castro inquired.

"S'up," Mak explained.

Baxter followed and nodded with the session musician's deference to the star.

When Emerson boarded he and Mak hugged and laughed and exchanged syllables unbound by sentences.

"Yo!"

"He's here!"

"Yup."

"You know."

"Do I."

"Hey."

"Rolling like the old days."

"Not quite."

"Little better."

"Nice customs."

"Check it."

"All cool?"

"Ad infinitum, Rex. Ad infinitum."

Castro, Emerson, Baxter, and I took seats at the table in the back of the plane, leaving Big Mak and his crew the four captain's chairs up front. Our flight attendants offered beverages and fruit. I took some bottled water and crackers.

I leaned in and whispered to Castro, "Why is he here?"

"Fin hooked us up. Mak needed a lift to Johannesburg to perform at this big concert to end hunger in Africa. By giving him a ride, we get to charge back half the cost of the plane to the event organizers."

"You mean we're taking food out of the mouths of starving children to pay for our jet fuel?"

"No, we're saving the charity more than half of what they'd have to pay to hire a whole plane just for Mak."

Three hours into the flight, when we'd had some drinks and everyone was relaxed and moving around the cabin, I asked Big Mak about the African hunger project he was traveling so far to support. How did it work? Who were the recipients? How were the funds distributed? Was there a lot of government interference? How did they get around the tax issues?

Big Mak was extremely savvy about finances. He had started out producing rap records in the cellar of a record store, built a label, sold half of it to a major without giving up any control, and become a millionaire by twenty-two. By thirty he had a clothing line, a film production company, two television reality shows, and his own men's fragrance. Big Mak had the fiscal acumen of a British banker and the aggressive acquisitiveness of a Wall Street lawyer. I expected him to give me a tutorial in African food management.

Instead he said, "I don't know shit about any of that. I'm going to land there and get driven to some drive-in theater where the concert's been going on all day. I'm going to walk from my car onto the stage, where I'm going to do one old hit and my new single to track, backed by a choir of two dozen township schoolkids. Then I walk off the stage, get back in my car, and get taken to meet Mandela. Snap snap, smile, shake hands, snap snap, smile, God bless you, sir, same to you, sir, and scram. We come back to the plane, we fly the fuck back to civilization. When people come to my house in South Beach, or my house in the Hamptons, or my house in Beverly Hills, or my office in Rockefeller Center, you know what's going to be over the mantel in each one? Mak and Mandela, brothers in glory. You got a picture with the Pope?"

"I don't, actually."

"Well, I'll see what I can do. Maybe call Quincy, hook you up there. You'd like that, right?"

"Sure."

"What the Pope is to you Irish, Mandela is to my people, right?"

"Got it."

I looked out the window at Africa passing below us and considered that in the eyes of status-hungry celebrities, the greatest moral leader of the last generation was only a higher class of Las Vegas greeter.

The flight lasted all day. I watched the moon rise over rivers and plains. I opened my computer and began treading through the accumulated e-mails of the last week. I had been out of range for most of our desert adventure, but we must have passed through a hot spot in Morocco where the dam opened and all the pent-up messages poured through.

There were fifteen from Simon. This was always unwelcome news. Since his deportation from America, Simon's paranoia had bloomed into something close to dementia. He thought people were trying to kill him. Somehow he had convinced himself that if he were dead, music companies with which he had been affiliated through the years would reap huge windfalls.

In our last conversation he had phoned me in the middle of the night to insist that someone had left a death threat on his phone machine. It took a long time to get him coherent enough that I could sort out what had happened. As I put it together, Simon had been driving in his car and a big truck had come tearing by, passing him on the wrong side. Simon had reacted by running off the road, up a patch of grass, and stopping just short of a stone wall. In his telling, the truck— a black truck, of course—had forced him off the road deliberately in an attempt to murder him. Having driven with Simon, I knew it was more likely that he had gone up on the grass out of unearned panic.

"And when I got home, there was a voice on my phone machine saying, 'You got away, fucker, but next time we will get you!' "

This had sounded concerning. Simon exaggerated like Baron Munchausen, but I had never known him to fabricate out of thin air. He might impugn, infer, and misinterpret, but he would not just make up something from nothing. I asked if I could hear the threatening message.

He called me back on his mobile phone and played it for me. It was garbled—a bad connection—but it did not to me sound unfriendly. A man's voice simply said, around a lot of buzzing and breaking, "Hey, Simon"—crackle buzz—"among those other"—hum buzz pop—"I'll get you later"—click.

"Simon," I said, "that wasn't a threat. It was someone saying he was sorry he missed you and he'd call back."

Simon was enraged. "You indifferent fool! Is that what you want to hear, or is that what you want *me* to hear? You know something about this, Jack? You got any idea who would profit from my being out of the way?"

"Oh, Simon, for God's sake . . ."

"Who is the little man with his fingers on the purse strings, Jack? Whose office do all my royalties flow through? You got poor Charlie's shares off him, didn't you? If I were out of the way you'd have the whole pie."

"You're stressed out, Simon. Let's end this conversation before one of us says something he'll regret."

"Too close to the bone, Jack? Who's your hit man? Huh? Who did you put in the black truck, Jack?"

I hung up. There was nothing I could do for Simon. In a way, I understood his pain. For years he had relied on the royalty stream from the old Ravons records as a cushion against insolvency. The CD boom had given those old albums a second life, and carried Simon through the eighties. Sales had slowed in the early nineties but the box set gave him a fiscal boost. Now, at the end of the century, even "Oh! Oh!" was not being licensed the way it used to be. Simon's annuity had been annulled. He was scared and needed someone to blame. I did not mind being accused of bad management, but his deciding I was trying to murder him was more than I was willing to bear. From that night on, I had refused Simon's calls.

Now I came face to face with fifteen Simon e-mail messages. The first, from five days earlier, when I was in Bamako, had no salutation and was straightforward:

"Please be informed that I immediately require copies of all of my record company and publishing royalty statements for the last twenty years. Sincerely, Simon Potts."

Within forty-eight hours seven more e-mails had arrived, each more hysterical than the last. The seventh read:

"It's me ringing your buzzer, Flynn. It's me who put that rock through your window. You can't hide up there forever. Come down and face me man to man, coward!!!"

I skipped ahead a few days. By the time I was recuperating in a bath in Tangier, Simon had become philosophical:

"The differences between us, Flynn, were fixed at birth. I am of the ruling class. You were born to the proletariat. You cling to petty trappings of 'success' because you desperately desire status. Having been born to the aristocracy, I have spent my life casting off what you long to put on. You are a servant who believes he can become a master by dressing in the master's old clothes. You are a footman who sneaks inside the carriage in the middle of the night and imagines himself a lord."

I skipped ahead another day. Now he was hysterical again and threatening to have me killed in self-defense.

I forwarded the whole chain to the FBI, and to my attorney. I did not think Simon would actually assassinate me but if by any chance he did, I wanted to be sure he would suffer for it.

I looked at my watch. We had been on this plane for hours and we still had six hours to go. I felt as if I would never get out of Africa alive.

That would show Simon.

I fell asleep and dreamed I was senior partner at Difford, Withers & Flynn, the father of four sons, enjoying my twenty-fifth wedding anniversary in my back garden at Barnes. When I woke it was night and we were descending into Johannesburg. The plane hit the runway, bounced once, and settled down. The doors opened and a customs official came aboard while we gathered our gear. We said good-bye to Big Mak and his aides, who departed for the charity concert at the drive-in theater.

To my surprise, Baxter left with them.

"Where are you going?" I asked him as he hoisted his backpack and hugged Emerson farewell.

"Going to meet Mandela, man," the drummer explained. "Came up while you were sleeping. Mak invited me along and Em said okay. You don't miss a chance like this, Jack. Not if you're black, anyway."

"I'd like to meet Mandela," I protested. It was true, and even more, I would have liked not to go on safari.

"Next time, Jack," Baxter said and took off after his new friends.

I wondered why he was getting off the hook when I was the one who had almost died. I promised myself, no more falling asleep.

"Don't leave anything behind," Castro said. "We're taking a different plane home."

The new shoes I had bought in Tangier were dressy, inappropriate for stalking game in the high grass. My traveling wardrobe was a mix of flashy new duds from the Villa Josephine and the few rough garments that had survived the Sahara. This trip had gone into double overtime and my wardrobe was insufficient to the commitment.

I thought back to losing my shoes under the palm tree in Spain while spying on Emerson's first wife in 1967. That had been nearly thirty years ago. How could it be true?

I expected we were bound for a hotel in the city. I was wrong. Instead we put ourselves and our luggage in a van that ferried us across the airport to another runway, where attendants pressed all of our baggage into the back of a small, narrow prop plane.

"What the hell is this?" I asked, not wanting to sit inside the beat-up aircraft on the ground, let alone in the sky.

"We got a leg to go, man," Castro said. "Jo'berg is as far as the big birds can fly. We're taking this spaceship out to the wild country."

"In the middle of the night? I have no desire to be Big Bopper to Emerson's Buddy Holly."

"It's almost morning, Flynn," Castro said. He pointed to a red ring on the horizon.

"Buck up, Jack," Emerson said happily. "We're going to glide into the African dawn!"

That's what we did, too. The old plane rattled and lurched and I was sure the weight of our bags would finish us off, but we cleared the trees at the end of the runway by three feet and wobbled into the sky. I smelled smoke but it was too late to protest. I resolved to shut up and die like an aviator.

For all my discontent there was a lovely moment when the left side of the sky out the window was filled with silver stars on a blue-black field, the center of the sky was violet, and the right side, the east, was exploding with streaks of gold and red.

Emerson saw me staring and leaned over the aisle and put his hand on my arm. "The world is full of beauty, Jack," he said.

I nodded. He might have enjoyed those colors even more if he had taken off his sunglasses.

We fluttered along, shaken by winds and spattered with light rain, for about an hour. Beneath us I could see only forests and fields. Castro consulted with the pilot, who indicated something below and began to descend quickly.

"What did he say?" I shouted at Castro.

"He says that's the landing strip!"

"What's the landing strip?"

"You see that meadow?"

"Yeah . . ."

"You see that bit of brown along the side of the meadow, near the trees?"

"No!"

"It's there. That's the runway."

We hit the ground so hard that the wheels wobbled and made a loud snap. Careening down the dirt path, we veered once toward the trees and then swept back onto the trail. We passed a water buffalo in the grass. The plane did not come to a halt as much as it wound to a stuttering stop, like a dying clock. I did not wait to be invited to pop the hatch and scamper to the ground.

The pilot got out and walked to the edge of the trees. He came back with two large rocks and planted them next to the wheels of his plane. Then he opened the back hatch and began piling our luggage on the grass.

"Where do we go from here, Gilligan?" I asked Castro.

"Be here now, Jack," Emerson instructed me. He had his shoulders thrown back and was smelling the air in deep gulps. "This is where our whole uncanny lives have brought us. Let's take it in."

We stood there absorbing the atmosphere while the pilot finished unloading our gear, removed the rocks from under his tires, and rolled down the field and back into the sky without saying a word of good-bye.

We watched him fly away and sat down in a field in southeast Africa with our travel bags and nothing else. I could see a cartoon thought balloon forming over the head of the water buffalo. It said, *Suckers*.

Castro tried to raise a phone signal. After about twenty minutes two green jeeps appeared in the distance.

"Here we go, then!" Castro said and took off his baseball cap and waved it in the air.

The jeeps pulled up to where we squatted in the high grass. They were customized with elaborate camouflage patterns and black *LIMPOPO RESERVE* logos riding on fields of tropical green. Each jeep had one white driver and one black guide. One of the guides got out and greeted us.

"Gentlemen! Welcome to Limpopo! I am David Makusu, chief of the hunt. Is one of you Mr. Castro?"

"I am Castro," Castro admitted. "This is Mr. Cutler and Mr. Flynn."

"Gentlemen," Makusu announced. "Have any of you been to Limpopo before?"

"I've been to Kenya," Castro said.

Makusu smiled. "Forgive me, brother, but here we look at the game reserves of Kenya the way a sailor who plies the great ocean might regard a little millpond."

I whispered to Emerson, "Five minutes and Castro's already whipping up ethnic hatreds."

The white drivers collected our bags and we rolled toward Limpopo. The road was a deep dirt lane running through the center of the grasslands. We spotted vultures in dead trees. A herd of zebras crossed in front of us and ran into a field. Two giraffes craned up from behind a bush to see what was passing. Castro and Emerson had cameras out and were clicking madly.

Makusu laughed and said, "Gentlemen! Don't waste all your film on the *road* to Limpopo. This is nothing to what awaits you!"

Much as I resented being dragged to Limpopo, I will admit that our rooms were fantastic. The hotel was a series of elaborate wood, grass, and glass cottages connected by winding wood walkways—docks, really—nested near the edge of a cliff dropping down to a river full of crocodiles, hippos, and water buffalo. There was a main dining hall and bar at the center of the compound, from which the wooden paths to the huts shot out like spokes. My room was beautiful, with a wide comfortable white bed inside and a futon under mosquito netting on an outside deck. There was a dining area, a kitchen sink, and showers inside and out. Meditative African music played from hidden speakers. I would have been very happy to climb into bed with a few volumes of Frantz Fanon and nod off to strains of gentle kora music, dreaming of the wretched of the earth.

Contradicting this ambition was a schedule of elaborate outdoor meals that seemed to be better suited to a cruise ship, and morning, afternoon, and evening safaris. These were photo opportunities only. No one who came to Limpopo would ever hurt an animal. I only wished the animals had signed a reciprocal agreement.

I managed to sleep for about an hour. I woke suddenly, sure that an intruder was in my room and about to be upon me. I rolled out of bed looking for a weapon, and a monkey leaped off the dresser and scampered screaming up into the beams of the ceiling. I shouted and then laughed. The monkey screamed at me from its safe height. It waved my reading glasses at me like a sword.

"Give me back those specs!" I ordered. The little ape clung to them and chattered at me angrily. Then he bounced from the beam to the immobile ceiling fan and from there out the door and into the trees, my glasses with him.

Teach me to not latch myself in, I admitted, and dressed and went down to see what there was to eat.

I was sitting by myself, holding a newspaper at arms' length trying to get the text in focus and enjoying some poached eggs, when Emerson and Castro dropped into the seats next to me and announced, "Midday safari departs in twenty minutes!"

I said, "What a coincidence, my midday siesta commences at exactly the same time."

"Don't be a pussy, Flynn," Castro instructed.

"We didn't come all this way to sleep," Emerson agreed.

I folded my newspaper.

A half hour later we were sitting on the raised second seat of a three-tiered jungle jeep, bouncing off the bumps of the Limpopo Reserve. Behind the wheel was a very pretty Dutch woman of about thirty who wore the resort uniform of camouflage shirt, matching baseball cap, kerchief, and shorts. Her name was Agatha Vandiver and there was no question that Emerson would try to seduce her before the day ended.

"How did you become a jungle girl, Agatha?" Emerson asked her as we pulled out of the compound and headed down a trail in the high grass.

"I'm working on my doctorate in veterinary medicine," she said while grinding the clutch like a cement mixer. "I am here for six months."

"Where are you studying?" I asked.

"University of Pennsylvania," she said. I think Emerson was disappointed to come all this way and find someone from so close to home.

"You get course credit for this?" I asked.

"I'm writing my thesis on the changing characteristics of young elephants."

"What?" Emerson said. "They're wearing long hair and bell-bottoms, are they?"

"Elephants have a very advanced social system," the driver explained. She really was pretty, I thought, with sun-streaked auburn hair and freckles. Her accented English was perfect. "Recently their social system is breaking down all over the continent. Young male elephants are behaving in uncharacteristic ways. It is a fascinating field."

She smiled, embarrassed, and added, "If you care about such things."

"I do care," Emerson said. "Deeply."

Seated next to Agatha, riding shotgun figuratively and literally, was a tall black African hunter with a shaved head, piercing eyes, and a rifle cradled across his lap. He was our guide, Peter, and it seemed to me that he was performing the role of native guide with the same practice and artifice he might bring to playing Othello.

"Be very quiet now," he informed us with a finger to his lips. "We will go among the sleeping lions."

Sure enough, we pulled into a field where eight or ten lions were snoozing in the midday sun like pensioners on a beach. Agatha turned off the motor and we sat craning our necks at the cats, who licked their lips, yawned, sniffed, checked us out without interest, rolled over, and went back to sleep.

"Would you like to get out and walk among them?" Peter asked.

"Not at all," I replied.

But Emerson and Castro were out of the jeep and looming between the dozing lions as if they were shopping at Selfridges. I climbed down from the elevated seat and joined them.

"We are not in a zoo, Emerson," I warned him. "These animals eat other animals for every meal. To them you are no different from a zebra, just not as quick."

He was not paying attention. We crept between the carnivores, oh wowing as we went. I looked back to be sure Peter had his rifle at hand just in case. I told myself that tourists did this every day, and then considered that the lions kill things every day, too, and they do it fast.

Back in the jeep and rolling over the fields, Castro and Emerson were ecstatic. I was not immune to the rarity of what we were doing, but I had spent too many years protecting Emerson from his own enthusiasms to be entirely relaxed. The danger with working for someone who at some level believes he is immortal is that he is likely to drag you over the edge with him before he finally learns he is wrong.

Peter the guide beguiled us with well-rehearsed stories about how the hippo is the deadliest of all the jungle beasts, how to stand if a hyena attacks, and which snakes and spiders would kill you instantly and which take a while. I was weighing all these options when Peter commanded Agatha the sexy driver, "Stop here!" and she hit the brakes and turned the wheel, swinging us to a halt with pizzazz.

The noble guide waved at us to stay seated and swung himself onto the ground. He advanced on a thick-barked tree, split by lightning.

"Aha!" he cried as he studied the bark. "Come and see this."

We gathered around him. He pointed at a black beetle about the size of my thumb which had burrowed into the wood. Peter said, "I thought I saw him in there! Mungi beetle, very old. Look at the dots on his shell. This old mungi has two hundred years. He was here before the white man came. Perhaps he will be here when the white men are all gone."

Peter said this with a jolly laugh and we all joined in but I thought it sounded like tourist-chummy bullshit. As we pulled away I whispered to Castro, "No way he spotted that bug in a hole in that tree from twenty yards in a passing jeep. This is all a routine, like Disneyland."

Castro smiled and took a swig from his canteen and wiped his mouth with the back of his wrist. We rolled down a dirt road with rising fields on our right and thick bushes trimming a river down a slope to our left. Peter held up his hand and Agatha hit the brakes.

Peter picked up his rifle and stepped out of the jeep. He said, "Tracks look like rhino. Very dangerous. I will go down to river and try to flush him out at curve by baobab tree down the bend. You meet me there in"–he looked at the sun–"forty minutes."

With that our brave mahout vanished into the bushes, taking his gun with him.

"Hope Peter doesn't come riding out of there on the horn of a rhino," Emerson said.

I said, "I have a feeling Peter's gone on coffee break." I leaned forward and spoke to Agatha behind the wheel. "How long will it take to drive to the baobab tree?"

"Ten minutes," she said in her Dutch accent. "Maybe fifteen. It will take Peter much longer going on foot up the river."

Castro asked what we were going to do with the extra half hour and Agatha pointed to a herd of elephants in the distance, walking circus-style, trunk to tail, at a distance of about half a mile across the great meadow to our right. She said, "We can park over there and watch the elephants go by."

That sounded pastoral to me. We headed toward the elephants, our jeep driving up and down ruts and crevices and around stumps, boulders, and thickets until we came to a stop facing the Dumbos, about forty feet from their parade. I sat on the raised third seat like it was a reviewing stand. Agatha turned off the motor and said, "Look at that wise old sybarite."

"You talking about me?" I asked.

"It's a poem called 'Elephant' by Irving Layton," she said. She moved her lips silently trying to remember and then announced, "Blows, ridicule, men's displeasure are wind beneath his ears."

Emerson and I nodded. If we'd had a tab of acid I'm sure we would have dropped it there. The sun was hot, the day was clear, and we were having a quiet moment in Africa, watching the wild elephants pass by.

One old gray matriarch about the size of a cement truck came out of the line and faced us. She raised her trunk to show her tusks. She stamped her front left foot and trumpeted.

"I don't think she likes us sitting here," I told the driver.

Agatha said, "She's just marking her space. Don't worry. An elephant will never attack a human unless it is boxed in on three sides and has no other place to go."

I said okay. There were at least a dozen babies among the herd, scampering to keep up and to stay with their mothers. The old matriarch kept waving her head and tusks at us. She took a few steps in our direction. I told Agatha that perhaps she should switch on the motor just in case.

Agatha turned and looked at me and smiled. She had full, cracked lips and freckled skin. She said, "It's not a worry, really."

Now the elephant began walking toward us, raising her head and flaring. There was a small white eucalyptus tree coming out of a red bush and she stood behind it. Emerson laughed and said look at the old fatty, trying to hide behind a little bush.

"She doesn't want us here," I said.

I do get sick of always being right. With shocking suddenness in an animal so large, the elephant raised her head, let loose a bugling blare, and charged toward us, ripping up the small trees as she clomped through them. We were stunned. More horrifying was that at the same instant all forty of the other elephants, young and old, male and female, turned out of their Animal Crackers profiles and began bearing down on us right behind him, howling and bellowing and kicking up earth as they came.

Agatha panicked. She twisted the key in the ignition and screamed, "Oh shit! Oh shit! Oh shit!" while Emerson tried to jump out of the jeep and Castro grabbed him by the belt and hauled him back in.

Time slowed down to where I could draw and exhale a breath between each second. My brain told me to be frightened but what I was seeing was too uncanny to convince my emotions that I was in real danger. A herd of wild elephants was charging me. I was about to be trampled and tusked. It was absurd. It was like something out of an old picture book. I was aware of the noise of the elephants pounding down the ground toward us, I was aware of the screaming of my companions, I felt the motor of the jeep turn over, and was cognizant of Agatha's frantic attempts to turn us around and away from the herd. The old matriarch was almost on top of us, her yellow tusks in the air and ready to shish kabob. I could see this was going to be a near thing—but all I could think was, I am going to be the first boy from my parish to die in an elephant attack! No one at home will believe it! They'll put a statue of me in the park! This, I considered, had to make up for being disbarred.

Time moved forward again and I grabbed the roll bar to keep from being flung from the jeep. The charging herd was kicking up a dust storm and our jeep was whirling around like it was about to be carried up the tornado. We burst forward with the lead elephant ten feet behind us. Emerson was holding on to the jeep with one hand and trying to get his camera to work with the other. Castro was screaming at Agatha the driver, who was screaming, too. She was swerving the jeep from side to side, trying to avoid trees and big rocks. We went down in a ditch and up on two wheels and I thought she'd kill us before the elephants did. We hit a log and everyone raised up off their seats, shouted, and landed back in the jeep.

Gradually we started to add distance between ourselves and the hurtling herd. When we were twenty feet from the lead elephant, Emerson started to laugh. He stood up on his seat like Admiral Nelson and majestically gave the finger to the receding beasts, who trumpeted their indignation.

Dinner that night was a wine-soaked celebration of our escape from a fate out of Hemingway. We regaled other resort guests with increasingly pulse-pounding details of our near-trampling. By the time Emerson went to bed, there were a hundred raging elephants and a lion or two goading them on.

I ended up sitting by the outdoor fire with Agatha the driver, who had begun the night as jolly as the rest of us but was, with the wine, revealing self-recrimination. She was supposed to be an elephant expert, and yet I had read them better than she. She was supposed to protect the tourists, yet she almost got her charges killed. No one at the hotel had reprimanded her, we had treated her as a comrade in our celebration, but she was making it tough on herself.

"You shouldn't feel badly," I told her. "You kept your head and saved us all. You drove that jeep like Steve McQueen, Agatha. From what you've told me, those elephants were acting in a completely uncharacteristic manner. Hell, it's got to be good for your doctoral thesis!"

She smiled. I asked whether we should open another bottle of wine and she nodded yes. I said that it was very good to have a plan for how your life is going to go, but know that life has surprises waiting that you will never see coming.

Agatha came back to my room with me and we lay on the open porch under mosquito netting and made love beneath an African moon. We fell asleep to the cooing of exotic birds and the rustle of the warm wind in the high branches all around us. When I left the Limpopo I got her number and promised to visit her in Pennsylvania when she returned to the university.

I don't know if Emerson got any actual musical inspiration in Africa, but he thought he did, so what's the difference? When we got home he wrote fifteen new songs that he claimed reflected the music he had heard in Senegal and the Sahara, in Morocco and Limpopo. To me, they sounded about as African as Bo Diddley, although, to be fair, Bo Diddley sounds pretty African.

We also came home with a lot of great photographs, which we all used to impress visitors to our offices. A month after we got back I was in the middle of a meeting with Emerson's latest record company A&R man when the young executive noticed a shot of Emerson, Castro, and me amid a family of sleeping lions.

"Holy cow, you guys really did go to Africa!"

"Of course we did, Jim, what did you think?"

The A&R man lowered his voice. "You don't know? Everybody assumed you were in rehab."

Charlie had many talents. He could sing, he could compose, and he could charm. He also had a talent for losing all his money. In the aftermath of the Disney fiasco I had managed to get him a new deal with a small San Francisco record label for an advance of twenty thousand dollars. Not much, but I used the news of that deal along with some suggestive hints that the Ravons were considering a reunion to also get him an eighty-thousand-dollar merchandising deal. A subsidiary of a major West Coast concert promoter was willing to advance Charlie four times as much for his T-shirts and posters as any record company would give him for his music. T-shirts were a cash business, and whoever you assigned your rights to would inevitably screw you, so the idea was to get as much money as you could up front and accept that you'd never see any more.

When I made the deal, Charlie was grateful beyond all measure. His gratitude lasted about as long as the money did.

Now the merchandising company was coming back to haunt us. Having failed to recoup even half their investment on a flop album and a tour canceled after only seven dates, the T-shirt dealers had chased Charlie down and told him to give them back their eighty grand or say good-bye to those fingers involved in making the D-minor chord.

"These cats are thugs, Jack!" he wailed at me over the phone line from California. "They ain't messin' around. You gotta get me out of this!"

"Cripes, Charlie, you spent *all* the money?"

"I got to live, Jack! I ain't like you, y'know, with all sorts of financial resources."

"Let me see if I can sort it out," I told him.

I got hold of the polite gangsters who owned the merch business and worked my way down to the rude gangsters who ran it. If I had had to, I might have just paid them off from my own pocket, but it's never wise to give money to strong-arm men. It gives them the idea you might be persuaded to give them more. I called Charlie back and told him we'd worked out a deal.

"You just have to go back out and stay out until you sell eighty thousand dollars' worth of T-shirts and tour books," I explained. "Castro and I can put a tour together. You haven't been to Canada in quite a while. We'll start out with clubs in Toronto and work our way across Montreal and Quebec City and end up in the Maritimes. If you're still in deficit then, we'll set up shows in New England."

"Christ, Jack," Charlie cried, "how long do I have to stay out?"

"Well, look, man, that depends on how fast the T-shirts go. I think we should price them to sell, myself. And we'll get some fake vintage Ravons shirts made up, too, and peddle those at a premium."

Charlie groaned down the telephone line. "I'm in the rag trade!"

"When the tour is over you'll come to New York and stay with me. Have a vacation."

"I'm going to freeze up there, Jack! You'll have to come looking for me with a team of sled dogs!"

"Hey, maybe we'll book you into Joe's Pub at the end of the tour. Record a live album. *Charlie Lydle Unplugged!*"

"I'm in the rag trade!"

I was beginning to wish I had stayed among the Tuaregs. Tensions in our office were running high. Wendy resented having been excluded from the boys' club camping trip to Africa, although she would have hated every moment of it. Castro never let a chance pass to talk loudly about all the adventures Emerson, he, and I had shared getting lost in the desert and dodging wild elephants.

The usual tension between my two lieutenants was getting worse. Each of them came to me to complain about the other, to say that he/she was messing up fragile negotiations, butting in where he/she did not belong, and offending with his/her oafishness and insensitivity all sorts of important people. Each hoarded the chance to talk with Emerson alone, and each tried to sabotage the other's ideas. I always told them the same thing: "Take it up with him/her. I don't want this stuff festering."

But it festered on. Castro and Wendy were like rival hunting dogs, dropping ducks at the feet of their indifferent master. Castro would pull Emerson aside after a show to pitch him on a movie soundtrack offer. Wendy would book two hours between interviews with him in a hotel suite so she could bend his ear toward a DVD deal. They were both stepping on my tail, but I let it pass. I suppose I figured that if they were each trying to top the other in the opportunities they scratched up for Emerson, it would only benefit the client in the end.

One day Wendy dropped a very big dead duck.

"I feel very strongly that Emerson should do *Behind the Music* to set up the new album."

Emerson was drinking tomato juice in a chair against the wall of my office while I sat behind my desk. Castro was leaning against the door. Wendy was marching up and down the rug.

"That's a freak show," Castro said. "Anyway, it's VH1. Emerson is an MTV artist."

"Are you drunk?" Wendy asked him. "MTV doesn't play anybody who shaves more than once a week. *Behind the Music* is really selling records. And if you do it, you can negotiate video rotation and multiple plays."

"That's the show about has-beens, right?" Emerson said. "The tragic fall of Milli Vanilli. How MC Hammer lost his house."

"Oh, and would you call Madonna a has-been?" Wendy asked. "How about Sting?"

"They're not on *Behind the Music*," Castro said.

"On top of things as usual, Ramon," she said. "Madonna just shot her episode. John Mellencamp and Billy Joel are both booked. This show sells records! I'm telling you, Em, it's a one-hour examination of your music and your career and they run these things, like, fifty times each. This is the era we're in now. Radio does not sell records anymore, television does."

"Who else has done it?" Emerson asked.

"Springsteen," Wendy said. "Bob Dylan."

"Total bullshit," Castro said.

"They're negotiating now! Look, this show is to the nineties what *Ed Sullivan* was to the sixties. We need to get in on it."

Emerson said, "I don't want anybody digging into my private life."

Wendy was on a tear. "It's all about providing a narrative, Emerson. We sculpt the story and present it to them. They flesh it out."

"So we can control this."

"Look, ultimately if you don't like the finished show, we deny them the sync rights. They can't run it without your music."

"What do you think, Jack?" Emerson asked me.

"I'd send the label in there first to make sure we know that the program will promote the new album and to negotiate a committed number of plays for the first video. Actually, make that the first two videos. If we can get that, I say proceed."

Wendy was delighted, Castro was crestfallen. I added, "And then, Emerson, make absolutely sure you do not give them anything that you cannot stand to see taken out of context, blown out of proportion, and rerun a hundred times."

With Wendy riding shotgun the label came back with a deal with VH1. Emerson would allow a film crew to shoot him working on his new album and interview him several times about the new record, his old records, and his career. They promised that Emerson's new album would be featured prominently throughout and would be the sole subject on the final act of the program.

We would provide the producers with vintage footage of Emerson's career, home movies, personal photographs, and access to some of his friends. Emerson drew the line at family. We also agreed to provide master use of his recordings gratis and to make best efforts to convince his music publisher to grant favorable terms.

Most important to me, *Behind the Music: Emerson Cutler* would not premiere before the third week of the following November, more than six months away. By that time I was confident Emerson's great African album would be in stores. To me it was nothing more than promotion for a record that was already a very long time coming and that we needed to be a substantial hit if Emerson was going to continue to be able to afford research trips to distant lands.

Over the next half year the *Behind the Music* cameras evolved from active nuisance to passive intrusion to just another aspect of working in the studio, like the tape operators and secretaries. Once or twice when the search for the elusive sounds became tense we asked them to leave, but as the recording dragged on and on and moved from studio to studio, I noticed that Emerson became anxious if a week passed and they did not come to film him. The cameras had become his audience and he wanted their approval.

I missed the days when promotion consisted of giving a bag of cash to a greasy man in a nylon jacket. It was faster, it required less energy, and although it is never comfortable to consort with criminals it was somehow less degrading.

On April Fool's Day I came back from the recording studio where Emerson was channeling Mali to a message that Agatha Vandiver, our African jeep driver, was in New York and wanted to see me. I called back the number and she picked up. I asked how she was doing with her thesis and she said it had slowed down. She was nearby and asked if we might meet for lunch. I cleared my calendar.

"I'm going to have a baby, Jack," she told me as soon as the waiter walked away.

"Well," I said, "that's good news. Congratulations."

We were seated in the window of Sal Anthony's, an Italian restaurant on Irving Place. "When are you due?"

"October. I don't need any help or expect anything from you, but I felt you should know."

How did I not understand what she was saying? It's inexcusable, of course. I think when one has a certain picture in his mind, it is very hard to stop seeing it, even when a different picture stands in front of you.

She looked at me expectantly. I looked back stupidly. I was probably smiling and thinking about whether to order the ravioli.

She gathered herself and said, "So, you don't have any hereditary diseases? No ancestral madness I should know about? Flat feet?"

The ravioli receded from my mind.

"Oh, Agatha. It's my baby?"

She looked nervous and then laughed. "That is why I am asking."

"Oh my God! I'm so sorry. I mean, I'm shocked. But I'm happy. I mean, are you happy?"

She nodded briskly.

"Well, what would you like to do? I have to help you financially, of course."

"No, you don't need to. This is my choice."

I am ashamed to say that the trained manager in me wondered if this might be a scam but the gentleman told him to pipe down.

"I know I want to have a child," she said, "and the doctors have told me that for me it may be difficult. That is why I choose to see this as a gift."

"Well, it is. I mean, I hope the baby looks like you and not like me. How far along are you?"

She looked a little hurt, like it might be a trick question. She said, "Just over two months. But I had the feeling right away, so I went and got checked. Of course, I could not keep working at Limpopo, so I came back to Pennsylvania."

She was such a beautiful woman. I was never going to find anyone better at my age. I said, "Come stay with me. I have a big place and I have help. You can have as much privacy as you want and everything you and the baby need. I know a great doctor, Niels Lauersen, he's written all the books on pregnancy and maternity. We're on a board together, I'll get us in to see him today."

She was surprised. Taken aback would not be too strong a description. She said, "I have a doctor in Pennsylvania. I like her. Jack, we don't really know each other."

"That's true, but look how much we have in common. Listen, think about it. That's all. I'm happy about this, Agatha. I will be with you through this time as much as you need me to be and I will step back when you ask."

We spent the rest of the afternoon talking and asking each other all the most basic questions. She was thirty-eight years old, which surprised me. She looked ten years younger. It relieved me, too. The disparity in our ages, while still severe, was not humiliating. She was fortyish, I was fiftyish. If you thought of it that way, it did not seem so bad.

She moved into my New York apartment. The summer of her pregnancy seemed to pass very slowly while it was going on, but collapsed into a montage of room-painting, baby-proofing, and meals by the television once my son was born. We never discussed whether Agatha would stay with me after the baby arrived. It was an unspoken assumption that grew every day as we found how well we fit together.

At the age of fifty-two I became a father for the second time. We named our little boy Benjamin. It was a long labor but Agatha stayed with her determination to give birth without painkillers or drugs of any kind. I was guzzling sedatives by the second hour.

Emerson made us a baby gift of his loft in SoHo. It was an act of almost unhinged generosity and I resisted instinctively, but he had worked it all out with our lawyers in advance. All I had to do was pick up the taxes. He was living now between Sagaponack and his mountaintop in Woodstock. When he stayed in the city, he always went to a hotel. "You can't bring up a family in that little hovel on Gramercy Park, Jack!" he insisted. "And I have no use for all that space I never visit."

I was determined to pour onto Ben all the attention I had failed to give Lucy when I was younger. I changed nappies, fell asleep with the baby on my belly, and roamed the three A.M. aisles of the local grocery store in my slippers and overcoat, looking for the right flavor of Similac. On days when I could get away with working from home, I would often strap Ben into a front-carrier and proceed to the park like a kangaroo, where I would push him on the swings and chat with the other mothers.

Emerson's African album, *River of Life,* **was released not long after** baby Ben, just in time to qualify for Grammy consideration. Wendy had arranged for the long-gestating *Behind the Music: Emerson Cutler* to premiere the same week that Grammy ballots went out. I had a small viewing party at the loft in SoHo to watch the show. Emerson came, as did Baxter the drummer and his wife, Castro, and Agatha's two sisters who had come to New York to see the baby. Wendy did not show up, which should have been a warning.

We had been promised from the start that we would have screeners of the *Behind the Music* episode two weeks before the program aired. As the premiere date got closer the producer swore to us that he was working around the clock in the edit room but would have something in our hands in time to get our reactions and notes. When we got within five days of the debut I began to smell a rat and sent Wendy to Los Angeles to go into the edit suite and make sure we were not being double-crossed. She called once to say that the show was still in pieces, she had seen a lot of great material, and was making them take out some bits that Emerson might find offensive.

"Is there anything I need to prepare him for?" I asked her.

"Overall it's going to sell a lot of records," she said. "But there are parts I'm negotiating to get out."

"Like what?"

"Well, right now Uta's in there."

"Miss Norway? What in the hell is she doing in Emerson's documentary?"

"It's tabloid shit from Scandinavian TV. I'm fighting to get it out."

"What else?"

"They interviewed Fred Zaras."

"Fuck me they did not."

"He's pretty measured. Says some nice things about Emerson."

"How did they even find him? Anything else?"

"Look, Jack, you knew going in the show was not going to be just a blow job. The important thing is that when all is said and done Emerson will come out, on balance, looking good. And we will sell a lot of albums off this. VH1 has already committed to heavy rotation for the first video."

"Wendy, if this is going south you have to warn me. I must prepare Emerson."

"It will be fine, Jack. Leave it to me."

That was the last I heard from her.

It was with some trepidation that Agatha and I welcomed our group of friends and family and our guest of honor Emerson to our home to watch the Sunday evening premiere of this documentary that had taken longer to bring into being than our child.

We gathered around the television like cavemen around a fire. At nine o'clock the screen lit up with a montage of Emerson through the years, bearded and clean-shaven, hippie and slick, moussed and permed, performing fingernail-splitting guitar solos to the open-mouthed delight of arenas filled with inspired fans. The guests clapped and nudged the real Emerson, who had the best seat on the couch.

A voice-over said, "Emerson Cutler is one of the true legends of British rock. His searing fretwork has been held up next to Clapton, Hendrix, and Beck. His soulful vocals compared to Mick Jagger, Rod Stewart, and Phil Collins."

"Phil Collins?" Emerson said. "I don't sing anything like Phil Collins."

We shushed him. The voice-over went on. "He has sold millions and made millions."

Here the unseen narrator dropped his voice like a court-appointed lawyer: "But for Emerson Cutler, success was a shortcut to personal destruction. He used and abused the women who loved him, he turned his back on the friends who took him to the top, and he looked for self-esteem not in the dexterity of his fretwork, but in the false highs of narcotics—and at the bottom of a whiskey bottle."

Fingers tightened on armrests. Emerson reeled back on his cushion.

I looked across at Baxter, who thrust his hands in his pockets like he was looking for a crucifix and holy water.

"Tonight, the harrowing story of Emerson Cutler, a superstar who rose to ultimate fame by betraying the gifts that got him there–*Behind the Music!*"

So it went for sixty torturous minutes. The thesis of the documentary was that Emerson had been a simple boy with a special talent, who had traded his gifts for life in the fast lane, along which expressway he also managed to dump the ruined carcasses of every man who stood behind him and any woman foolish enough to love him.

The first segment opened with some contract-fulfilling footage of Emerson in the recording studio working on *River of Life*. He wore headphones and sat hunched over his guitar, overdubbing a lead line. After blowing it, he turned to someone the camera did not reveal and said with petulance, "I can't [bleep] do this if people are going to be hikin' back and forth in there! I'm trying to play, all right? Now, if you don't need to be here, take a walk. Thank you!"

I looked at Emerson on the couch. He was rigid. The narration turned back the clock to black and white film of the very young Ravons rocking some British sock hop. Emerson played an impressive guitar solo, but you would never have known–the camera stayed focused on his strumming hand. Emerson and Charlie shared a microphone and shook their moptops. Dissolve to Charlie today:

"Ah, we had a great time, man. Girls, music, mates, and beer. Our life was a big laugh in the Ravons and Em was right in the middle of it. The chicks dug 'im, man. They really dug 'im."

Fade into still photo of Emerson signing autographs for delighted teenyboppers. Back to Charlie:

"Yeah, sure, he changed. We all changed. Em was smarter than the rest of us. He understood that if you were going to make a living at this you had to keep an eye on the money, too."

That was not what set Emerson to boiling over. It was when a middle-aged woman with hysterical blond hair and a surgically re-engineered face appeared in the middle of the screen. When she spoke, I recognized Kristin before the chyron told us.

"I was just a love-struck girl when I married Emerson," she intoned like she was repeating a memorized essay. "I didn't know anything about life. It never occurred to me that Emerson would have other girls on the side." Here she sniffled theatrically. "When I found out, it broke my heart. He told me I was a square, that everyone was sleeping with everyone nowadays and I should, too."

Someone off-camera asked how that made her feel.

"It made me feel awful! I told him I didn't want to be with anyone else and he just laughed and called me a silly little virgin."

"If there is one thing I never called you," Emerson shouted at the television, "it was a virgin!"

Kristin went on, overemoting like a new widow in a high school play:

"So finally, I did what he wanted. And . . . and . . . I didn't know . . . he had someone hiding there, taking pictures of me. Horrible pictures. And then his lawyer said if I contested the divorce, they'd show these pictures to my parents and ruin me!"

Although the narrator did not give the name of that blackmailing lawyer, he did announce, "Emerson's personal attorney forced Kristin Cutler to give Emerson his no-strings divorce. The attorney was later disbarred on drug charges. Kristin Cutler never got her day in court."

After that, the rest of the program could have accused Emerson of shooting the Pope and it would not have registered with us. Some of the guests made excuses to slip out the door. Castro and Baxter stayed. The midget video controversy was revivified and flaunted. When a bald and saggy Fred Zaras appeared on-screen in act four it was an anticlimax.

"The Emerson Cutler I knew as a young man had extraordinary gifts," Fred said with what I'm sure he hoped would read as saddened wisdom. "He was beloved of the muses and they showered him with blessings. He instinctively knew where the zeitgeist was going next. In those days after the breakup of the Beatles, with Elvis in Vegas and Dylan in seclusion, there was a moment when the idealism of the counterculture found its focus in Emerson Cutler."

I had been there and was pretty sure there was no such moment.

Emerson said, "Christ, Fred looks awful."

Fred went on. "Something in him could not bear the burden. It's almost as if he was afraid he was unworthy to represent the dreams of so many idealistic young people. So"–here Fred pretended to struggle for words—"he turned away from his gifts. He abandoned his old friends. And he cut off his access to the muse."

"Cut off your access right enough, you fat freeloader," Emerson said to the TV.

There was a short montage of some of Emerson's most unfortunate video moments—eighties excesses of hair gel, wardrobe, and choreography—over which the grim judgment of Fred Zaras intoned, "Few musicians of our generation had more talent than Emerson Cutler, and no one who had such talent squandered it so completely."

The bumper out to commercial was a shot of Emerson smiling while going over a sand dune. Then the announcer said, "When *Behind the Music* returns, how Emerson Cutler reconnected to his inspiration on a near-death journey to the dark continent."

"Ahhhh, fuck," I said as I killed the volume on the television. I turned to Emerson. "You want me to fire Wendy?"

Castro leaned forward like an anxious beagle.

"Nah," Emerson said. "Let's make her come out on the tour and suffer. I won't speak to her the whole time. Let her spin on the kabob for a couple of months."

He was oddly composed. He said to me, "You think people believe that about me, Jack? That I ripped off all my friends and blew my talent?"

"Of course people don't believe that," I told him. "The public neither thinks like that nor gives a hoot. They like the way you sing. They like going to your shows. When you have a new song on the radio that appeals to them, they buy it. If they like the new REM song more, they buy that instead. They don't care if you bought out Charlie's publishing or fired Gino the drummer they never heard of or had a bad divorce. They have problems of their own! I mean, I hate this fucking assassination job, but the truth is, it will probably sell a load of records. Simply because the people who watch it will say, 'Oh, I liked those songs! And his new album is out and it's his best in years? I might pick that up on the way home from the office tomorrow.' At the end of the day, that's really all that matters. The rest is fish wrap. More keyhole-peeking."

"That's one way to look at it," Emerson mumbled.

I was trying to make my friend feel better, of course, but I more or less believed what I was saying. The last segment of the program was fluff about how Emerson went to Africa to reconnect with his old inspiration and came back with *River of Life,* an album as fresh and exciting as the great work of his youth. There were home movies of our party in the Sahara and Dakar and at the game preserve, intercut with Emerson in the studio laying down the new songs. It was a five-minute commercial and, as it turned out, an effective one. *River of Life* went all the way to number five on the *Billboard* charts nine days after the premiere of *Behind the Music.* It was a big comeback for Emerson and somewhat mitigated his fury toward Wendy for walking him into the ambush. But he did make her come out on tour with him and refused to speak to her the entire time.

I was putting together Emerson's *River of Life* tour when Charlie's long, long trek through small clubs of the snow belt to pay back his merchandising advance finally shuddered to a close at a ski lodge in New England.

It had taken a year of work and over two hundred gigs, but he had finally sold enough T-shirts to settle his debts. Agatha and I drove up to see the last show in Brattleboro, Vermont. There were nearly a hundred people in the audience, and while many of them had simply wandered in because they had been skiing all day and this was the only entertainment around, half the room actually knew who Charlie was and paid attention.

"It's gotten better since that *Behind the Music*'s been running," Charlie told us over dinner in our room. "People yell out for the Ravons songs. Might we have sparked a revival, Jack?"

"Nice to think so," I said.

Charlie looked terrible. He was always thin, but now he looked frail, his head much too big for his shrunken neck and shoulders. His complexion was sallow and he was obviously exhausted. When I told him I was concerned, he said, "Ah, it's this bloody touring is all, man. Can't eat right, never sleep in the same place twice, always on a bus or plane. Now that it's over I'll do some exercise, get some rest. Be fit in no time."

Agatha and I insisted he drive back to New York with us the next day and spend a few days visiting. I reminded him that he had not yet met my son.

"Can't miss that," he said with a smile. "I need to have a few words with this young Benjamin concerning how best to deal with his pappy's eccentricities." He leaned over and told Agatha in a stage whisper, "You found out about the shackles and whips yet, Aggie?"

When Charlie had gone back to his own room Agatha told me, "He really looks very poorly, Jack. I'll bet he never sees a doctor. I'm going to ask Dr. Golub to see him while he's in New York."

"Charlie's a grown man, Agatha," I said. "You can't treat him like a little boy."

"But he is a little boy, Jack. He's a little lost boy who needs someone to make sure he eats right and doesn't get sick."

Agatha was young enough to be Charlie's daughter but she was right. When you got down to it we were all lost boys.

Dr. Golub had offices on Eleventh Street in the West Village. He was an older man with the almost extinct habits of a general practitioner. Agatha and I had discovered him through Wild Bill, the music mogul. Dr. Golub was the physician we went to for flu shots, for aches and pains, and for insurance physicals. He had not been sucked into the American medical industrial bureaucracy. You walked in, he looked down your throat and took your blood pressure, and you gave Nanette the nurse twenty dollars on the way out the door.

Agatha dragged Charlie to Dr. Golub's office on a Wednesday morning while I was arguing with promoters about the guarantees for Emerson's tour. Even with our increased record sales, I was getting a lot of pushback. Emerson had been off the road too long, I was told, it was too risky to book him into arenas. The promoters were arguing for a theater tour. If it sold well they could add nights. I pointed out that Emerson would rather play to twelve thousand people in a single show in an arena than play four shows in a theater to reach the same number. In reply I was asked, "And how's he going to like standing in a twelve-thousand-seat arena and seeing ten thousand empty seats? The market's rough, Jack. Play this one safe."

It is never wise to force promoters to take a risk they do not want to take. They have ways to screw you that can never be proven. Some of them would lose money just to prove themselves right. I played it their way. I put Emerson into large sheds in New York, Boston, San Francisco, and Los Angeles where I was sure he could sell out. In the rest of the country, we went for theaters and put extra nights on hold. We jacked up the ticket prices to make up some of the difference. The consumers interested in Emerson were over thirty-five. They had money. We worked out a deal with American Express to give them a thirty-day exclusive on advance tickets and they created a "Golden Circle" of seats priced at two hundred dollars for preferred customers and high rollers. It made me hesitate for a moment, but Castro said, "If we don't scoop up that money the scalpers will."

When I got home I complained about my day for a while and then asked Charlie how he had made out at Dr. Golub's.

"He says I'm run-down, man. Probably anemic. I've had this sore throat that won't go away. I think it's from singing so much but he took some blood. He wants to send me up to some lab on Fourteenth Street for more tests. I should probably just go back to California and rest up for a bit, Jack."

"Don't be silly," Agatha said. "We have plenty of room and Ben loves having you around. Stay here and recuperate. Wait for the test results."

After dinner Charlie pulled me aside and said urgently, "Jack, I got no insurance. I don't think I can do these tests."

"Don't be silly, man," I said. "I've got it covered."

For the next two weeks Charlie lay around my loft playing with Benjy, listening to music, and going from one medical facility to another. I was grateful to Agatha for being so generous with my old friend, although there were times when I would have liked it if he'd stayed in his room and not planted himself in the middle of our parlor night and day. Charlie loved watching HBO. He was oblivious to the effect that obscenities, nudity, and violence might have on little Ben. I came home one afternoon to find my son climbing over Charlie while on-screen a gang of mobsters hammered the head of a naked stripper with an oar.

"Maybe Ben shouldn't watch this, Charlie," I said.

"Oh?" He looked up at the TV. "Right you are, Papa. Benjy, go in the other room."

It was not Charlie's place to send my son out of his own living room. It was Charlie's place to turn off the television. I was about to tell him so when Agatha stepped in and called me into the kitchen.

"Dr. Golub doesn't like what he's seeing in Charlie's test results," she told me. "He's sending him to an oncologist on the Upper East Side."

"Really."

"Go a little easy on him, okay?"

"Of course."

I took some time out of the tour planning to go with Charlie on the next round of tests. We were back at Dr. Golub's office when he got the news.

"Charlie," he said, "here's the bad news and the good news. The bad news is that you have a squamous cell cancer at the base of your tongue."

"Shit," Charlie said. "Is it from smoking?"

"Might be. Otorhinolaryngological cancers, cancers of the head and neck, tend to occur more frequently in smokers and drinkers."

"I can quit."

"You will quit, Charlie," the doctor said, not unkindly. "The good news is, there is a seventy percent chance of recovery."

"Bad news?" Charlie asked.

"These cancers have high levels of recurrence down the line."

"Surgery?" Charlie asked.

"Sometimes. If it spreads into the jaw and throat you will want to go in after it. But it's also treated with radiation and with chemo-therapy."

"Okay," Charlie said. "Jack, could you write this down?" He was dazed. He knew he would want to remember exactly what the doctor said later. I borrowed some prescription paper and began taking notes.

"Can you just cut it out, Doc?" Charlie wanted to know.

The doctor said, "We have to see how far it's traveled. What we don't want to see is the cancer getting into your lymph system. That would cause me concern. How long have you had the sore throat?"

"Don't know," Charlie said. "I've been doing five shows a week all year, sometimes singing for two and a half hours a night. I always have a bit of a scratchy throat."

"You won't be doing any singing for a while, Charlie," the doctor said.

We made arrangements for more tests. Dr. Golub gave Charlie the names of cancer specialists and laid out the pros and cons of radiation vs. surgery vs. chemo. He told him he would have to approach this like a soldier going off to war. He could not be passive with cancer. He had to engage his fury in this battle. He had to determine to treat the can-cer like an invading army.

I asked how long it would take to beat it, best-case scenario. The doctor said six months would be extremely optimistic but it was better not to think of end-dates. "We are in this for the duration."

Charlie asked about alternative therapies. Here Dr. Golub turned severe. "Don't ever get cute with cancer," he said. "Don't think about New Age cures, don't go online and read about alternative therapies or experimental treatments. Don't look for a back way out, Charlie. Kill the monster before it kills you. That should be your only consideration."

Charlie nodded. The weight of the diagnosis was beginning to hit him. I took a prescription and some contact phone numbers from the doctor and we walked outside. We went over to Seventh Avenue and flagged a taxi and rode in silence.

"Don't think about the money, man," I said finally. "I've got it covered."

"I can't do that to you, Jack," Charlie said.

"I'm richer than you realize, Charlie," I told him. "I could spend a million dollars on your medical bills and it would not change my life by an inch. I am wealthy because you and Emerson hired me to be your manager thirty years ago. I pay all the bills."

"Thank you, Jack," Charlie said. He smiled a little bit and went back to looking out the taxi window.

I was still at home for the first week of Charlie's chemo and radiation treatments. I went with him when they gave him a subcutaneous injection of a drug called Ethyol, intended to protect the noncancerous parts of his body from fallout from the radiation. Beneath his leprechaun demeanor Charlie was a tough little bastard. When he got word that the cancer was in his lymph nodes—though not yet in his lymph system—he asked the doctors to give him the highest simultaneous doses of chemo and radiation possible.

"Take me right to the edge of killing me," he said. "And if that ain't enough, go farther. I'm gamblin' I can take more abuse than the cancer cells can." I brought Charlie home and he was violently sick all night.

Agatha and I both accompanied Charlie on his first visit to the Joshua and Zoey Feigenbaum Cancer Center on the East Side. He sat in what looked like a La-Z-Boy reclining lounge chair and was hooked up to a drip bag for three hours. Charlie sat back and waited for the miracle. After half an hour I told Agatha to go home. I had turned off my mobile phone. I was reading a sheaf of documents and contracts related to Emerson's tour. Advance ticket sales were slow.

"Hey, Jack," Charlie said lazily in the middle of hour two. He motioned with his eyes around the room. A dozen other patients were sitting back in big chairs with tubes running down to their arms. "Don't this joint look like a science fiction flick? All the humans hooked up to wires being kept alive by a big alien computer."

"We are living in the future, Charlie," I said.

"The only way to be, Jack." He smiled and tipped his head back and closed his eyes.

The chemo made Charlie vomit, but nothing prepared us for the radiation treatments. First, Charlie had to have his chest tattooed by a former Marine named Brian who explained that the small permanent triangles he was needling into Charlie's skin would ensure that the radiation was aimed right where it was supposed to be each time he got blasted. He was inking bull's-eyes onto Charlie's bosom. Before Brian turned on the juice he put Charlie's head into a radiation mask. This was molded from plaster to fit his face and wired with hard netting. Before the juice was switched on, the mask was bolted to a plank with Charlie's head inside. It looked medieval. I was certain that in a thousand years our descendants would count us as barbaric as the Incas.

Once his head had been bolted to the board, the white slab Charlie was lying on tilted up and a radiation machine like a giant hair dryer blasted him with rays intended to kill the cancer. It was so intense that burns like skid marks began to form on Charlie's back. Brian the Marine explained what they were: exit wounds.

As gruesome as all this was, Charlie did not suffer as terribly in the first week as he would later. I became very busy planning Emerson's tour and could not bring him in most of the time. I once sent an intern from the office and Agatha was appalled. From then on, she took him to the doctor's.

I had hired a car and driver—and after every appointment Charlie lay flopped in the front room listening to music or watching TV until the next day. He kept a saucepan by his side for the vomiting and a towel on his chest. Agatha cleaned up and kept watch over him like a mother with a sick boy home from school. Benjy would lean over the arm of the couch above Charlie's head and try to surprise him by yelling boo. Every time, Charlie pretended to be scared.

I was four days late leaving to join Emerson's tour. Agatha assured me that she could take care of Charlie without me. It was hard to leave both of them, and even harder, when I caught up with the tour, to put up with Emerson's complaints that his new musicians were not good enough, that the dates were poorly routed, and that the sound-man needed to be stood in front of a firing squad.

Emerson understood that his career was sliding southward and it drew all of his obnoxious qualities to the surface. Almost every person I have ever known who made a living as a rock and roll performer was afraid that he was on some level a fraud. In the case of Simon, his arrogance was so tightly wound around his insecurity that it was obvious to everyone. His wall of defensiveness demonstrated an interior wobbly with paranoia. Charlie always seemed to be easygoing, but I had lately begun to wonder if his self-sabotage with the Hollywood movie studio might not speak of a fear of success. Having chased the golden balloon for so long, perhaps Charlie was more comfortable being a beloved should-have-been than he would be living up to real stardom.

Not Emerson. Emerson was untroubled by self-doubt. He believed that he deserved everything he had and plenty he did not. As far as he was concerned, rock and roll was a scam he had mastered young and stayed atop with years of hard work. Emerson's self-esteem was impenetrable. The longer I knew him, the more I suspected that if his DNA were mapped we'd find out he was part cat.

When I caught up with the tour he was in a restaurant in Washington bitching about those fans he had left.

"People just come up and *talk* at you all the time," he said to Baxter right after I took a seat at the table and he nodded to me. "They feel a need to tell you their life story in double time as soon as you sit down next to them! I said the words 'chicken salad' in front of that mayor's mistress last night and she launched into a story about the chicken salad her grandmother used to make! They jump in on everything you say. They interrupt you and agree with you before you've made your point. They smile wider and talk faster and start telling you things they wouldn't tell their psychiatrist."

I had heard it all before. He began working on a cork wedged in a wine bottle and I tried to turn the conversation to Charlie's treatments, but Emerson was a little tipsy and had ears for no one else. It never would have occurred to him that anyone would have wanted him to stop talking:

"And it never lets up! It's everyone at the party and it's the guy who drives you to the boat and it's the kid driving the boat and it's the woman who greets you outside to walk you through the airport and the girl who escorts you to the chopper and then it's the helicopter pilot telling you about his missions in 'Nam the whole way back to the city. It's like I spend my whole life in a roomful of kindergarten kids with their hands in the air yelling call on me, call on me, call on me!"

Emerson shrugged. The party around the table laughed. He took another swig of wine and asked me how Charlie was doing. I said it was pretty rough and gave a brief description of the radiation mask and the tattoos and the burns on his back.

Emerson grimaced. He said, "Obviously I'll be there if he needs anything. I've been taking care of Charlie since we were fourteen. Couldn't get out of it now if I wanted to."

It was a magnanimous gesture but it was also his way of dismissing the subject. Emerson had just played a good concert and enjoyed a big meal and now he was holding forth on his hard-learned insights into the price of fame. He did not want Charlie's grave illness to come into the room and put things in proper perspective.

I was out with Emerson for the better part of ten weeks. There were breaks, of course, during which I flew home and helped Agatha deal with Charlie's treatments.

There is always a disconnect between tour-head—the mental state that comes with being on the road with a rock band—and adjusting to home life. When one whips back and forth between the two, seasickness is inevitable.

I knew Agatha had been under tremendous pressure, dealing with little Ben and with Charlie's illness. I gave her a ton of space. Still, she was angry with me all the time. When I was home from the tour, everything I did was wrong. If I engaged Charlie in talk about his treatments, Agatha would say it was inappropriate conversation for the dinner table. If I offered to help, to take him to the clinic, she assured me I did not know the right things to do. Charlie had had an allergic reaction to the chemo and if Agatha had not been there keeping a close eye, he might have died. Would I know the signs if that happened again? Would I know how to handle it?

I began to feel as if Charlie, Agatha, and Ben were the family and I was the guest overstaying his welcome.

Charlie, who was now as frail as a man can be, reached up his stick of an arm and grabbed me one day when she left the room after laying into me about something insignificant.

"Don't you know, Jack?" he whispered. "It's the third rule of wives. When they can't see you, they are sure you are goofing off and having fun. Doesn't matter if you're on the road running a big tour or making an album or performing surgery or outside the spacecraft trying to repair the solar panels. If she can't see you, you might as well be on the golf course with your mates."

I did not want to add to Charlie's miseries by making him feel responsible for this new pressure on Agatha's and my relationship, but it was clearly wearing on her. Here was a young, smart, vivacious woman, on her own, having adventures, tooling around Africa in a jeep. She meets an older man and gets pregnant. She comes looking for him and he sweeps her into a luxurious cage. Now she is dependent on this stranger. She has a child—that will turn anyone's head upside down. The man then vanishes for weeks at a time and leaves her to tend a grievously ill friend who is as much a stranger to her as the man, the home, and being dependent on someone else. I understood why she was at the end of her tether, but that did not make it easier to be the focus of her unhappiness.

These interludes of tension were my only respite from the obligations of Emerson's tour. I began to look forward to when it would be time to pick up my suitcase and say good-bye and get in the Music Express car for the airport. It used to be the time I felt most lonely.

Now it brought me relief. I was moving again. Hotels and airports had become my natural habitat. I found them consistent and comforting. I enjoyed being in the air, where the pilot was in charge and I had no decisions to make and I was unreachable.

Home was now where I felt displaced. Traveling was where I was at home.

The trouble with traveling is that sooner or later you must arrive. Emerson was playing a theater in Park City, Utah, and he was more miserable than usual. He had agreed to an opening act for this leg of the tour, a college radio act called Jiggle the Handle. As many of their fans were showing up at the concerts as his, and some of their audience were leaving during his set.

"They can't sing, they can't play, and they look like shit," Emerson said to me of Jiggle the Handle's appeal. "No wonder the kids love them. I mean, Christ, Flynn—how hard can it be for you guys to get this right? You know who my audience is! If you need to add a support act, make it someone compatible with me! You could have got Dr. John or Buddy Guy, someone my fans would get a kick out of seeing! But to subject my audience to these amateurs is just lazy! I better not find out this is some sort of kickback, a favor to their label or agent. If that's the case, I warn you, heads will roll."

The only favor being done here was Jiggle the Handle's manager letting Emerson play after his band, but I could not say that to my egotistical client. Over our many years together I had seen Emerson's graciousness recede as his sense of entitlement expanded.

When the Ravons were young, Emerson saw their success as a party to which all were invited. As he grew older, richer, and more successful, he would occasionally grumble about journalists and disc jockeys being leeches who rode on his back. Eventually he began to apply this epithet to the record company who profited from his work and the promoters who made themselves fat at the feast he provided. I told myself he was a man under pressure blowing off steam and anyway he wasn't all wrong.

But by 1999 everyone was a parasite. His driver who presumed to engage Emerson in uninvited conversation when he was sulking in the back, his housekeeper who acted as if she were part of the family, his cook who pretended not to remember that he hated carrots. They were all incompetents and coattail-riders dining out on their proximity to him. The lawyers whose bills he resented were leeches, too, and any record producer or engineer with the temerity to challenge his tempo or timing.

"Right," he would say when his judgment was questioned. "And how many number one records have *you* had?"

When he defended his music, this attitude had some merit. In time, however, Emerson began to use his musical success to shoot down challenges on any subject. If a television director suggested a change in lighting, Emerson would snicker and say, "Right, I think I know a *bit* about lighting. I did sell out six nights at the Albert Hall. You ever lit the Albert Hall, Joe?"

If a tailor suggested taking half an inch off his cuff, Emerson would say, "This was the way I wore it when I played for Charles and Diana at the palace, mate. This length was fine when I was on the cover of *GQ*. I think I know a bit about men's style."

I knew we had crossed a line when Emerson began adding his band, his fellow musicians, to the list of leeches. This happened after a concert in Seattle where the crowd was restless and did not ask for an encore, in spite of the lights being lowered to invite it. The whole way back to the hotel Emerson complained that he was sick of carrying these hired hacks and having to show them where to put their fingers on the frets and keyboards.

It was only a matter of time until I, with my percent of his profits, moved to the list of mooches, schnorrers, and succubae. But Emerson shocked even me when he decided that his fans were leeches, too, sucking his energy and taking advantage of his generosity and genius.

"Emerson," I said. We were in a cold locker room under a theater in Vancouver. The candles the promoter had lit to add a patina of New Age warmth to the surroundings instead made it look like a dungeon. "Those fans up there have paid sixty-five dollars a ticket, stood in line, and sat through a cold rain and a Canadian funk band for the privilege of standing and cheering every fart that comes out of your behind. You may very well feel nothing in common with them, but it is unfair to suggest that they are in any way taking advantage of you."

Emerson regarded me with slit-eyed displeasure. He was holding a thin slice of roast beef wrapped in a tube of bran bread. He let it fall from his fingers onto the concrete floor.

"They are sucking away pieces of my *soul*, Flynn. Can you even begin to comprehend what that feels like? I doubt it very much. I go up on that stage and open up my veins out there. I tear open my chest and show them my beating heart. And what do they do with it? They hold up green glow sticks and make fists in the air like fucking fascist cattle. I can put up with the promoters stealing the gate receipts and the record company feeding the food I pay for to their prostitutes and the journalists spying through the crack in the door and the fucking roadies bootlegging tapes from the soundboard and selling them on the black market. I can put up with the band, whose lazy incompetence is exceeded only by their unsubstantiated conceit. I can even bear you, my old friend and confidant, taking your commission on the gross while I pay all the inflated costs of this whole tedious exercise out of the net. All that I'm used to. What I have a hard time with is baring my soul, my pain, my heartbreak into the void only to have the void stroll out for a piss and a pretzel. That is a bit more than I signed up for, yeah?"

I could have argued with him all night and only made it worse. I said, "Well, then, I won't even bring up the itinerary for Mexico." That broke the tension enough that I could open the door and let in two dozen radio contest winners.

What I wanted to say—what I said to myself all the rest of that night as I rewrote the conversation in my imagination—was this: *We're all cogs in this machine, Em. We're all sucking at the breast of this monster. If you disappeared up your arsehole tomorrow and were never seen again, all of us parasites—crew, agents, promoters, management, press, musicians, and fans—could go out with Steve Winwood or Don Henley and the circus would not even slow down. You are as replaceable as anyone else.*

I never said that, of course. I understood that a lot of Emerson's ugliness was born of pain at his diminished professional circumstances. Anyway, when Emerson wanted to end an argument with me dramatically he would always resort to the same old line from a Mick Jagger song: "You gentlemen all work for me."

Charlie recovered from his cancer, but it was a long and terrible slog and Agatha had to take him through it alone while I was away, nursing Emerson's ego.

The chemo treatments that defeated Charlie's cancer almost killed him. His white blood cell count plummeted, he lost all sense of taste and smell, his teeth began to loosen and rot, and he developed sores, called thrush, on the inside of his mouth. Always skinny, Charlie was down to eighty-eight pounds when Emerson's tour ended and I came back to New York for good. Agatha had become a fierce mother bird protecting a weak chick.

"You have no idea how bad the medical care in this country is," Agatha told me as if it were my fault. "These hospitals, they want the beds. When Charlie was sickest they gave him a staph infection and then insisted on moving him into the intensive care unit. It sounds good but it is a euthanasia center, Jack. They sent in grief counselors to try to get me to schedule a time to gather his friends and turn off the machines! They wanted to order food and make it a going-away party!"

I told her I was sure she misunderstood, but she was certain and furious.

"You were not there! This is how the Americans do it now! This psychologist came to hold my hand and tell me that I had to let my husband go, it was cruel to keep him hanging on!"

That stopped me. I said, "They thought Charlie was your husband?"

"I had to tell them he was in order to sign the papers! If they had known he had no family they would have kept me out and killed him for sure. I tell you, Jack, these hospitals are factories. They are part of the funeral industry."

"You told them you were Charlie's wife?"

"What does that matter?"

"Well, legally . . ."

"So what? You are paying for all his treatments, there is no insurance company to defraud. I did what had to be done to stop these ghouls from turning off his life-support to cover up their own mistakes. I tried to bring in Dr. Golub to get him out of there but they would not allow him into the hospital because he is not insured to work in their facility. We had to use their doctors, and they rotate new ones through every three weeks, so you are always starting from scratch! What is wrong with this country?"

I had no answer that Agatha would have accepted. I had left her with this burden and it had taken the light from her eyes. She had gone to the extreme of hiring a private ambulance service and removing Charlie from the hospital while the nurse shouted at her that she would be responsible for the death of her husband. She brought Charlie home and with the help of Dr. Golub nursed him through his infections, got him hooked up to an IV, and was able to gradually move him back onto solid foods.

I was home now, and I took over as many of those duties as I could. Charlie slowly got better. When he was well enough he had surgery to remove some bad lymph nodes and give the doctors a chance to look around and make sure the radiation and chemo really had wiped out the cancer. He was given a clean bill of health, with the proviso that he come in for regular checkups.

"You saved my life, Jack," he said to me in the spring of 2000. "I was dead and you brought me back."

We were walking by the Hudson River. Charlie had gone from crutches to a cane, which he now swung around as he walked, like the same old shillelagh me father brought from Ireland.

"You brought yourself back, Charlie. You were right—you could take more abuse than the cancer could."

"Agatha is an angel, Jack. You better marry that girl."

"I keep asking."

"Well, it can't have helped, having me plopped down on the sofa all year. I'll be out of your hair now."

"I don't like the idea of you going back to California, Charlie. Your whole support system is here. How about I find you a place in our building? You could have your own pad. We'd be neighbors."

"Emerson had an idea," Charlie said. "There's a little house by a brook in Woodstock he's found. He wants me to come up there."

"Might be lonely," I said.

"Nah, it's a lovely village, isn't it? Full of sexually experienced sixties chicks and men who sell reefer. I could have a little recording studio in the house, get myself healthy in the country. And I'd be two hours up the road from you and Agatha and Benjy. There's a guest room, too! You could come up for weekends."

"You're going to get it together in the country, Charlie? Like Bombadil Glen? If you think I'm climbing up on your roof to screw in a weather vane . . ."

Some people who come face-to-face with death and survive spend the rest of their lives looking over their shoulder, dreading the next bad news. They get scared because they know what the end is going to be like and, knowing that, they can never enjoy themselves again. Charlie was the other kind. Having peered over the edge, he loved every day of life remaining. To him, it was all a gift.

By the time Ben was four, Agatha and I had discovered we had different assumptions about child-rearing. I wanted to keep Ben at home for as long as possible, to give him a strong sense of security and identity before he was forced to acclimate to the outside world. She was a confirmed socializer, who wanted to get the child into some sort of preschool. Agatha believed that if Ben was not stacking blocks and eating paste in a peer community by age four, he would mature into a misfit and probably end up climbing a bell tower with a rifle.

So we began searching the preschools of downtown Manhattan for a place where our child would be protected, given every advantage academic and social, and celebrated for the genius his mother and I recognized him to be. I wish Dante had lived to chronicle the experience of visiting all those kindergartens. It is beyond my capacity to enumerate the range of strangeness we saw.

We visited Aquarian day-care centers that insisted on a personal interview with the toddler before considering admission, who taught the fundamentals of yoga to four-year-olds and charged twenty-five thousand dollars a year. In reaction, I demanded we look at public schools, some of which were so dirty and underfunded that Agatha was reduced to tears, and others of which were so evangelically leftist that I ran to the parochial schools of the Greenwich Village area, which impressed me with having strong academic values without the upper-class snobbery of the private schools. The Catholic school children were of all races and denominations. What they had in common were parents who wanted them to excel. These were kids who got up before dawn in Harlem or Brooklyn or Staten Island and took long rides on buses and subways in search of a good education. Their parents were policemen, bookkeepers, secretaries, and schoolteachers who worked hard and sacrificed for their kids. It reminded me of how I grew up and it was what I wanted for Ben.

Agatha was unconvinced. Although the parochial schools we looked at assured us they welcomed Baptist, Muslim, and Hindu children along with Catholics, Agatha was afraid I was backsliding toward papism. She figured that if she let Ben enroll at St. Catherine's on Sixth Avenue, it was only a matter of time until father and son would be reciting the rosary on our knees at anti-abortion demonstrations. She became desperate to find an alternative.

"We have to go look at Horace and Goldman," she announced one evening at dinner.

"What is that?" I asked.

"School over on Hudson Street. K through eight. Katherine told me about it, both their kids went there and they loved it. It's a semi-public school."

"What does that mean? The curtains don't close all the way?"

"In the late sixties and early seventies a bunch of people in the West Village got together and decided the public schools were not meeting their needs. They negotiated with the city and got funding for a progressive grade school that's overseen by a board made up of parents. Katherine says it's the best of both worlds."

I said okay, we could take the tour.

Agatha and I were two of a dozen parents who passed through the corridors of Horace and Goldman School on a Tuesday afternoon later that month. The old building was yellow inside, from the film on the floor tiles to the light that squeezed through the dirty windows. One of the community mothers guided our tour, chattering on about how her daughter Aphro had spent her whole childhood at H&G and loved every minute. Aphro was now living in a van with her girlfriend in Santa Fe, making jewelry.

Classes were in session, if that term could be said to have any meaning in an institution where children roamed in and out of schoolrooms with untied shoes and crayons in their mouths.

We stepped into the back of one room, where an earnest woman in sweatpants and tennis shoes was projecting photographs of Auschwitz onto a screen for a dozen six-year-olds.

"The Nazis set up death camps to force labor out of and then murder Jews, homosexuals, and other minority groups," she explained. She clicked to the next slide and up came a photograph of Asian civilians behind a wire fence. "At the same time, the United States put loyal Japanese Americans into detention camps in California, simply because of their ancestry." She clicked through several pictures of Native American teenagers on an Indian reservation and settled on a shot of long-haired protesters raising their fists in a Washington, DC, football stadium in the late sixties.

"During the anti-Vietnam War protests in 1969 and 1971 right here in the United States, thousands of citizens exercising their right of peaceful assembly were herded into a makeshift concentration camp at RFK Stadium. I was one of them. It is the duty of you children to create a world in which this can never happen again."

As our tour continued, Agatha looked defensive, then brokenhearted. We ended up in the basement in what was called the gym but was just a cinder-block storage room. We were introduced to the new principal, Mr. Rallice, a thin man in a blue work shirt and jeans with designer eyeglasses, a Zapata mustache, and hair long on the back of his head to compensate for its absence on the top. Our tour guide explained in her introduction that Mr. Rallice had not actually assumed his duties yet. He had just been hired by the board of parents to take over for the outgoing principal, who had been canned for disrespecting the students' freedom to make personal choices about their grades. We were assured that Mr. Rallice had big ideas for H&G, some of which he would share with us now.

Mr. Rallice said thank you very much and went on to chat in a Public Radio voice about why Horace and Goldman was not a school that picked kids, it was a school that was picked *by* kids.

"We don't force your children to learn," Mr. Rallice explained. "We invite them to learn. We believe that each child is naturally inquisitive. One day she will come to school and want to learn all about math. We will guide her in her enthusiasm. Perhaps it will last for an hour, perhaps it will last for a month. Maybe it will last all year. We will be there to go as far and as fast as she feels comfortable. Then, one day, she gets bored with math and says, 'Today I want to learn to read.' Okay, then. Let's learn to read today. When she bumps into a problem with reading, we won't yell at her, we won't pressure her. We might say, 'Hey!

Who wants to paint a picture? Who wants to play an instrument? Who wants to learn Spanish?' By keeping a sense of joy in the learning, we believe we will unlock your child's potential and allow her to grow into the very best version of herself. Any questions?"

Normally in circumstances such as these Agatha would give me a signal to keep my mouth shut and be kind, but when I looked at her now she seemed miserable. She had so wanted this school to be the right fit that I felt obligated to see if perhaps we could not make it so.

"Mr. Rallice," I said, raising my hand.

"Call me Christopher."

"Christopher. I appreciate what you say about letting the child find his or her own way into schoolwork, but surely there's some point at which some sort of academic requirements kick in? Let's say my son gets to fifth grade and he still can't spell 'cat.' Does someone then say, 'Okay, kid, put down the lute, here come the flash cards'?"

Christopher Rallice looked at me as if I had suggested whipping the children with a strap.

"We never bully a child into learning at Horace and Goldman School, friend," he told me coolly. "If your child doesn't like spelling, he may simply grow up to be a secure, well-adjusted, and successful individual who doesn't happen to spell in the conventional manner. Would you love your child less for that?"

He looked for the next question. "Come on, Aggie," I whispered to my mortified partner. "We're going to enroll at St. Catherine's."

On our way up the stairs we ran into our tour guide, Aphro's mom.

"You're not leaving early!" she chastised us.

"I'll say we're not," I said. I failed to restrain myself. "If that prat downstairs is the best you can do for a principal, I'd hate to imagine what the last one must've done to get fired! Did she bake the children into pies?"

All geniality went out of our tour guide's face. "Class-conscious people sometimes react that way," she said with a bitterness that must have been lying in wait. "Perhaps you and your young second wife would be happier with one of the elite schools in the area." She pronounced "elite" like an accusation. "Or you can ship your child off somewhere, isn't that the English tradition?"

"Ah," I said, "I only had to open my mouth for the racism to rear its head."

"Racism?" she cried. Now the battle was on. "Leave it to an Englishman to think class distinctions are *racial*. I marched for civil rights, your lordship. I protested in the streets so that my children could grow up without any of your upper-class bullshit or arrogant sexist condescension. *That's* what this school is all about. And guess what—it was not made for people like you to come along and impose your antiquated judgmental prejudices on it."

Whatever this woman's problem was, it had nothing to do with me. I was headed for the door but Agatha took up the fight.

"Listen to yourself," Agatha told our accuser. "You don't know anything about us, where we come from, who we are, what we've been through, or what we believe, and yet you're ready in an instant to unleash all this venom at us. Why are you so filled with hate? And who lets you near their children?"

I grabbed Agatha and got her out of there before the fists started flying. As a veteran of the counterculture, a tattooed graduate of sex, drugs, and rock, a participant in both swinging London and smoky Laurel Canyon, and someone who had given my liver to liquor, my lungs to ganja, and the upper half of my auditory range to large concert speakers, I was by the 1990s really sick of the sixties and its hold on my generation. It had been thirty years, and it had not been all that good to begin with.

In the cab on the way home I saw that Agatha was not only upset about the school. She was angry with me. It defied logic. I reminded her that we had seen the same thing and had identical reactions.

"You get your way again, Jack," she said, teary-eyed. "Those people are ridiculous, we can't send Benjamin to a place like that. Catholic school wins. Jack wins. But why do you have to be smug about it? Why do you enjoy it so much? That silly woman on the stairs was harmless, you could have just let it pass. You had to rip into her, you had to show off, you had to make sure to stop and mock her on your way out the door."

"We can look at other schools," I said.

"Why bother? You'll get your way in the end."

I stopped talking. Anything I said was going to be wrong. A slow panic came into me. Agatha was pulling away. I was going to lose another family.

My first memory of the 9/11 attacks is seeing Britney Spears on the stage of Radio City Music Hall dancing in a leaf bikini while jungle natives writhed around her like King Kong's worshippers. At the climax of this frenzy, the show-stopping eleven o'clock number of the *2001 MTV Video Music Awards,* an actor dressed as a native draped a live if half-anesthetized boa constrictor over the singer's bare shoulders, and she finished her hoochie-coochie dance shimmying with the snake.

I was up in the balcony drinking free champagne with the rest of the music industry. From the reaction of the kids on the floor, Britney stole the show. I said to Hal Allyn, the man who signed the Ravons in America and now a corporate titan, "This has got to be the apocalypse, isn't it? Whatever rock and roll was, it wasn't this. Charo was more rock and roll than this!"

"You are an old man, Flynn," Allyn told me. "Elvis shook his hips like a holy roller, too."

I felt more at odds with the pop industry than I ever had before. I had never loved rock music the way that Emerson and Charlie did, but this was like working for Frederick's of Hollywood.

At home I was trying to hold together my relationship with Agatha. The tighter I tried to pull her, the more she pushed away. She had moved into the guest bedroom and insisted that I respect our separateness. That was the word she used. She was as committed as I was to giving Ben the security of two parents who he knew loved him, but she was less and less sure that the two of us made sense as a couple. I told her she was completely free to come and go as she wished, and insisted it was better for Ben if we all lived in the same place. It was big enough.

Britney's snake dance was on Thursday, September 6, 2001. The next day I took Ben for a beach weekend at a rented house on Fire Island. Agatha had other plans. This was the sort of careful exchange we had negotiated. I was gone for long periods when Emerson was on tour, and I made myself scarce for groups of days when he was not. It was awkward. Eventually all relationships are.

The summer sun was hanging on like a condemned man. I slathered my little boy with sunscreen and we spent three happy days at the beach. In the evenings we watched old monster movies and fell asleep in the same bed.

On Sunday afternoon I was sitting on the porch having cocktails with the gay couple at the house next door when I lost Ben. One minute he was digging in the sand and the next time I looked he was nowhere. I panicked and it spread to my neighbors. We ran to the water, crawled under the house, and shouted his name inside and out. I don't know a parent who has not had an experience like that. The fear is primal. After a half hour of searching, I saw Ben coming down the beach eating a chocolate ice-cream cone. A young man in an open sport shirt and swimming trunks was holding his hand and waving. He had found Ben wandering down the beach crying and taken it upon himself to figure out who had lost him and where he belonged. He had bought my son ice cream, got his name, and tried to find a telephone listing that matched. Failing that, he had marched him back the way he had come, looking for his folks.

I was relieved to have my child returned to me safely and touched by the great kindness and generosity of this young stranger. It was September 9, 2001. Later in the month I would see that young man's photograph in a magazine. He was one of the passengers who rebelled against the hijackers and brought down United Airlines Flight 93 in a field in Pennsylvania.

Am I descending to melodrama? That is inevitable. The events of September 11 radiated back and forth in time, making connections to people we otherwise would have encountered and forgotten.

On Monday, September 10, Ben started school at St. Catherine's Academy on Sixth Avenue in Greenwich Village. Agatha and I both got up at dawn to make him breakfast, go over the list of pencils, crayons, sandwich, and snack, dress him in his new uniform, make him a big breakfast, and walk him to school. We introduced ourselves to his teacher and nudged him toward a cluster of his new classmates. I became teary when we left him. I was waiting at the gate that afternoon when he got out.

The next morning I made breakfast while Agatha dressed Ben. We talked about the kids in his class and the picture he drew that his teacher had praised and hung on the wall. When it was time for him to leave, Agatha said, "Why don't you go back to bed for an hour? I can take him. You pick him up."

I took her up on the offer. I had felt winded all day Monday from rising at dawn. I had been a night owl too long to switch my system. I kissed Ben good-bye and started to go back to my bedroom. I decided to get shaving out of the way first. While I was rubbing lather on my face the phone rang.

Agatha said, "A plane has hit the World Trade Center. Go see."

I went into the kitchen and looked out the window. The tower on the right had a hole in it, from which brown smoke was rising. I could not see any sign of an airplane.

I went and turned on the local television news. The shot of the twin towers on my TV was almost exactly the same as the one out my window. The announcer was saying, ". . . a small commuter plane crashed into the north tower at the World Trade Center about ten minutes ago. No word yet on why the plane was so far off course. Private flights are prohibited over Manhattan."

I looked back at the smoking hole. Strange, I thought, to hit such a big building on such a clear day. I stood for a while watching the smoke and the damage. TV news helicopters were swarming around the damaged tower like dragonflies. I looked down to the street. People were hurrying by on their way to work, stopping at coffee carts to grab a bagel or doughnut, moving in and out of the subway. I began to wait for their reactions as they looked up and noticed the hole in the World Trade Center. The same thing happened again and again. A passerby would pause to buy a newspaper or bottle of water. His eyes would wander up, and he would do a double-take. He might nudge someone else, who would look to see what he had seen.

I went back to the bathroom and finished shaving. I dressed and came back into the kitchen and had a cup of tea and stared at the black hole some more.

All at once an explosion seemed to go off in the other tower. A row of windows burst open and black smoke blew out. My telephone rang and I grabbed it. It was Agatha, on the street.

"Another plane just hit!" she cried. "I saw it!"

"I don't think so, Agatha," I said. "I'm standing here looking at it. I think something blew up in the other building. Maybe leaking fuel started a fire . . ."

She was crying. She said, "Jack, I saw it."

"Did one of the news helicopters hit the building?"

She said, "It was another plane. A big one!" Then the phone went dead.

I tried to call her back. There was no signal. My cell phone did not work, either. The television announcers had lost their composure. They said, "A second airliner has slammed into the World Trade Center. Both towers are burning. The mayor's office is asking everyone to stay away from the World Trade Center area; if you are already there, start walking north. Do not look for a taxi, do not go into the subway, just walk north."

I walked out of my loft with just my wallet and keys. I decided not to take the elevator, to walk down the fire stairs. As I made my way, an upstairs neighbor came running past me screaming for his wife. He turned to me and said in a thick New York accent, "We're all toast, Jack! We're toast!"

I got outside and went up Broadway to Bleecker Street and turned left toward Sixth Avenue and Ben's school. No one was hurrying to work anymore. Commuters, waitresses, and parents walking their children to class were all standing, staring up at the two smoking towers. One woman was weeping loudly into a pay phone. No one else on the street was talking. No one was moving. They just stood staring.

I cut across Washington Square Park. Here I heard the sirens coming. Wave after wave of ambulances, police cars, and fire trucks were racing down Fifth Avenue, splitting ranks at the park like choreographed dancers and continuing down MacDougal and Mercer Streets, flying through the narrow lanes of the Village into SoHo toward the wounded buildings. I stopped for a moment to watch them.

I reached Sixth Avenue and cars were pulled up to the sidewalk, drivers standing with their doors open to let pedestrians hear the news reports. "Stay away from midtown, Times Square, the United Nations. Other planes may be heading to these destinations. All bridges and tunnels are closed; go to your homes and stay there. All roads in and out of Manhattan are closed; the governor says go to your homes."

"Christ," I whispered to a taxi driver who was standing outside his cab staring at the towers. "If they're telling me I can't get off the island, it makes me think I should bloody well try." He nodded. It was still very quiet everywhere. There was not a car horn, there were no raised voices.

And then someone shouted from a passing truck, "They just blew up the Pentagon!" and it was as if the volume, which had been set so low, came blasting back. All at once people were running, the motorists who had been parked got in their cars and lit out. Passersby hit their windows and asked for rides, strangers piled into any vehicle moving uptown.

I looked toward the steps of St. Catherine's School and saw Agatha coming down them with a confused Benjamin. I thanked God we had not missed each other. I ran to them. Ben said, "Why am I leaving school, Daddy?"

Then the street was filled with a procession of ghosts. An army of civilians covered in ash, filthy in their suits and neckties and work clothes, some of them bleeding from small injuries, were sleepwalking away from the towers, up the Avenue of the Americas, moving north. I picked up Ben and held him to me. We moved into the street and joined the march.

Ben asked me again, "Why am I leaving school?"

"There's been an accident, honey," I said in his ear. "A plane crashed into the World Trade Center." Ben craned his neck to see. We both looked at the buildings. The smoke was billowing now, it was hard to clearly make out the contours of the buildings. And then there was a shudder that ran through the ground as the first tower came down.

The fever for assassination set off by the murder of Kennedy and finally burned off by the shooting of John Lennon had been still for twenty years. The next psychopathic virus emerged in the nineties and set off a series of school shootings. Then came 9/11 and the suicide bomber became the new malignant prototype. In the years that followed, the emotionally dispossessed would bind their heads and venture out to immolate innocents with homemade bombs strapped to their own bodies.

Those who thirty years earlier would have tried to shoot a world leader now wanted to blow up a bus. The virus gave them a model for expressing their pathology. It came in on those planes that hit lower Manhattan. You could feel it crackling in the air.

By the time the second tower came down I was crossing Eighth Avenue with Ben in my arms. Agatha was looking back like Lot's wife. She screamed at me to cover his eyes. My car was in a garage on Twenty-fourth Street. I had left it there to have the wheels realigned. I prayed it would be in shape to drive. I got lucky. The place was open and my Volvo was intact. I paid the attendant and he gave me the keys. We strapped Ben in the backseat and started driving north on Eighth Avenue.

Traffic was heavy and slow. The roads were crowded with buses, trucks, and taxis, each one filled with as many hitchhikers as the axles could bear. The sidewalks were overflowing with the populations of the office buildings and evacuated subways, all trudging north like refugees, marching away from the catastrophe.

The police were shutting off side streets, directing traffic away from Times Square, and watching the sky. The entrances to Central Park were sealed by wooden barriers and paddy wagons. Cops with shotguns were being supplemented by National Guardsmen.

"Jack," Agatha said, "those old ladies look like they won't make it walking. We have to give them a ride." She rolled down the window and called to three elderly women who were propping each other up by the elbows, younger people shoving past them on every side. We got them into our car and moved Ben to the front to sit on his mother's lap. Agatha saw a woman pushing a man in a wheelchair and insisted we collect them, too. We got him in the front seat. Agatha and Ben climbed in the way-back.

The man and his daughter wanted to get out at Ninety-eighth Street. The ladies were going to Harlem. We became a taxi service, inching through the throngs at five miles an hour and listening to radio reports. Mostly it was rumors, warnings, and hysteria, with endless injunctions to not try to enter the tunnels or cross the bridges, the army had closed them off.

By the time we got to the Macombs Dam Bridge on the north end of Harlem, three hours had passed. Hundreds of people, almost all African-American, were walking across. There were no police barriers, no sign of any authorities at all. We drove slowly into the crowd, edging forward until we were a small boat in a sea of walkers. I did not feel as if we were in New York anymore. I felt like I was back in Mali. I felt the desperate world from which I had spent three decades insulating myself reach out and pull me back in.

We made it over the bridge in half an hour. I could see the Cross Bronx Expressway was stopped cold, thousands of cars frozen. "That's the entrance ramp to Route 80," I told Agatha when we were in front of Yankee Stadium. "We can take that all the way to Woodstock and stay with Emerson until we get a sense of what's really going on."

There was one overburdened policeman desperately trying to direct traffic as confused and panicked motorists poured toward him from all sides. No one was paying attention to his instructions. I drove past him and up the ramp onto the highway. Suddenly there was no traffic. Because the road was blocked south of us, we were almost alone. I did not know how long that would last, so I stepped on the gas.

"Is Ben strapped in?" I asked Agatha. "I think we just got a bit of luck."

We drove north, away from the city, past crisscrossed overpasses packed tight with stopped traffic. Every entry into Manhattan was closed and thousands of automobiles were frozen in place like model cars lined up on toy store shelves.

An hour up the highway I got back cell phone reception and reached Emerson.

"Oh Christ, Jack," he said, "I've been trying to call you! I spoke to Castro, he's in Montauk. Wendy is in California. No one knew where you were."

"I'm heading toward Woodstock right now with the family," I told him. "Any chance we could camp on your couch?"

"You can have my bed, man," Emerson said. "Thank God you're all okay."

We decided we'd better find an ATM machine to get some extra cash. We pulled off in a small upstate town and were surprised to find the banks and shops closed. There were handmade signs in the windows—*Pray for our country*. The flags were at half-mast.

It sounds absurd to say, but that was when I realized that this was not just something that happened to my neighborhood. This was Pearl Harbor. We saw a diner and figured we should feed Ben. The television was on in the corner, showing films of the planes hitting the towers in an endless loop. We sat Ben in a booth where he could not see it. The waitress brought us coffee and him a milk and paper and crayons.

Agatha and I ordered and looked at our little boy. He was humming, working on his drawing. He looked happy. Perhaps we had succeeded in blocking out the worst. Our food arrived. We ate without tasting anything. I looked down to see Ben's picture. It was the two buildings in flame and airplanes falling from the sky.

Emerson and his housekeeper Vera had prepared for us as if it were Thanksgiving. They had a warm dinner ready, the kitchen stocked with food for a little boy, and a fire roaring in the great stone fireplace that dominated Emerson's front room, an oak and rock den the size of a hunting lodge with a glass wall that looked out on a wild field rolling down the mountain to a grove of birch trees and a silver pond.

We settled into one of three overstuffed couches and Emerson, looking Scottish in big boots, tweed pants, and a seaman's sweater, sank down with his old Martin and began strumming folk songs. Agatha had had a shower and was wrapped in a robe decorated with Indian designs. She drank hot tea while Emerson and I tugged on mugs of brandy. Ben rolled on the floor playing with Emerson's King Charles spaniel.

"To the country squire," I said, raising my mug.

"I talked to Charlie," Emerson said. "He was as worried as I was. He'd like to come by if you're not too tired."

I had forgotten that Charlie was still in Woodstock, in the little house he had rented in town. I still pictured him in California. These days Agatha talked to him more than I did.

Charlie arrived carrying a box of fudge from a local candy store. He did not look like a man who had nearly died. He had a lot of white in his hair from his ordeal, but otherwise he looked like the same old Charlie, the rascal who could get away with telling a girl in a bikini, "I'd like to see more of you," or going up to a buxom woman and whispering, "May I offer you a tat?"

I'd have come away with a broken nose but Charlie always got a laugh, and sometimes got a lay. Emerson took out another guitar and he and Charlie led us in old songs, English and American. Agatha sang as loud as anyone. Ben fell asleep in her arms. We kept the television off and the murderous and tragic outside world at bay.

Eventually the drink made us philosophical. We talked about music, not as a dollars-and-cents business but as comfort and binder.

"The whole purpose of music," Charlie said, "is to be a light in the dark. It's for telling people they're not alone. You should walk onstage like all of us come in here, like you're walking into your best friend's living room."

Emerson smiled and shook his head. He said, "I don't agree, Charles. The audience doesn't want you to be like them. They want you to present a possibility of what they would like to be. A great song should be heroic. Can you imagine Bogart or John Wayne saying the lines? You have to walk onstage like the sheriff facing down a mob. Like a gunfighter."

Charlie laughed and began strumming his guitar and doing an imitation of John Wayne singing the old Little Feat song, "Willin'."

I been warped by the rain, driven by the snow
I'm drunk and dirty don't ya know
But I'm still . . . willin'.
Pilgrim.

We all laughed and he continued as Walter Brennan:

Out on the road late last night,
Seen my pretty Alice in every headlight
Alice. Dallas Alice.

We all tried to join in on the chorus but it fell apart in drunken laughter.

It sounds sacrilegious, but that evening, after the most terrible day, was one of the happiest I remember. I had got my loved ones away from the cataclysm and we were safe by the fire with my two oldest friends. It seemed to me when I fell asleep that night that Agatha and I could salvage our relationship, that I could persuade her to love me as I loved her, as we both loved our little boy. I would never be that happy again, and I would never be so foolish.

The next morning I left Agatha and Ben with Emerson and drove back down to the city. I had to check that our loft was secure, that the gas was off and the windows were closed and that in my hurry to leave I had locked the front door. Agatha had not even brought her handbag with her; she needed her credit cards and identification. She also wanted me to feed her fish and collect her parakeet. It was all I could do to convince her to stay behind with our boy.

Every old song on the car radio took on a double meaning that morning. Ray Charles singing his mournful "America the Beautiful" made me pull over to the side of the road. "A Day in the Life" became a meditation on mortality and the network news. Leonard Cohen's "Hallelujah" in all its incarnations became an anthem that month. Beefy policemen welled up when they heard James Taylor's "Fire and Rain," an agnostic's plea for strength and solace in the face of tragedy which ended with the line, "Sweet dreams and flying machines in pieces on the ground."

The radio was also filled with news and rumors. The country was crouched, waiting for the next assault. I knew from the reports that Manhattan was sealed off from traffic below Fourteenth Street, so I pulled into a parking garage on Forty-fourth and headed downtown. At Twenty-third Street there were police barriers. To continue I had to show identification proving I lived where I did. At Fourteenth Street the security was tighter. Proof of residence was not enough. I had to offer a pressing reason to be allowed home. "Left the dogs in my loft," I said. They let me through.

Walking through Greenwich Village, I was struck by how many people were wearing white surgical masks, a membrane of pla-cebo protection against the poisons in the air. I passed St. Vincent's

Hospital and walked down Seventh Avenue. Most stores were closed, but not all. The corner bodegas were doing normal business. About half the restaurants and cafés were open. What was eerie was that everyone was speaking in very low voices. The conversations were normal, they were discussing the Yankees and the stock market, but everyone spoke very quietly, as if they were at a wake.

Pasted on every wall, stuck to telephone poles and taped to mailboxes were xeroxed notices with photographs of the missing and handwritten requests asking for help.

JUANITA CALVERI–MISSING SINCE SEPT 11–PLEASE
CALL THIS NUMBER WITH ANY INFORMATION.

HAVE YOU SEEN MY SON? EDWARD BUCKLEY,
DEUTSCHE BANK EXECUTIVE. MAY BE HURT OR
INJURED. PLEASE CALL JOANNE BUCKLEY AT . . .

JOSEPH JACKSON, RESCUE WORKER ATTACHED TO
4TH PRECINCT. MISSING SINCE 9-11.

Row after row, like wanted posters, like pictures of the saints, imploring. Many of the photos were whatever the grieving family could pull down from the mantel–wedding pictures, prom photos, snapshots from barbecues and under the Christmas tree.

I turned down Washington Place and a little girl was sitting on the step of a townhouse selling lemonade. I bought a cup. She said, "The money's for the firemen." I gave her extra. I crossed Sixth Avenue and went through Washington Square. Under the arch I came face to face with a makeshift monument, a cathedral's worth of candles and plastic crucifixes and fences covered with the faces of the missing and the dead. I looked to where the towers had been. The two columns of smoke still stood like an accusation: the tablets of Moses written in clouds. This, I thought, is not going to go away for a very long time. This will be paid back in blood.

Houston Street was where the authority of the New York Police gave way to the U.S. Army. There were steam shovels, green dump trucks, military transports, and even two tanks forming a wall down the middle of the cross street that divided Greenwich Village from SoHo. Saying that I had to rescue my dogs did not get me through the guards at Mercer or Broadway. I moved down to Mott Street and said I had to collect my mother. I got to our loft and found it clean and intact. I poured the milk down the sink, turned off the air conditioner, and pulled the curtains on the window. I had a list from Agatha of clothes she and Ben would need, along with medicine from the bathroom, her favorite nightgown, and the chattering bird whom I would have chosen to liberate rather than carry all the way back uptown. If I wanted to win back Agatha's heart, though, I knew I had to return with her parakeet.

I saw that I had left out the shaving cream and razor I had been using just before the second plane hit. It felt like a month ago. I had left on the television in the living room and all the channels were in full frenzy. I found Agatha's pocketbook and money. I collected our passports and important papers. I put everything in a travel bag and took the birdcage in my other hand and turned out the lights and locked the apartment. Nothing was certain now.

When I got to Houston Street again I saw two locals in surgical masks walking their dogs, standing in front of a movie poster for an upcoming film in which Steve Martin would play a silly doctor. He was looking down at them in his surgical mask while they studied him in theirs.

This time when I went into Washington Square I was prepared for the candles and posters and photographs. I noticed something else. There were old men playing chess. There were young men playing Frisbee. There were locals exercising their pets in the dog run. I wished that one or two of the hundreds of news cameras fixed on the smoking ruins would pan up and show the rest of the country that all of New York was not on fire, all of Manhattan was not a war zone. To watch it on television you'd think this was London during the Blitz, but just blocks from where the firemen were digging and the wounded were being tended, life went on. People played with their pets and tossed Frisbees and ate lunch. Little girls sold lemonade.

When I got back to Woodstock that evening, Agatha told me that Charlie's landlady had another cottage for rent and Agatha wanted to take it. She had felt better in Woodstock, she said, than she had felt in years in New York. She needed a place of her own, somewhere to go on weekends. Someplace that was not in my name. She assured me that she and Ben would come back to the loft in SoHo with me. This was not instead of; this was in addition to. It told me that the clock was ticking on my chance to convince her to commit to me. It told me she was looking for a lifeboat.

We looked at the cottage and signed a year's lease. Then I brought Agatha and Ben back to the city. Benjy went back to St. Catherine's School. For the next month we drove up to Woodstock on the weekends, painting and buying secondhand furniture for the country house.

In October there was a parents' meeting to answer questions about the school's readiness for another terror attack. I wish I had gone alone. Agatha was in no shape to experience the full force of a roomful of anxious and accusatory New York parents. The meeting was in the basement of the school, which we entered through steps down from the sidewalk behind an iron rail. On weekends the basement served as a soup kitchen for homeless men, and it was designed with industrial efficiency, a room with bars on the windows, linoleum tiles, and a drain in the middle of the floor. It was a room that could be hosed down easily.

When we arrived, the parents were badgering the principal, a nun, about the school's vulnerability to terrorist attack.

The old sister was speaking calmly and methodically.

"Each child must bring in dry food, a large bottle of water, a coloring book, and some Handi Wipes and Band-Aids. Children are not allowed to have cell phones, I know that is controversial but that rule remains in place."

There was grumbling. A chubby man asked where the kids would be brought in case of an attack.

The principal recited her answer like a rosary. "We have talked to psychologists about this. They all say that what is best for the children in case of crisis is to be kept in one place. If we can stay in the school, it will be in this room. It is an old bomb shelter, you can see the Civil Defense emblem there below the clock. If we have to leave this building, we will go to the library on Eighth Street. If for some reason the library is inaccessible, our third option is the National Guard Armory on Fourteenth Street. You can call the school and someone will always be here to tell you where the children are."

"What about dirty bombs?" one mother shouted. "They must not go outside under any circumstances! How can you not know that?"

A Spanish man jumped at that mother and yelled, "Oh? What about anthrax? They have to be taken outside immediately!"

I turned to Agatha and whispered, "What about king cobras? The school better buy a mongoose."

She was distraught.

"I cannot let Ben come back here," she told me, shaking. She grabbed my arm. "I'm sorry, Jack. Ben and I are moving to Woodstock."

My dreams were undone.

I don't remember a longer winter than that one. Agatha moved into the little house in Woodstock and set about making it into a home for Ben and her. She painted and hammered and scrubbed. I came up on the weekends to help and to spend as much time as I could with my son.

There were three bedrooms in the cottage. Ben's was next to Agatha's, a converted sewing room on the ground floor. I was disappointed when I returned one Friday and she showed me how she had turned the guest room upstairs into my room. Agatha accepted and encouraged my weekend visits to be with our boy, but it was clear that I was not going to share her bed.

Going to Woodstock on the weekends became a comfort and refuge. New York City was a lake of anxiety while the World Trade Center rubble was being cleared and the dead were named and counted. By spring I had unplugged my television and put it in a closet. I set my bedside clock radio to a classical station. I did not need to begin every day with apocalyptic murmuring and loudmouths reading signs from the entrails of birds. If Caesar's wife had been alive in 2002 she would have had her own cable show with computer graphics demonstrating an artist's conception of the fountains of blood.

Agatha got swept up in it at her rural hideaway. She drew water from a well and climbed onto the roof to install solar panels. She was preparing to live off the land when the big attack came. I was upset one night to learn she had bought a shotgun and was taking target lessons at a shooting range in Kingston.

"I would rather have a gun and not need it," she told me, "than need it and not have it."

"You're speaking in someone else's voice, Agatha."

"I can't only be the Agatha you want me to be, Jack," she said. "Someday you will accept that."

It bothered me to have my son sleeping in the house with a gun. She said it was not loaded and the shells were locked in a strongbox in her closet. I did not ask what good that would do her if the mythical Taliban death squad came through the window in the middle of the night. I was glad she had that much sense. It annoyed me that in her isolation she had become a devoted listener to Howard Stern, the radio provocateur, and other flamethrowers of the airwaves. Agatha was not becoming a right-winger but she was taking on a lot of the "Let's not coddle these bastards, get them before they get us" attitude that I associated with the worst aspect of the American character—the bullyboy and big mouth. I did not want my son to grow up to be that sort of American man.

It will only get me in trouble to propose that many women take on the voices and attitudes of the men with whom they are living. (Does it get me off the hook to say that I blame this on patriarchal upbringing, not on the double X chromosome? No, I didn't think it would.) Living without a man, Agatha began to take on the views of the man on the radio.

Ben had settled happily into a local public school and Agatha was helping out at a women's shelter and driving into New Paltz to take classes at the State University of New York three days a week. When she was at college, Ben was looked after by Emerson's housekeeper Vera, a sweet-natured widow of Portuguese descent. When I arrived on a Friday in April, I collected Ben from Vera at Emerson's house.

I took my young son to the Little Bear Restaurant for Chinese food. Mommy was still at her class. Our table was by a window looking out on a rocky stream, moving fast with the waters from the spring rains and melting snow.

"Are you going to be here until Monday, Daddy?" he asked me while trying to wrap lo mein noodles around his spoon.

"Maybe, Benjy," I said. "I'd like to take you to school Monday, but I might have to go back late Sunday night. If I do, it will be after I've read you a story and put you to bed. Anyway, let's have fun now. We've got all night tonight and all tomorrow and into the night Sunday. Tell me about that boy in your class with the funny eyebrows."

"Are you going to sleep upstairs, Daddy?"

"Well, yes, honey, that's my room, isn't it? Do you want to sleep in my room tonight? We could have a campout like Bill and Ben the Flower Pot Men. Do you remember I told you about those silly fellows?"

"I remember." Ben was getting at something, wrapping an idea around his mind as he turned the noodles around his spoon.

"Daddy, how come when you stay over you sleep upstairs, but when Emerson stays over he sleeps with Mommy?"

Sometimes something goes into your ear and you want to reach up and pull it out again. You feel instantly that what was just said is going to attach itself and hurt you forever.

"When does Emerson stay over?" I asked him. I had been chewing on a stiff piece of pork. I spit the meat into my napkin and took a drink of water. "Ben? When does Emerson stay over?"

"Sometimes. When you're in the city. He stays in Mommy's room. One morning Mommy didn't wake up and I was late for school. I went to get her and Emerson was asleep in her bed. I woke her up and we had to run to get to school and she gave me a note for the teacher but she forgot to give me my lunch so my teacher made Jackie give me half of her sandwich."

I stared at my meal. Ben waited for me to say something. When I did not he said, "Mommy said Emerson is afraid of the dark so she lets him sleep with her."

"Ah," I said. "Well, that explains it. Emerson is a bit of a chicken. He's not brave like you and Daddy."

I felt my throat catch. I told Benjy to be a good boy, Daddy had to run to the bathroom for a minute. I went in and got control of myself. On the way home we stopped for ice cream and then at a toy store and then we got candy, too. I did everything I could think of to put off going to Agatha's house. Finally she called my cell phone and asked if everything was okay. I said everything was never okay.

I think Agatha understood as soon as she saw me that I knew about Emerson and her. I tried not to be hostile in front of Ben but I'm sure I was remote. When Ben had gone to bed and I was certain he was asleep, I told her. She did not act upset; she certainly didn't act guilty. She acted as if a burden had been lifted.

"I'm sorry you found out that way, Jack," she said. "It's not a big deal. Of course we end up seeing a lot of each other, being all the way up here . . ."

"So of course you figured it was no big deal to jump in bed with my oldest friend." I was trying to keep my voice down. Ben did not deserve to have memories of his parents doing this to each other. "A friend who you know treats women as interchangeable receptacles for his recreation. Emerson is a pig, right? You know that."

"The man you just called your best friend."

"I said oldest, not best. You mean nothing to him, you know. He's a spoiled child who wants whatever he's not allowed to have. Once he gets it, he loses interest."

Agatha looked at me coldly. She said, "I don't care. He means nothing to me, either. Now you can stop waiting for me to change my mind, Jack. Now you know—it is over between us and cannot be fixed. Benjy loves you. Give the love you had for me to him."

"Drop dead, Agatha. I don't need you to tell me to love my son. I am not sure this cozy setup is going to work anymore. From now on I want Ben to spend weekends in the city with me."

"So you only wanted him to feel the love of a mother and father together as long as you thought you might use that to get back in my bed?"

"I don't want to go back in your bed, Agatha. It's too crowded in there. And it's lonely."

You know what Emerson told me when I said I knew that he had slept with Agatha? He said, "Aw, sorry, man. It was just sport-fucking."

It was not when he said it that I slapped him across the face. It was right after he said it, when he smiled. His eyes flashed outrage and then faded and he said, "It won't happen again, man. She told me you and her were quits a long time ago. It was very stupid of me and I hope you can forgive me. Can you forgive me, Jack?"

The charm was so practiced he was not aware he was turning it on. I said, "I knew what you were like when I signed on with you, Emerson. But you can't pretend you don't know that this changes things between us."

He said, "Then I hope over time I can win back your trust."

Christ, I thought, every line that comes out of his mouth is like a bad pop lyric. I suppose that's why he's had such a long career.

Over the next year I was able to move forward with Emerson in a professional capacity by thinking of him as other—as someone exempt from normal human obligations. I could still be his manager, although I would never again consider him my friend.

Did Emerson feel bad that he had seduced the mother of my child and sabotaged any chance of my healing that relationship? That is hard to answer because of Emerson's unusual relationship with his conscience. For most of us, the conscience is a large black dog that barks in the night, disrupting our comfort and disturbing our sleep. Emerson was not like that. On the extremely rare occasions when Emerson felt any guilt at all, he quickly turned it to resentment against the person who made him feel guilty. Here was some profound ethical jujitsu. Some part of Emerson felt bad that he had taken advantage of Agatha and betrayed our long alliance. But it took him only about a day of guilt to begin to be angry with me for making him feel that way. Emerson was a stranger to shame and not long troubled by conscience. If I had not been so angry with him I might have admired the purity of his self-centeredness.

I suspect that Castro found out why Emerson and I grew more distant. I don't believe Wendy did. We kept the client working, but it was nothing larger than three-thousand-seaters now. He was not making any new fans and the old ones were starting to die off or drift away.

The record business was dying along with them. "Heritage artists" like Emerson made all their income on the road, raising their ticket prices every year to take advantage of the affluence of their dwindling faithful. Feeling detached from Emerson made it easier to treat him as an investment property. The smaller venues made touring cheaper. We did not need to carry truckloads of lights and hire fifty-man crews. Castro now supervised a reduced entourage for a diminished artist. Emerson did not even try to introduce new material into his sets anymore. It was too painful to watch half the crowd rush to the hot dog stands.

In 2003, Emerson, under the influence of a new girlfriend, asked me to explore reducing his tour's carbon footprint. Castro looked into it and learned that we could hire a tour bus and equipment truck that ran on ethanol and route the next leg through refueling stations. This proposal led to a mutiny by the drivers and roadies. They had worked out a whole system of barter with gasoline stations along the highways. They got fuel discounts that they could trade for upgrades at Holiday Inns and coupons they could redeem at restaurants. They also had girlfriends at many of the truck stops. Going green would have meant losing our crew, so Castro quietly scrapped the plan.

I began booking corporate shows for Emerson, Christmas parties for wealthy money management companies, and birthday bashes for dot-com arrivistes. The computer revolution had created a new barony of baby boom billionaires who wanted to pal around with rock stars and would pay top dollar to do so. Emerson was not above jamming on guitar in some silly rich man's private studio if it meant he could make use of his private jet. In 2004 we hit a new financial high and personal low when I got Emerson $700,000 to play the Miami bar mitzvah party of the son of an Israeli arms dealer. The grown-ups watched Emerson do a half-hour set of his biggest hits while the teen-agers danced to a disc jockey in the other room.

Our business relationship settled into muted cordiality. I preferred that to the old days of trying to manage his vicissitudes and ambitions. Now I just managed his work and his income.

In March 2005 Emerson called me at home on a Sunday, breaching our established etiquette. Whatever he wanted had to be very impor-tant to him.

"Jack," he said. "They're doing another Live Aid. Twenty-year an-niversary. This summer. I heard about it from Dave Stewart. You've got to get me on this show."

"I haven't heard anything about that," I said. "It sounds suspicious to me. Do the sacks of grain they dropped on Africa in '85 finally need a refill?"

"It's happening, Jack. McCartney, the Stones, the Who, Zeppelin, Pink Floyd. Everybody's going to be there. We missed the last one, I deserve to be on this."

"How do you figure? We missed the last one because I could not convince you to do it."

"Well, your memories of that may be slightly different but get me on this one. I need it."

I could not argue with that. County fairs and car shows were loom-ing. I made some calls and discovered that there was indeed going to be a sequel to Live Aid, around the G8 summit of the leading economic powers in the UK in the summer. The first Live Aid was a fund-raiser for African famine relief. The new show, to be called Live 8, had a more abstract ambition. It was designed as a consciousness-raising ex-ercise and lobbying effort to move the industrialized nations to forgive the debts of poor African countries, and also to raise funds from the Western governments to buy antiretroviral drugs to combat the African AIDS epidemic.

The plan was for eight concerts to be staged simultaneously around the world in July, with the central event being in Hyde Park, in the middle of London. To Emerson this was more than a career boost. He saw it as a chance to set right something that had gone wrong for him a long time ago. He was convinced that turning his back on Live

Aid had excluded him from the old boys' club of British rock. He had never won the acclaim that came to Clapton and Bowie, let alone the worship that went to Lennon and Hendrix. He was awarded no honors by Buckingham Palace. He was not in the Rock and Roll Hall of Fame. He had never even made peace with the punk and new wave generation. In spite of all his hits and all his millions and all his many years of success, Emerson was afraid he had missed his train. He had settled on his refusal to perform at Live Aid as the reason.

It was very difficult to figure out who was in charge of the new concert. Bono and Bob Geldof were the consciences and public faces, but there was no Bill Graham running the show itself. Instead there was a network of concert promoters, talent agencies, corporate underwriters, and media companies. I finally spoke with an American from an online service who had bought the digital rights and seemed to have some sort of veto power over second-tier talent. I flew to Philadelphia to talk with him.

"I can't do Emerson, Jack," he told me as if he had ever met either of us before. "Too many old Brits as it is. I need Eminem, I need Usher. I don't need another—no offense—Jickey over sixty."

"Emerson feels very strongly about this," I insisted. "You may remember his album *River of Life*. He has spent a tremendous amount of time in Africa. These issues are personal to him."

"Oh yeah, yeah," the Internet man said. He was young and fit and looked like he had had a skin peel. "I remember that *Behind the Music* when he got lost in the jungle or whatever it was. That gives me an idea. We need some white acts to play on the African part of the show, right now we got a lot of people nobody ever heard of down there. You think Emerson would want to go to Africa to play? Maybe do a duet with one of the natives?"

"No," I said. "Obviously Emerson loves Africa, that's why he wants to be on the show, but I must insist he be onstage in London, in Hyde Park. He is a Londoner. He was born there, he formed the Ravons there. It can be early in the day. It doesn't have to be in a prime spot. He doesn't even need to be on very long. But Emerson needs to be onstage in London."

"You might have just solved this for both of us, Jack," he said. What a silly little man he was. I had spent my life tolerating silly little men like this. "Emerson Cutler by himself, sorry—no go. But a Ravons re-union, that might be worth clearing fifteen minutes. They never have played together since the sixties, right?"

"No, but I don't know if it's really feasible . . ."

"Yeah, no, I get that. Fin Finnerty is an old pal of mine, you know. It could be really emotional. Cutler ripped the other guys off, right? Stole their publishing and shit? For them to bury the hatchet and get back together for the higher cause of debt relief would be a moment, wouldn't it? I'll tell you what, Jack. You get all four Ravons to agree to play their three biggest hits onstage and I'll put them on the bill in Hyde Park."

I was improvising now. I was not sure if Emerson would agree to this, but if he would there could be advantages beyond Live 8.

"The Ravons have turned down millions of dollars to reunite," I lied. "There are many personal issues. If they did agree to put them aside for the greater cause, I would need to know that they were going on in prime time, after sundown, and they would need at least a half hour."

"Jack, you're funny. You get all four Ravons to clean up and come to Hyde Park and I will put them on for fifteen minutes in the after-noon. That's a favor, Jack. They don't want to do it, fine. I will still con-sider adding Emerson to the African stage but he better say yes quick because this show is filling up."

I said I would check with Emerson. I went to talk to him in person. He had sold his house in Woodstock. He was at Sagaponack. I laid out the case for reuniting with the Ravons. I did not mince words or pre-tend that they were interested in him otherwise.

"It's the last card, Emerson," I said. "It's time to play it."

He nodded. "It might be fun," he said.

"You want me to call the others?" I asked.

"No, get me their numbers. I'll do it. I formed the Ravons, Jack. And I broke them up. They should hear this from me."

By the time I passed my sixtieth birthday, age had unleashed all its insults on me.

I was forty-four when my eyes began to go. I started playing the trombone with menus in ill-lit restaurants until I would have needed the ape-arms of Tug Bitler to see the entrées.

At forty-eight I had developed a choking habit that scared me and everyone around me until we all got used to dealing with it. If I ate something stringy—corned beef, pot roast, duck—I would often find a small piece lodged in some pocket in my gullet. I would stop talking, stop chewing, and sit in hope that it would slip down into my stomach. Agatha learned to read when this happened and she would cover for me in front of company. If the impediment did not pass on its own, I would have to excuse myself, go into the bathroom, and stick my fingers down my throat until the chunk flew out. One hostess in whose lavatory I ejected some venison spread the story that I was bulimic.

My physician sent me to an eye, nose, and throat specialist, who poked around my tonsils and said hmmm and packed me off to an esophagus expert, who filled me to the brim with barium and then X-rayed every angle of my neck, chest, and jaw. He left me sitting in a backless hospital gown on a cold bench for a very long time before he came back with the slippery X-rays, to pronounce my obstruction invisible and therefore beyond his purview.

I was fifty when I finally found someone who could dismantle the tollbooth at my trachea. It was, unlikely as this sounds, a proctologist who was about to put me under for a colonoscopy. Making small talk as the anesthesia took hold, I asked if he could recommend anyone to clear my throat's obstruction. He said, "Oh, a web! I can clip that out while you're under if you want me to."

I was fading fast—I was not legally compos mentis but at a certain age you begin to value doctors who don't spend their whole careers looking in the rearview mirror for lawyers. I said, "Sure, Doc. Go to it. Snip away."

I woke what seemed a moment later to a mildly raw throat and a nurse who commanded me to take a few moments before trying to sit up. In the recovery room I thought I heard her tell me that the doctor went down my throat with his plumbing snake as soon as he pulled it out of my ass and pronounced both procedures completely successful. I was still foggy and I insisted three times she assure me that the physician had not used the same probe in my throat that he had used in my rectum. She said blandly that this was a professional facility and everything was sterile. After that I never had another choking incident and I could swallow anything smaller than a ham without chewing.

Bad back, sore knees, receding gums, mild hearing loss, thinning hair, sinus infections, and lines in my face added to my physical tribulations as my fifties wound toward inexorable infirmity. I knew this was natural. My Catholic upbringing prepared me for the decay of the flesh. Tell a child regularly from an early age that he is dust and to dust he shall return and he will grow up unsurprised at the eventual erosion of physical authority.

Under the advice of many doctors over many years I had adopted various exercise routines. I had run, I had swum, I had biked, and for a while in the eighties I even had a Nautilus machine in the guest room. By sixty, though, I was trying to make a habit of minor virtue. I joined a gym very close to my apartment and visited it for a half hour every morning from Monday through Friday. I stuck to the regime for an entire autumn, winter, and spring. If I had a late night and missed a morning, I tried to make it up that evening. My cardiologist was almost as impressed with me as I was with myself.

This pride collapsed the night before I had to leave for London for Live 8. I had missed my workout that morning because of last-minute meetings and, knowing I would be away from my routine for at least a week, I headed out for the health club as soon as I finished packing my suitcase at nine P.M.

At my locker I realized that I had forgotten to bring white athletic socks. I looked down at my thin black dress socks. If I wore them I would look like a silly old man to the young and well-built singles who packed the gym in the evening hours. In the morning when I usually went the clientele were fewer and less fit, including four or five regulars as old as me. The hell with it, I decided, I am a silly old man. If any of these preening Adonisi have nothing better to do than smile at my black socks, they are welcome. I laced up my trainers and headed into the gym.

I was very surprised that in spite of my effort to be unselfconscious, I was sure that the young men and women around all the exercise equipment were in fact staring at me, smirking, and giggling.

I told myself I was being paranoid. No one is looking at your socks, I insisted. I took a seat on one of the weight machines and began a stretching exercise. An obnoxious fitness instructor whom I usually avoided came over, to try to sell me his skills as a personal trainer, I supposed. I grabbed the levers and began to pump. He leaned over and said in my ear, "Too hot in here for ya, big guy?"

I had no idea what that meant. He grinned like an idiot. I was pumping faster than I should have, trying to fan him off. I hoped I could maintain my pace until he left; it would be shameful to exhaust myself in front of him. Looking away to avoid his eyes, I fixed on my reflection in a wall-sized mirror across the room. It took me a moment to comprehend what I saw.

All over the gymnasium young fit athletes of both sexes were looking askance at a red-faced white-haired old man who was frantically levering a weight machine while dressed in a sweatshirt, white trainers, black socks–and his white underpants.

I had had nightmares like this. I pumped harder, trying to wake up. I tried to understand. I had been so concerned with turning down and obscuring my dress socks that I had, in my distraction, walked out of the locker room and into the gymnasium without any pants. I stopped exercising and leaned forward on my knees, breathing hard. People around me averted their eyes. I took a towel, wrapped it around my waist, and trudged back to the locker room. I dressed without washing and walked out of the building, never to return.

None of my physical maladies had bothered me for longer than it took to get to the doctor, but this mental lapse terrified me. I had seen Emerson fret over the fading of his looks, but I was never handsome, so I was not vain that way. I watched how desperately Emerson conspired to disguise the decline of his talent, but I had no such talent to protect. I knew that Emerson relied on aphrodisiacs prescribed and proscribed along with erectile dysfunction pills, to compensate for the diminution of his virility. To me the slightening of the libido that came with the years was mostly the easing of a distraction.

But my mind had always been my gift, the seat of what made me exceptional and the source of my self-esteem. My vanity was founded on possessing a quick intelligence. I could forgive myself the public humiliation of walking into a roomful of men and women in my underpants, but what it implied about the coming disintegration of my mental functions filled me with terror.

I hardly slept that night. A car arrived before dawn to take me to the airport for London. When I found my seat on the plane the flight attendant saw that I was worried. She genuflected at my armrest and whispered, "Are you frightened of flying, sir?"

"Oh no," I told her. "I've got better things to be scared of now."

The evening before the Live 8 concert I drove over to Hyde Park with Charlie. There was a security stand set up near the Stanhope Gate. I produced an envelope filled with parking, stage, and meal passes and we were allowed to drive up the Serpentine into the busy backstage area. It was like driving into a fort and fuel dump set up in the desert by an advancing army. We proceeded into a truck lot ringed on the south by service tents and production offices and on the north by the back of the giant stage, which rose up like the screen at an American drive-in movie. Roadies were rolling equipment cases along an infrastructure of ramps while men and women wearing headsets and clutching clipboards hurried up wooden staircases to the proscenium.

I tried to drive through the next gate, into the Talent Area, where I was told by a large Scottish man in a poncho to park my car with the trucks and walk in. We did. The Talent Area looked like an empty fairgrounds waiting for the elephants to arrive. There were cheap plastic chairs and picnic tables, some perforated by big umbrellas, and a few potted palms that looked like they had been lifted from a student production of *The King and I* leaning against trellises set up around the entrance to Paul McCartney's Quonset hut, which was twice as big as anyone else's. Fair enough, I figured. He started it.

Outside the security perimeter of the Talent Area was a grand two-story wood and glass turnip of a structure erected by the BBC to serve as a base for their coverage of the event. From the top of their toadstool they could look out on the crowd beyond the final fence, or peek into the stars' yard. In a narrow tunnel between the BBC tower and the side of the stage was a kennel of small interview trailers for the lesser press and TV partners from around the world.

This was a gauntlet into which few major stars would suffer to set foot.

"What's that music?" Charlie asked me. "Is that someone playing live or is that a tape?"

I listened. The echoing din had the monotony of a recording, but the voices singing over it were too irregular to be anything but human. We made our way up one of the backstage staircases to an observation deck above the stage and saw Madonna overseeing a choreography rehearsal with what looked to be the entire cast of a Broadway musical. The diva was displeased and the dancers were paying for it.

So were the members of Pink Floyd, who were with us on the platform, sulking. We said hello and they explained that they were supposed to have taken the stage to rehearse their big reunion moment an hour ago, but the Material Girl refused to respect seniority. Charlie asked if they had seen Emerson anywhere and Floyd's keyboard player said yes, he was talking to Simon on the other side of the stage.

"Ah," Charlie said. "Speaking of reunions!" We made our way over to where Emerson and Simon were chatting away as if not a day had passed since they had been sharing a van across Germany.

Charlie slipped up behind Simon and tapped him on the shoulder. When Simon turned, Charlie planted a kiss on the end of his nose.

"Hello, you old jazzbo!" Charlie squealed.

"If it isn't the imp of the perverse," Simon snorted. He smiled at Charlie and put out his hand but when he saw me he turned sober.

"How are you, Simon?" I asked.

"I'm very fine indeed, Flynn. You look like you've been eating well."

"Yes, the genetic bomb has exploded, I'm afraid."

That was it for camaraderie. Simon gave his attention back to Emerson and Charlie. He said, "I don't want to do any of the obvious crap. We're here for a bigger cause. Our repertoire should reflect that."

Emerson was bearing with him. He said, "I take your point, Simon, but at these multi-act events, it's probably best to give the people the biggest songs you have."

"I'm up for anything," Charlie said. "As long as I get a piece of the publishing!"

Simon threw a cigarette on the floor and stepped on it. "Think about it, that's all I'm asking," he said, and he left without looking at me again.

Emerson turned to me. "Simon seems to think an excerpt from his failed rock opera will really cheer up the Africans."

Charlie said, "Haven't those poor people suffered enough?"

When they were certain Simon was out of earshot, Charlie said to Emerson, "What do you figure? Prozac?"

"He does seem to be on an even keel," Emerson answered. "I would be inclined to credit psychopharmaceuticals."

"Science's gift to psychos," Charlie said.

"And we who must work with them," Emerson replied.

My eyes fell on a tall, silver-haired man with a deep tan, an expensive suit, and an open shirt, who was laughing nearby with two top managers, a famous promoter, and the wife of a rock legend. I had seen this same man backstage at Madison Square Garden, the Grammys, and the Rock and Roll Hall of Fame dinner, but I could never put together who he was. Everyone seemed to know him and he had apparently unlimited access—but whenever I asked about him I was told, "Oh, he's just a nice guy," or "He's a big fan, everybody likes him." I knew all the billionaires who followed rock stars around, shedding money on them in exchange for snorting up their coolness. He was not one of those. It bothered me that everyone seemed to know this fellow except for me.

I decided to crack the case. I walked up to where he was standing and nodded greeting to my peers.

"Tony, Edward," I said. "Vivian, very good to see you." I put out my hand to the silver man. "Jack Flynn," I told him. "I think we've met before."

The silver man displayed an impeccable smile and took my hand and said, "Good to see you, Jack!"

He was unfathomable. The next day I got to the park at nine in the morning and the silver man was already in the Talent Area, greeting the giants of the music world with affectionate hugs and leaning to whisper in their offered ears. Everyone knew what he did except me. The silver man was introducing Elton John to a startlingly attractive redhead whose lips and eyes seemed too big for her head and whose long frame seemed too lean to support her enormous breasts.

I was looking around for Fin, who had not checked into the hotel last night and who had not, as far as I knew, played drums professionally in thirty years. Whatever the differences in their levels of success, Emerson, Simon, and Charlie had all worked at their musical craft since the breakup of the Ravons. I was not sure that Fin had, and I needed to convince myself that he was not going to fall apart under the attention of four hundred thousand fans and the TV eye of the world.

I spotted him coming around the corner in a white suit and black shirt. His head was crew-cut, almost shaved, and he was laughing. Fin must have been sixty like the rest of us, but he looked twenty years younger. I waved to him and he smiled back, but then he spotted the silver man and veered away to grab his arm and ruffle his hair.

When he had kissed the voluptuous redhead on both cheeks and finally peeled away, he came to me and embraced me and told me how much he was looking forward to playing with the Ravons again.

"If you can make your way down to that truck in the grove of trees beyond the security check-in, you might get a chance to actually rehearse with them before going onstage," I told him. "I know Emerson is very anxious to run through the songs."

"Four tunes!" Fin laughed. "We can play 'em in our sleep!"

"It's the audience falling asleep I worry about," I told him. "Listen, who is that guy?" I pointed to the silver man. "I overheard one of Elton's band asking him about some pills; is he a drug dealer?"

"That's Art Gardner!" Fin said with a laugh.

"And who's Art Gardner, then?" Why did everyone know but me?

"Come on, you know him, Jack!"

"I'm senile; remind me."

Fin lowered his voice. "He's the hair guy."

"The hair guy? You mean like 'Let the Sunshine In'? He wrote that?"

"No, Jack." Fin looked at me like he was sure I must be pulling his leg. "He does hair." Fin pointed to the crown of his head. "Like, you know, cosmetic stuff."

"Oh, you are fucking kidding me."

"You know Art Gardner! He does everybody! You check out any fifty-, sixty-year-old rock star with a quiff like James Dean and you'll see Art Gardner on his permanent guest list."

"It makes sense now."

I looked back at the woman on the silver man's arm.

"Do you think she's been . . . ?"

"Enhanced? Of course she has, man. Come on. She's a walking display case."

"We've lived too long, Fin."

"Not yet we haven't."

"Will you please go down there and at least sit behind the drums for a while so Emerson will believe that you have thought about this gig?"

"You bet. Are the guys here?"

"They will be within half an hour."

"Coolio."

"How are you earning your living these days, anyway? Are you still representing dead celebrities for commercial endorsements?"

"Not so much. I'm easing out of that."

"What is the value of an endorsement from a dead person? Surely the public realizes that if the celebrity is deceased he does not actually use and probably never used the product. Why would an advertiser want to use John Lennon to sell a computer he never heard of or Bob Marley to promote a mobile phone?"

"It's all about selling an environment people want to be part of."

"Get thee behind me, Finnerty."

"Anyway, now I'm into giving back. You know about carbon credits, Jack? This global warming is real. We need to fix the atmosphere or we're all going to be dead celebrities soon."

"What's the angle, Fin?"

"I'm part of an environmental alliance who sell carbon credits. You use a private jet, right? Okay, that eats up a ton of gasoline, throws off a lot of pollution, chews up the atmosphere. We compute for you how much damage you're doing, and sell you carbon credits, which we use to plant trees in Brazil and Madagascar. To offset the damage you're doing and rebuild the ecological balance."

"Holy crap, Fin, you're selling indulgences! I get to sin and I pay you for a paper that makes it okay. You should expand into usury!"

"You can laugh, Jack, but this is serious. My group is building a new rain forest to clean up this air we all breathe."

"I've never heard such malarkey! You don't really plant those trees! I'll bet you've got one big field somewhere and you planted a row of saplings and every sucker who signs up for your carbon credits gets a photograph of the same bunch of palms! Tell me the truth."

"It's all monitored and audited by an independent environmental group."

"In Madagascar! Go practice your drums, Fin, play for your sins."

The Ravons were going to perform in the middle of the afternoon, after Paul McCartney and U2 opened the concert and long before the Who and Pink Floyd got to take advantage of the falling darkness and the rising stage lights. Emerson had made a halfhearted protest that they deserved a better slot but he knew that it had taken a full band reunion and all of my negotiating skills to get the Ravons on the Hyde Park bill at all. The concert organizers had been trying as late as a week before to convince me to move them to Germany. I had made the case to Emerson that it was better for us to go on in the slow middle section and steal the show than to be lost in the superstar finale.

When all four of the band members were present I left them in a trailer behind the artist compound to run though their four songs with tiny practice amps and a cocktail drum kit. I got out of there as quickly as courtesy allowed. Castro stayed to manage the tension and egos. Wendy the flack kept trying to sneak in with radio interviewers, print journalists, TV crews, and photographers, each of whom she insisted was the single most important person in the entire press pit. I explained diplomatically that if she ruined the band's one chance to rehearse before playing their first show in thirty-five years for a worldwide audience of a billion people I would bury her up to her neck, put her head in a birdcage, and let her eyeballs be pecked out by a mad parrot. It did not stop her but it gave her pause.

Let me pull the emergency brake here for one quick footnote. When I used the term "a billion people" with Wendy I was indulging in hyperbole. It is my pet peeve that whenever there is a big international television event–the Olympics, the World Cup, the Academy Awards–commentators routinely claim that a billion people are watching. I recall one Oscar telecast where the host welcomed "literally billions of viewers around the world." Now stop and consider this. There are, as I write this, six billion people in the world, twice the number as when the Ravons broke up in 1969. Half live in poverty, at least a fifth in extreme poverty. Do the producers of, for example, the Grammy Awards really believe that in the jungles of South America thousands of peasants are making the long foot trek to the nearest village with a communal television? Are the remote hamlets of China banging together satellite dishes from old gasoline cans in order to gather the clan and see if Tim McGraw beats Brooks & Dunn for Country Record of the Year? If these shows were that big a deal, they would at least win their time slots.

But we have all gotten used to audience inflation, so if the press around Live 8 bought the organizers' rhetoric that a billion people would be watching, who was I to prick the balloon? All I wanted was to focus the attention of my band of sixty-year-olds who had not played a show together in more than half their long, long lives.

I had two hours to wander the backstage area and commune with my fellow members of the fraternity of old rock managers. As always happened when we got together with drinks in our hands, we reiterated our creed of grievances against the thuggish record labels:

"Nobody ever works out what royalties mean as pennies per record! You got eighteen percent? Yeah? Eighteen percent of *what*?"

"Now they're asking not just for the universe, but for the universe 'known and unknown.' The bastards are trying to get our earnings in other dimensions!"

"You can't possibly agree to sign away the rights to something that hasn't been invented yet!"

These were dark times for the record companies. The digitalization of recorded music had given them a windfall with the compact disc, but now with the widespread use of computer communications young fans were duplicating and sharing music online with no revenue going back to the label or the artist. CD sales were plummeting. The label chiefs, rapacious as ever and driven to new ruthlessness by their dilemma, were demanding that artists give them a percentage of their income from touring, TV shirts, and music publishing.

The general attitude among the managers was, *Screw you! It would*

*make more sense for me to give the concert promoters a percent of my
record sales! At least they pay me on time!*

It was making for bad feelings all around. Recently an album had
gone to number one on the American charts with sales of sixty thousand copies. A decade earlier, that would not have gotten you into the
top ten. Touring was still a lucrative business, at least for acts with audiences old enough to pay the rising price of concert tickets. Emerson
made almost all his money on the road now. Sentimentally I was sorry
to see the labels go, but I could not pretend they had not brought it on
themselves. They kept jacking up the prices on music and stealing from
the artists until robbing them back seemed morally justified.

We'd had a great run.

I went back to tell the Ravons they were twenty minutes out and
found practice over, a Radio One reporter in their trailer with Wendy,
and Charlie holding forth on the pros and cons of digital downloading:

"It doesn't bother me at all, man," Charlie was telling the journalist's digital recorder. "Music should be free. Only way to keep the gift
from eating you up is to just let it pass through you. Let the music
come in and go out. You don't control it. You don't shape it, you don't
own it. Just open your ears and your eyes and your heart and let it pass
through and then give it away. Do that and the music will take care of
you. But if you try and hold on to it, if you try to own it, it will poison
you. If you try to own it, it will end up owning you."

Simon and Emerson were holding their tongues. I knew them well
enough to know what they were thinking: Easy to be all for giving it
away when nobody's buying it anyway, Charlie. Some of us still like
getting paid for our work.

"Fifteen minutes to stage, gents," I told them. Emerson looked a little stunned. The abstract idea of a Ravons reunion was becoming real.

I went outside the trailer to wait for them and tried to reach Agatha
by phone. I had sent her two tickets to bring Ben to London for the
show and visit his grandmother. My mum was ninety-one. She still had
her senses but she spent more of the day sleeping than awake. I had
never told her that Agatha and I had split. I kept thinking she would
be gone soon and why burden her, but she hung on. I knew that my es-
tranged family had arrived in England and checked into the Park Lane
Hotel, but I had not seen them here at the concert. I worried that they

were impeded at one of the many security checkpoints or had come in at the wrong end of the park and were stuck in the throngs beyond the barriers.

I was walking to the stage with the Ravons when my mobile buzzed and I saw it was Agatha.

"Are you here?" I asked.

"We're at Hamleys," Agatha told me. "Ben insisted on looking for new weapons for that Action Man doll you bought him."

"The Ravons are about to play, Aggie!" I said. "We're walking to the stage right now! Aren't you coming?"

"Has Madonna played yet?" she wanted to know. "We'll be there in time for Madonna."

I lost reception as we started up the steps to the stage. Agatha had no intention of seeing Emerson. I think she thought it was weak of me to still associate with him. I did not doubt that she was right.

We stood waiting in the wings of the stage with a collection of well-credentialed wives, agents, celebrities, and show business executives. A young female singer who had recently had an international number one was finishing up a sing-along version of a Bob Marley song. She came off to polite applause and a well-known film star went out and made a speech about the wildfire spread of AIDS in Africa. A British television comedian nudged up to the Ravons and said, "Hullo, boys! I'm doing the honors! Now, I just want to make sure I have it right—you're Simon, you're Charlie. You we all know. And you are . . ."

"Dan Finnerty," Fin announced. "Drummer with the Ravons since 1967."

"Right, got it," the comedian said. "Wasn't sure you made it. I have to tell you, boys, I nicked my older sister's copy of 'Voodoo Doll.' Got my first humjob to that record."

"There's an inspiring image," Simon said.

"Glad we could help, man." Charlie smiled.

"If you could find a way to slip the name Lola Swotksi into the lyric tonight," the comedian said, "I'd like to think she'd hear it and remember. Oh, there's the signal. We're up, boys."

He went out onto the stage and began telling the audience the same story he had just told us. I looked at my charges. Emerson wore a tight, frozen smile and did not blink. Fin had his eyes almost closed; he was doing paradiddles on a flight case with his drumsticks. Simon looked ruthlessly upbeat. Charlie seemed relaxed and happy, as if he were back by the pool in California in the seventies, smoking pot under a starry sky.

"They taught the Beatles to harmonize, they taught the Stones to play the blues, and they got me my first lesson in love—please welcome back to London, for the first time in thirty-five years—the Ravons!"

Everything moved in slow motion as the four musicians made their way across the huge stage and picked up their instruments. Fin was chewing gum like a desperate beaver eating its way through a log. He waited for Emerson to look back at him and then counted off the first song. It was "Voodoo Doll." I could not tell if they were playing it right or not. I had the ocean in my ears. I looked out at the crowd and they were bopping in the boiling July sun, waving their hands, shirtless and sunburned and happy to be there. I looked around at the backstage VIPs swaying in the wings and on the makeshift balconies behind the speaker columns. They seemed to be respectfully interested. I looked at Charlie. He was concentrating on his guitar but at the last second he moved up to his microphone to add harmonies to Emerson's first chorus. And I looked at Simon.

Here I stopped being frightened and became amazed. Simon was bouncing around and grinning like Gerry of the Pacemakers cross-bred with Freddie of the Dreamers and given a tank full of lithium. This was not the Simon I had known for nearly forty years, this was someone happy.

Emerson looked confused when Simon hopped over to the center microphone as the second chorus came around. I think he was afraid he was going to attack him. Instead, Simon leaned in to Emerson's mike to sing along on the "Vooo-doooooo Doll!" refrain. Emerson looked relieved and confused. Charlie saw that expression and began laughing. As Emerson went into his guitar solo Charlie strolled over to where Simon was bopping and joined him in a bit of bunny-hopping choreography. Fin had his head down and was desperately keeping time.

Emerson played the same solo on "Voodoo Doll" every time he performed the song, but this time, standing at the edge of the stage leaning into a young crowd who had not seen him before, he added a wild, fast run down the neck at the end, drawing cheers and fists in the air. He whirled around and raced back to the microphone for the last verse and chorus, Charlie and Simon flanking him like Pips to his Gladys Knight.

The crowd went crazy. It took me a moment to convince myself I was not wishing it to be so. Even the big shots and insiders up on the backstage catwalk were shouting and whistling. The Ravons jumped into their second song, "Mary vs. Mary," and played it like they knew this was their last great day. Now Simon was singing right in Emerson's microphone, spewing spittle on his face. I looked across the stage at Castro, crouched down in the opposite wing, who smiled and shrugged. Fin looked up and realized that the set was going over well. His whitened teeth gleamed in the sunlight bouncing off his crash cymbal.

One of the concert organizers grabbed my sleeve. "They're great, Flynn, but they have to cut a song. We're way over time."

"Shit, don't tell us that now, man," I shouted in his ear. "They've got two songs left."

"No choice! One more and then the TV feed cuts away to Philadelphia."

Across the stage someone was telling Castro the same thing. When "Mary" ended he skidded onto the stage and whispered the word to Emerson and Simon. Charlie relayed it to Fin. The television cameras panned across the cheering crowd, who went twice as wild when they saw the cameras. The Ravons had a hasty conference and then Emerson told the audience, "This is a great day for a great cause. I'm very very happy to be here with my oldest and dearest friends. Now we're going to leave you with a song we have never played before."

This was news to me; we had gone over the set list twenty times— the Ravons' four biggest hits and out. What had they hatched in that trailer?

Simon began rumbling through a two-steps-up, one-step-down bass pattern and Charlie chimed in on a ringing acoustic guitar. Fin tapped out a pattern on his hi-hat and kick drum. Emerson nodded to Simon and began tolling out a mournful guitar figure. I knew this song from somewhere but I could not place it until Emerson began singing, "In a smoke-stained world, we're just making out, we're just making out . . ."

They were doing Simon's song "Evangeline," the sing-along dirge that had won the attention of the German spies. It had never been a hit single, and while Simon Potts aficionados would recognize it, Simon Potts aficionados had to be a statistically tiny percentage of the fans swaying and holding up their arms in front of the stage. By learning his song and performing it for the biggest audience of his life, Emerson made a gesture to Simon of magnanimity and brotherhood that caused a tear to run down even my skeptical old face.

They extended the song to six minutes, effectively swiping back the time the promoters had tried to subtract from them. They went down a storm. When it was over the four old men stood with their arms around each other's waists and shoulders and basked in the cheering of the biggest crowd they had ever played for. How happy they were that everything had worked out in the end.

If a future generation wants to understand what England was like in the early days of the twenty-first century, look at the five days that began with Live 8. British rock, which had shaped our nation in the imaginations of millions the world over, came together in Hyde Park to bring global attention to the epidemics of disease and economic oppression that were engulfing Africa. Here were McCartney, Townshend, Elton, and a dozen other old generals of the British Invasion summoning the troops for one more crusade. If it had ended there, it would have been a cultural event, but many of the musicians and concertgoers moved up to Scotland, where Prime Minister Tony Blair, himself a reformed rock and roll singer, was hosting the G8 summit at the Gleneagles Hotel.

President Bush of the United States, President Chirac of France, President Putin of Russia, Prime Minister Koizumi of Japan, Chancellor Schröder of Germany, Prime Minister Berlusconi of Italy, and Prime Minister Martin of Canada found themselves listening to the arguments of Bono and Bob Geldof while the news cameras rolled and Prime Minister Blair, the man responsible for Mick Jagger's knighthood, egged them on.

The rock stars and their supporters won from the world leaders a series of concessions and promises, including cancellation of forty billion dollars in debt owed to the industrialized world by eighteen of the poorest countries. To me it seemed more than amazing. It actually seemed preposterous. After decades of empty-headed sentimentality and revolutionary posturing, rock stars were at this late date accomplishing something concrete in the political world.

"Don't be such an old grump, Jack," Charlie chided me. "We're the establishment now! All those geezers paying their taxes and working in banks are the kids who used to be sleeping at Glastonbury. You didn't think they'd forget, did you?"

"Charlie, I didn't believe they could remember their house keys. But I'm delighted to be proved wrong."

We were sitting on the couch in Charlie's newly rented flat in Camden Town, watching the morning news with Agatha while Ben played with his Action Man figure on the floor. Charlie had been threatening to move home to England since shortly after 9/11. Now he had stumbled on an affordable space. He said that by New Year's he would pack up his Woodstock house and come home to stay. Agatha, Ben, and I had come over to check out Charlie's new pad, a first-floor walk-up just off the main road, with a brick wall out front and flowers struggling to rise in a window box. Charlie was moving back to London, he told us, to live out his days among people who drove on the proper side of the street. Agatha had agreed to an early breakfast before she and Ben flew back to America.

Everything in the four days since Live 8 had been giddy. The Ravons' performance had gotten them tremendous press and offers to tour. Bootleg videos of "Evangeline" were lighting up the online services. The band had agreed to allow the song to be released on an all-star charity album that the Ravons would not have been invited to be part of a week earlier. Now they were going to be lined up alongside Coldplay, U2, and REM to fly the flag for Africa.

In between Live 8 and Gleneagles, Tony Blair had flown to Singapore, where the Olympic committee was meeting, to make a last-minute personal pitch for the 2012 games to be held in London. It was widely assumed and reported that France had the deal sewn up. When word came from Singapore that Blair's appeal had worked and the games were coming to London after all, celebrating crowds flowed into Trafalgar Square waving banners and shooting off streams of champagne. At that moment Blair could have won election as King.

"It's a nice time to be in London," Agatha said.

"Maybe our long circle is coming to its close, Jack," Charlie said. "Maybe it's time for all of us to come home."

I looked at Agatha. Charlie ruffled Ben's hair and said, "I don't suppose I could interest me old mate Benjamin in going down to the canal to see the boats? And maybe get an ice cream?" Ben picked up Action Man and followed Uncle Charlie out the door.

When they left I resumed my old pitch to the mother of my son.

"The boy loves it when the family's together, Aggie," I said. "You saw how he was at Mum's."

"It's unfair of you to use Ben's happiness against me, Jack," Agatha said. "He is a well-adjusted child. He's fine with the way things are. If we got back together, it might very well be worse for him."

"Kingston's a nice place for a boy to grow up, Aggie. He'd be close to his grandma. Close to Richmond Park and the deer. Mum's not got long, we could try it for a year or two. Be an adventure."

"What are you talking about, Jack?" She stood up and looked down at me sitting on the couch. "I'm not moving Ben to England! He's almost ten years old, he's in the middle of school. You and I are his parents. That will always bind us together, but we are not a couple anymore and I wish you'd stop pretending we could be."

"Well, we could be."

"We're not, Jack. I'm sorry."

She went to wash the breakfast dishes and I tried to think of another argument. I was overwhelmed by the certainty that this was my last chance at fixing what I had done wrong in my life. If Agatha and Ben would stay with me, there would be happy years ahead. If they left, I would be old soon and alone forever.

Charlie returned with Ben. Agatha announced that they had to get back to the hotel to pack and check out. I said I would walk them down and get them a cab. Agatha said no, they were going to walk through Camden and look for a Hansen-Godfrey hairbrush. She said they would get the train at King's Cross and avoid the morning traffic. I started to protest but realized that Agatha would not tolerate another argument from me this morning.

"Okay," I said, "but I'll be at the hotel at noon to bring you to the airport. You're not getting out of that one."

I hugged Ben and kissed Agatha good-bye. When they were gone Charlie said, "She's the one for you, Jack. You know that."

"She does not agree."

"She'll come around if you stay on her, man."

"I always thought I'd end up back here, too, you know, Charlie.

I never put it in words, but I imagined that when all our adventures were over I'd be sitting in the house in Kingston, looking at my photo album, finally reading all of those books I bought. Now I worry that that day's never going to come. I fear I am going to stay out there until I die. What if the carnival we ran away with never lets us go?"

"We'd be circus clowns without portfolio. Now listen, as a man who is much poorer than you and one statistically expected to depart much sooner, may I politely ask we table this talk of death and decay and discuss how to make me a lot of money in the time I have remaining?"

"Well, codger, if the early e-mails are any indication, interest in the reunited Ravons is somewhat greater than it has been at any time since the Queen Mother was still menstruating. I don't know how Emerson is going to feel about this, but he certainly enjoyed Hyde Park."

"And I've got songs, Jack. I got dozens just waiting to be fleshed out. How much is Emerson writing these days?"

"Lately he is perhaps not as prolific as you."

"Faker! He hasn't written a tune this year, I can tell. Well, I am prepared to cut him some cowrites if he acts now on this onetime offer."

"Don't count your royalties yet, Charlie," I warned him. "Simon's still mad as a squirrel, Fin barely got through the three songs before his arms fell off, and Em is more than capable of seeing Live 8 as a nice boost for his public image and solo career. We also have to be serious about your health. I know you're feeling good now, but nothing is worth setting you back."

"I'm mended, Jack. The doctors can't believe it. I'm the poster boy for remission."

Charlie went into the bedroom and came back with a big old Gretsch Country Gentleman guitar. "Check this out," he said. He sat down on the couch next to me and began strumming a modified Chuck Berry riff.

He sang, "I never went to bed with an ugly woman but I woke up with one or two. I never misled an honest woman but I might have confused a few. The wives will kill us if they ever find out! The wives will kill us if we open our mouths! If they ever catch on, the wives will kill us! A wop bop a loo bop, Ruth and Phyllis!"

He let the last chord ring and looked up at me happily. "That's a hit, Jack!"

"You had me right up to 'Ruth and Phyllis,' old bean," I said.

"Aw, whaddayou know, ya pencil pusher? All right, how about this?"

Charlie sang me a pretty good rocker called "Kiss Me" and a heart-tugging ballad called "The Right Girl" and a rollicking knees-up number called "If You See Kay."

I told him he had lots of good ideas but that did not mean Emerson would go for putting the band back together. We would have to wait for all the offers and evaluate them.

The television had continued to play with the sound turned down. Charlie was looking past me, at the screen. He made a little noise and went over and turned up the volume.

A blond woman newsreader was in front of a photograph of smoke coming out of a tube station and people running in the street.

". . . eastbound Circle Line number 204 traveling between Liverpool Street and Adgate. Unconfirmed reports from witnesses say that the explosion shook the platform. Survivors covered with blood and torn clothing are said to be making their way out of the tunnels on foot while rescue workers attempt to reach the trains with medical and fire-fighting equipment. We stress that these reports are unconfirmed . . ."

I began dialing Agatha's mobile phone number. I could not get a connection, just a fast beep.

"Did she say she was going to the Camden station?" I asked Charlie.

"It's going to be fine, Jack. She wasn't heading that way."

"She said she was going to look for a hairbrush and get the train at King's Cross, Charlie. The Circle Line goes through King's Cross."

The news came quickly now. Two more bombs had exploded on trains, one on a westbound Circle Line heading for Paddington, the other on the southbound Piccadilly line leaving King's Cross for Russell Square.

"Mary Mother of God," I said. I kept punching in Agatha's number. There was no signal at all.

"The odds against them being on one of those trains, Jack . . ." Charlie said, but he was white. I ran out of the flat and down to the street. Word was already spreading. I felt like I was back in New York on September 11. At least that day I had Ben in my arms, I could cover his eyes. Who was there to cover his eyes now?

I ran through Camden, past the markets and news merchants, the nightclubs and chemists and fruit stands. My heart was like an animal in a trap. I ran all the way to King's Cross, past ambulances and fire trucks, past police barricades and screaming women, past businessmen sitting in the street holding bloody handkerchiefs to their eyes and necks.

Everything was black, white, and gray, like an old photograph. There were pools of water on the ground but it was sunny. I began seeing cracks everywhere, in the pavement, in the street, in the buildings. Were they always there? Was the world splitting open? I tried reciting old prayers from childhood, the Hail Holy Queen, the Miserere. I implored heaven to help my wife and child but I stumbled on the words. I circled back, I could not remember. I saw rescue workers carrying stretchers down into the tube and hurried after them. A policeman grabbed my arm and told me I had to go back behind the line. I shook him off and ran after the stretchers. Something crashed into me. It was a soldier. He pinned me against a wall and put a baton to my neck and leaned in to my eyes and shouted at me, "You keep running and you will be shot! If you need help, go back behind the line and find a medic. If you are not hurt, walk home now!"

I could not make words come. The cop I had shaken off came and put his hand on the soldier's arm. "He's okay," the cop said. "You have to leave this area, sir. We need to keep it clear so the firefighters can get in."

I nodded and they let me go. I walked back past the barriers to where a crowd was gathered, watching like mourners. I blamed myself for not heeding September 11. That tragedy had flown in front of our window and we escaped harm. We ran through the New York streets carrying our baby and got away safe. Why had I not accepted that warning? After the World Trade Center I promised myself I would stop working, stop flying. I intended to be done with the madness of the wider world. But I let jealousy and the habit of useless ambition blind me. I gave up on my family and went back into the world. I acted as if I were immune to the viciousness of history. I knew I had been ungrateful. I knew that God had lost patience with me.

I saw a coffee shop sign–Nero. I remembered how Ben always insisted that the sign said "Nerd." If my son was dead every reminder of his life would be a nail in my chest. I went in and sat in the window and watched the pandemonium in the street through the glass. No one came to take my order, so I just sat. My mobile was still out; the circuits were either overloaded or some government emergency agency had shut down all the cell phones. Perhaps the bombs were activated by mobile phone signals. I had read that happened in the Middle East. We were all in the Middle East now.

I don't know how long I sat in that window staring at the disaster and I am not clear on what I saw with my own eyes and what I saw on TV later. At some point my phone rang and I leaped on it, hitting all the wrong buttons. It was my cousin Mary, with my mother, checking to see if I was all right. I said I was fine. She asked about Agatha and Benjy. I could not find words. I finally managed to say, "Oh, they must be at the airport by now, I should go out there and see them off," when I saw the Action Man doll moving past the window outside. There were Agatha and Ben, searching through the mayhem. I rapped hard on the glass. Ben saw me first and tugged at Agatha's sleeve. I told my cousin everything was fine, I'd call back soon, and raced out onto the sidewalk and grabbed them and hugged Agatha and held our little boy between us.

"We went back to Charlie's," she said. "He told us you were down here. The phones are all out."

All I cared was that they were alive. Although I had done nothing to deserve it, someone had saved me again. Understanding passed into me like light and I knew at once and completely that it did not matter if my son and his mother lived with me, as long as they were safe and happy. It did not matter how much they loved me, or even if they loved me at all. All I needed was to love them completely. All I needed was to have them to love.

Everyone wanted the Ravons. Concert promoters and agencies from Europe, the United States, Canada, Japan, and Latin America all made inquiries, sent offers, and laid out business plans. A reunion tour suddenly had the prospect of earning, with sponsorships, licensing, and merchandising, upward of fifty million dollars.

Castro and Wendy were wetting themselves with excitement. Each of them was getting calls from connections trying to go around the back door and get straight to Emerson. Sometimes they told me about these approaches and sometimes they conveniently forgot, waiting for a long plane ride to drop a hint in Emerson's ear.

I was used to such skulduggery. It was inevitable in organizations such as ours where middle management hung on for years with no room for advancement. Castro and Wendy were earning too much to ever quit, but they had outgrown their roles. He was too old to be a road manager, she knew too much to be a publicist. They had come to resent not earning a percentage of what Emerson earned, as I did. That's the trouble with giving people big titles. Instead of being grateful, they come to believe they really are who you have agreed to pretend they are.

Some management organizations make it a point to flush out the lifers every six or seven years, to avoid their becoming entrenched. I understood the wisdom of such calculations, but I was softhearted. Whatever their eccentricities, Castro and Wendy shared with me the experience of dealing with Emerson on a daily basis. They knew his temperament, and he was comfortable with them. To try to break in new people now would inevitably mean that many of Wendy's and Castro's day-to-day duties would fall on me. I had dealt with those duties for years—I didn't want them back.

So I appeased my squabbling lieutenants as best I could. Castro's contract now stipulated that he get a hundred premium tickets for each of Emerson's concerts, which he scalped through his lawyer's office—a perk worth ten thousand dollars a show. Wendy had negotiated into her last deal that she get a producer's royalty on any Emerson Cutler TV show, film, or long-form DVD—in spite of her role on most video projects being simply to stand around dialing phone calls and making Emerson nervous.

They both spent a lot of time bitching about each other to me. I knew that the two of them also bitched about me to each other. All of that was okay—it kept them from mouthing off about private matters to outsiders. We were no more dysfunctional than any other family with adult children.

These new offers, though, these fifty-million-dollar mirages, added a fierceness to Wendy and Castro's calculations. They knew better than anyone except me that Emerson's earning power had been on the wane. To some degree that had been mitigated by inflation, the abrupt rise in the price of concert tickets, the discovery that prosperous baby boomers would pay grand opera prices for rock and roll shows, and Emerson's embrace of product endorsements. These new revenue streams had kept our profits afloat, but now we were faced with a saturated market and the hard truth that we had milked out our audience. Emerson was too old to get on Top 40 or the video channels. He had not had a real hit in ten years and the way the industry was set up now, he would never have a hit again. Emerson had a large residual audience of people over forty, but he had been playing to them for decades. There was no new story to tell. There was no reason for people who had seen Emerson Cutler in concert six times to buy a ticket to see him a seventh time. The Ravons reunion would be a new story. It was what we all needed.

Emerson said no before I finished asking the question.

"I can't go back, Jack," he said blithely. "Never have, never will. The Live 8 thing was lovely, but it was a one-off."

"Could you stop talking to me as if you were giving a press conference, Emerson?" I said. We were sitting on the deck of a sailboat he had rented for the summer, moored at the dock of his house on Long Island. "A lot of people have put serious work into putting these offers together. You owe them the respect of listening before you say no."

He reached over and hit a lever on the sideboard and a hidden drawer popped open. He scooped out a dovetailed joint and lit up. He was wearing loose khaki trousers and an unbuttoned short-sleeve shirt printed with the faces of famous jazz musicians. He was shoeless and working on a tan. He took a drag on the pot and said, "Okay, make the pitch."

"The Ravons set on Live 8 really woke up something in the television audience," I said. "Kids who don't know much about you saw a new band they could relate to. Old fans were reminded of what they liked about you in the first place. You know, a lot of people think you're Californian. They didn't know about the Ravons, didn't even know you were English."

"A lot of stupid people," Emerson said.

"Well, guess what, Emerson? Stupid people buy tickets, too. Come on. I know it's the center of *our* lives, but we have to accept that most of the punters don't know who sings the songs they hear on the radio, they just know if they like them. We have to reintroduce you to the general audience, the people who are not longtime fans, the people who have never bought a ticket to one of your shows. And with the Ravons we have the chance to reinvigorate the base, give the people who have been loyal to you something they've been hoping for for years."

He knew I was beating around the bush. He said, "What's the money?"

"All in? Could be fifty million. Could be more."

That impressed him. I pushed: "Let me put that in perspective. Let's say we say no to this. Fair enough. Your call. We say no to this, we go out next year and it's theaters. Two-thousand-seaters. That's in the good markets, New York and LA. Middle America, we either get on a double bill or we're playing large clubs. The money, not even close. Not even a fraction. On the other hand, we do this Ravons tour, you're selling out arenas, lots of press, multiple nights. Strong possibility of an HBO special. Spring and summer, everything first class. Then it's over. And guess what? We immediately hit the promoters up for an Emerson solo tour one year later. The money stays up there, the fans are back—new lease on life all around."

Emerson sat blowing smoke toward the rigging. I looked out at the ocean. A windy day, lots of sailboats. Couple of windsurfers.

Emerson said, "What does Wendy think?"

"She'll hang herself if you don't do it. Castro, too."

"Yeah, they've been making noises. No one laid it out financially, though."

"That's why I'm here."

"You really think I need to do this."

"You want to keep being able to rent antique schooners with secret compartments for your pot? You need to do this."

"What's the split with Simon?"

"Well, Simon still owns a third of the brand, so he has to be taken care of. On the other hand, we're obviously going to be using your crew, your gear, your trucks, your staging. I think we can work this out so you get half off the top for absorbing those costs. Fin gets paid a flat fee out of that–he won't say no to a million dollars. You, Simon, and Charlie split the remaining fifty percent equally."

Emerson wet his fingers with his lips and then squeezed out the tip of his joint carefully. He flipped it over the rail into the ocean.

"Why would we give Charlie an equal cut?" he said. "He doesn't have any equity in the Ravons."

"That's true, he doesn't have legal equity, but he is an essential part of the band. There is no Ravons reunion without Charlie. I assumed you'd want to take care of him."

"Of course I want to take care of him, Flynn. For God's sake. I've been taking care of him for thirty years. I think offering him a million dollars with no exposure would be taking care of him pretty nicely, don't you? Considering that he's destitute and more or less living off me anyway. I don't think a million dollars is particularly insulting, do you?"

"It's hard for me to feel comfortable with a scenario where Simon makes nine or ten million dollars and Charlie makes one."

"Simon was smart enough and mean enough to not sell off his shares in the band. Fair play to him. He's not worth it but I suppose you're telling me I have to accept it. However, in the interests of fairness I'll tell you what. Offer Simon six million, flat out, and Charlie two. I'll take anything left over, if there is anything left over, and I will assume all the risk, all the expenses, and provide all of the personnel, expertise, and equipment for this gigantic undertaking. If they don't like those terms they can all fuck off back to B. B. King's."

"You want to think that over for a day or two before I make the calls?"

"If I think it over, Flynn, I will decide not to do it at all. Remember the workers in the vineyard, old altar boy. It does not cheat a man who is being paid an honest wage if someone else is paid even more. You sure Charlie's well enough to do this?"

"He's in remission a long time now. He swears he's feeling great."

"God bless him."

"A million okay for Fin?"

Emerson sat forward, pulled off his sunglasses, and looked at me with cold eyes. I decided that someone had bought him cheap pot; it was making him edgy.

He said, "Fin is not part of this. That is not negotiable. He was useless at Live 8. He's not a musician anymore, he's a suit."

"These offers are for the full band."

"Fin was not an original Ravon. He was never even a legal member of the group. Hell's bells, Jack, he's not even English. No one will notice if Fin's there or not. Baxter is the drummer. That's nonnegotiable. That's a deal-breaker."

I had my orders. I walked down the gangplank.

Wendy and Castro were ringing my mobile phone as soon as I set foot on dry land. They were not interested in any of the details. All they cared about was that he said yes. I knew that they traded in gossip as a commodity, but I begged them to keep the lid on until I reached out to Simon and Charlie. This could still blow up.

I drove up to Woodstock to see Charlie. He was supposed to be packing up to move back to London but he never seemed to get it done. I suspected he was sleeping with his landlady. His cottage looked like the home of Winnie the Pooh. There were spirit nets dangling from the windows and large plants all around. He was very thin, but otherwise looked so healthy that I wondered how he could have come so close to death that the hospital was lobbying to turn off the machines. He welcomed me into his little green house and pointed to a white desk in the corner on which he had mounted a computer with a large freestanding screen.

"You've discovered the World Wide Web, Charlie," I said with a laugh. "You, the last Luddite!"

It had taken Charlie years to master even the answering machine. Until about 1990 whenever he left me a message he would speak as if he were dictating a letter:

> Hello, Jack—
> I find myself a bit short at tax time and it occurs to me that you may be holding some funds I am due for Japanese royalties on the Ravons box set. I know our Asian fans are enthusiastic and frankly I could use the dosh.
> > Yours very kindly,
> > Charlie L.

These messages always made me laugh and—perhaps Charlie designed it this way—usually caused me to cough up a check to which he
was not entitled. To see him with a full computer setup reminded me
that the times really had a-changed.

"It's the best, Jack," he said. "I record on it, I keep a diary, I talk
to fans. You can sell music on it, you know. People leave messages on
my web site lookin' for my old records that are out of print and I just
download 'em and send 'em away."

"You're charging for this, right?"

"Well, yeah, I ain't stupid."

"Strictly speaking, Charlie, you shouldn't do that. You're bootlegging your own old LPs. The labels still own the rights."

"Let 'em try to catch me! I'm the Scarecrow of Romney Marsh up
here, Jack. I'm Robin Hood in Sherwood Forest. Rob from the rich and
give to the poor. Anyway, they're my records, it's my music, they never
paid me any royalties, and now they don't even keep 'em in release.
That's how I look at it."

"I can't argue."

Charlie grinned. "Tell you a secret, Jack. Sometimes I get a request
for an old song I don't have a copy of, so you know what I do? I sit
right down over there and make a new version and send 'em that."

"Every time, Charlie?"

"Yep. They send me two dollars and I knock off a tune. I'm buskin'
again, Jack. Just like when I was a boy. Only now I'm buskin' across
the whole world."

"You've hooked into the ley lines."

"Ain't I?"

I told Charlie I had some good news. We'd been getting offers for
a Ravons tour and Emerson was open to the idea. No one had asked
Simon, and Simon was unpredictable, but I was going to try. What
did Charlie think?

"I'd love it, man. You know that. How big a tour we talkin'
about?"

"Could be pretty big. The USA and Europe. Could go on from April
until August. You think you're in shape for that? Want to check with
your doctors?"

"Fuckin' doctors almost killed me the last time, Jack. I ain't askin' them for nothin' but some blank prescription paper. What kind of money?"

"Don't get your hopes up, man, but I think this could be over a million. Maybe two."

"Dollars or pounds?"

"Dollars."

"That what the others would get, too, Jack?"

Leave it to Charlie. Under the Hobbit manner was the mind of a street hustler.

"Well, man, you know you sold off your rights to the band name. From a business perspective, it would be structured like an Emerson tour, with him taking on all the financial risk and supplying all the crew and support. He would guarantee your salary, and Simon's. In the eyes of the world, of course, it's three total equals."

Charlie chewed this over. He clicked on his computer. A map came up. "You been on Google Earth yet, Jack? It's the best thing invented since the electric guitar." Charlie began moving around the satellite map of Europe. "Look at this—here's Norway, there's Sweden—look, I can swoop down here—now turn up this way, you're shooting right down past Finland and—look, Jack—St. Petersburg. You can see the streets. You can see the river. Did you know it was so close? Now up we go . . ." He pulled back to a continental elevation and moved his cursor across the North Atlantic. "And here we are. There's Boston, there's New York City. Follow the Hudson River and here is Woodstock." He pushed in closer until the streets of the town appeared and the roofs of the houses. "And Jack, here we are. That's the Native American shop, this is the stream right here, and this little chimney poking up is you and me."

Charlie looked away from the screen into my eyes, delighted. "It's like being an angel, Jack! I can sit here and go anywhere in the world. Nobody can see me, but I can see them."

I asked him what he wanted to do about the tour.

"Well, Jack, I'd love to play music with Emerson and Simon again. Love to travel around with you. Maybe we could even play St. Petersburg, I'd like that very much. You think that's possible?"

"Might be. I know we have offers from Scandinavia and Berlin."

"So go back, see what old Simon says, and try to figure out if Emerson might want to cut me just a little bit more of the pie."

"You know, Charlie, I'm going to get you as much as I can."

"I know you will, Jack! But old Em's been living with the richies so long he's begun to get a little silly about money. You know how to remind him where he comes from."

I was almost out the door when I realized that Charlie had not asked about Fin. "Listen," I said, "Emerson wants Baxter to be the drummer on this tour. I know you and Fin are close but—"

Charlie said, "Fin's not a real Ravon, Jack. He'll understand."

I left Charlie's house and drove to the top of a hill looking for cell phone reception. When I finally found a signal I got hold of Castro and told him Charlie was pretty much in but would want more money. Now came the tough part. Simon still hated me, and he was more than capable of screwing up this opportunity out of spite and self-righteousness. Taking the money and doing the tour might mean less to him than being able to brag to journalists that he turned it down. Castro begged me to let him approach Simon. He said they were in touch. I was happy to be off the hook. I figured if Castro blew it I could always come in and clean up.

Two days later he called me at four A.M. from England.

"Jack? You asleep? Sorry. I just left Simon. He's in!"

I rolled over and reached for the light, knocking a glass of water off the nightstand.

"He okay with the deal?" I asked.

"More or less. Nothing we can't work out. Here's the hitch."

Uh-oh.

"He wants Emerson and Charlie to come to London to meet with him and discuss it in person. This is an ego thing with him. He says the Ravons are a British band and why should he go to America to talk to them."

"Because everyone else lives in America would be one reason."

"It's not worth fighting over, Jack. We need to do this, show respect, assuage his insecurities, and then we're home free."

"All right, fine. I'll get Emerson there."

"And Charlie."

"Of course, and Charlie."

"Cool. When do you want to set it up?"

"It's four in the morning, Ramon. Call me in the office later."

"We did it, man! We did it! The Ravons are reunited!"

"Yippee." I hung up the phone and dreamed I was flying all over the planet, like an angel on Google Earth.

Six days later I was on a private jet skimming over the Atlantic with Emerson, Charlie, and Wendy, who shouted like something had bit her every time we hit an air bump.

Emerson had not resisted Simon's demand that we have the great band meeting in England. At this point in his long and well-traveled life, a Gulfstream was to Emerson just another hotel room. In fact, he would have been all right with a standard first-class ticket. It was Charlie, the simple woodsman, who said when I told him we had to go to London, "We're not flying commercial, are we, Jack?" Since the September 11 attacks, "commercial" had become for rock stars as déclassé as flying coach, although I have to admit I was surprised that Charlie was so quick to readjust his temperament to assume the entitlements of the upper one percent. This could be a long tour.

If the division of money became a problem when we got to the meeting, I had made a private resolution to toss the commissions I was entitled to for Charlie and Simon back into the pot. This would increase their take by 15 percent each. I expected that the magnanimity of that gesture would put an end to quibbles over decimals.

We landed in London and checked into the Charlotte Street Hotel. I showered and ordered eggs from room service before we reconvened in a private conference room with a fireplace. Simon showed up with a petite fortyish Asian woman whom he introduced as "Willi." Whether she was an assistant, manager, or inamorata was unclear and never explained. Simon's hair was still long but had turned completely white, which gave him the look of a wicked schoolmaster from a Victorian novel. He greeted me with overdone sweetness and extravagant good manners.

"How *are* you, Jack? *So* good to see you."

"Same here, Simon. You look very fit."

"You look *very* healthy, Jack."

Charlie had to be right: Prozac. Charlie rolled in, hair still wet from the bath, and wrapped his arms around Simon, who lifted him off the floor. Next came Castro, out of breath and sweating, carrying loads of papers and charts. Finally the prince arrived. Emerson breezed in like a tennis pro, a pale jacket and light blue shirt setting off his suntan. Wendy followed behind him, trying to flick something out of his hair.

"The boys are back in town!" Emerson said with a laugh, putting one hand on the back of Charlie's neck and the other on Simon's shoulder. He was introduced to Willi and kissed her hand. We all found seats on couches and chairs while Wendy passed around tea and bottled water and Castro locked the door.

"First," I said, "I can't tell you how pleased I am to see the three of you together like this. The Ravons changed my life. The Ravons changed a lot of lives. I don't think the band has ever been given the full credit you deserve for playing such an important role in the development of sixties rock, which of course paved the way for everything that has come after. For everyone who was there then and has dreamed of seeing it again, and most of all for all the millions of fans too young to have caught it the first time—I want to start by thanking you, Simon, Charlie, and Emerson, for entertaining the idea of coming together again."

The three Ravons nodded and smiled and the other people in the room said, "Hear! Hear!"

We got down to business. Castro laid out large sheets of paper with possible tour routings, Wendy addressed TV and film opportunities, I ran all the offers and numbers by them on a computer plugged into a PowerPoint display. I showed how much we could earn if we took everything on the table but how we might reduce our risk and preserve our health by being a bit more moderate.

We talked about who should write the tour book and whether to go with one giant touring company or a combination of smaller ones. We talked about the pros and cons of trying to hit the Far East and Australia. We talked about insurance and inoculations and tax exposures and how to protect against them. We discussed forming an offshore holding company to handle the profits from ticket sales, and a second

one to bank merchandising money. We had lunch delivered at one
o'clock and then spent an hour on whether it was better to come out
with a single-disc Greatest Hits package or a new box set, the pros and
cons of a TV campaign to sell it, and whether there was any chance
of the Ravons recording a couple of new tracks for such a collection.
After a lively debate, they decided that rather than get bogged down
trying to come up with new songs, they should add to any Best Of
package two of the performances from Live 8. When Wendy said that
if they did that, they would have to give a percentage of each CD sold
to the Live 8 Charity, they decided that maybe they could rerecord one
of their old hits instead.

By suppertime we had moved through all the top-line agenda
points. Simon and Emerson were talking set list and pulling out song
titles I had never heard, making each other laugh. Charlie was a little
distant but I attributed that to jet lag and his shaky health.

"I suppose that's it for the key points," I said. I closed my computer.
"This will be the first of many, many meetings. Anyone feel like going
out for Thai?"

"There is one more item, Jack," Simon said.

Oh God, I thought, here it comes. He's going to make some ridiculous demand that we perform one of his leaden opuses or paint the
stage black or he's going to inform us that Willi here plays melodica
and he wants her to do a solo each night. I glanced over at Castro,
who looked nervous, and Wendy, who was searching her handbag for
a cigarette.

Simon said precisely, "It's about the band's management."

It had not occurred to me that Simon might want to bring his own
manager aboard. As I was not planning to commission him, it didn't
matter to me. I just hoped it would not be someone preposterous.

Emerson said, "I'm afraid the other boys want a change for this
tour, Jack."

I did not understand what he was talking about.

"You and Emerson have made a lot, Jack," Charlie said. "This is Simon's and my last shot."

Why were the three of them talking as if they all knew something
I did not? I looked at Wendy and Castro. They were white. I realized
what was going on.

"Are you fucking firing me?" I said.

"If you want to be brutal about it," Simon told me with a slight smile, "yes."

"Can't say fired, Jack," Charlie put in. "Strictly speaking, you were never hired for this."

I looked at Emerson. He smiled in the sheepish, head-down, eyes-up manner he used when he ran into a groupie he had abandoned. He said, "It stinks, Jack, but I'm just one of three this time. I'm afraid the boys don't feel right if it's my manager in charge of a Ravons tour."

That was too ridiculous to argue with. All I could say was, "And who do you suppose will guide this wagon train without me?"

Simon could not wait to tell me. "Ramon and Wendy know what to do. They do it already."

Ah, of course. I saw it all. Et tu, Castro. Well, why not? He stole Emerson from me once before. I had been wrong about Castro and Wendy having no place up to go. There was one place.

I should have understood when Wendy came to me to conspire against Castro and Castro came to me to conspire against Wendy and I refused them both, that of course they would then come together to conspire against me. To expect otherwise was nothing but vanity, the illusion that all of them would consider me indispensable. We are all self-centered creatures. In the end the only person any of us considers indispensable is himself.

Wendy looked terrified. Castro looked at the door. I found myself working to suppress a laugh. I knew how this went. A big star gets sick of paying his manager 15 percent of what he makes. He begins to think, Why should I pay anyone a percentage of my money? There are plenty of people around who would do this for a flat salary, just for the bragging rights to be able to call themselves my manager.

And it's true. There are a lot of people like that. I was looking at two of them.

"Listen, Jack," Emerson said. "You don't want to do this anymore. You've told me that over and over. And it's such a big chance for the guys."

Charlie said, "Ramon has a lot of ideas about digital opportunities, monetizing our legacy."

"Well, then," I said, rising. "Who am I to stand in the doorway or block up the hall?"

Emerson, Castro, and Wendy glanced at each other.

"It doesn't mean you and I can't work together in the future, Jack," Emerson said.

"Oh, you bet it does, Emerson," I said. "But I'm sure your new management team has explained to you that I will continue to commission royalties and residuals from the work I have already done. That would include every recording you've made since, when was it–1971? I'm sure there will be enough left over to fairly compensate Ramon and Wendy."

I could tell by his expression that Emerson had assumed that when he fired me, he was done paying me. Castro and Wendy had failed to correct that mistake. It would cost them all.

Charlie tried to lighten the mood by suggesting we all go out and get that Thai food. "Emerson, you're paying!"

I said I'd take a rain check and went straight to the front desk and told the clerk that I was checking out, to prepare my bill and call me a car while I went to get my luggage. Emerson, Charlie, and Simon did not come out of the conference room.

Those three people came into my life together and they were going out the same way. That was fair. Let them go. They deserved all the misery they would visit on each other until Mr. LaSalle knocked on the dressing room door and presented his bill for services rendered.

The human ego is a construct of extreme elasticity. No matter how it is twisted out of shape or for how long, it will snap right back in no time. When the Ravons launched their reunion tour, Charlie and Simon were blessed with what—each in his different way—they had longed for for more than thirty years. Over those decades they had been humbled, obscured, and reduced in all their circumstances. They had scrambled for low-paying gigs, struggled at times to pay their bills, and labored along the cluttered rain gutters of the tower of song. The whole time, thirty-five years, longer than the entire lives of some acclaimed musicians, they had been haunted by the great What If. They watched as their prodigal brother Emerson gathered the fame and wealth they could only covet. They lived for years, sometimes, on the royalty scraps of old Ravons records sold by his illuminated name on the cover. And at night they dreamed of what their lives might have been if the band had stayed together, if they had shared a ration of his success.

From the dissolution of the Ravons in 1970 until their unexpected resurrection three and half decades later, Simon and Charlie lived with the vision of an alternative world in which they shared the fruits of Emerson's glory. I knew both of them well enough to understand that when their hardships had been worst, the imagined life on the other side of the mirror looked more real to them than the lives to which they were bound.

How long do you suppose it took them to forget all that when the Ravons reunited? For Simon, about as long as it took to arrive at rehearsals and start complaining about the size of his hotel room. Charlie—having a better heart and the greater capacity for irony—held out all the way until the end of the first gig.

By the time the Ravons Reunited Tour moved from a Toronto rehearsal open to VIPs and radio contest winners to the first paid preview show in Hartford to the official press opening and after-party in Boston, Charlie and Simon had shed the humbling lessons of their years in the minor league and were making up for lost time with all the greed and self-aggrandizement of nineteenth-century Belgians being carried through the Congo on mounted chairs.

Simon hated the way he looked on the monitors above the stage and slathered on makeup until he resembled the Mummy. He fired three cameramen for making him look bad. The last of these retaliated by initiating a crew-wide ritual of peeing into the canister of throat spray with which Simon spritzed his mouth throughout each concert.

Charlie berated the monitor mixer for what he insisted was persistent feedback. They could not convince him that what he was hearing was the echo of the PA bouncing off the back of the arena walls. That was inevitable and unfixable, but Charlie had never played arenas in the modern age and refused to believe it was not something the engineers were screwing up.

Simon took to demanding four suites in each hotel. Upon check-in he would be escorted from one to the other before waving a hand and selecting the least offensive.

Charlie became picky about the private jet that carried the band from city to city. He would march up to the cockpit and insult the pilot's flying skills if his ears popped.

I was not there. I heard the stories from everyone working on the tour. Many of those involved in the enterprise, from riggers to caterers, professed to miss my hand on the wheel and checked in to let me know it wasn't the same without me. Among those sentimentalists, some were sincere, some enjoyed the opportunity to spread ugly rumors about their bosses, and some nursed grudges against me and called under the guise of regret to gloat. Whatever degree of loyalty to me they professed, none had passed up the paycheck.

Charlie himself checked in with me from time to time to assure me that I was missed. He knew I could never begrudge him a long-overdue payday, although he never suggested it might result in his repaying any of the loans I had made to him through the fallow years. I understood that, though. Part of Charlie saw the millions I made from Emerson over the decades as payment enough. Part of me agreed with him.

Even Emerson checked in with the occasional e-mail. Or I should say, Emerson occasionally dictated an e-mail to his assistant, who typed it and sent it to me under the subject line "From E to JF." The messages were along these lines:

"Great version of Mary v. Mary in Delaware. Thought of you. Come out soon. Love—E."

Or:

"Four encores in St. Louie! If there'd been a German shepherd in the hall someone would have shot him. When this is over I'm buying you dinner and telling you ALL the stories."

I did not reply to these. They did not demand it. They were tidbits tossed off like guitar picks chucked into a sea of outstretched hands.

But as the tour rolled on I read between the lines a repressed frustration, an implication that in my absence Emerson had at last begun to comprehend what I had provided him.

"Another sold-out stop on the Egos Unlimited Express. Room service bills would pay off African debt. Next time—Holiday Inns for all."

"Moira the wardrobe girl broke down in tears when I asked her to let out my waistband. Promised to do sit-ups but then got the real story. Our Open-Minded Friend has been abusing her verbally. Miss your pastoral wisdom."

"Where are you, Flynn? Painting the Pope's ceiling? Come out to LA and SF as my guest. It's lonely in the middle!"

This last one was signed:

"Your old friend, Emerson."

He was like an astronaut who realized too late that he had lost his radiation shields.

Simon was lording it over everyone. He berated the roadies, mocked the local arena staffs, insulted the promoters, and in every interview unleashed his contempt for the giant conglomerate that owned the tour. He made sure the record showed that he resented the corruption of the music, which at its best was ennobling and liberating, by the tawdry sale of T-shirts, posters, and trinkets. To read his press you would have thought that Simon spent each evening's intermission with a wooden staff in his hand, driving pigeon-sellers from his sanctuary.

The true object of his resentment was anyone who got a bigger cut of the merchandising than he did.

Simon's ingratitude toward the touring company that was under-writing the opportunity for his indignity caused headaches for Castro and Wendy. As the new management team, they were the daily inter-face between the band and their angry sponsors. I was not so generous as to not enjoy that.

Charlie's sins were less public. After each show he would return to his suite with an entourage of mostly female admirers and instruct the hotel kitchen to send up every item on the room service menu, from which he would pick and sample and leave most of it moldering. As a cancer patient in remission he was supposed to be following strict rules about rest and diet, but he ignored them all, except when he needed an excuse to skip out of a band meeting or rehearsal.

His illness was also an excuse for Charlie to give Simon his proxy vote to lay down certain mandates he did not want to take the blame for:

No one in the crew could begin to eat dinner until Charlie, Simon, or Emerson had either served themselves from the backstage buffet or raised their hands to grant the others permission to go ahead.

The onstage support musicians were to dress in matching black slacks and shirts, have no spotlights, and make no extravagant ges-tures, facial expressions, or poses onstage that might pull focus from the principals.

All roadies who worked on the stage during the concert were to shave, shower, and deodorize between sound check and showtime.

My favorite story was that under Castro's innovative tutelage the band had discovered a new revenue stream. For two thousand dollars a head, a select group of high-rolling fans were allowed to come in and watch sound check each night and have their photos taken with the Ravons. For ten thousand dollars, you got to get up and sing one of their hits with them. I laughed out loud at the description of Simon trying to maintain his dignity while the sexy third wife of another man with too much money shimmied up to the microphone to sing "Mary vs. Mary" or even, as I'm told happened for one lucky bar mitzvah boy in Ohio, "Open-Minded Friend."

While the great reunion tour rolled on without me, I checked into

an experimental alcohol treatment program in Montana that promised to train the problem drinker to moderate his intake by keeping
strict count of fluid ounces on a scale of proofs and percentages. The
complexity of the measurement system was navigated by an enam-
eled wallet-sized card that enumerated the allowable doses of wines
and spirits that a participant could imbibe in any week. The program
promised to facilitate conservative social drinking while setting up a
system of alarms and tripwires along the border of overindulgence. A
drunkard's dream!

The logic—irresistible to any alcoholic—was that dieters were not
asked to give up food altogether, only to limit their intake of bad calo-
ries. So drinkers should be able to enjoy drink in moderation, as long
as they adhered to a strict discipline of self-limitation. It all sounded
great and I gladly laid down ten grand for a two-week course. I went
through the system without a hitch, graduated with A-plus grades,
imbibed to exactly my limit for nearly ten full days afterward, and was
putting away a fifth an evening again in no time.

I had been through so many treatments over the years that I did not
see it as a failure. I considered that I had successfully given my liver a
four-week trial separation from its abusive lover King Alcohol, after
which they enjoyed a touching reconciliation. Perhaps next year we'd
do it again.

Although I was curious to see the revived Ravons, I did not want to see Castro and Wendy and I did not particularly want the band to know I was coming. Call it pride, caution, or cowardice, I wanted to sniff the air before going back into the monster's cave. There was no one on the crew I trusted to sneak me in without blowing my cover, so I resolved to do something I had not done in years: buy my own concert ticket.

I called the ticket agency with my credit card in front of me and a pen in my hand and negotiated the purchase of one ticket for the Ravons concert in San Diego. A decent seat halfway back on the side cost me $347 plus trumped-up facility fees, state and local taxes, delivery costs, and an added stipend to assuage the burden of their actually sending me a ticket, rather than just transmitting an e-mail receipt for me to print myself and scan at the turnstile. It was a penalty for making them do any work at all.

Having labored the other side of the counter for so many years, I knew that most of these charges were arbitrary and some were fake. Everyone in the industry admired the enterprising Canadian promoter who had for years deducted from the payments of every band who played Toronto a "city performance tax." This went on until some zealous tour accountant made a couple of phone calls and discovered that Toronto had no such tax. The promoter had made it up and pocketed tens of thousands of dollars along the way. Such was the nature of our business that after the promoter had paid his debt to society, the biggest stars, the very acts from whom he had embezzled the most, vied for his services. Anyone that savvy was someone they wanted on their team.

I actually put my hand in my own pocket and shelled out nearly four hundred bucks for a single concert ticket thinking, Bloody hell! Who would pay this kind of money to hear the Ravons? It works out to twenty-five dollars a song!

I arrived at the San Diego Sports Arena (I refused to call any of these halls by their transient corporate names—the Schick Pavilion, the Izod Center, the Slim-Fast Stadium, the Listerine Bowl) with the punters, parked in the public parking lot—another rip-off—and allowed myself to be frisked and electronically billy-clubbed on the way to have my ticket read and walk up two broken escalators with a herd of white-haired men and the potbellied women who loved them on the long march to my so-so seat. From my position at three o'clock in the oblong arena I looked out across a sea of balding heads that called to mind a cathedral filled with tonsured monks.

The house PA played a loop of songs selected to provide a context in which anticipation of the Ravons would be amped up, while not setting a standard they could not meet. We were not going to hear "Gimme Shelter" or "Baba O'Riley"—nothing actually magnificent. Rather, "Strange Brew" by Cream, "Something in the Air" by Thunderclap Newman, "She's Not There" by the Zombies, "Itchycoo Park" by Small Faces, and "Gimme Some Lovin'" by the Spencer Davis Group filled the hall with the implication that we were all on a spaceship back to sixties London and time to strap in for touchdown.

At eight-thirty the house lights dimmed. The slow, macho chug of Muddy Waters's "Mannish Boy" announced that something historic was swaggering forth. The middle-aged audience rose to their feet cheering as a wall of flashbulbs exploded and the silhouettes of the Ravons, ageless as long as we could not really see them, blasted into "Voodoo Doll."

I confess, I was thrilled. At least for a minute or two. I forgot what I knew of the hidden strings and secret levers and joined in the collective adrenaline rush as all of us in the auditorium conspired to pretend that the Ravons were eternally young and so we must be, too. It was a lovely self-hypnosis while it lasted. When it faded I looked around the hall and saw an army of men in their fifties on their feet and determined to believe that they were witnessing a musical miracle of age resisted and time suspended. Then I looked at the stage and saw my old friends and shipmates. Emerson was as always perfectly groomed and professional, immaculate. Charlie by his side sang his heart out on harmony and looked full of joy. Simon was self-absorbed and majestic in the haughty manner of a French nobleman being trundled toward the guillotine.

In the shadows behind them were a whole orchestra of backup musicians: two keyboard players, two female singers, a bonus guitarist, and Baxter Selwyn behind what looked like a corral of drums circling him to repel invaders. Alongside Baxter a second percussionist peered out from the spaces between congas, bongos, steel drums, a bell tree, and what looked like a hat rack hung with pots and pans.

Emerson began to thank the roaring crowd for its welcome but Simon stepped forward to cut him off.

"We are the Ravons from London, England!" Simon announced. "Are you with us?"

The hall reverberated with bellows of support. Emerson took a step back from his microphone. Simon said, "This song is about California!" and began playing "Karma Suit Ya" while Emerson and Charlie exchanged surprised glances and then fell in behind him.

As the show continued and everyone got used to being there, large chunks of the audience sat down. The floor sections immediately in front of the stage remained standing until an extended blues jam broke out about sixty minutes in, at which point all but the most enthusiastic took a load off their feet and checked their BlackBerrys. By that point Simon was overplaying with a ferocity rarely witnessed since the seventies heyday of progressive rock. In his perspiring intensity, he appeared to begin to decompose. It looked on the video screens like pieces were falling off him. Simon was sliding and shimmying as he played, as if he had a snake for a spine. Sweat poured down his brow, causing his makeup to run and his hair to flatten against his skull. The flesh of his face seemed to be dropping away to reveal a serpent head.

My eyes moved to Charlie, who had started the concert in a flush of energy and apparent good health, but who was now slumping. His two lead vocals had been positioned early in the show, when he still had most of his voice and vigor. By the one-hour mark the lights on him had been brought down by half. He was barely strumming his guitar, and his harmonies had been taken over by the guitarist in the shadows at the back.

Sometimes we put off knowing what we don't want to know. This was the first time I recognized that Charlie was going to die, and it would be pretty soon.

After ninety minutes the Ravons finished with a one-two-three blast of short and beloved classics that returned the room to its feet. They then stood with their sweaty arms around each other to acknowledge the ovation and take their bows. Charlie was beaming, although it seemed to me that Emerson and Simon were supporting him between them as they waved to the crowd.

While the Ravons made their exit, my eyes followed the cheering audience across the arena and up into the rafters. The room was lit by five thousand tiny white eyes. The crowd was holding up mobile phones, taking photos and movies of the Ravons. I thought back to the sixties, when the fans used to raise their hands in peace signs and sometimes clenched fists of solidarity with the musicians onstage. In the seventies they held up candles and lighters, making each concert hall a galaxy of little stars. In the eighties those lights went out and for a while crowds demonstrated their enthusiasm by doing the Wave, an orbiting demonstration of coordinated goonishness more suitable to a sports event than a musical performance and indicative of the spirit of that silly decade. In the nineties younger bands had mosh pits and stage diving, but for us seniors there was only cheap irony—devil horns made by holding up fists with the index finger and pinky extended, and a "We are not worthy" bowing gesture borrowed from the Wayne's World movies. The new century had introduced new rituals of tribute to the altar of music and technology, new gestures of supplication to the dying god of rock from his aging worshippers. Now the rooms where the Ravons performed were illuminated by thousands of tiny camera lights to make the musicians immortal or, depending on your theology, steal their souls.

Charlie bounced back for the encores revived. I hoped he was not using cocaine to get there but I would not put it past him. When the show was over I was happy for him that he was enjoying a return to the spotlight before the inevitable imposed itself. When the last song had ended the lights came up. I saw twenty people I knew shutting down the soundboard and starting the long night's work of dismantling the stage. I considered going back to say hello to the band. I had come this far.

Then I saw Castro in the wings, pointing to some problem with an overhead lamp and hectoring a technician, and I thought, I don't want to have to be nice to Castro tonight. Then I thought, I don't actually want to have to be nice to any of them tonight. And then I thought, I don't have to.

I walked out with the crowd and collected my automobile and went home. I flipped around my satellite radio looking for something to raise my mood. I landed on a young British band doing a cover of a Stones song: "I'm free to do what I want any old time." It was almost what I was looking for.

The trade papers said that the Ravons earned seventy million dol-
lars from their reunion tour. Whatever the real figure was, it was a
lot more than Emerson could earn on his own. Castro and Wendy,
the new management team, made a mistake I would not have made
and immediately announced that the Ravons would be back again the
next spring. They should have let it rest a year or two but they were
insecure and anxious to grab the big offers while the promoters were
still heated up. It was no problem booking the tour, but it turned out
to be tougher than they expected to sell all the tickets. Those who
cared most about the Ravons had just seen them, in what they had
been told was a once-in-a-lifetime opportunity. To be immediately
informed that in fact it was twice, three, or four times in a lifetime
caused resentment among Emerson's core fans and indifference in
the larger rock community. The press and radio who had covered
the novelty of the Ravons' first lap around the track had no interest
in the second. The shows did okay, but in many markets the upper
tiers were empty and Castro was forced to renegotiate with the disappointed promoters, taking less than he had been promised.

Charlie was not part of the second tour. His cancer had come back,
making it impossible for him to travel and perform. Different members
of the inner circle had different impressions of whether he agreed and
wanted out or was pushed against his will. I later learned that he tried
to negotiate a piece of the tour for himself, but Castro reminded him
that he had no legal partnership in the Ravons' corporation or rights to
the name. He was given a six-figure payout and the consolation prize
of a block of twenty tickets to every show that he could use, give away,
or scalp.

Castro and Wendy recognized that Emerson had needed Charlie for the first tour, to sell the press and old fans on this being a true reunion. Having established that, and with the press having gone away, "The Ravons" was now a lucrative brand name that Emerson could occupy with any musicians he wanted. Simon had been smart enough to hold on to his minority stake—his paranoia had paid off in that regard—but I thought that he had still better watch his back.

Emerson actually telephoned me himself to invite me to the final show of the second tour, a multi-act charity performance at London's O2 Arena. I told him I would not be able to get to England that week but it was very kind of him to call. I knew that for Emerson to pick up the phone and dial a number with his own finger, to put himself out that way, was the equivalent of a normal person giving five pints of blood. He said he was going to be in New York at Christmas and he would very much like to have dinner with me. I said of course and we set a date.

When that day came the city was trampled in tourists, partygoers, and Christmas shoppers. I suggested he come by my apartment and we order in. He showed up five minutes early, alone, with a wrapped gift for me. It was a large framed photograph taken at the Alibi Club in 1968. I was sitting at a table covered in empty bottles and half-filled glasses along with Charlie, Fin, Emerson, Tug, and Simon. We all looked half gassed and silly. Charlie was pulling a face. There were some pretty girls sitting with us, too, none of whom I could now remember.

"What a crew!" I said. "Where did you find this, Emerson?"

"Cat named Bobby Groot, do you remember him? Used to hang around with Ilsa the She Wolf? He's got a gallery now. Brought it down to the O2 show. Look over here."

Emerson pointed to half-focused figures at the table behind us, in the corner of the frame.

"Bloody hell—is that George Harrison?"

"And Brian Jones."

"Bet Bobby Groot wishes he'd shot them instead of us!"

I did not have a present for Emerson. I escorted him into the living room and gave him a seat and a glass of wine while I went back to a closet in the guest room and looked for a Christmas gift I could repurpose. A label boss had sent me an impressive bottle of Texas mescal, complete with drowned worm in the bottom. I grabbed a blank Christmas card, scribbled on it, *To Emerson—Here's the Xmas Spirit!–Jack,* taped it to the bottle, and went back into the front room and handed it to him. He laughed and thanked me and we made small talk while my housekeeper laid out a proper English dinner of ham, roast parsnips, and Christmas pudding flamed with brandy.

"Get a load of this, Jack!" Emerson said when we sat down to eat. "You'd think you were a Brit!"

"Couldn't find any spotted dick with custard, though," I told him. "But I believe there is a dusty old bottle of Tia Maria under the sink."

"I don't have any desire to go that far back."

I thanked the housekeeper and told her she could leave, while Emerson tucked in.

"Have you spoken to Charlie?" he wanted to know.

"E-mails mostly," I said. "You know he's back in Camden. Paid off his flat with some of the tour money. He's going in for all these experimental, alternative, holistic treatments. I just hope he isn't getting suckered by quacks."

"Bloody fucking e-mail," Emerson said. "I hate all that crap."

"Cheaper than phone calls," I said. "You've fallen out of love with the computer age?"

Now real emotion came into my old friend's face. "It's awful, Jack. They've got little cameras in their phones and they sneak pictures of you at the beach or the gym and post them for the world to see. Any stupid or embarrassing thing you said in some drunken interview thirty years ago is right there for your child to read. And on top of that, anyone can make up anything they want. It doesn't have to be true, there's no editorial control. These Web sites, these horrible blogs. They don't talk about the music, they just go on about 'Emerson can't sing anymore,' 'Looks like he had a hair transplant,' 'I saw them in Altoona and he was out of key the whole night.' They bitch about the ticket prices. Don't come! There's this one prick always talks about my having a fat arse. I run six miles a day and have a thirty-one-inch waist! And you can't do anything about it! These lies stay up forever and anyone, I mean any real fan or some young kid just getting interested in music, anyone who Googles 'Emerson Cutler' or 'Ravons' is subjected to all this . . . this swill."

Emerson's eyes were red. The Internet was murdering him. Access to the unfiltered thoughts of his audience was ruining the self-image he had spent a lifetime cultivating. All this time Emerson thought he had them fooled. All this time, he thought they loved him. When an audience loses its illusions about a performer, it is a shame. When a performer loses his illusions about the audience, it is a tragedy.

"Look at me, Jack." Emerson stood up from the table and patted his belly. "How many men my age look like I do?"

"One in a million," I told him.

He sat down. "Fucking right."

Emerson was a very good-looking, very well preserved man soon to be sixty-five years old. He had most of his hair and a superb dye job. His face was lined lightly, his skin was good, his teeth were better than mine had been when I was twenty-five. He dressed beautifully. His face was fuller now around the jaw and the flesh above his eyes drooped. The smile lines around his mouth had begun to look jowly, but anyone seeing him for the first time would think him handsome. The problem was that no one was ever seeing him for the first time. Almost everyone he met was familiar with photos of him from the seventies or videos from the eighties, and by that measure he could not stack up. Good-looking as he was, he was worse-looking than he used to be. Emerson was stuck in a competition with his younger self that he could never win.

He regained his composure. "Anyway, the hell with all that nonsense. Listen, Jack, I need your advice."

Here Emerson reached for the bottle of Texas mescal I had given him. With a nod at me he broke the seal, unscrewed the top, and poured us each a glass with ceremonial gravity. He handed one to me and lifted the other in a toast. I nodded and took a sip. It made a fiery contrast to the British dinner we had just digested.

Emerson swallowed, shook his head, and smiled. Then he explained, "Castro wants to license two of the Ravons' songs to *Rock Band.* Have you heard about this? It's a computer game. Apparently every thirteen-year-old boy in America has one. They sit with a plastic guitar and learn to play along with classic songs. There's a pretty decent fee, and a royalty attached, but here's the big thing. These young kids are going out and buying CDs by the artists they learn about on

the game. All of a sudden Lynyrd Skynyrd and Black Sabbath are selling like mad to junior high school kids, because of this game. What
do you think? It sounded naff to me at first, but radio doesn't play me
anymore and Castro is sure this is a pathway to a whole new audience."

"Well," I told him, "Castro's usually on top of these things. All I'd
hold out for is, does it have to be two Ravons songs? How about one
Ravons and one more recent Emerson solo number? What about
'Ragged Religion,' that has a good riff, nice soloing. Don't let them lock
you in the sixties."

Emerson took an envelope from his pocket and began writing
down what I'd said. He must really be getting old, I thought, to not be
sure he could remember that.

He put away his pen. "See, Jack, that's why I need to be able to talk
to you. Castro is good at bringing in offers, he's a good road manager
and all, but I need someone who sees the bigger picture. You know
I always wanted you to be with us for the Ravons tour. I was furious
with the others for not wanting to pay you what you deserved, but
they had me two to one and—you know—they were greedy fuckers. But
that's over now. We did the Ravons to death, Simon can go invade
Ukraine, for all I care, I never want to see that twat again. What do
you think of you and me picking up where we left off?"

It was nice to hear anyway. A year earlier I might even have considered it. But now I had gotten used to living without working and it did
not bother me a bit. I had plenty of money, my real friends still liked
me, and the frauds were out of my life.

"Kind of you to ask, Em," I said. "But I've come to realize that you
did me a favor. I'm too old to do this anymore." This was a bit of a dig—
Emerson was the same age.

He didn't know what to say. He took a long swig of whiskey. He let
it settle in before he spoke.

"All right, Jack, I get it. You got fucked over and we both know it.
I'm as sorry as I can be. It was a mistake, all right? It was my mistake
and I regret it."

"Thank you for saying that, Emerson, but it's okay. I don't need an
apology. We had a great run. It's a long way from Difford, Withers &
Flack to this elegant loft in Manhattan and servants laying out dinner

for us. I have nothing but good feelings about you and our journey together. But that journey is complete." I raised my glass to him and emptied it.

"Okay," he said, "I know what this is about. It's about Agatha. Jack, you have no idea how awful I feel about that. I have no excuse. All I can tell you is, it was a frightening time, we were in a state of shock, the country was under attack, we didn't know if we were going to live another day, and we were stoned. If I could go back in time and make it not happen, I would. But I can't. I can only tell you that I hate myself for doing that to you and I am truly, truly sorry."

He put away some more mescal and I matched him. If this was going to be my final conversation with Emerson, we might as well go all out.

"Emerson," I said, "Agatha has nothing to do with it. I don't want to work for you anymore. I don't need the money, I don't need the aggravation, the music business is dying, and so are we. Enough! Why go on if going on means dropping from congestive heart failure in some hotel in Las Vegas after the second show? I don't need any more. The only thing I value now is time, and time is in short supply."

Emerson's expression registered anger, then incomprehension, and then settled into a sadness that made him look all of his years.

"But what will happen to me?"

"Emerson, you're very rich. You can do whatever you want to do, including keep playing music. Only one person out of every million has what you have. Can't that be enough?"

"I'm an artist, Jack. You never understood what that really means." And here he said what he always said when he ran out of other excuses: "I am in pain every day of my life."

I finally got to say, "Emerson, welcome to the human race."

We broke up then. We made vague plans to go see Charlie together in the new year. I walked him to the door and we hugged and I went back and sat at the dining room table with the dirty dishes and the empty mescal bottle, which I contemplated with the melancholy profundity only a drunk can summon.

Emerson's sort of fame intoxicates the star just like a bottle of mescal. It fills him with confidence in his own power, it makes him glib and cocky, it loosens his tongue and his libido. Give him half an audience and he will climb up on a table and declaim.

But there is a worm in the bottom of that bottle. And the more you drink the mescal of fame, the deeper that worm burrows into you. The worm crawls up your spine and settles at the base of your skull and whispers, *Watch it there, pal. Don't slip up. All those people are looking at you—they're going to find you out. You copied that lyric from an old poetry book, they're going to find out. You lifted that lick from a Hawaiian record, they're going to find out. You can't even tune your guitar, you're not as smart as they think you are, you shouldn't be a famous star. They're going to all find out.*

The bigger you get, the more of that mescal you drink, the louder the worm in your skull starts to sound. So you begin hiding from people, trying to protect yourself from being exposed. You buy a big house and you lock the door, but they're still all over you—so you build a fence but they still get in. You start to panic. You seal yourself off from your fans, those parasites. You seal yourself off from your friends, those freeloaders. Your wife—she just married you for your money. Your kids—can't let them find out you're a fake.

You start bricking up the room around you to save yourself, to protect your privacy, to keep everyone from finding out who you really are. The more success you get, the higher and closer you build that wall around you. Until no light can come in. And no music can get out. And it's just you in there. With the worm.

When I was living in California in the early seventies I read a Kurt Vonnegut book about a man who goes mad because he reads a science fiction story that tells him that the reason his life is unhappy is because everyone in the world is a robot, except for twenty real people whom the robots endlessly maneuver into bumping into each other. This idea made more sense to me the older I got. People I had crossed paths with in my youth came around again and again, often in new jobs, sometimes in new countries, almost always with new wives. I began to feel that we were a shrinking company of real humans on a planet of androids.

Kurt Vonnegut died a few months before Charlie Lydle. So did Ingmar Bergman, Norman Mailer, Marlon Brando, Robert Altman, and James Brown—a whole faculty of cultural luminaries who influenced my generation and me. The Hound of Heaven had our scent. It seemed as if once a week I got word that another friend had been diagnosed with cancer or suffered a heart attack. The dogs were getting close.

Ungrateful underlings had forced the original head of Tropic Records into retirement at the turn of the millennium. Wild Bill had retreated to a house on a hilltop in Jamaica. Now he was dying of colon cancer and had returned to New York for treatment. With nostalgia and hypocrisy, the same people who had pushed him out were honoring him with tribute dinners and induction into the Rock and Roll Hall of Fame. He accepted the accolades with good manners and laughed all the way to the undertaker.

I was surprised to see him leaning on a cane and looking frail at a secret dinner meeting called by his old subordinate Hal Allyn, the Ravons' first American A&R man and the producer of Emerson's first solo album.

"How are you, Bill?" I asked him, taking a seat beside him in the back of the room.

"I'm dying, Jack, how 'bout you?"

"Since the day I was born, Bill," I told him. "Since the day I was born."

"You want to buy a house in Jamaica cheap?"

"You'll need it for your convalescence."

"Not as much as I need to sell it so I'll have some dough to leave my kids. You been there, right? Take it off my hands."

I said I'd think about it.

Hal Allyn was not much changed from the ambitious hustler I had met forty years before. He was still chunky, still wore black-frame eyeglasses. He no longer laughed all the time. As far as I could tell he no longer laughed at all.

Over the decades Allyn had become CEO of what was now the largest record company in the world. The collapse of the recorded music business prompted dozens of labels to fold into four, and three of those were run by whoever was left in the office after the hustlers and sharks had sailed off into the sunset on their golden parachutes.

Hal Allyn was the exception. He was still hungry. He had gathered a dozen labels under his corporate umbrella and now cast his eye on his last remaining rivals. He intended to have them all in the end. Seeing Hal and his peers in one room made me think of Fred Zaras's theory of the warring tribes of cannibal amoebas.

Where other record chiefs saw doom, Allyn saw opportunity. In this he was a bit like the outgoing Republican administration, who had turned the fear that washed through America after 9/11 into a tide on which to sail their legislative agenda.

My entrée to this gathering of old moguls was Allyn's right-hand man, Danny Finnerty—his president of new media. The heads of two of the three other majors were gathered with us upstairs in a second-floor parlor at Allyn's beach house in Southampton. We had all agreed to keep the meeting strictly private, as this was the sort of get-together that made the careers of trust-busting attorneys general and online conspiracy theorists.

Although I was not in the same income bracket as these titans,

Fin had assured me that I was revered as a wise elder. So was my old friend Bill with the cane and the colostomy bag.

Allyn started the evening by welcoming everyone, thanking them for coming all the way out to the beach, and reiterating that this get-together was strictly hush-hush and off the record.

Then he handed the floor to Fin, who gave a glowing and optimistic assessment of how many digital downloads his label was selling, what a surprisingly large percent of this year's profits would come from sales of single songs through the Internet, and how anyone who thought the record business was finished was going to look pretty foolish in a few years.

I leaned over to Bill and whispered, "Do you think it's true?"

Bill struggled to his feet and said to me quietly, "Take a walk with me out on the piazza." I followed him onto a raised porch with a view of the ocean. He took out a cigarette and lit in.

"I can smoke all I want now," he said. "Lung cancer would be an improvement. So, you want to buy my house?"

"You think Fin's full of shit about digital sales?"

"Of course he is. Even when they talk about digital profits, it's not really downloads. They lump in all the money they make from granting digital licenses to Yahoo, Pandora, Rhapsody, video games. They put all that in the pot to create the illusion that kids are paying millions to download songs instead of taking them for free. It's all nonsense anyway. Unlike my beautiful home in Jamaica, which is a once-in-a-lifetime bargain."

"You don't believe selling songs for a dollar over the Internet can catch on? No overhead. No trucks, no pressing. I'll bet they still take a packaging deduction even though there's no package. Could work."

"Listen, Flynn," the old man said. "I started in this business in 1946. Working in a record store called Maynard's Music in a black neighborhood in Miami. This was in the days of 78s, one song on each side of a big fat platter. We sold jazz, jump blues, R&B to a discriminating clientele.

"One day Maynard comes to me and says, 'Great news! That song everybody wants, "Moppin' the Shop."' This was a record out of a little label in Kansas City that had blown up on radio. The label couldn't press 'em fast enough to meet demand. Maynard says, 'This is wonderful! Saturday we're gettin' two hundred copies. Put a sign in the window!'

"I said, 'Maynard, what are you so happy about? You pay a hundred bucks to get these records, you sell them for a dollar each, even if you sell all two hundred in one day, you only make a hundred dollars. That's your biggest day of the year? That's no business.'

"He says, 'Okay, smart guy, what do you suggest? Raising the price? My customers will just go over to Sears, where records are forty-nine cents.'

"I said, 'No, Maynard. Here's what you do. You got a basement full of shit, old records you can't return, right? You got a closet full of albums gathering dust.' You remember those old albums, like photo albums that held seven 78s each. People would buy symphonies in little pieces that way, or a collection of 'Italian Love Songs.'"

I told him I remembered. That's why we still call collections of music "albums."

Wild Bill went on. "I told Maynard to let me take all the old shit records in the basement and put them in all the empty albums in the closet. We leave one slot for 'Moppin' the Shop.' Then I'll make a sign that says, *Available Saturday, Seven Hits for Seven Dollars. Includes 'Moppin' the Shop'!* That's what I did. Saturday morning there was a line down the block. We opened the door and sold all two hundred copies of 'Moppin' the Shop' before noon. But instead of making two hundred times one dollar, Maynard made two hundred times seven dollars. Get it?"

I said I got it. Bill said, "Everything we ever did, the LP, the cassette, the eight-track, the CD, was all based on that simple principle. Trick the rubes into paying for twelve songs to get the one they want."

Bill pointed through the open door at Fin, still holding forth inside on the splendor of digital downloads. He leaned on me and said in my ear, "One dollar a song was a shit idea for a business in 1946 and it's a shit idea for a business now."

We made our way back into the room, where Danny had finished and Hal Allyn was getting down to the real nitty-gritty.

"Friends," Hal said. "I want to present to you now the salvation and future of the music business." He reached dramatically behind the bar and pulled out what looked like a small car radio.

"This is . . . the Black Box."

Some of the people in the room seemed to know what he was talking about. I did not.

He explained, "This only works if we all go in together. Now think of this. How much would a consumer pay for one device"—he pointed to the prototype, the Black Box—"that you buy and it gives you permanent unlimited access to every song ever recorded on every major record label for the last one hundred years?"

He let the audacity of the offer sink in.

"Do you think people would pay a thousand dollars for that? Ten thousand? How much did you pay for your new flat-screen TV system? Now, suppose the Black Box were priced at two hundred dollars. How many of them do you think we'd sell? Remember, once you buy it you never have to pay for music again. Everything from Beethoven to the Beatles is yours for free forever. At two hundred dollars, might people not buy one for the living room, one for the bedroom, one for each car? I think they would. At two hundred a pop, I believe that in three years we could sell one hundred million Black Boxes in the United States alone. And then we go global."

A fellow from one of the other majors raised his hand. He said, "But once someone has the Black Box, why would he ever buy another CD?"

Allyn smiled. He said, "I don't fucking care! Do the math. A hundred million people times two hundred dollars gives us twenty billion dollars in new revenue in two years! Divide that four ways and put it against your fiscal projections. Huh? This is the fire sale, this is 'Everything must go.' People will still buy new music through digital downloads, they can even store them in the Black Box to keep it up to date, but this monetizes our entire back catalog in one fell swoop. And, of course, we will come out with new models every couple of years. Eventually we'll load in movies, TV shows, we'll have a blue Black Box and a white Black Box and a pink Black Box. But guess what? That's for the next guys. For us, the Black Box is the doorway out of here."

The enormity of the opportunity before them descended upon these captains of the music industry, who silently contemplated what their own profit-sharing and bonuses would work out to with a twenty-billion-dollar windfall. Might the public not pay *three* hundred for every record ever made? Three twenty-five? These were calculations to make a grown CEO swoon.

I spoke up from the back of the room. I said, "Hal? What about the artists?"

"New-technology clause," Allyn said, "they don't get a vote."

"No, I mean, how do you propose paying the artists? How do we calculate royalties on an evacuation sale?"

Allyn acted like I had brought up the Starving Children of India at an all-you-can-eat buffet. He said, "We will do everything we can to fairly compensate the artists."

I pressed him, "But what does that mean? There are no individual units sold, no way of monitoring which songs are played. It seems to me that you're leaving the artists out of the equation."

Fin was looking at me like he would do anything if I would please shut up.

"I thought you were out of management," Allyn said.

"I am indeed. But I'm not out of ethics."

Allyn looked at Fin, who was trying to crawl under the carpet. Allyn said to me, "Well, I'm sure all of us appreciate having the ethical perspective brought to the fore. Those of us who actually have jobs sometimes lose track of our obligations to moral abstracts, especially at a time when pretty much all of our resources are being stolen from us. Thanks, Jack, for reminding us of the higher virtues."

I wandered out on the porch again while the other label bosses got into an argument about whether their pieces of the Black Box should be divided equally or according to market share.

Danny Finnerty followed me.

"Shit, Flynn, why'd you do that? I brought you in here because we thought you might be a good guy to *run* this!"

"You're joking."

"No way. To make this work, we're going to have to sell it to the managers. Hal figured that's your peer group, you know all those guys, they trust you. They all know you're a super-smart and honorable man."

"So of course I'd be the natural choice to convince them to sell out their clients' futures."

"Jack. What future?"

Hal Allyn joined us at the rail. Fin split immediately. Hal looked at me with his old smile. "You put me on the spot in there, Flynn."

"Someone had to ask it," I said.

"Indeed they did. Got it out of the way. So what do you think? Would you want to have a role in making this real?"

"I don't think so, Hal. I'm an old man, I've been working all my life. I think I might want to enjoy the time I have left."

We looked out at the sea. I said, "And I still am not sure I've forgiven you for talking Emerson into leaving the Ravons. That was a dirty trick."

He laughed. "You should say a prayer of thanks for that every day, Flynn. If I hadn't pried Emerson out of that silly group you wouldn't be rich enough to turn down my offer."

I conceded that might be true. Allyn's smile fell away. He leaned in to my face. "You know the trouble with you, Jack? You like artists, don't you? See, I don't like artists. I think artists are selfish."

"Of course you do, Hal. You resent those greedy artists demanding a tenth of the money their music generates and leaving you with a lousy ninety percent."

Hal Allyn shook hands with me and went back to his other guests. I considered whether what he'd said to me was true. After all the years and all the insults and abuses, did I still like artists after all?

No, I decided, not very much. I didn't like artists very much at all. It was only that I liked ticks like Hal Allyn even less.

I was done. The next day I met Wild Bill for lunch and we negotiated my purchase of his house in Jamaica.

"They'll never find you there, Jack," he told me.

"Bill," I said, "that's what I'm counting on."

My mother died in her sleep two months after her ninety-second birthday. I suppose you cannot ask for an easier passing or a longer life, but when my cousin Mary called to tell me I shook like a baby. My experience with grief is that we move through the sadness fast enough, but the emotional imbalance that follows the loss of a loved one can knock your compass out of whack for a year or more. It's when we think grief has passed and we're back to normal that we decide we hate our siblings, or fall in love with the housekeeper, or punch the boss, or cash in all our stocks and move to the South Seas to paint. It is when we think grief has subsided that it really turns us inside out.

I went back to the house in Kingston to clean it out and settle the estate. I offered to sign it over to my cousin but she did not want to stay. She had done her duty by her mother and mine and now she was anxious to move on. I offered to buy her a flat by the ocean in Brighton and she leaped at it.

"I found this," she told me. It was a framed and faded photograph of the two of us smiling with our mothers at the seashore when I was about twelve and she was about five.

"That was fifty years ago, Jackie," my cousin said.

I ran my hand over the glass and asked her, "How is that possible?"

I stayed in the house for nearly a month. I went through all the closets and drawers. I slept in my parents' bed. I burned old letters and records. I found scrapbooks my mother had filled with articles about me and the Ravons. I read those carefully and burned them, too.

I would call the States to talk with Ben about school and sports. It was almost my only contact with the outside world. Agatha became concerned. She said she was afraid I was fading away over there. I told her I was just an old pensioner taking my time closing up the family home. What did I have to rush back to?

I fell into the rhythms of walking into the village each morning to get breakfast and buy the paper. As I emptied out the house it seemed to get bigger and bigger until it grew from my mother's cramped quarters to a barren manor. When the place had been empty for a week I had to either go ahead and put it on the market or move in and make it my own. That made no sense. The winter rains had started. I knew I was better situated in Jamaica. But I also knew that when I left this house, I would never again have a real home. I considered that and came to a realization. If I stayed here I wouldn't, either.

When I got back to Manhattan I had a message to call a man named Bob Kasdan about the death of Fred Zaras.

My God, I thought, the saints really are marching in.

I called the number, which turned out to be a left-wing bookstore in Greenwich Village. Kasdan was the owner. He explained that Fred had been working in the store, where he spent most of his time arguing with customers and expounding on his theories. Apparently the new century had not been kind to Fred. In spite of his enjoying a season of academic notoriety in the early nineties, when his theories of the emerging megastates seemed confirmed by the collapse of apartheid and the fall of communism, Fred had of course managed to offend everyone who offered to publish him, invited him to lecture, or gave him a forum on radio or cable TV. Although he had a small cult of devotees with whom he communicated on the Internet, Fred had spent his last ten years in the employ of Joe Hill Books on Carmine Street. I got the impression from Kasdan that the job was less to do with heavy lifting or working the cash register than a sort of endowed chair from a sympathetic admirer.

"I know Fred had been close with Emerson Cutler once," Kasdan told me. "We're organizing a memorial. I wondered if you thought Mr. Cutler might wish to speak, or even send a taped message."

"When is it?" I asked. I no longer worked for Emerson but I was still going to be his bad cop.

"Tuesday night here at the bookstore."

"I will ask Emerson, but he's recording in England right now, so I think it's unlikely."

"I understand."

"I might come by, though. If that's all right."

"Oh, of course. Fred spoke of you often. That's how I knew to call you."

"Really."

"He said you were a man of intelligence and personal integrity in a sea of fools."

"Really?"

I thanked him and hung up. I was startled to find myself weeping. For some reason I could not locate, hearing that the lunatic Fred Zaras spoke kindly of me so many years after we parted on bad terms meant a great deal to me.

The following Tuesday I made my way to the bookstore on Carmine Street where Fred had spent his last years. I was afraid I would be the only one there, but there must have been forty people. Fred had found friends and even a few followers.

I had gone through the motions of calling Emerson, Charlie, and Simon. Emerson said he'd send flowers but he did not. Charlie was too ill to come to New York from England. Simon said that Fred was dead and so if he came it would only be for the sake of the other people in the room and he did not know them.

Among the speakers there was an ideological split between those who felt it was a tragedy that so brilliant an author had given up writing to work in a shop, and those who believed he had done a brave thing by putting aside an effete pursuit in favor of honest labor.

My favorite eulogy was by a college-age youth who said that at the time of his death Fred was developing his theory of the "Neuro-Electric Halo," which boiled down to a hypothesis that brains are like televisions hooked up to a variety of antennae and frequencies. Our thoughts are electrical impulses and currents flowing down neural paths. If two people in close physical proximity have the same sort of aerials, if they are tuned to the same channel, thoughts may jump back and forth between them. Fred thought that this was a scientific phenomenon that would explain ESP, déjà vu, premonitions, and perhaps even communication with the spirit world, or, as Fred had described it, "Distress signals from beacons in decay."

So many speakers mentioned Fred's early friendship with Emerson

Cutler and the Ravons that I finally felt compelled to go to the rostrum and say a few words.

"My name is Jack Flynn," I said, "and for many years I managed Emerson Cutler and other artists who were fond of Fred. I spoke to Emerson just this evening, and he asked me to please convey to all of you how much Fred meant to him, and how much he appreciated the kindness and camaraderie that he clearly found with all of you."

That was all I had wanted to say. I looked for a way to wrap up.

"Fred was very important to us early on," I said. "Emerson has said to me that Fred did something very extraordinary. He explained Emerson's music to Emerson himself. He helped him bring what had been an instinctive, perhaps subconscious talent into a place where Emerson could control it. He helped Emerson turn a random gift into a craft, a skill he could manage and access."

I had paddled out far from shore and had no idea how I was going to get back. I said, "Fred and Emerson had a falling-out, you know. I don't remember what it was about. But I think, hearing all of you speak and knowing of the interesting work Fred got into later, the truth was that Fred needed to do his own writing, he needed to explore his own passions and enthusiasms—not simply decipher another artist's work. I know that Emerson was very shocked and sad to hear of Fred's death. And . . ." I really needed a close. "Perhaps we will all meet again in the Neuro-Electric Halo."

I stayed awhile after the service, drinking punch with the other mourners. Kasdan, the man who owned the bookstore, asked me if I knew that Fred's great work, *The Rise of the Super-States,* existed only because of Emerson Cutler.

I did know that, of course. Emerson's generous settlement with Fred had given him the money to publish his manifesto. But that was not the story Fred had told his audience at Joe Hill Books. According to the legend Fred expounded, he had finished a version of the Emerson biography, which a number of publishers rejected because half of it was Fred's theories about how mankind was splitting into seven mega-nations and the old national boundaries were going to go out the window.

More than one publisher said that if Fred would lose all the crap about the shifting of the anthropological plates, they would be happy to put out the book about the rock star. Fred stormed out of many such meetings in many huffs.

Finally, according to Fred, some enterprising junior editor at a small paperback house went to the effort of taking scissors and glue and cutting Fred's opus into two halves, the Emerson half and the Global Amoeba half. He xeroxed both halves into clean copies and presented them to Fred with the notion of bringing out both books, for which Fred would be paid the magnanimous combined fee of twenty thousand dollars, exactly what they would have paid him for the Emerson book alone.

The proposed irony was that the Emerson book never cleared the publisher's legal department. According to this myth, Emerson had denied Fred the right to quote any of his lyrics and otherwise obstructed the project. Left with no way to print the Emerson book, the publisher sought to salvage something of his investment and brought out *The Rise of the Super-States*, launching Fred into the ionosphere of political theory and prophetic prognostication.

It was all nonsense, of course, but I am sure that after he told the story a few dozen times Fred came to believe it himself. That his opus got respectful reviews and earned Fred a following among a subgroup of college students and people who gathered in radical bookstores was all the validation he needed to feel his work had been a success.

I thanked Kasdan for filling me in and marveled at the strange order of the universe. "By the way," I said, "what did Fred die of?"

Kasdan said, "Malnutrition."

"My God."

"He could afford food, he just wouldn't eat anything other than cookies, candy, and soda pop. We all pestered him about it."

"Damn those Oreos," I said. "Got him at last."

I went out of the store and walked down Bleecker Street. As I stood waiting for the light to change a bird dropped a turd on the sidewalk right next to me.

I said, "That you, Fred?" Then I felt bad for saying it.

No matter how broke or low-down he was, Charlie could always find a girlfriend. In the last stages of his cancer he had been blessed to take up with a registered nurse he met during radiation treatments. She moved into his flat in Camden and she took care of him through good days and bad.

Lately we had been e-mailing almost every day. I tried to convince him to come visit me in Jamaica, but he kept putting it off until he finished his next round of treatments. He sometimes sounded frail, sometimes alert and funny. I knew how ill Charlie was, but I was still shocked when, after I hadn't heard from him for two weeks, his girlfriend phoned and told me, "He's almost out of time, Mr. Flynn. He's been asking for you. If you did intend to try and see him again, it has to be soon."

I booked a flight to London.

I had not flown on the new Virgin Upper Class and would not have done it then if it was not the best they had available. It was an overnight flight and I was prepared to suffer through it in discomfort, but to my surprise that section of the plane looked like something from a Kubrick film.

The seats were arranged like an open zipper, each turned to two o'clock and divided by a high wall from the seat next to it. We were all hidden in our own little pods.

Once I settled in, a TV screen swung out on an arm and offered me a choice of dozens of films and television programs. When I was ready to sleep, the seat reclined all the way back to a flat bed. I thought of how far air travel had come since I sat smoking and sweating on that propeller transport to Spain in 1967. I sorted through the music options and selected the Blue Danube.

When we landed in London I walked straight past the passport line and up to the IRIS gate. This was an innovation for frequent travelers that allowed those accepted into it to bypass customs. Two sliding doors opened and I stepped into the booth. I was instructed electronically to stare into a black screen. Invisible lasers read my retinas, a slip of paper like a bank receipt with my name and date of arrival rolled out of a slot, and the doors on the other side of the booth swung open. I stepped into England without showing a passport or speaking to a human being.

If IRIS had been installed at the English Channel forty years ago, I thought, I'd still be a solicitor today.

I had decided to go straight from the airport to Charlie's flat. The urgency in his girlfriend's voice had put the panic into me. The driver fed the address into his robot-voiced GPS system and found the house. The front door was open. I climbed the stairs and knocked and introduced myself to Charlie's angel.

"Charlie," she called, as I followed her into the front room. "Look who's here!"

Charlie was almost all head; his body had shriveled away to a pile of sticks. Worse, he was seated in a wheelchair, facing the window. He looked around to see me and registered no surprise at all.

"Hullo, Jack," he said with a smile. He reached out a bony hand. "What brings you here?"

"Came in to do some business," I said, bringing up a stool next to him. I tapped his wheelchair. "What's all this, then?"

"Don't get around much anymore, Jack," Charlie said. "Annie blagged this from the hospital. Naughty girl."

He looked at me seriously. "I won't walk again, Jack. Doctor told Annie and she told me. This skateboard is going to be my leaving trunk."

I squeezed his wrist and held it. "I didn't know it was this bad, old man."

"Ah, no, you just happened to be passin' by Camden Town on your way to Montego Bay." We both laughed. "Thank you, Jack. Thank you for coming all this way to see me off."

I asked if he had spoken to Simon or Emerson. "Once or twice. Em's been helping out with the bills. I told him, 'Make sure you notify G. T. LaSalle, you and the others are off the hook.'"

We sat there for a long time, watching the sky turn colors. We'd talk and then sit quietly and then talk again. We repeated for Charlie's girlfriend our well-worn routines about the Ravons, how the crowds used to go so wild that the police had to shoot their dogs, the time we climbed over the roof of Sacré-Coeur, terrible tales of Tug Bitler. We laughed about Simon's proposed rock operas and Emerson's early gift for getting out of ever carrying any equipment.

And, I thought, in the end I love them all. Whatever used to enrage or annoy me now seemed like the follies of children whose only sin was struggling too young to achieve the wisdom it takes a lifetime to earn.

"What are you listening to these days, Charlie?" I asked him.

He pointed toward an old record player within reach of his arm. He struggled to haul a fat maroon box up into his lap from the floor. It had a flip top, revealing six vinyl LPs in brightly colored sleeves.

"Shakespeare," Charlie said. "Some oldies but goodies."

"He's a heritage artist, I understand."

It was one of the boxes from the *Living Shakespeare* collection Charlie had given us all when the Ravons had their first hit. Tattered and beaten, it looked like it had come through a war.

"The big hits are missin'. No *Hamlet* or *Macbeth*. But I been groovin' to some of his more obscure numbers."

"Shakespeare's cut-out bin."

"Yeah, Shakespeare's *Cahoots,* Shakespeare's *Here, My Dear.* You ever read *Cymbeline,* Jack?"

"I'm getting around to it."

"Better than you'd think. Get this." Charlie closed his eyes and sang gently, "Golden lads and girls all must / As chimney sweepers come to dust."

He opened his eyes and smiled. "Pretty good, eh? Lyrics by Bill Shake, music by Charlie Lydle. Why didn't we think of this years ago, Jack? I could have set twelve Shakespeare poems to music—they're all public domain, y'know—and every schoolkid who had to memorize one would have bought my LP!"

"It's still a good plan, Charlie. I could roll an Apple Mac up here and you could do the whole thing on GarageBand."

"It's a deal, Jack. You'll manage me again?"

"As long as my cut comes off the gross."

"Fuckin' bread-head."

It was getting cool. I got up to shut the window and Charlie said to leave it open a little longer. The weather was changing.

"You still believe in God, Jack?" Charlie asked me.

"Sure I do," I said. "You're the one who told me about the big ball of sex, and how He expects us to use it up so we can leave it behind."

"I forgot about that. I may have to revise my theology to see if we can get a bit of bonking across the Jordan."

"You lived a good life, Charlie," I said. "You are a good man."

"I'll tell ya, Jack. All those years we'd travel around, drinkin' and chasin' women. And if I talked about God someone always said, 'Hey, I'll believe it when I see it. Show me a miracle or pipe down and drink your bitter.'"

He squeezed my hand.

Charlie said, "We were always waitin' for Him to show us a miracle. To make it easy. And now, Jack, I sit in this window. And I look outside and I see people just goin' about their day, boys kissin' their sweethearts, kids riding bikes, folks going to work and school. And I would give anything to be able to do what they can do. To be healthy, to be young. To walk."

He looked out his window at the world passing.

"We were always waitin' for the miracle, and it was right in front of us the whole time."

Charlie squeezed my shoulder and leaned toward my ear. He whispered, "We're it, Jack. We are the miracle."

I kissed him on the top of the head and told him it was true. We were the miracle.

ACKNOWLEDGMENTS

This book would not exist without the counsel, wisdom, and wisecracks of Jeff Rosen.

Thanks for expert advice and patient suggestions to Tony Dimitriades, Elvis Costello, and Robyn Hitchcock.

Gratitude to all the men in the back of the Mexican restaurant on Houston Street, especially Willie Nile and Richard Lloyd. Michael Golub was my medical guide. Dr. Mary Flynn checked the hospital charts. That silhouette on the shade may be T Bone Burnett.

Jimmy Buffett graciously loaned me his house in Key West to write a big chunk of this story. I repaid him by appropriating some of his endless insights and adventures. Travels with him and Tom Freston, Jonathan Brandstein, Kino Bachelier, and Chris Blackwell (minister without passport) inspired some of the tall tales here.

Joanne Cipolla Moore gave me her house in Maine to finish the novel and was the first person to read it. I can never adequately thank Judy McGrath for encouraging me to moonlight.

Josh Feigenbaum and Allen Toussaint helped me navigate New Orleans. Rosanne Cash filled in details about touring behind the Iron Curtain. Robert Plant was my ambassador to the Tuaregs. Bob Neuwirth, James Taylor, and Ahmet Ertegun each made observations to me that went straight into the text.

Allen Klein spent many hours tutoring me on how the music industry really worked, lessons not taught in business school. Bill Curbishly made valuable suggestions, although some were anatomically impossible. Ed Bicknell was a great source of classic music biz scams. Ed also introduced me to Peter Grant, whose ghost came around while I worked on this. The spirit of Neil Aspinall visited, too. The mold from which those cats were cast is no longer in operation.

Many other friends and fellow travelers show up in bits of this story, but it would be inappropriate to list the names of people who might regret the association.

Scott Moyers drove me to distraction by resigning as my editor, only to drive me back by reappearing the next week as my agent—along with the unflappable Jeff Posternak and the wizardly Andrew Wylie. Talk about a supergroup. This book was heading over a waterfall when David Rosenthal and Sarah Hochman pulled it back.

Love to Susan, Kate, Sarah, and Frank. Gratitude always to Mark and Dave. Blessings to all on Sir John Rogersons Quay and upstairs at the Clarence. Special thanks to Steve Ionata for talking me into the youth fare flight to England in tenth grade. I never got over it.

As I type this I'm looking at an old photo on my wall of Ronnie Lane outside his house in North London. I'm lucky to have known him. I'm lucky to have known all of them.

Bill Flanagan
New York, 2009

ABOUT THE AUTHOR

Bill Flanagan has written several books, including the novels *New Bedlam* and *A&R*. His work has appeared in *Esquire*, *Vanity Fair*, *GQ*, *Rolling Stone*, *Spy*, and many other publications, and he is an on-air essayist for CBS News *Sunday Morning*. He is the executive vice president and editorial director of MTV Networks. He lives in New York City with his wife and their three children.